BACKLASH

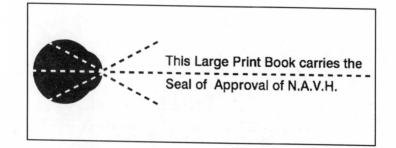

This Large Print Book carries the
Seal of Approval of N.A.V.H.

BACKLASH

A THRILLER

BRAD THOR

THORNDIKE PRESS
A part of Gale, a Cengage Company

Farmington Hills, Mich • San Francisco • New York • Waterville, Maine
Meriden, Conn • Mason, Ohio • Chicago

LIBRARY OF CONGRESS CIP DATA ON FILE.
CATALOGUING IN PUBLICATION FOR THIS BOOK
IS AVAILABLE FROM THE LIBRARY OF CONGRESS

ISBN-13: 978-1-4328-6653-2 (hardcover alk. paper)

Published in 2019 by arrangement with Emily Bestler Books/Atria Books, an imprint of Simon & Schuster, Inc.

Printed in the United States of America
1 2 3 4 5 6 7 23 22 21 20 19

For Robert C. O'Brien
Patriot. Diplomat. Friend.

There will be killing till the score is paid.

— HOMER, *THE ODYSSEY*

CHAPTER 1

Murmansk Oblast
Russia

The transport plane, like everything else in Russia, was a piece of shit. For years, mechanics had swapped out its worn scavenged parts with even older parts. Cracks had been filled with epoxy. Leaking tubes and frayed wires had been wrapped with tape. A crash had been inevitable.

A booming noise, like a horseshoe thrown into a dryer, had been coming from the left engine. The pilot had throttled back, but the noise had only gotten worse.

He and the copilot had scanned their instruments, searching for clues, but hadn't found any. Everything, right down to the cabin pressure, had appeared normal.

But suddenly, the interior had begun filling with smoke. Seconds later, the left engine died, followed by the right.

As the pilot restarted them, an explosion

erupted from the right engine. Seeing the exhaust temperature spike, he immediately ordered the copilot to activate the extinguisher. They had to keep the fire from spreading to the rest of the aircraft, even if it meant shutting the right engine down permanently.

The copilot pulled the fire extinguisher handle as ordered, but they had another problem. The left engine, which had successfully been restarted, wasn't producing enough thrust. They were falling at a rate of more than one thousand feet per minute. Over the blaring of cockpit alarms, the pilot put out a distress call.

They were flying in bad weather over one of the most remote, most inhospitable regions in the country. It was unlikely anyone would receive the transmission.

The pilot never got a chance to repeat his Mayday. The avionics and electrical system were next to go.

After trying to get the auxiliary power unit back online, the pilot instructed the crew to prepare for the worst. They were going down. Hard.

All this risk, he thought, *all this danger, just to deliver one man — a man chained in back like an animal.*

A Russian Special Forces team had

boarded him with a hood over his head. No one had seen his face. The entire crew had assumed he was a criminal of some sort; maybe even a terrorist. They had been informed that he was dangerous. Under no circumstances were any of them to speak with or get anywhere near the prisoner.

But that was before they knew the plane was going to crash.

Moving quickly to the rear of the aircraft, the plane's loadmaster approached the large Spetsnaz soldier sitting nearest the prisoner.

"You need to put an oxygen mask on him," he said in Russian.

The operative, who *already* had *his* mask on, looked at the hooded prisoner, adjusted the submachine gun on his lap, and shook his head.

"*Nyet,*" he stated. *No.*

Career Russian Air Force, the loadmaster was used to transporting elite operators. He was also used to their bullshit.

"I'm not asking you," he replied. "I'm *ordering* you."

The soldier shot a sideways glance at the intelligence officer sitting nearby.

The plane was losing altitude. The smoke in the cabin was getting worse. The officer nodded back. *Do it.*

The ape reached over, snatched off the

11

hood, and affixed a mask over the prisoner's face. Then he replaced the hood and, satisfied, leaned back in his seat.

"Now unshackle his arms so he can brace for impact," the loadmaster continued. It enabled only a minor altering of the body's position, but in a crash it could mean the difference between life and death. Whatever the prisoner had done, surely he didn't deserve to die, at least not like this.

Pissed off, the soldier glanced over again at the intelligence officer. Once more, the man nodded.

Producing a set of keys, the Spetsnaz operative reached down and opened the padlock securing the prisoner's handcuffs to his belly chain. Grabbing the man's arms, he raised them and placed them against the seat in front of him.

"His feet as well," the loadmaster ordered. "He must be able to rapidly evacuate the aircraft."

The soldier didn't need to look to his superior a third time. The intelligence officer answered for their entire team.

"The only way that man walks off this plane is with one of us," he said from behind his mask.

The loadmaster gave up. He had done what he could and knew it was pointless to argue any further. They were out of time.

"Make sure your weapons are secure," he directed, as he turned to make his way to his jump seat.

Suddenly, the plane shuddered and the nose pitched forward. The crewman lunged for the nearest seat and buckled himself in as anything not locked down went hurtling through the cabin like a missile.

With no instruments and no visibility, they were flying blind. The pilot and copilot fought to regain control of the aircraft.

Fifteen hundred feet above the ground, the pilots managed to pull the nose back up and slow their descent. But with no thrust from the remaining engine, they were still falling. They had to find someplace to land.

Peering through the weather, the pilot could see they were flying over a dense forest. Ahead was a clearing of some sort. It might have been a field or a frozen lake. All he could tell was that it appeared to be devoid of trees.

"There," the pilot said.

"There's not enough length. It's too short."

"That's where we're landing," the pilot insisted. "Extend the landing gear. Prepare for impact."

The copilot obeyed and engaged the

emergency landing gear extension system. With no electricity with which to activate the PA, he turned and shouted back into the cabin, "Brace! Brace! Brace!"

The command was acknowledged by the loadmaster, who then yelled over and over in Russian from his seat, "Heads down! Stay down! Heads down! Stay down!"

Only a few hundred feet above the ground, the pilot pulled back on the yoke to lift the aircraft's nose in an attempt to slow it down, but he misjudged the distance.

The belly of the plane scraped across the tops of the tall snow-laden trees. The left landing gear was snapped off, followed by the right.

Just before the clearing, one of the wing-tips was clipped, and the plane went into a violent roll.

CHAPTER 2

Governors Island Lake
Winnipesaukee
Gilford, New Hampshire
Police Chief Tom Tullis had seen plenty of dead bodies over his career.

But this was a record for him at a single crime scene.

During the height of the summer, the popular resort town of Gilford could swell to as many as twenty thousand inhabitants. Off-season, like now, the number of full-time residents was only seventy-three hundred. Either way, four corpses were four too many.

Pulling out his cell phone, the tall, crew-cut-sporting cop texted his wife. They were supposed to meet for lunch. That was impossible now. He told her not to expect him for dinner either. It was going to be a late night.

Returning the phone to his duty belt, he

15

focused on the bodies — two men and two women. They had all been shot, either in the head, the chest, or both. Judging from a quick scan of the walls and windows, no rounds had missed their targets. That told him the shooter was skilled.

Interestingly, three of the four victims were armed. One of the women had a Sig Sauer P365 in her purse, the other a Glock 17 in her briefcase. One of the two men carried a Heckler & Koch pistol at his hip. No one had drawn their weapons. That told Tullis something else. Either the victims had known their killer, or they had all been taken by surprise. Considering who the victims were, he doubted it was the latter.

The woman with the Sig Sauer had credentials identifying her as a former Boston Police Detective, eligible to carry concealed nationwide. The woman with the Glock had no such credentials, but in the "Live Free or Die" state of New Hampshire it was legal to carry without a permit. Not that she would ever have had trouble getting one.

Seeing the name on her driver's license, Tullis had instantly recognized her. She had made a lot of headlines when the President had elevated her to Deputy Director of the CIA.

The gun-carrying male victim had ID that

16

claimed he was an active military member. United States Navy.

What the hell were they all doing here? the Chief wondered. *And who had killed them?*

He suspected the key might lie with the final victim.

Just off the dining room, facing a large TV, a hospital bed had been set up in the den. In it, shot once between the eyes, was a man who appeared to be somewhere in his eighties. He was the only victim Tullis and his team hadn't yet identified. The Chief had some decisions to make.

Judging from the postmortem lividity of the bodies, they had been dead for at least two days, maybe more. The killer's trail would already be going cold.

As a seasoned law enforcement officer, Tullis knew the importance of doing everything by the book. He needed to secure not only the house but also the grounds.

Going the extra step, he decided to shut down the lone bridge that connected the 504-acre Governors Island to the mainland and to request Marine Patrol units to cover the shoreline.

This wasn't some murder-suicide where the husband had shot the wife and the pool boy before turning the gun on himself. And it wasn't some drug deal gone bad. This was

17

a high-profile case; exactly the kind of case no town ever wanted — especially a tourism-dependent town like Gilford.

Getting on the radio, the Chief told the dispatcher to send the entire shift. He then instructed her to call in all available off-duty officers. They were going to need as much manpower as possible.

The next step was to alert the State Attorney General's Office in Concord. Per protocol, they would mobilize a Major Crime Unit team from the State Police to come up and lead the investigation. Before he made that call, though, he decided to place another.

It wasn't a by-the-book move. In fact, Tullis was way overstepping his authority.

But if it meant protecting Gilford and the town's hardworking men and women who so depended on the tourist trade, that was one scenario in which the Chief was willing to bend the rules.

CHAPTER 3

Laconia Municipal Airport
Gilford, New Hampshire

When the call came in to Langley, the Director of Central Intelligence, Bob Mc-Gee, happened to be in a meeting with the Director of the FBI, Gary Militante.

Though the DCI's assistant was hesitant to interrupt, she knew she had to make her boss aware of the call. McGee put it on speakerphone. He and Militante were stunned by what they heard.

The FBI Director introduced himself, gave Tullis his personal cell phone number, and asked to be texted as many pictures from the crime scene as possible — pictures of the bodies, the IDs, the weapons, all of it. Minutes later, his phone began vibrating.

As the photos poured in, McGee kept his emotions in check. With professional detachment, he narrated who and what they were looking at, right down to the body in the hospital bed — retired CIA operative Reed Carlton, the man who had founded the Agency's Counter Terrorism Center.

Militante had the same questions as Tullis. "What were they all doing in New Hampshire, and who would have wanted them dead?"

It was a long story, which McGee promised to explain in-flight. He wanted a look at the crime scene for himself — and the only way he'd have any legal access to it was if the FBI was attached.

Before he and Militante could leave, though, there was an additional person he needed to reach.

He tried three times, but his calls all ended up in voicemail. *Why the hell wasn't he picking up?*

After sending a quick text, McGee grabbed his jacket and headed downstairs with the FBI Director and their security details for the two-minute ride to 84VA, the Agency's helipad a mile west of Langley.

Once they boarded their respective helicopters, it was a short flight to Joint Base Andrews, where an Embraer Praetor 600 was fueled and waiting.

The jet was a recent addition to the CIA's fleet. Fast and able to take off using less than five thousand feet of runway, it was perfect for the trip to Gilford.

When they landed, a phalanx of SUVs was waiting for them. The detail leaders hated movements like this — no warning, no planning, and little to no coordination with elements on the ground. Nevertheless, both directors had insisted that the trip was necessary and that time was of the essence.

From Laconia Municipal, it was only four miles to Governors Island. They were met at the airport by Gilford PD and given an escort through town and over the bridge to the crime scene.

Stepping out of one of the SUVs, McGee took a deep breath. The air was cold and smelled of pine. A hint of wood smoke drifted from a chimney somewhere unseen.

McGee looked like a marshal from an old Western. He was a tall man in his late fifties with gray hair and a gray mustache. A testament to his Army career, his shoes were shined, his suit was immaculate and his shirt was crisply pressed.

He wore no jewelry other than a Rolex Submariner — a gift to himself when he left Delta Force decades ago and signed on with the CIA's paramilitary branch.

McGee was old-school, known for being tough, direct, and unflappable. He hated politics, which had made him a good choice to head the CIA.

The nation's once proud intelligence service was being choked to death by bureaucracy. It was packed with talented people willing to give everything for their country, but they were being held back by risk-averse middle managers more concerned with their next promotion than with doing what needed to be done.

Familiar with the Agency from the ground up, the President had put McGee in charge of cleaning out the deadwood. And he had gone after it root and branch.

But McGee had quickly realized that mucking out the Agency's Augean stables was indeed a Herculean task — one that was going to take much longer than any of them had envisioned.

In the meantime, the threats against America were growing — becoming deadlier, more destabilizing, and more intricate.

As red tape slowed Langley down, America's enemies were speeding up. Something needed to be done — something radical.

With the President's approval, McGee had agreed to a bold new plan, as well as a major sacrifice.

The plan was to outsource the CIA's most clandestine work. It would go to a private intelligence agency outside the bureaucracy's grasp. There, safe from government red tape, sensitive operations could receive the support and commitment they deserved.

It was viewed as a temporary fix while Langley was undergoing its gut rehab — a rehab that would have to go all the way down to the studs.

The private intelligence agency charged with taking over the darkest slice of the CIA's pie was The Carlton Group, founded by the aforementioned, now deceased, Reed Carlton.

And as to McGee's sacrifice, it was personified by another victim at the scene.

With his blessing, Lydia Ryan had left her position as CIA Deputy Director in order to run The Carlton Group.

That was the backdrop against which Bob McGee stepped out of the SUV, breathed in the chilly New England air, and prepared himself for the horror he was about to see inside.

Tullis met the two directors at the front steps and solemnly shook their hands. Then, after having them sign into the crime scene log, he distributed paper booties and latex gloves. The protection details didn't get any. They would have to wait outside — the fewer people coming in and out, the better.

The Police Chief was about to show the

two men inside, when one of his officers came up carrying a clear plastic evidence bag.

"We found something back in the trees near the end of the driveway," the patrolman said, holding it up. Inside was a phone.

McGee recognized it immediately. Or, more specifically, he recognized its case.

Made from a rigid thermoplastic, the distinct Magpul cell phone case was popular with military operators. Its styling mimicked the company's rugged rifle magazines. On the back, a distinct Nordic symbol had been customized. The Chief stepped off the porch for a closer examination.

As he did, the FBI Director saw the look on his CIA colleague's face. Slowly, he mouthed a name. *Harvath?*

McGee nodded.

Their bad situation had just gotten worse.

CHAPTER 4

Murmansk Oblast

When Scot Harvath regained consciousness, his ears were ringing. There was the distinct, metallic taste of blood in his mouth, probably from having bitten his tongue during the crash. *The crash.*

Slowly, he opened his eyes, but he couldn't see anything. The hood was still over his head. Reaching up, he began to pull it off, half-expecting one of his captors to knock his hand away. No one touched him.

His sandy-brown hair was matted, and his blue eyes struggled to focus.

Removing the oxygen mask, he looked around. The aircraft's fuselage had been severed into three pieces. In some places, seats were missing. In others, entire rows had disappeared.

He glanced to his right, but the soldier who had been next to him was gone, along with the seat he had been sitting in.

25

A strong odor of jet fuel filled the air. It was mixed with the smell of smoke and melting plastic. Some part of the plane was on fire.

Under normal circumstances, he would have moved slowly — assessing the damage and making sure that he didn't have a spinal injury — but these weren't normal circumstances. He needed to get out.

Planting his feet, he stood. But when he tried to step into the aisle, he couldn't. His Spetsnaz minder had locked his ankle chain to the leg of his chair.

Sitting back down, he attempted to jerk himself free, first by kicking out his legs and then by reaching down and trying to pull the chain loose. It didn't work.

Searching around his seat, he looked for anything he could use to help him escape. There was nothing. Without a key, he was fucked.

Though he had been sedated on and off over the last several days, images began to flood his mind. As they did, an unbearable pain began to build in his chest and his heart rate started to climb.

Taking a deep breath, his training kicked in, and he forced himself to relax. There was no question that unspeakable things had happened. Worse things, though, were

26

on the horizon if he didn't get control of the situation.

As one of America's top intelligence operatives, he had been a prime target for the Russians. His knowledge of spy networks, covert operations, and classified programs was invaluable. But that wasn't the only reason they wanted him.

Year after year, he had been behind some of the most successful operations against the Russian military and Russian intelligence. As such, he had ranked very near the top of a little-known, clandestine kill list maintained in Moscow.

But as badly as the Russians wanted him, and as much as they had risked to grab him, he knew the United States would risk even more to get him back. He just had to remain alive and one step ahead until then.

Scanning the cabin, he saw one of the crew pinned beneath a nearby cargo container that had broken free. The legs of his uniform were stained with blood. Over the ringing in his ears, he could hear the man moaning.

Harvath recognized him. It was the loadmaster who had insisted that he be allowed to brace for impact. When his hood had been removed to put his oxygen mask on, he had only caught a quick flash, but he remembered the man's face. Without his help, Harvath might not have survived the crash.

Pinned next to the loadmaster was the body of his missing Spetsnaz minder. He was neither moaning nor moving.

From everything else he could see, he and the loadmaster were the only two survivors in this section of the plane. That was the good news. The bad news was that the temperature was rapidly dropping.

Looking through one of the ruptures in the fuselage, he saw nothing but snow and ice outside. Wherever they were it was cold. *Really* cold.

Harvath had no clue as to his location. He'd had a bag over his head since being taken in New Hampshire. He assumed, though, that they were somewhere in Russia.

Nevertheless, he hadn't made it into his forties and survived a plane crash only to turn around and freeze to death. If he and the loadmaster were going to make it, they were going to have to work together.

Harvath called out to get his attention. "I can help you," he said in his choppy Russian.

For a moment, the airman stopped moaning and looked over at him. He then just shook his head.

"Hey!" Harvath yelled. "Hey!"

When the man turned his agony-stricken face back in his direction, Harvath sniffed the air around him in an exaggerated fashion.

It took the loadmaster a moment, but he finally realized what the prisoner was trying to draw his attention to — *fire.*

The man strained against the cargo container pinning his legs, but it was beyond his ability to move.

"I can help you," Harvath repeated.

"You?" the man replied in Russian. "How?"

Pointing at the Spetsnaz operative crushed by the container, Harvath searched for the word, then held up his shackles and said, *"Klyuch." Key.*

Toss me the key and I'll help you. The loadmaster considered the offer. Of course, the prisoner could be lying, but the Russian airman didn't have much choice.

Patting down the soldier, he found the keys and, using what little of his strength remained, tossed them in the prisoner's direction.

The throw came up short. Harvath leaned out as far as he could into the aisle, the shackles tearing into his ankles, but he missed it and the keys landed on the floor several feet away.

"Damn it," he muttered under his breath.

"*Prahsteetyeh*," said the loadmaster. *I'm sorry.*

Glancing around, Harvath saw a nylon tie-down strap with a heavy metal clamp. He couldn't tell if was within reach or not.

Getting down onto his stomach, he lengthened his body to its max, struggling to create every millimeter of reach possible, but the strap remained just inches beyond his grasp.

He searched for something handy — a screwdriver, a pen or pencil, anything — even a rolled-up magazine. Then an idea hit him.

Returning to his seat, he grabbed his oxygen mask and pulled out the hose. Tying it to his hood, he attached the two together. They weren't long enough to reach the keys, but they might be long enough to reach the tie-down strap.

Kneeling, he took aim and tossed the hood toward the buckle. It landed right on top of it. Slowly, he retracted the oxygen tube and pulled it in.

With the buckle in hand, he began gathering up the strap, which turned out to be much longer than he needed.

He had reeled most of it in when he noticed something else. The opposite end was stuck.

"Damn it," he repeated.

When the strap went taut, he began yanking on it, twisting and pulling from every possible angle. When that didn't work, he started flipping it like a whip.

"Let loose, *motherfucker*," he cursed as he cracked the strap, sending a ripple down its length, and then yanked it backward with all of his might.

It turned out to be the right combination, as the buckle on the opposite end was freed from its entrapment and came screaming backward like a bullet. If Harvath hadn't ducked, it would have hit him right in the face.

Realigning himself, he pitched the strap into the aisle and pulled back the keys the loadmaster had thrown.

Finding the one he needed, he unlocked his wrists and then bent down and unlocked his feet. He was almost free.

Removing the remaining chains, he made his way over to where the loadmaster was pinned. But before he could even think about helping him, he needed to make sure the soldier lying next to him was dead.

Harvath placed two fingers where the

man's jaw met his neck. There was no pulse.

In his holster, the soldier carried a nine-millimeter Grach pistol. It now belonged to Harvath. After checking to make sure a round was chambered, he put his shoulder against the cargo container and pushed.

The metal box barely budged. He was going to need a fulcrum and a lever of some sort to lift it. And judging by how much the loadmaster's left leg was bleeding, he was going to need to find a tourniquet as well.

But before he could help him, he had to sweep the rest of the wreckage. If there were any threats remaining, those would need to be dealt with first.

Grabbing a thick rag, he folded it several times and pressed down on the wound. He was searching his mind for the correct words to say to the man in Russian about keeping the pressure on, when he saw a flash of movement outside.

CHAPTER 5

Harvath only had time to react. Bringing the pistol up, he applied pressure to the trigger and fired three shots, just as he had been trained — two to the chest, one to the head. The Spetsnaz operative outside fell dead in the snow.

Sliding behind the cargo container, Harvath took cover. The loadmaster stared at him, wide-eyed. Harvath didn't know if it was from the shock of the gunfire or from the blood loss — probably both.

Ejecting the Grach's magazine, he looked to see how many more rounds he had. There were fifteen, plus one in the chamber.

Leaning over, he pulled a spare magazine and a flashlight from the dead soldier next to the loadmaster. Dressed in hospital-style scrubs, he didn't have any pockets, nor did he have a tight-enough waistband to tuck them into. He would have to carry them in his hand.

If any of the other operatives had survived, and were even partially ambulatory, the sound of the gunshots was going to draw them in like a tractor beam. There was only one thing Russians liked more than drinking or fucking, and that was fighting.

Harvath had gotten lucky. Seeing the operative outside first had been a gift. He didn't expect to get another one. He needed to go on the offensive. But to be successful, he needed information.

Looking down at the loadmaster, he asked, "How many men?"

The man's condition was worsening. "Four crew," he replied weakly in Russian. "Six passengers."

That sounded right. A pilot, a copilot, the loadmaster, and maybe a navigator or flight officer of some sort would have composed the crew. As for the six passengers, Harvath had been traveling with the same group since being taken. There were four Special Forces soldiers accompanying him, plus one intelligence officer — *Josef.*

At the thought of the man's name, his rage again began to build. It was like acid eating away at him. He wanted to let it loose, to vomit it out in every direction and kill every Russian in sight. But instead, he warned himself, *Not now. Keep your shit together.*

Laboring to remain calm, he focused on the situation and ran a count. Two of the soldiers were down — one had died in the crash and the other he had just shot outside. The loadmaster was pinned beneath the container. That meant six potential threats remained. Each had to be accounted for and, if necessary, neutralized. Raising his pistol, he slipped out from behind the container.

The fuselage was difficult to traverse. It was on its side and strewn with debris. There were sharp, jagged pieces of metal everywhere.

As he picked his way through, he kept his eyes peeled for survivors, as well as warm pieces of clothing. He found neither.

At the front of the tail section, he had to step outside to get to the next portion of the plane. Carefully, he leaped down onto the ground.

Immediately, he was hit with a blast of razor-sharp snow. It was driven by one of the coldest, bitterest winds he had ever felt.

As the crystals raked his exposed skin, he knew he would have only minutes in this temperature — five tops — before numbness would commence and the cold would begin to overtake him.

In the fading light, the crash wreckage was

scattered as far as the eye could see. It looked to Harvath as if they were in the middle of a snow-covered field, surrounded by forest. He could make out where the plane had torn through the trees. A long scar of burning debris and snapped pines led back into the woods.

Hip-deep in the snow, he crossed to the next section of fuselage and climbed inside. Because this section faced upwind, the freezing air blew through with a vengeance.

With the spare magazine clenched between his teeth, he held the flashlight away from his body in case anyone saw the beam and wanted to take a shot at him. A few moments later, he found another Spetsnaz operative.

The motionless man was still strapped into his seat. His head hung at an obscene angle, his neck probably broken. Harvath grabbed him by the hair and lifted up his head so he could look into his face.

He didn't know the soldiers' names. They had only used call signs around him — words in Russian he didn't understand. What he did understand, though, was what they had done.

After handcuffing him at the house on Governors Island, this Spetsnaz operative had delivered a searing blow to his kidney.

Harvath's knees had buckled. No sooner had he hit the floor than the Russian had grabbed a fistful of hair. Yanking his head up, he had forced him to watch as Josef had murdered Lara, Lydia, Reed, and the Navy Corpsman.

Harvath had thought they were going to kill him, too. And for a moment, he had wanted to die — right there with Lara, whom he loved more than anything in the world. But then he had been jabbed with a needle and everything went black.

When they brought him back around, it was obvious that he had been moved. They were in a dank, cold basement someplace. He didn't know where, or how long he had been out.

He had a splitting headache, his clothes had been removed, and he had been tied to a chair. A video camera had been set up. Half an hour later, Josef had come down the stairs and the interrogation had begun.

Whenever he hesitated, whenever he refused to answer a question, it was the man with the broken neck who had struck him. In the beginning, Josef was playing good cop; trying to build rapport. It wasn't until they boarded a private jet that things had gotten really ugly.

Letting the dead man's head drop, Harvath placed his fingers against his neck, just in case there was a pulse. There wasn't. "You got off easy," he said, sizing up the Russian.

The other two soldiers had been monsters — barrel-chested thugs, well over six feet tall. This one was closer to his height and build of a muscular five feet ten.

Wearing nothing but scrubs and the equivalent of prison slippers, Harvath had already begun shaking from the cold. He needed to conserve whatever heat he had left and quickly stripped off the Russian's uniform.

Snatching an American, especially one of Harvath's stature, was an act of war — particularly when carried out on U.S. soil. It would have been a completely black operation.

If Harvath had to guess, everything they needed — civilian clothing, fake IDs, credit cards, even weapons — had been arranged via Russian mafia contacts in the United States.

Once the private jet had touched down, the soldiers had changed out of their American street clothes and into cold-weather military uniforms. The man with the broken neck was wearing long underwear, wool socks — the works. Harvath took all of it.

The only thing the Spetsnaz operative

wasn't wearing was a coat. They had boarded with them, though, so there had to be at least one somewhere.

Buttoning up the clothes with stiffening fingers, he pulled on the man's boots and laced them up. Then he continued his search.

Picking his way through the wreckage, he came upon a small crew closet.

It had been jammed shut by one of the rows of seats that had come loose during the crash. Harvath had to burn precious calories to shove the seats out of the way, but it was worth it.

Inside was a thinly insulated Russian Air Force jacket with a faux fur collar. He pulled it on and zipped it up. There were no gloves in the pockets, but there was a beret. It wouldn't keep his ears warm, but it would help retain some heat and was better than nothing.

He was about to close the closet when he heard a noise from the other side. Without hesitating, he put two rounds through the door. The plane's flight officer fell down dead on the other side.

Closing the door, Harvath saw what he had done. He hadn't intended to kill any of the flight crew unless absolutely necessary. Though Russian military, they weren't directly responsible for what had happened. That responsibility lay with Josef, his Spetsnaz operatives, and whoever had tasked them with kidnapping Harvath and murdering the people he cared about.

But after everything that had happened, he had zero capacity for remorse. Russia, and every Russian in it, was his enemy now.

Pushing forward into the wind, he cleared the rest of this section of the fuselage. There were no additional survivors.

Trudging through the snow, he arrived at the final section of the plane — the nose. It included the badly damaged cockpit, which was consumed by flames. From what he could see, the pilot and copilot were both dead and still strapped into their seats. The fire was too hot, though, for him to get any closer. Getting his hands on a map, a radio, or some sort of flight plan was out of the question.

Staying in this part of the plane was also out of the question. As much as he needed the warmth, the thickening toxic smoke forced him out.

Stepping into the snow, he pushed back toward the tail section, making sure to keep his eyes open for Josef and the remaining Spetsnaz operative.

He had no idea where they were. For all

he knew, they had been torn from the plane during the crash.

Sweeping back through the center segment of the aircraft, he hurriedly gathered up anything he could safely burn to keep warm, including a heavy aircraft manual the size of a phone book and two wooden pallets.

When he returned to the tail section, he checked on the loadmaster. The Russian's pulse was thready. His eyes were glassy and his skin was ashen. He had lost far too much blood. Nevertheless, Harvath was determined to do what he could to save him.

Dragging over a sheet of metal, he set it as close to the loadmaster as he dared and used it to build a fire on. There was a shovel clamped to the wall. After breaking down the pallets, he found a small piece of flaming wreckage outside, scooped it up, and brought it in to get the wood burning.

Tearing the dry pages out of the technical manual, he crumpled them into balls and tossed them in to stoke the fire higher. As soon as it was burning good and hot, he set his attention to helping the man who had saved his life. He had to stop the bleeding.

None of the soldiers had been carrying tourniquets, so Harvath was forced to improvise. Grabbing two carabiners from the vest of the Spetsnaz corpse nearby, he collected several strips of cargo netting. It was a spit and baling wire solution, but it was all he had.

Using one of the carabiners as a windlass, he applied the improvised tourniquet to the man's left leg, cinched it down, and employed a length of wire and the other carabiner to hold everything in place. Then, adding even more fuel to the fire, he moved in closer to warm up.

Because of the angle of the tail section, the wind here wasn't blowing straight through, but that was a small blessing at best. Outside, the temperature continued to plunge. Harvath needed to figure out some way to help better wall them off from the cold. He also needed to find blankets and a way to get IV fluids into the loadmaster. There had to be some sort of medical kit on the plane. Whether it had survived the crash was another question entirely.

In addition, he still needed a lever and fulcrum to raise the container off the man's crushed legs, to gather up any food and water he could find, and come up with some sort of a pack in which he could carry as many supplies as possible that would aid in his escape.

It was a long list. The sooner he got

started on it, the better — for both of them. He had no idea how soon a rescue team would arrive.

"I return," he said, in his limited Russian. The loadmaster didn't respond.

It was a bad sign. Even so, Harvath had promised the man that he would help him.

Further back, near the cargo ramp, he opened a series of metal cabinets. Each contained a range of equipment, but none that he needed. If there was a med kit on board, it wasn't in this part of the plane. Maybe it was kept up near the cockpit. And if so, it was a lost cause.

Harvath did, though, find what resembled some kind of moving blanket. His luck, at least in part, was holding out.

Removing it, he turned to hurry back to the loadmaster. But as he did, he came face-to-face with the remaining Spetsnaz soldier. The man was bleeding from a gash above his left eye and had a suppressed ASM-Val rifle pointed right at him.

"Zamerzat!" the man ordered, blood dripping down his face. *Don't move.*

CHAPTER 6

Governors Island
Gilford, New Hampshire

"Whoever the killer was," said Chief Tullis, "he or she knew what they were doing."

"You think this was done by one person?" asked McGee.

"Not necessarily. Based on the footprints outside, there were likely multiple assailants. The victims, though, were all lined up, on their knees, and shot execution-style. Judging by the wounds, we believe it was done by the same shooter with the same weapon."

Pointing at the bodies, he continued, "Based on the shot placement, specifically rounds being directed to the head, the chest, or both — the killer appears to have training. None of the shots went wide. We didn't dig anything out of the walls, the ceiling, or the floorboards. No rounds went through any of the windows. Cool, calm, and collected. If I had to guess, I'd say the killer had probably done this sort of thing before.

"Then there are the cameras. Most of the seasonal properties up here have them in case of burglary or vandalism. This house has four and should have showed us anyone coming or going."

"But?"

"We can't review any of the footage."

"Why not?"

"It was recorded to a DVR in a crawl space above the front hall closet. It has been smashed, and the hard drive is missing."

Before he had even landed, there was no doubt in McGee's mind that this was a professional hit. His two most pressing questions at this point were *Who was the hitter?* and *Where was Harvath?*

"How about the adjoining properties?" he asked. "How many of them have cameras?"

"Several," the Chief answered. "I already have officers working on accessing the footage."

"How soon will your team start in on hair, prints, and fibers?" asked Militante.

"All of that gets handled by the AG and the State Police. Our job is to secure the crime scene and preserve all possible evidence."

"If there's any assistance the FBI can give, all you have to do is ask."

"Thank you," Tullis responded. "I'm sure the Major Crime Unit will appreciate that."

While McGee knew that forensics were often key in solving homicides, they didn't have that kind of time. Whoever did this already had a big head start. In fact, if it was a professional, he or she was probably already out of the country. Time and distance were two of their biggest impediments — and those would only grow.

"What else have you found?" he asked.

"The shooter," the Chief stated as he held up another evidence bag, "appears to have policed up all of the brass, except for one."

McGee accepted the bag from him and, along with Militante, studied the shell casing.

"Nine millimeter," the FBI Director concluded. "Popular round. Likely consistent with the gunshot wounds of the victims."

The CIA Director nodded and handed the bag back to Tullis, who set it back on the table.

"Now it's your turn," replied the Chief.

Militante knew the police officer wasn't speaking to him. He glanced at McGee, who had turned away and was staring out the window at the flat, gray lake.

"This was supposed to be a safe house," the DCI revealed.

Tullis wasn't surprised. With what he knew of the CIA, anything was possible. "Who were you keeping safe?"

"The man in the hospital bed."

"Who was he?"

"One of the best our business ever saw."

It was evident from his voice that the DCI held the man in high esteem. Out of respect, the Chief allowed a moment of silence to pass before continuing. "What was his name?"

McGee turned to face the den, and with it, the hospital bed. "Reed Carlton."

"Was he CIA?"

"He was. Served decades as a case officer, ran stations around the world, and helped establish the Counter Terrorism Center. They broke the mold with him. No mission was ever too tough or too dangerous."

Tullis looked at the body lying in the hospital bed. "Whom were you protecting him from?"

The DCI grinned. "Everyone."

The Chief raised an eyebrow. "So he had enemies."

"Lots of them."

"Why the hospital bed? What was wrong with him?"

"He had Alzheimer's."

"My mother had Alzheimer's," Tullis responded. "It's a terrible disease. Why wasn't he in a hospital or an assisted living situation?"

"Part of the disease," the CIA Director explained, "can involve the brakes coming off. Patients can say things they shouldn't."

Remembering his own ordeal, the Chief mused, "Tell me about it."

"Reed had a lot of very sensitive information stored in his head. Some of those things, if they fell into the wrong hands, could have been harmful to the United States."

"The CIA could have hidden him anywhere in the world, though. Why Governors Island?"

It was a reasonable question, but it hadn't been the CIA's call. It had been Harvath's. He had been not only Reed Carlton's protégé but also his heir apparent and in charge of all of his affairs.

"Reed summered here as a boy," the DCI recounted. "His grandparents had a cottage on the island. The hope was that he'd be comfortable here — maybe even relive some of his oldest memories."

"I wish you had let us know," said Tullis, the compassion evident in his voice. "We could have looked in on him. Added extra patrols. My officers would have taken a lot of pride in helping to protect a man like Mr. Carlton."

The DCI turned to face him. "I don't doubt it. Thank you. In the end, we felt the fewer people that knew he was here, the better. It's how we do things."

"In secret."

McGee nodded.

Chief Tullis regretted causing more pain, but he needed additional information. "I know it's difficult, but what can you tell me about the other victims?"

The knot in McGee's stomach hadn't gone. In fact, it had only tightened. "Lydia Ryan worked for me at the CIA. She was one of the best field operatives I have ever known."

"Any idea what was she was doing here?"

"She worked for Reed."

"As in *used* to work for him? Back at the CIA?" Tullis asked.

McGee shook his head. "When the time came, Reed retired from the CIA. He gave it a good try. He played golf, took a couple of cruises, even joined a group of ex–case officers who got together weekly for lunch, but the lifestyle didn't agree with him. He missed being in the game.

"By the time he tried to come back, though, the things he disliked about the Agency — particularly the bureaucracy — had only gotten worse. So, he decided to see what he could do from the outside and started his own company, The Carlton Group.

"Things went well for several years until he was diagnosed with Alzheimer's. When that happened, he recruited Lydia to become the company's new director."

"What kind of company was it?"

"It's a private intelligence agency."

The Chief looked at him. "Is that like private contracting?"

"Kind of," the DCI acknowledged. "They hire ex-intelligence and ex–special operations people to assist CIA missions."

Tullis was intrigued. "What kind of missions?"

"I'm not able to discuss that."

"Why not?"

"The operations that The Carlton Group were involved with are classified."

That didn't surprise the Chief. "What can you tell me about the other two victims?"

Gesturing toward the male corpse, McGee said, "Navy Corpsman. He was part of a rotating team. There was always someone in the house with medical expertise, keeping an eye on Reed."

"Were they always armed?"

"Just in case."

Tullis made a mental note of that and then, gesturing toward the final victim, inquired, "Do you recognize her?"

"I do. Her name was Lara Cordero."

"She was carrying credentials identifying her as ex–Boston PD. Did she also work for The Carlton Group?"

The DCI shook his head. "No."

"Any idea what she was doing here?"

"She was friends with Reed. And with Lydia."

Tullis hadn't handled a lot of murders, but he had conducted a lot of interrogations. He could tell when someone wasn't being fully truthful.

"So, just up for a visit, then?"

"I guess so," replied the CIA Director.

"Huh," said Tullis as he removed a spiral notebook from his pocket. Flipping several pages in, he scanned his notes. "Based on the suitcase and clothing in the guest room, we assumed the Corpsman was staying here in the house. Lydia Ryan and Lara Cordero, though, had key cards for rooms at a nearby hotel.

"Ryan's room was single occupancy, but Lara Cordero checked in with a man, a man

51

whose clothes are still in their room and who hasn't been seen for at least the last two days. Any idea who that might be?"

The knot in McGee's stomach ratcheted ten degrees tighter. Pointing at the evidence bag containing the cell phone, he asked, "Is it on?"

The Chief nodded. "It is. It even has some battery left, but it's locked."

The CIA Director didn't care. He had people who could open it. Though he had recognized the case, he just wanted to be certain it was Harvath's.

Taking out his own cell phone, he pulled up his call log and redialed the number he had been calling and texting before leaving Langley.

It took only a moment for the call to connect.

As the phone inside the evidence bag began to vibrate, one of McGee's worst fears was confirmed.

CHAPTER 7

The CIA Director was no stranger to death, but identifying the bodies of three close friends had taken a toll. He needed to get some air and clear his head. Until he did, he wasn't going to be able to think straight.

Tullis could sense the DCI needed a break and suggested they all step outside. One of his officers had just made a run into town for coffee.

"Hope black is okay," he said as he handed him a cup.

McGee, who was leaning against one of the patrol vehicles and studying the house, thanked him.

The pair stood in silence for several moments as the steam rose from their cups.

"What can you tell me about this Scot Harvath?" Tullis finally asked.

McGee chose his words carefully. Harvath was one of the country's most valuable intelligence assets. "He's one of the good guys. And tough as hell. He reminds me a lot of Carlton."

The Chief let that sit for a moment. He didn't want to ask his next question, but he had to. "Is Harvath capable of what happened inside?"

"Absolutely not."

"You sound pretty certain."

"I'm *positive*," McGee declared. "And if you knew him, you'd be positive, too."

"Then help me out. Who is he? Tell me about him."

The only reason McGee was here was that Tullis had extended him a professional courtesy. The CIA had no jurisdiction. And short of some as-yet-undiscovered federal nexus or an official request for help, neither did the FBI. The least McGee could do was cooperate. "Where do you want to start?" he asked.

"How about we start with his full name?"

"Scot Thomas Harvath."

Tullis had his spiral notebook back out, along with his pen. "And what was his relationship to the victims?"

"He worked for Reed Carlton."

"At The Carlton Group?" the Chief asked.

"Yes."

"In what capacity?"

McGee raised his cup and took a sip of

coffee. "I believe he was Director of Operations."

"You don't know for certain?"

"It's complicated. Harvath wasn't big on titles. All I know is that Lydia carried out the day-to-day business, while Harvath took care of the ops side of the house."

"Which entailed what?"

"He dealt with the assignments. Staffing them. Executing them. That sort of thing."

Tullis took a few notes and then asked, "Tell me about his background."

"He was a Navy SEAL for many years."

"Which team?"

"If I remember correctly, he started out at Team Two — the cold-weather specialists — and ended up at SEAL Team Six. He caught the eye of the Secret Service and did some work for them, then ended up at the CIA doing contract work before joining Reed's operation."

"What kind of contract work?"

"I can't discuss that."

The Chief made several more notes. "Any PTSD?"

McGee shook his head. "The joke in our industry is that guys like Harvath don't get PTSD, they give it."

"So no issues that you are aware of."

"Zero."

"Any medications?"

"None that I know of."

"What was his relationship with Cordero?" asked Tullis. "Were they romantically involved?"

"Yes."

"Married?"

McGee shook his head once again.

"Engaged?"

"Not that I know of."

"So were they boyfriend-girlfriend?" the cop probed. "Or was it more casual? A friends-with-benefits sort of thing?"

"They had been dating for a while. In fact, Lara had recently moved in with him."

"Where was that?"

"Virginia, right on the Chesapeake. Just down from Mount Vernon."

"Any problems? Any stress in their relationship that you knew of?"

McGee looked at him. "No."

"How about at work? Any problems between him and Carlton?"

"No."

"Any problems between him and Lydia Ryan?"

"No."

"Was there anything beyond business going on between him and Lydia Ryan?"

"Absolutely not," the CIA Director asserted, getting annoyed. "I'm telling you, Harvath's not the killer."

Tullis looked up from his notebook. "I have to ask these questions. I'm just doing my job."

McGee took another sip of his coffee. He needed to remain professional. "I know. I'm sorry."

"You've lost people. I understand. But what I need *you* to understand is that until we're able to rule him out, Harvath is going to remain a person of interest in this case. Based on everything you've told me, you must want his name cleared as soon as possible."

"I do," McGee replied. "Absolutely."

"We have that in common, then."

"What else can I do to help?"

The Chief trailed backward in his notes until he found what he was looking for. "When Harvath checked into the hotel with Cordero, he listed the make, model, color, and tag number of the car he was driving. It was a rental, picked up from Hertz at Manchester-Boston Regional Airport, about an hour and fifteen minutes south of here. It hasn't been seen either.

"The AG's people will likely issue a subpoena for the rental agreement. In the meantime, if you can provide a photo of

Harvath, as well as his Social Security number, a copy of his driver's license, as well as any credit card and banking information, you'd be giving the investigation a huge leg up."

McGee's mind, partially cleared, was already two steps ahead. "By law, I can't give you anything from his file, not without a subpoena. But as a private citizen, concerned over his whereabouts, I might be able to get you a photograph."

"That'd be very helpful."

"In the meantime, how thoroughly have you searched the area?"

Tullis pointed to the K9 SUV parked halfway down the drive. "We secured a piece of his clothing from the hotel. So far, our canine unit hasn't had any luck."

McGee knew that detecting viable scent differed from dog to dog. It normally depended on the handler and how the animal had been trained. The longer the scent was in the wild, though, the harder it was for most dogs to pick up, much less track.

"Any blood or sign of a struggle outside?" he asked.

"None," answered Tullis.

"Have you checked the shoreline?"

"I have two Marine Patrols working the

water. So far, nothing there either."

McGee wasn't quite sure how to process that information. On one hand, it sounded as if Harvath hadn't crawled off somewhere and was lying in the woods dying. On the other hand, how the hell had he been able to walk out of a situation like this? Either he was in pursuit of the killer, or he himself was the killer, which was absolutely a nonstarter.

There was, though, a third possibility: that everyone inside the cottage had been killed as part of an operation to snatch Harvath.

But why kill them? Why be so heavy-handed, so excessive? As the question entered McGee's mind, he was reminded of the North Korean dictator having his half-brother assassinated in plain sight, in the middle of the Kuala Lumpur International Airport. Then there were Russia's high-profile assassinations of former spies living in the UK. The Saudis had been arrogant enough to send a fifteen-man hit team, complete with their own forensic pathologist and a bone saw, through Turkish customs to murder a dissident journalist at their embassy in Istanbul.

None of the perpetrators had been afraid to operate on foreign soil, and none had chosen to be understated with their methods. Subtlety and the dark arts no longer seemed to go hand in glove. The world was indeed a dangerous place — and getting more so all the time.

McGee was confident that he had heard and seen enough. He was ready to leave. The sooner he was on the jet, the sooner he could begin relaying instructions back to Langley. Wherever Harvath was, he was going to find him. He only hoped that when he did, Harvath was still alive.

Looking over to where the FBI Director had been chatting with one of the detectives, he saw both men approaching.

"Good news," the detective said. "We finally made contact with the owners of the home across the street. They have a hide-a-key in back and have given us permission to enter and review their security footage."

"That *is* good news," Tullis replied. "Maybe we just caught a break."

CHAPTER 8

Murmansk Oblast

"Hands!" the Spetsnaz soldier shouted in Russian.

Harvath was cradling the moving blanket, and underneath it, out of view, his pistol. Instead of dropping the blanket, he dropped to the floor, repeatedly pressing the trigger as he did.

The rounds struck the Russian in the stomach and in the chest. And as he fell, he fired back.

Harvath rolled as the bullets tore up the fuselage around him. They came dangerously close, but fortunately none found their target.

When the shooting stopped, Harvath stood up and, keeping his pistol pointed at the soldier, approached.

The man was in rough shape. Bleeding badly, he had dropped his rifle when he'd hit the ground. Harvath now kicked it away.

This soldier was the worst of the muscle from New Hampshire. He was the one who had forced everyone, except the Old Man, who was bedridden, onto their knees, in advance of being executed.

When Lara had reached out to Harvath, this Spetsnaz operative had punched her in the gut. Helpless, his hands cuffed behind his back, Harvath had watched in agony as she doubled over in pain.

The Russian then grabbed her by the throat and yanked her to her feet, only to body-slam her to the ground. When she tried to get up, he viciously kicked her in the ribs.

Next to Josef, this was the man Harvath had most wanted to get his hands on — and not in a gentle way.

He could have just put a bullet in his head, ended it, and walked away. But he didn't. Harvath wanted revenge.

Drawing his boot back, he kicked the man in the side harder than he had ever kicked anyone in his life. Then he did it again, and again, and again, knocking the wind out of him and shattering his rib cage. It was only the beginning.

Kneeling down as the man gasped for air, Harvath wrapped his left hand around the Russian's throat and began to squeeze, slowly cutting off his oxygen supply.

A bloody froth appeared at the corners of the soldier's mouth as he fought to suck in air. Harvath kept applying pressure.

He dialed it up until the man's eyes began to bulge and his skin started to turn blue. Once that had happened, he pushed down as hard as he could, crushing the man's windpipe. But his bloodlust wasn't satisfied. Not yet.

Grabbing the man by the hair, he gave in to his rage and pistol-whipped him with the Grach.

Back and forth he swung the weapon, harder and harder with each blow. He struck him for Lara. He struck him for Lydia. He struck him for Reed Carlton. Even the Navy Corpsman.

Totally out of control, he went from pistol-whipping to bludgeoning.

He didn't stop swinging until he couldn't lift the pistol anymore. By then, he had beaten the soldier to death.

With his body trembling, his lungs heaving for air, and every ounce of his strength gone, he collapsed against the wall.

Rivulets of sweat ran down his face. Part of him wanted to throw up. Another part of him wanted to revive the Russian, just so he could beat him some more.

Revenge was a bitter medicine. It didn't cure suffering. It didn't provide closure. It only hollowed you out further.

Harvath didn't care. In his world, you didn't let wrongs go unanswered — not wrongs like this, and especially not when you had the ability to do something.

Vengeance was a necessary function of a civilized world, particularly at its margins, in its most remote and wild regions. Evildoers, unwilling to submit to the rule of law, needed to lie awake in their beds at night worried about when justice would eventually come for them. If laws and standards were not worth enforcing, then they certainly couldn't be worth following.

The Russians wanted to enjoy the peace and prosperity of a civilized world, without the encumbrances of following any of its laws. They wanted their sovereign territory respected, their system of government respected, their ability for self-determination respected, and on and on.

What they didn't want was to be forced to play by the same rules as everyone else. They fomented revolutions, invaded and annexed other sovereign nations, violated international agreements, murdered journalists, murdered dissidents, and strove to subvert democratic elections and other democratic processes throughout the Western world.

If the Russians were allowed to sit at the global table without adhering to any international norms, why would the totalitarian regimes of the Middle East, Africa, or Asia bother to comply? It was much easier to amass wealth and hold on to power by subverting rather than by respecting the rule of law.

But bad behavior, be it by an Osama bin Laden, a Saddam Hussein, or a Muammar Gaddafi, couldn't simply be wished away. There was no moral equivalence among systems of government, their leaders, or cultures. Any society that did not respect human rights or the rule of law could not consider itself the equal of those that did. Cancer was cancer. Only by tackling it head-on could you hope to beat it.

And in a sense, that had always been Harvath's job — going after cancer. When everything else failed, he was called in to kill it, by any means necessary.

Sometimes he was given a strict set of rules by which to operate. Other times, things were so bad that his superiors agreed to look the other way, as long as he got the job done. And he always got the job done, just as he would get *this* job done.

With his strength returning, he reached down and unsheathed the man's knife. Then, leaning forward, he grabbed him by the hair and began slicing.

When rescuers eventually showed up, Harvath wanted it to be clear what had happened here. The Russians were not only superstitious but also congenital gossips. The tale would make its way through their military and intelligence services. By the time it was done being told, he would be credited not only with killing some of their most elite operators but with bringing down the plane as well. If nothing else, they would think twice about ever coming for an American like him again.

After swapping out the magazine in his pistol, he checked the man's wrist. This was the asshole who, on top of everything else, had also stolen his watch.

Sure enough, there it was — his Bell & Ross Diver. Removing it, Harvath put it in his pocket and finished patting down the dead soldier, helping himself to anything of value, including his rifle. Gathering up the blanket, he then returned to the loadmaster.

Though he hadn't been gone long, he found the man worse than when he had left him.

In his hand, the loadmaster held a tattered picture of his family. Even if Harvath had found something to use as a lever, he wasn't going to make it. All he could do at this point was make him comfortable.

Draping the blanket over him, he stoked the fire and sat down next to him. It was bad enough he was going to die; he shouldn't have to die alone. His to-do list could wait.

As he listened to the wind howling outside, he kept one hand on his pistol, one hand on his flashlight, and both eyes on the ruptures in the fuselage. There was one last passenger still unaccounted for: the one in charge of the operation, the man who had given everyone else their orders, the most important passenger of all: Josef.

As he sat there, all the horrific images from New Hampshire began to flood back into his mind, but he didn't have the energy for them. His focus needed to be on staying alive. The biggest part of that strategy depended on information.

Reaching over to the loadmaster, he gently put his hand on the man's shoulder. "I'm sorry," he said to him in Russian, and he meant it.

The man opened his eyes halfway and looked at him. *"Spasiba,"* he responded.

Thank you. He knew the prisoner had done all he could for him.

"Where are we?" Harvath asked in Russian.

In response, the loadmaster simply shrugged. He had no idea.

Harvath held out his hand and pantomimed an airplane taking off. Pointing at the imaginary ground beneath it, he asked "Where? What city?"

"Murmansk," the man mumbled. Fortunately, it was loud enough for Harvath to understand.

Pointing his pretend airplane down, he repeated his question. "Where? What city?"

"Loukhi."

Harvath had a basic grasp of Russian geography, but didn't know Loukhi.

He repeated the name to make sure he was pronouncing it correctly. The loadmaster nodded in response.

Resetting his airplane, Harvath pantomimed taking off and then crashing. Once again, he asked the same question. "Where? What city?"

The Russian shrugged, his eyes shutting.

Harvath gently squeezed his shoulder to get his attention. "Where?" he repeated. "What city?"

"Ja ne znaju," the loadmaster replied,

struggling to open his eyes. *I don't know.*

"Direction?" Harvath asked, pantomiming the plane taking off and landing. "Murmansk to Loukhi. Which direction?"

"Yug," the man whispered. *South.*

Pantomiming the plane's takeoff to its crash, he bracketed the distance with his fingers and said, "Distance. How many?"

The man's eyes had closed again.

Harvath was losing him. "Time," he stated. "How many?"

There was no response.

Applying pressure to his shoulder, Harvath tried to rouse him once more, but without any luck. He tapped him lightly on the cheek. Nothing. The loadmaster had lost consciousness.

Opening each of the man's eyelids, Harvath used his flashlight to test his pupils. Neither constricted. His brain was shutting down.

"You're going to be okay," Harvath lied. "Don't fight it. Just relax." He had no idea if the man could hear him, much less understand what he was saying. It didn't matter. Harvath kept talking, watching as the Russian's breaths became shallower and farther apart. He didn't have much longer.

Unable to do anything but await the inevitable, Harvath's mind turned to a checklist of things he needed to accomplish in order to survive.

In the SEALs, he had undergone extensive SERE training. SERE was an acronym for Survival, Evasion, Resistance, and Escape. If you were caught behind enemy lines, the goal was to keep you alive and help you get to safety. If Harvath hoped to survive and get back home, he was going to have to remember every single thing he had ever been taught in SERE school. And even then, there were no guarantees.

At the moment, his primary focus was survival. Having eliminated the immediate human threats, his most pressing environmental threat was the cold.

Even with the fire, the temperature inside the cabin was continuing to drop. He needed to find a way to seal it off from the outside.

Using his flashlight, he did a quick scan of his surroundings, but nothing presented itself. Heavy tarps or plastic sheeting of some sort were what the situation called for. But unless some were hiding in one of the remaining lockers he hadn't opened in the tail, he was screwed.

He could stack wreckage until his strength gave out, but it would never act as an effective barrier. Like water flooding a leaky boat, the cold would exploit every single opening until it overwhelmed him. He had to come up with a better plan.

Looking down at the loadmaster, he watched him exhale, and then waited for him to take another breath. It never came. He had expired. And with him, so had any moral responsibilities Harvath had left.

Taking the blanket from the man, Harvath wrapped it around himself and got busy trying to survive.

CHAPTER 9

It turned out that the solution to his most critical problem had been staring Harvath right in the face. He didn't need to seal the cabin off from the cold. He only needed to seal *himself* off from it. The cargo container that had crushed the loadmaster's legs would provide the perfect shelter.

Opening the doors, he discovered it was filled with mining equipment. Like most everything else he had come across on the plane, it was totally useless. He dragged pieces out until there was enough room for him to comfortably fit inside.

Tearing loose insulation from the walls of the cabin, he packed as much into the container as possible, creating a nest.

Next, he moved the fire closer to the opening and propped up a couple of sheets of metal behind it to help direct the heat toward him.

As the icy wind blasted the exterior of the

aircraft, he conducted one last sweep for supplies. The entire time, though, he kept one hand on his weapon. There was that one final passenger, the man in charge of the operation, whom he assumed to be an intelligence officer — likely Russian military intelligence, also known as the GRU — still unaccounted for.

Searching the loadmaster and the dead Spetsnaz operative next to him as he had done to the one in the back, he pocketed anything of value that he found — cash, watches, jewelry, and even a couple of condoms.

There was no galley area, but he did find a coffee station. The pot must have gone missing in the crash, so he opened the condoms. Using them as bladders, he filled them with as much of the water as he could and tied them off at the top. Like the missing pot, there wasn't any coffee either. There was, though, a tin with some loose tea, which he took, along with a metal canteen cup.

The most significant discovery came in the final locker. It was just wide enough for the loadmaster to have hung his winter parka. There was a knit cap and a pair of gloves in one of the sleeves.

As Harvath hurriedly put them on, he

looked down and saw a gray sling pack. Pulling it out, he realized that it was a Russian Air Force survival or "ditch" kit. Underneath was a portable emergency locator transmitter — ELT for short.

Carrying everything back to the cargo container, he piled it all neatly inside. Now, there was only one more thing he had to do.

With several lengths of wire he had scrounged, he rigged random pieces of debris and laid a series of trip wires. If anyone else was still alive and was thinking about coming for him, he wanted as much notice as possible. Once that task was complete, he returned to his improvised shelter and the warmth of the fire.

Despite the hat, gloves, and new parka he had just donned, his body was still trembling with cold. He needed to get something warm into his system.

Filling his metal cup with water, he set it as close to the fire as he could and then turned his attention to the ELT.

The first thing he noticed was that it was pretty old. It probably didn't even operate on the current frequency for distress signals. Based on the tag taped to the side, it hadn't been serviced in a long time. The battery was almost certainly dead.

The best thing about it was that it was a portable, manually activated unit. That meant the chances of there being an additional ELT, automatically activated by the crash and currently broadcasting their exact location to COSPAS — the Russian Space System for the Search of Vessels in Distress — were next to zero. Despite how unreliable their technology was, the Russians weren't into redundancy. Any rescue team was going to have to find the crash site the old-fashioned way — they were going to have to hunt for it. Just to be safe, he broke off the ELT's antenna and set the equipment aside.

Next, he checked out the contents of the ditch kit. Inside was a flare gun case, as well as four olive drab, vacuum-sealed pouches covered in Cyrillic writing. His ability to read Russian was almost as bad as his ability to speak it. At best, he could make out only the most basic words.

From what he could understand, the two largest pouches were individual food rations called Individualnovo Ratsiona Pitanee, or IRPs for short. They were the Russian military's version of American MREs — meals ready-to-eat.

These were Cold Climate/Mountain Operation versions, which were calorie-dense, and meant to see a soldier through an entire twenty-four-hour period.

Harvath couldn't remember the last time he had eaten. It had been at least three days.

All he wanted to do was rip open the packaging, but he had been trained better than that. In a survival situation, every item you came in contact with could be potentially life-saving or life-threatening. Nothing should ever be taken for granted.

Slow is smooth, and smooth is fast went a popular SEAL mantra, which he now heard echoing in his brain.

Taking off his gloves, he felt along the edge of the packaging, looking for a notch or someplace to tear back the cover. There wasn't one.

Removing a folding knife he had taken off the dead Spetsnaz operative next to the cargo container, he carefully made an incision in the packaging, closed the knife, and returned it to his pocket. He then peeled back the plastic.

It was sharp in spots, and he took care not to cut himself. He remembered a buddy of his growing up in California who had sliced his hand opening a tin of coffee. It resulted in an infection that was so serious, doctors had wanted to amputate the hand to stop the infection from spreading to his heart.

Luckily, he had been at one of the best hospitals in the world, and they had ultimately discovered the right combination of antibiotics.

That kind of luck, though, wouldn't be in the cards for him. Not as a fugitive on the run inside Russia. If he got sick, he couldn't just walk into some hospital, much less one on a par with anything to be found in the United States. No, it was critical that he stay healthy. His health and his training were his two greatest assets.

Sitting cross-legged, he removed the food items and laid the amazing array of provisions on the ground in front of him.

There were six sleeves of crackers or some kind of shortbread-style cookies, with about ten in each. There were also five bars of dark chocolate, a small tin of processed cheese, a pudding-sized cup filled with a chocolate-hazelnut spread, two bags of hard candies that appeared to be caramel, a cherry-flavored drink mix, one multivitamin, two servings of instant coffee, a tea bag, two pouches of dried muesli with dehydrated milk, a nut-and-fruit bar, and a packet of applesauce.

In addition, there were three Army-green

plastic spoons, six antiseptic wet naps —
half were formulated for cleaning utensils
and the other half for cleansing human skin
— three paper napkins, paper sleeves of
pepper and salt, and six rather large packets
of sugar with twenty grams in each.

An ingenious piece of lightweight ma-
chined metal, no bigger and not much
thicker than a playing card, was included
and could be bent into a tiny camp stove
that stood on three legs. Along with it came
three hexamine fire tablets, five stormproof
matches, and a striker.

Assembling the stove and placing a hexamine tab in the center, Harvath ignored
the stormproof matches and used a lighter
he'd taken off one of the dead soldiers to
ignite it. He used his glove to draw his
canteen cup back from next to the fire and
placed it atop the camp stove in hopes of
bringing the water to a quicker boil.

Turning his attention to the tin filled with
processed cheese, he grabbed the tab and
carefully pulled back the lid. He then raised
it to his nose and inhaled. It smelled deli-
cious. Picking up a spoon, he dug in. It was
one of the best things he had ever tasted.

Licking the spoon clean, he opened a
sleeve of crackers and tackled the chocolate-
hazelnut spread next. He was ravenous.

Everything tasted so good.

Though he assumed the water from the coffee station was potable, he didn't want to take any chances. He let the water in his cup come to a good, rolling boil for several minutes before removing it from the flame, adding the tea bag, and setting it aside to cool.

There were six purification tablets, each individually wrapped in foil, and each good for purifying a liter apiece. Popping one out, he untied the larger of his two water-filled condoms and dropped it in. He didn't expect to tap that water source until he left the plane. By then, any potential contaminants would be neutralized.

Two thermostabilized entrees, one pork and one beef, as well as flameless ration heaters, were also included. The heaters were something the U.S. military used too, but they had come a long way from the water-activated systems Harvath used to know. Because they gave off highly flammable hydrogen gas, the old versions had been forbidden on planes and in submarines.

Like their predecessors, the new, air-activated flameless ration heaters allowed precooked food to be warmed up, in its pouch, via heat from a chemical reaction —

the idea being that if a campfire wasn't advisable or available, soldiers could still enjoy a hot meal. There was, though, something else the heaters could be used for.

Their chemical reaction was identical to that of disposable hand and foot warmers. That was because they all used the same main ingredient — iron powder.

When exposed to air, and assisted by sodium chloride, activated charcoal, and vermiculite, iron powder produces iron oxide — rust — and, most important, *heat*. How much heat depended upon how much iron powder was used. Hand and foot warmers used less and could reach 163 degrees. MRE heaters used more and could reach 200 degrees.

The point here was that Harvath had stumbled onto two, albeit temporary, portable forms of instant heat. There were likely two more in the other IRP. In the end, even one of them might end up being the difference between life and death once he struck off from the wreckage. They weighed next to nothing, and he knew he would never regret having them along.

In addition to the entrees, there were two pâté appetizers, both pork, apparently. One appeared to have been made with pig brains, the other with pig's liver. Harvath opted for the liver. Pulling open the pouch, he went after the salty protein with his spoon.

He had to force himself to go slowly. His stomach would have shrunk over the past three days, and eating too much too quickly could make him throw up.

By the time he was done with the pâté, his tea had cooled enough to drink. He took that slowly as well. As soon as he began drinking, his mind began flashing back to what had happened on the private jet.

CHAPTER 10

Whatever drug his Russian abductors had been using to knock him out, they had an equally powerful antidote to return him to consciousness.

It produced an instant migraine and was like having red-hot coat hangers rip your brain out through your eyes. There was no pain he had ever experienced anywhere near it. That was only the warm-up, though.

His interrogator was a Russian in his late fifties who had introduced himself simply as Josef. Tall and fit, Josef had gray hair that was cut in a trendy, long-on-top, skin-tight-fade-on-the-sides style that was more appropriate for a man in his twenties. He looked like a douchebag, and Harvath had told him so.

What made the insult even funnier was that despite his impressive command of English, Josef was unfamiliar with the term. Harvath had to explain it to him, and did so in such a way that the Spetsnaz operatives understood it as well.

When Josef finally clicked on the equivalent word in Russian and mumbled it aloud, his men chuckled. So did Harvath. It was, without a doubt, a terrible haircut.

For a moment, Josef appeared to have a sense of humor and laughed right along with everyone else. Nothing about his demeanor suggested what was about to happen next.

In a flash, the Russian pulled out an electrical cord and started beating Harvath with it. The blows fell again and again, lashing his chest and shoulders, stomach and thighs. Secured to a chair, he had no way to fend off the painful attack.

It was meant to show dominance and sow fear. Josef was making it perfectly clear who was in charge and who wasn't. He intended to break his captive, by any means necessary.

For his part, Harvath had already made up his mind back in New Hampshire that he was going to kill Josef. The only question was how badly he would make him suffer first. The beating with the cord only strengthened his resolve and lengthened the pain he would make the Russian endure.

And that went double for whoever, higher

up the chain, had tasked Josef. Harvath didn't care if the trail led right to the President of Russia himself. Anyone and everyone involved would pay, *dearly.*

Over the last three days, Harvath hadn't had much time to piece things together. Most of the time, he had been drugged. When he wasn't drugged, he was being beaten and interrogated. They had even waterboarded him.

It was a tactic he had used on prisoners himself. He knew how effective it was. Even though he had undergone it in training, it was still a horrible procedure to be on the receiving end of.

Upon being placed inside the private jet, he had hoped that part of the nightmare was over. But when he saw the four-liter water jugs stacked in the galley, he knew that it had only just begun.

The flight to what he now knew had been Murmansk was brutal. He had blacked out several times. And, on at least one occasion, he had lost more than just consciousness. Judging by the pads stuck to his chest, the automated external defibrillator, and the vial of epinephrine nearby, he had flatlined.

His memories were fuzzy. What he remembered best was how it had all started.

Josef and his men had shown up at the

cottage in New Hampshire out of the blue. Harvath had gone there with Lara to visit Reed Carlton, whom he affectionately referred to as the "Old Man."

He was also there to wrap up some loose business ends with Lydia, one of which involved a meeting with a diplomat from the Polish embassy in D.C.

Artur Kopec was a double agent, working for his own country's foreign intelligence service as well as the Russians. He was a drunk, nearing the end of his career, who had lied, cheated, manipulated, and schemed to get one final, plum posting.

Early on, he had actually been a capable intelligence officer. But as his star had risen, so, too, had his opportunities for corruption. Unfortunately for him, and for Poland, he had chosen self-enrichment over patriotism.

He and Reed Carlton went way back — back to the days of the Cold War. They had undertaken great risks together, bled together, and buried friends together, all in the name of defeating Communism and advancing the cause of freedom.

But once Carlton learned that his old ally had been co-opted, he was left with only three choices: kill him, report him, or use him. He opted for door number three.

Kopec was so sure of himself and so confident in his tradecraft that he believed no one would ever find out he was working for the Russians on the side. He might have been able to fool everybody else, but he hadn't been able to fool Carlton.

Instead, the American spymaster had decided to use the cocksure Pole to America's benefit. Over the years, Carlton fed him a steady diet of quality intelligence — "one old friend to another."

It was stuff that, if the Russians didn't already know it, they would eventually.

The quality of it, plus his access to such a renowned, well-connected CIA officer, made Kopec a star back in Moscow. That had all been part of Carlton's plan as well. The more they believed the veracity and reliability of Kopec's reporting, the easier they were to manipulate. That was how Carlton had used him.

In addition to feeding him a diet of grade-A intel, when it suited the United States, he'd mix in some things that were absolutely false, things he knew the Russians would believe to be true.

The reasons were myriad. Sometimes, the CIA just needed the Russians to be confused. Sometimes, they needed them to act. Sometimes, Carlton just wanted to fuck with them.

When his health began to fail, the Old Man handed the reins over to Harvath. He explained what a valuable asset Kopec had been but allowed Harvath to make up his own mind about what to do with him. Harvath chose door number three as well — using the unwitting Polish intelligence officer in ways even Carlton hadn't considered. All of that, though, was over now. It had ended with the assault on the cottage on Governors Island.

When it came to intelligence gathering, the Russians ran a brutish operation that somehow succeeded despite itself. They were not thoughtful, meticulous savants. They were rats with terrible eyesight and even worse noses. Luck and bravado, more often than talent or hard work, usually carried the day.

Despite their failings, they had eventually caught wind that Reed Carlton was ill. They wanted Kopec to confirm it for them. So did Harvath.

He wanted them to believe that Carlton was so far gone that he was of no value and no threat to them whatsoever. His hope was that if Kopec reported back to Moscow that Carlton didn't have much time left, and had lost his mental faculties, they would write him off. The last thing Harvath wanted was for the Russians to uncover his whereabouts and attempt to snatch him. But little did he know that Carlton wasn't the only person the Russians were interested in.

Playing the distraught former comrade-in-arms, the flabby, white-haired Kopec had kept asking to see his old friend. Once Harvath had felt the time was right, Lydia Ryan had set it up. Never in a million years would he have believed the Russians could set up a snatch operation that quickly. But that was what had happened, and Harvath should have been ready for it.

Kopec had flown up from D.C. on a commercial flight into Portland International Jetport in Maine. A private car service was waiting for him at the airport and had driven him the rest of the way to the island. The car waited for him in the driveway.

When his visit with Carlton was over, he and Harvath chatted, and then Kopec got into the car and drove away, presumably back to the airport.

Harvath had watched him drive off and then returned inside to chat with Lydia. They discussed a couple of items before Harvath saw Lara through the window outside. She had been on a hike and had just gotten back.

Pausing his conversation with Lydia, he had stepped outside to join Lara, and that was when all hell had broken loose.

CHAPTER 11

Having seen the Russians before he did, Lara had yelled for him to "Run!" but by then it was too late. They quickly surrounded her, and Josef put a gun to her head.

In retrospect, maybe Harvath should have gone for his weapon. Maybe he should have tried to shoot his way out. If they had taken him down, perhaps he could have taken a couple of them with him.

Maybe Lydia and the Corpsman would have joined in. Maybe neighbors would have heard the shots and called the police. Maybe his taking a risk would have saved the others. They were questions that would haunt him for the rest of his life.

The one question he didn't need answered was why he had acted as he did — why hadn't he pulled his weapon and risked everything?

Years before he had met Lara, there had

been someone else, someone as near to perfect as he had ever known. But because of him, she had taken a bullet to the head.

An assassin, looking to settle a terrible score, had targeted her out of revenge. Miraculously, she had survived, but in almost constant, unimaginable pain. Her one last act of love for Harvath was to leave him, so he could start over again with someone who could give him what she knew she never could — a family.

He had been racked with guilt and heart-broken on top of it. He would have done anything to ease her suffering. He would have taken it all upon himself if he could have, but that just wasn't possible.

Instead, all Harvath could do was relive over and over again what had happened to her, finding new ways each time to blame himself. It was a terrible form of self-torture.

Slowly, though, his pain at losing her began to dissipate, though the guilt for what he had caused would never fully go away.

As a kind of perverse therapy, he threw himself into his work. He became more brutal with those who had committed evil, blurring the line between him and them. It wasn't healthy. And although he told himself he could compartmentalize anything, this thing he couldn't.

To compensate, he had done what everyone else he'd ever known in his line of work did — he had retreated further into himself, shrinking his circle of friends, drinking more, and playing it all off with a graveyard humor common in men who stared death in the face and kicked it in the balls for a living.

"Better to be lucky than good," he would crack, echoing a flippant saying in the Special Operations community.

All the while, though, he knew that he was taking greater risks and that at some point it was going to catch up with him.

But Lara had changed that. His relationship with her had calmed his recklessness. She had given him something worth living for.

Now, though, his guilt was back. The more he thought about what had happened in New Hampshire, the deeper he spiraled.

Whether outside the house or in, Josef was always planning to kill Lara and everyone else. Harvath knew that. There was nothing he could have done to change it. But even so, he blamed himself.

He blamed himself for being the beacon that had drawn Josef there. He blamed himself for bringing Lara along. And most of all, he blamed himself for not thinking more quickly, for not finding some way to protect her.

The stew of rage and recrimination was eating away at him, now opening the door wider to his vengefulness and darkening his heart.

The more he fanned the flames of hate, the greater the threat to his humanity grew. If he allowed that part of himself to be extinguished, there was no coming back. He would become the abyss he was staring into.

He needed to snap out of it and turn his mind to something else — most important, getting the hell out of Russia alive.

Setting down the tea, he reviewed the remaining items in the ditch kit. Picking up the bag marked with a first aid cross, he sliced it open and dumped out the contents.

It contained a suture kit, more water purification tablets, Russian aspirin, blood-clotting gauze, an Israeli-style wrap bandage, tweezers, six Russian-style Band-Aids of varying sizes, two antibacterial wipes, a small tube of antiseptic ointment, and an electrolyte drink mix.

The fourth and final pouch in the ditch kit was emblazoned with words Harvath didn't know. Opening it up, he looked inside.

As soon as he saw the signal mirror, he knew exactly what this bag was — a SERE kit.

In addition to the mirror, there was a compass, a whistle, more storm-proof matches, more water purification tablets, a small notebook and pen, a silk scarf printed with panels containing survival instructions, more hextabs, a flint and striker, a packet of sunscreen, and some mosquito wipes.

Opening the flare gun case, he examined its contents. In keeping with similar setups from the Soviet days, the kit included the pistol itself and four flares, beneath which was a conversion tube. When inserted into the barrel, it allowed for firing of .45 or 410 ammunition. Two cardboard boxes with five rounds of each were also included.

It was a clever piece of equipment, but not something Harvath anticipated needing. Thanks to the Spetsnaz operatives onboard, he had access to much more effective firearms.

That said, the flare gun might come in handy, so he set it aside. Opening the aspirin container, he popped two in his mouth, picked his tea back up, and took a sip to wash them down.

As he took another sip, he gazed at all of his supplies. They didn't seem to be nearly enough, but they were much better than nothing. He was alive, and aside from the beatings he had suffered, he was walking away from a major plane crash unscathed. For all intents and purposes, he was ahead in this game. *But for how long?*

It was the number-one question in his mind at this moment. Had the pilot's Mayday been received? How long until the plane was missed? And after that, how long until a search was launched? That was the equation Harvath was most concerned with. How long should he stay with the wreckage, getting warm and assembling his escape kit, before fleeing?

The light was completely gone now and the storm was howling outside. If he struck off before morning, he was as good as dead. The only thing he had going for him was that there was no way the Russians would launch a rescue operation in weather like this. They wouldn't risk losing more aircraft. They would wait until the storm had passed.

For the moment, Harvath was safe. But the sooner he got moving the better.

After stoking the fire, he wrapped himself tighter in the blanket, his pistol in one hand, his flashlight in the other. Closing his eyes, he told himself he was only going to grab a few hours of sleep.

He was exhausted and instantly drifted off.

CHAPTER 12

Governors Island
Gilford, New Hampshire

"Pause it," Bob McGee said, pointing at the TV screen. "Right there."

They were at the house across the street, reviewing security footage.

"Whose vehicle is that?" he asked.

"The caretaker's," said Chief Tullis.

"And he's the one who found the bodies?" Militante asked.

The police officer nodded. "The lease your man Harvath signed requires the owners to maintain the property. We've had a lot of weather up here, so he was bringing by extra salt for the driveway. According to his statement, he was checking the gutters around the house for ice damming when he saw the victims through one of the windows."

"Which is when he called 911?"

Tullis nodded. "Six-eighteen this morning," he stated, reading from his notebook.

"Okay," replied McGee. "Keep rewinding."

They watched footage from the past two days. Only a handful of cars passed the security camera. None of them drove into or out of Reed Carlton's driveway.

Then a silver four-door Chevrolet was seen leaving the property.

"Stop," said the CIA Director.

The Police Chief complied, pressing the Pause button once again. Checking his notes, he read off a series of letters and numbers.

McGee peered at the screen and studied the car leaving Carlton's driveway. "I can't make out the plate."

"Or the driver," Militante added.

Tullis rewound and advanced the footage, pausing at different spots, trying to get a good view. From the vantage point of this camera, shooting across the street, the image just wasn't sharp enough. "Maybe they can enhance this at the lab in Concord. For now, though, what we can see is that the make, model, and color of the vehicle we're looking at are a match for the one Harvath registered at the hotel."

"Keep going backward," the CIA Director ordered. "Slowly."

Chief Tullis activated the remote. Based on the condition of the corpses, they were looking at footage from the day of the murders.

"Stop!" McGee ordered.

Onscreen, they could see that the driver's window of the silver sedan had been rolled down and the driver's arm was sticking out.

"Roll it back a few more frames and then push Play."

Tullis did as he was asked.

From across the street, they could make out only the bottom of Reed Carlton's driveway. But it was enough.

As the Police Chief hit Play, they all watched as the car appeared in view, the driver thrust his arm out the window, and then snapped it back in.

"What side of the driveway did they find the cell phone on?" asked Militante as Tullis paused the feed again.

The Chief walked up to the TV, rewound the video, and pressed Pause. Everyone could see the driver throwing something. Tullis put his finger on the object and drew a line from it into the trees.

Leaning in, the CIA Director saw that the driver was wearing what appeared to be a chunky, rubber-strapped diver's watch, similar to the one that Lara had given

Harvath for his birthday. Sport watches were common among military types and fitness buffs, but Harvath's was different. Made by Bell & Ross, it was square with a blue face and a thick blue strap. But at this distance, without magnification, it was impossible to be certain.

Nevertheless, seeing Harvath's cell phone being chucked out the window of Harvath's rental car by a driver wearing the same kind of watch shook him. He tried to keep the exclamation to himself, but the word still escaped his lips. "Fuck."

Without needing to be asked, Tullis activated the DVR and scrolled back even further.

When a black Lincoln Town Car was seen exiting the driveway, he pushed Pause and examined the time code. The vehicle had left the property just before Harvath's car. There was less than an hour between them.

"Any idea who that was?" Militante asked.

The Chief shook his head. They shuttled back and forth through the immediate footage without luck. The vehicle had tinted rear windows and its license plate was blurry. It appeared to be a livery of sorts.

McGee signaled to continue rewinding.

They scrolled back far enough to see the Town Car arrive. It appeared to have been

at the cottage for a few hours. The only other activity was Harvath's car arriving, preceded by the vehicle Lydia Ryan had rented and registered at the hotel. Other than those, no one else entered or left the driveway.

"What other footage do you have access to?" Militante asked. "What about red light cameras? Speed cameras? That sort of thing?"

"In New Hampshire," Tullis responded, "the government isn't allowed to spy on citizens."

It was a good policy — the *right* policy in a free country. Nevertheless, in a world obsessed with surveillance, it seemed out of step.

"There is one exception," he clarified.

"What's that?"

"Our EZ Pass tolls."

"Where, I'm assuming," said McG "you capture a photo of the driver as v as the vehicle license plate as they j through?"

The Chief nodded.

"Can you get us a copy of that foot asked Militante.

The lead detective, who was standir the fireplace, shook his head. "We have access to it."

"Who does?"

"It all goes through the State Police."

"Fine," said the FBI Director. "Let's put in a request. In the meantime," he added, removing a thumb drive, "I want to download all of the footage of those vehicles coming and going from the property."

The detective looked at his boss, who was reading a text that had just come in on his phone. Looking up, Tullis nodded his approval on the footage. Then, turning to Mc-Gee, he motioned for the CIA Director to follow him back to the kitchen.

Once there, he opened the sliding glass door and the two men stepped out onto the rear deck so that he could have a smoke.

Tullis pulled out a pack of Marlboros and searched for his lighter. As he did, he noticed McGee looking at the cigarettes. Shaking one out of the pack, he offered it to him, but the CIA Director waved it away.

"I don't smoke," he said.

"Suit yourself," Tullis replied. Removing a cigarette, he placed it between his lips and lit it.

McGee watched as the Chief took a long drag and drew the smoke deep down into his lungs. He could almost see the stress leaving his body. He remembered the sensation.

Even though he had gone cold turkey years ago, the cravings had never completely gone away. That said, he hadn't wanted a cigarette this badly in a long time.

Exhaling a cloud of smoke, Tullis stated, "The Major Crime Unit team is going to be here in forty-five minutes. The AG and the Investigative Services Bureau back in Concord will want to review the evidence, but a decision has already been made regarding Harvath."

"What kind of decision?"

"They think he snapped."

"They what?"

The Chief held up his hand. "They're naming him as their lead suspect. A BOLO is going to go to law enforcement. An APB has already gone out on the vehicle."

"Damn it," said McGee.

"It gets worse," Tullis went on. "There's talk about a press conference. They want to share some of the details with the public in the hope of apprehending him as quickly as possible."

"I *told* you. He isn't the guy. This is an unbelievable waste of resources. Not only that, but consider the damage you'll be doing to this man's good name. He has given everything to this country. And then some."

"It's out of my hands. This is the AG and

the State Police we're talking about. And besides, you need to see it from their side."

"Actually," the CIA Director countered, "I don't. The only side that matters is the truth."

"That's what they're trying to get to."

"By outing this guy on TV? Claiming, without any proof, that he's got some sort of PTSD? And that he went on a killing spree? That's bullshit."

"So you keep telling me, but the evidence is what the evidence is," said Tullis.

"It's not good. I'll give you that. But right now it's all circumstantial."

"But it places him at the scene at the time of the murders. And now we have footage of him leaving the scene and ditching his phone as he does."

"We can't tell it's Harvath in that vehicle," McGee argued, defending his friend.

"You think it's somebody posing as Harvath?"

"Maybe."

The Chief took another puff of his cigarette. "Let's say you're right. Why throw the phone into the trees?"

"To set him up. To make it look like he had ditched the phone so he couldn't be tracked."

"But what if that's exactly what he did?"

McGee shook his head. "That's not Harvath. And it's *definitely* not how he was trained."

"I don't understand."

"If he was worried about being tracked, he would have used the phone as a decoy to send you on a wild goose chase."

"How?" asked Tullis.

"All he'd have to do is select a vehicle going in the opposite direction. He could have found one at any gas station or truck stop. While there, he might overhear a conversation, or start one up himself and discover a driver headed to Texas or California. It wouldn't be hard to hide a phone so that its signal could continue to ping passing cell towers."

"And send law enforcement chasing a bogus trail of bread crumbs."

"Precisely," replied McGee.

The Chief took another drag of his cigarette. "Or . . ." he said, his voice trailing off.

"*Or* what?"

"Or maybe he wasn't willing to go to all that trouble. Maybe he thought he already had enough of a head start. Or, after he snapped, realizing what he had done, he just ran."

"Is that what you think?"

"What I think doesn't matter," Tullis

remarked, exhaling another cloud of smoke. "What matters is what the AG's team thinks. And I guarantee you, this is high on their list."

Tullis was right. He wasn't the person McGee needed to convince. If he wanted to help Harvath by heading off a news conference or anything else, he was going to have to deal with the AG. Or, more specifically, he was going to have to convince Militante and the FBI to deal with the AG. Absent the Federal nexus, though, it was going to be a very difficult, if not impossible, case to make.

Thanking the Chief, he stepped back inside to brief Militante. As he passed through the kitchen, his mind was going at full speed. There had to be something they could use as leverage.

Then, just as he set foot in the living room, it came to him.

CHAPTER 13

Russian Military Intelligence
Moscow

Ponstantin Minayev glared at his deputy for a solid ten seconds without responding. He was a terrifying man, given to fits of anger and extreme violence. Delivering bad news to him was never pleasant. Doing so any time after midmorning, when he began his drinking, was a nightmare.

The deputy stood uncomfortably on the worn carpet in front of his boss's scarred wooden desk. The large office smelled like stale cigarettes, cheap counterfeit American cologne, and dog shit. Of course it wasn't really dog shit, it was worse. It was a dog shit *sandwich.*

Minayev was an old-school Russian, proud of his peasant lineage and how he had risen through the ranks. He prided himself on his work ethic and was famous for eating at his desk, never once having set foot in the GRU cafeteria.

Each day he arrived at headquarters with a sack lunch consisting of two thick slabs of farmer's bread and one of the worst-smelling cheeses ever produced.

The scent fell somewhere between rotting human flesh and roadkill. It was so bad that it was banned on all public transport in Russia.

Though none would ever have had the courage to say so to his face, being summoned to Minayev's office was referred to as paying a visit to the "devil's asshole."

The joke had been around for so long, no one could say whether it was in reference to the odor or to the General's temperament.

"What do you mean the plane *fucking* vanished?" he bellowed.

His deputy had learned early on to stick to facts. He wasn't paid to give analysis. "It disappeared from radar somewhere over Murmansk Oblast."

"Where exactly?"

The deputy removed a printout from his briefing folder, stepped forward, and placed it upon his boss's desk.

Minayev reviewed the report. "Is this a mistake?" he asked, pointing to the attached map — a large portion of which was covered with a thick red circle.

"No, sir."

"This is the fucking search area?"

"Yes, sir."

The General rubbed his meaty face with his even meatier hand. "Are you kidding me?"

It was a rhetorical question. The deputy knew better than to respond.

"Wasn't the aircraft outfitted with an emergency locator transmitter?"

The young man checked his notes. "Yes, a portable version that must be manually activated by survivors."

"And?"

"And there has been no activation."

Minayev was not happy. "What about search planes?"

"They can't take off until the weather improves."

"Fine. How about one of our satellites with infrared?"

The deputy drew in a sharp breath of air between his teeth.

The General cocked a bushy eyebrow. "What's wrong with satellites?"

"Nothing. But the Air Force would have to request it. Technically, that flight never happened. And, as far as anyone is concerned, our people had nothing to do with it."

His deputy was correct. It was a black flight. There was no record of it, or of its passengers. The Kremlin had been crystal clear.

They wanted all knowledge of the operation kept to as few people and as few agencies as possible. Plausible deniability for Russia was paramount.

As head of the GRU's special missions group, Minayev had had the idea to snatch Scot Harvath in New Hampshire, smuggle him out of the United States, and render him to Russia.

A festering, debilitating thorn in their side for years, he had interrupted countless critical operations and had been responsible for the deaths and suspected disappearances of untold numbers of operators.

The plan was to wring as much intelligence out of him as they could and then kill him.

The order had come from the Russian President himself. In fact, it was he who wanted the honor of *doing* the killing. That was why Minayev had told Josef to leave Harvath's face unmarred.

He could abuse his body, break his bones — pretty much whatever he wanted — but when the GRU handed him over to the President, he had to be recognizable.

The General wanted there to be no mistake in what he had accomplished and whom he had delivered to the President. This would be a high point in his career, and he was going to take it all the way to the bank.

When pleased, the President could make men's wildest dreams come true. Minayev had watched lesser men deliver lesser achievements and be handsomely rewarded.

Having just turned sixty, he had spent more than forty years in the Russian military. No one could argue that he hadn't served his country. Now, he wanted it to serve him.

He needed investors and government approval to launch a timber company, which would exploit the rich forests of Siberia. This was a dream that the President could make a reality, if he was so moved. The General had every intention of "moving" him. This news about the plane vanishing from radar, though, threatened everything.

Everything on the aircraft was replaceable: its crew, the Spetsnaz team, even Josef — one of the absolute best operatives the General had ever trained and put in the field. They were all replaceable. The only person on that plane who wasn't replaceable was the American — Harvath.

If this operation went south, the closest Minayev would come to becoming a timber baron was being beaten to death with an axe handle and buried in a shallow forest grave. In that regard, the Russian President had also been very clear. He was not a man you disappointed — ever.

"We also don't have a satellite with infra-red capabilities on station," his deputy explained. "I checked."

The General could feel his blood pressure rising.

"Retasking one," the deputy continued, "would raise a lot of questions, and not only in Russia. With the Chinese, the Europeans, and especially the Americans all monitoring the positions of our satellites, altering an orbit would draw unwanted attention.

"What's more, we'd be pulling in an additional agency from which there'd be pushback. They'd want to know what was so important about a transport plane that it required such valuable and immediate attention."

His deputy was right. They couldn't risk it. "How long until the storm is forecast to pass?" he asked.

"A day. Possibly two."

"What are the chances of anyone surviving in that weather, provided they even survived the crash?"

It was another rhetorical question, but the deputy answered anyway. "Not very good."

Minayev agreed. But if anyone could survive something like that, it was Josef.

He was a man of extraordinary focus. He would kill and eat his own men if that's what it took to complete the mission.

"How many search teams are standing by?" the General asked.

"Four. As soon as they can get airborne, they will. Each one will take a section of the search area. Once the aircraft is located, a rescue team will be sent in to —"

"No rescue team," Minayev interrupted. "We will send our own people in."

"Understood. Whom did you have in mind?"

"Wagner."

The deputy blanched. Wagner was the call sign of a former Spetsnaz commander, Kazimir Teplov.

A twisted devotee of the Third Reich, Teplov was alleged to have selected the call sign himself — an homage to one of Hitler's favorite composers.

The private mercenary company Teplov created bore the same name and was shot through with Nazi symbolism and ideology. Many of its members subscribed to Rodnovery, a brutish, cultlike religion that paid homage to Nazi paganism in general and the Nazi Schutzstaffel, also known as the SS, in particular. It had sprung up during the collapse of the Soviet Union and its logo was reminiscent of a highly stylized swastika.

As private military corporations were technically illegal in Russia, they were referred to as "ghost soldiers." The deputy preferred the term "shock troops," since there was no barbarity they weren't willing to carry out. And as such, they were useful, especially when it came to off-the-books operations where plausible deniability was paramount.

They were the Kremlin's "little green men," multitudes of highly paid former special forces officers sent abroad to places like Syria, Ukraine, and Crimea to carry out Moscow's bidding without leaving any direct fingerprints.

In fact, when Minayev had first discussed his plan with the Kremlin, the President had suggested he use Wagner for the operation, but the General had politely demurred.

Having been repeatedly pitted against less capable adversaries, Wagner's people had begun to believe in their own invincibility. That kind of arrogance bred carelessness.

Minayev wanted men he knew and whose

training he had personally overseen. He wanted men he trusted and who were loyal to him. His future was riding on this operation.

He also hadn't wanted to give up the prized intelligence asset he was coordinating with in the United States — not to a cowboy like Wagner.

Minayev had been correct to keep the entire operation within his own control. It had been perfectly executed. Harvath had been grabbed, exfiltrated, and brought to Russia.

But despite all of his careful planning, the operation had now fallen short. Never in a million years would he have foreseen the flight from Murmansk to the GRU interrogation facility as being the weak link that would unravel it all.

If there were survivors, though, the operation might still be salvaged. The key was getting to them as quickly and as quietly as possible. Like it or not, Wagner was his best option.

"Should we update the Kremlin?" the deputy asked.

"Are you out of your mind?" the General replied. "Absolutely not. Until we have more information, we tell them nothing. Do you understand?"

The deputy nodded.

"Good," said Minayev. "Now go track down Teplov. I don't care where he is or what he is doing. I want him on a secure line within the next twenty minutes."

CHAPTER 14

Murmansk Oblast

Harvath awoke with a start. There had been a *crash* — like the sound of a heavy piece of debris falling over. *Was it one of the pieces he had rigged with a trip wire? Had someone crept into the tail section? Was it Josef?*

Throwing off the blanket, he leaped to his feet and stood near the opening of the container, listening. It was dark and the storm was still howling.

He had blown well past the "couple of hours" he had allotted himself to sleep. Instead, he had been out for most of the night. His body was repairing itself, but he had lost precious time.

Like the wreckage outside, his fire had burned down. It was nearly pitch black.

Suddenly, he regretted not having dragged a little more of the mining equipment out of the container — just enough to create a space where he could have taken cover in case he had to fight from inside.

His ears strained to pick up any sound that might explain what he had heard.

Had it just been the wind? It seemed stronger than when he had gone to sleep. Maybe a gust had knocked something over.

That was the most logical assumption. But he had been trained never to assume anything.

For a moment, he wondered if maybe his mind had played a trick on him. Maybe he hadn't heard anything at all. Then there was another sound.

This time it was unmistakable. It was a *thud* and sounded as if something had struck the exterior of the fuselage.

But how could something be both inside and outside his section of the plane? In a fraction of a second, he had his answer.

Instantly, the hair stood up on the back of his neck, and his grip tightened around his pistol.

They had probably been out there for hours, circling the wreckage, studying it, as they waited for the fires to die. Now, there was nothing holding them back.

Leaning out of the container, into the darkness of the tail section, Harvath activated his flashlight.

Eight pairs of yellow eyes stared back at him. They had come to feed on the dead.

The dead, though, were frozen solid by now. Not much of a meal. Harvath, on the other hand, was warm. Nice and warm.

Russian wolves were fearless predators and had no qualms about taking down humans. While they preferred women and children, they would take a man if hungry enough.

The fact that Harvath's presence, much less the bright beam from his flashlight, hadn't frightened them off told him that they were hungry enough. They were only feet away and, in unison, began to growl.

Their lips were pulled back, revealing long, sharp teeth. Saliva dripped from their mouths.

None of them moved. They all stood together, staring at him; staring into the beam of his flashlight. He was no stranger to wolves and knew what they were planning.

Their job was to keep him occupied, distracted, so that the alpha could flank him and take him down. That wasn't going to happen.

Raising his pistol, he began to fire. The wolves attempted to scatter, but there was no place for them to go except back the way they had come in.

The only other breach in the fuselage was to his left, where he had seen the Spetsnaz soldier earlier and shot him.

He expected the alpha to charge at him from there, but the attack never came. Possibly, the gunfire had scared him off.

Stepping out from the container, he moved forward to where he had lit up eight sets of eyes.

Two wolves lay dead, another lay dying, and at least three trails of blood led out of the wreckage and into the snow.

It wasn't exactly shooting fish in a barrel, but having them bunched up inside the fuselage had given him an advantage. In an open space, if they had set upon him all at once, he wouldn't have been so lucky.

The question that remained was how many of them were still out there.

Harvath hoped not to find out. As long as they left him alone, he'd return the favor. Right now, he needed to make up for lost time.

His plan had been to leave at first light, storm or no storm. There was still much to do.

After restarting his fire, he went down his list. First was to fashion a pair of snowshoes, which he did over the next hour via metal tubing, cargo netting, wire, and duct tape.

They weren't pretty, but they didn't have to be. All they had to do was distribute his weight evenly so he could stay on top of the snow rather than sinking down into it.

Once the snowshoes were complete, he packed up the ditch kit with all the supplies he had gathered.

Under his parka, he wore a chest rig with extra magazines for the rifle. He tucked one of the pistols into the outer pocket of his parka and slid the other into the holster on his thigh.

In his other pockets he carried the folding knife, batteries, an extra flashlight, and as much additional ammo as he could find. No matter what might get thrown at him, he didn't intend to go down without a fight. A *big* one.

With everything set, he drained the last of the water from the coffee station into his depleted condom, added a purification tablet just to be safe, and then cooked himself a hot breakfast.

He pulled the blanket tightly around him as he alternated between spoonfuls of warm muesli and sips of hot coffee from an additional cup he had found. He knew all too well that the rest of the day was going to suck. Right now, at this moment, was the warmest he was going to be. He took breakfast slowly, savoring every bite and sip.

Getting to safety was going to be a massive undertaking. It would be like trying to solve a blackboard-sized equation, where three quarters of it had been erased. The key was in starting with what parts you knew to be true.

Though he wasn't certain exactly where he was, he knew that they had taken off from Murmansk. He also knew the geography of Russia well enough to know that the nearest friendly country was Finland.

It was all he had to go on, so he had decided to head in that direction — due west. He would course correct as circumstances dictated. In a survival situation, it was important to have a goal.

Staying put in hopes of a rescue by American forces was out of the question. They likely didn't even know he had been kidnapped, much less that he had crash-landed in Russia. The only person who could save him was him.

So, once his breakfast was finished, he packed up his gear and made ready to leave, but not without taking care of one last thing.

Starting with the Spetsnaz operative behind the cargo container, he took out his fixed-blade knife and set about collecting the rest of his scalps.

The body of the dead soldier outside, as well as the man with the broken neck in the center section of the fuselage, had been torn apart by the wolves, but there was still enough left for Harvath to get what he needed.

He hung all four scalps on a piece of wire in the tail section.

Then, just as first light was breaking, he strapped on his snowshoes, picked up his pack and rifle, and headed out into the storm.

CHAPTER 15

The arrival of daylight did little to improve the weather. It was still freezing. But if there was one thing SEALs were taught to withstand, it was the cold.

Harvath had spent more time in the frigid water of San Diego Bay than he cared to remember. After that, he had gone to the U.S. Navy's facility in Alaska, where he endured extensive training in winter warfare and cold-weather survival.

It was no wonder to him that so many Navy SEALs moved to warm climates once they left the service. By then, they had seen more cold than most people do in a lifetime.

Sometimes, he wondered where he'd be if he hadn't chosen a career that kept him glued to D.C. He was a big fan of the Florida Keys and the Greek islands. He also loved Park City, Utah, and the Swiss Alps. He didn't have a "special" place he saw himself in. He had even moved to Boston for a time simply to be closer to Lara and her little boy, Marco.

Just the thought of her sent a wave of remorse through his body. He couldn't believe she was gone. And not only was she gone, she was gone because of him. Once again, someone he loved had been marked for death, and it had been his fault. He vowed never to let that happen again.

Struggling through the snow, the visibility next to nothing, he made it into the trees at the edge of the clearing. Pushing Lara from his mind, he concentrated on his most important priority — putting as much distance between himself and the crash site as possible.

When a rescue team finally did show up, and when they realized the plane was carrying a prisoner who had disappeared, someone was going to start doing some math. Average speed per hour of a healthy adult male in snow would be multiplied by the estimated hours that had elapsed since the crash. A circle would be drawn on a map, and the hunt would be on.

Scenes of a Russian Tommy Lee Jones from *The Fugitive* telling his men to conduct a hard-target search of every "gas station, residence, warehouse, farmhouse, henhouse, outhouse, and doghouse" within that radius played across his mind.

He figured that at best, in the current conditions, he was making three miles an hour on his improvised snowshoes. How long he could keep it up was the question. At some point, he was going to have to stop to rest.

Then there was the issue of where he'd spend the night. He needed not only someplace where he could keep warm but also someplace from which he could defend himself. The image of the pack of hungry wolves wasn't far from his mind. He had imagined something on his six o'clock ever since leaving the crash site. Even in this storm, he was keeping his eyes and ears open. The idea that they could be only feet behind him, ready to pounce, wasn't very comforting.

The upside to the weather, though, was that wind and blowing snow would help to cover his tracks. Without a visible trail, any manhunt would be forced to spread its resources in all directions, leaving more gaps for him to slip through. But Harvath hoped to be long gone before any search even started.

To do that, first he needed to find a road. Then he needed to find a vehicle. From there, everything else would work itself out.

All he had to do was get to the border. *Goals,* he reminded himself. *Stay alive. Stay ahead of the Russians. Don't freeze. Make it to Finland.*

Being careful not to drop it in the snow, he checked his heading on the survival compass and pressed on.

Snowshoeing had one big plus and one big minus. The minus was that it burned a lot of calories. The plus was that burning that many calories was like carrying an onboard furnace. In fact, he had to unzip his parka to vent some of the heat.

The Russian gear he had on wasn't nearly as high-tech as American cold-weather clothing. If he got soaked from too much sweat, he might not be able to get dry. Even being slightly damp would accelerate heat loss if he was forced to remain outside without a shelter.

Harvath checked his watch. Moving through the forest, he tried to keep his pace consistent. After two hours, be began encountering hills, some much steeper than others. Though his hips and legs were aching, he pushed on. An hour after that, it was all he could do to keep going. He was forced to take a break.

Pausing under a large pine, he propped his rifle against his pack, took off the snowshoes, and gave them a quick inspection.

They had held up remarkably well and needed only a few minor adjustments, which he made before attending to anything else. That was something else he had learned in the SEALs. The instructors had been fanatical about it. Even when returning from a grueling mission when all you wanted was a hot meal and an even hotter shower, you always took care of your gear first. It was a lesson that had become a part of him.

With the snowshoes taken care of, he gave his weapons a quick once-over and wiped down the rifle. Only then, with all of that complete, could he see to everything else.

Under the pine, he was able to get out of the weather, which was a welcome relief. Walking for hours with icy crystals being blown into your eyes was a special kind of torture.

From where he sat, he could see that the intensity of the storm had begun to lessen. Visibility was starting to improve. He knew better than to tempt the fates by celebrating, but inside he allowed himself a quick thought that maybe things were breaking in his direction.

Removing his tiny, foldable camping stove,

he ignited a hextab and scooped up some snow in his canteen cup. He needed to rehydrate, as well as to replenish the water in the condoms. In addition to burning a lot of calories, snowshoeing also depleted a lot of fluids.

As the first batch of snow began to melt, he added some of the cherry drink mix from the IRP, along with some of the electrolyte powder from the med pouch, to form his own version of survival Gatorade.

Making sure the liquid wasn't too hot, he stirred it with a spoon and then raised the metal cup to his lips.

It tasted better than he had expected, and he quickly drank it down.

He was convinced that the reason sports drinks were referred to as "thirst quenchers" was that the moment their salts and sugars hit your taste buds, your body knew the relief it had been begging for was on its way. That's what this felt like to Harvath.

After chugging it down, he quickly whipped up another batch. Judging by how much he had been sweating, it was no surprise that he needed to replenish himself.

He took the second cup more slowly, savoring it as he had his breakfast. There was no sound other than the wind and the occasional clumps of snow falling through the boughs of the trees. In any other circumstance, it might have been peaceful, beautiful even.

Removing his compass, he marked which direction was west and then finished off his drink.

Packing his cup with snow again, he placed it on the little stove and stood up to take a leak.

His urine, no surprise, was dark, and proved what he already knew — he hadn't been hydrating enough. It was a luxury he couldn't afford at the moment. Though it wasn't healthy, he had to push himself in order to stay ahead of anyone who might be coming after him. The alternative — getting captured — wasn't an option.

Sliding back under the tree, he spent the next fifteen minutes melting snow and refilling the condoms. Before tying them off, he added what was left in the drink mix and electrolyte packages to each, along with some of his sugar and a little bit of his salt.

Steadily consuming that mixture would allow him to go harder, longer. It would also reduce the likelihood of cramps and headaches. He had to start thinking of it as a marathon, not a sprint. There was no telling how far he'd need to travel before he would feel safe enough to stop.

With his makeshift bladders topped off, he extinguished his fire and repacked his gear. Putting the snowshoes back on, he checked his compass one last time and then headed out.

As the storm continued to recede and the curtains of snow parted, he began to notice signs of life throughout the forest. A couple of blue hares came into view, as well as a red fox. Then, half an hour later, he spotted a lynx, and suddenly, it was decision time.

Fresh meat was a godsend in a survival situation. It also came with a certain amount of risk.

Topping Harvath's risk list was that the shot from his rifle could give him away. The odds that anyone was going to hear it, though, seemed pretty remote, especially as the weapon was suppressed and its retort would be considerably reduced.

He had a day's worth of food left, two if he stretched it. He was going to need every single calorie to stay alive, and to stay ahead of his pursuers. The moment he stopped putting fuel in his tank was the moment his mileage would start to drop.

What's more, there was no telling if the weather was going to continue to improve, or if what he was seeing was the precursor to something even worse. This part of Russia was renowned for terrible storms that could bring both bitter cold and mountains of snow.

He decided the risk was worth it.

Unslinging his pack, he lay down in the snow, picked up his rifle, and balanced it on top.

Without even thinking, his mind went into marksmanship mode, focusing on the big three: breath control, sight alignment, and trigger press.

He wasn't going to take the animal back to a taxidermist, so he didn't care where his shot landed as long as it did the job.

Wanting the easiest target, he abandoned a head shot and focused on a lung shot, just behind the cat's shoulder.

Sucking in a deep breath, he tried to oxygenate his blood and get his respiration under control. Because of how strenuous the snowshoeing had been, his heart was thudding in his chest. It was like running in a marathon and abruptly having to stop in the middle of the race to perform surgery.

The conditions weren't terrible. The animal was in range; visibility — at least for the moment — was decent; and the wind was in his favor.

Lining up the front and rear sights, he

took one more breath, exhaled, and applied pressure to the trigger.

CHAPTER 16

The subsonic, 9×39 mm round didn't produce the loud "crack" most people associated with gunfire. It was designed to be quieter, especially when coupled with a suppressor. The tradeoff, though, was less muzzle velocity — the speed with which the bullet left the gun.

But while it was moving more slowly and packing less punch, it still had an effective lethal range of more than five hundred meters, perfect for Harvath's purposes.

Still peering through his sights, he watched as the bullet struck the lynx and the animal went down.

Then it got back up and took off.

Harvath was confused. It had been a clean shot and should have dropped the cat right there.

He prepared to fire a second time, but the voice in the back of his head said "No."

As a kid, he had read, and watched,

everything he could get his hands on about the great American mountain men. Jim Bridger, Jedediah Smith, Jeremiah Johnson, and Jim Beckwourth were some of his favorites. He remembered even asking his father if there'd been a rule that only men whose names started with J could be mountain men.

He also remembered something else — and it was that something else that stopped him from taking a second shot. In one of those books, or in one of the many movies he had seen, some grizzled old mountain man had passed on a key piece of survival information to a newcomer: Only shoot once. If you shoot again, the Indians will be able to find you.

So, instead of taking a second shot, Harvath decide to track the animal. It had gone down pretty hard, and he was relatively certain it couldn't have gotten too far away. He just hoped it hadn't scrambled up a tree.

Flicking the lever above the trigger guard, he rendered the weapon safe and got to his feet.

Dusting the snow off his pack, he put it on, and then slung his rifle across his chest. He wanted to be able to get to it quickly, just in case the cat had any fight left and decided to come at him. If that happened,

Indians be damned, he *would* fire again.

Slogging through the snow, he arrived minutes later at the spot where he had shot the lynx. There was a bright patch of blood on the ground and a trail leading off into the distance. It wouldn't be hard to track.

Harvath took a quick check of his compass. The animal was headed south. He needed to be going west.

He wasn't crazy about having to divert, but he not only needed the food, it was also the right thing to do. If you wounded an animal, you tracked it and finished the job. You didn't let it suffer.

His father, a SEAL instructor, had drummed that into him. It was not only the morally correct thing to do, but there was this notion that if you left the animal to die, you were inviting a host of bad things to happen.

What those things were, his father never explained. It stemmed from an American Indian belief that if you were worthy, the Great Spirit would provide. And as it did provide, you should take only what you needed. The land and all things in it and on it should always be respected.

His father had been a fascinating font of wisdom. A rugged individualist, he probably would have made a good mountain man. A lover of American Westerns and standing up for the underdog, he also would have made a great gunslinger — riding into town, righting wrongs, and then riding off into the sunset.

All of those things were what likely had drawn the elder Harvath to the SEAL community. They were unquestionably what had developed his son's character and path in life as well.

It was a shame that the two men hadn't realized how similar they were before the elder Harvath had died in a training accident. Perhaps it was because they were so similar that they had often been so at odds.

Following the blood trail, Harvath made sure to constantly scan the area around him, as well as look up into the trees. Lynx were highly intelligent predators. They were known for ambushing their prey and could take down adult deer weighing more than three hundred pounds. The last thing he needed was to miss that the cat had doubled back. He had no desire to be attacked.

Soon enough, he noticed that the blood spatters had changed direction and were heading uphill. He raised his gaze toward the top of the ridge, but there was no sign of the lynx.

Adrenaline and an animal's will to live

notwithstanding, it was starting to look as if Harvath's shot hadn't been that well placed after all.

Ready for any even deeper burn in his legs, he leaned into his snowshoes and began to climb. It was like scaling the back of an icy wave.

Several times during the ascent, he was overcome with the feeling that he was being followed — convinced that someone or something was on his tail. But each time he stopped and turned around, there was nothing there.

Once at the top, he noticed more blood and that the spatters were coming closer together. Based on the length of the lynx's stride, he could tell that the animal was slowing down. It wouldn't be long now.

When he finally caught up to it, the majestic cat was an incredible sight to see. It was a healthy, full-grown male, at least sixty pounds in weight. Black-tipped ears and a short, black-tipped tail offset its dappled, silver-gray fur.

Short clouds of labored breath escaped from its mouth and rose into the cold like puffs of steam from a dying locomotive. The wound, which Harvath had been sure was a lung shot, had been off by several inches.

While only a bad carpenter blames his

tools, he assumed the sights on the rifle had been damaged in the plane crash. It would explain what had happened to the lynx and, fortunately, why the Spetsnaz operative's bullets had failed to hit him inside the wreckage.

He watched as the cat's breathing continued to slow. Its eyes appeared fixed on him, yet they seemed to look right past him at the same time. The animal didn't hiss or growl as they were known to do.

Harvath hadn't thought much about what he was going to do once he found his quarry. Would he take that second shot? Or would he find some other way to humanely finish the animal off?

In the end, the lynx made the decision for him. The cat exhaled one final time, releasing its spirit with its last breath.

After making sure the animal was dead, he took out his knife and went to work.

Lynx was a lean meat that was alleged to taste like pork or chicken. Harvath couldn't say for sure, as he had never tried it. What he did know was that, like rabbit and squirrel, it didn't have a lot of fat. In a survival situation, that could be a problem. You could actually get too much lean protein.

Splitting the animal open, he worked quickly. The only internal organs he was interested in were the liver and kidneys. Everything else went into a guts pile. It was messy work, but he was grateful for the food.

He was about to skin the carcass when the hair on the back of his neck stood up, just as it had at the wreckage. He didn't need to turn around to know why. The growling of the wolves was all he needed to hear.

CHAPTER 17

Gray wolves were the greatest predators of the lynx. Whether the pack had come for Harvath or for his kill didn't make a difference. He wasn't going to let them have either.

Grabbing the rifle, he spun and began firing.

He was amazed at how close they had gotten before his Spidey sense had kicked in. He was also amazed by how many of them there were. He had never seen a pack this big. It was a sea of teeth, and claws, and fur.

As he had back at the crash site, he kept his shots controlled, moving back and forth, focusing on the wolves closest to him. And all the while expecting to be flanked.

Though the suppressor dampened the sound of the rounds leaving the rifle, it was still loud enough to scare most of the wolves into halting their advance.

The other great thing was that the bullets he was firing had an air pocket in the tip that caused them to tumble when they hit soft tissue.

At this range, not only was he able to hit his targets without relying on the screwed-up sights, but it was as if each wolf he shot had been hit with a mini buzz saw. The rounds chewed right through them.

Standing his ground, one snowshoe on the lynx to prevent it from being dragged away, he waited to see if the wolves would regroup and come back at him. As he did, he un-zipped his parka, indexed a thirty-round magazine from the rig on his chest, and reloaded. Never once did he take his eyes off his surroundings.

He tucked the depleted mag into his outer pocket, breathing a little bit easier now that he was topped up on ammo.

Scanning the dead wolves that littered the snow in front of him, the same question from earlier popped back into his mind. *Where was the alpha?*

He had a feeling he'd know soon enough.

In the meantime, he needed to make a choice — wait the pack out and see if they dispersed, or run his ammo down by taking out as many of them as possible.

If he didn't make a stand against the pack

here, they'd keep coming for him. But every round of ammo he expended now was a round he might wish he had later, especially if the Russians ended up coming for him.

As the wolves glared and growled only yards away, he made his choice and opened fire.

He dropped three and was trying to line up a fourth when the pack turned and disappeared into the trees.

Their sudden retreat was followed by an unsettling quiet. Next to the ringing in his ears, the only thing he could hear was the blowing of the wind.

While he couldn't see them, he knew better than to assume they had completely given up. If this was the same pack, they had been stalking him for hours. He needed to find some way to put distance between him and them.

Removing his snowshoe from the carcass, he slung his pack. Then, with one hand on the pistol grip of his rifle, he reached down with his other hand and grabbed the lynx.

Dragging the cat next to him, he sidestepped up to the very top of the ridge and looked over the side. It was steep, which might be a plus, or could be a minus.

It would be a plus if it was too steep, or the snow too deep, for the pack to follow him. It would be a minus if it turned out to be too difficult for him to traverse and he ended up injuring himself. Or worse.

Because of the limited visibility, it was impossible to see how far the slope descended and where it stopped. But as Harvath didn't have the luxury of any alternative routes, this was it.

Swinging the lynx over his shoulders, he took a deep breath and stepped over the edge.

The blowing snow had significantly built up on the opposite side and was quite deep. The incline was also much steeper than he had anticipated.

As soon as he put his snowshoe down, a large sheet of icy snow cracked and broke away.

This whole thing was a deathtrap, but so was going back the way he had come. Avalanche versus wolves — his own Scylla and Charybdis.

Adopting a technique called "side-hilling," he pushed the uphill side of each snowshoe into the slope as he traversed across its face in a zigzag pattern.

It was monotonous, but he didn't have a choice. He couldn't go straight down. It was too steep.

What he really needed to help maintain

his balance was a pair of poles. He kept his eyes peeled and eventually found two sturdy branches that would do the trick.

Tying the legs of the lynx together, he continued, stopping every so often to glance behind him, while constantly listening for any danger.

The good news was that the wolves seemed to have given up, and the snowpack was holding. Half an hour later, the slope leveled off.

Though the snow was still blowing, some of it had tapered off at this elevation. He appeared to be in a valley of some sort with a frozen river running through it.

The ice, where patches of snow had been blown away, was clear, and he could see water moving beneath it. Confirming with his compass that the river ran somewhat westerly, he decided to follow it, hoping that it would lead to civilization.

As he drove his legs forward, he looked for possible places to build a shelter. There were only a few more hours of daylight left. If he had to dig out a snow cave, he wanted the job done before dark. Engineering a fire in such a way that it would keep him warm while also keeping predators at bay and not giving his position away to any search-and-rescue aircraft was going to be an undertaking.

It was a good thing to keep his mind occupied. Too often his thoughts had drifted to Lara, Lydia, and the Old Man, and the rage would threaten to overtake him. One foot in front of the other, he'd remind himself, drawing his focus back to what he needed to accomplish simply to stay alive.

He was fortunate that he had food and water covered. That meant heat and shelter could be at the very top of his to-do list.

As far as what kind of shelter he might create, there were several options. If he wanted to carve blocks of packed snow, he could build an igloo. He could also dig out a snow cave or snow trench. There were enough evergreen trees around that he might build a lean-to with a fire in front if he chose.

The problem with lean-tos, though, was that they were largely exposed. They could be nice and toasty with a fire going in front, but if the wind shifted or a storm intensified, they could become rather inhospitable.

No matter what shelter he chose, he was going to have to hoist the lynx carcass, along with any garbage from his IRP, into the trees, to keep predators away.

The best scenario would be to find an

empty cave that he could move right into. So far, though, the topography wasn't cooperating. He hadn't seen so much as a rocky overhang that he could shore up and spend the night beneath. It was pretty clear that wherever he ended up overnighting, he was going to have to build his shelter from scratch.

Up ahead, the river looked as if it took a ninety-degree turn before disappearing from sight. If he hadn't found a good spot by the time he got there, that was where he'd dig in for the night. He simply couldn't go any farther. It was only by sheer force of will that he had made it this far.

One of the hardest things about snowshoeing was the wider stance. Even if you were as fit as Harvath, hadn't had your body abused by Russian captors, and were pushing only a fraction as hard, the first day out was brutal on your body.

He knew that the pain he was feeling now was nothing compared to what he was going to be feeling in the morning. Overnight, as the lactic acid built up in his muscles, things would only get worse.

It wasn't a pleasant thought, but he had been sore and tired and cold enough times to know he could handle it. It was why SEALs were put through Hell Week. The idea was to push them past the breaking point so if — God forbid — they were ever in this kind of situation, they would persevere.

And that was exactly what Harvath intended to do. Failure was not an option. The *only* option, no matter how bad things became, was success.

It was the mindset that had been drilled into him in the SEALs, and especially at SERE school. He needed to set small, achievable goals — a shelter, a fire, a meal — and then appreciate and build upon his successes. *Everything* was about state of mind and how he chose to perceive his situation. The people who felt powerless were the ones who wouldn't make it.

Coming around the bend in the river, Harvath needed a moment to realize what he was looking at. As soon as he did, he froze in his tracks.

CHAPTER 18

Reston, Virginia

It was when Chief Tullis had mentioned the Investigative Services Bureau of the New Hampshire State Police that the piece McGee needed had fallen into place.

In December of the prior year, a disturbed man had contacted the CIA via its website and had threatened to shoot the Governor of New Hampshire.

In addition to reaching out to the Governor's office and the FBI, the Agency had also gotten in touch with a little-known division of the Investigative Services Bureau known as the Terrorism Intelligence Unit. Working with officers there, the CIA was able to keep the New Hampshire authorities informed of their investigation, which found that the suspect had no known connections to international terrorism. The FBI had also come to the same conclusion on the domestic front.

The investigation had been given high priority, and had been conducted thoroughly, professionally, and quickly. It also, as it turned out, had earned the CIA and FBI a favor from the Governor. He agreed to put the press conference announcing Harvath as their prime suspect on hold.

He insisted, though, that a notice be put out to law enforcement. If Harvath had snapped and then turned around and shot a cop, he didn't want blood on his hands. McGee understood, and Militante helped the State Police draft the alert.

With that task complete, they had convoyed back to the airport with their security details, boarded the Agency's private plane, and flown back to Andrews Air Force Base.

In flight, McGee had contacted the White House and had requested an emergency meeting with the President. He would need to be briefed. And after being briefed, he would need to authorize what the CIA Director wanted to do next.

The FBI's Hostage Recovery Fusion Cell was a multiagency task force, based at FBI headquarters, that pooled resources, data, and intelligence in an effort to recover Americans who had been kidnapped abroad.

There were obvious reasons he needed the

President's approval to activate this cell, most glaring among them that there was zero evidence that Harvath had been kidnapped.

But that's exactly what McGee's gut was telling him — this had been a snatch operation.

The question, though, was who was behind it. Harvath had a list of enemies longer than his arm, all of them extremely violent.

It could have been Islamic militants, organized crime, even the Russians, all of whom Harvath had tangled with on behalf of the United States.

The Russians had the most skill, and a particular axe to grind with him, but McGee was skeptical. Even though Harvath had foiled their ambitions more than once, they would have known grabbing him on American soil like this would be an act of war. The reprisals they had already suffered for their prior bad actions would be nothing in comparison to what the U.S. would do in response to something like this.

The CIA Director felt certain that an undertaking this brazen, with such an incredible downside, had to have been carried out by a nonstate actor. It was the only thing that made sense.

Nevertheless, before the plane had even

landed, he had pulled together a trusted team at Langley to comb through Harvath's past assignments, all the way back to his SEAL days, to see if anything jumped out at them.

Accessing Harvath's jobs for The Carlton Group was another matter. They had other clients besides the CIA. McGee was going to need somebody inside whom he could trust, someone with access to all of the files. There was only one person who filled that bill.

In any other situation, the request could have been made via a secure teleconference or an encrypted email. Today, though, it needed to be made in person. No one at The Carlton Group was yet aware of the murders. It was going to hit the entire organization hard, but no one harder than the man McGee was about to meet.

The man known in international intelligence circles as "The Troll," The Carlton Group's Chief Technology Officer, met the CIA Director at the elevator. Because of primordial dwarfism, he stood barely three feet tall.

With him were his ever-present guardians — Argos and Draco — a pair of white two-hundred-plus-pound Ovcharkas, also known as Caucasian Sheep Dogs. In the dangerous, cutthroat world he inhabited, the dogs were both a bulwark against attack and a reminder of the powerful enemies he had made.

Before joining The Carlton Group, the little man had enjoyed an extremely lucrative career trafficking in the purchase and sale of highly sensitive black-market intelligence. He was a hacker and IT specialist par excellence. What he lacked in physical stature he had more than made up for in brainpower and ambition. He was also a man of particular appetites whose predilections would put some of the world's grandest bon vivants to shame.

His given name had been abandoned to a past fraught with heartache, pain, and abandonment. A quiet supporter of orphans and orphanages in far-flung corners of the world, he had taken for himself the name of the patron saint of children, so his small circle of friends and colleagues at The Carlton Group knew him as Nicholas.

When the CIA Director and his retinue stepped out of the elevator, the little man could read the expression on his face. Something very bad had happened.

McGee suggested they conduct their meeting in Lydia Ryan's office, as it was more comfortable than the Sensitive Compartmented Information Facility, or SCIF, that Nicholas called his own.

Agreeing, the little man led the way.

When they arrived at Lydia's office, Mc-Gee's security detail did a quick sweep and then retreated into the hall.

"Take a seat," Nicholas said, gesturing toward one of the long leather couches. "Can I get you something to drink?"

"Coffee," McGee replied, as he scratched Argos and Draco behind the ears. He had gotten to know them quite well since Nicholas had joined the firm.

There was the sound of ice cubes being dropped into glasses, followed by bourbon being poured.

Putting the cork back in the bottle, Nicholas turned from the liquor cart and waddled over to the couch with two tumblers. "We're out of coffee," he said as he handed them over.

Once he had climbed up onto the couch, he took one for himself and asked, "Why do I get the feeling I'm going to need this?"

McGee had already decided he wasn't going to pull any punches. "Lydia has been killed. So has Reed. And so has the Corpsman who was on duty."

Nicholas was in shock. "When? How?" was all he could manage to say.

"As best we can tell, a few days ago. They were all shot inside the cottage in New Hampshire. Lara Cordero was there, too. She's also dead."

The blood drained from the little man's face as he braced for what he was certain was coming next.

The CIA Director's following sentence, though, surprised him. "There was no sign of Harvath."

Emotion overcoming him, Nicholas fought it back and took a long sip of his bourbon. As he raised it to his small mouth, the large glass trembled in his hand.

McGee wasn't good at consoling people. There were a bunch of things he could have said, but he was afraid they might sound hollow, or, worse, phony. Instead, he kept his thoughts to himself.

He knew that Harvath and Nicholas shared a special bond. They were kindred spirits. Once on opposite sides of the fight, they had been drawn together somehow. Theirs was an extremely unlikely friendship, but it was a friendship nonetheless. And it was deep. Harvath reserved for Nicholas an esteem that he had extended only to men with whom he had been in combat. For Nicholas, Harvath represented something he had never truly enjoyed — family.

Having dribbled a little of the liquor down his chin, Nicholas reached up with the back of his hand and wiped it off. Then he raised the glass again and drained what remained. McGee followed suit.

Handing over his empty tumbler, the little man motioned to the bar cart and asked, "Do you mind?"

The CIA Director didn't. Getting up, he took both glasses over, filled them up, and then returned to the leather couch, handing Nicholas his.

"Who did it?" Nicholas asked.

McGee leaned back, exhaled a tired breath, and shook his head. "I don't know."

"Who do you think did it?"

Again, he shook his head. "I don't have any idea."

Nicholas took another long sip of bourbon before asking, "He isn't a suspect, is he?"

The CIA Director nodded. "According to local law enforcement, he is. Their working theory is that Harvath has some kind of PTSD and snapped."

"That's ridiculous."

"Of course it's ridiculous."

"No," Nicholas replied, lowering his glass. "I mean it's *fucking* ridiculous. Do you have any idea why he and Lara went up there?"

"I assume to see Reed."

156

The little man looked at him, his eyes wide in disbelief. "They didn't tell you?"

"Tell me what?"

"Of course not," said Nicholas, shaking his head. "Nobody was supposed to know. At least not right away."

"Nobody was supposed to know what?"

Setting his glass down, he filled his guest in. "Scot and Lara had gone up there to get married. They hired a local minister to do the ceremony. Reed had been getting worse, and they wanted him to be part of it. The plan was to have a proper wedding with Lara's parents and everyone else a few months down the road."

"Jesus," said McGee, leaning forward. "Who else knew?"

Nicholas shrugged. "Only Lydia. She had to be up there already to see Carlton. Afterward, she was going to take a few days off. I assumed that's why I hadn't heard anything from her."

"Who else might have known that they were going to be at the cottage?"

The little man thought for a moment. "I heard them talking about an old intelligence asset that Reed used to run. The asset knew that Reed was sick and wanted to see him one last time. Lydia was trying to put something together, but she wanted Harvath

157

to be there for it too."

"Did this asset have a name?"

"Just a codename," Nicholas replied. "*Matterhorn. Does that ring a bell?*"

Very slowly, as the color in his face drained, McGee nodded.

CHAPTER 19

Donbass Region
Ukraine

Kazimir Teplov, the man known as Wagner, stood atop an armored personnel carrier, a rifle hanging at his side, and yelled to his team. "Let's go! Hurry it up. I want the plane loaded this year!"

He had handpicked his best men, all seasoned special operations veterans, and all winter warfare experts.

The call had come directly from Minayev. The head of the GRU's special missions group had made it crystal clear that this assignment was a top national priority. And by *top national priority,* it was automatically understood to mean that it was a top Kremlin priority.

The mission parameters, though, were interesting, if not downright unusual.

Whenever the government had used Wagner before, it had always been for assignments outside the country. This was an operation *inside* Russia.

The Russian military, though, had its own elite soldiers. There could be only one reason that the Kremlin wanted mercenaries: deniability.

But with all the active military and intelligence personnel devoted to the Russian state and its President, it was hard to imagine what could require such extraordinary measures.

Even over the encrypted line, Minayev had been reluctant to say. He would meet the plane at Alakurtti Air Base and explain everything there. He had provided only broad brushstrokes — expected terrain, weather conditions, size of force required, and equipment suggestions.

If Teplov had to guess, there was some sort of coup afoot. Though hard to imagine, it wasn't an impossibility. The fact that a mercenary team was being called in suggested that the Russian military couldn't be trusted.

He ran through a potential list of plotters in his mind, men in the Army's high command capable of such a thing. There were more than a few of them.

The plotters, though, couldn't have had much support, because Minayev wanted the operational footprint kept small. His request had been for two dozen men. More than that, he claimed, would be unnecessary.

Teplov didn't like it. Assembling and equipping a team without knowing all the details was dangerous. These were his men, not Minayev's. The ultimate responsibility for a successful outcome would fall to him.

By the same token, Teplov respected the General's experience. The man had not risen to where he was by accident. He was both tough and highly intelligent. And despite Teplov's success in the field, the older man had seen more action in a lifetime than he would see in two. He would defer to the GRU chieftain's judgment. For now.

In addition to twenty-four of his best men, he had marshaled his best equipment, and then doubled the amount of ammunition they might need. Everything else would be up to the gods.

He had then briefed his team on what he knew. They were flying to an air base north of St. Petersburg for an operation of indeterminate length, the objective of which had yet to be revealed.

The men were professionals. They had worked on countless missions where the details were unknown until the last moment. Even now, none of them questioned

161

why they were being deployed on Russian soil. They were almost fanatical in their loyalty to their leader, and would follow him anywhere.

Teplov hoped he wasn't making a mistake.

CHAPTER 20

Murmansk Oblast

It was as if God himself had set down a tiny jewel in the middle of the vast, unforgiving Russian wilderness. And while it tore at his painfully frozen skin, Harvath smiled.

The question of where he would shelter for the night had been answered.

On the opposite bank sat a small, weather-beaten cabin.

No smoke rose from its chimney. Drifts of snow reached up to its windows. There were no signs of life anywhere. It appeared uninhabited.

Now all Harvath had to do was get across the ice.

Fording an unfamiliar river was dangerous enough. Fording a frozen one took the danger to another level.

The fact that he had been able to see water moving under the surface concerned him. It was practically guaranteed that the thickness wasn't anywhere near what he'd like it to be. His options, though, were limited.

He could take his chances and cross here. He could keep walking, hoping to find the "perfect" point to cross. Or, he could give up altogether, stay on this side of the river, and get to work building a shelter.

Compared to sleeping outside in subzero temperatures, the cabin was the Ritz Carlton. It would provide shelter not only from the elements but also from predators. And though it didn't look like much, there was no telling what supplies he might find inside.

There was also the possibility of a road, which he could trace back to civilization. His choice was clear. He needed to cross. The only question was where — upriver or down?

Based on the abrupt right angle the water took, he decided that was the worst place. The water was being forced around a corner, which meant there'd be a lot of churn and the ice would be at its thinnest. He decided to push farther down the bank.

A few hundred yards later, he stopped. This seemed as good a place as any.

Dropping the lynx carcass and his pack, he took a good look around and listened for any sound of danger. All he could hear was the sound of the wind, accompanied by the groaning of the frozen river, and beneath it, ever so faintly, the rushing of the frigid water.

Glancing at it, he was suddenly reminded of a fly-fishing trip he'd been on years ago. They had been working a fast-moving stream with a strong current they had to lean into. One of their party had slipped and fallen. Despite the belt meant to cinch them tight, his waders quickly filled with water as he was swept away.

They barely made it to him in time. The man had almost drowned. It was something Harvath had never forgotten.

Looking across the ice to the opposite bank, he decided to repack his gear. He wanted the most critical pieces on his person. Everything else — the pack, the rifle, and the lynx — he would tow behind him via a piece of cord he had salvaged from the wreckage.

If he fell through, he wanted as little as possible weighing him down and, God forbid, dragging him under the ice with the current.

Within moments of removing his gloves, his hands began to stiffen. He worked as fast as he could, stopping only to take short breaks to warm them.

When everything was ready and he had his gloves back on, he stepped carefully out onto the ice and stood there listening.

The wind still howled, the frigid water still rushed, and the ice still groaned, but no more so than before. *Good sign.*

He had strapped the pack to the lynx carcass and now set the bundle down on the ice next to him. He had about five feet of cord left over to use as a towline. He would have preferred more, but it was better than nothing.

The problem was whether to tie it around his waist with a quick-release knot or pull his gear along by hand.

He still had his makeshift poles and wanted to hold on to them. Most of the river was covered with snow, and he could use them to probe the ice as he moved forward. He decided to tie the cord around his waist.

Once it was in place and the knot secure, he began lightly placing one snowshoe in front of the other.

The farther he got out across the river, the harder his heart pounded. The ice felt as if it was flexing underneath him. His decision to make the crossing was going to be either really smart or really stupid. He'd know in less than fifty feet.

Like a dentist examining a mouth full of decaying teeth, he used his poles to cautiously pick his way toward the opposite bank.

With each step he took, he reminded himself to breathe. Everything was okay. He was almost there. He was going to make it.

That was when he heard the crack.

CHAPTER 21

It wasn't a particularly loud crack. It was more like someone had snapped a piece of kindling. Nevertheless, it stopped him in his tracks, and he stood stock-still.

As his eyes swept the area around him, his ears struggled to pick up any further hints of danger. It took only a moment.

The sound resembled a string of light-bulbs being crushed, as if they were being driven over by a heavy truck. It was quiet at first, but was quickly growing louder. He didn't need to see through the snow to know the ice was spiderwebbing.

His mind panicked and urged him to run, but he ignored it. Instead, he listened to his training.

Casting his poles away, he quickly flattened himself on top of the ice, arms and leg spread wide in an effort to distribute his weight as evenly as possible.

The cracking stopped. All he could hear

now was his heart hammering inside his chest.

He tried to kick off his snowshoes, but it was no use. They were too firmly affixed. Instead, he had to turn both of his legs out at uncomfortable angles in order to belly-crawl the rest of the way across the ice.

Using his forearms to pull himself along, he dared move only inches at a time, but at least he was moving, and fortunately, the ice was holding up.

Arm over arm he crawled, dragging his equipment behind him. The snow piled up in front of it like a plow, making it harder and harder to tow.

He was doing everything with his upper body. With his feet off the ice because of the sides of the snowshoes, all he could do was drag his legs behind him. It only added to the pain he was already feeling in his hip sockets, but he pushed it from his mind and forced himself on.

Less than twenty feet from the bank, he had to stop. His lungs, seared by the arctic air, were burning. His body was out of adrenaline. He needed to catch his breath and regain his strength.

Spreading his arms and legs like a starfish once more, he lay back down. As he did, a wave of fatigue swept over him.

He was beyond tired. What he was feeling now might have been even worse than what he had felt in Hell Week. All he wanted to do was close his eyes.

Instead, he forced himself to look at his objective. Even with the snow, he could see the edge of the riverbank. It was so close — only fifteen feet away. He was almost there.

You can do this, he told himself. *Just a little bit more. You've got to get off this ice. It isn't safe here. Start moving.*

Coming up onto his right elbow, he reached his arm out and pulled himself forward. But as he did, the ice cracked and gave away beneath him.

Before he knew what had happened, he was fully submerged under the freezing cold water.

Don't lose the hole! Don't lose the hole! his mind screamed.

As his arms pulled in wide, powerful strokes, trying to help him resurface, the cord around his waist went taut and pulled him back down.

His gear had fallen in too and was acting not only like a heavy stone but also like a sail that had caught the wind of the current and was now threatening to drag him down-river, *beneath* the ice.

Cut it loose! his mind yelled. *Hurry!*

170

Reaching down, he yanked the short end of the knot, and instantly the water ripped his gear and the lynx away.

He kicked and stroked for the surface, the hole still within his grasp. The snowshoes and his heavy winter boots, though, acted like cement blocks tied to his ankles.

Pull, damn it! Pull! his mind shouted.

Summoning one last burst of strength, he pulled as hard as he could and broke the surface.

Grabbing the edge of the ice, he latched onto it with a death grip. He knew that if he lost hold, he'd slip back down and drown.

Now, all he had to do was get out — something much easier said than done.

His snowshoes, though a latticework of cargo netting, had caught the current's attention and were threatening to pull him back under. There was no way he could unlace his boots and slip out of them in time.

Adding to his predicament, his clothes were soaked through. He simply didn't possess enough strength to fight against the current and pull himself out of the hole. Something had to give, and he knew immediately what it was — his parka.

It felt as if it had taken on an additional fifty pounds of water. He needed to get rid of it. It was the only way he was going to survive.

Terrified of what might happen when he let go, he managed to get one arm fully up onto the ice. Wedging himself against the edge as tightly as he could, he released his opposite hand, unzipped the parka, and struggled out of the sleeve.

As soon as he did, the current caught it and began pulling at it, trying to drag him under.

He wanted to take a breather, to muster what little strength he might have left, but the current was relentless. He had to switch arms and let the rest of the coat free — *now*.

Repeating the process, he pinned himself against the ice and allowed the river to rip the parka the rest of the way from him.

In an instant, it was sucked down into the water and disappeared beneath the ice. He knew that if he didn't climb out of the hole immediately, it was only a matter of seconds before he followed.

With the current firmly gripping his snowshoes, he clamped both his forearms onto the ice and pulled.

An excruciating pain tore through his back and shoulders — a pain that, once again, he ignored.

He pulled and kept on pulling until he

could feel his chest on the ice, then the middle of his abdomen, followed by his waist.

Once his thighs had cleared the opening, he tried to pull himself the rest of the way out, but he couldn't get enough purchase.

Risking a further fracturing of the surface and the very real possibility he would end up back in the river, he rolled over onto his back and used the momentum to pop his legs out of the water.

The gamble paid off.

His legs, followed by his boots and snowshoes, came shooting up in an icy spray and landed hard on the ice.

He thought for sure the force with which they struck had done him in, but nothing further happened. The ice held.

Without energy enough to roll back onto his stomach, he started inching backward, using the palms of his waterlogged gloves to propel him.

He didn't stop until he reached the bank.

Once there, it took every ounce of discipline he had not to close his eyes, even for just a moment, and rest. He knew that if he did, he would never wake up. Soaking wet, with no coat in the bitter cold, he would die from exposure right there. He had to get up and get moving.

He could see the cabin. There was only one way he was going to make it.

Rocking up into a sitting position, his frozen hands no better than crude clubs, he hammered away at the bindings of his makeshift snowshoes. He kept it up until the first came loose, and then the second.

Kicking them off, he rejected a lotus-laced voice enjoining him to close his eyes, just for a moment — just long enough to regain his strength. Rather than succumb, he forced himself to stand.

Though he had no strength left whatsoever, he still managed to stumble forward. The snow was deep, but free of the snowshoes, his steps felt wonderful. It was a minuscule relief, but reward enough to keep him going. At this point, anything that got him to the cabin was welcome.

Based on the feeling in his extremities, coupled with his collapsing vision, he knew hypothermia was setting in. Part of him was beginning to doubt that he could make it to the cabin at all, but he shut that part right down and banished it from his consciousness.

He told himself that his mission was to make it to that cabin. His life depended on it. He had come too far to fail. He would *not* fail. He would make it. Success was the only option.

Gritting his chattering teeth and wrapping his arms around his shuddering body, he picked up his pace.

As the cabin got closer and closer, he spun wild fantasies of what was waiting for him inside. The first thing he imagined was a roaring fire. Next was a warm bed. After that, he saw a long wooden table set with all kinds of food. At its head, he saw Lara — sweet, beautiful Lara, wearing a sundress, with a glass of white wine in her hand, just like his favorite picture of her, taken on his dock and kept in a silver frame in his bedroom back in Virginia.

He was well aware that he was losing his mind. But the image of her kept him going, so he allowed it to continue.

Nearing the cabin, he saw Lara standing at the front door, smiling. Her hair was tied back, showing her long neck. He wanted so much for this vision to be real.

He felt the ground rising beneath his boots. The cabin was uphill from the river-bank. It made the trek even more difficult. He struggled to stay upright, not to lean too far in any direction and topple over into the snow. He knew that if he did, he no longer had the energy to get back up.

Keeping his eyes on Lara, he battled

forward. She looked so gorgeous. And just beyond her, through the open door, he could see that she had a big, beautiful fire going. She had been cooking as well. He could smell it. It smelled like roast beef.

There was also music. She was an opera fan. It sounded like "Nessun Dorma" from *Turandot,* which she played over and over at home.

As he arrived at the entrance, Lara stood back and beckoned him in. The table was fully set. A bottle of wine had been opened. She loved fresh flowers, and in the center was a pitcher filled with irises. He assumed she had picked them herself from someplace nearby.

Stepping up to the threshold, he paused for a moment to lean against the door frame and catch his breath. She stood patiently and waited for him. *He had made it.*

She smiled in that way that drove him crazy. She could have been a model — tall, with a beautiful body and the most captivating eyes he had ever seen.

She beckoned him to join her and get out of the cold. Placing his hand upon the door handle, he pushed it open and stepped inside.

The wind rushed in behind him, chasing away the scent of cooking and extinguishing the fire. It blew away the flowers, the table settings, and the wine.

All that remained was Lara, sitting by the hearth, wrapped in furs. He closed the door behind him to seal out the cold and went to her.

"The fire has gone out," she said from her chair. "You need to relight it."

He watched as she pointed to an old metal box. Inside were matches. From the stacks next to the fireplace, he gathered up tinder and kindling. When he had them going, he added several logs to the fire.

"Take off your clothes," she commanded, in that voice that drove him wilder than her smile.

He didn't want the dream to end, so he obeyed.

As he removed his wet clothing, she pointed to the cot against the wall. "Wrap yourself in the blankets."

Doing as she asked, he wrapped them around his body and joined her at the fire.

"More logs," she ordered, and once again he obeyed.

With the fire burning hot and bright, she gestured for him to sit down in front of it.

The warmth of the flames felt good — almost as good as having her so close.

"Close your eyes," she told him.

He looked up at her but couldn't see her face.

"You're safe now," she whispered. "Sleep."

He didn't want to sleep. He wanted to pull her to him and breathe her in. But she had cast a spell on him, and, powerless to resist, he felt his eyelids begin to close.

The last thing he remembered was Lara helping him lie down as he fell into a dark pit of deep and dreamless sleep.

CHAPTER 22

When Harvath awoke, it was to the fading echo of Lara's voice. "Don't let the fire die," she warned.

Shaking the cobwebs from his head, he allowed his eyes a moment to adjust to the darkness.

The only light in the cabin came from the glowing embers in the fireplace. He had no idea how long he had been asleep.

Glancing to the left of the fireplace, he saw the seated figure wrapped in furs. Even without sufficient light, he could tell it wasn't Lara, although they both had one very big thing in common. They were both deceased.

It was probably the cabin's owner. Based on the way the man was dressed, as well as the rusty devices hanging on the walls, he was a trapper.

He appeared to be somewhere in his seventies, although appearances in Russia, especially when it came to age, were often deceiving. He looked to be one of the Sámi, the collection of indigenous people sometimes known as Laplanders, who inhabit northern Sweden, Norway, Finland, and this part of Russia. Under the Soviets, they had been very badly treated, even forcibly removed from their lands. The resentment and hostility lingered to this day.

Getting up from the floor, Harvath moved in for a closer look.

There was no apparent trauma. The man had probably died from a heart attack. How long ago was anyone's guess. The subzero temperatures would have helped to preserve the body.

Turning his attention to the fire, he threw on a couple of logs. They were well seasoned and caught instantly. With the increasing heat and additional light, he could reconnoiter the rest of the space.

The first thing he noticed were his boots and the pile of wet clothes nearby. He remembered falling through the ice, but not much after that. It was as if he had witnessed it at a distance, as if it had happened to someone else.

He knew what hypothermia and severe cold could do to a person. He was incredibly fortunate not only to have survived the river but also to have made it to the cabin. How he'd had the presence of mind to get a fire going and get out of his wet clothes was beyond him. Somebody, somewhere, he figured, was watching out for him.

In a space that appeared to be used for preparing food, he found a bucket of water almost completely frozen. What small portion had thawed had probably done so in response to the gradual warming of the cabin from the fireplace. Until this moment, he'd had no idea how thirsty he was.

Raising the bucket to his mouth, he drank all of the liquid water. Then he took the bucket over and placed it near the fire so the rest of the ice could melt.

Returning to the food prep area, he opened its lone cupboard and did a quick inventory. There wasn't much. A few cans of what looked to be vegetables, plus a little tea and coffee, sat on the shelf. He'd lost more in the river than what was stored here. There had to be more.

Propped next to the front door was an old pump-action shotgun known as a Baikal, along with a box of shells. He placed both down on the table and kept looking.

He found a small toolbox, an old flashlight, kitchen items, and a few pieces of clothing, including some heavy wool socks.

Tossing the blankets back on the cot, he put on the clothes and spread out his wet items to dry in front of the fire. He was almost beginning to feel human.

Removing a hammer from the toolbox, he knocked off a piece of the ice from the pail, placed it in a saucepan he had found, and stuck it directly into the fire to boil. After everything he had been through, hot tea would be a welcome luxury.

Setting the hammer down, he examined the rest of the odds and ends in the toolbox. There was a small container of oil, as well as some twine, screws, nails, pliers, duct tape, an adjustable wrench, and a screwdriver with multiple heads. What was missing were many of the tools necessary for the fur trapper to ply his trade — including skis or snowshoes.

By the looks of the cabin, he didn't skin any game inside. There had to be an outbuilding of some sort. At first light, Harvath would take a look around the property. In the meantime, he continued his tour of the interior.

The one thing he hoped to find, though, eluded him. There was no map, nothing that would tell him where the hell he was. The only printed materials he turned up were two vintage Russian paperbacks and a stack of out-of-date magazines. He tried not to let his disappointment get him down.

Glancing at his watch, he tried to estimate how much more time he had before daybreak. His best guess was that there were a couple of hours left. Once the sun was up, and he had done his quick look around outside, gathering whatever additional supplies there were, he would head out. Staying any longer was out of the question. He had to keep moving. Sitting still meant capture. And capture meant death.

In order to keep moving, though, he needed heavy outerwear. Not only was his coat gone but there was no way his boots were going to be dry by sunrise. The trapper, on the other hand, was fully outfitted.

By all appearances, the man had either been on his way out of the cabin or back in when he sat down by the fireplace and died. He was wearing an anorak, hat, mittens, leggings, and boots, all of them made from reindeer fur.

As respectfully as possible, Harvath lifted the trapper from the chair and moved him to the bed. There, he worked quickly.

While he didn't mind stripping dead Spetsnaz soldiers, this felt different. It felt wrong somehow.

Be that as it may, he didn't have a choice.

This was about survival — something no longer relevant to the deceased trapper.

After removing the man's clothes, Harvath solemnly wrapped him in one of the remaining blankets and, after observing a moment of silence, placed him outside.

"Thank you," he said before closing the door. "I owe you."

Returning to the fireplace, he saw that his water had come to a boil. Using a thick piece of cloth to protect his hand, he removed the saucepan by its handle and set it aside. Filling an infuser with loose leaves of black tea, he placed it in an enamel mug and poured the water over it.

The tea had a distinctly smoky aroma, which was popular across Russia. It was referred to as *Caravan* tea.

It was originally imported from China via camel train, and the smokiness was caused by exposure to caravan campfires over the tea's eighteen-month journey. In the modern era, drying the leaves with smoke created the flavor.

The closest comparison was Chinese Lapsang Souchong — a tea Lara loved, but whose name Harvath had always felt sounded too pretentious for him to say. Literature professors could order Lapsang Souchong. Navy SEALs? Not so much.

That didn't mean he didn't enjoy drinking it. Whenever Lara made it at home, he was happy to have a cup, especially in fall or winter. The rest of the time, though, he was strictly a coffee guy.

Lara loved to tease him about it, often when they were out with friends. Reluctantly, he would admit to drinking tea, but only the "chai" popular in the Muslim world, and only because it was part of Islamic culture and therefore part of his job when overseas.

As the steam rose from his mug, he closed his eyes and could see Lara standing in his kitchen. She had a row of hand-painted tins lined up on his counter, each with a different kind of tea. Making him close his eyes, she liked to hold different ones under his nose to see if he could guess what they were. The only one he ever nailed consistently was the Lapsang.

Remembering her frustration brought a smile to his face. But it was immediately wiped away by a tidal wave of guilt.

Never again would he be able to tease her, or hold her, or tell her how much he loved her. She was gone, and it was *his* fault.

Looking down into his tea, he wished the cup was filled with something stronger — much stronger. Something that would allow him to forget, if only for a little while, what had happened.

"How does a Russian," he wondered aloud about the dead man, "even in the middle of nowhere, not have a bottle of vodka?"

He waited, but of course the man outside didn't answer.

Walking over to the cupboard, Harvath attempted to identify the cans of food.

As best he could tell, there were carrots, beets, potatoes, and something that might be pickled cabbage. They offered some nutritional value, but not much. He tried not to think of all the food he had lost in the river.

Instead, he worked on being thankful for what he had — the cabin, a fire, and dry clothes immediately came to mind.

Looking over at the corpse, he also realized that he was thankful to be alive. He wasn't out of the woods, not by a long shot, but he was alive. And as long as he was alive, there was hope.

But hope for what? *Escape? Revenge?* Were those the only things worth living for?

He neither knew nor cared. It was his training and his instinct to survive that were pushing him, dictating what should be done next.

There was a kerosene lamp hanging from one of the rafters. Taking it down, he gave it a shake and sloshed the liquid around inside. *Full.*

He set it on the table next to the shotgun and walked over to the fireplace for the matches. *Small tasks,* he reminded himself. *Small victories.* That was the key to staying positive and staying alive in a survival situation. Everything came down to attitude. With the right attitude, anything was possible.

Adjusting the wick, he lit the lamp and lowered its glass chimney. It was amazing how much light it produced. Out of caution, he decided to drape the blankets over the windows. Even the flame from a lone, flickering candle could be seen from miles away.

Returning to the table, he emptied the box, as well as the shotgun, and examined each of the shells. They were the correct gauge, and all appeared to be in good shape.

After placing them aside, he fieldstripped the shotgun, cleaning and lubricating it as best he could with the materials he had available.

It didn't require much work. The Baikal's owner had taken good care of it. Reassembling the weapon, he loaded it and leaned it up against the wall.

Brewing another cup of tea, he dumped a can of potatoes into the saucepan. And as he got to work on breakfast, he tried to keep his mind on being thankful.

Once the sun was up, there was no telling what his day was going to bring.

CHAPTER 23

Washington, D.C.

Spies who stayed in the game too long tended to make mistakes. Artur Kopec had been in the game too long.

The old spy was on his last posting. It was a plum assignment for the Agencja Wywiadu, Poland's foreign intelligence service. Based in the Polish embassy, he enjoyed official cover and diplomatic immunity, which was why Bob McGee had put Nicholas in charge of snatching him.

To his credit, Kopec didn't fight. He was too old, too tired, and too out of shape to put up any resistance.

To *his* credit, Nicholas had done the deed himself and had shown up in person. Along with him, of course, were his dogs, as well as several of The Carlton Group's top operatives.

It was a sign of respect, something Kopec appreciated. Why, though, the little man had gone to such extremes was beyond him. He was old friends with Reed Carlton, quite enamored with Lydia Ryan, and fond of Scot Harvath. A call suggesting any of them needed anything would have brought him to their offices posthaste.

Nicholas, though, had a shockproof bullshit detector. And now that he knew who Kopec was, he knew he was full of it.

Yesterday, when McGee had asked to meet with Nicholas in Lydia's office, it wasn't just so they could be more comfortable. In case anything ever happened to her, she had given her former boss and mentor the code to her safe. Inside was an array of sealed envelopes, hard drives, paper files, journals, and binders full of information.

Removing one such binder, McGee had handed it to Nicholas as he explained who the Polish intelligence operative really was.

Codenamed Matterhorn, Artur Kopec was one of America's greatest weapons against the Russians.

He was a double agent. He worked for Poland, but his deeper loyalty was to his paymasters in Russia. Over the years, he had grown rich feeding Moscow sensitive intelligence, particularly about NATO and its member states.

Reed Carlton had uncovered him, but

instead of turning Kopec in, he had convinced the United States to turn the Polish spy to their advantage.

The two had worked together on multiple allied assignments and had developed a strong affinity for each other. There was even trust between them. But once the Pole's duplicity had become known, all of that was over.

Carlton being Carlton, the experienced spymaster had figured out a way to use their friendship to his advantage. Not only did he maintain his relationship with Kopec but he also continued to share information with him.

For the plan to be successful, though, the information had to be authentic and, at times, even damaging to NATO and the West. It was the only way to ensure that Moscow continued to place high value on the intel the Pole gave them. Which was exactly what had happened.

Kopec was considered a source of such high quality that eventually his reporting was briefed directly to the Russian President himself. He was their "golden bird." Carlton had built a covert pipeline right into the Kremlin.

It was quite a feat. But Carlton hadn't stopped there.

In an effort to rattle the Russians and to erode confidence in their sources, he had leaked the existence of Matterhorn. It wasn't anything in great detail, simply that a high-level Western asset being run by Russian intelligence as a double agent was actually a triple, feeding them bogus information.

It drove the Russians crazy. None of their intelligence operatives knew who had the rotten source. They wasted countless man-hours interrogating their assets, fraying relationships, and creating an all-around toxic environment of distrust and suspicion.

The best thing about it was that Kopec didn't even know he was being used. No matter how many times his handler had quizzed him, his answers had never wavered. No one in Russian intelligence had any reason to distrust him.

So, having survived the crucible, Matterhorn had become even more valuable to both Russia and the United States.

This meant that whatever Nicholas decided to do with him, he had to be very careful.

"Wait," the little man had said, confused. "How is this my call?"

In addition to the binder on Matterhorn, McGee had removed one additional item from the safe — an envelope with McGee's name on it.

Inside was a cover letter from Ryan, along with a sheaf of legal documents signed by Reed Carlton.

Nicholas had always assumed that if anything happened to Lydia Ryan, leadership of the organization would pass to Scot Harvath. And if anything happened to Harvath, control would pass to the company's Chief Financial Officer.

Based on the documents McGee now showed him, he had been right on the first two candidates in the line of succession, but when it came to the third, Carlton had someone much different from the CFO in mind.

Nicholas was stunned. "He wanted me to take charge? Of all this?"

"He obviously thought you were up to the task."

Nicholas didn't know what to say. He didn't actually need to say anything. Carlton had shown tremendous faith in him. McGee knew Nicholas wouldn't disappoint any of them — especially Harvath, whose life depended on the decisions they needed to make.

The moment Nicholas had revealed that Kopec had been at the safe house, McGee had his answer to who had been behind the attack. It was the Russians. He was certain of it. But before he could move forward, they needed proof, and Kopec was the key.

Nicholas and McGee had then discussed strategies, some more radical than others. Each posed considerable risk.

In the end, Nicholas chose the least elegant but most direct path. They didn't have time to screw around. Harvath was worth a thousand Matterhorns.

Now, here he was, face-to-face with Kopec — two master craftsmen, skilled in the art of deception.

Nicholas, with his short, dark hair and close-cropped beard, stared at the jowly, clean-shaven Pole, with his white hair and bulbous nose.

Physically, they couldn't have been more different, but appetite-wise, they had much in common, which was exactly how Nicholas had lured him out into the open.

As a diplomat, discretion was top of the list for someone like Kopec. With only a couple of hours of hacking, Nicholas had been able to learn that in addition to being overweight, the Pole suffered from alcoholism and cataracts, and had a two-pack-a-day smoking habit, high blood pressure, high cholesterol, and symptoms indicative of the onset of diabetes.

The only reason the Polish government didn't know this was that he was bribing a doctor to keep all of it out of his official file and away from the attention of his supervisors.

Artur Kopec was a man with many secrets — exactly the kind of target Nicholas liked. Secrets were vulnerabilities, points upon which pressure could be applied and, if necessary, into which blades could be thrust.

For the moment, though, they wanted Kopec to believe that despite the manner in which he had been picked up, he was safe, among friends.

"I don't understand," said the Pole as he was shown into Lydia's office. Nicholas then commanded the dogs to lie down, and the guards were dismissed.

"Neither do we," the little man responded, walking over to the bar cart. "Vodka?"

Kopec nodded. "Neat."

Nicholas prepared their drinks and, as he had done with McGee, handed both to his guest as he leaped up onto the couch to join him.

"I'm sorry for the drama," said the little man as he reached out and accepted his glass. "You were being watched."

"I was? By whom?"

"By whom? Everybody. Do you not know what has happened?"

Kopec looked at Nicholas, completely clueless. "I have no idea."

This time, the little man believed him. "Reed and Lydia are dead."

"Dead?" he replied, shock written across his face. "What happened?"

"We don't have all the details yet. I understand you went to visit Reed not too long ago?"

"Is that why I'm here?"

Nicholas took a sip of his drink and nodded. "There's video of you leaving his cottage in New Hampshire shortly before the murders took place."

"Murders?" he replied, even more agitated.

"Along with his nurse and Harvath's wife."

"Harvath was married?"

Nicholas nodded. "They had gotten married earlier that day, before you arrived. Harvath wanted to do it before Reed had fully slipped away."

"He didn't mention it."

The little man smiled. It was good to have Kopec on record as having been there. "Harvath isn't much of a talker," he replied. "More of a doer."

Kopec sat expressionless, drink in hand.

"What happened to him? To his wife?"

"The wife is dead. Reed's nurse is also dead."

"Oh my God. I'm so sorry. What about Harvath?"

"We don't know. That's what I was hoping you could tell us."

The Pole looked at him, confused. "Me?"

"Like I said, *everybody* is looking for you, Artur — the FBI, CIA, DSS, all of them. But they didn't find you. I did."

"Is that good?"

Nicholas smiled again. "I think you can end up being the hero in all of this. There could even be a White House visit and possibly a Presidential Medal of Freedom."

It was an attractive offer, and one that appealed to his vanity, but it would take a lot more than a medal and a visit with the American President to pay for the villa he wanted in the south of France.

That required cash, and lots of it — which was where the Russians came in. As long as he continued to do what he was told, they would continue to keep the money flowing.

Those payments were his retirement plan. He had no intention of taking a flamethrower to the goose that laid the golden eggs.

"There's no need for a medal," he replied.

"All I want to do is help."

For an intelligence operative, Kopec was a terrible liar. Nevertheless, Nicholas played along. "Who knew you were going up to New Hampshire?"

The Pole pretended to think for a moment. "Everything was coordinated through Lydia. I assumed she and Harvath were the only ones who knew."

"Did you tell anyone else about the trip?"

"No," Kopec replied with a shake of his head. "Not a soul."

More lies.

Nicholas wanted to put a bullet in him. Or, better yet, he wanted to set the dogs on him, wait for his confession, and *then* put a bullet in him.

But that wasn't what he and McGee had agreed to. If nothing else, Nicholas was a man of his word. It was time to stop playing games.

Removing a folder from behind one of the cushions, he handed it to Kopec and said, "There's something we need to talk about."

CHAPTER 24

Alakurtti Air Base
Murmansk Oblast

The Alakurtti Air Base was located near the southern boundary of the Murmansk Oblast, fifty kilometers from the Finnish border. It was home to Russia's Fourth Naval Bomber Regiment and the 485th Independent Helicopter Regiment.

General Minayev was already waiting for Teplov when his enormous cargo plane from Ukraine touched down and taxied into the hangar.

Though it was a highly secure military airfield, Minayev preferred to keep the presence of the Wagner mercenaries as quiet as possible. Not even a ground crew had been allowed inside.

When the aircraft's loading ramp dropped, the first thing the General saw was Teplov.

He was the picture of an elite Russian commando — tall and muscular, with thick veins that snaked under his skin like ropes. His body was marbleized with scar tissue, a testament to his years of combat.

Calling out orders to his men, he stepped down the ramp and greeted Minayev. "What's the latest?"

"Follow me," the General replied, returning the mercenary's salute.

At the rear of the hangar was a large ready room that had been temporarily converted into an operations center. It was staffed by a handful of trusted GRU personnel Minayev had brought along from Moscow.

Tacked to one of the walls was a large map of the Murmansk Oblast. A grid, marked out in red grease pencil, defined a search area. Teplov helped himself to a cup of coffee and then stood back to study the map.

"What are we looking for?"

"One of our transport planes," said Minayev, picking up a picture of the Antonov An-74 aircraft and taping it to the wall next to the map, "took off from Murmansk two days ago and disappeared in bad weather."

"No emergency beacon?"

"It carried a manual beacon. Never activated."

"What was this plane transporting?"

The General picked up another photograph, this one of a man in restraints, and taped it beneath. "An American intelligence operative."

Teplov looked at the name under the photograph. "Scot Harvath. Should I know him?"

"The Kremlin knows him. That's all that matters."

"What can you tell me about him?"

Minayev handed over a file. "It's all in there. Most important, he's a former U.S. Navy SEAL with advanced winter warfare training."

"So is this a rescue or a recovery operation?"

"You won't know until you get there."

Eyeballing the search area again, the mercenary replied, "If that's your haystack, I'm going to need a lot more men."

"Our biggest problem has been the weather. All aircraft have been grounded, but now the storm is beginning to pass. We expect the search to start within the next couple of hours. Once the plane has been located, you and your men will be sent in.

"Your job is to ascertain the situation on the ground, report everything back to me, and then await further instructions."

Teplov nodded as he skimmed through Harvath's file. "Out of curiosity, who was accompanying the prisoner?"

"A four-man GRU Spetsnaz team."

"Led by whom?"

"Kozak."

The mercenary looked up from the file. "*Josef* Kozak?"

Minayev nodded. He knew that the two had not only served together but were also good friends. In fact, it was a rather poorly kept secret that when Teplov had started Wagner, he had done all he could to woo Josef away from the GRU to come work for him. "I'm sorry," the General offered.

"Don't be sorry," he replied. "Josef Kozak is one of the toughest, meanest bastards I have ever known. You don't write off a man like that without a corpse. Trust me."

Minayev agreed. Josef was one of his best operatives. The chances, though, of surviving a crash, much less the brutal conditions in the Oblast, weren't very high. "I have two helicopters standing by — Arctic Mi-8s. One will be for cargo, the other for personnel. As soon as we get word, I want you and your team in the air. I don't want to waste any more time."

"Yes, sir."

"And no matter what you encounter on scene, there is only one objective: *Harvath*. Everything and everyone else is secondary. If he's alive, bring him back alive. If he's dead, I want the body. Is that clear?"

"Completely."

Minayev paused to make sure he had the mercenary's undivided attention. He even addressed him by his call sign. "Understand me, Wagner. There is absolutely no room for error. When you reach for a tool, it had better be a scalpel and *not* a fucking hammer. This isn't Syria, Ukraine, or Venezuela, where you're being sent in to spill blood and break things. This is Russia, and this assignment is a national security imperative. Work quickly, work quietly, and above all else, do not fail. Because if you do, I personally guarantee that it's the last thing you will ever do."

CHAPTER 25

Murmansk Oblast

First light found Harvath fed, dressed, and caffeinated. After his breakfast of potatoes, he had indulged himself in a cup of coffee before putting on all of the dead trapper's outerwear. The clothing was snug, but warm.

Outside, it was still windy and snowing, but less so than before. Visibility was improving.

Harvath had walked only a few feet from the cabin when he began to make out the contours of another structure set farther back. From it, he could hear a faint rattling that resembled wind chimes.

He was careful to maintain his bearings. If the weather took a turn, he didn't want to lose his way back. His survival training had been replete with tales of people who had gotten lost in the snow, only to freeze to death feet away from their shelters.

The drifts were deep and difficult to trek through. It was hard to know how much had fallen since he had arrived, but it had to have been several feet.

As he neared the structure, he could finally take it all in. It was more a shed than anything else. Long, narrow, and leaning to one side, it was constructed of the same wooden planks as the cabin.

Hung from the roofline at the front were strings of bleached-white bones and broken antlers. The wind banged them into each other, like some sort of haunted xylophone.

The rough-hewn double doors were unlocked. Pushing one open, he ducked beneath the low frame and stepped inside. Just as he had suspected, it was the trapper's workshop.

It was cluttered with junk, the floor stained with blood. Even in the deep cold, the space smelled earthy and stale.

In addition to a small cast-iron stove, there were two workbenches, one under each of the shed's dirty windows. Upon them were all manner of tools, traps, and skinning accessories. Underneath were crates and boxes. A pile of animal pelts sat stacked in the corner.

Harvath took out the old flashlight he'd found in the cabin and began searching the place in earnest.

Halfway through, hanging on a peg, he made an incredible discovery — *snowmobile keys.* He didn't waste any more time in the shed. If there was a snowmobile somewhere outside, he didn't want to wait to find it.

Tucking the keys into his pocket, he put the fur mittens back on and stepped back outside.

Next to the shed was a lean-to. It was nothing more than an additional piece of roofing supported by poles. It was open to the elements and a large drift had piled up beneath it. Harvath began scooping away the snow, most of which was powder.

A couple of moments later, he hit a blue plastic tarp. Working the edges, he kept digging until he had removed enough of the snow to peel it back. Underneath was the trapper's sled — a Finnish brand of utility snowmobile known as a Lynx Yeti.

After fully removing the tarp, he straddled the machine and unscrewed its gas cap. He rocked the sled from side to side and listened to the fuel sloshing around inside. It sounded like about half a tank, maybe less. Replacing the cap, he made sure the kill switch was engaged, inserted the key, and attempted to turn it over.

Snowmobile technology had come a long

way. The Yeti had a four-stroke engine with grip-warmers, a two-speed gearbox — which included reverse — a twelve-volt power outlet, and an electric starter. Unlike sleds of old, there was no pull cord.

Under optimal circumstances, push-button starters were a breeze. When circumstances were less than optimal, though, you started having problems.

No matter what Harvath did, he couldn't get the machine to start. In fact, he couldn't get any signs of life out of it whatsoever.

Opening the front housing, he made sure nothing was missing and that everything was connected. It all looked good. The only thing he could think of was that the battery was either too cold or was completely out of juice. As with the body of the dead trapper, there was no telling how long the snowmobile had been sitting here.

Removing the battery, he took it back to the cabin to warm up, and then returned to the workshop to continue his search.

The effort turned out to be more fruitful than he had hoped. Hidden in all the junk were some real finds. In addition to spools of wire for snare traps, there was a container of smoked bear meat, a pair of old wooden snowshoes, and a small, plastic bin containing electronics.

Popping the lid, he removed a small Russian GPS device, a portable battery booster, a flexible, portable solar panel, and several different cords.

He tried to power on the GPS, but it was dead. The battery booster was dead, too. Taking a look out the window, he tried to ascertain how much power he'd be able to pull with the panel. Probably not much, but it was worth a try.

Before leaving the shed, he used what wood was available to start a small fire in the cast-iron stove. He needed it good and warm inside for his plan to work.

Returning to the cabin, he set up the solar panel outside, facing south. Then, running its cable back through the window, he attached it to the portable battery booster. Whether it would work or not, only time would tell.

He put another log on the fire and then went back to the shed. Under the lean-to, behind the snowmobile, was a woodpile. He made three trips.

Once he had a good stack next to the stove, he used the trapper's axe to split the logs into small enough pieces that they would fit inside.

That was the easy part. Now he turned himself to the hard part, dragging the snowmobile into the shed.

If the trapper owned a shovel, Harvath couldn't find it. He looked everywhere, but there was no sign of one.

Alternating between a decrepit Russian broom and a splintered piece of plank, he cut a path through the deep snow. It was a colossal pain in the ass.

His body was already aching from everything he had been through. More exertion only made it worse.

Dragging the sled was something straight out of the Labors of Hercules. The fucking thing just didn't want to move.

He talked nicely to it. He talked dirty to it. He threatened it, cajoled it, and made it wild promises. He picked it up in back and dropped it. He picked it up in front and dropped it. Hitting it in the middle, he rocked it from side to side.

Then, all of a sudden, it slowly started to move.

The burn of snowshoeing had nothing on dragging the Yeti. Whereas that burn had been largely confined to his legs and hips, now everything was on fire, including his arms and especially his back. It was like doing all of his least favorite gym exercises — squats, rows, deadlifts — all at the same time.

With each pull on the snowmobile, he let out a loud grunt, then paused, sucked in another breath of freezing-cold air, and repeated the process all over again.

His progress was painfully slow, but inch by muscle-searing inch he got the sled to where he wanted it to be.

At the entrance to the shed, he allowed himself a moment to sit and rest. As soon as the voice in his head suggested he close his eyes for a few seconds, he got back to his feet. Throwing open both doors, he dragged the snowmobile the rest of the way into the shed.

He pulled it as close as he could to the stove and then gave up. "That's as far as I'm willing to go on the first date," he said, closing the doors and walking back to stoke the fire.

Having been exposed to a possibly long bout of extreme cold, the Yeti could have other problems beyond a dead battery. But getting the sled warmed up would make it that much easier to start.

As he loaded more wood into the stove, he wondered how visible the smoke was from its stack. With the weather starting to lift, the Russians would be itching to get search planes into the air. He was still way too close to the wreckage for comfort.

The one thing he had going for him, though, was that the storm had erased his tracks. There was no way they'd be able to track him. They'd have to send men in every single direction.

It seemed highly unlikely, but until a few days ago, so did the idea of the Russians kidnapping him on U.S. soil.

Closing the stove door, he remembered the blue tarp outside. Perhaps wood smoke wouldn't be noticeable, but a bright blue sheet of plastic had a good chance of catching a pilot's attention.

Exiting the shed, he walked around to the side and gathered up the tarp. It was there that he noticed something sticking out of the snow right next to the woodpile, something he hadn't seen earlier because he was so focused on the sled. The trapper did have a stash of vodka after all.

He bent down and pulled one of the bottles from the drift. It was a cheap Siberian vodka from Surgut, but it was still vodka.

First a snowmobile, now booze. If the GPS was operable, he had hit the better-to-be-lucky-than-good Triple Crown. But if his years in the field had taught him anything, it was that things usually got worse, often much worse, before they ever got better.

CHAPTER 26

Bouncing back and forth between the shed and the cabin wasn't very efficient, but both fires needed to be tended. Unfortunately, even with the cast-iron stove going full blast, the poorly insulated workshop remained drafty and quite cold. So cold, in fact, that Harvath was concerned about whether he could sufficiently warm the snowmobile. Without taking it apart, there was no way of knowing what if any damage had been caused by the extreme arctic air.

The battery, though, seemed to be doing better. Resting near but not too near the fireplace, its temperature had greatly improved.

Outside, the sun had grown more visible as the storm died and the clouds began breaking up. That meant good news for the solar panel. Though all it needed was daylight, direct sunlight packed the biggest punch.

Not wanting to drain a moment of energy from the booster pack, he resisted the urge to turn it on and check its meter. He figured, at best, he was going to get one shot with it. The challenge was to pick his moment. If he tried too soon, he could blow all his gains. But if he waited too long, he was going to lose precious time.

Once search aircraft were airborne, their number-one goal would be to find the crash site. As soon as the site was located, a rescue team would be launched. But until the Russians had done a thorough search of the wreckage and the surrounding area, no one would be looking for him. That meant he had time; the only question was how much.

The other person they'd be looking for was Josef. For all he knew, the man was lying dead only a few hundred yards from the plane. Not that it mattered. One man or two, the search was going to be intense. Of that, he was positive.

On his first trip back to the cabin, he had downed several cups of melted water from the pail. Shoveling snow and dragging a snowmobile, he had worked up a powerful thirst. He had also worked up a powerful appetite.

Slicing up some of the bear meat, he placed it in the saucepan with a can of carrots and some more water. It wouldn't be the best meal he had ever eaten, but he had eaten worse — much worse.

Placing the saucepan near the fire to heat, he got to work loading up the gear he'd be taking with him. It didn't take long, as there wasn't much to pack. Everything went into a sturdy canvas rucksack he had discovered in the workshop.

After zipping over to the shed to check on the fire there, he returned to the cabin, tested his "stew," and decided to pour himself a drink.

Among the kitchen items he had found was a small etched glass. No doubt the trapper had used it for the same purpose Harvath was now. Unscrewing the cap, he filled it with ice-cold vodka.

The spirit burned going down, but it was followed by a numbing warmth that quickly spread to the rest of his body. The vodka was the closest thing he'd had to a painkiller since popping the two Russian aspirins back at the wreckage.

He was covered in bruises and lacerations from the beatings he had taken. For the most part, he had been able to ignore the pain. It was when he sat down to rest that it was inescapable. The vodka, though, helped, and he poured himself another glass.

Two would have to be the limit. He was still in extreme danger. Deadening his senses any further would have been a big mistake.

Alcohol was also a depressant, and the only thing that came racing back into his moments of rest more acutely than his physical pain was his anguish.

One drink was bad enough. Two, though, and his walls would start to lower. Abetted by any more vodka, he knew it was a steep, slippery slope into a dark, emotional pit. The luxury of guilt and self-loathing was a gift he'd give himself once he made it out of Russia — and only after he gave Lara, Lydia, and the Old Man the gift of revenge.

Sipping on the second vodka, his listened to the logs crackle in the fireplace. It was a sound that often put him at ease, something he associated with home. But not here. Every snap, every hiss and pop of the wood was amplified, a reminder that sand was slipping through the hourglass.

For someone experienced in making life-or-death decisions in the heat of battle, the indecision about when to attempt his escape was an almost unbearable weight. The snowmobile, the solar charger, and the GPS unit had been strokes of unbelievably good fortune, but only if he used them successfully. If he fucked this up, he deserved whatever happened next.

As soon as the thought entered his mind, he pushed it out. That kind of thinking, fueled by his pain and exhaustion, would get him killed. He needed to stay focused. Small achievements. Small victories.

Crossing to the fireplace, he stirred the contents of the saucepan and reminded himself of every positive thing that had happened. Even after he lost everything in the river, there had been more waiting for him on the other side.

The trapper and his cabin had offered up a shotgun, dry clothes, food, and a snowmobile with the potential to get him to the Finnish border. Though it presented its own set of challenges, his situation was unquestionably better now than it had been when he had first set off from the wreckage. He was going to make it, but only if he kept his head straight. *The only easy day was yesterday,* he reminded himself.

Removing his bear meat stew from the fire, he set it aside to cool and checked the temperature of the battery. Not that it would have made any difference, but it would have been nice to know how long it had been since its last charge. When your mind was fighting to remain positive, chalking up items in the *good news* column was like piling up gold in a vault.

As he prepared to eat, he drained the vodka from his glass and set the bottle outside the door in the snow. Even though he had an almost iron will, he didn't want the temptation. Out of sight, out of mind — at least for now.

The older the bear, the gamier the meat. With his first bite, he could tell he was in old-age territory. There were a lot of ingredients that might have improved the taste — Worcestershire sauce, balsamic vinegar, even orange juice — none of which he had. But instead of focusing on the terrible taste, he tried to remain grateful for the nourishment and focus on what his next steps were going to be.

The snowmobile didn't have a full tank of gas, but he had found one jerry can of reserve. Unless there were others he had missed, it had to be enough fuel to get the trapper to civilization. If he could get the sled started, and with it the GPS, he hoped to definitively answer the question.

But civilization didn't mean redemption. Civilization represented opportunity. Depending on how far it was to Finland, he could either revert to his original idea of stealing a car, or, if he could handle the prolonged cold, steal enough gas to get him to the border. Either way, fuel was going to be an issue.

Driving up to a gas station was out of the question. It didn't matter that one of the things not lost in the river was the currency he had taken off the dead Spetsnaz operatives. He had to avoid all interactions. It took only one grocery store clerk, one hotel manager, or one gas station attendant to blow the whistle on him. His SERE trainers had been adamant: Only mix with locals as an absolute last resort. And when you do, don't mix, but rather disappear among them.

Harvath knew a few things about the Russians. They were tough and proud, more enamored of their past than their future. Their "best" days as a nation were always those behind them, never those yet to come. The desire, among the very young and the very old alike, to return to Communism was startling.

That said, there was an overall distrust of, and even a disdain for, government. It was well-placed.

Little had changed in Russia since the collapse of the Soviet Union. The country was still being run as it had been during the Cold War. But instead of a Politburo, a handful of former KGB people now controlled everything, and they used that control to line their own pockets at the expense of the Russian people.

The contempt that Russians had for their government only grew the farther you traveled from Moscow. Out in remote areas, the evidence of the Kremlin's failures was everywhere: lack of basic services, crime, corruption, and desperation. Across the country, standards of living, life expectancy, and literacy were all decreasing.

Russian President Fedor Peshkov and his cronies had grown astronomically wealthy by raping the country. It was a modern kleptocracy. They lived like royalty, and there was nothing the average Russian could do.

Every election was rigged, and those journalists, dissidents, or political opponents of Peshkov who did stand up were quickly knocked down, or worse.

In Russia, you learned not to question Peshkov or his allies. Survival existed along one path — the path of least resistance. No one in today's Russia had ever taken on the government and survived, much less won.

But as much as the citizens of Russia detested Peshkov, Harvath was under no illusion as to where their loyalties lay. Their pride came from a deep sense of nationalism, something Peshkov was expert at manipulating.

Not a week went by that he didn't accuse America of being the source of his nation's woes. It was straight out of the Soviet playbook.

An ex-KGB man himself, Peshkov was masterful at pointing the finger overseas in order to distract from his problems at home. If he didn't continually blame "capitalism" or "American arrogance" or "American imperialism" or any of the other bogeymen he laid at the feet of the United States, the Russian people might start wondering if he and his government were to blame for their crappy existence.

On the run in almost any other nation, Harvath might have been more hopeful of soliciting aid from sympathetic locals. The history of snitching, even on family members — along with the consequences for not snitching — were so entrenched in the Russian psyche, though, that it barely seemed worth considering. An American evading authorities represented only one of two things: a big reward, or a big punishment. And even the most clueless Russian, in the deepest of the sticks, was wise enough to know what would happen if they didn't do right by the powers that be.

With that in mind, Harvath's plan was simple: stay out of sight and as far away from civilization as possible. The only exception was for supplies, and even then, his search would be limited to the very outskirts of any town or village.

Cleaning out the saucepan, he put on water for tea. While it heated, he would check the situation in the shed. There was one thing more he needed to add to his supplies before he could leave.

CHAPTER 27

The final item Harvath was missing was a length of tube or a hose — anything that would allow him to siphon gas from any vehicles he found along his way. Short of stumbling across full cans that he could just up and run with, this was his plan for replenishing fuel.

Without having powered up the GPS, he had no way of knowing how much fuel he was going to need. His goal was to stop as infrequently as possible — get in, get what he needed, and get going. That was the plan. Whether it would actually work remained to be seen.

After an extensive pass back through the workshop, Harvath found neither a hose nor any tubing. That was a problem. "Hoping" to find a siphon somewhere along the way was stupid. Hope was not a plan.

Think, he admonished himself. There had to be something. Then it hit him. He already

With that in mind, Harvath's plan was simple: stay out of sight and as far away from civilization as possible. The only exception was for supplies, and even then, his search would be limited to the very outskirts of any town or village.

Cleaning out the saucepan, he put on water for tea. While it heated, he would check the situation in the shed. There was one thing more he needed to add to his supplies before he could leave.

CHAPTER 27

The final item Harvath was missing was a length of tube or a hose — anything that would allow him to siphon gas from any vehicles he found along his way. Short of stumbling across full cans that he could just up and run with, this was his plan for replenishing fuel.

Without having powered up the GPS, he had no way of knowing how much fuel he was going to need. His goal was to stop as infrequently as possible — get in, get what he needed, and get going. That was the plan. Whether it would actually work remained to be seen.

After an extensive pass back through the workshop, Harvath found neither a hose nor any tubing. That was a problem. "Hoping" to find a siphon somewhere along the way was stupid. Hope was not a plan.

Think, he admonished himself. There had to be something. Then it hit him. He already

gear, including the snowmobile battery, to the workshop. The last thing he did was to disconnect the booster pack, coil up its cable, and retrieve the solar panel.

Before exiting the cabin, he extinguished the fire and gave the place a final inspection — a "dummy check," as they called it in the military — to make sure he wasn't forgetting anything.

Confident that he had everything, he brought the trapper's corpse back inside and placed it gently on the cot. Standing there, he thanked the man once more. If not for what he had built and stored here, Harvath probably wouldn't have made it.

Stepping outside, he made sure to close the cabin door firmly behind him. The trapper deserved to rest in peace, not to have his door blown in and his corpse turned into a carrion feast.

Back at the shed, he installed the snowmobile battery. Making sure the kill switch was firmly attached, he turned the key and hit the starter. *Nothing.*

Getting out the booster pack, he attached the jumper cables to the corresponding battery terminals. Taking a deep breath, he powered on the booster pack.

For a moment, nothing happened. Then, the green charge level lights began to cycle.

Power!

Reaching for the snowmobile's start button, he applied pressure. Instantly, the machine roared to life.

Harvath couldn't believe it. It had worked. *All* of it. He let out a cheer.

This wasn't a small victory, it was a *huge* victory. It felt as if he had been injected with a syringe full of adrenaline. Instinctively, he grabbed for the throttle and revved the engine. The growl was music to his ears.

He sat there for several more moments, revving the engine and charging the battery back up.

Once he felt comfortable enough, he unclamped the booster, closed the engine cover, packed everything up, and opened the double shed doors.

Returning to the sled, he gave it some gas and navigated out into the snow. He drove slowly, getting a feel for the machine as he warmed up its engine and pumped life into the battery. Then came the real moment of truth.

Coming to a stop, he removed the GPS unit from inside his anorak. Plugging it into the twelve-volt outlet, he powered it on and snapped it into the holder above the handlebars.

It took a moment for the device to make

satellite contact, but once it did, Harvath's chance of survival skyrocketed.

He had a topographic picture of everything around him: what his elevation was, where the river ran, and multiple waypoints selected by the trapper, which likely marked the position of his traps. But more important, as Harvath zoomed out, he could finally pinpoint his location.

He was in a densely forested area north of the Arctic Circle, more than 120 kilometers from the Finnish border. According to the GPS, the nearest inhabited area was forty kilometers away. After that, it was nothing but ice, trees, and snow for farther than the eye could see.

Marked on the trapper's digital map with what looked like the Russian word for "home," the town didn't appear to be much more than a provincial backwater. That was a good thing. Such a small, out-of-the-way location probably wouldn't have much of a law enforcement presence.

As Harvath prepared to get going, there was one critical piece of gear he hadn't been able to find in the cabin or the workshop — eye protection. Snowmobiling through the bitterly cold wind with no goggles, or even sunglasses, was going to be painful. There was also the possibility that if he pushed it too hard, he could damage his vision. But he had zero choice. It was a chance he was just going to have to take.

Though he hadn't yet seen any search planes, he could almost feel them closing in on him from above.

Hopping off the sled only long enough to extinguish the fire in the stove and close the shed doors, he hopped back on and let the GPS be his guide. The feeling of power and movement was exhilarating, but so, too, was his very real sense of fear.

He had at least seventy-five miles to go. A lot could happen over the course of those miles. He was by no means home free. Not yet. That wouldn't be the case until he had safely crossed the border into Finland. And at this point, he still had no idea how that was going to happen.

Would it be by snowmobile? If so, how much ground could he cover before it got too cold to keep going and he had to stop for the night? Was stopping for the night even an option? No matter how bad the cold was, didn't it make sense to push on? But once the Russians did start looking for him, wouldn't the beam from his snowmobile headlight, cutting through the darkness, give him away? And, if he did decide to stop for the night, what if the snowmobile refused to start again in the morning? What then? He couldn't expect to stumble across another abandoned cabin within snowmobile-dragging distance.

His best bet was to steal a car, or a truck of some sort. Actually, his best bet was to steal a car or truck that had a trailer, onto which he could load the snowmobile. He wasn't going to be crossing at any official border checkpoint. The more remote the location, the better his chances, and that meant no roads and lots of snow. Like it or not, the sled was his key to getting out of Russia.

Nevertheless, he knew circumstances, more than anything else, were going to dictate how everything would go down. It was the nature of what he did for a living. You couldn't control everything. In fact, you couldn't control most things. What made him an exceptional operative was his ability to change from moment to moment and adjust to the facts on the ground. He was an expert at adapting and overcoming. No matter what happened, no matter what was thrown at him between here and the Finnish border, he would adapt and overcome. Success was the only option.

With its wide, specially designed skis and higher-profile track, the Yeti was built for deep snow.

Hunching low, to keep as much of his face as possible behind the short windscreen, he prepared to punch the gas. But all of a sudden, he saw a flash of movement out of the corner of his eye.

Before he knew what had happened, he was struck from behind and knocked off the sled. Then a new pain began.

had a length of tubing back in the cabin.

Stoking the cast-iron stove, he picked up an old water bottle he'd come across and headed back. Once inside the cabin, he opened the plastic bin and pulled out the wall cord for the booster pack. The rubber insulation was, in effect, nothing more than a four-foot-long tube.

Fully cutting off the end that plugged into the booster, he then carefully sliced through the insulation at the other end, making sure not to cut through any of the wires inside. Then he placed the plug on the floor, stepped on it, and pulled off the insulation.

It worked perfectly. He had his tubing.

Though he would have preferred a much wider pipe through which to siphon, it was better than nothing.

Opening the toolbox, he removed a sharply pointed awl, probably used to poke holes in leather. Unscrewing the cap from the 1.5-liter water bottle, he pierced a hole through it and then widened it with a screwdriver. He only needed it to be slightly narrower than the insulation tubing.

Screwing the cap back onto the bottle, he threaded in one end of the tubing and smiled. That was it. He'd done it.

In order to give his siphon a test, he placed the water pail atop the fireplace mantel. Into it he placed the free end of the tubing. Holding the water bottle below the mantel, he began to squeeze it.

He heard bubbles in the pail and then seconds later saw the bottle begin to fill with water. He couldn't believe it. It was slow, but it actually worked.

Without the water bottle, he would have been forced to suck on the tubing himself. That only ended one way — with a mouth full of gas. It wasn't necessarily fatal, but it was a level of miserable that no human being should ever have to experience. This was yet another small victory, and he was proud of it. He took it as a sign that he was going to make it, that the snowmobile was going to start and he was going to get the hell out of here.

Draining the tube and bottle, he returned the pail to where it had been and brewed another mug of tea — likely his last one for a while.

He had everything he needed at this point, and it was time to move. The storm had all but passed, and that meant planes were likely already in the sky looking for the wreckage. Half of the day's light was already gone. The sooner he got going, the better. Adding a few more items to his canvas rucksack, he began transferring all of his

CHAPTER 28

FBI Headquarters
Washington, D.C.
The Hostage Recovery Fusion Cell was buzzing with activity. Normally, a presidential "hostage" briefing would take place at the White House. President Paul Porter, though, wanted to thank the men and women of the Fusion Cell personally.

There were fifty of them, drawn from across a broad spectrum of government agencies, working together to achieve one common goal — bringing a very important American home safely.

Each of the desks in the war room–like setting represented a different agency: Treasury, Justice, State, Defense, CIA, NSA, DHS, and others. Their job was to draw in information from their respective organizations and share it with the other team members, thereby developing the most current, accurate picture possible.

Overseeing the operation was Special Presidential Envoy for Hostage Affairs, or SPEHA, Brendan Rogers.

Rogers was a hard-charging former Navy JAG officer turned corporate attorney who had turned over his practice to his partners when the President had asked him to accept the SPEHA position. Though it was a pretty significant pay cut for a man in his late forties with a hefty mortgage and two kids in college, he had never said no when called upon by his country.

To be honest, Rogers relished the challenge. Interacting with some of the world's worst dictators and bad actors was exciting. They ran the gamut from despotic regimes to criminal cartels and terrorist organizations. Getting Americans safely back home to their families was more rewarding to him than any litigation he had ever prevailed in.

Though he went to some absolute shithole places and carried out some of the toughest, most tension-filled negotiations anyone had ever seen, he loved the job. And part of the reason he loved it so was that he was good at it. He hoped, for Scot Harvath's sake, that his winning streak continued.

Since accepting the SPEHA position, Rogers had helped secure the release of more than twenty-two Americans held in such places as North Korea, Iran, Venezuela, Afghanistan, Chechnya, and Mexico. Harvath's situation, though, was extremely difficult.

After the President had thanked everyone out on the floor, the principals adjourned to a secure conference room for the Harvath briefing.

Rogers knew the President was a detail guy who liked to ask questions, and he had prepared a detailed update.

"Mr. President," he said. "Again, let me welcome you to the Hostage Fusion Recovery Cell. I know I speak for the entire team when I tell you what an honor it is to have you here. We have some of the best, brightest, and most patriotic people working in government here. Your recognition of their commitment to bringing American hostages home safely is much appreciated."

"It's the least I can do," replied the President. "I know you all have been working around the clock. Why don't you bring me up to speed."

"Yes, sir," Rogers stated. On his laptop, he activated a piece of video and projected it on the monitors around the room. "This is security footage from the day of the attack. It comes from the neighbor across the street from the safe house on Governors Island.

We've sped it up, but here you see former Deputy Director of the CIA Lydia Ryan arriving, followed later by Scot Harvath and Lara Cordero. Later that day, a black Lincoln Town Car shows up. That's where I'd like to start."

Porter nodded, and the SPEHA continued. "The Town Car was carrying a lone male passenger. He has been identified as a Polish intelligence officer working out of their embassy here in D.C. His name is Artur Kopec, and apparently he had prior relationships with Lydia Ryan and Reed Carlton. As you can see, Kopec gets out of the car, goes into the cottage for about three hours, exits the cottage, and leaves via the Town Car.

"It has been explained to me by DCI McGee that Kopec is a known Russian asset. The Russians, though, are unaware that we possess this information. Therefore, CIA wants this knowledge, and the man's identity, kept a secret." Looking over at CIA Director McGee, he sought clarification. "Is all of that correct?"

"Yes," replied McGee.

The President piped up with his first question. "Would it help if the rest of your team knew the man's identity?"

Rogers thought about it for a moment.

"We're a clearinghouse for intel and analysis. That's why we exist. Is it imperative anyone outside this room know who the man is? I can't say, but the more information they have, the better they can do their jobs."

Porter looked to his CIA Director. It was obviously an invitation to chime in. "Kopec is highly valuable. However, getting Harvath back is our top priority. If we have to burn Kopec in the process, we're prepared to do that. He might, though, be able to help us."

"How?"

"We're working on it," McGee responded. "All that matters is that we don't want to burn him if we don't have to."

"But we're confident that he's the leak?" asked the President. "We're certain he's the one who revealed the location of the safe house and led the hit team there?"

"We're one hundred percent confident that he provided the information," Nicholas replied. "Whether he knew what was going to happen after providing the information is still being looked into."

Porter glanced at his FBI Director. "Where is he now?"

Militante, who had no idea, shrugged. The President then turned to McGee, who gave a quick shake of his head as if to say, *You don't want to know.*

It was Nicholas who stepped back in and ended the line of questioning. "Let's just say we have eyes on him and he's not going anywhere."

Before the President could ask another question on the subject, Rogers advanced to a new series of photos and picked back up with his briefing.

"So the team kills everyone in the house but Harvath. One of them, who may have been wearing Harvath's watch, gets in Harvath's rental car, drives to the end of the driveway, and throws Harvath's cell phone out the window, then drives off.

"Based on other cameras we were able to collect footage from, the rental car crosses the bridge from Governors Island to the mainland, makes a beeline for the interstate, and heads north on I-93. It was later abandoned near Franconia Notch State Park, about seventy-nine miles south of the Pittsburg-Chartierville Border Crossing. Which brings us to the secondary vehicle, the one we believe the hit team used."

The SPEHA brought up a new series of pictures and videos and continued speaking. "Kopec flew commercial from Reagan National to Portland, Maine, which is about ninety miles away from Governors Island.

"He was met at the Portland airport by a car service with instructions to bring him to the cottage on Governors Island. FBI has interviewed the driver, but he wasn't much help. He says the passenger was pleasant enough, but that's about all he remembers. They drove in silence most of the way there and back. The passenger made a few phone calls in a foreign language, which the driver couldn't place. He thought it sounded Eastern European."

"What about the second vehicle?" Nicholas asked.

"Panel van, rented at the Portland airport the day before," said Rogers, as he picked back up with a video feed from the counter. It showed a tall, muscular man in his late thirties. "He presented a credit card, proof of insurance, even an American driver's license — all of which, we know now, were fakes. Highly sophisticated, backstopped fakes, but fakes nonetheless.

"The next day, this panel van can be seen on multiple cameras. It begins by following the Town Car from Portland airport all the way to Governors Island. When the Town Car turns into the safe house driveway, moments later you can see the van drive past and keep going. Unfortunately, wherever it came to a stop and parked, none of the other homes there have cameras.

"Then, several hours later, as Harvath's rental car is seen leaving the island and heading north, the panel van is about ten minutes behind it. U.S. Customs and Border Patrol found it abandoned the next day, less than a mile from the border.

"At that point, the trail went completely cold. Even the Canadians were unable to generate any leads. Then they got a hit on the car rental counter footage we sent them. Two days ago, a private jet left Montréal-Trudeau International. Someone at the Canadian Security Intelligence Service decided to go back, sweep FBO security footage, and run it through facial recognition. Our car renter popped up, along with four other men. At that point, they were traveling on Finnish passports with several large pieces of luggage, a couple of which could have been used to smuggle Harvath on board. They had —"

"But no one saw Harvath," interrupted the President.

"No, sir," replied Rogers.

"Okay, continue."

"The jet's crew had filed a flight plan for Ivalo, the northernmost city in Finland. Considering the number of people on board, plus the fuel capacity, it was at right about the outer range of the aircraft. According to the Finnish government, the plane was forty-five minutes from its destination when the pilot radioed in a change. They claimed they were going to St. Petersburg, Russia, instead — but that's not where they went."

"Where'd they go?"

"A bored Finnish air defense officer continued tracking the aircraft. It ended up landing in Murmansk."

"What's in Murmansk?" the FBI Director asked.

"Lots of polar bears and terrible food," Nicholas replied.

"Do we have any satellite imagery?" asked President Porter. "Any visuals on who got off that plane?"

"No, we didn't have anything on station," Rogers answered. "Even if we had, a severe weather system was beginning to build, and it would have been difficult to get definitive imagery."

"So that's it?"

"Not exactly. After we received the FBO footage from Canadian Intelligence, we shared it with our other Five Eyes partners. MI6 came back with a hit."

"What kind of *hit*?"

"Four of the men were identified as active

Spetsnaz soldiers. The fifth, though, is the most interesting," explained Rogers as he brought up a photo. "Meet Josef Ilya Kozak. Also Spetsnaz, but, more important, a colonel in Russian Military Intelligence — specifically, the GRU's special missions group."

The President stared at the man's picture. He had a drawn, gaunt face, punctuated by dull, lifeless eyes. The photo looked as if it had been snapped at the moment the man's soul had been taken from his body. He had a disturbing aura about him. It wasn't cruelty. It was more than that. The man looked evil. Everyone in the room sensed it.

"So," said Porter, "if I may?"

"Of course," replied Rogers, ceding the floor.

"We have Kopec, a known Russian asset, who was followed to the safe house by at least one, and presumably more, Russian Special Forces operatives. In the house, four Americans are brutally murdered and one goes missing. Two vehicles associated with the attack are found abandoned, one very near the Canadian border. A private jet with Special Forces operatives, including a GRU colonel, posing as Finns leaves Montréal, allegedly headed for Finland. Then forty-five minutes before touchdown, the plane claims to be diverting to St. Petersburg, but lands in Murmansk once it believes the Finns are no longer paying attention to it. Do I have that about right?"

"Yes, sir," answered Rogers. "But there's something else. It may not be connected, but considering what we know, it could be. And if it is, it's big."

CHAPTER 29

Crash Site
Murmansk Oblast

The scene from the air was horrific. The plane had torn a jagged scar through the forest and landed in three broken pieces on the edge of a clearing. There were no signs of life on the ground.

When the two black-and-neon-orange helicopters touched down, Teplov was the first off. From the moment the call had come in that the plane had been located, the hairs on the back of his neck had been standing up. He had no idea why. For some reason, his sixth sense, honed over decades in battle, was trying to warn him.

He divided his men into groups. His team took the tail section. Just before they were about to make entry through the rupture in the side of the fuselage, they found a body — or at least what was left of one.

Because of the shredded uniform, it appeared to be one of Josef's Spetsnaz operatives. The man had been torn apart, and the skin covering the top of his head was missing. Who or what had done it, he had no idea. Pulling the butt of his rifle into his shoulder, Teplov cautiously led his men into the plane.

Immediately upon entering, he saw four scalps hung along a thick piece of wire, and the hair on the back of his neck stood up even further. It was like something out of a horror movie.

Just in front of them, a cargo container appeared to have been turned into a temporary shelter. His men searched inside, but it was empty. Behind the container, though, they found two bodies.

The first was one of the flight crew. His legs had been pinned beneath the container and his pants were stained with blood. Wrapped around one of his thighs was a makeshift tourniquet. It was hard to tell if the man had fashioned it himself or if someone had done it for him. Regardless, what was apparent was that he had bled out.

Next to him was another of Josef's Spetsnaz operatives. As with his colleague outside, his scalp had been removed, but his body was still intact. Again, he was uncertain if the operative had frozen to death, died in the crash, or suffered some other fate.

Around them lay the carcasses of several wolves. They were large, but underweight.

It had been one of the longest, most brutal winters in memory. There were stories of starving wolf packs banding together in hordes to attack villages and even towns. Polar bears, unable to find food, had done the same. Throughout the Murmansk Oblast, Russians were living in fear of coming face-to-face with one of these vicious, wild creatures.

Suddenly, the radio crackled to life. From the front section of the wreckage came a report that the pilot and copilot had been found in the cockpit, burned beyond recognition.

The team in the middle section reported two corpses as well. The first was a flight crew member who had been shot. The other was a man with an apparent broken neck. He had been stripped of his clothes and his scalp had also been cut away.

Teplov didn't need to see the body to wager that it was another of Josef's Spetsnaz operatives.

Heading deeper into the tail section, one of his men found a set of empty shackles. Then, they found the body of the fourth and final soldier.

The man's face had been caved in, beaten to a congealed, bloody pulp. Looking at the blood spatters along the interior of the fuselage, it was obvious that whatever had been used to bludgeon the man, the killer had swung the weapon in wide arcs and with extreme force over and over again. It was an act of excessive violence, an act of pure rage. His scalp was also missing.

The scalps had been a message. Someone was taking revenge. That someone was Harvath.

Getting on the radio, Teplov ordered two of his best shooters to break off their search of the wreckage and get to the helicopters. Unless he was lying dead somewhere out in the snow, Harvath was already on the run. And while he might have had a head start, Teplov had both superior numbers and superior equipment. Harvath wouldn't stay hidden for long. Teplov was going to find him.

CHAPTER 30

Harvath's mind instantly went into fight mode. He had landed hard on his rucksack, with his chest and stomach fully exposed. He looked like a turtle that couldn't right itself.

The large jet-black alpha wolf had come out of nowhere. It ripped and tore at him, sinking its long, sharp teeth into every part of his body that it could.

Using one arm to fend off the massive beast, he tried to reach for the shotgun, but it was pinned underneath him. The animal seemed to sense what was happening and intensified its attack, going for Harvath's throat.

Drawing back his free hand, Harvath delivered an uppercut, punching the wolf right underneath the jaw. He followed it up with a strike to the side of the animal's head. He did it again and again and again.

He kept punching until the beast jumped

off him and backed away. Harvath knew that the retreat was only temporary. It would last just long enough for the wolf to shake off the pain and then come back at him. He would have enough time to make only one move.

Getting to his feet was out of the question. He would have to fight from the ground.

In the fraction of a second that it took for him to commit to what he was going to do and make ready for the attack, the animal struck again.

On his belt, beneath the trapper's anorak, he had hung one of the dead man's best knives. It was long and incredibly sharp, and when the wolf leaped at him he drove the blade in all the way to hilt, just below the creature's breastbone.

The alpha, though mortally wounded, fought back viciously. It seemed determined to kill the man who had taken so many of its extended pack.

As the wolf slashed at him and tried to clamp its jaws around his throat, Harvath twisted the knife and drove it even deeper into the animal's chest cavity. Slicing open its left ventricle, he drove his knee up into its belly, grabbed a fistful of the scruff around its neck, and yanked its mouth away from his neck.

Rolling to his left, he pushed the dying animal off him. He was covered in blood, though whose, he had no idea. Before he could assess his injuries, he had a bigger problem to deal with — the rest of the pack.

He had been so focused on the alpha that he hadn't even noticed the others. Now that he could risk a look, he saw that they had him surrounded. Growling, their mouths dripping with saliva, they appeared ready to attack. None of them, though, were making the first move. With their alpha dead, they were waiting for a new alpha to step up and take charge. Harvath took full advantage of the situation.

Pushing himself up onto his feet, he unsheathed the shotgun, pointed it at the nearest group of wolves, and blasted away. And as soon as the first wolves dropped, he took off running.

He hadn't attached the snowmobile's kill switch cord to his clothing, nor had he wrapped it around his wrist. When the wolf had attacked, he had been revving the gas. When he had gotten knocked off, the sled had rocketed forward.

That was both a blessing and a curse. It was a curse because now he had to struggle through deep snow to get to it, but it was also a blessing, in that he could hear it was still running.

Turning, he cycled the shotgun and fired, then pumped and fired again, killing two wolves that were right behind him and practically biting at his heels.

As the animals fell, Harvath turned back and jumped onto the sled. It had come to a stop with its nose jammed against a tree. Throwing it into reverse, he backed up and fired again at the wolves. Then, tucking the hot shotgun beneath his leg, he turned the Yeti's skis, slammed the gear selector into forward, and pinned the throttle.

He risked one look over his shoulder. The issue of who would be the new alpha seemed to have settled itself. Another enormous black wolf was leading the chase after him. It was unbelievable how fucking fast they were. Harvath gave the snowmobile even more gas.

Eventually, they receded into the distance. But even then, he kept going full speed for quite some time.

When he finally felt it was safe to stop, he did so. His eyes were burning, and as they teared from the wind, the tears turned quickly to ice. It was as if somebody had sprayed bleach in his face. It hurt like hell.

He needed to assess his injuries, which

was difficult because he had so much of the alpha's blood on him.

In addition, he knew the wolf had punctured his clothing several times and had succeeded in injuring him. The question was, how badly.

Reloading the shotgun and laying it over the handlebars, he removed his anorak and examined his new wounds. They were bad.

He had bite wounds to his chest and abdomen, as well as a gash along his upper left arm that was bleeding heavily. He attended to the bleeding first.

Dousing the wound with vodka, he selected the cleanest piece of clothing in his rucksack and used it as a bandage, securing it in place around his arm with duct tape.

Next he focused on the bite wounds. The first thing he did was to gently press on them to encourage bleeding. It was counterintuitive, but bites from dogs and wolves were often highly infectious. Encouraging the punctures to bleed was supposed to help flush out the bacteria.

As he had with the gash on his arm, he then cleansed the wounds with vodka and covered them with small pieces of cloth, which he held in place with duct tape.

By the time he carefully put the anorak back on, his body was trembling with cold.

He helped himself to a long slug of the multipurpose vodka before returning it to his backpack and securing the shotgun where he could get to it quickly if he needed to.

Off in the distance, he thought he could make out the sound of a helicopter. It was hard to hear over the noise from the Yeti's engine. He didn't dare shut it off, though, for fear that he wouldn't be able to start it again.

If there were helicopters in the area, that meant they had likely found the crash site. And if they had found the crash site, they had found the dead Spetsnaz operatives and everything else he had left behind. If they weren't already looking for him, they would be soon, and a helicopter would all but guarantee they'd find him — unless he could get out of sight.

He needed to get to that town on the GPS, find someplace to hole up, and figure out how he was going to get across the border.

He also needed antibiotics. Eight hours was the window. If he waited any longer than that, the risk of infection multiplied.

If he got stuck hiding someplace, even out in the wilderness, while waiting for a search party to pass and he got sick, he could die before he ever saw Finland and freedom.

Fuck, he thought to himself. Siphoning gas was risky enough. Stealing a vehicle was even more dangerous. But trying to get his hands on medicine? That was a whole other set of problems he didn't need. He had a serious decision to make.

Hitting the gas, he decided to wait until he got to town to settle on a plan.

CHAPTER 31

He stayed in the trees as much as possible.
Using the thick tree cover, he hoped to hide
himself and the snowmobile's tracks. He
also made sure to keep the sled's light off.
Whenever he thought he heard a helicopter
nearby, which was happening more and
more often, he would seek cover and come
to a full stop. Nothing attracted the human
eye like movement. The harder he could
make it for the search teams, the better.

When the helicopters were out of range,
he would gun the snowmobile, covering as
much distance as possible as quickly as possible. As he arrived at the outskirts of the
town, the sun had already begun to set.

It was bordered by a wide river, which
wasn't iced over. There was one bridge on
the southernmost edge of the town. He
could either hide his snowmobile in the
trees on this side or take it across and try to
find someplace on the other side. He chose

to take it across.

As the light faded, the already frigid temperatures continued to drop. On one of the streets up ahead he saw the headlights of a passing vehicle. Other than that, the only visible lights were from inside houses where locals were preparing dinner.

Harvath assumed that, as in Alaska, in such a remote area, a snowmobile passing through town didn't even warrant a second look. And even if someone did glance outside, they wouldn't have been able to see much of his face, bundled up as he was in the trapper's fur outerwear.

As he moved past houses, he kept his eyes open for opportunity — cars left running, dwellings that were uninhabited, as well as gasoline and other supplies. He also kept his eyes peeled for anything resembling local police or military.

Not only did the fading light provide him a certain level of camouflage but it also helped hide the bloodstains covering his anorak. One good, clear look at him would have raised a ton of questions. Better no one see him at all. That was the way he preferred it — especially now.

Making his way through the snow-covered back streets, he kept on the lookout for signs of a pharmacy or doctor's office — even a veterinarian's would have done the trick.

Like the surrounding landscape, the town was bleak. If hopelessness were an actual color, this place would be all fifty shades of it.

It was exactly what he pictured when he thought of life during the interminably long, dark winters north of the Arctic Circle. He was astounded by the fact that the Finns could be so close, yet so different. The Russian psyche did not lend itself to upbeat, sunny optimism. The sooner he was out of here, the better.

More important than where he could steal the antibiotics he needed was where he could stay warm and hidden for the night. Though he had kept his eyes peeled for signs of an uninhabited dwelling, he wasn't finding any. Every home appeared to be spoken for.

If the trapper had a primary residence in town, it wasn't marked on the GPS. Following the signal, it led Harvath to a sparse, central square with a rundown, kitschy, tropical-themed café. Its mascot was a pelican wearing a parka.

Behind the frost-covered windows, he could see people drinking and having a good time. Though he could barely make it out over the noise from his engine, it sounded as if there was music playing as well. No matter how bad the weather was, alcohol and other people tended to make things better. It was a comfort that he would need to remain a stranger to.

Pushing through the town center, he found what he was looking for on the other side. It was a drab, one-story building that billed itself as a medical "clinic." As best he could tell, the clinic practiced family medicine, specializing in infants to senior citizens, and also handled "minor" dental emergencies. There was a number to call for appointments, as well as one for after hours. Harvath drove his snowmobile around back.

There had been no vehicles in front, nor were there any at the rear of the building. None of the lights were on, either. It looked as if everyone had left for the evening.

Figuring he could hike back to the café and steal a car if he needed to, Harvath decided to shut off the snowmobile's engine. Erring on the side of caution, though, he broke out the spare jerry can and filled the sled's gas tank. The needle had been hovering just above empty since he arrived. *Be prepared* was more than just a motto in his book. It was a way of life. There was no telling what kind of an exit he might have to make out of town. Better to do it on a full tank of gas.

After tucking the GPS and its power cord into his rucksack, he did a quick sweep of the building for alarm sensors. Not seeing any, he knocked on the back door. When no one answered, he raised his boot and kicked it in.

The frame splintered and the door gave way. Pushing the pieces of wood back in place to hide the damage, he gathered up his rucksack and shotgun and then hurried inside, carefully closing the door behind him.

For several moments he stood and listened. There was no one there but him.

The heat must have been turned down for the night. It was quite chilly inside. Locating the thermostat, he turned it way up. Somewhere, an old furnace groaned noisily to life. The place reeked of antiseptic.

There were two examination rooms, a small procedure suite, a break room, a waiting room, and a front office. Starving, Harvath hit the break room first. He helped himself to a yogurt and a bottle of Sprite Cucumber he found in a small refrigerator.

In a cabinet above the sink were tea, coffee, sugar, and two tins of cookies. He grabbed all of it and stuffed it into his pack. Then he headed for the procedure room.

Careful not to alert anyone outside to his presence, he kept the lights off and used only the dull-beamed flashlight he had taken from the trapper's cabin. It was enough to see by, and that was all that mattered.

Along the near wall was a medical storage cabinet. He gave the handle a try, but it was locked. Removing a screwdriver from his rucksack, he pried it open and shined his light over the contents.

Reading the contents of canned goods or IRPs was the absolute outer limit of his Russian vocabulary. That meant deciphering the Cyrillic names of medicines was completely out of the question. He didn't have a clue what he was looking at.

The last thing he wanted to do was ingest or inject himself with something that not only wouldn't help but could very well make things worse. There had to be some way to figure this out. Picking up the shotgun, he headed toward the front office.

It was an enclosed space that sat behind the counter facing the waiting room. It looked like any other doctor's office or minute clinic he had ever been to. And like those places, it had a computer.

As backward as it was, Russia had a high level of connectivity to the Internet, even in some of its most remote areas. If he could get online, he could not only search for the correct spelling of the drugs he needed but also send a covert message back to the United States for help.

The moment he sat down at the computer he realized that he was out of luck. The keyboard was completely in Cyrillic. *Damn it.*

Leaning back in the chair, he tried to come up with a plan. He knew how to read a handful of words only because he had memorized them, not because he had learned the Cyrillic alphabet. But maybe, like a Rosetta stone, it might be enough. He had to give it a shot.

Pressing the Power button, he waited for the decades-old computer to boot up.

Once it had, he was greeted with another disappointment — a password request.

He tried 0000 and 1234, neither of which worked. He turned the keyboard over, hoping to find a sticky note with the password. There was nothing there. He opened the desk drawers. Nothing still. He ran his hand under the desk and came up empty.

It was a doctor's office, albeit a Russian one, so he shouldn't have been surprised that they took computer security seriously. He was going to have to figure out another plan.

Standing up, he walked over to a long bookshelf and, aided by his flashlight, studied the titles. In the era of Google Translate, the likelihood of finding an English-Russian dictionary to help with translating medical articles was basically zero.

His pessimism was proven correct. Every book, textbook, journal, and manual was in Russian. There was only one other thing he could think to do.

Unlike clinics back in the United States, this one still relied on paper charts. Opening one of the many office file cabinets, he grabbed a stack of charts, carried them over to the desk, and set them down.

There was a particular word he knew the Cyrillic for. His friend Nicholas, who had grown up speaking Russian, used it all the time: собака. Dog.

The only reason he could imagine the word appearing in a medical file would be because a patient had been bitten. Nine out of ten times, oral antibiotics would be prescribed. Only in cases where it wasn't known if the dog had been vaccinated would a course of rabies injections be necessary. He felt confident that if he could find one dog bite case, or, better yet, two, he could figure out the name of the medication he was looking for.

Before he started reading the files he opened a large, leather ledger sitting next to the phone. It was the clinic's appointment book. As each day wrapped up, someone had drawn a slash through the date. Based on what he could understand, the first appointment was tomorrow morning at 0800. That gave him literally all night to wade through the files if he wanted. It was more than enough time.

Taking off the anorak, he made himself comfortable. There had been a small task lamp in the break room, and he went and got it. Draping a dishtowel from the break room over it, he was able to dim the light enough that he felt comfortable using it to work by. He had no idea how much juice was left in his flashlight, nor how long his search was going to take.

Just like American doctors, Russian doctors had terrible handwriting, too. Using a blank piece of paper, he went through line by line. He was about a quarter of the way through the files when he found what he was looking for.

Two brothers had both had some sort of incident with a dog. Their charts were right next to each other. In both cases they had been prescribed антибиотики.

Harvath was pretty certain this was what he was looking for. After writing the word down on the blank sheet of paper, he headed for the medicine cabinet in the procedure room.

But when he stepped into the hallway, someone was waiting for him. And that someone had a very large-caliber weapon pointed right at him.

Chapter 32

"Who are you?" the woman demanded in Russian. "What are you doing here?"

She was dressed in a dark-green down parka, black snow pants, and winter boots. In her hands, she held a bolt-action hunting rifle with a large scope.

Harvath hadn't even heard her come in the rear door, probably because the furnace was so loud. Stupidly, he had his shotgun over his shoulder. At this range, if he reached for it, she'd put a hole in him so big you could drive a tank through it.

Keeping his hands where she could see them, he held out the piece of paper with the word *antibiotic* written in Cyrillic.

"Who are you?" she repeated.

"I am not a threat," he replied in his broken Russian.

"Last chance," she stated, as she took a tighter grip on her rifle. "Who are you?"

"*Menya zovut* Scot." *My name is Scot.*

"What are you doing here? Why did you break into my clinic?"

She was going too fast. He couldn't understand what she was saying. "My Russian is terrible. Please. Do you speak English?" he asked.

Moments passed as she tried to decide whether she wanted to engage with him in his language rather than hers. Finally, in English she said, "What are you doing in my clinic?"

"I'm injured."

"I can see that. You have blood all over you. Why did you break my door?"

"I'm sorry. I needed medicine."

"So you just broke in?" she replied.

"You have every right to be angry."

"Of course I do. This is *my* clinic."

"Again, I'm sorry, but —"

He had begun to lower his hands and she stiffened, applying pressure to the trigger. "Keep them up," she commanded.

Harvath put them back up. "I'm not a threat. I won't hurt you."

"Is that so? Then why don't you tell me why my uncle's snowmobile is parked outside, why you're wearing his clothes, why you're carrying his shotgun, and why you're covered in blood?"

Harvath was stunned. "The fur trapper?

He was your uncle?" He could see some resemblance in her face, a hint of Sámi around the eyes — but not much.

She was blonde, with high cheekbones, a thin, delicate nose, and full pink lips. She looked more Caucasian than anything else.

"What do you mean *was*?" she demanded. "What happened? What did you do to him?"

"Nothing," Harvath insisted. "He saved my life. Unfortunately, I couldn't do the same for him."

The woman, though obviously distraught at hearing a family member had passed, kept the gun pointed right at him, waiting for him to continue.

"I was in a plane crash. The only survivor. I can't even remember how long I was walking before I found your uncle's cabin, but I was on the other side of the river. When I tried to cross, I fell through the ice and almost drowned. Somehow, I made it inside and was able to start a fire before I passed out. When I woke up, I realized he had been sitting in a chair near me the entire time, but it was only what remained of him. He had passed away days, maybe even weeks before I arrived at the cabin. I don't know what happened. Maybe it was a heart attack or something like that. All I know is that it's because of him that I'm alive."

"And the blood? Are you actually injured? Or did that come from someone else?"

"May I?" he asked, gesturing that he wanted to lift up his shirt and show her.

She nodded, and Harvath lifted up his shirt. With his free hand, he began peeling away the pieces of duct tape that had been covering his bite wounds.

Her eyes grew wide. "What did that to you?"

"Wolves."

"That explains the bite marks, and perhaps the bruising was suffered during the crash, but it doesn't explain the lacerations. They look like they were caused by some sort of a whip, like you have been tortured."

Harvath lowered his shirt but didn't respond.

When he failed to provide an explanation, she pressed him. "I still don't understand why you had to break into my clinic. The evening telephone number is written outside. You could have stopped anyone in town and they would have brought me to you. Why do this?"

It was the moment of truth. Harvath had to decide if he was going to bring her into his confidence or not. His espionage training, all of the lessons the Old Man had drilled into him, told him to lie. His gut and his hard-won experience, though, implored him to tell her the truth. He decided to go with the truth.

"Three days ago, maybe four, my wife was murdered and I was taken captive. Two other people I cared for very much were also killed. The men who did this put me in shackles and loaded me onto a plane. When we landed in Murmansk, we changed planes. It was the second plane that crashed."

The woman didn't believe him. "Something like that would have been all over the news. Whenever a boat or plane goes missing, they always ask us to keep an eye out — especially our woodsmen, the hunters and trappers."

"If your government is anything like mine, the flight would have been kept very quiet," he said. "It would have been off the books."

"Why?"

"Because sending a team to kidnap an American citizen on American soil is an act of war."

She didn't know how to respond. It was an absolutely outrageous claim, but nothing about the man's demeanor suggested he was lying. In fact, he struck her as serious. *Deadly serious.*

"What did you do that made them take

such a risk?"

Harvath shook his head. "It's a long list."

"Name one thing."

"The suicide bomber that leaped the fence and detonated just outside the White House, did you hear about that?"

"Yes. It was a Muslim terrorist."

Harvath kept going. "How about the assassination of the American Secretary of Defense in Turkey?"

"Also Muslim terrorists."

He smiled. "All Muslims, yes. But they were recruited and trained by the same man. He had been a student at Beslan during the terrible school siege and hostage crisis. His father had been the principal, his mother an art teacher.

"After it was all over, Moscow had combed through the survivors. They had interviewed all of them. It was an experiment of sorts. Their hope was that the trauma those students had experienced could be weaponized. Only one child showed any promise, and he was off the charts.

"They poured everything they had into training him. He worked with all of the best Moscow had to offer — spies, Spetsnaz, everything. I heard someone refer to him as Russia's Jason Bourne. It's a bit of an exaggeration, but he was incredibly valuable to the GRU."

"What happened to him?" she asked.

"I tracked him down and then put him in a deep, dark hole."

"And so that's why you were kidnapped?"

He shrugged. "That's just one reason. There are plenty of others — things that never made it into newspapers or onto television. Like I said, it's a long list, but what connects them all is me. I have a tendency to prevent Moscow from getting what it wants."

There was a beat, and then the woman said, "Good," as she lowered her rifle.

"Good?"

"You have your reasons for not liking Moscow. So do I."

"What do you mean by that?"

"I have lost someone, too," she said, coming in for a closer look at his wounds. "My husband."

"I'm sorry."

"Don't be. He knew what he was doing."

"How did he die?"

"He was a medic for a mercenary group. He was killed fighting in Syria — a place I don't think Russia should ever have been. But the Kremlin was paying his company a fortune.

"I told him that I didn't care about the money, that I didn't want him taking such risks. He had other plans, though. He wanted us to move to Moscow. He planned to open a private security company with a couple of his friends. But he couldn't do it without the money. And now he's dead, and I'm alone."

"I'm sorry about your uncle as well," Harvath offered.

"Thank you. But back to what you're doing here," she said, changing the subject as she had him lift his shirt back up. "Your plan was to break in here, steal some antibiotics, and then what?"

Harvath winced as she touched the skin near one of the punctures. "I don't know. From what I can tell, we're not far from the Finnish border."

The woman shook her head and smiled. "In these temperatures? It may not look far on a map, but there aren't enough reindeer skins in the entire Oblast to keep you from freezing to death out there."

"It's a plan," he replied, trying to ignore the pain and smiling back. "I didn't say it was a good one."

Lowering his shirt, she took a step back and said, "You definitely need antibiotics. I'd also recommend we begin a course of rabies injections. And judging by your other injuries, I believe painkillers would also be in order."

Harvath appreciated her assistance, but there was something he needed even more. "Can you help me get to the border? If you can, I promise to make it worth your while."

CHAPTER 33

After two hours of searching, Teplov's men had found Josef. His back was broken and he was suffering from frostbite and severe hypothermia, but he was alive.

As the transport plane had tumbled through the forest, breaking apart, he had been sucked out. Unable to walk, he had clawed a trench in the snow and had used seat cushions and other debris to insulate himself. Dragging himself inside, he had done the only thing he could do at that point — he had waited for rescue.

When word of Josef's discovery broke over the radio, Teplov had rushed to his friend's location. He was relieved to see him alive, if just barely. The man, though, was hovering on the edge of consciousness and obviously in great pain.

Despite Minayev's earlier orders about the allocation of resources, Teplov redirected the cargo helicopter and two of his mercenaries to transport Josef back to the air base for emergency medical attention.

Before they took off, Teplov tried to ask him if he knew what had happened and where Harvath might be. Josef was unable to answer.

Shielding his face from the hail of crystalline snow, he stood back and watched as the helicopter lifted off and disappeared into the distance.

The revelation that Josef was still alive had only deepened his resolve to track down Harvath. A couple of hours later, they had a lead.

As the area was so heavily wooded, Teplov and his team had to be dropped some distance away and snowshoe in. But it had been worth it.

Inside a cabin, they had found the body of an old Sámi with a blanket pulled up over his face. His clothes were missing, but in a pile on the floor near the fireplace was a damp Spetsnaz uniform. Harvath had been here.

In addition to helping himself to the old man's clothes and canned food, he also appeared to have helped himself to the Sámi's snowmobile.

Blowing snow had almost completely erased the tracks — only a whisper of a trail remained. Teplov and his men followed it.

A couple of hundred meters into the trees, there was another carnage of wolves.

Several lay dead by what looked like shotgun blasts. Another — a much larger black wolf — looked as if it had been gutted with some kind of blade. The snow was covered with blood.

Marking the direction the snowmobile had taken from there, Teplov radioed one helicopter to go search, and the other, which had returned from dropping off Josef, to pick him and his men up where they had been dropped off.

As they trekked back to the landing zone, Teplov consulted his GPS unit. Harvath was headed west, likely for the border. He had a snowmobile, a shotgun, and a modicum of other supplies. Did he have enough, though, to get him all the way? What's more, what kind of shape was he in?

Considering how far he had come from the crash site and how much havoc he had caused, Teplov decided he was doing well enough to be dangerous.

The only other question he had was how long Harvath had been on the run with the snowmobile. If he could answer that, it would go a long way toward tracking him down.

Night was falling, and Teplov had no idea how much fuel Harvath had. It was going to get much colder. If he was going to resupply or rest for the night, where might he do that?

Teplov consulted his GPS. If Harvath maintained his course, the nearest habitation was a town approximately forty kilometers away.

He had to have known that he would stand out significantly from the local population. Merely putting on someone else's clothing wouldn't be enough to disguise him. The people of the Oblast could recognize an outsider quite easily. That would go double for an American.

Harvath's only chance was to stay out of sight. He would be looking for a farm, another cabin, or some sort of abandoned property where he could get warm and, if need be, get food for himself and fuel for the snowmobile.

At the very least, Teplov now knew how Harvath was traveling and in which direction. That was a dramatic improvement.

Finding the needle was the easy part. Identifying the haystack was where the challenge lay.

But now he had his haystack. All he and his men needed to do was to get out their pitchforks and rip it apart. Scot Harvath didn't stand a chance.

CHAPTER 34

Above the Atlantic

The Gulfstream G650 ER extended-range jet was capable of Mach 0.925, more than seven hundred miles per hour. But, in addition to its speed, its fuel capacity had made it The Carlton Group's preferred aircraft.

Fully fueled, it had a range of seventy-five hundred nautical miles. That meant it could do Hong Kong to New York nonstop. At about half the distance, Washington, D.C., to Helsinki, Finland, was even easier.

In addition to its range and speed, the aircraft was incredibly luxurious. It boasted a premium leather couch, handcrafted oversized reclining seats, sixteen panoramic windows, designer carpeting, fold-out flatscreen displays, LED lighting, a bathroom with a shower, and a full galley with a convection oven, wet bar, and even an espresso machine.

The private plane could sleep ten people

and had voluminous cargo space — key requirements when sending a high-end tactical team downrange.

"This is a joke, right?" said the voice of Tyler Staelin as he opened the oven. "Who stocks a seventy-million-dollar plane with fucking pizza?"

The five-foot-ten Staelin was a former Tier One operator from the "Unit," or Delta Force, as it was more popularly known. Hailing from downstate Illinois, the experienced thirty-nine-year-old played double duty as the team's medic. An avid reader, he never travelled with less than three books.

"I did," replied Chase Palmer. "Nobody wanted to take responsibility for catering, so I stepped up. Next time, don't ignore my texts."

A native Texan in his early thirties, Chase looked so similar to Harvath that the two were often asked if they were brothers.

He had been the youngest operator ever admitted to Delta, and his exploits were legendary — filling multiple hard drives at the Department of Defense. His teammates had loosely nicknamed him "AK," for Ass Kicker, but after he had used an empty AK-47 to bluff six enemy fighters into surrender in Afghanistan, it stuck.

"You never texted me," Staelin asserted as

he pulled out his phone and scrolled through his messages. When he got to the ones from Chase, his expression changed. "My bad."

"Apology accepted. By the way, there's a warming drawer behind you. You might want to take a peek."

Staelin did, and a smile spread across his face. "Sirloins?"

"You're welcome," Chase replied.

Normally, Harvath handled this stuff. He was a detail guy, and secretly they all believed he was a bit of a control freak. He liked to act as if he didn't care about what anyone thought, but they knew better. Harvath was a good man who cared deeply about the people around him. That was yet another reason why the events of the last several days had been so difficult.

The news that the Old Man, Lydia Ryan, and Lara Cordero had been murdered came as a shock to the entire team. The fact that Harvath had gone missing and that police in New Hampshire were actually considering him a suspect made them all want to throat-punch somebody. Then, Nicholas had called them into HQ for a briefing.

At each seat at the conference table, he had placed a copy of the Old Man's succession plan. Like Nicholas, Carlton had also been a no-bullshit, detail guy.

It was unnecessary. If Nicholas had said "Reed and Lydia are gone. We don't know where Harvath is. Until further notice, I have been left in charge," the team would have believed him.

But because of his dishonorable past, Nicholas often felt unworthy around them. He respected their courage and integrity, and worked hard to earn their respect in return. In so doing, he committed to always being one hundred percent transparent with them, and held nothing back in his briefings.

After detailing Kopec's presence at the safe house, how they believed the murders had unfolded, and then how they suspected Harvath had been smuggled into Canada and then out to Russia via a private jet, he began to get into the pertinent details on their mission.

The NSA had picked up chatter about a Russian Air Force transport plane that had disappeared in bad weather. The plane had taken off from the same airport Harvath had landed at, shortly after his arrival. While coincidental, it wasn't conclusive. That's where the next piece of intelligence was so valuable.

Sources in Ukraine stated that right after

the plane was reported missing, Kazimir Teplov, head of the Wagner Group, hastily assembled his best men and flew them, along with a ton of equipment, back to Russia. Specifically, they had flown to Alakurtti Air Base south of Murmansk and, according to the Finns, were there awaiting orders to begin some sort of operation. The kicker was that whatever these orders were, they had to do with the missing transport plane.

"U.S. Intelligence believes Harvath was on the plane that disappeared," Nicholas had revealed. "We believe that Moscow is trying to keep the situation as quiet as possible, so instead of using active military and law enforcement personnel, they have brought in Russian mercenaries."

It was one shocking revelation stacked upon another.

The United States Joint Special Operations Command had a quick reaction force known as a "Zero-Three-Hundred" team on standby in Germany. They were SEALs from DEVGRU, ready to HAHO jump in as soon as Harvath's location was pinpointed.

As a demonstration of how serious the President was about getting Harvath back, U.S. F-22 Raptor all-weather stealth tactical fighters had been moved to a base in northern Sweden, and an LC-130 Hercules "Ski-bird" aircraft was being repositioned from Greenland.

The LC-130 was particularly special, as it was equipped with retractable skis, allowing it to land on snowfields, ice fields, and even frozen bodies of water. To assist in slushy snow or for short takeoffs, the Skibird was one of the few aircraft in the world to be equipped with rockets.

If they had to, they were prepared to send the LC-130 into Russian air space, escorted by F-22s, to bring Harvath home.

There was also talk of having the USS *Delaware,* a Virginia class nuclear-powered attack submarine, slip into the White Sea in order to insert an additional covert operations team just off the Kola Peninsula. Everything was being considered. Nothing was off the table.

The Carlton Group's job was to employ a lighter touch. If they could get in, get Harvath, and get out without the Russians' knowing, that was the President's first choice.

Though he would have killed to be on the assignment, Nicholas's physical limitations made him a liability. Snow and rugged terrain disagreed with him.

Besides, his role as de facto head of the

organization meant he had to remain in D.C. and act as a liaison with all of the other players, including the White House, the Pentagon, the CIA, the FBI, and the NSA. He was thankful Rogers was helping to co-ordinate efforts through the Hostage Recovery Fusion Cell.

It had been decided, almost immediately, that a kinetic operation was called for. The Russians were unlikely to give Harvath up, no matter how much diplomatic pressure was applied.

Even so, Rogers had been tasked with co-ordinating a parallel track. With Nicholas's help, they had come up with an aggressive strategy in hopes of negotiating Harvath's release.

In the meantime, The Carlton Group team would head to Finland and prepare to cross over into Russia.

The passengers onboard the private jet looked like something out of a hard-core action movie.

In addition to Staelin and Chase, there was the former Fifth Special Forces Group operative Jack Gage — a massive six-foot-three man who clocked in at two hundred and fifty pounds. Between his physique and thick, dark beard, he looked like a pirate on steroids, or some sort of professional wrestler. He was a slave to chewing tobacco, a habit he surprisingly hadn't picked up in the Army, but rather growing up in Minnesota, of all places.

There were also two no-longer-active United States Force Recon Marines on the team — Matt Morrison and Mike Haney. Morrison, a thirty-one-year-old from Alabama, was tall, good-looking, and always ready for a fight. His teammates liked to joke that he had been born with the looks of male stripper and the IQ of the pole. It was an unfair characterization, but as they at least recognized his superior physical attributes, he let the rest of their barbs slide.

The other Marine, Mike Haney, was never knocked for being dumb. In the field, the six-foot-tall leatherneck from Northern California was in charge of all their operational technology. Radios, drones, satellite phones — if it had a battery, Haney was responsible for it. At forty years old, with one of the longest service records on the team, he carried a wealth of experience. He was both an exceptional operator and highly skilled as a leader.

Rounding out the team were Tim Barton and Sloane Ashby. Barton had been with the Navy's elite SEAL Team known as DEVGRU, formerly called SEAL Team Six.

If Gage was built like a professional wrestler, Barton was built like a college wrestler. He was short — only five feet six — but barrel-chested and absolutely fearless. Whenever the team needed a volunteer, the redhead's hand was always the first to go up. Somewhat OCD, he preferred everything to be in its place — a trait that earned him regular but good-natured ribbing from his teammates.

Sloane Ashby, like Harvath, had been handpicked by the Old Man. The moment he had met her, he knew he had to have her for The Carlton Group. As she was a very attractive blonde in her late twenties, most people never saw past her looks. She had graduated top of her class at Northwestern University, was an accomplished athlete, and had paid her own way through college via the ROTC.

When she enlisted in the Army, she had done so only on the guarantee that she would see combat. She was an amazing soldier. In fact, she had racked up so many kills in Afghanistan that she reached a certain a level of notoriety. The Taliban and Al Qaeda put a price on her head, and a popular magazine did an unauthorized feature on her. As soon as that happened, the Department of Defense pulled her from combat.

She fought to be allowed to go to Iraq, but the answer was an emphatic *no.* Instead, she was sent to Fort Bragg, where she helped to train Delta Force's elite all-female unit known as the Athena Project. It was a waste to put such an exceptional operator out to pasture. When Reed Carlton offered her a chance to get back into the thick of the action, she jumped at it.

Sloane could kick doors with the best of them, and that was precisely what she did. Joining The Carlton Group was one of the best decisions she had ever made. From the moment she signed on, it had been everything the Old Man had promised it would be, and more. She was doing exactly the kind of work she had been born to do.

As the jet raced toward Finland, the team members wandered in and out of the galley to grab food, energy drinks, or cups of coffee. Some slept, some read books, and others watched movies or listened to music.

While there was much of the good-natured back-and-forth they had developed as a team, there was also something missing — *Harvath.*

He was their leader, and it felt not only odd not having him along, but it was also somewhat unnerving. The idea that he, an

apex predator who had killed, they liked to joke, more people than cancer, could be captured was difficult to swallow. It meant that he was fallible, human.

He had been Superman to them. But Superman had been captured. And if Superman could be captured, none of them were safe.

They had to get him back — not only because he was their leader but because he was their brother. And because you didn't let the fucking Russians, of all people, kidnap Superman. That wasn't how things worked. Not in their world. If he was still alive, they were going to find him and bring him home.

CHAPTER 35

Russian Embassy
Washington, D.C.

"Mr. Ambassador," said SPEHA Rogers as he strode across the office and shook the man's hand. "Thank you for seeing me."

"I'm sorry for putting you off," replied Egor Sazanov. "I didn't want you to come all this way and not have answers for you."

"I practically live at the State Department these days, so I'm not that far away."

The Russian Ambassador smiled. "How about a drink?"

"I'd love one. Thank you."

Rogers and Sazanov had previously worked together when a young American had been taken hostage by a Muslim terror organization in Chechnya. The SPEHA had found him to be a good partner, honest and diligent. He was charming and had an excellent command of English. Rogers could see him as Russia's Foreign Minister or maybe even its President one day.

The Ambassador's office was filled with heavy wooden furniture and dark, sky-blue Kuba rugs from Azerbaijan. Tiny flourishes of gold leaf could be seen along the ceiling. As worldly as the Ambassador was, there wasn't a single book anywhere in the room.

He showed his guest to a seating area and gestured for his assistant to leave them alone and close the door behind him.

Sazanov was a fan of high-end bourbons and still had the special bottle Rogers had given him as a thank-you.

"Ice, correct?" he asked as he uncorked the Pappy Van Winkle's Family Reserve 20 Year.

The SPEHA nodded.

Usually he drank his neat, but he knew that the Ambassador was an ice aficionado.

In addition to his love of American bourbons, the Russian had become quite enamored of the huge pieces of crystal-clear ice served at upscale bars around D.C. He had made it his personal mission to learn how to do it himself. He quizzed every bartender, bought every silicone mold they suggested, and tried every kind of water, from bottled to boiled.

The end product was a perfect cube that looked as if it had been laser-cut from a pristine glacier.

As a Sinatra fan as well, Sazanov had ordered custom rocks glasses with the faux country club logo Frank had designed himself.

It seemed a waste to pour one of the best bourbons in the world over a huge chunk of ice, but Rogers was the consummate diplomat. He thanked his host, they clinked glasses, and each took a sip.

The Ambassador savored it and closed his eyes. "You need to tell me where you found this. I want to send some bottles back to Moscow."

Rogers chuckled. "You don't find Pappy like this. It finds you. Kind of like being struck by lightning."

Sazanov opened his eyes and smiled. "Please. How did you find it?"

The SPEHA decided to give up his secret. "The Vice President knows a private collector. After you were so generous in helping get our citizen back, I asked him to make a call."

"The Vice President of the United States?"

"The man himself."

"I did not know. That is an incredible honor."

Rogers took another sip and said, "If you can help us with our current situation, I

think we can help find a lot more Pappy for you."

Instantly, the expression on the Russian's face changed, and he lowered his glass. "I am sorry, Brendan. I went to the very top. We don't have him. No one at the FSB, the GRU, or the Kremlin knows anything about his disappearance."

The SPEHA believed him. More specifically, he believed that's what the Ambassador had been told. In fact, he had expected it.

Taking another sip of bourbon, he set his glass down on the table, removed a folder from his briefcase, and handed it to Sazanov.

"What's this?" the Russian asked.

"A glimpse into what we've been able to piece together so far. I think you should take a look at it."

The man did, starting with a detailed executive summary of what the Americans believed had happened to their operative, Scot Harvath. It was followed by a series of photographs. Attached to each was a short bio. The Americans had identified four Spetsnaz operatives as well as a GRU colonel.

Unless the Americans were lying to him, it appeared his own government hadn't told him the truth. "How did you come by all of this?" he asked.

"I'm sorry, Mr. Ambassador," answered Rogers, "but I am not authorized to discuss sources and methods."

Sazanov closed the folder. "What *are* you authorized to discuss?"

"We'd like to find an immediate and peaceful resolution to this matter. I'm authorized to discuss any steps that might get us there."

"I'm listening."

"Get Harvath back to us in the next twenty-four hours, and we won't ask any questions. Maybe he was taken by a terrorist organization. Maybe he was taken by the Russian mafia. As long as he's returned, we won't challenge the story.

"And just so we're clear, if you want to use a third-party nation — Germany, China, Syria, Belarus, or even the Iranians — we don't care. We just want Harvath back. In fact, President Porter will publicly praise any third party and give them credit, if that's the route you choose to take."

The Ambassador looked at his watch. "I am going to have to make another round of phone calls."

"I understand," said the SPEHA. "But before you do, there's something else I need to share with you."

Withdrawing another folder from his briefcase, the SPEHA handed it to his host. "Your President has approximately forty billion dollars in personal assets hidden outside of Russia. As of twenty minutes ago, half of them have been frozen. Inside that folder, you'll find a full list.

"If Harvath is back to us within twenty-four hours, we'll unfreeze everything. If he's not, your President will never see that money again. What's more, we'll go public so that the entire world, but especially the Russian people, see the extent to which he has pillaged your country."

Sazanov's temper flared. "This is blackmail."

"This is business," Rogers said, stone-faced. "Nothing more. Nothing less. And, to demonstrate that we're not completely unreasonable, if your government provides us with proof of life within the next eight hours, we will unfreeze five billion of your president's assets."

"You don't understand how Russia works. I'm going to get blamed for this."

"You're not going to get the blame. You're going to get the credit. As far as anyone is concerned, unfreezing the five billion in exchange for proof of life was your idea."

The Ambassador shook his head. "Don't throw me your bones. I don't want them."

"Egor, you're a good man. The kind of man Russia needs."

"Excuse me?"

"We think you're someone we can work with."

Sazanov held up his hand. "Wait. What are you talking about?"

"If you help make this happen, the United States will be in your debt."

"In my debt *how*?"

Rogers smiled. "You have a long political career ahead of you in Russia. We want to help you be successful."

"*You* want to help *me*. That's interesting. Okay, I'm listening."

"We can work out the details later, but suffice it to say that there's a laundry list of items your government wants from the United States. Some of which we'd be willing to agree to. We would make sure the press covered you coming and going from the White House. Maybe you and a key cabinet member would be seen golfing. Then you —"

"I don't like golf," the Ambassador replied. "I prefer sailing. Like your President Kennedy."

"That's perfect. The Treasury Secretary

loves to sail. The fact is that we could help promote you not only as a diplomat Americans trust but also as someone who helps get results for the Russian people."

Sazanov shook his head. "The Foreign Minister, much less the Russian President, would never allow me to steal their thunder. I could never take credit."

"I agree," replied the SPEHA. "But the best part is, you wouldn't have to. Based on the press reports alone, people would recognize that it was you who was doing the heavy lifting. Your best course of action would be to downplay your involvement, show humility. Let the American President declare how much he appreciated your role in bringing Russia and the United States together.

"We will help see to it that you are recognized as one of the most successful Ambassadors to have ever served Russia. Believe me, being seen as a diplomat whom America respects and listens to can go a long way for you back home."

The Russian took another sip of his bourbon. He liked what he was hearing. It was an interesting proposition.

It was also fraught with incredible danger. If President Peshkov developed the slightest suspicion that he was cooperating with the

Americans, he was as good as dead. Diplomats, journalists, dissidents — no one was safe. That was how Russia, at least under its current President, operated. Sazanov had everything to lose.

He also had everything to gain. An offer like this, the backing of the world's most powerful nation, wouldn't come around a second time.

Still, the Russian was wise enough to not jump too quickly. "I appreciate the confidence your nation has in me," he said. "Let me think about it."

Rogers understood.

Draining the rest of the bourbon from his glass, he stood and extended his hand. The two men shook.

"Just don't take too long," the SPEHA said. "If you do, both of our nations are going to regret it."

CHAPTER 36

Murmansk Oblast

Harvath was on edge. He disliked not having a plan. As the doctor thoroughly cleaned and dressed his wounds, he tried to build rapport by asking her questions.

Her name was Christina. She had attended medical school in the city of Archangel at the Northern State Medical University. As part of her training, she had studied abroad in London. After returning home, she had taken over the clinic.

The town, known as Nivsky, had been founded in 1929 as a settlement for laborers building a nearby hydroelectric plant. Not much happened in Nivsky. Its people were proud, worked hard, and hoped for better lives for their children.

Christina and her husband had met at medical school, where he was studying military medicine. They had no children.

She was about ten years younger than

Harvath, and in addition to being very pretty, she was also very athletic. In the winter, she did a lot of snowshoeing and cross-country skiing. The rest of the year, when the Oblast wasn't frozen solid, she was into hiking and mountain biking.

The rifle she had been carrying was a Russian-made Molot-Oruzhie. Though they were far enough from the ice not to worry about polar bears, the wolves had been a big problem. Everyone in town was carrying some sort of firearm. Considering how much drinking went on in Nivsky, Christina expressed surprise that there hadn't been any "friendly fire" incidents yet.

Harvath smiled at her joke. She hadn't responded to his request to get him to the border, and he wasn't going to push her — yet. He knew she was thinking about it.

"When was the last time you ate?" she asked.

"Besides the yogurt I found in your fridge?"

She nodded.

"I had some of your uncle's smoked bear meat and a can of carrots earlier today."

The woman shuddered. "Are you hungry?"

Harvath nodded. He was ravenous.

Christina walked up to the front office,

returned with a paper takeout menu, and handed it to him. It was from the bar and café he had passed on his way through the center of town. His inability to read Russian was negated by the fact that there were pictures of everything.

"Is this for real?" he asked, pointing at one of the items.

"The cheeseburger?" she replied. "It's actually quite good. Even better if you get it with bacon."

"Perfect. I'll take two of them. And a slice of the chocolate cake."

The woman laughed. "And to drink?"

"A Diet Coke."

"Because you're concerned about calories."

Harvath smiled. "Obviously."

She shook her head, walked over to the phone on the wall, and dialed the number.

He paid attention as she placed the order, alert for any sign that she was giving him away to the authorities. There was nothing, though — not in the way she spoke or in what she said — to give him any concern.

"Twenty minutes," she stated as she hung up the phone and turned back to face him.

One of the few things he had not lost when he plunged into the icy river was the money he had taken off the dead Spetsnaz soldiers. He peeled off several bills and handed them to her. "For the food and the medical care." Then, peeling off several more, added, "And for the damage to your door."

Christina accepted his offer, and then took the rest of his money as well. "If I'm going to help get you to the border, we're going to need additional supplies. I think it's better if I do the shopping. Your Russian really is terrible."

Harvath was incredibly relieved. His odds of escape had just improved dramatically. He wanted to throw his arms around her. Instead, he maintained his professional composure. "Thank you," he said.

"Don't thank me yet. Wait till we're at the border."

Once again, he smiled. "Fair enough."

Over the last several days he had endured physical, psychological, and emotional torture. He hadn't thought he'd ever be able to smile again. Now, he'd done so twice in less than five minutes.

"What can I do for you in return?" he asked.

"I don't know," she replied. "Maybe nothing. I haven't thought that far ahead."

"How far ahead *have* you thought?"

"Dinner, as well as hiding my uncle's

snowmobile before people start wondering why he's back and no one has seen him."

Good point. "What can I do?"

"First, I'm going to give you an antibiotic injection," she replied. "Then I'm going to give you day one of your rabies vaccination, which is one dose of rabies vaccine, plus a one-time shot of rabies immune globulin, which loads rabies antibodies into your system."

"What about follow-on shots?"

"You'll need three more rabies shots — on the third, seventh, and fourteenth days from exposure. I'll put together everything you need, so you can take it with you. I assume you're not afraid of injecting yourself?"

"I can handle an injection."

"Good, because if the wolf that attacked you was rabid and you did nothing, it would be a death sentence. Rabies is over 99 percent fatal. By the time a victim notices symptoms, it's too late."

"Then I'm glad I found your clinic."

"And how lucky for you my door was *open.*"

Before he could respond, she had swabbed his left arm with an alcohol-soaked cotton ball and jabbed him with the antibiotic shot. There was no preamble. There wasn't even an "On three" where she tricked him and pricked him on "two." She just jabbed the needle into his arm as if she wanted to pay him back for kicking the door in, and also, maybe, as if she wanted to see if he could take it.

"I hope I didn't bend your needle," he said, flexing the muscles in his arm after she withdrew it.

Taking his joke in stride, Christina examined it and replied, "I think we can still use it for your next two shots. I'll just rinse it under some water."

For a second, Harvath thought she was being serious. Then he saw her discard it into a sharps container and prep two more syringes.

"When was the last time you had a tetanus shot?" she asked.

"I can't remember."

"Within the last ten years?"

Harvath thought for a moment. "I'm not sure."

Christina prepared an additional shot and then brought everything over on a tray and set it next to him.

She started to prep his right arm for the rabies vaccination, but he stopped her. His right arm was his dominant arm, and he didn't need it getting sore. He was in bad enough shape already.

"Can you inject that someplace else?" he asked. "I want to keep that arm as functional as possible."

"The rabies vaccine has to go into a deltoid, but I can use your left arm again," she replied. After swabbing the area, she gave him the shot.

"You're getting better at this," he remarked. "That one didn't hurt at all."

"Make sure you leave a five-star review," she quipped before motioning for him to remove his leggings and roll over onto his stomach.

He did as she asked and she swabbed his left butt cheek. "This is the tetanus injection."

"Give it your best shot," he replied.

She rolled her eyes, administered the medication, and then prepped the fourth and final syringe, along with another cotton ball soaked in alcohol.

"This is the immune globulin, and it's going to hurt," she said as she swabbed a spot on his right cheek.

"Seriously?" he asked, turning his head to look over his shoulder at her.

"I'm only kidding," she replied as she gave him the injection. "Hopefully, there's no more pain in your future."

It was a nice sentiment, but Harvath feared that there was a lot more pain to come. In fact, the closer they got to the border, the more dangerous things were going to get.

CHAPTER 37

Nivsky
Murmansk Oblast

There was nothing subtle about Teplov. He always wanted to make a big statement. *Step in. Scare the shit out of people. Take charge.* That was how he rolled.

So instead of landing the helicopters on the soccer field outside of town, he had them land right in the middle of the town square.

The thunderous, beating blades of the enormous birds sent tremors through buildings for blocks around. Their rotor wash pelted cars with shards of ice and frozen snow. The men of Wagner had arrived.

Hopping out of his helo, Teplov immediately began barking orders. He wanted his men and cargo unloaded immediately.

The patrons inside the Frosty Pelican, their faces pressed up against the windows, couldn't believe what they were seeing. They watched as one of the giant helicopters disgorged soldiers who were dressed from head to toe in winter camouflage. The other helicopter spat out snowmobiles and crates of equipment. It was like a scene out of the American movie *Red Dawn*. It was as if they were being invaded. And in a sense, they were.

Shortly before touching down, an encrypted call had come in from Minayev. After isolating it to Teplov's headset, the two had conducted a brief conversation, with the GRU General doing most of the talking. President Peshkov had put an eight-hour window on finding Harvath. He not only wanted him found, he had demanded immediate, verifiable proof of life.

When Teplov asked what had caused the increased urgency, Minayev had snapped at him. Reminding him who was in charge, he had told him to do his "fucking job" or else.

Something had gone wrong. And, as shit always rolled downhill, Teplov had the unenviable position of being at the very bottom.

Before Minayev hung up on him, Teplov had asked if there were any restrictions on him and his men. Specifically, was there anything the Kremlin wouldn't allow, as long as they tracked Harvath down? The

General's answer was succinct and to the point — *Do whatever it takes.*

For all intents and purposes, the town of Nivsky now belonged to Teplov. If Harvath was here — and he had good reason to believe he was — his mercenaries would find him.

But to do so, he was going to need to enlist the locals. Judging by the number of eyeballs watching him from the Frosty Pelican, he had found the perfect place to start. Whistling over a handful of his men, he headed toward the establishment.

Like the Nazi SS, whose strategies he not only studied but revered, Teplov was a voracious consumer of data. Via a quick Internet search on the way in, he had learned how much the average citizen of the Oblast earned, how much they saved, and how much they carried in debt. Establishing a bounty on Harvath had been simple.

Fifteen thousand American dollars was more than twice the average annual salary. The townspeople would be cutting each other's throats to find Harvath and turn him in.

In addition to motivating the locals, they would block the roads in and out, while teams went house to house conducting searches.

During World War II, SS troops worked with Italian fascist units to root out American spies and saboteurs who were hiding in the snowy forests and Alpine villages near the Brenner Pass. The exercises were called *rastrellamento* — Italian for "raking up."

Though each *rastrellamento* covered a much greater area and involved far more soldiers, Teplov was confident that the same concept would work in Nivsky. It came down to offering a very big carrot, backed up with a very big stick.

As he entered the bar, the customers fell silent. Teplov pulled out a picture of Harvath and held it up so everyone could see it.

"We are looking for a man — an American spy — who has murdered four Russian soldiers and at least one Russian Air Force member. He was on a plane that crashed approximately seventy-five kilometers east of here. We have reason to believe he is now traveling via snowmobile and headed for the border.

"The Russian government is offering a reward of fifteen thousand U.S. dollars — that's nearly a hundred thousand rubles — for information leading to his capture. This man is armed and considered very dangerous. If you see him, do not approach him. My men and I will be staying in your town until we find him.

"We will be conducting house-to-house searches. If anyone is found to be sheltering this man, they will be prosecuted as an accomplice to murder and an enemy of the state. If anyone so much as gives him a crust of bread, they will also be prosecuted as an accomplice to murder and an enemy of the state.

"If you suspect that your neighbor or someone you know is aiding this American, you must report it to me or one of my men immediately. Failure to do so will result in the harshest of punishments.

"At both ends of town, we are establishing checkpoints. It will be necessary to provide your government-issued identification when entering and leaving. We are also creating a registry of vehicles.

"To that end, let's begin with the five SUVs parked immediately outside. Will the owners please identify themselves by raising their hands?"

Teplov waited until the hands went up and then sent his men to collect the keys from four of them. The man with the worst vehicle would be allowed to keep his. He would function as a chauffeur for the others.

Immediately, the men began to protest.

One even refused to hand over his keys. Teplov used that as an opportunity to teach the townspeople a lesson.

When he nodded his head, two of his men dragged the resister out of the bar and beat him in front of the windows for all to see. They left him bloody and unconscious in the snow.

Returning inside, they commandeered the Xerox machine in the office and made hundreds of copies of Harvath's photo. They made sure everyone in the place had one before leaving with tape, staple guns, and the rest of the copies.

As they exited, Teplov kept an eye on the crowd until his men were safely out the door. If anyone was going to do something stupid, like throw a bottle, this was when it normally happened. No one did.

Once the Wagner men had moved away from the entrance, several of the patrons rushed outside to retrieve their beaten friend. Christina, who had been there to pick up her order, rushed outside with them.

Careful to make sure his head and neck were supported, they carried him back inside, laid him down, and covered him with a coat to help warm him up.

Everyone was aghast at what the soldiers had done. "This isn't the Soviet Union," one said. "They cannot do that to us," said another. "We have our rights!" exclaimed a third person.

Christina, though, knew differently. "Rights" were whatever the oligarchs in Moscow decided they were. They could be given and they could be taken away at a moment's notice.

She also knew that those men were not soldiers — not in the traditional sense. They weren't current members of the Russian Army. They were mercenaries. She had recognized the patch they were all wearing on their parkas. It was just like the one her husband had worn as part of his uniform. They belonged to Wagner.

And if Wagner was here in Nivsky, it could mean only one thing — the Kremlin was keeping the hunt for Harvath a secret.

Why they would do that she didn't know. She also didn't care. She had seen the condition of Harvath's body. She had also just seen the brutality they were capable of firsthand.

The Wagner men were dangerous. They were also about to close off the town and begin a house-to-house search. With four SUVs and several snowmobiles, they would be able to cover a lot of ground in a short time. She needed to get back to Harvath as soon as possible.

But with all eyes on her as the town's doctor, she first needed to tend to the man who had been so savagely attacked.

CHAPTER 38

"Get your things," said Christina as she burst through the back door of the clinic and began gathering up supplies. "We're leaving. Right now."

"I heard the helicopters," replied Harvath, already dressed and ready to go. "What's going on?"

"They know you're here. They're passing around your photo and are closing off the town."

He implored her to take a breath. "Who knows I'm here?"

"Mercenaries. Wagner, the company my husband worked for."

Harvath was familiar with them. Most were ex-Spetsnaz. "How many did you see?"

"Around twenty. Maybe more."

"How were they equipped?"

"White uniforms. Helmets with night vision. They were carrying rifles. And pistols, too."

"How do they plan to close off the town?"

"They are blocking the road at both ends. Anyone coming in or going out will be checked. They are offering a reward for your capture."

"How much?"

"Fifteen thousand dollars, American. That's a lot of money around here."

He didn't doubt it. He knew enough about Russia to have an idea what the average person earned, especially someone who didn't live in Moscow or St. Petersburg.

"How are we going to get out?" he asked.

It was a good question — one her mind had been working overtime on. "Driving is impossible," she replied. "I'm afraid the snowmobile is, too. We'll have to figure something else out, but we can't stay here. They're right behind me. We need to get going. *Now.*"

The *"Now"* kicked Harvath into high gear.

Christina had struck him as a calm, very competent medical professional, someone capable of staying cool under pressure. When she intimated it was time to haul ass, he took it seriously.

Having upward of twenty, and possibly more, former Spetsnaz soldiers on his tail wasn't something he relished. He had made it this far because of good training, good luck, and one hell of a head start.

The head start was now all but gone. All he had left was his training and whatever good luck ended up in his path.

Before she had left to pick up the food, he had asked her to help him send a message back to the United States. Without revealing completely how the process worked, he had assured her that it couldn't be traced back to her and that there was no risk.

Knowing how the Russian Internet was used to hunt down anyone who opposed the Kremlin, it didn't sound safe to her. Nevertheless, she had said she'd think about it and they could discuss it when she got back.

Now, as Harvath asked her again, she looked at him like he was crazy.

"It'll take two seconds," he said.

"Do you want to get caught?" she asked. "Because I don't. They made it very clear what will happen to anyone who is discovered assisting you."

Of course Harvath didn't want to get caught. He wanted to get to the border. But he also wanted to summon the cavalry.

Knowing the best-trained, best-equipped military on the planet was speeding to his rescue wouldn't necessarily improve his odds in the short run, but it would be a hell of a morale booster. It also meant that all he had to do was stay alive until they could get to him. They would handle getting him out.

As Christina turned on her heel and headed out the back door, he abandoned any hope of hopping on her computer. No matter how little time he thought he needed to transmit his message, he couldn't do it without her help.

Outside, her tiny 4×4 was idling in the cold. Before hopping inside, she pointed to a shed and said, "It's unlocked. Put the snowmobile in there."

Harvath did as he was told.

Fortunately, the machine fired right up and he didn't need to drag it. Not that he could have if he had wanted to. His entire body was aching. He would have set the fucking thing on fire before dragging it into a shed to hide it.

Throwing his rucksack into the back of the 4×4, he hopped into the passenger seat with the pump-action Baikal and literally rode "shotgun."

"What's the plan?" he asked, scanning the street in both directions as she pulled away from the medical clinic.

"You're a bit like cancer," she said, handing him his takeout. "The Wagner mercenaries know the town has it — they just don't know where exactly to look for it."

"Okay," Harvath replied, unwrapping the first bacon cheeseburger, not sure where she was going with her analogy.

"When doctors begin to focus in on where the cancer is, they start to get excited. It makes sense. They can't kill it until they've located it. So once a location makes itself known, all attention goes to that one point."

"So?"

"So I think we should give the mercenaries a location."

"What do you have in mind?" he asked as he took his first bite.

"If they're any good, which I'm assuming they are, my clinic is high on their list of places to check for a fugitive who survived a plane crash. Once they get there, they'll see my back door has been kicked in and the heat has been turned up. They'll find bloody gauze pads, as well as fresh sterile wipes in the garbage. It won't take long for them to put two and two together.

"Expanding their search, they'll find the snowmobile in the shed. They might not get to it right away, but at some point someone will tie it to my uncle. When that happens, they'll start connecting dots. The cabin you stayed in was, obviously, within walking distance of the crash. If they haven't already, they'll search his home here, on the outskirts of Nivsky."

"And that's what you want to give them?"

Christina shook her head. "At some point, very soon, they're going to check it out. When they do, I want to leave a false trail. I want them to think you were there, but have gone in a completely different direction."

She was a strategic thinker, and he appreciated that about her. Setting up some sort of red herring at the uncle's house could buy them valuable time.

"What are you thinking?" he asked.

"I don't know yet. Finish eating. We can talk about it when we get there."

Harvath, who had been chowing through the first burger as quickly as he could while continuing to scan for threats, took out the Diet Coke and drained half of it in one long sip.

It reminded him of some low-rolling death-row inmate's last meal. He just hoped it wouldn't be his.

CHAPTER 39

The trapper's home was nothing like his cabin. It was a modern, orange brick structure clad with red roofing tiles. Wrought-iron railings bracketed a set of three concrete steps in front, which perfectly matched the house's glossy black gutters. An artsy piece of metal sheeting was bolted above the door to provide a modicum of protection from the elements when people were entering or leaving.

Inside, the rooms were small but cozy — probably just the right amount of space for an older man who lived alone and was often gone. It smelled like potting soil and old newspaper.

There were books, a television set, and even a record player. Framed family photos lined an entire bookshelf; many of them included Christina.

"I'm sorry again about your uncle," he said.

"It's how he wanted to die — out there in the wilderness. We were the only family each other had left. I think if it hadn't been for me, he would have sold this place, gone into the woods, and never come back."

"Are these your parents?" he asked, pointing to one of the pictures.

"Yes. And my aunt. They're all deceased now."

"I'm sorry," Harvath repeated.

The woman shrugged. "Life in Russia is tough. Life in rural Russia is even tougher. They all smoked and drank way too much. None of them, except for my uncle, ever got any exercise."

She sounded cold and detached, but Harvath could see the emotion in her eyes. It wasn't easy being the only one left. Harvath could relate.

Off the living room was a small kitchen. Stepping away from him, Christina ducked inside and began inventorying supplies.

As Harvath continued poking around the living room, she suggested he start a fire in the fireplace. "Not too big," she cautioned. "We want to make sure it's burned down by the time anyone gets here. Let them think we have a bigger head start than we do."

It was a good idea. After he got the fire

going, he called out to her and asked what he could do next.

"My uncle was a vain man who colored his hair. There should be a kit in the bathroom. Leave any packaging in the trash, but flush the actual coloring down the toilet, after you spill some at the sink. They'll think you're trying to change your appearance. Run the shower and leave towels on the floor. If you want to shave, do it quickly. I'll grab some extra clothes from the closet."

The woman was a natural. Not everything she had suggested would work, but every time their pursuers were forced to stop, scratch their heads, and evaluate, it was an additional moment they fell behind.

Hitting the bathroom, he decided against the shave. Instead, he invested ninety seconds in a hot shower. It was one of the best showers he could ever remember taking.

With hot food in his stomach and hot water on his skin, it was the first time since the plane crash that he had felt truly warm. He had a feeling it wasn't going to last.

Climbing out, he quickly dried himself off and then wrapped the towel around his waist, below the bite wounds.

He had taken off his bandages before getting in the shower. All of them were bloodstained. Christina hadn't sewn him up. Part of healing from a wolf attack was leaving the wounds open so they could seep. That meant no stiches and no staples.

He was just about to put his bandages back on when Christina knocked and pushed open the bathroom door.

"Leave those," she said, stepping inside with her bag. "I brought more. I don't know how smart those Wagner assholes are, but I like reinforcing that you're injured. Leaving more bloody bandages will continue to make them think they have the upper hand."

After she had redressed his wounds, she placed two pain pills next to the sink and stepped out so that he could finish up.

Searching for the hair dye, he found a brand new toothbrush and brushed his teeth. It was another terrific feeling, something he had long taken for granted.

After leaving a few drops around the sink and dumping the dye chemicals down the toilet, he cast aside the packaging and swallowed the pills.

Getting dressed, he walked back out to the living room and found Christina, hands on hips, slowly scanning the bookshelves.

"What are you looking for?" he asked.

"Bread crumbs to help create that false trail we discussed in the car."

Finally, she found it. Removing a large

atlas of the Murmansk Oblast, Christina carried it to the dining room table, beckoned Harvath over, and began flipping through its brightly colored pages.

When she got to the map she wanted, she stopped and tapped it with her finger. "This one."

Harvath examined the image. It showed Russian rail lines as they ran along the western edge of the Oblast.

Reaching for a ballpoint pen, she picked a spot on the border with Finland, about three hundred kilometers northwest of Nivsky, and circled it.

"Why there?" he asked.

"Because we're going in the other direction," she replied, as she tore the page out of the atlas and tucked it in her pocket.

He then watched as she returned the book to the shelf, though not as neatly as he had found it. Once more, he was impressed with her thinking.

"For somebody who's not sure how smart those Wagner assholes are, you're giving them a lot of credit."

"You don't think it will work?" she answered.

"I think it's a long shot. First, they have to find the atlas. Next they have to notice the page is missing. Then they have to source another copy of the same atlas. I'm assuming it's popular?"

The woman nodded. "Practically everybody in town has one."

"Okay," Harvath went on. "Next, someone has to notice the impression left behind by your pen. If this person knows anything, they'll lay a piece of paper down and rub it with a pencil. That'll let them know where you made your circle on the missing page. They marry that up with an intact atlas, and the wild-goose chase is on. Did I miss anything?"

Christina smiled at him. "Very well done."

"You know that's not normal."

"What are you talking about?"

"The way your mind works. Most people don't think two steps ahead, much less three."

"Well, I'm definitely not normal, and absolutely not like most people."

Harvath smiled back. "There is one problem, though. The snowmobile."

"What about it?"

"There's no way I could have covered the distance from the crash site to here so quickly — not on foot. I am assuming they found your uncle's cabin and the snowmobile tracks, which explains why they're here. This was the closest town.

"I am also going to assume that they know I have a GPS device and that's how I got here. Their proof will come when they find the snowmobile in the shed behind your clinic. There's an attachment on the handlebars for it."

Christina hadn't considered that. "You could leave the GPS unit here. Then the missing page from the atlas would be believable. Let them think you are going completely off the grid."

"Or, better yet, that I believe the grid will completely be going off."

Now he had her completely confused. "I don't understand."

"Your uncle's GPS device isn't a tracker. It doesn't send out a signal telling people where it is. Therefore, there'd be no reason for me to get rid of it. It's too valuable. But if the GPS system stops working, then it's worthless. At that point, I *would* need a map."

"I still don't understand. When was the last time the GPS system ever stopped working?"

"Last year. During NATO training exercises in Scandinavia, Finland accused Russia of jamming the GPS signal in their northern airspace. If I was concerned that they'd do it to prevent me from escaping, or from being rescued, I'd want a paper map as a backup."

"So then my plan is good."

"It is," replied Harvath. "I think we can make it better."

"How so?"

"With an Internet search of the same area. Does your uncle have a laptop or a tablet in the house?"

She shook her head. "He didn't like technology. Didn't trust it. The GPS device was as far as he would go."

"Then we'll have to run the risk of overplaying our hand," he said as he walked over to the shelf, pulled the atlas back out and then placed it on the table next to the ballpoint pen. "I don't want to take any chances that they miss it."

She didn't disagree.

"So what's the plan?" he asked.

"There's a Sámi village about twenty kilometers west of here."

Harvath did a rough conversion in his head. *Twelve miles.* "But if the roads are shut down, how are we going to get there?"

"That depends. How much stamina do you have left?"

"Don't worry about me. I'll be fine."

"Good, because we're going to have to ski."

"Downhill or cross-country?"

She smiled at him again. "If it was all downhill, I wouldn't ask about your stamina."

"What about there not being enough reindeer skins to survive in this weather?"

"That was when we were talking about you going all the way to the border. Right now, all we have to do is get you to the village."

Back out in the open, in the freezing cold, at night. Harvath wasn't looking forward to it. "And then what?"

"I'm working on it."

"What about gear? Skis?"

"You can use my husband's equipment. It's all here, in the garage," she said, leading the way through the kitchen to a door in the back. Turning on the light, she pointed to some boxes and some things hanging on the opposite wall. "My uncle didn't think it was healthy for me to be holding on to his things."

"Where are your skis?"

"At my house, but there's no time. I'll show you on the GPS where you're going and whom to ask for. Sini speaks English. She'll take care of you."

"You're not coming?"

"I'll be there as soon as I can. First I need

327

to deal with those Wagner assholes. If I'm right, they're going to be calling me any minute about a break-in at the clinic."

"Before I go, I need you to promise me you'll do something," he replied.

"We've already wasted too much time. You need to hurry up and get out of here."

"I'm not going unless you promise me."

She couldn't believe this guy. Two dozen former Russian Spetsnaz soldiers with helicopters, snowmobiles, and stolen SUVs were all looking for him, yet he wasn't going to flee until he got a promise from her. She couldn't decide if he was incredibly brave or just incredibly insane.

In the interest of getting him moving, she agreed. And while he geared up, she created a route on the GPS and wrote down everything he needed to do.

Then, standing outside in the snow, he handed her a small, folded piece of paper. "This is all you have to do."

She looked at it. "Are you serious?"

"As serious as cancer," he said, as he turned and skied off into the woods.

CHAPTER 40

A litany of things had been flying through Christina's mind as she maneuvered home. She had to remind herself not to speed. Though they were a tight-knit community, loyalty wasn't guaranteed — not with soldiers in town offering rewards for information and beating people who resisted.

It reminded her of the stories her grandparents used to tell of life under communism. The most dangerous people weren't the apparatchiks or the secret police. The most dangerous people were your neighbors, your coworkers, the babushka who swept the street. The reign of communist terror was successful at preventing another revolution because it was impossible to organize. You didn't know who you could trust. Every person on every corner was a potential informant. Christina needed to be very careful.

She left the car outside, so the engine

would cool more rapidly. She didn't want to give away that she just arrived. When the Wagner thugs came calling, she wanted her alibi to be airtight. She had worked late, called in a takeout order, and had gone straight home.

Gathering up Harvath's takeout containers, she brought them inside and spread them out across her kitchen counter. The meal had come with fries, which he had neglected, so she helped herself as she downed two quick shots of vodka to steady her nerves.

If anyone came calling, it was important that she appear to have been home, alone, drinking.

She had just poured a large glass of wine, from a half-empty bottle, when her bell rang. There was little doubt in her mind who it was.

Fries in hand, she walked up to the front door and opened it. Standing outside were three Wagner mercenaries. Front and center was the man in charge — the one from the bar who had held up Harvath's picture and had given all the orders.

He was tall, with blond hair and several prominent facial scars. "Doctor Volkova?"

"Yes?" she replied, a half-eaten French fry in her mouth.

"My name is Colonel Kazimir Teplov. I am sorry to disturb you. May we come in?"

"What do you want?"

"It's somewhat cold outside. If you wouldn't mind I'd rather do this inside."

Taking a moment to finish chewing her French fry, she then stood back and allowed the men to enter.

The rifle Teplov had been carrying at the bar was gone. From what she could see, he had only the sidearm holstered at his thigh. The two goons behind him, however, were not only carrying rifles, but appeared jumpy, ready to fire if anyone so much as sneezed.

"Thank you," said Teplov, as he and his men stepped into her home. "As I said, my name is —"

"Kazimir Teplov. I know. I was in the bar when you and your people arrived."

"Is that so?" he asked.

"It is so. By the way, the man your soldiers beat unconscious, were you aware that he served honorably in the Russian Navy? And that he is also our auto mechanic."

"I did not know that. I'm sorry. It was a most unfortunate incident."

Christina despised this guy and was having a very hard time disguising it. "So, Mr. Teplov, what can I do for you?"

"It's Colonel Teplov."

"Is it?" she asked, pointing at the patch on his shoulder. "Because I didn't know that Wagner mercenaries retained their rank from prior service in the Russian Armed Forces."

Teplov smiled. "You know who we are."

"Oh, I know all about you."

"And how did you come by this knowledge?"

Walking over to her kitchen counter, she picked up her wine, crossed her arms just as she took a long sip, and said, "Because I'm a Wagner widow."

For a moment, Teplov's mask slipped. He was genuinely surprised. "Who was your husband?"

"Demyan Volkov," she responded. "He was killed in Syria. Latakia Province."

"I'm very sorry for your loss."

"So am I. What is it you want, Mr. Teplov?"

He looked at the food containers. "Did I interrupt something?"

"Why do you ask?"

He walked over and read the receipt taped to the top of one of the containers. "Two bacon cheeseburgers, chocolate cake, French fries? Sounds like a lot of food for a woman your size."

"Are you accusing me of something, Mr.

332

Teplov?"

He paused and, looking at her, replied, "Should I be?"

"That depends. If you asked the new girl what I normally order, she would tell you it's always salads. Sometimes, though, I get fish or chicken. If you ask someone who isn't new, they'll tell you the same thing, but they'll add that several times a year, I come in and order a very large, very unhealthy meal.

"When that happens, it tends to be on a significant anniversary — the day I met my husband, the day he died, the day we got married, or the day we had our first date, which today happens to be the anniversary of."

"Again, I'm truly sorry," said Teplov. "I didn't know."

Extending her wineglass in a mock toast, she then brought it back in and took an even longer slug. "What they won't tell you," she said, once she had swallowed, "because none of them know, is that after I bring the food home and eat it, I drink way more than I should — usually several bottles. The next day I am pretty useless."

He had no reason to doubt the veracity of her account, so he decided to cut to the chase. Taking out the photo of Harvath he had shown around the bar, he presented it to her. "Have you seen this man? We believe he may be hiding somewhere here in town."

"I have not," she answered.

"Would you mind if my men took a look around your house? As I explained in the bar, the American is armed and very dangerous."

Christina raised her palms. "I don't know why he'd be here, but go ahead. Be my guest."

Teplov nodded and his men commenced their investigation. Turning his attention back to her, he said, "We were concerned you might be in danger."

"In danger? Of what?"

"During our search for the fugitive, some of my men passed by your clinic. Were you aware that the back door had been kicked in?"

"Kicked in by whom? When?"

"We don't know. We assume it was the American and that it happened within the last couple of hours."

"Was anything stolen?" she asked, trying to appear concerned.

"We found some bloody gauze pads in the trash as well as an empty antibiotic vial, plus two for rabies. Have you had cause to treat anyone for rabies recently?"

Christina shook her head. "I have not."

"Interesting."

She had no idea if he believed her or not, but the alcohol had emboldened her. "Where would your fugitive have been bitten by a dog?"

Teplov held up his index finger. "Not a dog. Wolves."

"Jesus," she replied.

"You don't like wolves," he said with a smile.

"Can't stand them. They've been preying on people in the Oblast all winter. None of us go anywhere without a rifle. So far, though, they haven't attacked people in Nivsky. Where did this happen?"

"A hundred kilometers east of here."

"Wonderful. In addition to a murderer, we also have killer wolves on our doorstep," she said, before changing the subject. "How bad is the back door to my clinic. Was there any other damage?"

"None that my men have reported."

"Anything stolen? Besides the things you found in the trash?"

"They couldn't tell," he responded. "It sounds like some sort of cabinet used for storing medicines was broken into."

"Damn it," she cursed. Then, downing what remained in her wineglass, she grabbed her parka, which had been hanging over one of the kitchen chairs.

"What are you doing?" demanded Teplov.

"What does it look like I'm doing? Someone broke into my clinic. I need to know how bad the damage is."

"I don't think you should be driving."

"Pardon me, but who's the soldier and who's the doctor?" she asked.

"Fair enough," said Teplov. "But you're part of the Wagner family. It's our duty to look out for you. The American could be anywhere."

There was no point in arguing with them. She would accept an escort, but she wasn't going to get in a car with them. "I'm okay to drive. You can follow me to the clinic if you wish. Are your men ready to go?"

Teplov called out to his men. Moments later, they materialized and gave him the thumbs-up. They hadn't uncovered any sign of the American. The house was clean.

Locking the door behind them, Christina hopped into her 4×4 and headed back to her clinic.

She drove fast, but not too fast. She was well aware that if Teplov was the top man, and he had come out to her house, then she was his top lead. That meant that every moment she kept him and his men tied up was another moment that helped Harvath get farther away.

She just hoped that she had understood Harvath's directions correctly.

CHAPTER 41

"Hit!" Nicholas exclaimed from the desk he had been given in the center of the room. "Hit! Hit! Hit!"

His dogs, which the FBI Director had allowed in the building as "service animals," leaped to attention. Growling, they scanned for threats until Nicholas commanded them to lie down.

"What do you have?" the SPEHA asked as he rushed over. "Is it Harvath?" After his meeting with the Russian Ambassador, he could use some good news.

Nicholas had a smile on his face that stretched from ear to ear. "It's his rescue protocol. And the code is one hundred percent his," he said, pointing to his screen.

On it was an Instagram account with only a few thousand followers, all of them fakes. It had been set up as a digital dead drop.

The Carlton Group paid a trusted source in Iceland to update it with posts about makeup, fashion tips, and celebrity gossip. When Harvath, or someone operating under his authority, popped up and commented on the most recent entry, Nicholas was overjoyed. Rogers, on the other hand, was pragmatic.

"I know you're excited," he said. "Slow it down for me, though. What are we looking at?"

Nicholas was all too happy to explain. "Like the CIA, The Carlton Group has developed situation-dependent communication protocols. They run the gamut from transmitting SITREPs while under surveillance in friendly nations, to an operative transmitting a distress signal from inside a hostile country. We just received the latter from Harvath."

"You're positive it's him?"

Nicholas nodded. "No question. It's his authentication code and everything."

The SPEHA stared at the Instagram comment. "You can be absolutely sure, just from this?"

Nicholas nodded again, emphatically. "Harvath set all of this up himself. Using Instagram was his idea, as were all the code words. He also built in a way for us to immediately know if the message was being sent under duress."

"Under duress?"

"That someone was forcing him to write it," Nicholas explained. "That doesn't appear to be the case here."

"So what do we have?"

"First, he's alive. He's *fucking* alive. Thank God."

"And next?" Rogers asked.

"He posted from Russia. Specifically Nivsky, a town in the Murmansk Oblast. But he's on the move."

"On the move where?"

"West," stated Nicholas. "He's trying to get to the border with Finland."

"That's fantastic," said the SPEHA. "How do we get in touch with him?"

Nicholas looked up from the screen. "He doesn't have access to a means of secure communication."

"Then how do we pinpoint his location?"

"We can't. All we have is his last known location. I can only imagine what it took to get this message out to us."

"Agreed," stated Rogers. "Okay, listen up, people," he called out to the Fusion Cell. "According to what we just learned, we may have found our man. He does appear to be in Russia. He's on the run. Our starting point is a town called Nivsky, in the Murmansk Oblast, heading west. All hands on deck. I want to fix his precise location. Start pulling SIGINT, geospatial, all of it. I'll be damned if the Russians are going to beat us. Let's move!"

CHAPTER 42

Murmansk Oblast

Seven kilometers in, all Harvath wanted to do was puke his guts out. Part of it was the cheeseburgers, but another part was how fast he was moving. He wanted to get as far away from the mercenaries as fast as possible.

He was pushing himself too hard. He knew that. But if he didn't make it to that village, if he got caught by a Wagner snowmobile or helicopter patrol, he'd never breathe free air again. He had to push it as hard as he could.

In addition to extra food, Christina had put medical supplies and clothing in his rucksack. Mercifully, she had also affixed a water bladder to it. Given how close the enemy was there could be no stopping to melt snow into water.

The temperature tonight felt worse than anything he had experienced since the crash. Christina, however, had assured him he could make it. He was wearing her husband's winter gear and was insulated from head to toe. Even his eyes were protected by a set of goggles.

The pace he was keeping, though, had him sweating. He could feel the rivulets of salty perspiration rolling down his face and down his back.

Whenever his mind suggested that he stop, if only for a moment to catch his breath, he redoubled his efforts and pressed forward. Now wasn't the time. Stopping equaled capture.

Fortunately, he hadn't heard any helicopters overhead. Perhaps Wagner was convinced that he was holed up in one of the houses in town and had decided to give them a rest. If so, that was a good thing.

Nevertheless, he made sure to stay in the woods and to use the tree cover to full advantage. Wagner likely had access to thermal imagers that could pinpoint him based on his body heat. There was no reason to make things any easier for them than he had to.

Pushing through the deep snow, he slowed only to take quick sips of water and to check his GPS.

From time to time, he had trouble getting

a signal, and when that happened, he had no choice but to ski back out toward the edge of the woods where he could get a good view of the night sky and reconnect with the satellites.

But as soon as he had reestablished the signal and had confirmed his heading, he skied back into the trees.

Even with the small course adjustments, the trip felt as if it was taking a lot longer than Christina had said it would. He knew that was just his fatigue talking, though — the unhelpful part of his brain that always spoke up when he was exhausted and wanted to sabotage his progress.

As he had done with his guilt and grief over losing Lara, he slammed an iron door shut on that part of his psyche and pressed on.

Movement and concealment were all that mattered. He needed to get to that village.

When he reached the ten-kilometer mark, he paused for the world's shortest rest. He was only one-third of the way there.

He believed that if he sat down, even with the help of his poles, he wouldn't be able to get up. So, he contented himself with leaning against a tree. Almost instantly, his legs began to cramp.

Bending down to massage them, he took

his weight off the tree, which released a pile of snow from the boughs high above. *Somebody* was trying to tell him something. Stopping was a bad idea.

He took a long drink of water, hoping to ease the cramps. After clearing the snow from his pack, and his shotgun, he pushed on again.

To fuel his trek, he allowed himself to tap into an emotion he had been trying to hold at bay — his rage.

He knew behind which door it hid and he didn't just crack it, he kicked it wide open. Instantly, it crashed into his bloodstream like liquid lava, taking him over.

It was the darkest energy from the darkest part of his soul. More addictive than any drug, more powerful than any other emotion, rage lay beyond reason, beyond any sense of right or wrong. Rage was primal. And though he had been taught to never let it take control, he gave himself over to it, fully.

He saw everything from the cottage in New Hampshire unfold once more in his mind's eye. He saw the brutal executions and the lives leaving the bodies of the people he loved. He saw the men responsible. He saw his own role — unable to stop any of it — and pure, toxic hate rose within him once more.

His mind shifted to the Spetsnaz soldiers at the crash site — those who had already been dead and those he had killed. He saw himself taking their scalps and stringing them along a piece of wire — his small and unsatisfying act of revenge. Carving off pieces of those men was an end-zone dance. Hanging those scalps up was a "fuck you" to the men who would eventually come upon them.

The only real sense of satisfaction he would get would be when he tracked down the men who were ultimately responsible for what had happened. It didn't matter if it took him days, months, or even years. All he knew was that he wouldn't stop until he had found them and had taken from them just as much as if not more than they had taken from him.

With the molten rage pumping through him, he pushed his way through the snow.

He eventually developed a rhythm. Kilometer after kilometer fell away behind him, until the terrain began to angle upward.

It wasn't a very steep ascent, but it was agonizing, reengaging many of the muscles he had torn down while snowshoeing. There wasn't enough rage left in his tank to propel him at the clip he had been going.

And as the rage started to ebb away, it was replaced by something else — fear. *He wasn't going to make it.*

Each push of his skis came at greater cost — each required more energy, each was more painful, and each carried him over a shorter distance. He had gone from moving feet to moving only inches. And whether or not it was a trick of his exhausted mind, the incline felt as if it were growing.

If ever he needed his rage to spur him on, it was now, but he couldn't summon it. Leaning forward, he used his poles to drag himself up the hillside.

Millimeter by millimeter he climbed, refusing to give up. He could feel the muscle fibers tearing in his back and shoulders, arms and legs. His body, already badly broken, didn't have much left to give.

Once again, the voice of the saboteur came to him, urging him to drop his pack, to stop, rest, give up. He tried not to listen, but the voice only grew louder, its arguments more convincing. There was nothing he could do to close it off. He was too weak to fight. So, he did the only thing he had left in him — he negotiated with it.

He cajoled and bargained, but never stopped moving. He allowed the voice to run wild, to persuade him why it was right

347

and he was wrong. Eventually, he suc-
cumbed.

He was almost at the top when he realized
that he had lied to Christina. His stamina
was for shit. The stress of being on the run,
the bitter arctic cold, the grueling physical
exertion, had eaten it all away.

He couldn't go any farther. This was it.
He needed to rest, maybe even to sleep, if
only for just a little while.

Planting his skis, he stuck his poles in the
snow, unslung his shotgun, and dropped it
alongside him. He followed with his pack,
but as he tried to get out of the straps, he
stumbled.

He landed with his legs twisted beneath
him and one of the skis missing. He didn't
care. All he wanted to do was to close his
eyes. It would be a death sentence, however,
to fall asleep out here in the cold.

A feeling of warmth was spreading across
his body. Along with it whispered the voice
of the saboteur, encouraging him to give in.

It felt so good to be still, to be off his feet.
Through breaks in the snow-covered trees
he could see an occasional star. They were
the same stars he had pointed out to Lara
while sitting on his dock back home in
Virginia.

He had begun to teach Lara's son, Marco,

the names of the constellations, the same way his father had taught him. It was in those small, simple moments that they had come closest to being a family — the thing Harvath had wanted more than almost anything else.

Now, lying here in the snow, he had a reason to stay put. He had convinced himself to keep staring up into the night sky — that once he had seen enough stars to identify a constellation, he would start moving again. It was an homage to Lara, a eulogy of sorts. No matter how cold or how tired he got, he wouldn't move until he had done so.

"Sit up," a voice suddenly said.

It was hard to hear it over the wind.

"Sit up," it repeated.

It was Lara's voice.

"Stop playing games. Get moving."

He ignored her. He knew her voice wasn't real. He was losing his mind again.

Maybe, he thought to himself, *things would make more sense if I just closed my eyes for a little bit.*

And so, despite every rational circuit in his brain telling him not to, he gave in to the saboteur and allowed his lids to close.

CHAPTER 43

Nivsky
Murmansk Oblast

Christina made a big deal about the back door to her clinic having been kicked in, letting loose with several choice words not necessarily befitting a doctor.

Teplov, who had been on her bumper the entire way from her house, had followed her inside. He watched her, closely, to see what she did.

After bitching about the damage in back, she went straight to the room with the cabinet where the drugs were stored.

It was obvious it had been broken into. Inventorying the contents, she appeared relieved.

"What is it?" Teplov asked. "What do you see?"

"I see my narcotics. Fortunately, none of them were taken."

"Anything else?"

"As you mentioned, a vial of antibiotics is missing, along with the first two doses of a typical rabies vaccine, plus the follow-ons."

"The *follow-ons*?"

"Yes, the doses that would be need to be given on the third, seventh, and fourteenth days from exposure."

"Interesting," mumbled Teplov, lost in thought.

"Why? Because your American understands what a course of rabies vaccination entails?"

"No," said the mercenary, coming back around. "What's interesting is that he stole the entire course. Either he's planning on hanging around for the next two weeks, or he's concerned with how soon he might be rescued."

Christina was nonplussed. "That's your problem. I want to know who's paying for the damage to my back door and the stolen medicines."

"I hope you have insurance."

"Exactly what Wagner told me when my husband was killed."

Without waiting for the man to respond, she left the room and went to check the rest of the clinic.

"Doctor Volkova," he called out after her. "Doctor Volkova."

She turned and faced him in the hallway. "If you cooperate with us, the Kremlin has a 'Heroes' fund," he said. "Perhaps we can get your husband recognized as a hero of the Russian Federation. It comes with a modest stipend."

"Fuck you," she replied.

"Excuse me?"

"You heard me. *Fuck you.* I am here. I *am* cooperating. And regardless of what Wagner or the Kremlin says, my husband *is* a hero."

Teplov was taken aback. "I didn't mean to suggest that he —"

"I don't want to talk about it anymore. Do you understand me?"

The mercenary nodded and Christina continued her search.

In one of the examination rooms, she pointed out the bloody gauze pads. Then, in the office up front, she drew Teplov's attention to the fact that the computer had been left on. Something, she explained, that clinic staff never did.

Looking through the break room, she noted that there were several small food items missing. The more honest she was, the quicker she believed Teplov would lose interest in her.

It was trending in that direction when one of his men entered the clinic through the

352

"As you mentioned, a vial of antibiotics is missing, along with the first two doses of a typical rabies vaccine, plus the follow-ons."

"The *follow-ons*?"

"Yes, the doses that would be need to be given on the third, seventh, and fourteenth days from exposure."

"Interesting," mumbled Teplov, lost in thought.

"Why? Because your American understands what a course of rabies vaccination entails?"

"No," said the mercenary, coming back around. "What's interesting is that he stole the entire course. Either he's planning on hanging around for the next two weeks, or he's concerned with how soon he might be rescued."

Christina was nonplussed. "That's your problem. I want to know who's paying for the damage to my back door and the stolen medicines."

"I hope you have insurance."

"Exactly what Wagner told me when my husband was killed."

Without waiting for the man to respond, she left the room and went to check the rest of the clinic.

"Doctor Volkova," he called out after her. "Doctor Volkova."

She turned and faced him in the hallway. "If you cooperate with us, the Kremlin has a 'Heroes' fund," he said. "Perhaps we can get your husband recognized as a hero of the Russian Federation. It comes with a modest stipend."

"Fuck you," she replied.

"Excuse me?"

"You heard me. *Fuck you.* I am here. I *am* cooperating. And regardless of what Wagner or the Kremlin says, my husband *is* a hero."

Teplov was taken aback. "I didn't mean to suggest that he —"

"I don't want to talk about it anymore. Do you understand me?"

The mercenary nodded and Christina continued her search.

In one of the examination rooms, she pointed out the bloody gauze pads. Then, in the office up front, she drew Teplov's attention to the fact that the computer had been left on. Something, she explained, that clinic staff never did.

Looking through the break room, she noted that there were several small food items missing. The more honest she was, the quicker she believed Teplov would lose interest in her.

It was trending in that direction when one of his men entered the clinic through the back and asked to speak with his boss in private.

When they were done, Teplov rejoined her.

"I wonder if you could come outside with me for a moment," he said.

"What for?"

"It won't take long. There's something I need you to identify, please."

It didn't sound like she had a choice. So, as the man stood back to let her pass, she zipped up her parka and walked toward the back door.

Outside, a couple of the Wagner men had opened the shed and discovered the snowmobile.

"Do you recognize this?" Teplov asked.

Ever since she'd had Harvath put the machine in the shed, she had expected the question. "I do," she replied. "That's my uncle's snowmobile. But what's it doing here?"

"Doctor Volkova, when was the last time you saw your uncle?"

She took a moment as she tried to remember. "It has been at least three weeks."

"And how was his health?"

"Why do you ask?"

"Just answer the question, please," the man commanded.

"He had emphysema and an irregular

353

heartbeat. What is his snowmobile doing in my shed? If you know something, *tell* me. Where is my uncle?"

Teplov was a soldier, not a clergyman or a counselor. His bedside manner was sorely underdeveloped. "Doctor Volkova, I'm sorry to have to tell you this, but your uncle is dead."

"Dead? How?"

"We don't know."

"What does this have to do with my clinic being broken into? Is the American you're looking for connected to this? Did he murder my uncle?"

He held up his hand. "We don't know."

"Well, what the hell *do* you know?"

Teplov tried to calm her down. "Your uncle was a fur trapper and had a cabin, correct?"

She nodded.

"We think the American, Harvath, found your uncle's cabin and may have stayed there for a short time. We believe he helped himself to clothing and other supplies and then used your uncle's snowmobile to come here."

"But did he *murder* my uncle?" she repeated.

"We found your uncle in his bed, with the blanket pulled up over his head. We couldn't what do you see?"

"I see my uncle's house," she replied, playing it as cool as possible.

"Yes, but is anything missing? Is anything out of place?"

It was now that she was especially glad he'd had the two shots of vodka. Teplov didn't know what he was looking for. As a result, he was asking her.

Whatever she told him, as long as she was believable, would dictate where his search went next.

"Is it okay for me to look around?" she asked.

"Absolutely."

She headed for the bathroom and Teplov followed.

Pointing at the wet towels and bloody bandages, she remarked, "It looks like your American was trying to clean up."

"What can you infer about his injuries?"

She told the truth. "You don't suture canine bites. You let them ooze. Your fugitive seems to be doing that, which suggests he definitely has medical training."

"Anything else?"

She shook her head and stepped out.

Leading Teplov into the bedroom, she looked through the closet, the dresser drawers, and the nightstands before declaring

find any signs of trauma."

"Then how did he die?"

Teplov shrugged. "We don't know."

"So he stole my uncle's snowmobile, rode into Nivsky, and just happened to break into *my* clinic? How is that possible?"

"We assume that he either found a map, or judging by that," Teplov said, pointing at the bracket mounted to the handlebars, "a GPS device. Do you know what your uncle used for navigation?"

"GPS," she replied, telling the truth. "All of the hunters and trappers use them."

"That confirms what we thought."

"But how did this Horvath —"

"Harvath," he stated, correcting her.

"How did this *Harvath* make the connection between me and my uncle?"

"There's likely no connection at all. Just coincidence. He's injured and needed medical supplies. That's why he came here."

"So where did he go? I'm assuming your men searched the clinic."

"They did and he isn't here. I have other men searching the nearby buildings."

"Do you think he might come back?"

"To your clinic?" asked Teplov. "No. I think he got what he came for."

"Rabies vaccine, a couple of tins of cookies, coffee, tea, and sugar?"

"He's a fugitive. They tend to travel very light."

"Whatever you say," she replied. "Can I work on getting somebody out here to fix my door?"

"Not yet," said the mercenary. "First we need to talk about where Harvath may be headed."

CHAPTER 44

An escort sat in the car with Christina w Teplov and several of his men swept uncle's house. Once they had deemed safe, they had her come inside.

"Was he here?" she asked as she wa escorted into the living room.

Teplov nodded and held his hand over the coals in the fireplace. "It looks like it."

"Sir!" one of the mercenaries called out, as he emerged from the bathroom carrying the hair dye kit and handed it to his boss.

Teplov examined it and said, "Spread the word that we believe the subject has changed his hair color to . . . midnight raven."

"Sir?" the operative replied.

"Black," he growled. "Harvath has changed his fucking hair color to black."

As the soldier stepped away and took out his radio to pass the word, Teplov looked at Christina. "Same question as at the clinic them untouched. She did the same thing in the kitchen. In the dining room, she paused.

"What is it?" asked Teplov.

"Nothing," she replied.

He had seen what she was looking at — a pen on the dining table. He walked over and picked it up.

"Why did this catch your eye?"

"Look around you. My uncle was a neat freak. It's an insufferable character trait."

"You disapproved?"

"He's my elder, my uncle. I don't get to approve or disapprove. But it was a source of tension between us. His need to have everything in its place bordered on unhealthy."

It was a lie. Her uncle wasn't a "neat freak." He was just an older man with few possessions who kept his home in order. The neat freak label was useful, though, in pointing the mercenary in the direction she needed him to go.

"Interesting," said Teplov, as he picked up the pen, walked it over to the desk near the bookshelves, and placed it in the leather cup with the others. "What else do you see?"

She took her time looking around. She absolutely wanted to draw his attention to the atlas, but of all the cards she had to play, this one was the most critical.

After a protracted search, she walked back into the kitchen, pulled a small, etched glass from the cupboard, and took a bottle of chilled vodka from the freezer.

As Teplov watched, she poured a tall shot and knocked it back. When it looked as if she was setting up a second, he stopped her.

"We're almost done here. Why don't you wait until you're back home?"

Christina glared at him. "My uncle's dead, but at least you're consistent. That's exactly the level of empathy I'd expect from Wagner."

He didn't know what she wanted and he was running out of patience with this woman.

While driving to the clinic, he had contacted his offices in Moscow and had verified that she was who she said and that her husband had died while employed by his company. Even so, there was something about her that bothered him. He didn't trust her.

Nevertheless, for the moment, he had to humor her.

"I'm sorry. Is there someone I can contact for you?"

She put on an all-too-obvious fake smile and shook her head. "There's no one to contact. You and President Peshkov killed my husband. And now, somehow, the two of you have figured out a way to kill the only other family member I had left."

Teplov didn't know what to say.

"Okay if I have one more?" Christina asked as she poured another shot and, without waiting for his response, tossed it back.

Setting the bottle down, she left the kitchen and walked back into the living room. She looked through her uncle's desk and then, with her hands on her hips, she stood staring at the bookcase.

Teplov was watching her. As with the pen, he again noticed that something had caught her eye. What, though, he couldn't tell.

Before he could ask her what it was, she pointed to a large atlas covered in green fabric. It was out of place, its spine unaligned with its neighbors, as if someone had failed to properly put it back.

Teplov stepped forward and removed it. Casually, he flipped through several pages and then tossed the book on the couch.

Damn it, Christina thought to herself.

"Did I miss something?" Teplov suddenly asked, returning to the book.

It was as if he had read her mind. Nevertheless, she needed to play dumb. "You asked me to look for things that were out of place."

"Interesting that you chose this atlas."

"Why is that interesting?"

"I don't know yet," he said, as this time, he flipped through the pages much more carefully. When he got to the part where she had removed one of the maps, he stopped.

Christina felt a bad feeling growing in the pit of her stomach.

"There appears to be a page missing," Teplov declared. "That doesn't seem like something a neat freak would do, much less a man who owned his own GPS."

He looked at her and Christina stared right back at him. The alcohol was continuing to embolden her.

"Doctor Volkova," he asked, "why would your uncle pull pages out of such a beautiful atlas?"

Christina shrugged. "He was an old man. They do weird things."

"I agree," said Teplov, as he produced the missing page and held it up. "My men found this buried between the seats of your car."

She wanted to curse, but the words wouldn't come. Despite the circumstance, all she could think of was Harvath. She had failed him, but she knew that as bad as things now were, she still might be able to buy him a few more minutes with which to escape.

But before she could say anything, Teplov approached her, drew back his fist, and punched her in the stomach, knocking the wind out of her.

As she doubled over in pain, he grabbed a fistful of her hair and painfully jerked back her head.

"Out of respect for your deceased husband, I'm going to give you one, and only one, chance," he hissed. "Where the fuck is Harvath?"

CHAPTER 45

On Approach
Finnish Air Space

"We heard from Harvath," Nicholas explained as The Carlton Group jet was about to land at Helsinki Airport.

"Thank God," replied Sloane Ashby, who had taken the call over the plane's encrypted satellite phone. "Where is he? Is he okay?"

"What's going on?" Chase asked.

"Harvath made contact," she answered as she put the call on speaker and everyone moved closer. "We're all listening now. What do we know?"

"There's not much," Nicholas replied. "Apparently, he was in the Russian town of Nivsky, headed west."

Haney pulled up a map on his laptop. "Nivsky. Got it," he said, projecting the image onto the screens in the cabin. "About 250 kilometers south of the city of Murmansk and, as the crow flies, about eighty kilometers due east of the Finnish border."

"In other words," stated Staelin, "deep in Indian country."

"What else do you have?" asked Barton, as he adjusted the pitch on his seat so it matched the seat across from him. "Is he traveling by car? On foot? Is he injured?"

"That's all we know," said Nicholas. "The message came in as a comment on Instagram using one of our prearranged codes. It was posted from an account belonging to a doctor in Nivsky — Christina Volkova. She appears to be in charge of a medical clinic there. If she's helping Harvath, it might explain why there wasn't a lot of detail. He'd want to protect her and limit her exposure."

"What's the plan, then?" asked Matt Morrison, as the plane eased out of its descent and began to climb.

"We're diverting you to Lapland Air Command in Rovaniemi. There, you'll meet up with a representative from the Ministry of Defense who will travel north with you to Sodankylä."

Haney found it on his map. "It's practically a straight shot from Nivsky — just an additional eighty klicks after crossing the Finnish border."

"It's also," Nicholas added, "home to a

battalion of the Finnish Army's Jaeger Brigade."

"Those guys are badass," stated Gage. "We trained with them when I was in Fifth Group."

"So did we," said Haney, pointing at himself and Morrison. "They know their stuff when it comes to arctic warfare and equipment."

"That's why President Porter has asked for their help," Nicholas continued. "The Finns, though, are skittish about supporting an incursion into Russia. They don't want to provoke a confrontation, which means the scope of their involvement is still being worked out. Be ready for a lot of last-minute decisions.

"Now, to give them top cover, this is being treated as a downed pilot exercise. The Zero-Three-Hundred team is being moved to Luleå in northern Sweden, where they will be on call with the Skibird and F-22 Raptors."

"The Finns wouldn't allow them in?" asked Sloane.

"Like I said, they're skittish. And on this issue, the President agrees. The Russians have a lot of eyes in Finland, particularly when it comes to movements of military equipment. While we can hide some SEALs from DEVGRU, we can't hide F-22s and a Skibird. Moscow would know something was up. It's much better for our purposes if we slide in under the radar."

"How exactly are we going to slide into Russia?" asked Barton.

"That's Jaeger's area of expertise. First, we have to pinpoint Harvath's location. Best-case scenario, he makes contact again and is able to give us his precise coordinates. In the meantime, we're working on getting a satellite overhead.

"The Finns have also stepped up. As the most forested country in Europe, their 832-mile border with Russia is notoriously difficult to patrol. They have invested a lot in new drone technology and are going to make some of their best equipment available to us."

"So in the meantime," asked Morrison, "we just wait?"

"Negative," replied Nicholas. "Our goal is to get you outfitted and inserted into Russia ASAP. We don't want to wait for Harvath to come to you. We want you to go to him."

The team was in agreement and there was a chorus of "Roger that," which resonated through the cabin.

Being one of the older, most experienced team members, Staelin was one of its most pragmatic. In his estimation, this operation was going to either be a stunning success or an unimaginable failure that would be taught throughout the Special Operations community as a "what not to do."

Though they were paid handsomely to take on high-risk, short-notice assignments, this one gave him a really bad feeling.

Normally with hostage scenarios, you found out where the subject was being held and you inserted a spotter team. While they kept 24/7 watch on the location to make sure the hostage wasn't moved, an exact replica of the target was constructed back in the United States. There, a takedown team rehearsed until they knew every door, window, stairwell, and flagpole on the property.

When it came time for the assault, the operators were as familiar with the location as they were with their own homes.

They also knew that hostage-takers often were under orders to kill the hostage if any rescue attempt was made. It created an added layer of danger, and stress, but that's what made them the best. They were completely focused, high-end professional athletes, able to turn on a dime and adjust to real-time changes on the field. Nobody did these kinds of things better than they did.

Nevertheless, this kind of operation was nothing but wild cards. With each unknown, the odds of failure rose exponentially. To say what they were about to do was exceedingly risky would be a gross understatement.

Haney felt the same way. In fact, he had pulled Staelin aside, shortly after takeoff, to share his reservations.

As the senior operatives, the mission planning and decision-making would come down to them. It was a tremendous responsibility, but one they were more than capable of taking on.

With all of the unknowns, there was one thing they did know, one thing they agreed on: that no matter how dangerous, no matter how bad the odds, Harvath would risk it all to come for them. He was one of them, their brother. They weren't going to leave him behind enemy lines.

"So," said Nicholas, wrapping up. "Does anyone else have any questions?"

Staelin leaned in toward the phone, wanting to make sure he was perfectly heard. "Just one thing," he said. "What are the rules of engagement?"

"There aren't any."

"So weapons free?"

"Weapons free," Nicholas confirmed,

granting approval to engage any target with lethal force. "The only thing that matters is bringing Harvath back."

CHAPTER 46

Murmansk Oblast

Harvath was delirious. He couldn't remember if he'd heard the dogs first or had felt the rough hands as they yanked him to his feet. They were carrying guns.

He did remember someone making a big deal about his shotgun and snatching it up so that he couldn't reach it.

In a sense, he was relieved to have been captured. He hoped they'd put a bullet in his head and just be done with him, but in the back of his mind he knew that wasn't likely.

His brain was foggy and his eyesight was almost nonexistent. It was nearly impossible to tell what was going on.

One of the men, yelling in Russian, slapped him around. He had suffered worse in his SERE training. The more the man yelled, the more the dogs barked. Someone patted him down. They then took off his skis and tied him up. After that, he had blacked out.

When he awoke, he could still hear the dogs. They were someplace close. Did Wagner even have dogs? It was possible, he supposed. Plenty of military units used them. But dogs meant any escape was next to impossible. It sounded as if they had a lot of them.

His vision was slow to return. He attempted to move his arms and to his surprise, he was no longer tied down.

When his eyes adjusted to the darkness, he could see that he was in a cabin of some sort. It smelled like clay and chimney smoke. A fire crackled in the fireplace.

Most of his clothing had been removed. He was lying in a bed, with a compress laid across his head. A fire burned warm and bright nearby.

At a small table, an older woman sat with her back to him, humming. Next to a leather satchel were what looked like plastic Ziplocs filled with dried herbs. He had no idea where he was or what had happened.

His head felt as if it had been split open with an axe. He tried to sit up, but that only made it worse. Closing his eyes, he fell back against his pillow.

When he opened them again, the woman

was standing over him. A large cup was in her hand. "Drink," she said in English, offering it to him.

Seeing the distress he was in, she set the cup aside and propped him up. Then, she held the cup up to his mouth so he could drink.

It was a broth of some sort. *"Spaseba,"* he said, after he had finished.

"It's okay. I speak English."

"Where am I?"

"In the woods."

"In the woods where?"

"Outside the village of Adjágas," she replied. "You're safe here."

Adjágas, though, wasn't the village he was supposed to be in. "I need to get to Friddja," he said, trying to get up.

"Relax," she responded, easing him back down. "Everything is going to be okay."

"You don't understand."

"I think I do," she said, removing the note Christina had written and handing it to him. "I'm Sini."

"Where'd you get that?" he asked, taking a better look around the room. Near the front door he could see his rucksack, along with his shotgun.

"The men who found you in the snow, they were trying to figure out who you were.

373

They searched your pockets."

"Why did they bring me here?"

"They're from Adjágas. They were on their way home from a hunt. Their dogs were tired. It was better to come here and then send word to me in Friddja."

"I remember being tied up."

Sini nodded. "You were in bad shape. They wrapped you in blankets and secured you to one of their sleds so you wouldn't roll off."

She had a kind, craggy face and a gentle voice. Harvath reached for the cup and she held it to his lips again so he could drink.

When he had finished, he asked, "What about Christina? Have you heard anything from her?"

Sini shook her head.

He looked at his watch and tried to figure out how long it had been since he had left Nivsky. "I can't stay here."

The Sámi woman smiled. "It's late. It's also very cold outside and you are in no condition to travel. Let's wait until morning. Maybe Christina will be here. We can discuss everything then."

Harvath didn't have the will to fight. He also didn't have the strength to charge back out into the snow — not tonight at least. So he gave in.

"May I?" Sini asked, pointing at the blanket that covered him.

He nodded and she pulled it down in order to reexamine his wounds. Slowly, using the items on the table, she began replacing the poultices she had applied to him earlier.

"Are you a doctor, too?" he asked.

"No," she replied. "In my language, I'm called *noaidi,* a healer."

"Your English is very good. Where did you learn it?"

"I grew up in the Swedish part of Lapland. We all studied English in school."

"How did you end up in Russia?"

"It was part of my calling as a *noaidi.* I'm originally from here. We left because of communist persecution. Eventually, I felt compelled to come back."

"And Christina? How do you know each other?"

"The Sámi people embrace both traditional and modern medicine. Christina has always been good about coming out if there's a situation I can't handle. I guess you could say that we began as colleagues, but now are close friends. She's a very special person."

Harvath agreed. Christina was special.

Pulling his blankets back up, Sini removed

his compress and walked into the kitchen to prepare another, along with a special kind of tea.

Returning with the new compress, she laid it across his forehead. "Your body has absorbed a lot of punishment. It needs rest. This will help you sleep," she said, as she raised the cup, now filled with tea, to his mouth.

Harvath was grateful for the broth, the poultices, and especially the rescue. He knew he was not one hundred percent and that his body needed repairing. He also knew that he couldn't stay here. He needed to get moving. For the moment, though, he'd gladly take anything she offered that would help him recover.

"Is there anything else I can do for you?" she asked.

He looked around the room once more. "Is there a computer or a cell phone? Maybe a radio of some sort?"

The Sámi woman smiled and shook her head. "We still do things the old way here. Word travels fast, but it travels by foot."

Pointing at his shotgun, he asked, "Would you please bring that to me? I dropped it in the snow and need to clean it."

"It will be fine until tomorrow. Like I said, you're safe here. Nothing is going to happen to you."

He didn't doubt her sincerity, but she had no clue about the two dozen mercenaries who had landed in Nivsky and were actively hunting him. He needed to get across the border. But it wasn't going to happen tonight.

At best, he'd be well enough to strike off in the morning. And while he didn't like having to operate during daylight hours, if Sini and her friends were willing to help him, he might be able to make it to the border. Already, a plan was beginning to form in his mind.

Tomorrow, though, was a long way off. There were still many hours of darkness to go. And under the cover of darkness was where some of the worst things were known to happen.

CHAPTER 47

Teplov had dragged Christina out of the house by her hair. He didn't care who saw. The more the better as far as he was concerned. Just as at the bar, it would send a message. She had lied to him, repeatedly, and in so doing had only made things worse for herself.

As intelligent as she was, it baffled him that she never thought they would check her vehicle. She should have burned the page she tore from the atlas, not shoved it down between the seats.

It didn't matter. All that mattered was that Teplov and his men knew where Harvath was headed and that they had been saved from a massive wild-goose chase.

Now, they were going to get a chance to drag her through the center of town before putting her on one of the helicopters. Seeing their beloved Doctor Volkova dealt with so sternly would help solidify any cooperation they might need going forward.

And God help her if they needed it. If she had lied to him again, the beating she had received inside her uncle's house was nothing compared to what would be coming. If they went through all the trouble to load the bird and fly out to Friddja, only to find no one had even seen Harvath, there'd be hell to pay.

Teplov had radioed ahead. He knew whom he wanted with him and how to make the biggest spectacle in order to draw the most attention.

He planned on leaving a sizable stay-behind contingent, just in case Doctor Volkova had lied again. The contingent would continue searching for Harvath in and around town.

The fresh ski tracks they had found outside the uncle's house, though, were a good sign. They led in the direction of the village he was allegedly headed toward.

He had sent his men to follow them, but with the wind and blowing snow, the tracks had quickly disappeared. Their best hope now was to fly overhead and catch Harvath en route, or to isolate him on the ground in Friddja and capture him there.

The moment they arrived at the town square, the cargo helicopter came alive. As its engine began to roar and its rotors started to spin, townspeople, including all of the patrons inside the bar and café, were drawn to the windows around the square. He had their attention.

They had previously witnessed the beating his men had doled out to the bar patron who had refused to cooperate. Now they would see their doctor, beaten and bloody, dragged out of a vehicle, placed in the helicopter, and flown away.

It was yet another SS tactic he found useful. You always dealt harshly with those who showed initial resistance. Afterward, it was often necessary to make an example of a highly respected member of the community — someone whom people looked up to and who was seen as being above reproach.

Pulling up outside, he saw all the patrons, just as before, glued to the windows. He parked his SUV right in front and had his men remove Doctor Volkova.

She refused to comply as they tried to parade her forward. Teplov ordered his men to let her be.

When they stood aside, he walked over and punched her in her lower back. Her knees buckled and she fell to the ground, where she spat blood into the snow.

People inside the bar and the café gasped.

It was barbaric, what was happening outside. None of them, though, dared to react. They had no doubt that the soldiers would shoot them dead on the spot. Instead, they did the only thing they could do. They cowered inside and watched it all unfold.

Teplov grabbed Christina by the hair and pulled up her head so everyone inside could see her face. Several of them turned away in horror, unable to watch what was happening.

Letting go of her head, Teplov stood and commanded his men to walk her to the helicopter. If she refused to walk, she was to be beaten until she complied.

Christina had suffered enough. When the soldiers helped her to her feet, she did exactly as she was told. With a man holding each of her arms, she allowed them to guide her forward and then up the ramp.

Once Teplov and his people were all present and accounted for, the spinning of the rotors increased and the helicopter lifted off, throwing snow and ice in all directions and pelting all the vehicles parked around the square.

It banked to the north, hovered briefly over the uncle's home, and then made its way west toward the Sámi village of Friddja.

As the helicopter slowly flew, the crew

scanned their instruments for any signs of Harvath. Attached inside, heavy black ropes sat coiled on the floor, ready to be kicked out the doors if the Wagner mercenaries needed to rappel down and grab him.

When out of the darkness the village appeared up ahead, the men checked their weapons and prepared their night vision goggles.

As with the Nazi SS, to be a member of Wagner, recruits not only had to have been tops in their previous military units, but they also had to have "pure" Russian blood. They had to have demonstrated obedience and an absolute commitment to Russia, the Russian President, and the Russian people.

The Wagner motto was identical to that of the SS: *My honor is loyalty.* Teplov led the men in a recital of their oath. "We swear to you, O Russia, fidelity and bravery. We solemnly pledge obedience to the death to you, and to those named as our leaders."

Inside the helicopter, the men exploded in the Russian battle cry, popular since the days of the Imperial Russian Army, *"Ura! Ura! Ura!"*

If Harvath was down there, Teplov had no doubt that his fired-up, highly disciplined, and highly experienced men would find him.

CHAPTER 48

Harvath hadn't been asleep that long when he heard the helicopter pass. Instantly, he shot straight up in bed.

Sini, who was sitting nearby and watching her patient, had heard it, too.

"What is it?" she asked.

"Bad news," replied Harvath. "Very bad news."

The letter from Christina had explained that he was in trouble, but that it wasn't his fault and that he could be trusted. Her only request had been for Sini to see to his injuries and to keep him safe until she could get there.

The Sámi woman saw Harvath eyeing the shotgun. This time she didn't argue with him. Walking over to the door, she picked it up and carefully brought it to him.

"What else do you need?"

"A rag," he replied. "And some oil if you have it."

Sini hunted the items down and carried them over to Harvath. She watched as he unloaded the weapon and expertly took it apart, examining each piece, rubbing some with the cloth, and applying small drops of oil where necessary.

Then, as quickly as he had broken the shotgun down, he reassembled it, loaded the rounds, and racked one into the chamber.

His confidence with the weapon spoke to a certain level of expertise. The injuries to his body, as well as his detached demeanor, suggested to her a man all too familiar with violence. His concern over the helicopter suggested he was being pursued by the state.

"That helicopter is looking for you," she said. "Isn't it?"

Harvath nodded.

"And you think they will come here?"

"I know they will."

"Why?" she asked. "What happened?"

"I don't have time to explain. How far are we from Friddja?"

"You think that is where the helicopter is going?"

It had to be. There was no other reason he could think of for it to be out here.

But, if it was heading for Friddja, that could only mean one thing — Christina had

384

given him up. There was no way they could have tracked him through the snow. Any trail he left was quickly covered over. It had to have been Christina.

Though he barely knew her, he doubted she had given him up willingly. The soldiers from Wagner had proven their brutality outside the bar in Nivsky. It wasn't a stretch to believe they would have beaten Christina as well if they thought she had information they needed.

"The men in that helicopter are mercenaries. They beat a man back in town unconscious because he refused to give them his vehicle. If they are headed to Friddja, it's because they figured out Christina was helping me and they forced her to talk. When they get there, and can't find me, they're going to come here. We need to get moving. Now, how far away is Friddja?"

"*Poronkusema,*" she replied. "One *poronkusema.*"

"I don't know that word," he said, as he removed the poultices and began pulling his clothes on.

"In this area, we herd reindeer. Reindeer can't walk and urinate at the same time. They have to stop. A *poronkusema* is the average distance between stops," said Sini as she tried to come up with an equivalent

385

he would understand. "Somewhere between nine and ten kilometers. We'll say nine and a half."

It was way too close. "Who knows you're here?"

"My husband, of course. Why?"

"Who else?"

"No one. Just him."

"What did you tell him?" he asked.

"I didn't tell him anything," she said. "Jompá, one of the brothers who rescued you, put together a new dog team and came to get me. When he arrived, he showed me the letter they had found in your pocket.

"He told us the story of how they had found you in the snow. He asked me to come back to Adjágas with him. That was all. I told my husband to send Christina as soon as she arrived."

"Are we in Jompá's home right now?"

She nodded. "He is at his brother's."

"Okay. Listen to me very carefully. All of you are in danger because of me."

"We could hide you until —"

"You can't hide me. These men can smell a lie from a mile away. And once that happens they will hurt you. All of you."

"So what are we supposed to do?"

"Tell them the truth, all of it — that they found me in the snow, that you gave me medical attention, and that when I heard the helicopter, I fled."

"But Christina asked me to take care of you, to keep you safe."

"I am very grateful for all that you have done," he said, lacing up his boots, then putting on his coat and zipping it up.

"I'm sorry," Sini replied. "I wish there was more that we could do. I know Jompá and his brother will feel the same."

"You need to go be with them. Please tell them that I said thank you. You saved my life."

"Where will you go? It's freezing out there."

"I'll figure something out. Where are my skis?"

"Just outside," she said, "along with your poles."

Removing the bladder from his rucksack, he handed it to her. "Can you fill this for me please while I put them on?"

Sini did as he requested. Then, putting on her own coat, she stepped outside and handed it to him.

He thanked her and asked one last question. "Which way is Friddja? That's the way they'll be coming from."

She raised her arm and pointed. "That way," she said. "Through the trees. You can't miss the path." She then watched as he skied off in the opposite direction.

It was completely black and only took a matter of seconds before he was swallowed up by the darkness.

In her heart, Sini wanted to believe that he would make it, but in her head she knew that wasn't going to happen. A man in his condition, alone in the bitterly cold wilderness, hunted by mercenaries with a helicopter, didn't stand a chance.

The woman, though, didn't know Scot Harvath.

Chapter 49

As smoke rose from the chimneys and stove pipes of Friddja's snow-covered houses, the arctic helicopter touched down on the edge of the village, spooking a herd of reindeer kept in a pen nearby.

Squeezing the back of Christina's neck, Teplov pushed her out the door and ordered her to identify the dwelling where she was supposed to meet Harvath. She resisted until the pain became unbearable. Only then did she point it out.

After two snowmobiles had raced down the helicopter's loading ramp to secure the perimeter, Teplov ordered his men to move in and encircle the house.

Just as in Nivsky, residents had gathered at windows and even more had poured outside to see what all the commotion was about. Sini's husband, Mokci, made the mistake of opening his door just as one of

Teplov's goons had stepped up to kick it open.

For his trouble, Mokci caught a rifle butt in the mouth and was shoved back inside. He fell to the floor as the assault team spilled in searching for Harvath.

Standing outside, Teplov took satisfaction in the villagers' shocked and indignant reactions. He, along with several more men, watched and waited for someone to make the mistake of picking up a rifle, but none of them did. *Mission accomplished.*

Moments later, the assault team leader stepped back outside and signaled the all clear. Harvath was not inside.

Trying to keep his anger under control, Teplov marched Christina up to the house and pushed her through the door.

When she saw Mokci sitting in a chair, blood gushing from his face, her professional instincts kicked in and she rushed to help him. Teplov didn't stop her.

She found a clean towel and had him hold it to his mouth and apply pressure. In the meantime, she asked and was granted permission to retrieve a piece of ice from outside. When she came back in, she wrapped it in another clean towel and had Mokci hold that against his wound.

He was almost an identical male version

of his wife — small, but sturdy with a kind, weathered face, dark hair, and brown eyes.

"What is wrong with you people?" Christina demanded as she turned to face Teplov. "That was completely unnecessary."

"Shut up," the mercenary ordered, as he grabbed the Sámi man's face and examined it by twisting it from one side to the other. "He'll be fine."

"You might have broken his jaw."

"I told you to shut up," he barked, focusing on Mokci. "Where's the American?"

"What American?" Mokci blubbered through a quickly swelling and still bleeding lip.

"The one Doctor Volkova sent here. The one who was supposed to meet with your wife."

"I don't know what you're talking about."

Teplov could tell by the way the man refused to make eye contact that he was hiding something. Drawing his cupped hand back, he aimed for his left ear and slapped him as hard as he could in the side of the head.

The blow was so intense, it knocked the Sámi out of his chair and down onto the floor, where he screamed in pain.

"Stop it!" Christina shouted. "First you try to break his jaw and now you're trying to rupture his eardrum. He said he doesn't know."

Teplov spun on her and grabbed her by the throat. "I'm not going to tell you again. Shut. Up."

Casting her aside, he nodded at his men, who picked Mokci up and placed him back in his chair. Tears were streaming down his face.

"I haven't done anything wrong," the man pleaded.

"That wasn't what I asked you," retorted Teplov. "I asked you where the American is."

"I told you. I don't know what you're talking about. I have not seen any American. No American has been here."

Teplov, scanning the main living area, demanded, "What about your wife?"

"What about her?"

"She is a *noaidi*, is she not?"

Mokci nodded.

"Where is she?"

"Adjágas," he replied. "A village not far from here."

Teplov looked at one of his men, who located it on his map and showed him. "Why?"

"Someone was ill."

"*Someone* who?"

"I don't know."

Teplov raised his hand to strike him again. Mokci cowered and told him everything he knew. "A man named Jompá said he and his brother had found a man, more dead than alive, in the snow. They brought him back to Adjágas and then Jompá came here to get Sini. That's all I know. I am telling you the truth."

"How long ago?"

"Several hours at least."

"And do you know what house in Adjágas belongs to this Jompá?"

The Sámi man hesitated and that was the only confirmation Teplov needed.

Over the radio, he sent the two snowmobiles on ahead. Before they boarded the helicopter and took off, he wanted to conduct a search of the village. He had too much riding on this to lose Harvath just because the Sámis had heard the helicopter coming and were smart enough to have hidden him in another house.

It wouldn't have been the first time something like that had happened. It wouldn't matter, though. He would turn over every rock, look under every branch, and search every house in the Oblast until he found him. There was no way Harvath was going to make it to the border.

CHAPTER 50

Once out of sight of Adjágas, Harvath cut into the woods. Because of all of the heavy snow, there were broken pine boughs scattered around.

He skied in circles, joined back up with his tracks on the main trail, then returned to the woods where he removed a length of rope from his rucksack and tied it around his waist.

Spotting the perfect pine bough — wide, but not too heavy — he tied it to the other end and dragged it behind him in an attempt to partially cover his tracks.

On a scale of one to ten, the results were a four, but it was better than nothing. He hoped that, in the dark, it would be enough. He only needed a little head start.

Soundlessly, he moved through the trees, making his way back toward the village as quickly as he could. The only hope he had of being successful was via the element of surprise.

His mind was moving as fast as, if not faster than, his skis. There were a lot of unanswered questions, vital equations, he was trying to solve.

First and foremost, *How many men were on that helicopter?* Had the full two dozen been sent, or had some been left behind to continue searching for him in Nivsky? If Harvath had to wager, he'd be willing to bet that they had left some behind. That still didn't fully answer his question, though.

His next question was, *What was his objective?* Obviously, it was making his escape. But what was that going to look like? There was no way to know until the opportunity revealed itself.

He couldn't outrun their helicopter. And if they had brought snowmobiles along, which they probably had, he couldn't outrun those either.

That meant that he was either going to have to convince them that he was no longer running, or make it so they couldn't chase him.

At the very least, he'd do enough damage to force them to fall back, regroup, and be very nervous about coming after him.

They would, of course, come after him, but if they did so with trepidation, he would have secured the upper hand.

Injecting fear into the hearts of battle-hardened special forces soldiers, Russians or otherwise, was no easy feat. It was quite a tall order, but one that — if he was lucky — he might just be able to pull off.

For that to happen, though, a lot had to take place between now and his eventual escape. And all of it had to go right. One single screwup on his part would mean either death or capture, which he was certain were pretty much the same thing.

Arriving back in Adjágas, the first thing he did was to ditch the pine bough. He followed that up by hiding his skiing equipment in a crawl space beneath one of the cabins.

Now, his only liability was his boots. They left very distinct prints. But as he had done when trying to disguise his ski tracks, all he could do was hope that in the chaos of the moment, with loads of adrenaline pumping through them, that none of the mercenaries noticed.

Hope, though, wasn't a plan. In fact, he needed to do everything he could to make sure his tracks would not stick out.

Staying away from fresh snow, he trod only where the villagers themselves had walked, altering how he placed his feet so as not to leave a full print.

The boots were rigid. They not only hurt his feet, they also slowed him down. Nevertheless, it was worth it. He hadn't come this far to leave a trail that would lead right to him. The element of surprise, right now, was the only thing he had going for him.

Arriving at Jompá's cabin, he peered into one of the windows. Sini was nowhere to be seen. Coming back around, he tried the door and, as he had expected in such a small village, it was unlocked.

Stepping inside, he closed the door behind him, removed the flashlight from his pocket, and set it on the floor so as not to draw attention from anyone outside.

Unshouldering his rucksack, he pulled out the box of shotgun shells he had taken from the trapper's cabin and made a tough decision — how many could he part with? He settled on half.

Giving up ammo, especially when you didn't know how many of the enemy you were facing, normally wasn't the best idea. But in this case, the rounds could end up acting as a force multiplier.

After retrieving a glass jar he had seen earlier in the kitchen, he took out his knife and began opening the shells, making sure all of the powder went inside and that all of his buckshot was accounted for.

It took him several more minutes to complete his improvised explosive device, but when it was done, he felt confident that it was more than up to the task. The only problem remaining was where to place it.

He lacked the materials necessary to create a fuse with a delay. If he set it up at the front door, it would go off the minute someone set foot inside and only affect the first person through. To be worth it, it had to kill, or at the very least injure, as many of the Wagner mercenaries as possible. He decided to set it up farther inside and use the bed as bait.

Christina had been right about playing up his injuries. The more blood and bandages they saw, the more their confidence grew that he was weak and unable to put up a decent fight. If he was lucky, a booby-trap would be one of the last things they'd be thinking about.

All of Sini's supplies were still scattered about. After setting up the bed to make it look as if someone was sleeping in it, he placed other items nearby so that to anyone entering, it would appear that he was in even worse shape.

By the time they got close enough to realize that the bed was empty, it would be too late. They would have already hit the trip wire.

At least that was the plan. He had constructed several IEDs in his day that had worked, as well as several that hadn't. It seemed that the more he needed them, the greater the odds were that they would fail. He hoped that tonight, that wouldn't be the case.

After doing one last sweep to make sure everything was perfect, he backed out of the cabin and closed the door. Far in the distance, he could hear snowmobiles.

All of a sudden, he got another idea. Slinging the rucksack and his shotgun, he ran off toward the trail Sini had pointed to earlier, the one that led to Friddja.

And as he ran, he said a silent prayer that not only were the snowmobiles taking that route, but that he could get to the right spot before they did.

CHAPTER 51

Harvath ran as fast as he could up the trail. He didn't care if he was leaving footprints in the snow or not. All that mattered was speed.

As he ran, he kept his eyes peeled for the ideal place to set his trap. Finally, he found it.

The two trees were thick enough and were positioned perfectly on either side of the trail.

Rummaging through his rucksack, he pulled out the second spool of wire he had taken from the trapper. It was a heavier gauge than he had just used to set the trip wire for his IED. Because of the amount of force it was going to have to withstand, it needed to be.

While he would have loved to have been equipped to kill multiple birds with one stone, he knew that wasn't going to happen. The trail was too narrow for the mercenaries to be riding in anything other than single file.

Harvath only had enough wire for two traps. The best he could hope to do was to take out the men piloting the first and second snowmobiles. After that, he'd be reliant on his shotgun.

He worked quickly, guesstimating where precisely to set the first wire, and then making sure it was as secure as humanly possible. Clipping the wire, he ran about five meters farther down the trail, where he set the second trap. This one was even more difficult.

Based on what Christina had seen while picking up his dinner in Nivsky, he knew the mercenaries would be wearing night vision goggles. That meant he would have to camouflage himself. He couldn't arm the second trap, though, until the first snowmobiler had raced past, and even then, he had to remain hidden. He needed a spring, something he could activate from his hiding place without revealing his presence.

He found exactly what he needed in the shape of a younger, more pliable tree, which even in the deep arctic cold he was able to bend. He tied it down using a piece of cord and an adjacent tree trunk.

With his wires set, he stashed his rucksack

and then dug a place in the snow, which he covered with several pine branches. Holding his knife in one hand and the shotgun in the other, he made ready. He could hear the snowmobiles. They were close, almost there.

He was about to lose his only advantage — the element of surprise. Once the first rider hit the first trap, the mercenaries would know they were under attack. The tricky part for him would be timing the leap from his hiding spot. Fortunately, he had a halfway decent view of the trail and would be able to make that call on the fly.

Straining his ears, he tried to discern how many snowmobiles were approaching. It was an impossible task. All he could tell was that it sounded like more than one. He had no way of knowing how many men he was about to face.

Lying there in the snow, he would have given a decade's worth of paychecks for a few claymores or a box of hand grenades. There was precious little cover available beyond tree trunks. If this turned into an all-out gunfight, he was going to be in trouble.

He had to win it before they could get in it. That meant he had to be fast as hell and on the money with each shot.

Reminding himself of the old maxim for

coming out on top in a gunfight, he repeated, "Slow is smooth and smooth is fast."

The snowmobiles were hauling ass. He could hear the whine of their engines as they raced toward him. That was a good sign — the faster, the better.

They were seconds away now. Ten. Maybe twenty.

Extending his knife out from under the cover of his hide site, he let it hover just above the taut cord that would spring the second trap. His heart was pounding and he took several deep breaths in order to help it calm down.

When the first snowmobile came blazing past, he slashed the cord. The young tree did exactly what it was supposed to do, pulling the wire wrapped around a much sturdier tree taut. What Harvath hadn't been expecting, though, was that the second rider would be following so closely behind the first.

There was a loud *twang* as the snowmobiler hit the wire, which was hung across the trail like a clothesline at chest height, and he was instantly decapitated.

His sled went sailing into the woods, hitting several trees before landing mangled and upside down.

The lead rider must have noticed something had happened — maybe, out of the corner of his eye, he had seen the beam of his colleague's headlight as it bounced off into the forest — because just as his machine drew even with the other trap, he turned and looked behind him.

Either Harvath had set it too low, or this guy was too tall, because instead of having his head sliced clean off, the wire cut off his arm and sliced into his torso.

He was thrown clear of the snowmobile, which managed to stay on the trail until it glided to a stop.

Harvath looked and listened, but there were no other snowmobiles. Leaping from his hide, he ran from the woods and up to the trail to the mercenary who lay bleeding out in the snow.

He could have shot the man from where he was, but he was unsure how far the sound would carry and how close the rest of them were. Instead, he slung his shotgun and closed in on him with his knife.

Even before he drew even with the man, he knew there was no saving him. Not even a tourniquet would have made a difference. In addition to losing his arm and slicing open his chest, the wire must have snapped up as he was thrown from the snowmobile and cut into his neck, severing a major artery. He was spurting blood like an out-of-control sprinkler.

Harvath made sure to not get too close and kept one eye on the man's hands. The mercenary, though, didn't attempt to reach for his weapon.

Under the glow from the night vision goggles, Harvath watched as the life left the man's eyes. There was no need to plunge his knife into him. The job had already been done. Harvath's challenge now was to figure out what to do next.

He didn't bother to wait for the good idea fairy to strike. Instead he raced back to retrieve his rucksack and stripped the two dead mercenaries of anything of value to his survival. In that category, there was a ton.

He helped himself not only to their weapons, but also to their ammo-packed chest rigs, four fragmentation grenades, the decapitated man's winter coveralls, which, because of how his body had landed, had only minimal bloodstains, and best of all, one of their helmets rigged with night vision goggles.

In almost any other situation, he would have booby-trapped the bodies with the frag grenades. He was afraid, though, that one the villagers might come along and get hurt. So leaving the dead soldiers where they were, he gathered up the rest of his equipment and ran down the trail to the remaining snowmobile.

He secured the gear as best he could and was preparing to take off when he heard a sound that shook him to his core.

The helicopter was coming.

CHAPTER 52

It was make or break time. When that helicopter landed, he had no idea how many men would be pouring out of it or how they'd be equipped. Would they be on foot? On skis? Or all on snowmobiles? There was no way of knowing.

What he felt certain about, though, was that they had located Sini's house in Friddja. That meant either Christina had described it to them, or more than likely, they had brought her along to make the identification in person.

Once they had found Sini's, they had probably found her husband, which was why they were inbound to Adjágas.

And just as he suspected that Christina had been dragged along, the Wagner mercenaries had probably brought Sini's husband as well. His job would be to help them identify Jompá's cabin.

What the mercenaries planned to do with

their hostages was anyone's guess. Harvath knew they were not going to let Christina go — not after she had aided his escape. This left him with a serious problem.

Either they were going to hand her over to the GRU, who at best would throw her in prison, and at worst would execute her, or the mercenaries would rape and then beat her to death, leaving her body for the wolves. None of those were acceptable outcomes in his book.

She had helped him and he needed to help her. He just prayed to God that she was on that helicopter. He didn't want to have to go back to Nivsky to find her.

Based on the possibility of hostages being among the mercenaries, his mindset flipped from ambush to rescue. That didn't mean, though, that he couldn't kill every last Wagner soldier on that helo, it just meant he had to make sure no harm came to Christina and, if he was present, Sini's husband.

If he knew exactly where the helicopter would land, he might have been able to find concealment nearby and, using the night vision goggles, catch a glimpse of who, and how many, got off. But as it stood, he had no clue.

All he knew was that they would search Jompá's cabin first. That's where they expected to find him. With the bird coming in fast, he kicked it into high gear.

He hid the snowmobile and his rucksack at the edge of the village, covering them with broken pine boughs. Then, he strapped on as much gear as he could carry, shouldered all the guns, and rushed toward the cabin.

He knew where he was going to end up, but before he got there, he needed to establish several alternative positions — places where he could predeploy weapons and ammunition.

Moving through the shadows behind the cabins, he picked his spots carefully. He wanted to be able to quickly access the gear, but also to remain hidden. And, if he found himself in a running gun battle, he wanted at least some cover.

With everything set, he moved to his final position.

Each cabin in Adjágas was different, but most of them were built with crawl spaces underneath — similar to the one where he had hidden his skis.

One of them was rather dilapidated, but had an excellent view of Jompá's. Even better, it was uninhabited.

Clearing some of the snow away, he was able to dig a hole wide enough to allow him to squeeze underneath. It was only then that he realized how structurally unsound the cabin was.

The floor above had rotted through in places and it sat on beams atop short, stacked stone pillars. He had the sense that just bumping one could bring the entire cabin crashing down on him.

The space was so small, he had to balance the AK-15 rifle on his forearms and belly crawl to get into position. Had he been even the slightest bit claustrophobic, it would have been impossible.

At the far end of the crawl space, he set his rifle aside and pushed away enough of the snow to be able to see Jompá's. The range was perfect and there was nothing obstructing his view. The only drawback was going to be his muzzle flash. As soon as he started firing, it was going to be obvious where it was coming from.

Backing up, deeper into the crawl space, and firing from there was out of the question. As he backed up, his line of sight became impaired and he couldn't fully see the target. He was going to have to risk shooting from where he was and follow the three Bs: be fast, be accurate, and be the hell out of there.

He hoped there'd be enough chaos that

he could get in all the shots he needed. But he knew better than to think like that. Murphy, of the eponymous law, always found a way to screw things up.

For his own good, he needed to resist becoming greedy. Staying one second too long in that crawl space could mean death. If at all possible, he had to be on the way out before they even began shooting back at him. It wouldn't be easy, but he didn't get to choose the circumstances. He only got to choose how he was going to react to them.

Outside, he could hear the *thump, thump, thump* of the helicopter's blades as it arrived and hovered somewhere overhead. The rotor wash sent snow and ice flying in all directions as it illuminated its powerful searchlight and lit up Jompá's cabin. Even at his distance, the light was practically blinding for Harvath.

Shielding his eyes, he was able to watch as ropes were dropped and a team of six operators in total rappelled down.

This wasn't what he had planned for. He had expected them to set down someplace and come in on foot. *Fuck,* he thought to himself. *Now what?*

There was only one thing he could do — what he was trained to do: *adapt and overcome.*

411

Though he hated to do it, he backed up, turned around, and scrambled back in the direction from which he had entered the crawl space.

He didn't need to see them to know there were snipers onboard providing overwatch for the operators. The moment he started firing, they'd be putting rounds all over him. The deadly difference, though, was that they'd be shooting from above, through a rotting floor, rather than trying to skip rounds off the ground and maybe hit a target hidden in a crawl space.

The presence of the helicopter was a game changer. It also provided a potential opportunity.

Harvath had less than a minute, thirty seconds at best. The moment the mercenaries triggered his IED, all bets were off.

Moving as fast as he could, he popped out of the crawl space, flipped up the night vision goggles on his helmet, and leaped to his feet. It was critical that he time his next move precisely.

Based on the searchlight, he knew exactly where the helicopter was. He made sure to keep the corner of the cabin between him and the snipers. They couldn't shoot what they didn't even know was there.

Already, the fire selector on the battle rifle

he had taken from one of the dead Wagner snowmobilers was set to semiauto. Wrapping the sling around his arm for stability, he didn't need to double-check that the weapons were hot. He had already chambered rounds in all of them.

The enormous helicopter continued to blast the village with whirling sheets of ice and snow, as its searchlight illuminated Jompá's cabin with its white-hot beam.

Harvath had done countless entries over his career. Though he was tempted to stick his head out and see what was going on, he stayed right where he was.

There was only the front entrance, nothing in back. They would have seen that as they had flown over and before they had rappelled down.

Right now they'd be lining up in a stack, ready to kick in the door. After which they would charge in, searching the room for threats, their weapons sweeping left and right when . . .

BOOM.

The explosion wasn't the loudest Harvath had ever heard. But it was significant.

While all attention in the helicopter was on the IED that had just gone off inside Jompá's house Harvath swung out from behind the corner of the dilapidated cabin

413

facing it and began firing.

He focused on the helicopter's searchlight, and it took him a total of four shots to knock it out.

The instant the light went dark, he swung his barrel and dumped four more of the 7.62×39 rounds into the door area, where there was indeed a sniper.

After killing the sniper, he shifted to the pilot's window, fired four additional rounds, and then targeted the bird's engine with the rest of the ammunition in his mag.

If Christina was onboard, he prayed that she was strapped in. Having run the weapon dry, he ejected the empty magazine, and pulling a fresh one from his chest rig, rammed it home and cycled the bolt.

But before he could reengage, the helicopter banked hard away from him. Smoke was billowing from its exhaust and it was losing altitude. Harvath didn't need to see any more to know the big Mi-8 was going down.

Snapping his eyes to Jompá's house, he saw two Wagner mercenaries, each dragging an injured comrade out of the burning cabin.

He didn't give his next move a second thought. Taking aim, he pressed his trigger and lit all four of them up.

Changing magazines, he heard a clap of

thunder as the helicopter snapped through the trees of the forest beyond the village and slammed into the ground.

It was a bad crash, but based on how low the helo had been, he knew it was survivable.

Disguised in Wagner winter whites and carrying a Wagner-issued weapon, he flipped down the night vision goggles on his helmet and went to finish what they had started. His first stop — Jompá's.

As the villagers slowly popped their heads out to see what had happened, Harvath waved them back inside. He didn't need them making this any more dangerous than it already was.

Out of the corner of his eye, standing outside one of the cabins, he saw Sini. And she saw him.

Harvath didn't need to ask for her help. She understood what was happening. Immediately, she began shouting in Sámi and gesturing for people to get back inside their homes.

The killing had only just begun.

CHAPTER 53

Slinging his rifle, Harvath pulled the pistol he had taken off the dead snowmobiler and quickly approached Jompá's cabin.

The minute he was in range, he head-shot every Wagner mercenary he saw — just to be sure. He wanted to be absolutely certain that they were dead.

After he drilled the four at the door, he took a quick peek inside. Blood and pieces of flesh from the other two operatives were splattered everywhere. The IED had done its job. Nevertheless, each of the bodies inside received a head-shot as well. Now, he needed to get to the helicopter.

Taking a quick peek outside to make sure no one was lying in wait, he stepped through the doorway, helped himself to fresh magazines and extra frag grenades from the dead men.

One of the mercenaries had been carrying two incendiary grenades and Harvath grabbed those as well. They were used for destroying equipment and could burn at four thousand degrees for forty seconds.

As he had with the snowmobilers back on the trail, he decided against booby-trapping the bodies.

Shoving everything into his pockets, he left the bodies alone and ran for the snowmobile. Along the way, he picked up his other guns and ammunition. There was no telling what he was going to encounter at the downed chopper.

After tossing away the branches, he secured his rucksack and equipment, fired up the snowmobile, and took off.

He had a general idea of where the crash had happened, but didn't know what the terrain was like or how close he was going to be able to get to it.

Using his night vision goggles to see by, he kept the headlight turned off. It was bad enough that the loud whine of the engine would give away his approach — he didn't intend to add a visual beacon on top of it.

About half a klick into the forest, he began to see light in the distance. It had to be coming from the downed helicopter. He kept going, getting as close as he felt comfortable, then killed the engine and went in the rest of the way on foot.

The snow, as it was everywhere else in this godforsaken country, was deep and he struggled to push through it. If he never saw a single flake of it again, it would be too soon.

As he moved, he made sure to take advantage of the natural camouflage of the trees. There was no telling who had survived the crash. Any number of them could be headed his way, or worse, preparing an ambush.

Every few yards, he stopped and listened. But even as he closed in on the chopper, he didn't hear anything. It was still — deathly still.

Cresting a small rise, he saw the helicopter beneath him. It was down in a gulley, lying on its side. All around, the tall pine trees had been snapped like toothpicks. The helo's rotors had been shorn off and there were pieces of wreckage strewn everywhere. Using a tree for cover, he crouched down. For several moments, he watched and waited.

No one moved. No one made a sound. He had a bad feeling that Christina might be dead. He wouldn't know, though, until he got down there.

Picking the route that provided the most protection, he slowly descended into the gulley.

It reminded him of an operation he had conducted in Norway, on similar terrain and in similar conditions. There had been an ambush and it had turned into a bloodbath. Gripping his rifle, he kept his eyes open, stopping every few feet to listen.

The only sounds he heard were the last gasps of the helicopter's mechanical and electrical systems, punctuated every so often by the hiss of hydraulic fluid as it spat from a severed hose somewhere.

Once in the gulley, he carefully approached the helo from its nose. Peering through the shattered cockpit windscreen, his AK-15 up and at the ready, he could see the pilot and copilot. They were both dead.

It was hard to see any deeper inside — some piece of cargo was obstructing the view. He kept moving.

With the bird lying on its side, the helicopter's porthole-style windows were pointing either up toward the sky or down toward the ground. He'd have to climb on top of the helo if he wanted to look through the windows. He decided to make a complete loop of the aircraft and quietly slid around to the back.

The tail had been sheared off coming through the trees and tossed somewhere in the woods. From where he stood, he couldn't see any sign of it, nor its rotor.

The rear cargo doors, mounted at the back of the fuselage and underneath where the tail had been, were still intact, but badly damaged and partially ajar.

Harvath didn't like it. Even though they looked as if they had been forced open because of the crash, he proceeded with caution.

Sneaking a glance under one of the hinges and not seeing anything, he risked a look around the door itself. There was no one inside — at least not anyone alive.

Cargo lay scattered everywhere and there was a strong smell of spilled gasoline. Unlike jet fuel, which needed to be aerosolized first, gasoline was highly flammable. The presence of frayed electrical wires, some of which were actively sparking, was bad news.

Off to the side, he saw multiple jerry cans — likely for the snowmobiles — that had ruptured. What he didn't see was any sign of Christina. Climbing over and around all the debris, he moved toward the cockpit.

At the forward doors, wearing harnesses, he found the two Wagner snipers on either side of the chopper. One of them was the one he had been shooting at. Judging by the man's wounds, he had hit him at least three times. The other looked as if he had died on impact.

It appeared that Christina hadn't been brought along after all. That could only mean that they were holding her back in Nivsky. *Damn it.*

Shoving the large container aside that had earlier blocked his view, he quickly went through the cabinets near the cockpit. He didn't want to leave anything behind that could be of value.

Gathering what few things he had found, he walked them to the rear, tossed them out the cargo doors, and then examined the jerry cans. Most of them were in bad shape.

Only two of them were salvageable, so, slinging his rifle over his shoulder, he picked them up and carried them outside.

When he did, he saw Christina standing there waiting for him. Next to her was a Sámi man, his face badly beaten. And behind both of them, holding a gun, was a very large Wagner mercenary. Based on the description Christina had given of him earlier, this had to be the one from the bar — the one who was in charge.

"Hands up," Teplov said, pointing his gun right at him.

This time, Harvath didn't have a pistol hidden under a blanket he could use. There was no choice for him but to comply. Setting the cans down, he did as the man instructed.

CHAPTER 54

Sodankylä, Finland

Tero Hulkkonen, from the Ministry of Defense, had met The Carlton Group jet on the tarmac at Lapland Air Command in Rovaniemi. He had an NH90 tactical transport helicopter, its rotors hot, standing by. As soon as the team had transferred their equipment, they lifted off and headed for the Jaeger Garrison 125 kilometers northnortheast in Sodankylä.

The helo landed in a heavily fenced area on the far side of the base. It reminded Chase, Sloane, and Staelin of the Delta Force compound at Fort Bragg. In fact, it was the first thing they mentioned when they hopped off the bird and began unloading their gear. Alternatively, the first thing Haney, Morrison, and Barton remarked on was how "fucking cold" it was.

The base commander, Colonel Jani Laakso, had set them up in a private barracks contiguous to their ops center. Once the team had stowed their gear, they met up with the Colonel and their MoD liaison in one of the op center's secure conference rooms.

A few trays of hot food had been brought over from the mess hall. There was coffee and bottled water. None of The Carlton Group members bitched about dietary restrictions. They were professionals and had been trained to show respect to their hosts, especially when forging a relationship. What's more, they had all been subjected to significantly worse cuisine. Finnish food was absolutely gourmet compared to meals they'd had in places like Somalia, Pakistan, Mozambique, and Yemen.

Everyone loaded up a plate, grabbed a coffee or water, and sat down at the long wooden table. After their flight, they were wiped out, and not in the mood to do much talking. The team was relieved when a reconnaissance specialist was shown in, the lights were dimmed, and a briefing began on a flatscreen at the front of the room.

The specialist brought them up to speed on everything the Finns knew about the terrain, Russian capabilities, and continuing efforts to pinpoint Harvath. It was nothing they didn't already know from their own experience, as well as the work they had done on the plane.

When the presentation was complete, Colonel Laakso thanked the specialist and then asked if anyone had any questions. There were none.

The Colonel promised that if there were any developments, someone would come get the team leader, whom the team members had all agreed on the plane would be Haney.

They thanked the Colonel for his hospitality and, as he and the specialist left the room, Hulkkonen from the Ministry of Defense took over.

He had just finished reading a message on his phone, and now tucked the device into his pocket. "So, the position of the Finnish government, and thereby the Finnish Defense Forces, remains that we can help you up to the border, but we cannot violate sovereign Russian territory."

"We wish your position was different," Haney replied, "but we understand and we appreciate any and all assistance you can give us. Obviously, our one and only goal is to get our teammate safely home."

"Have you had any updates?" Hulkkonen asked. "Any more specific idea as to what route he is traveling, other than west from

Nivsky?"

Haney shook his head. "Not yet. We're hopeful, though, that we'll have something soon."

"Us, too. In the meantime, here's the plan. You try to get some rest. At 0600, we'll serve breakfast in this room while we conduct another briefing. Then, we'll go over potential mission parameters and get you outfitted with cold weather gear, skis, and whatever else you may need."

"And after that?"

"We plan to move you up to one of our border outposts. There's a 'hole' of sorts that the Russians are unaware of. It will allow you to get across the border without raising any alarm."

"The plan is for us to ski eighty klicks into Russia?" Staelin asked, a bit taken aback.

"No, not the full eighty. I'm working out the details now. I'll have more for you by tomorrow."

"What about access to Finnish airspace? If we want to HALO a team in?" Haney asked, referring to a High Altitude Low Opening parachute jump and thinking about the Zero-Three-Hundred team on deck at the Luleå Air Base in northern Sweden.

"That request is looking better. I haven't

426

heard of any final approval yet, but from what I understand, as long as your aircraft remains within our airspace, we do not have a problem with that. This is a 'downed pilot' exercise, so it would be natural to rehearse airborne reconnaissance.

"If, during this rehearsal, a door opened and 'items' were separated from the aircraft, we'd prefer not to know about it. Does that sound fair to you?"

"Very," Haney replied.

"Okay, then. I will be staying here on base as well and will see you all at 0600. If you need anything in the meantime, you have my cell phone number."

They said good night to Hulkkonen and, after finishing their food, shuffled back to the barracks.

The building was divided into a series of rooms with private bathrooms. As the lone female on the team, Sloane got her own. The rest had to double up. Not a single person bitched. Not only was there central heating and indoor plumbing, they all knew that Harvath was having a much rougher night.

Haney encouraged everyone to grab a shower and get to bed. While he waited his turn, he typed out a quick SITREP and sent it to Nicholas back in the United States.

There wasn't much to report, but it was a policy the Old Man had set himself. Even if there was no news, he still wanted to regularly hear from his people in the field. And if you failed to report in, there had better be a damn good reason for it, or there was going to be hell to pay. As a result, they all had become compulsive report writers.

The word "compulsive" was exactly what sprang to Haney's mind as Barton exited the bathroom in a towel and a pair of flip-flops.

"You remembered to bring shower shoes?" he asked.

"You didn't?" replied the former SEAL, shaking his head.

Haney had pounded so much ground as a Marine that his feet resembled a Hobbit's. He wasn't concerned.

Powering down his laptop, he grabbed his dopp kit and headed for the shower.

Once in the bathroom, he closed the door and got undressed. Pulling back the curtain, he saw the shower was not only spotless, but had a head that could be adjusted to pulse and give you a massage.

Haney turned on the hot water full blast, but then changed his mind. Out of a sense of solidarity with Harvath, he flipped the temperature selector to cold.

It was good not to get too comfortable in the field. That's when complacency set in.

Freezing his ass off, Haney took one of the shortest showers of his life. It reminded him of how bitterly cold it was outside and what Harvath was going through right at this very moment.

When he hit his bunk, he was thankful for the blanket, which he pulled up tight under his chin.

Before he drifted off to sleep, he said a prayer for Harvath. He vowed that if God would keep him alive, he and the rest of the team would do everything it took to get him out.

It wasn't the first time Haney had made a deal with God. Often, in his life, there was blood, bullets, or both, but God had never let him down. And he didn't believe that God would this time either. The only thing he needed was a sign.

CHAPTER 55

The "sign" came a few hours later when Haney's encrypted cell phone awoke him. He knew who it was just by the ring. They all had ringtones for each other. Partly as a joke, but partly because he respected him as one "bad motherfucker," his ringtone for Nicholas was the theme song from *Shaft*.

Before even opening his eyes, he had grabbed his phone, activated the call, and pressed it up against his ear.

"Haney," he said, blinking at his watch to see what time it was.

"I think we've got a fix on Harvath," the little man stated.

"Where?" he asked, throwing back the blanket and getting out of bed.

"What's up?" asked Barton, his head still on his pillow.

"We may have a fix on Harvath," he replied.

"The National Reconnaissance Office had

a satellite searching the area over Murmansk Oblast. They picked up something outside Nivsky."

"They've got Harvath?"

"If it's not Harvath, then the Russians have got another very big problem on their hands."

"What did you see?" Haney asked.

"I'm transferring the imagery now. Hulkkonen and the Colonel are going to meet you in the ops center," Nicholas answered. "We'll pick back up via conference call there."

Haney hung up and quickly got dressed. As he exited the room, Barton was right on his heels. Haney wanted to tell him that it might be nothing and that the operator should go back and get some sleep, but he knew it was no use. If their positions had been reversed, Haney would have insisted on coming along as well.

When they got to the operations center, the Colonel was already there. One of his techs patched in Nicholas via a secure video link and put his image up on one of the large screens on the opposite wall. He looked like a giant and Haney told him so as Barton brought over cups of fresh coffee.

As soon as Hulkkonen had arrived, Nicholas explained what the NRO believed it had picked up.

After the message had come in from Harvath, they had worked like crazy to get a satellite over Nivsky. The presence of the two helicopters in the town square told them the Russians were onto him.

From there, they started looking for vehicles traveling west. There were only a handful, but nothing definitive. There was also one person traveling via what had to have been skis, and even a couple of dog teams in the area. Again, there was nothing definitive.

"That," said Nicholas, as he switched from the still images he had been feeding to the op center's screens to infrared video, "was when this happened."

They all watched as there was a commotion in the square and people and equipment, including two snowmobiles, were loaded onto one of the helicopters and it lifted off.

The satellite followed the bird as it traveled toward a speck of a village Nicholas identified as "Friddja," about twenty klicks west.

There, the bird touched down and disgorged the two snowmobiles and all the people who had gotten on in Nivsky. One person, it appeared, was being dragged, or at least forced, by the presence of figures on either side.

A handful of other figures then got into a stack formation and made entry into one of the houses. Moments later, several more followed.

A short time later, they emerged with an additional person.

As the snowmobiles raced off, several figures went house to house. Then, all the figures got back onto the helicopter and flew to the next village, ten klicks over.

This, Nicholas explained, was another indigenous Sámi village, called Adjágas.

They watched as the snowmobiles approached, only to have both of their riders knocked off and a mysterious figure appear out of the woods.

"That's got to be Harvath," exclaimed Haney.

"Like I said," replied Nicholas. "If it isn't, then the Russians have another *very* big problem on their hands. Keep watching."

All eyes were glued to the screens as the rest of it unfolded. They sat riveted as six figures rappelled out of the helo only to hit a house and have something explode inside. Then as the survivors were dragging out their injured, they were all engaged by sniper fire from the same mysterious figure, who moments later began firing at the helicopter and caused it to crash.

The footage began getting crackly and then went dark as the satellite passed out of its window.

"That is definitely Harvath," Barton stated.

"We agree."

The Colonel had one of his people pop up a map. "Adjágas is close, only about sixty kilometers from the border."

Haney recalled Staelin's complaint about potentially having to ski eighty kilometers. He wondered if he'd feel any better knowing it had been cut to sixty.

Turning to Hulkkonen, he said, "Based on this new information, I'd like your government's permission to scramble our aircraft out of Luleå Air Base in Sweden and for it to enter Finnish airspace."

"As part of our joint training exercise," he responded.

Haney nodded and the man pulled out his cell phone, walking away so he could converse with his superiors discreetly.

Looking back at Nicholas, and careful not to implicate the U.S. President directly, even in front of an ally, he asked, "Has the White House seen this?"

"He has. They want final approval over

whatever the plan is, but you're the ones on the ground, so you get to set the board."

Haney looked at the Colonel. "Mr. Hulkkonen mentioned that there's a hole, a blind spot of some sort, we can exploit at the border."

"That is correct."

"He also said we'd have to go in via foot, or at least on skis, but perhaps not the entire way. What did he mean by that?"

The Colonel looked at the Ministry of Defense representative and then returned his attention to Haney. "We have an asset in that area. Someone who might be able to help."

"Someone who can provide transport?"

"Yes, but it's complicated."

"It's *always* complicated," Haney said.

"But in this case, even more so."

"Why?"

"Because," said the Colonel, "the asset hates Americans."

CHAPTER 56

Murmansk Oblast
All this? All the cold, all the pain, and all the miles just for this? Just to get captured? Harvath was pissed. He was pissed at himself. He was pissed at his circumstances. He was pissed at everything. In fact, he was more than pissed. He was *fucking* angry.

And his anger was calling up something deeper, something much more deadly. His anger was calling back up his rage.

"Very slowly," Teplov ordered, well aware of the type of man he was dealing with. "Let the rifle fall to the ground."

Reluctantly, Harvath did as he was ordered.

"Now the chest rig."

His rage building, Harvath unclasped it and tossed it to the side.

"Remove the whites. And your coat. *Slowly.*"

Trying to come up with a way out of this,

436

Harvath did as the man instructed and let them drop to the ground.

"Now turn around," the Russian commanded.

As Harvath turned, the intense, bitter cold bit through his remaining clothes and into his flesh. And though his eyes should have been fixed on the Russian and his gun, he couldn't help but glance at Christina.

He wanted to convey to her that everything was going to be okay, that he would protect her, but she couldn't see his eyes. They were hidden behind the night vision goggles suspended over his helmet.

Somehow, as if Teplov could read his mind, the Russian commanded, "Take off the helmet."

Flipping the goggles up, he unfastened the chinstrap and tossed the helmet aside. He didn't like losing his edge, but now they were on even ground. The Russian wasn't wearing night vision either.

As his eyes adjusted, he quickly shifted them to Christina. She looked terrible — beaten, defeated. The Sámi man standing next to her looked even worse.

But they had survived the crash. And they hadn't survived just to be killed now. Harvath had to do something. But what? He needed to buy himself more time, so he attempted to engage his captor.

Apropos of nothing, he raised the issue that had been burning him up, "After my plane went down, there was one person I couldn't find — a man named Josef."

Teplov smiled. "He made an impression on you, did he?"

"A big one," Harvath stated, the hatred revealing itself across his face. "In fact, I promised him that I'd be the last person he ever saw before he died. Did I succeed?"

"We found him in the woods, beyond the wreckage. His back was broken, and he was suffering from hypothermia, but he is still alive. So it looks like you failed."

"For now."

The Russian's grin broadened. "On your knees."

Harvath held out his arms as if to say, "Cuff me."

Teplov, though, was too smart for that and not in the mood for games. "Mr. Harvath," he said. "It's quite cold and we all know how this is going to end. Let's not drag this out. On your knees."

Harvath refused to move.

Adjusting his pistol, Teplov fired into the ground just next to him.

"On your knees," he repeated. "Or I'll put my next shot *in* one of your knees."

Disabling Harvath would make it difficult to get him out of the gulley and back to the village, but something told him the Russian wouldn't care. Harvath had no doubt that he'd shoot him. So, with no other choice, he began to bend his knees.

Just as he did, there was an enormous explosion as the fumes from the ruptured gas cans inside the helicopter ignited.

The force of the blast threw Harvath more than twenty feet away, almost impaling him on a piece of severed rotor blade.

Leaping to his feet, he spun and saw his captor. Teplov had also been thrown a considerable distance and appeared to have come into violent contact with a tree. He was much slower in getting up. Christina and the Sámi man were lying nearby. Neither one of them was moving.

Harvath scanned for a weapon, but didn't see one. Knowing he wasn't going to get another chance, he put his head down like a running back and charged.

Hitting Teplov was like running into a wall. The man was a good half a foot taller and weighed at least seventy more pounds. As he struck him, the big Russian just absorbed it. Then Teplov began to rain down his own blows.

Fists, knees, and elbows flew. Harvath

couldn't believe how fast the man was. Every time he thought he saw an opening, the Russian closed it and struck him again.

Harvath could taste blood. Whether it was coming from his mouth or his nose, he had no idea. It was probably both.

What he did know was that he couldn't keep going for much longer. He didn't have the strength.

He managed to land a decent jab, cross, hook combination, but the Russian wasn't even fazed. He just kept coming.

Harvath angled to take out one of Teplov's knees, but every time he did, the man seemed to sense what was coming and got out of the way. And as he did, Harvath would catch another elbow, often to the head, in the process.

He was bleeding, short of breath, and almost completely out of energy. He needed to end this fight, *now*.

Pretending he was going for Teplov's knee again, he stopped halfway through the move. The Russian, though, had already set in motion the changing of his footwork and couldn't pull it back. He had left himself wide open.

Stepping in, Harvath delivered an absolutely searing kick to the man's groin. The big Russian doubled over in pain. And as he came forward, Harvath met him with the biggest uppercut he had ever thrown.

There was the sound of breaking bone and he didn't know if it had come from his hand or Teplov's jaw. The Russian's head was so hard that it was like hitting a cinderblock.

Harvath's punch was followed by a spray of blood from Teplov's mouth as his head snapped back.

He couldn't have timed or delivered the strike any better than he had. It should have been a knockout blow. But it wasn't.

Teplov's eyes looked unfocused and he must have realized that he had almost been rendered unconscious, because out of nowhere, he pulled a knife.

Harvath leaped back, but barely in time, as the blade sliced through his clothing, just missing his skin.

With blood pouring from his face, Teplov advanced.

From the way he was holding and moving the knife, it was apparent he was very skilled.

He came at Harvath fast, thrusting and slashing. It was everything Harvath could do to fend off the blows and not get cut.

He was at a serious disadvantage. Teplov was driving him backward, through the wreckage-strewn snow, and he couldn't see where he was going.

With his long arms, the Russian was able to keep the knife out well in front of his large body. It was absolutely impossible for Harvath to land any blows to the man's head or body. His only options were to either trap the knife and wrench it away, or create another feint, and this time actually drive his boot into one of the Russian's knees.

Considering how skilled and how fast Teplov was with the knife, Harvath decided to go for the man's knee — the right one.

But no sooner had he made the decision than he hit a piece of debris and stumbled. He tried to catch himself, but only caught a handful of air as the knife sang past and sliced off the top of his glove, missing his index finger by a millimeter.

As he fell backward, the Russian kept coming, lunging for him and incorporating himself into the fall.

Harvath hit the ground with the taller, heavier, and considerably stronger Teplov right on top of him.

The Russian switched the knife into his left hand and wrapped his right around Harvath's throat and began to squeeze.

Harvath tried to summon every grappling and ground fighting technique he had ever learned, but none of them worked

As he struggled in the snow, the Russian increased the pressure of his choke on him. Harvath was starting to see stars — little points of light — as his vision dimmed. Then he saw the man pull back the knife and raise it into the air.

There appeared to be a glint in the blade. Maybe it was light from the burning helicopter, or perhaps it was a trick caused by the oxygen being cut off from his brain. But he thought he saw something. Movement.

Before he brought the knife plunging down, Teplov increased his impossibly tight hold on Harvath's throat even further.

With the last ounces of strength he had remaining, he attempted to drive his knee up and into the Russian. The moment he did, he heard a crack — and everything went black.

CHAPTER 57

Like a bungee jump in reverse, oxygen filled his body and Harvath was snapped back up onto the bridge of his consciousness.

Upon opening his eyes, he found himself staring right into the same face again. But something was different. Teplov's eyes were lifeless.

He was no longer straddling Harvath, trying to plunge the knife into him. Instead, he had fallen partway to the side. Harvath pushed him the rest of the way off and rolled away from him.

As he did, he could see that a piece of the back of the man's head was missing. *What the hell had happened?*

Scrambling away from the body, he struggled to get to his feet.

"Easy. Go slow," a voice said. It was Christina's.

Turning, he saw her walking toward him, his AK-15 in her hands. The crack he had heard wasn't from bones or cartilage snapping, but from the rifle. She had shot Teplov and in so doing had saved his life.

"Are you okay?" he asked.

"I'll be fine," she replied. "We need to get moving, though. The copilot put out a distress call. Reinforcements are coming."

Harvath had gotten lucky bringing down the first helicopter. He didn't expect to get that lucky again. What's more, he had lost the element of surprise. The second Wagner helo would be coming in hot and probably shooting at anything that moved. They needed to be gone before it arrived.

He found his helmet, with the night vision goggles still intact, but there was no sign of his coat, so he stripped Teplov of his and put it on, along with the man's gloves. While he did, Christina went to get Sini's husband, Mokci.

The man had taken some shrapnel in the explosion, but he was conscious and fully ambulatory.

Joining them, Harvath asked Christina to translate that Sini was back in Adjágas, that she was unharmed, and that there was a snowmobile nearby. They would all ride back together.

As Mokci nodded, Harvath accepted the AK-15 from Christina. He then pointed the

445

way out of the gulley and told them he would catch up.

"Why?" asked Christina. "What are you doing?"

"Just go," he insisted, not wanting her to see. "I'll be right behind you."

Once they were out of sight, Harvath scalped what was left of Teplov's head and used the Russian's own knife to nail the bloody trophy to the nearest tree. He wanted the rest of those Wagner fucks to know who was responsible for killing their boss.

It would also, like the scalps he had left at the airplane crash site, add to their fear of him. Fear slowed people down. It made them pause and think twice. Even the shortest of pauses might make the difference between capture and escape.

The final thing he did was to make an exception to his "no booby-trap" rule. They were far enough from the village, and he knew the mercenaries would be on-site shortly. The gulley was narrow and, as he rigged Teplov's facedown body with multiple frag grenades, he hoped to kill or injure as many of them as possible.

When everything was set, he chased after Christina and Mokci and reached them about halfway to the snowmobile.

It was difficult to move in the deep snow,

but he urged them to pick up their pace. They needed to hurry.

With each step, he pushed himself to come up with a plan. Where would Teplov's men be drawn first? To the downed chopper? Or, would they do a quick overflight of the village and see the bodies of their dead colleagues outside Jompá's cabin and start there?

Either way, it didn't matter. Not counting Teplov and the pilots on the first helicopter, Harvath had taken out eight Wagner mercenaries. If they really had arrived in Nivsky with two dozen, there could be as many as fourteen more speeding their way toward him.

They had enough men to drop ropes and rappel teams down at both Jompá's and the crash site, while still keeping men in reserve. The helicopter could then fly a safe distance away and await further instructions.

If there was a way to create a diversion, it wasn't springing to mind. His brain was all but spent. There had to be something else, though. Yet the only thing he could think of was the warning Lara had yelled to him outside the safe house in New Hampshire: "Run!"

But where was he going to run? The border? There might be enough gas in the snowmobile to make it. He still had his GPS. It was only sixty kilometers, give or take based on the terrain. It might be worth a try. If anyone with Wagner figured it out, though, he was as good as dead.

It didn't matter whether they had a team on board who could rappel down. All they'd need would be a single sniper. They could pinpoint his heat signature with thermal imaging and that would be that.

His thoughts then turned to Christina. She was as good as dead if she stayed behind. He had to take her with him. How he'd get *both* of them out, though, was unimaginable at the moment. He just knew he had to do it.

Suddenly, something bubbled back up in his mind. When Sini had been taking care of him, he had begun to formulate a possible way to escape — *if* she and her friends might be willing to help. Now, the plan seemed to take a more definite shape. They would still need some sort of diversion.

Arriving at the snowmobile, Harvath told Christina to sit behind him with the extra weapons. Mokci would sit behind her and wear his rucksack. He had just picked it up and was about to hand it over when he saw the Sámi man already had a bag.

"Where'd that come from?" he asked.

Christina asked and translated his response. "He said it belonged to Teplov. After the crash, he had gone back inside the helicopter to bring it out. It seemed rather important."

Harvath asked to see the bag and Mokci handed it over.

Inside, wrapped in plastic, were stacks of currency — including U.S. dollars — probably designated as petty cash to be used for bribes, as well as the reward promised at the bar in Nivsky for Harvath's capture. There had to be at least $100,000 worth.

He continued to dig. In addition to a few chocolate bars and personal items, he found a weatherproof notebook, detailed topographic maps, and a small SERE kit containing a signal mirror, stormproof matches, tinder, chem lights, a handcuff key, razorblade, lock picks, and a small compass like the one he had taken from the plane. The real payoff, though, came next.

Rapidly searching the outer pockets, he found a med kit, Teplov's GPS device, and in the last pouch, hit the jackpot — a satellite phone.

Closing it all up, he put the backpack on over his chest, fired up the snowmobile, and when they were all on board, hit the gas and raced as fast as the sled would carry them back to the village.

On the outskirts of Adjágas, Harvath killed
the engine. They left the snowmobile in the
woods and crept the rest of the way on foot.
It was better if no one knew that they were
there.

The Wagner thugs were going to turn
every house inside out. They were also going to sweat the inhabitants — hard.

With their boss and so many of their
comrades dead, anyone holding out on
them was going to get a severe beating and
possibly worse. The mercenaries could get
out of control and end up murdering everyone in the village and burning every house
to the ground. Harvath couldn't let that
happen.

As he had warned Sini earlier, you
couldn't lie to these mercenaries. You had
to tell them the absolute truth. If they did
that, they might be able to escape any
brutality. That meant he had to give them a
good story — a true story.

He also needed to leave a trail that would
take the mercenaries away from the village
and, if possible, throw them off his scent. In
other words, he needed a distraction. But
first, he needed help.

They snuck up behind the cabin of Olá,

Jompá's brother, and stopped. Peering around the corner, he scanned the area with his night vision goggles. There was no one to be seen. The bodies of the dead mercenaries still lay in the snow. No one had touched them and according to Mokci, no one would. The Russians would have to claim their own dead. The Sámis, partly out of superstition and partly out of not wanting anything to do with what had happened, wouldn't go near them.

That was good news for Harvath. Pulling Christina aside, he told her what he needed her to do and handed her Teplov's backpack full of cash. Then, as she and Mokci slipped inside, he headed for the Wagner corpses.

Without having to worry that one of the villagers might roll one of the dead mercenaries over, he was able to set additional traps. Using frag grenades, he booby-trapped them all. No matter which body was touched first, it was guaranteed to be a deadly result.

Though he couldn't see them, he could feel the villagers' eyes on him. After he was done, he disappeared into the woods and rigged the corpses of the dead snowmobilers, before doubling back to the cabin where he had left Christina and Mokci.

Peering through the rear window, he

waited for her signal. When she flashed him the thumbs-up, he pulled out Teplov's satellite phone, extended the antenna, and powered it up.

"Please work," he said under his breath, knowing this might be the only chance he got.

As he waited, he pulled out his GPS device courtesy of Christina's uncle and powered that up as well. The clock was running out. Everything now depended on the groundwork being laid inside the cabin.

CHAPTER 58

Hostage Recovery Fusion Cell
Washington, D.C.

"Quiet!" Nicholas yelled to the room, as he stood on top of his desk to get everyone's attention. Instantly, the dogs were on guard and he had to give them the command to relax.

The room fell silent instantly and when it did, he returned his attention to his phone. "Say again, please?" he asked. It was a terrible connection and kept going in and out.

"Norseman," Harvath repeated, using his call sign, as was their protocol for this type of emergency transmission.

A series of coded challenge questions and answers then went back and forth, ending with, "Tim has a metal roof. I repeat. Tim has a metal roof."

"*Tim has a metal roof.* Good copy," said Nicholas, acknowledging the final coded response. *"Would you like to hear the specials?"*

"Negative. My wife and I are ready to place our order."

Nicholas looked at SPEHA Rogers, who had appeared at his desk, and pantomimed for the man to grab a pen and paper to take down the following information. Harvath had authenticated that it was him, that he was calling on comms he couldn't trust, and that he was going to need to get pulled out plus one — a woman.

"I'm ready," said the little man.

Harvath rattled off two strings of letters and numbers, which Nicholas repeated back to him. Rogers wrote them down and was about to race over to the NSA desk, which was coordinating with the National Reconnaissance Office, when Nicholas stopped him.

"Subtract one from the latitude coordinates and add two to the longitude."

Rogers nodded and headed off.

There was a lot that Nicholas wanted to ask, but for Harvath's sake, he had to keep things as short and to the point as possible. "Have you eaten with us before?"

"Twice."

Harvath was being professional, delivering the coded information calmly, but Nicholas could sense a distinct underlying tension in his voice.

"Are you free to take a quick survey about that experience?"

"Negative," said Harvath. "A lot of people want to use this phone."

"We'll get this order placed right away for you."

Nicholas was about to add, "So good to hear your voice," when the call went dead.

"Hello?" the little man said. "Hello? Can you hear me?"

Confirming that the call had indeed been terminated, he hopped down from the desk, just as the SPEHA hurried back over.

"What did he say?"

Nicholas ran through everything Harvath had relayed in their brief conversation.

"Do we know who is chasing him?" Rogers asked. "Russian military? Russian law enforcement? Both?"

"He didn't say."

"How about the identity of the woman? Do we know who she is?"

"We don't know that either, but if I had to guess, it's the doctor we saw the Instagram post from."

"What about how he's traveling? Is he on foot?"

Nicholas shook his head. "No, definitely

not on foot."

"By vehicle then?"

"I think so."

"Do we know what kind? Is it a car? A truck?"

Once again, Nicholas shook his head. "He could have given me a code, but he didn't. All we know is that whatever it is, he and the woman are traveling separately."

"Why? What purpose do you think that would serve?"

"Maybe there are checkpoints and one has to act as a decoy or something. I don't know. He didn't say."

Rogers could tell Nicholas was getting frustrated with him. "I'm just trying to help. Don't worry. We'll get to work on what we have. Did he say when he'd be back in touch?"

"No. The call went dead."

The SPEHA put his hand on the little man's shoulder. "I've never met him, but based on what everyone has told me, he's going to make it."

Nicholas agreed. If anyone could beat the odds, it was Harvath. But if there was one thing he had learned in their business, it was that if you weren't cheating, you weren't trying.

They needed to make sure that they were

doing everything to stack the deck in Harvath's favor. It was time to go all in.

CHAPTER 59

Murmansk Oblast

"Tell him that I'm freezing my balls off out here and that if he doesn't open the door and let us in, I'm going to burn his fucking house down," said Haney. *"With him in it."*

The Jaeger soldier, whom the Finns had reluctantly sent along, relayed the message in perfect Russian, though with just a little added tact.

"Fine," the asset agreed, "but make sure they hide their equipment around back. I don't want anyone to know they're here."

The Finn translated, and while Haney and Staelin stood guard in front, the rest of the team went around back and shrugged off their gear.

Once they had all deposited their equipment, Barton and Gage offered to take first watch.

Haney had been instructed to get right to the point. And once inside, he did just that.

He spoke slowly so the Jaeger soldier could translate and, because the subject matter was somber, he made sure to adopt a respectful tone.

"United States President Paul Porter extends his deepest condolences to you and your family. He hopes you will accept my country's sympathies for what happened to your brother during the Soviet-Afghan War. We deeply regret that it was an American weapon, provided by the United States to the mujahideen, which caused his death."

Haney, along with the rest of The Carlton Group team, studied the older man's visage, searching for any hint of softening, or of forgiveness.

He was a stone-faced, flinty bastard, well into his seventies if he was a day. His hate for the United States oozed from every pore. The only country he hated as much was Russia, which was why he had agreed to work against it, in the service of the Finns.

His codename was Pavel. That was all the Jaeger commander was comfortable sharing. Haney was fine with that. He wasn't here to make friends. He was here to rescue one.

Both the United States President and the Secretary of State had given Haney permission to make the in-person apology. "Just don't gild the lily," the Secretary of State had warned him.

Haney didn't care. He would have told Pavel that the U.S. had faked the moon landing if it meant securing the Russian's cooperation. As the team saw it, there really was no way to pull this off without him.

Upon confirmation from Nicholas that Harvath was alive and they had a location for him, the team had been flown to the border on Army Aviation MD500 "Little Bird"–style helicopters.

The Jaegers had sent one of their intelligence specialists, Aleksi, along to help manage the meeting with Pavel and to make sure that the Americans didn't "screw it up."

Pavel was one of many cooperators the Finns had within Russia. They functioned not only as human trip wires, alerting Finland to Russian troop movements, but also as guerilla fighters ready to harass the Russian military and provide assistance to Finnish soldiers and intelligence officers should war ever break out.

Pavel, though, was more than just a prized agent-in-place for Finland. He had highly specialized training that made him invaluable in the effort to recover Harvath. It was training the United States was willing to pay top dollar for.

And to that end, Haney opened his backpack and removed multiple bricks of U.S. currency and set them on the table. "In addition to President Porter, we also bring salutations from another notable American, Mr. Benjamin Franklin."

The Russian and the Jaeger soldier watched as Haney continued pulling money out and stacking it on the table.

"He wants to know how much that is," said Aleksi.

"Two hundred and fifty thousand dollars," Haney replied. "He gets half now and the other half when we get back."

It was a fortune, especially in this part of Russia, and the old Russian's face lit up as the Finn translated. He had his hands around the throat of a golden goose that could lay diamond-encrusted eggs. He wasn't about to let go.

"Two hundred and fifty thousand dollars for his help," the Jaeger soldier translated. "How much in reparations? For the loss of his brother at the hands of an American shoulder-fired missile?"

Haney had known that was coming, and he smiled. "Please explain," he stated, "that my country doesn't pay reparations in situations like that."

As soon as the words had been translated into Russian, Pavel began to put on a show of shock and dismay. His lousy acting was akin to that of a soccer star who had been tapped by another player's foot and who fell down on the field, writhing in phony agony.

"But," Haney continued, "because we value his cooperation and want to have a good relationship, we're willing to negotiate something."

"How about we don't kill him?" Staelin asked, so that only Haney could hear. "How about that for a counteroffer?"

Staelin hated dealing with people like this. It was part of the job, but he had never liked it. The moment you opened your wallet, they wanted everything and more from inside. The fact that they were negotiating with the United States only made people greedier. They figured the U.S. could afford to give them whatever they asked for.

Aleksi listened to Pavel and then said, "He wants $10 million for the loss of his brother."

Haney had been ready for an opener like that and simply replied, "No." He didn't offer a counter.

The old Russian sat there trying to figure out what to do. If he wasn't careful, his golden goose would slip out of his grasp and leave him with nothing.

He dropped quickly down to "$5 million" and passed the request on through Aleksi.

Haney continued smiling and tried to keep his tone respectful. "Mr. Pavel, I am authorized to offer you an additional $250,000. It will be delivered to you once we are safely out of the country. That's my best offer."

The Russian listened to the translation and stared at his American counterpart long and hard. Finally, he blinked, and the blink was followed by a smile.

He leaned over and spoke to Aleksi, who replied, "He'll take it."

Pavel then got up from the table and walked over to his kitchen. Assembling a tray, he returned with glasses for everyone and a bottle of vodka.

Haney looked at the Jaeger soldier. "Should we be doing this?"

Aleksi shrugged. "It's tradition. It's how they seal the deal. Plus, he's a pretty serious alcoholic."

"He's what?" Haney asked, taken aback. That was a part of Pavel's history that hadn't been shared by the Finns.

"Alcoholism is quite common in Russia, especially in Murmansk Oblast. If you attempt to stop him from drinking, it could blow your entire operation."

"Are you nuts?" he asked, careful not to raise his voice. "The American government can't agree to pay some drunk $250,000."

"It just did," replied Aleksi. "And before you start having second thoughts, let me remind you that not only did you ask for this, but you don't have any choice. This is the best way to get to Harvath."

To get to Harvath, though, they were going to have to survive the trip. And as he watched Pavel pour a tall shot of vodka, that was now one of his biggest concerns.

CHAPTER 60

"Here," Christina said, as she pointed at a spot on Teplov's topographic map. "Jompá and his brother Olá were just out there yesterday. They said the wind has been so strong that the surface is completely swept clean. The lake looks like a black mirror."

Harvath prayed they were right. The only thing that could possibly give them away would be footprints. But as long as there was no snow on top of the ice, they might just make it.

He had to give Christina credit. She had been an exceptional saleswoman. Jompá and Olá had every reason to say no, but using the money from Teplov's backpack and leveraging her relationship with their village, she had convinced them to say yes.

As instructed, she had left Sini and Mokci out of it. In fact, as the husband and wife had been reunited, a plan was hatched to get them on their way, unseen, back to their own village.

The Wagner thugs were mercenaries, not detectives. They'd be anxious to pick up Harvath's trail. Retracing their colleagues' footsteps back to Friddja, hoping to find a witness to interrogate, was too much work.

Harvath quickly studied the map and asked, "Where's the rendezvous?"

She placed her finger on a spot, up a river, two kilometers inland. "It's a small hunting camp, part of a chain, shared by the Sámi. Jompá and Olá will meet us there."

Memorizing the map, Harvath fired up the snowmobile. He needed to let Nicholas know where they were headed, but more important, he needed to get the hell out of there before the Wagner assholes arrived. The call would have to wait.

As soon as he felt Christina wrap her arms around his waist, he hit the gas and took off.

Driving a car under night vision, even down a gravel road, was tough enough. Navigating a snowmobile, at high speed, through a forest, though, was like playing Russian roulette.

Harvath clipped so many trees along the way that he was positive that the Audubon Society was going to put him on a hit list.

The sled's fiberglass body got beat to shit.

The rest of it, thanks be to the "escape gods," remained in working order. Nothing critical was damaged.

Just as he had done when he had fled the trapper's cabin, whenever he hit an open piece of ground, he pinned the throttle.

The sled screamed beneath them and raced forward. As its skis jerked and bumped over the frozen terrain, the frigid air smelled to him like freedom. Suddenly, all he could think about was home.

Every atom in his body ached to be free, to be back in America, and to be back among the people he loved.

Making himself more aerodynamic, he dropped his shoulders, put his head down, and leaned over the handlebars, urging the snowmobile on. They couldn't get to their destination fast enough.

Soon, the ground began to slope downward, and through the trees up ahead, he could see it. Through his night vision goggles, it looked like an oblong, asphalt parking lot.

As he sped out of the forest, he made sure to leave plenty of visible tracks along the shore before speeding out onto the ice. There, he flipped the goggles up so he could see the surface unaided. It looked like a piece of polished black marble.

Flipping the goggles back down, he cruised to the other side of the small lake, being careful to avoid the thinner ice, and found the perfect spot to unload Christina and their gear.

Here, the woods came right down to the shore. As soon as they set foot in the snow, they'd be in the forest and their path would be difficult if not impossible to detect.

After unloading everything and making sure Christina was safe, he got back on the snowmobile.

"Be careful," she warned him.

"I've already been swimming once on this trip," he replied. "I don't plan on doing it again."

Hitting the gas, he spun on the ice, got control of the sled, and then steered toward what looked like the most logical spot.

Several streams, two of which were quite wide, fed the little lake. They came together and pushed fresh, warmer water underneath the ice. That was where he intended to carry out his diversion.

Bringing the snowmobile to a halt, he pulled out his satellite phone, extended its antenna again, and powered it up. He had no idea if the Russians were tracking its calls or not.

Speaking quickly, he delivered another

coded message to Nicholas, which relayed his location as well as how he and Christina planned to make their escape.

Then, after turning off the phone and putting it back in his coat pocket, he pulled out the two incendiary grenades.

He had gone over the plan several times in his head. The most important part was the placement of the devices. At four thousand degrees each, he needed to be extremely careful how he used them.

Snapping a chem light, he tied its lanyard to the back of the sled, activated the snowmobile's headlight, and then, with the incendiary grenades right where he wanted them, he pulled the pin of the one in front and then the one in back, before moving backward on the unstable ice so as not to be sucked in.

He knew better than to look at the bright light from the burning phosphorus, which could damage his retinas. Turning his head away, he shot an indirect glance to the side as the white-hot thermite rapidly melted the ice around the snowmobile.

There were loud cracks, like windows being broken, as the ice beneath the snowmobile began to melt rapidly.

In less than a minute, the sled had fallen

through, swallowed up by the cold, black water.

Harvath had never used an incendiary grenade to melt ice before and was impressed by how fast it worked.

Retreating to the shore, he stood with Christina for a moment, watching the eerie glow of the snowmobile's headlight beneath the surface.

"How long do you think that will last?"

"In these temperatures?" he replied. "Not very long. That's why I tied the chem light to the back. That won't be much better, but it was worth a try. Ready to go?"

When she nodded, they shouldered their equipment and headed upstream toward the camp.

It was a rough push. The snow was deep, it was bitterly cold, and they were both tired and in pain. But they kept going.

She was in excellent shape and Harvath admired her. Anyone else would have slowed him down. Not once, though, did he have to encourage her to hurry up.

Every several minutes, they paused and listened. But all they heard were the sounds of the forest. Water rolled beneath the iced-over stream. Wind blew through the trees, shaking their boughs.

It was getting stronger, and he suspected

another storm might be coming. Foul weather could work to their advantage, providing cover, but if bad enough, it could also hamper their progress.

Approaching the camp from the south, Harvath dropped everything but his rifle and had Christina hang back in the trees. He wanted her to wait there until he had made sure it was safe to come out.

It only took him a few minutes to clear the camp and determine that there were no threats.

Rejoining her, he helped pick up their gear and then pointed out where he wanted them to go.

There wasn't a lot of shelter to choose from, but right off the bat he crossed the traditional tents off the list.

Made of reindeer skins, they were probably decent for keeping warm, *if* you lit a fire inside. They, though, weren't going to be lighting any fires.

Instead, Harvath steered them toward a small shed with a metal roof. Known as a *banya*, the freestanding sauna was the perfect place to hide, especially if what you were hiding from was thermal imagining.

Once the two of them had piled in with all their gear, he closed the door, and they tried to get warm.

471

Pulling out the heavy blankets Jompá had given them, he wrapped one around Christina and one around himself.

He looked longingly at the sauna's rocks, which sat atop a rudimentary stove. There was nothing he would have loved more than to have loaded it with wood and dropped in a match. The little structure would have heated up in seconds. So, too, though, would the stovepipe.

Out in the middle of nowhere, its heat signature would have been the equivalent of slicing through the night sky with a Hollywood movie premiere searchlight. Until Jompá and Olá had arrived, he wasn't going to take any risks.

They were both shivering. Christina opened her blanket, pulled him close, and pressed her body against his in an attempt to conserve warmth.

Her touch sent a jolt of electricity through him, but right behind it came a crashing wave of guilt.

Christina was an extremely attractive woman. She was also lonely, and in part vulnerable — like him. No doubt, if they had both agreed, they could have had each other right there. But that wasn't what Harvath wanted. He wanted Lara and she was gone.

He stood with Christina for several more minutes until they both started to warm up. Then, he gently stepped away. Things were complicated enough without adding to the confusion.

The only thing he wanted to be thinking about was getting them both out of Russia alive.

CHAPTER 61

"Not in the dark," Aleksi translated. "Not on a lake he has never landed on before. We have to wait until morning. In the daylight, he can conduct a flyover and inspect the area to make sure there are no obstructions."

Haney had worked with plenty of bush pilots. He knew the drill. That didn't mean he liked it.

Harvath was so close. They could be on top of him in less than half an hour of flight time. The old Pilatus airplane the Russian pilot kept in the hangar outside was capable of carrying their entire team. It was outfitted with skis so that it could land on ice or snow, exactly like the Skibird the United States had repositioned from Greenland. The Pilatus, though, was much smaller and classified as a STOL — Short Takeoff and Landing — aircraft, which meant it needed even less runway.

Even so, based on the new coordinates Nicholas had provided, the lake Harvath was at now was too small. There was another, longer lake a few miles away that would work perfectly. Harvath, though, would have to get there. That's what Haney and the rest of the team were worried about.

"So what are we going to do?" Staelin asked, as he and Haney stepped to the other side of the room to talk.

"We wait."

"*Wait?* That's bullshit. We need to get moving. Now."

Haney looked at him. "You're the guy who was bitching about skiing all the way to Nivsky."

"But we're not going to Nivsky," he said, pointing at the map. "We're linking up with Harvath here. If we leave now, we can be there in two hours. Two and a half tops."

"If you were skiing hard, over flat terrain and minimal snowpack — none of which you would be. Then there's Wagner and their Mi-8. The minute you get picked up on any sort of imaging system, it's game over."

"They'll be too busy looking for Harvath. They won't expect us to come in from the west."

Haney shook his head. "Wouldn't you be

expecting us? Don't underestimate these guys. They're good. The only reason Harvath is still alive is that he's better.

"Then there's the problem of the Alakurtti Air Base. We could almost hit it with a nine iron from here. Wagner wouldn't need to waste any manpower. Their pilot could simply call it in — a column of heavily armed skiers, moving through the nearby forest, under cover of darkness. I'm guessing they'd send someone to check that out. What do you think?"

"I think it would probably get a pretty substantial response," replied Staelin.

"Which is why we're not doing it."

"I understand, but we can't just sit here."

Haney appreciated his doggedness. They all felt the same way about Harvath, and part of what made them all so good at their jobs was never taking "no" for an answer. They were always pushing back, always looking for different and better ways to achieve their missions. Never had it been more important for any of them than right now. But Haney's job was to examine their list of options and select the best one.

"Waiting sucks," Haney agreed. "I get it. It's even worse knowing that Harvath is so close. For the moment, though, he's okay."

"For the moment," the former Delta Force

operator stated.

"Listen, the best thing we can do for him is to get some rest and be ready for wheels up before first light."

Staelin wasn't done yet. "What about the Zero-Three-Hundred team?"

Haney consulted the most recent message he had received. "Finland has agreed to open their airspace. The Zero-Three-Hundred team, along with U.S. aircraft, is being spun up in Sweden right now. But in all likelihood, we're going to get to Harvath first. If we do, then we pick him up, we get him out, and no one's the wiser."

It was a solid plan, but even the most solid of plans could go sideways. "What's our contingency?"

"I'm working on it," said Haney. "We should have another satellite on station shortly. Once we get a look at the latest imagery, we'll be able to make some more decisions. In the meantime, why don't you grab a piece of floor with everyone else and try to get some shut-eye."

Staelin knew he'd be no good to Harvath, or anyone else on the team, if he wasn't at his best, and so he gave in.

But it was more than just being at his best for the team. He didn't know why, but he had felt apprehensive ever since they entered Russia.

Something told him that he was going to need everything he had to get through this assignment.

CHAPTER 62

White House
Washington, D.C.

Nicholas and SPEHA Rogers had made the short drive from the Fusion Cell at FBI Headquarters to 1600 Pennsylvania Avenue together. This was the first time the little man had been on the White House grounds, much less inside one of its buildings. It was difficult for him not to feel a sense of awe.

President Paul Porter met them in the dining room, just beyond the Oval Office and his personal study, as he was wrapping up his dinner. "Can I get either of you anything?" he asked, knowing how hard they had been working.

"No, thank you," the pair replied.

"How about some coffee?" he then asked. Before the men had answered, he rang for the steward and placed the request.

They made small talk until the steward arrived. Once he had cleared the President's dinner dishes and had left the room, they got down to business.

"So how soon until we pick him up?" Porter asked.

"If all goes well," Nicholas replied, "a few hours. But that's only half the battle. Then, the team will need to get him back over the border and into Finland."

"Do we have a plan for that?"

"Yes, sir. Several actually. Per our agreement, the ultimate call will be made in conjunction with the team leader on the ground."

"Understood. What's the weather looking like?"

"Not good," said Nicholas. "It's going to get rough again. The question is whether we can beat it."

"When will you know?"

"Unfortunately, not until we're right up against it. A few minutes on either side might end up making all the difference. We're going to need to move fast."

"And you want to run the operation out of the Situation Room downstairs, correct?" asked Porter.

"Yes, sir. As I said, this is going to come down to fast decision-making with only minutes or seconds to spare. We believe it's critical that it be done here and that you be in attendance."

"Without question. We'll set it up."

"Thank you, sir."

The President then turned to Rogers. "Now, tell me about this grand fallback plan in case everything goes wrong."

Rogers cleared his throat and spent the next five minutes laying out his proposal. Porter listened intently, interrupting only a handful of times when he thought his SPEHA was being too vague, or too optimistic. Each time he did, though, he was impressed by the thoroughness of the man's reply.

When Rogers had finished laying everything out, the President picked up his coffee cup and leaned back in his chair. It was a lot to ponder — especially as it was packed end-to-end with risks, not the least of which was an all-out war between the United States and Russia.

It was also an offer the Russian President might not be able to refuse. When they had gone after Harvath, they realized how valuable he was. What they hadn't realized was what it would ultimately cost.

Could they crack the diplomatic door enough for the Russian President to save face? If tossed a quiet lifeline, would he take it?

There was no telling. Time and time again, Peshkov took stances and pursued courses that, by all accounts, were completely against Russia's, as well as his own, self-interest.

And time and again the United States had struck back in response to his aggression. Yet, in one form or another, the aggression had continued. It was as if the Russian President had a screw loose. But even that was too simple a metaphor.

For years, the brightest minds in U.S. intelligence had been trying to figure him out, and for years they had been continually frustrated. The man simply defied any profile they came up with. He was the enigma of all enigmas.

This time, though, they were trying something different. It was simple, and perhaps, that's what had been missing in all of their past engagements.

Porter hoped that his visitors were correct, that their plan was as well thought through and airtight as it appeared, because the alternative was almost unthinkable.

"All right," he said, leaning forward and setting his cup down in its saucer. "We're going to move forward with this plan. I want to be perfectly clear, though. We all need to be prepared for what happens if it doesn't work. So, if you're not fully confident — if there's some other idea you've been holding in reserve — now's the time to get it on the table. Once we pull the trigger, there's no putting this bullet back in the gun."

He paused to let his words sink in. Slowly, he looked at Rogers and then Nicholas. Neither of the men seemed eager to offer any alternative.

"That's it then," the President decreed. "Let's start calling everybody in. In the meantime, I'll make sure they get you everything you need."

"Thank you, Mr. President," Rogers said as he stood and shook Porter's hand.

Nicholas followed suit.

As he watched the men leave the room, the President was gripped by a singular thought. What they were about to launch would go down as one of the most courageous rescues in history, or it would be viewed as one of America's greatest mistakes.

Either way it would be pinned to him and to his legacy. He wouldn't lose sleep over that, though. That wasn't why he had accepted this job. He had accepted it because someone needed to be willing to stand up and do the right thing for the nation, no matter what the personal cost. All he cared about was getting Harvath home.

He prayed to God that they had made the right decision.

CHAPTER 63

Murmansk Oblast

Harvath had stood at the door listening, his blanket still wrapped around him, while Christina had curled up on one of the sauna's benches and fallen asleep.

Standing still went against everything he had ever been taught. All of his training had hammered into him that the key to escaping and evading enemy forces was to keep moving.

Waiting for Jompá and Olá to show was beginning to feel like a mistake. So much so, that part of him wanted to take his chances in the snow, to wake up Christina and run for the Finnish border. The other part of him, though — the rational, sane, experienced part — told him to stay put, take a deep breath, and relax.

He needed to dial his anxiety down, to think of something else that would move him off code red to at least code orange, or maybe even code yellow.

Normally on an operation, he didn't allow his mind to wander. He had become an expert at compartmentalization, and could remain focused, no matter how badly his mind wanted to wander. But for a few moments, he allowed himself to wonder what he might do once he made it out.

He knew one thing for sure: whatever he did, it wouldn't involve snow and it definitely wouldn't involve cold. There was a little hotel he liked in the Florida Keys. He had taken solace there before. Maybe that's where he would go — warm sand, warm water, and a bottomless bar bill.

He couldn't go home, at least he couldn't stay there — not for long. Home was Lara. Her clothes were hanging in the closet, her makeup in the bathroom, her fancy teas all organized in the kitchen.

At some point, he would have to make his peace with what had happened, but not until he had settled the bill. It would happen on his time, and only when he was ready. There was no other way it would work.

Leaving the sound and smell of the ocean, he brought his mind back to the here and now.

As the sauna had no windows, he had felt

okay snapping a couple of chem lights and using them to dimly illuminate the tiny space.

He looked at Christina. She had been through a ton. He had been trained for this kind of grueling exhaustion, she hadn't. It was good to see her sleeping. The more rest she could get, the better. The biggest push was still ahead.

He knew she could handle it, though. She was amazingly resilient. When he had explained all of the risks that faced them, she had smiled and simply said, "Let's go."

It wasn't hard to understand why, but she had explained it to him nonetheless.

There was nothing left for her in Nivsky, nothing left in Russia, except pain. She had made up her mind to go with him the moment she had agreed to help him. He was an answer to a question she didn't even know she had.

It didn't matter what lay ahead. All that mattered was that she keep moving forward and put Russia behind her.

She knew all too well how her country operated. Everything good came at a heavy price. It was why so many of its people were so miserable. Nothing good ever really happened to average Russians, there were just shades of "less worse."

Living abroad had given her a taste of what could be. She just hadn't had the courage then to stay abroad. And while England wasn't the United States, she had gotten a taste of Western culture and understood what it meant.

The United States was still a land of opportunity. The only limits there were the ones you placed on yourself. Whatever she wanted to do, she could do it.

In Harvath's opinion, she had nailed it. In fact, she had nailed it in a way that only someone who didn't have those advantages and freedoms could. It eased his mind that involving her had been the right thing to do. Somehow, all of this seemed destined to have happened.

That said, they still had much to do before they could consider themselves free.

Looking at his watch, he tried to anticipate how much time remained before Nicholas would be able to see him again via satellite. Several times, he had heard the distant rumble of what sounded like the Wagner helicopter, but it had yet to make it this far out. In a way, that was a victory. And despite its being small, he knew he should celebrate it. So far, so good.

Christina must have had incredible hearing, because at the first, far off barking of the dogs, she stirred and sat up.

"Jompá and Olá?" she asked, rubbing her eyes.

"It sounds like it," he replied, picking up the rifle. "We should get ready to move."

Together, they packed up their gear except for a little bit of food, which they split between them.

They ate quickly and in silence. By the time the dog teams pulled up outside, they were ready to go.

With Christina translating, Harvath showed Jompá and Olá the spot on the map where he wanted them to be taken to.

The men nodded. The lake was known for its fishing and there was another Sámi village not far from there. Two Sámi coming to trade shouldn't be an unusual sight. All that was left was to load Harvath and Christina onto the sleds.

Pulling back the reindeer hides, the brothers exposed the large slabs of frozen moose meat they had brought with them. They would be uncomfortable to hide beneath, but they would effectively shield them from any thermal imaging.

Harvath's initial plan had been to purchase from Jompá and Olá two live reindeer that were scheduled for slaughter, have the brothers hollow, or "cape," them out, and for him and Christina to be transported to the rendezvous inside those.

It would have been a warm, but somewhat disgusting way to travel. The weight, though, the brothers had explained, was too much for the dogs to pull, so they had settled on their current solution.

To help insulate their passengers from the cold, they had brought extra reindeer hides along.

Laying Harvath and Christina down, they helped bundle them up and then lowered the moose meat down over them.

Fortunately, there was a small, wooden framing system atop which the slabs set, but it didn't leave a lot of room. Both Harvath and Christina had to turn their heads to the side or tuck their chins into their chests to avoid their noses pressing directly against the meat.

Once everything was set, Jompá and Olá called out to their teams, the dogs started barking, and the sleds lurched forward.

Over thousands of years, the Sámi had built up an amazing tolerance for the cold. Whereas Christina had warned Harvath that there was only so much distance he could travel before succumbing to exposure, Jompá and Olá could far outlast him. The dogs also moved a hell of a lot faster than a man on skis or snowshoes.

While he hated not being able to see what was going on, Harvath tried to relax and enjoy the ride. If everything went according to plan, they'd be across the border and into Finland in a matter of hours.

By the same token, he knew that very seldom did everything go according to plan. In fact, the better things seemed to be progressing, the greater the likelihood that something bad was right around the corner. It was how Murphy worked.

He gripped the rifle a little tighter. In addition to the shotgun lying on his other side, he also had a pistol. Christina had a pistol, too, as well as a rifle.

Doing a quick mental inventory, he tallied up how many frag grenades he had left and then how many rounds of ammunition they had between them.

In the end, he hoped they wouldn't need any of it, but if they did, he prayed that it would be enough.

CHAPTER 64

Pavel, the bush pilot, made his money chartering his old plane to anyone capable of paying. Mostly, he flew hunters and fisherman. Occasionally, he got an arctic research team or a group of mining company executives. No matter who the client was, the seats were removable and the cabin could be reconfigured to handle the load.

It was a tight fit, and would be even tighter on the way back with Harvath and the woman, but they had managed to get themselves and all of their gear loaded.

Haney's concern over the pilot's drinking remained. Though Aleksi had convinced him to lay off the booze, when he rose to do his preflight check of the aircraft, he didn't appear to have sobered up much. He probably kept a bottle in his bedroom, the bathroom, or both. In fact, Haney was willing to bet there was one aboard the plane as well.

"Did you remember to pack a parachute?" Staelin joked, as they watched the wobbly pilot walk around the Pilatus, manually testing the flaps and rudder.

"I did," Barton deadpanned, as he slid past carrying bladders full of fresh water.

Haney chuckled. Sipping on a fresh cup of coffee, he stomped his boots in the snow and tried to warm up. "You ready for this?"

"As ready as I'm going to be," answered Staelin. "What's the latest on Harvath?"

"Everything's on track. NRO is monitoring two dog sleds heading toward the LZ."

"What about the weather?"

"We're going to have to move fast," Haney replied. "The front is already closing in and visibility is dropping."

Staelin used his chin to gesture toward the pilot. "Can we rely on this guy?"

"Aleksi says yes, but I don't trust anyone I don't know. That's why I'm riding up front with him in the copilot's seat."

"Have you ever flown a plane before?"

Haney nodded. "Just haven't done any takeoffs or landings."

"That's reassuring."

"Relax. We're going to be fine."

"I'll relax when we've got Harvath and we're out of Russia," Staelin replied. "Speaking of which, what do we know about those mercenaries who are after him?"

"As far as we know, they're still looking. The last report I received was that the helicopter had landed at Alakurtti for refueling and probably a crew change."

"So we've got no idea if they've given up or are still in the hunt?"

"They're still in the hunt. There are men on the ground at and around the village where the other Mi-8 went down."

"And our rules of engagement still stand?"

Haney nodded. "They still stand. Weapons free."

"Roger that. When do you want to do the final briefing?"

Looking at his watch, the team leader said, "Let's gather everybody up and do it now."

It took several minutes, but once Staelin had pulled the team together, he handed the floor over to Haney. He reviewed the mission parameters, the rules of engagement, and all the latest intelligence. He then opened it up for questions. There were none.

After a comms check, he gave the team the ten-minute warning and grabbed Aleksi to have a final chat with the pilot.

The Finnish soldier would not be coming with them. His government had forbidden it. They had no desire to be part of an act of war on Russian soil, no matter how justified.

Haney didn't like not having a translator along. Pavel didn't speak a word of English. Even though they were asking for trouble, it was the hand they had been dealt. They were lucky the Finns had gone along with them this far. As long as the Russian and his plane could fly, they'd take everything else as it came.

Anxious to be gone before sunrise as well, Aleksi bade the team good fortune, clamped into his bindings, and skied back into the forest toward the border.

As he did, the first flakes of snow from the storm began to fall. Haney and his crew were now on their own.

CHAPTER 65

Alakurtti Air Base

With the Wagner disaster, as well as President Peshkov breathing down his neck for proof of life on Harvath, General Minayev hadn't gotten any sleep, which only served to make him more disagreeable than usual. When the Mi-8 flared and touched down, he was already outside, waiting impatiently on the tarmac.

As soon as Teplov's second in command, a man named Garin, hopped out, Minayev grabbed him and dragged him to the operations center at the back of the restricted hangar.

Once there, he cleared everyone else out and then began shouting. "What the fuck happened? Thirteen dead. *Thirteen!* Including Teplov! And he took down a Russian Air Force helicopter! One *fucking* man did all of this?"

"Yes, sir."

"And he's scalping people? *Scalping?* What is he, a fucking maniac?"

"Apparently."

Minayev waited for him to expound, to provide a little additional insight based on what he had seen, but the man didn't offer anything further.

"Damn it!" the General shouted. "Fucking damn it!"

Garin knew Minayev's reputation for biting the heads off his subordinates. It was better to give the shortest answer possible and not to step out on a rhetorical limb. Speak when spoken to, and always keep your opinion to yourself around him, even when he asked for it.

"Where is Harvath now?" the General asked. "Right this very second."

"We don't know."

"Where do you think he is?"

"I'm sorry, sir. I don't have enough information at this time to answer your question."

"Damn it, Garin! Don't play games with me. Where the fuck do you think he is? Answer me. That's an order."

At this point, the Wagner mercenary had no choice but to obey. "He's either dead or on his way to the border with Finland."

Minayev wanted to put a bullet in him.

"That's the dumbest fucking answer I have ever heard. Did you come up with that on your own?"

"Sir, let me explain."

"This had better be good."

"Harvath stole one of our snowmobiles. We believe that is how he was able to get away from the village before we could get there.

"We found tracks near the helicopter crash. It looks like he parked the snowmobile and came in on foot. After shooting and scalping Colonel Teplov, he hiked back to the snowmobile with two other people. We think it was Dr. Volkova from Nivsky and the husband of the healer she was supposed to meet in Friddja."

"He only has a snowmobile, but *you* have had a helicopter. So where the fuck is he?"

"The reason we think he may be dead is that we followed a set of fresh tracks to a lake southwest of the village. There was a hole in the ice — one big enough that the snowmobile could have fallen through — and we could see some sort of light under the water."

"So he fell through? Are you positive?"

"No, not at all."

"Then why is there light coming from the bottom of that fucking lake?" Minayev demanded.

Garin remained composed, hoping his calm might prove contagious. "It could be intentional. Meant as a diversion. Maybe he wants us to think he fell through. Until we get a cold-water dive team out there, we can't be sure."

"I will requisition one."

"Thank you."

The General then locked his eyes on him. "And if it *is* a diversion?"

"Then we need to be focusing all of our attention on the border," said Garin. "That's where I believe he will be going."

"The border is over thirteen hundred kilometers long. Just where exactly are we supposed to fucking look?"

"Not *where,* sir," the mercenary replied. "But rather, *for what.*"

"Okay," Minayev responded. "*For what* are we looking? And before you answer, understand that I'm out of *fucking* patience. This had better be informed. *Very* informed."

"Yes, sir," said Garin, confident that his information was just that. "We have been interrogating the villagers. Apparently, two brothers were returning from a hunt when they found Harvath unconscious in the snow. They brought him back to one of their cabins — the one that ended up being booby-trapped. And while the owner stayed with Harvath, the other brother went and collected the healer woman from Friddja, the next village over."

This was good information indeed. The General removed a cigarette and lit it. "And what did the two brothers have to say about all of this?"

"Nothing. We can't find them. They're gone."

"What do you mean *they're gone*?" he stated, exhaling a cloud of smoke.

"When we went to question them, they had already left."

"Meaning they just walked into the woods and vanished? Or maybe they fell into your fucking ice hole and are down there swimming around with Harvath, the snowmobile, and all the fish."

Garin ignored his sarcasm. "According to the villagers, whenever the brothers have a successful hunt, they keep some of the meat and the rest they go and trade."

"Go and trade *where*?"

"With any number of other Sámi villages."

Minayev took another puff of his cigarette as he tried to recall how many indigenous villages there were in the Oblast. There were more than a few. Nevertheless, he couldn't figure out how this information was useful, and was just about to say so, when Garin continued.

"While we may not know where they're traveling," he said, "we know how. This is where the *what* comes in. The two brothers are using dog teams. As soon as we can get the helicopter refueled and get a new crew assigned, that will be the focus of our search. They may be helping Harvath."

The General smiled. This he could work with. The Kremlin would be pleased. "New crew or old crew, as soon as that helicopter is refueled, you're lifting off. Is that clear?"

"But General Minayev, the —"

"Is that clear?" he barked.

"Yes, sir," said Garin.

"Good. Now get the fuck out of here. And don't come back without Harvath — even if you have to chase him into fucking Finland."

CHAPTER 66

Jompá and Olá stopped only once to rest the dogs and check their heading. Hearing no sound of helicopters, they lifted the frozen slabs of meat to allow Harvath and Christina a chance to get out of the sleds and stretch their legs.

It was snowing and the wind was blowing even harder than before. With the rifle slung over his shoulder, Harvath removed the satellite phone from his pocket and dialed Nicholas as he walked.

They kept the call short. Harvath provided him with an update on their progress and Nicholas confirmed their location via the live satellite footage they were watching in the White House Situation Room.

Nicholas also let him know that the plane with the team was airborne and that there was no sign of any Russian activity in his immediate area.

Good news, thought Harvath. *For the*

moment.

After he and Christina had climbed back into the sleds, Jompá and Olá replaced the slabs, covered everything with reindeer hides, and then mushed their dogs toward the landing zone.

Harvath's senses were on fire the entire way. As close as they were to escaping, there were still so many things that could go wrong.

Some of the most intense battles he'd ever been in were en route to an extraction. They were all-or-nothing scenarios. The bad guys knew it was their last chance to take you out. You knew that if you didn't succeed, you weren't going home. Both sides had everything to lose and winning came down to who fought the hardest.

Even so, you could fight like hell and still lose. Sometimes it was nothing more than a numbers game. That was always the biggest risk when you were fighting on someone else's territory. Better to get in and out without being seen and without engaging the enemy.

That was Harvath's biggest concern right now — getting out without being seen. He'd been able to stay one step ahead almost the entire time he had been in Russia. If he could just continue that streak a little longer, he'd be home free.

He hadn't asked to come here. He hadn't asked for Lara, Lydia, and Reed to be murdered. He hadn't asked for any of it. All he wanted now, after everything he had been through, was to get across that border. But as he had spent a lifetime learning the hard way, circumstances often seemed to conspire against him.

As the sled sliced through the snow, he forced himself to relax as he breathed deeply. *Stay calm,* he repeated in his mind. *Almost there.*

But as he said those last two words to himself, he knew that it was a lie. He wasn't *almost there.* In fact, he was far from it.

At the moment that thought entered his mind — as if he had the power to conjure up the worst possible demon to come and torment him even further — he heard something. He heard it over the barking of the dogs and the creaking of the sled. Though it was faint, he knew exactly what it was — a *helicopter.*

"Fuck," he whispered, as the sound of its rotors grew louder.

He had no doubt that it was Wagner, and within moments, it was hovering almost directly overhead. Jompá and Olá, though, kept going.

Harvath heard the helicopter change position and hover out in front of them. The pilot was sending the mushers a message: *Stop.*

Jompá and Olá had no other option. That's what they did.

The frozen slabs of meat should have hidden their presence from any thermal imaging. This had to be about something else. Someone in the village had talked.

Harvath, though, had expected that. What he hadn't expected was that the Wagner mercenaries would devote time and resources to scouring the countryside for a couple of Sámis known to be gone at odd hours and for days at a time, hunting and trading with other villages.

Sinking the snowmobile had been meant to throw them off his trail, but maybe it had ended up leading them right to him.

He didn't have time to figure out what had happened. He needed to make a plan to deal with this threat — right here, right now.

The helicopter was too loud for him to yell back to Christina. It was almost too loud for him to communicate with Jompá. Almost.

Though Harvath's Russian was pretty bad, he knew enough to get what he needed in this situation.

"*Shto ty vídish?*" he shouted. *What do you see?*

"*Odin vertolet,*" the man shouted back, so that Harvath would be sure to hear him. "*Dva verevki.*" *One helicopter. Two ropes.*

This wasn't a reconnaissance. It was an interdiction. They were going to have a team rappel, inspect the sleds, and question Jompá and Olá.

Harvath planted his feet and brought his knees up against the slab of meat. "*Skol'ko soldat?*" *How many soldiers?*

"*Chetyre.*" *Four.*

Two for each sled, Harvath thought to himself.

He tried, in vain, to listen for the approach of footsteps. But between the roar of the helicopter blades and the dogs barking, it was impossible.

Suddenly, though, he could hear the helicopter ascend and then move off to the side. It was still close, but not directly in front of them, nor immediately overhead. The mercenaries were obviously concerned about what they were about to face. And having already lost one helo, they didn't intend to lose another.

As the Wagner men neared his sled, they began yelling at Jompá in Russian.

"Dva ostalos," the Sámi said for Harvath's benefit. *"Dva verno." Two left. Two right.*

With his face hidden behind the ruff of his anorak, the mercenaries couldn't see him feeding one last clue to Harvath. It was the last thing he was able to utter before the men were right on top of them.

Harvath gripped his weapons as an icy calm settled over him. Now that trouble had arrived, he was in his element.

His challenge was to affix in his mind, without having seen them, where all the players were — the four mercenaries on the ground, the helicopter and its likely snipers, Christina, Jompá, and Olá.

He was about to engage in an incredibly dangerous gamble, but there was no alternative. It was kill or be taken prisoner, and he had already made it quite clear where he stood on that proposition. He was going to kill whoever got in his way, and he would keep killing until he had escaped. He was going home and *nobody* was going to stop him.

Though the clouds had dampened its first rays, the sun had begun to rise. To his left and to his right, Harvath was able to see beneath the edges of the reindeer hides covering the sled.

He could make out two pairs of legs. Both

were wearing the same winter whites as all the other Wagner thugs.

Once he had both his weapons in place, he said a quick prayer, exhaled, and pressed the triggers.

CHAPTER 67

Using his legs to upend the frozen slab and the reindeer skins, he let them fall to the ground as he came out shooting.

He put two more rounds into the injured men on either side of his sled, killing them both, and then quickly rolled to his left to engage the men behind him before they could get to Christina.

As he did, the snipers in the helicopter let loose with a withering barrage of fire. Jompá, who had crouched down behind the sled for cover, fell bleeding into the snow.

Harvath kept his attention on Olá's sled and the two men there. One of them had his weapon pointed right at him. Harvath fired before the man could get off a shot, double-tapping the mercenary in the chest and putting an additional round underneath his chin and up into his brain.

Before the man had even hit the ground, Harvath had his colleague in his sights and was already lighting him up.

He ripped a zipper of lead from the man's left rear buttock, up through his ribcage, and into the back of his head, splattering brain, blood, bone, and bits of helmet everywhere.

All the while, the snipers continued to fire, unable to get an accurate fix on him. Curtains of snow obstructed their view, as powerful gusts of wind buffeted the helo.

Rolling back behind the sled, Harvath ejected his magazine, slammed home a fresh one, and dragged Jompá closer, hoping to save him. There was nothing Harvath could do for him, though. The man was dead.

Popping up from behind the sled, and using the oblong slab of moose on the other side for concealment, he went full auto and emptied his magazine into the cockpit of the helicopter, before disappearing back down again.

Doing another magazine change, he scanned his surroundings. They were out in the open, which was an absolute death sentence when dealing with a helicopter. They needed to get to the trees.

He called out to Christina and Olá, but neither of them replied. He prayed it was only because they couldn't hear him.

Rising into a crouch, he popped up once

more and began firing as he ran back to the second sled.

Sliding in next to it like a baseball player stealing home, he ejected the magazine from his AK-15 and rocked in another.

"Christina!" he yelled over the sound of the helicopter as it swung around in an attempt to provide its snipers with a better angle. "Christina!"

Peeking behind the sled, he saw Olá lying facedown in the snow, bleeding. Harvath didn't need to roll him over to know that, like his brother, he was also dead. The snipers had taken both of them out.

"I can't get out," Christina shouted. "The slab won't move. It's stuck."

Lifting up the reindeer hide, he peered underneath and saw the problem. The edge was jammed between two of the bed's supports.

"I'm going to lift it. When I do, roll toward me as fast as you can. Okay?"

Christina nodded.

"On three," yelled Harvath, as he planted his boots and leaned into the slab. "One. Two. *Three!*"

It was incredibly heavy, just like the one he had hidden under. He was only able to raise it a few inches, but it was enough for

Christina to get out, pulling her rifle behind her.

Before she could even thank him, she saw Olá. She tried to go to him, but Harvath stopped her.

"They're both dead," he said. "We need to get to the trees."

"How?"

"You go first and I'll cover you. Ready?"

Christina nodded and once again, Harvath counted to three and yelled for her to run.

As she took off, he popped up from behind the sled and began firing, successfully putting several rounds into the side of the helo, forcing it to swing away from them.

Once he saw that she was safe, he pointed at the helicopter and instructed her to start shooting. The moment she did, he ran back to Jompá's sled. He needed his rucksack.

Sliding again to safety, he reached inside and pulled it out. Now, all he had to do was make it to the trees.

The helicopter, though, had shifted into a new position, one that was going to make it very difficult for Christina to engage from her position.

He was getting ready to jump up and fire at it himself when she stepped out from behind the trees and began shooting.

It was an incredibly courageous move, and

one that he didn't waste. Hopping to his feet, he ran faster than he could ever remember having run in his life.

He got to her just as her weapon ran dry and together they bolted into the trees as the snipers began to return fire.

The bullets tore off pieces of bark and sent snow flying all around them. Up ahead, Harvath could see a small rock outcropping. He pointed at it and shouted for her to keep running. "No matter what, don't stop!"

She did as he ordered and didn't notice until she got there that he had stopped to return fire on the helicopter.

It seemed like a suicide mission to her. Hovering above the trees, the snipers rained down bullets, slicing through the branches and coming very close to hitting, and likely even killing him.

Harvath, though, was equally dangerous to the helicopter. He not only found his target, but also put no fewer than two rounds through its belly.

Whether those rounds penetrated into the cabin and took out any of the mercenaries on board, he couldn't be sure. What he did know was that he had burned through precious ammo, but once again had succeeded in beating the helicopter back and forcing it to break contact.

As the helo temporarily disengaged, Harvath rushed for the outcropping.

"We're not going to have long," he said, as he changed magazines and tried to catch his breath.

"They can't get to us here, can they?" Christina asked.

"Not with the helicopter. They'll come in on foot. At least one group from uphill, so they can shoot down on us. Another will come in on one of our flanks."

"What are we going to do?"

"We're going to fight," he replied, pulling the few magazines he had left from his rucksack and handing one to her.

"But I don't know how," she insisted, and for the first time, he saw the fear written across her face.

He stopped what he was doing and looked at her. "Listen to me," he said. "I'm not going to let anything happen to you. Do you understand?"

She believed him and, slowly, she nodded.

Turning his attention back to his preparations, he pulled the satellite phone from his coat pocket, extended the antenna, and powered it up.

He waited for several moments, but the device failed to acquire a signal. There was too much tree cover. He had no way of giving Nicholas an update on their situation.

As he powered the device off and returned it to his pocket, he heard the helicopter stop and hover up the slope from where they were. The pilots must have found a big enough break in the trees, through which men could rappel.

After inspecting and reloading Christina's rifle, he handed it back to her. "Get ready," he said. "They're coming."

Chapter 68

"I don't care what's going on down there," Haney said, his face a steely, don't-fuck-with-me mask. "You land this plane right now."

When Pavel refused to comply, Staelin, who was sitting right behind him, pulled out his H&K pistol and pressed the barrel right up against the back of the bush pilot's head.

During his initial flyover to check for obstructions on the ice, they had passed over the top of the Wagner helicopter and had seen shots being fired. It had frightened Pavel enough that he was now trying to abort the landing.

But as Haney and Staelin were making perfectly clear, despite the language barrier, they weren't aborting anything.

Resigning himself to what he was being forced to do, the pilot swung the plane around, decreased its airspeed, and prepared to land.

The Pilatus touched down with only a light skip of its skis on the snow. It was one of the best landings any of them had ever experienced. Pavel might have been a terrible alcoholic, but he was a terrific pilot.

When he tried to pull back on the throttle to slow down, Haney put his hand over Pavel's and pushed it forward, forcing him to speed up.

With his free hand, Haney pointed at the very end of the ice. Bullets be damned, that's where they were headed. He wanted the team dropped off as close to Harvath as possible. The bush pilot did the only thing he could do — he obeyed.

When they were almost at the shore, Haney allowed Pavel to finally slow the aircraft down. He even allowed him to turn it around, so that it was ready for takeoff when they returned.

As the team raced to unload their gear, Haney gave the Russian a final warning. Whether the man could understand his English or not didn't matter. He could understand his tone.

"Don't you fucking go anywhere," he ordered, poking his finger into the man's chest. "Remember, we know where you live."

The look on the bush pilot's face made it clear that the message had been received. Reaching over, he killed the plane's engine and held his hands up in mock surrender.

Hopping onto the ice, Haney slung his large pack, clicked into his ski bindings, and hailed the tactical operations center of the Joint Special Operations Command at Fort Bragg in North Carolina as they raced toward the woods.

To limit the number of cooks in the kitchen, JSOC had been assigned to coordinate this phase of Harvath's rescue.

Haney engaged in a very quick back-and-forth. He let them know that they had landed safely and were inbound to Harvath. JSOC let Haney know what Harvath's last position was and what kind of force was arrayed against him.

Everyone else on The Carlton Group team was listening to the report over their headsets. There was no need for Haney to repeat any of it.

On point, Sloane Ashby had a wrist-top computer strapped to the outside of the left sleeve of her winter whites. The technology had gotten to the point where she didn't need to peel off her gloves and punch in

Harvath's location. It was being done for her by JSOC via satellite. Her job was to lead her team to him.

It was a good piece of technology to have, especially as the snow continued to fall and visibility worsened. The only downside to it, though, was the very real possibility of losing the link due to heavy cloud cover.

Knowing that Harvath was under fire, they all pushed themselves at top speed to get to him.

The plan had been for the dog sleds to transport him and the woman to the forest at the edge of the frozen lake. Once the plane had landed, the team would jump out, link up with them in the woods, and escort them back to the aircraft. They would then fly back to Pavel's and disappear across the border. That was the best-case scenario.

The list of worst-case scenarios was endless. It included everything from Harvath and the woman being injured and needing to be carried, to Harvath being recaptured and the team needing to go inland to break him out and bring him back. The one thing they had all agreed on was that they were absolutely not leaving Russia without him.

Up at the front of their column, Sloane continued setting a blistering pace. But then something happened.

From somewhere out in front of them, they began to hear gunfire. And all at once, they took an impossibly hard pace and kicked it up. *Way up.*

CHAPTER 69

In the SEAL teams, Harvath had had a good buddy from Texas. On a long deployment, when they were mind-numbingly bored, he had made the mistake of asking him what he thought the greatest state in the union was. He should have known what the man's answer would be.

The SEAL held forth for well over an hour about how Texas, hands down, was the greatest state in the Union.

Texans were a special breed. In fact, they were some of the toughest warriors Harvath had ever encountered. As a glutton for punishment, Harvath had followed up by asking his friend what he thought the second-greatest state in the union was. The answer had surprised him.

"Tennessee," the SEAL said.

"Why?" Harvath had asked.

"Because if it wasn't for Tennessee there'd be no Davy Crockett and if it wasn't for

Davy Crockett, there'd be no Texas."

Crockett, of course, had been part of the Texas Revolution and had been killed by Mexican troops at the Battle of the Alamo.

A student of military history, Harvath had always wondered what it must have been like to have been at the Alamo, to have been completely surrounded, and to have fought against such overwhelming odds.

He assumed it must have been akin to the three hundred Spartans who had held back the Persian army at the Gates of Thermopylae, or even the Allied forces that had landed on the beaches of Normandy and had pushed the Nazis all the way back to their downfall in Berlin.

The point was that some of the most important battles in history had been won not by those with the greatest number of troops, but rather those with the largest commitment to winning the fight.

And now, low on ammunition and sitting in what was shaping up to be his own Alamo, Harvath was determined to show the same commitment.

The overhang above them made it impossible to see who or what was coming downhill. Only when they pressed themselves against the rocks to either side could they even grab a partial glimpse of what was hap-

pening. And, if anyone ran up toward them from below, they were completely exposed and vulnerable.

Having warned Christina that the mercenaries were incoming, he picked up his rifle and made ready.

As he had done earlier, he once again did the math. Four dead Wagner operatives at the sleds meant there could be ten left — eight if they had maintained their two snipers aboard the helicopter.

Either way, those were bad odds and Harvath knew it. It was also the kind of battle a true warrior wished for. Only against an overwhelming force could you ever really prove that you had what it took.

The one thing about Harvath, though, was that no matter how many times he had proved it, he always felt as if he had to prove it again.

Maybe it was a hangover from his SEAL father, who never seemed happy with anything he had done. Maybe it was something else.

Maybe, like his father, Harvath was always trying to push himself just a bit further than anyone else was willing or able to go.

Whatever the answer, it didn't seem to matter much as he saw the first mercenary approach and he readied his rifle. Then, when the shot presented itself, he took it. And the moment he did, everything around them exploded.

The Wagner mercenaries had done an excellent job figuring out exactly where he and Christina were taking cover. As their rounds slammed into the overhang and the large rocks that acted as its wings, sharp chips went flying in all directions, hitting both Harvath and Christina in the face. It was like standing behind a revved-up jet as someone dumped a box of razorblades into one of the turbines.

Sticking the barrel of his weapon through a space between the rocks, he pressed his trigger and sprayed his assailants with a ton of lead.

It forced the mercenaries back, but only for a moment. Before he knew it, the barrage was back on and he and Christina were dodging bullets and more flying pieces of stone.

He was beginning to grow concerned about their ability to battle their way out of this. He could fight, but he could only kill what he could see. Their position provided only a few vantage points. And Christina, as tough and as willing as she was, didn't have the training to go up against ex-Spetsnaz soldiers. At best, she might be able to hold them off by firing in their direction, but only until her ammo ran out.

The mercenaries were incredibly adept at using the trees for cover. Harvath had yet to put one down. Every time he actually caught sight of one and took a shot, his target disappeared — and not the way he liked, as in a spray of blood. Nevertheless he kept shooting.

With Christina keeping an eye on their flank, he worried about being overrun from above. He couldn't pop his head out to look uphill without possibly getting it blown off.

At the same time, he knew what he had heard. The Wagner helicopter had hovered up the slope and it hadn't done so to admire the view. Any second, men were going to pour over the overhang — or worse, they were first going to send a grenade.

Seeing movement again in the trees to his right, he fired and blew through the last two rounds in his magazine.

Letting the spent magazine drop to the ground, he inserted a fresh one and called Christina over to him.

"I need to poke my head out and look uphill," he said. "When I do, I want you to spray all of the trees over there. Just swing your barrel back and forth and keep shooting. Can you do that?"

Christina nodded and when Harvath gave the signal, she stuck her rifle out and began firing.

As she did, Harvath peered over the overhang and risked a look up the ridge. It was a scene straight out of a nightmare — multiple Wagner mercenaries were quickly closing in on them.

Without proper cover or concealment, there was no way Harvath would be able to repel their attack.

They couldn't stay here. As dangerous as it was to move off into the trees, it was more dangerous to stay put and wait for their position to be overrun.

Helping Christina swap out magazines, he explained to her what they needed to do and prepared her for how to make it happen.

He would give her the biggest head start possible and hold them off as long as he could.

He told her to run, and not to stop running until she couldn't hear the gunfire anymore.

"What about you?" she asked.

"I'll be right behind you."

She knew that wasn't true. He was going to stay and fight in order to buy her time to get away. She was afraid he wouldn't make it. She didn't want to let him do that.

"We can both run," she said.

"No," Harvath replied. "There isn't time. You need to go. Now."

Another volley of gunfire tore up the rocks around them. Harvath spun and fired back.

When he turned back around, he said, "We'll do it like before. When I count to three, I want you to run."

He was just about to start counting, when a pair of mercenaries appeared atop the overhang behind him.

"Look out!" Christina screamed.

CHAPTER 70

One moment the mercenaries appeared on the overhang and the next moment they fell down dead at Harvath's feet. Neither he nor Christina, though, had killed them. Somebody else in the forest had fired the shots.

What's more, they had come from suppressed weapons — something Harvath was intimately familiar with.

Tier One operators used them not only to dampen noise and help reduce muzzle flash, but also to know which gunshots were being fired by their teammates.

The sound was unmistakable and hearing it now could only mean one thing. There were friendlies close by.

Scrapping his plan to abandon their position, he warned Christina not to shoot anyone, unless she was absolutely certain she was targeting Wagner mercenaries.

She asked how she would know the difference, when all of a sudden there was a flash of white behind one of the trees below them. It was followed by another and another.

A small force, carrying suppressed rifles, was quickly working its way up toward them.

Their winter whites were more sophisticated and less splotchy than Wagner's.

Harvath was just pointing out the difference to Christina when several of them raised their weapons, pointed them in their direction, and began firing.

Instinctively, Harvath and Christina dropped to the ground. As they did, two more dead Wagner mercenaries dropped over the edge of the overhang.

The force then split into three teams, two of which branched off to the sides, forming a perimeter as they continued to engage the enemy, while the third headed right for them.

When the leader turned his head and revealed the muted American flag on his helmet, Harvath felt flooded with a sense of both relief and overwhelming pride. He wanted to wrap the man in the biggest bear hug he had ever given. Even before the operative had pulled down his face mask, he knew exactly who it was.

"Friendlies!" Haney called out.

Harvath helped cover them as they hurried up to the outcrop.

"Somebody here order a pizza?" Staelin asked, pressing himself against the rocks next to Christina.

"Hours ago," quipped Harvath, who was so glad to see them. "What took you so long?"

"Traffic was terrible."

Harvath couldn't wait to hear all about it. Patting Staelin on the helmet, he ran his gloved hand over its American flag patch.

"We've got a plane waiting," Haney stated, as he kept his weapon up and continued to scan for threats. "It's a couple of klicks away. Are you both capable of walking?"

"Affirmative," answered Harvath.

Haney was attempting to call in a SITREP to JSOC when all around them a tidal wave of bullets crashed down and showered them with more sharp pieces of chipped rock.

"What the fuck?" Haney angrily demanded. "How many more of those assholes are out there?"

"Can't tell," Staelin responded, as he looked for targets to fire on. "Harvath picked the one spot in the entire Oblast with zero lines of sight."

"I was in a hurry," Harvath said in his defense, subtly giving his colleague the finger. "But I counted four on our flank."

"Plus the four above you," Haney stated, unshouldering his backpack. "Whom we neutralized."

"What's the plan, boss?" Staelin asked.

Unzipping the pack, Haney withdrew a two-foot-long, olive-drab-colored tube and said, "I'm going to need some cover fire in a moment."

"Roger that. Just say when."

Harvath pulled Christina closer to him. The back blast from the M72 Light Anti-Tank Weapon, or LAW, could be pretty intense. You didn't want to be anywhere within its path.

The LAW was a one-time-use, shoulder-fired, 66 millimeter, anti-armor rocket launcher that weighed five and a half pounds. It was, essentially, a mini bazooka.

Pulling the retaining pin from the back, Haney removed the rear cap and then the one up front. Extending the collapsed tube to its full, locked length — causing the front and rear sights to automatically pop up — he slid the safety forward. The weapon was now armed and ready to fire.

"Going hot," said Haney, as he checked to make sure no one was behind him in the exhaust area. Placing the weapon on his shoulder, he called out, "Back blast area clear?"

"Clear," Harvath and Staelin responded.

"Cover fire in three. Two. *One.*"

Harvath and Staelin trained their rifles on the trees from where the Wagner mercenaries had been firing and unleashed a storm of lead of their own. As they did, Haney leaned out from behind the rocks, sighted in where he believed the Russians to be, and fired the LAW.

The projectile erupted from the rocket launcher and went screaming through the trees.

When it connected with its target, it exploded, sending snow, bark, and body parts in all directions.

Haney looked at his buddies and said, "First rule of a gunfight? Bring a Marine with an antitank weapon."

"Oorah," Staelin replied, grunting the USMC battle cry.

"If we're done fucking around," asked Harvath, "can we go now? I'd kind of like to get the hell out of here."

"No matter what I do for you," said Haney, rolling the spent launcher tube in the snow to cool it off, before putting it back in his pack and zipping it up, "I never get a thank-you."

"You'll get my thank-you when we're on the plane."

As Chase, Sloane, and Barton hung back to cover their six o'clock, Morrison and Gage led the march downhill, while Haney and Staelin stayed in tight with Harvath and Christina.

Not a single gunshot was heard. The LAW had done its job. If any of the Wagner mercenaries had survived, they hadn't been in any shape to give chase or to fight back.

At the bottom of the hill, where the trees started thinning out, and just within sight of the dog sleds and the dead Sámis, Haney was finally able to get a satellite signal.

As he relayed a quick SITREP back to JSOC, he watched as Christina said something to Harvath. Nodding in agreement, the pair walked cautiously into the open. It took him a moment to realize what was going on, and then he saw it. The dogs were still harnessed to the sleds.

One by one, Harvath and Christina unfastened them. But instead of running off, back to the village, they lay down next to Jompá and Olá and refused to move.

"What are we doing, Harvath?" Haney asked, as he walked up behind them, his report to JSOC complete.

"The dogs don't want to leave."

"Guess what?" the Marine replied. "*I do*. In fact, I never even wanted to come to this godforsaken place. But I did it, for you. So, you'll forgive me for not caring about a bunch of fucking dogs. When they get hungry enough, they'll go home. As for us, we need to get moving."

The Marine wasn't wrong. The dogs could make up their own minds. Harvath had made up his.

"Let's go."

As the team clicked into their skis, Sloane and Chase each unstrapped a pair of snowshoes from their packs and handed them to Scot and Christina.

"Snowshoes," Harvath groaned. "Love these."

Sloane, who loved to bust Harvath's balls, was about to tease him, until they all froze.

Coming in fast over the trees was a Wagner helicopter.

CHAPTER 71

"Reinforcements!" Garin yelled into his headset to Minayev back at Alakurtti Air Base. "He's escaping! Send *everyone.*"

As the helicopter made a pass over the scene below, the Wagner commander was stunned to see at least nine individuals, all of them armed. Somehow, a rescue team had made it to Harvath. He was furious.

Turning to his snipers, he ordered, "Stop them. And if you can't stop them, kill them. *All* of them."

The snipers nodded and as the helicopter came around again, they fired repeatedly, chewing up the snow near Harvath and his rescuers, who dove for cover.

As the helo banked above the trees to swing out and prep for another pass, they saw one of the figures — a man dressed in Wagner winter white whom Garin assumed to be Harvath — get back to his feet and raise a defiant middle finger as they flew out of view.

"How many more LAWs do you have in your backpack?" Harvath demanded, as he lowered his finger.

"One," said Haney, as he got back onto his skis.

"I want it."

"For the helo?"

"You're damn right *for the helo*," Harvath replied.

The Marine was reluctant. "How many fingers am I holding up?"

"How many fingers *am I* holding up," replied Harvath, raising his middle finger again and directing it at Haney.

"I guess you've earned it," said the Marine as he handed him his backpack. "But what if this doesn't work?"

"Then you'd better have a hell of a Plan B in place. For right now, let's get everybody out of sight."

The team did as he asked, moving deeper into the trees. Harvath remained up front, concealing himself as best he could.

When the Wagner helicopter returned, it came in low and fast with its snipers hanging out the windows, itching to unloose their weapons on anyone they saw.

The problem, though, was that there was

no one to see. Everyone had vanished, likely into the woods.

The helicopter was just about past when a lone individual suddenly materialized. Garin spotted him, his defiant middle finger raised high once more.

"It's him!" he shouted. "Right there! That's him!"

Pulling back on the speed, the pilot aggressively banked the helicopter in an attempt to line the snipers up for a shot.

It was exactly what Harvath needed.

Sighting in the cabin area behind the cockpit, he gave it just enough lead, depressed the Fire button, and sent the projectile skyward. It couldn't have been a more perfect shot.

Upon piercing the Mi-8, the warhead detonated and the helicopter exploded in a roiling fireball.

As it came crashing to the ground, the team cheered.

Harvath, though, knew they weren't safe yet. They still had to make it back to the plane — and even then, he wouldn't feel completely relieved until they were out of Russia.

Rapidly organizing the team, Haney had Sloane return to the point position and lead them toward the lake.

With just his first steps in the snowshoes, Harvath was reminded of how much agony his body was in.

He could have asked Staelin, who functioned as the team's medic, for a painkiller, but he didn't want to slow them down. It could wait until they got to the plane. Or at least, that's what he had thought.

Out of nowhere, they heard the sound of an engine coming to life, powering up, and then speeding away.

Harvath didn't need to ask what they were hearing. The look on Haney's face said it all.

"Is that our ride leaving?" Harvath asked.

"That motherfucker," the Marine cursed. "I knew we shouldn't have trusted him."

"Who's *him*?"

"Pavel," Haney replied. "A local alcoholic and chickenshit bush pilot who's an asset of the Finns."

"You left a foreign asset sitting there with a fully functioning aircraft? You didn't even pull the master fuse?"

"I had no idea how quickly we'd need to take off. I didn't want to screw around with his plane."

"So what are we going to do now?" asked Harvath.

Without missing a beat, the Marine stated,

"We're walking out. It's just a little over fifty kilometers."

"I knew this was going to happen," said Staelin.

"That's enough," replied Haney as he looked over at Sloane and said, "Pick the nearest spot the Finns told us we'd be safe to cross the border and plot us a course."

"Roger that," she replied, punching her ski poles into the snow and turning her attention to her wrist-top GPS device.

In the meantime, Haney transmitted a new SITREP to JSOC and told them to stand by for the updated route information, which was slow in coming.

"Sloane," he said. "What's taking so long?"

"All of a sudden, my GPS is all wonky," she responded.

"What do you mean *wonky*?"

"Wonky meaning it's not working."

"Is it the weather?" the Marine asked.

"I don't know."

Harvath, though, did know. "It's not the weather. The signal is being jammed. And if the signal is being jammed, that means Russian military is inbound."

"Wait," said Haney. "How do you know?"

"The Russians have been perfecting their GPS jamming. During the last set of NATO training exercises in Norway, they turned everything upside down."

"If that's what's going on here, how do you know they're inbound?"

"Because the system has a particular radius. The jammer is usually mounted on a ship or a vehicle of some sort. As we're not close enough to the water and there are no passable roads anywhere near us, I'm guessing it's on a plane or a helicopter."

"We're not far from Alakurtti Air Base," said Haney. "They're known for their helicopter regiment that specializes in electronic jamming."

"There you go," replied Harvath. "So what's Plan B?"

As team leader, the Marine rapidly weighed their options.

But when he didn't answer right away, Harvath began to feel uncomfortable. "There *is* a Plan B, right?"

"There's *one hell of* a Plan B. But the President needs to sign off on it."

Pretending his hand was a telephone, Harvath lifted it to his ear and said, "Then you'd better get hold of him fast because the Russians aren't going to stop at killing our GPS. They're going to flood this area with troops and either capture or kill all of us."

CHAPTER 72

White House Situation Room
Washington, D.C.

When JSOC relayed Haney's request to the President, Porter immediately turned to Nicholas and SPEHA Rogers. "Are we officially out of options? Because as we discussed, this has the ultimate downside risk."

Rogers looked at Nicholas and then back to the President. "The team on the ground has maps. They know where they are and can attempt to land nav to the border, but . . ." he said, as his voice trailed off.

Porter raised an eyebrow. "*But* what?"

"But there's a reason the Russians are jamming their GPS," stated Nicholas. "They want to slow them down, so they can capture them. Not only will they have Harvath, but seven more Americans who will be accused of espionage and God knows what else. At this point, we're out of options. We need to pull the trigger on Plan B."

"Do you agree?" the President asked Rogers.

"Yes, sir," the SPEHA replied. "I do."

With his mind on everything that had gone wrong in the failed Iranian hostage rescue of the 1980s, Porter looked to the Chairman of the Joint Chiefs. "Can we successfully execute in this kind of weather?"

"We won't be able to have the Zero-three-hundred team parachute in. It's too dangerous. Everything else, though, we can do," the Chairman replied.

"Show of hands," the President then called out, addressing the rest of the national security personnel seated around the long mahogany table.

Every single hand went up.

Turning his attention back to the monitor with the live feed from JSOC, the President transmitted his order. "Launch Operation Gray Garden."

After confirmation from JSOC, it was time to start the next phase of their plan.

"We have a total of three calls to make," said Porter. "Who goes first?"

"I do," replied Nicholas. "Once Matterhorn has the information, he will transmit it directly to Moscow."

"Then," said Rogers, "I will reach out to the Russian Ambassador and communicate our offer, which he will also transmit directly to Moscow."

"After which, I will call President Peshkov and ask him for his answer," stated Porter.

"Yes, sir," responded the SPEHA. "At that point, the ball will be completely in his court. It's his call."

"And if he says *no*?"

"If he says no," Nicholas answered, "Then we buckle up, because things are going to get very bumpy."

CHAPTER 73

Murmansk Oblast

If the Russians were coming, Haney had decided it was better to dig in and make a stand than to try to outrun them.

Retracing their path to the lake, they chose the spot they had originally marked out for Harvath. Unlike the outcropping where they had found him, this location provided excellent fields of fire and could be much better defended.

With Harvath and Christina running on fumes, it took twice as long to get there as Haney had expected. Once there, he told Harvath to stand down. The man had been through enough. He didn't need to now man a post.

Staelin saw to both of them — Christina first, because Harvath insisted. When it came to his needs, he refused to take anything stronger than Ibuprofen and Tylenol. Until they were safely out, he didn't want anything fogging up his head.

And as for laying his rifle down and not manning a post, there was no way that was happening either. This was his fight and he was going to see it through until the very end.

When Haney had explained "Plan B" to him, he admired not just its audacity, but also its cleverness. If it ended up working, he owed Nicholas and whoever SPEHA Rogers was the best steak dinner in D.C.

As the wind and the snow continued getting worse, his concern began to grow. It was bad enough that he was surrounded by seven teammates who had all risked their lives to save him, but to add to their ranks? He didn't like all of this being done on his behalf. Upping the risk and enlisting more lives to save his felt wrong.

He was the one who was supposed to risk everything to go in and get people out. Not vice versa.

With all of his experience and all of his training, he should have been able to handle this. It was who he was. He should have been able to get himself and Christina across the border without risking anyone else's life — just as he should have been able to save Lara, Lydia, and the Old Man.

Now, Jompá and Olá, the men who had

pulled him from the frigid snow, were dead. Theirs were just another two entries on a long list of people who had died because of him. Why, he wondered, was he still alive? What possible purpose could his life even serve?

He was slipping down a razorblade-threaded rabbit hole of survivor's guilt when Chase Palmer signaled for everyone to be silent. He had heard something.

Harvath listened but didn't hear anything. His ears had been around a little longer than Chase's and had been subjected to a lot more explosions and gunfights.

In a couple of moments, though, he began to hear it as well. *Helicopters* — plural.

"Everybody grab some ground," Haney ordered.

The team was huddled together where part of the forest had eroded, behind several fallen trees.

As they all lay down, Haney added, "Everybody stay frosty."

"Seriously?" Staelin remarked, as he blew a cloud of warm breath into the air.

"One more peep out of you," whispered the Marine, "and you'll be walking all the way home. Are we clear?"

"Good copy," the Delta Force operative acknowledged, shooting him a smile and a thumbs-up.

No one moved a muscle as the sound of the helicopters grew louder.

Gage, the Green Beret, had the best view of what was headed their way. "Fuck me," he said. "I'm looking at two Mi-8s, plus a pair of Mi-24 helicopter gunships."

"Fuck *us*," Sloane responded.

"There'll be no *fucking*," Haney sternly responded, "unless it's *us* fucking *them*. Is that understood?"

"Oorah!" Staelin grunted while everyone else joined in a chorus of "Roger that."

"Got any more tricks up your sleeve?" Harvath asked.

"Nope. I'm all out," said Haney.

"So what's the plan?"

"The plan," the Marine explained, "is that we hold our position and wait for extraction."

Harvath looked at Christina and saw that the fear from earlier had returned. Reaching over, he put his gloved hand reassuringly on her arm. "Everything is going to be okay," he said.

She didn't speak. She didn't even try to force a smile. She gave him one quick nod and that was it.

He let his hand linger for a moment longer and then turned his attention to his rifle.

Drawing back the charging handle, he made sure a round was chambered and that the weapon's safety was off.

Around him, the other operators quietly conducted similar drills.

"Hey. About that *no fucking* rule?" Gage asked, breaking the silence.

"What about it?" Haney replied.

"Things are starting to get romantic."

Crawling over to see what he was talking about, the Marine peered through a space between the downed tree trunks and watched as the Mi-8s touched down.

"Jesus," he muttered as the helicopters disgorged their occupants.

"What's going on?" Harvath asked.

Haney waved him over to see for himself.

As Harvath stared at the troops massing in the snow, Haney turned and addressed the team.

"Okay, listen up," he said. "In addition to the two heavily armed Mi-24s, the Mi-8s just vomited up an entire platoon of soldiers. By my count, there are at least thirty of them. And if they're dropping here, that probably means they suspect we're nearby. So stay alert and stay ready."

"Only thirty?" Morrison mused, as he made sure the rounds were seated in all of his magazines. "That'd be a pretty short gunfight."

Though Harvath appreciated his sense of humor, the thirty Russian Army soldiers from Alakurtti Air Base had them outgunned by more than three to one. They also had four helicopters, two of which could blast the piles of logs they were hiding behind into matchsticks in the blink of an eye. It would be a short fight all right. In fact, it'd be a slaughter.

"What are the rules here?" Barton asked, his extra mags unpacked and stacked neatly in front of him.

"We're still weapons free," Haney confirmed, as he went to call in an update to JSOC. "But let's not start anything we can't finish."

They all made sure to remain on the ground. If they popped any part of their bodies above the logs, their heat signature could be detected by one of the helos, or by one of the soldiers on the ground if they were carrying handheld units.

"Shit," said Haney. "I'm having trouble getting a satellite signal again."

"Is it the Russians?" Harvath asked. "Do you think they're affecting our comms as well?"

"Our system is antijam. I think it's the weather — too much cloud cover. We'll have to go old school and hope our ride's in range," he said. Pointing at Chase, he began relaying instructions. "Power up the Falcon and see if you can reach Hurricane Two-Two on any of the designated frequencies. Let them know we need assistance ASAP."

"Roger that," Chase replied, as he reached for his backpack and removed the Multiband Multi Mission Radio he was lugging as a backup. Hurricane Two-Two was the call sign for their ticket out.

As Chase set up the radio, Haney kept trying to get a satellite signal on his device. And while they worked on comms, Harvath and Gage attempted to keep an eye on the Russian soldiers. But with the weather, it was becoming increasingly difficult to see what they were up to.

All of the soldiers were on skis, were wearing whites, and were carrying an array of weaponry. They divided into eight four-man fire teams and then began skiing off in different directions. One was headed right for them.

"Hurricane Two-Two, this is Nemesis Zero-One," Chase said into the handset. "Do you copy? Over."

He waited for a reply and then tried again.

"Hurricane Two-Two, this is Nemesis Zero-One. We need immediate extraction.

550

Do you copy? Over."

When, through the static, a faint voice finally replied, it sounded weak and far away — as if it was coming from the bottom of a well.

"Nemesis Zero-One, this is Hurricane Two-Two. We read you. What is your status? Over."

After letting Haney know that he had established contact, Chase had a back-and-forth with Hurricane Two-Two, answering some questions and giving a quick SITREP.

"Acknowledged," said Hurricane Two-Two when Chase had finished. "Nemesis Zero-One, stand by. Over."

"Roger that," said Chase. "Nemesis Zero-One, standing by. Over."

Peering through his rangefinder at the approaching Russian soldiers, Gage provided an update. "Two hundred meters and closing."

"Good copy," said Haney, acknowledging the information. "Two hundred meters."

Gage was an exceptional distance shooter and carried an H&K 417 rifle with a twenty-inch barrel. Its effective range was eight hundred meters — more than four times the distance of the approaching threat.

"Are we going to let the air out of these guys?" he asked.

"Negative," Haney replied. "Hold."

"Roger that. Holding."

"What's the status of Hurricane Two-Two?" Haney then asked.

Chase held up the handset. "I'm still standing by."

Harvath didn't like how long this was taking.

"One hundred seventy-five meters," Gage reported.

"Copy that," replied the Marine. "One hundred seventy-five meters."

"Still nothing," Chase stated.

Harvath needed to remember that this wasn't his team right now. It was Haney's. And as such, Haney was in charge. Nevertheless, he couldn't help but wonder if they should have tried to make it out on foot.

"One hundred fifty meters," announced Gage.

"Roger that," Haney replied. "One hundred fifty meters."

"Heads up," said Sloane. "We've got activity just south of us. One of the other fire teams has changed direction and is now coming up this way."

"Range?"

"Approximately one hundred meters."

"I've got clean shots here," Gage stated.

"Me too," replied Sloane.

"Negative," Haney ordered. "We hold."

Harvath looked at him, but the Marine had already shifted his focus to Chase. "Tell Hurricane Two-Two right now that —"

But the young operator held his hand up and cut him off as he listened intently to the voice on his handset.

A fraction of a second later, he said, "Roger that, Hurricane Two-Two. Good copy. Nemesis Zero-One out."

Then, turning to his teammates, he declared, "Angels inbound. Thirty seconds."

No one spoke. No one moved. Lying on the frigid ground, they watched the approaching Russian soldiers and strained their ears for the telltale sound of their rescue.

Ten seconds passed. Then twenty. At exactly thirty seconds, a pair of F-22 Raptors flew in incredibly low and blisteringly fast. Hitting supersonic, they broke the sound barrier.

The boom was so powerful, the earth trembled and snow was knocked off trees for as far as the eye could see. It sounded as if a rip was being torn through the fabric of the sky. All of the Russians dove for cover.

If the intent had been to scare the hell out of them, it had worked. Even with the reduced visibility, Gage and Sloane could tell the nearest fire teams were calling their superiors, asking what had happened and awaiting instructions as to what to do next.

Collectively, Harvath and the rest of the team held their breath. This was the moment of truth.

President Porter had proven he was willing to violate Russian airspace. President Peshkov now had to decide whether he was willing to let it stand.

In the last five minutes, Peshkov would have received intelligence through Artur Kopec's handler that the Americans had a team on the ground and had recovered Harvath. Egor Sazanov, his Ambassador to the United States, would have phoned the Foreign Minister and shared the good news that the entirety of Peshkov's frozen assets was poised to be thawed.

Then, just before the American jets had crossed into Russia, the U.S. President himself would have called. He would have explained what he wanted and, more important, what he was willing to do to get it. The choice after that was up to Peshkov.

And it became apparent, very quickly, that he had made it.

CHAPTER 74

Harvath and the team watched as, one by one, the Russian troops turned around and returned to the ice.

There, covered by the Mi-24 gunships, they climbed back aboard their Mi-8 helicopters and took off.

All the while, the F-22 Raptors stayed on station, circling overhead, ready for anything they might be called on to do. Never once did a single Russian intercept aircraft appear to address the incursion. Whatever word had come down from on high, Peshkov had made it clear that no action was to be taken.

As a SEAL, Harvath had been inside more C130s than he cared to remember. But never had one sounded as sweet as the one that came roaring in on approach, landed, and taxied to the edge of the frozen lake.

The propeller engines on the Hercules aircraft were known as the "Four Fans of

Freedom," which couldn't have been more appropriate than at this moment.

They continued thundering as the rear cargo ramp dropped and the Zero-Three-Hundred team raced out onto the ice, riding cold-weather ATVs.

When they got to him, Harvath insisted on snowshoeing the rest of the way to the aircraft. Despite all that had happened, he wasn't going to leave his teammates. He encouraged Christina to accept a ride, which she did.

When they reached the ramp, a pair of Air Force Pararescue Jumpers, more commonly known as PJs, was waiting. They stepped forward to give Harvath a hand, but he waved them off. He didn't need any help getting on the aircraft.

C130s were essentially enormous cargo planes. There was the cockpit, a bathroom, and maybe a galley. After that, it was just open space configured for the mission.

In the Skibird, the center aisle was about ten feet wide and reserved for cargo. Along the sides, suspended from bright orange nylon webbing, were seats made from the same material, which flipped down.

At the far end, an enormous American flag had been hung. Upon seeing it, Harvath was filled with emotion.

The PJs were the medical component of the operation and they tried to steer Harvath and Christina to two stretchers upfront. Once more, he told the PJs to assist Christina and promised that he would join them in a moment. Until everyone was on board, he wasn't going to stand down.

Popping out of their skis, Haney, Staelin, Chase, Sloane, Morrison, Gage, and Barton climbed into the aircraft and stowed their gear.

They were followed by the DEVGRU SEALs of the Zero-Three-Hundred team. Once their ATVs were lashed down and everyone was ready, the Skibird's loadmaster radioed the pilots that they were ready for takeoff.

Before the engines were even powered up, one of the PJs had already started an IV on Harvath with a saline drip. It was standard procedure and would make administering any meds much easier. There was also the concern, after everything he had been through, that Harvath was severely dehydrated, which the IV would help to reverse.

Taking seats alongside the stretcher, his friends sat down with him.

"We did it," said Haney. "It's over."

Harvath understood what the Marine was trying to say, but it wasn't over. Not for him.

And not by a long shot. The only thing he could think to say was "Thank you."

"Don't thank us until we're out of here," replied Staelin, as they felt the big LC-130 shudder as it turned and set up for takeoff.

"Fuck that," joked Barton. "I'll take my thank-you now."

"Me too," added Gage. "Do you have any idea the amount of shit I had to rearrange to be here?"

"I didn't even want to come," replied Chase.

"At least they told you the truth," snarked Sloane. "They told me that I'd be rescuing the President."

Harvath didn't think he had it in him, but he smiled nevertheless. He then looked at Morrison. "What about you?"

"I can't lie," said the younger Force Recon Marine. "I came for the vodka."

Harvath raised the arm with the IV and pointed toward his rucksack. "Open it," he said.

Morrison did and inside found the remainder of the bottle of vodka Harvath had found at the trapper cabin. Pulling it out, he held it up. The team cheered.

"First drink goes to Christina," Harvath ordered. "That belonged to her uncle, and the two of them saved my life."

Morrison handed the bottle to one of the PJs, who unscrewed the cap and handed it to Christina.

Sitting up on her stretcher, she smiled and held it aloft. *"Za Vstrechu,"* she said, taking a swig. *To our meeting.*

The bottle was then handed to Harvath. This time, he had no difficulty finding words. "To those who are no longer with us," he said, as he took a drink and passed it along.

Each of his teammates repeated his toast as they took a sip. Outside, the thrum of the engines increased as the throttles were pushed forward.

"I've got an idea," said Haney, just as the brakes were being released. "How about we ask our new pilot to swing by Pavel's house so we can kick his ass?"

Once again, a cheer rose from the team.

Harvath had always loved his teammates, but he had never really known how much until right now. They had all fought and bled together. But when he had been dragged into hell, they had rushed in to drag him back out.

It wasn't about money, medals, or fame. It was about loyalty, friendship, and honor.

Even if no one ever knew what had happened here, *they* would know. They would know *what* they had done and *why* they had done it. Integrity was all the reward any of them would ever need.

Harvath only wished that his own integrity had been enough to prevent his wife and two of his dearest friends from being murdered.

Before he could get sucked into that line of thinking, the huge aircraft lurched forward and began racing down the ice.

When it seemed it had reached its maximum speed, yet still couldn't achieve lift, the rockets on the sides kicked in and the nose of the plane began to rise. As the LC-130 became airborne, another cheer went up.

The F-22 Raptors accompanied the plane out of Russia and into Finnish airspace, and then all the way back to Luleå in northern Sweden.

Along the way, it was Christina who convinced Harvath to accept something more than he had already taken to deaden the pain of his injuries.

He had agreed, but on one condition. Turning to Haney and Staelin, he had made them promise that as soon as they landed in Luleå, they would all board The Carlton Group jet and head straight home. No detours to Landstuhl or any other overseas medical centers for treatment. They would fly directly back to the United States and Christina would be coming with them. Haney and Staelin had immediately agreed.

Unbeknownst to Harvath, those had been their specific orders.

CHAPTER 75

Death was never easy. It was messy and complicated on the best of days. On the worst of days, it was tragic, heartbreaking, and incredibly unfair.

After arriving in Sweden, Harvath had spent almost the entire plane ride back to the United States asleep, or pretending to be. He wasn't in the mood to talk. What's more, his body desperately needed the rest.

When the jet touched down at Andrews Air Force Base, instead of Dulles International, it wasn't hard to guess who was waiting for him. The amount of security alone gave it away.

Inside the hangar, an enormous American flag had been hung to welcome Harvath and the team home.

Harvath took his time pulling himself together, allowing his teammates to deplane first. He had no idea how many of them, if any, had met the President of the United

States before. Finally, when he couldn't wait anymore, he led Christina down the airstairs.

The small receiving line was composed of President Paul Porter, CIA Director Bob McGee, Nicholas — minus his dogs — and a fourth man whom Harvath didn't recognize.

Starting with the President, Harvath shook hands and introduced Christina.

"On behalf of the United States," Porter said to her, "I want to thank you for helping bring Scot home."

"It is my honor Mr. President," she replied, a bit awestruck that the President of the United States had come to meet them personally.

"It's good to have you back," Porter then said to Harvath.

"Thank you, sir. It's good to be back."

That was all Harvath had in him. The President wasn't offended. He realized how much the man had been through. The fact that he had walked off the plane under his own power was a testament to how tough he was.

Graciously, Porter passed him off to McGee, adding, "You and I will catch up soon."

"Yes, sir," Harvath replied, as he thanked the President once more before shaking hands with the CIA Director and introducing him to Christina.

"Welcome home," said McGee, to both of them.

Next up was Nicholas, who greeted Harvath warmly before engaging Christina in Russian.

Harvath waited a couple beats and when the little man didn't break off his chat, he reached out and introduced himself to the last man in line.

"Brendan Rogers," the SPEHA said, shaking hands. "Very glad to have you back home."

"Thank you for everything you did to make it happen," Harvath responded. "I owe you and Nicholas a steak dinner at some point."

"You don't owe me anything. I was just doing my job. Although I would like to be able to chat with you about your experience, if that would be okay."

"Now?"

"No," Rogers said, with an exaggerated shake of his head. "You work on getting acclimated. We can talk when you're ready."

"Thank you."

As Nicholas continued to speak with Christina, Rogers explained what they had arranged for her.

He had come not only to welcome Harvath home, but also to personally escort Christina to a farm in Virginia where she would be looked after while all of her paperwork was being processed. For her role in helping Harvath escape, she was being given full U.S. citizenship, as well as a substantial reward.

"Start-up funds," Rogers said. "With which she can begin her new life."

They chatted for a few more minutes before Nicholas finally broke off and introduced her to the SPEHA.

Once they had met, Harvath said to her, "I don't think I can ever repay you."

"You don't have to," she replied.

"I do, though. You gave up everything to help me."

"I'm going to be all right."

"I know you are," he said, as they hugged.

As their hug ended, she smiled at him warmly.

"For your safety," Harvath continued, "Rogers and his people are going to keep you out of sight for a while. As soon as I can, I'll come see you. Okay?"

"That sounds nice. I'd like that. And for *your* safety, don't forget to get the rest of your rabies shots."

With that, the SPEHA led Christina over

to the Diplomatic Security Service protective team that would be taking care of her. Once those introductions were made, they all exited the hangar together to a pair of waiting SUVs.

Turning around, Harvath watched as President Porter posed for pictures with the team, eventually waving him over to join in. There, in front of the giant red, white, and blue American flag, they commemorated their successful mission.

After shaking hands with everyone once more, Porter was whisked away by his Secret Service detail.

As the team pulled their gear from the plane, Harvath pitched in and helped. One by one, he thanked them.

Once they had completely unloaded, Nicholas directed them toward the vehicles he had waiting. Harvath, though, wasn't included. The CIA Director had other plans for him.

"We'd like to get you to the hospital and have you looked over," said McGee. "After they run some tests, we can —"

"I'm fine," Harvath interrupted. "I don't need a hospital. I'd rather just go home."

"I understand. Unfortunately, we can't do that. Not yet. I need to debrief you first."

A debriefing was the absolute last thing

he wanted to do. What he wanted was to be left alone. He wanted to go home, get drunk, and not talk to anyone for a week — or maybe forever.

But while he didn't like the idea of a debriefing, he knew why it had to happen. He had been under the control of and interrogated by a hostile foreign power. The CIA and the President needed to know what questions he had been asked and, more important, what he had said in response. He didn't have a choice. Better to get it over with.

"Okay," Harvath said, giving in. "Where? Back at Langley?"

McGee shook his head. "We'd like to make you a little more comfortable than that."

"More comfortable" than Langley turned out to be an Agency safe house a short helicopter flight away on Maryland's Eastern Shore.

It had a nice view of the water, was tastefully decorated in a nautical motif, and smelled like steamed crab. There Harvath, McGee, and a CIA psychiatrist named Dr. Levi spent the next four days, watched over by a small security contingent.

The home had a large, comfortably furnished den, which was well lit and had been wired for both sound and video. While someone else might have been self-conscious about being under such scrutiny, Harvath didn't care. He had long lived by the maxim from Mark Twain — as long as you told the truth, you didn't have to worry about remembering anything.

He answered every question that was put to him and asked many of his own.

McGee and Levi drilled down on everything, endlessly circling back and asking him to repeat details he had provided minutes or even days before.

Both men were impressed that Harvath had held out as long as he had. Everyone, though, breaks. Harvath had been close, but had had the presence of mind to feed them falsehoods that they wouldn't be able to verify until they were back in Russia. The crash of the military transport plane had turned out to be a blessing in more ways than one.

Beyond learning what techniques the Russians used and what intelligence they had wanted Harvath to reveal, they were deeply interested in his ordeal and how he had survived. No doubt, he was going to end up as a case study at the Agency, as well as in all of the SERE schools.

The questions they continued to ask ran the gamut from his relationship with Kopec and what had happened at the safe house in New Hampshire, to how he had discovered the trapper's cabin, what he had done after breaking into Christina's clinic in Nivsky, and why he had chosen to assault the Wagner mercenaries the way he had.

As someone uncomfortable with praise, he was even more uncomfortable with talking about himself. Many times he couldn't give them a *why*. He did what he did because it was either the way he had been trained or the only option he saw available. There wasn't necessarily a lot of high-level thinking going on. In fact, a lot of it was gut-level.

The worst parts were when McGee stepped out of the room and left him alone with Levi. The man loved two things — golf and cars. He used both in an attempt to build a rapport with Harvath. Harvath wasn't interested.

When the doctor couldn't get him to open up, he took more direct routes — literally asking Harvath how he was feeling, what regrets he may have had, and what he thought he was going to do moving forward.

It was pretty intrusive stuff and frankly none of Levi's business. He worked for The

Carlton Group, not the CIA. If he chose to throw his hat in the ring for any future contracts, they could discuss his fitness then. Wanting to pick apart his current "emotional well-being," as Levi put it, was a nonstarter. He made it clear that there was a bright line and that Levi better back up off it.

The only saving grace of the debrief was that one of the men on McGee's detail, a guy named Preisler, was a hell of a cook. Steaks, pasta, all sorts of breakfasts, it seemed there was nothing he couldn't pull off. For a former door-kicker, he was a formidable chef.

The other thing Harvath had appreciated was that when the debrief was done for the day, it was done for the day. There were no prohibitions on Harvath's having a couple of drinks. As long as he wasn't under the influence when they had him on the record, they didn't care what he did. In fact, they went out of their way to give him his space and leave him alone.

Though Levi likely had a hand in it, you didn't need to be a shrink to realize that after everything Harvath had been through, he was going to need some time to be by himself. He was even allowed to leave the house and walk down to the water without anyone accompanying him.

While he would have preferred his own house, his own dock, and his own slice of the Potomac, the view of the Chesapeake from here wasn't terrible. And though he had to put on a coat, at least there wasn't any ice or snow.

On their last night, Levi walked down lugging a cooler and dropped it on the dock next to Harvath. After helping himself to a beer, he sat down and looked out over the water. Harvath waited for him to say something, but the man didn't make a sound.

They sat like that for a good ten minutes before Harvath broke the silence. "What else is in the cooler?"

"I wasn't sure what you were drinking, so I put a little bit of everything in there," the doc replied.

Leaning over, Harvath flipped up the lid and grabbed the bourbon, plus a couple of fresh ice cubes. He dropped them into his glass and then poured himself several fingers.

"Cheers," said Levi.

Harvath raised his glass without looking at him.

"Scot, right now we're off the clock. None of this is official and nothing is going into my notes. Okay?"

Harvath sipped his drink.

"You've been through some unbelievable trauma," the shrink continued. "In my experience, people tend to go in either of two directions from here. They quit and usually fall into a life of substance abuse, which often ends in suicide, or they allow themselves time to grieve, time to heal, and they come back better, stronger."

It was an observation, not a question, so Harvath didn't feel compelled to respond.

"With just the little bit I know about you from your file," offered Levi, "and what I have seen of you here, I think you can come back much stronger. It has to be your choice, though. That's why if there's anything you want to talk to me about, anything at all, I want you to know that you can."

Levi might have been a nice guy, but Harvath wasn't here to make friends. There was nothing he needed to "get off his chest." All he wanted to do was to be left alone. In furtherance of that goal, he remained silent.

Walking back up to house, Levi found McGee sitting on the porch, smoking a cigar.

"It didn't work, did it?" the CIA Director stated.

The doc shook his head. "No, it didn't."

"I told you it wouldn't. That's not how a

guy like Harvath operates."

"And I'm telling you, you have a malfunctioning weapon on your hands. If you let him go, I won't be held responsible for what he does."

"His wife is being buried the day after tomorrow. We can't keep him here. We have to let him go."

"At least put a surveillance team on him; follow him — for his own good."

Not a chance, thought McGee as he blew a cloud of smoke into the air. "Anything else?"

"No. I'm driving home tonight. My report will be on your desk in the morning."

The CIA Director nodded, turned back toward the water, and took another puff from his cigar. His concern wasn't that Harvath was "malfunctioning." In fact, based on everything he'd seen, Harvath, all things considered, was functioning better than anyone would have assumed.

No, his concern ran deeper, to something more visceral.

Inside every human being was a very dark, very cold place. Sealed behind a heavy iron door, the cold dark was populated by the worst demons known to man.

But crack that door — even just an inch — and out all of the demons would fly. And once they had escaped, there would be no bringing them back until they had fed.

What they would feed upon was what worried McGee the most. In the case of Harvath's demons, only one thing would satiate them.

Revenge.

CHAPTER 76

Harvath didn't know what was harder, facing Lara's parents and explaining how they had secretly gotten married at Reed Carlton's bedside, or facing Lara's little boy and not being able to explain to him why he couldn't save his mom.

The service was gut wrenching. It was a full-on police funeral, where Harvath was highly disliked and seen as the guy who had convinced Lara to leave the force and move to D.C. In everyone's mind, he was the reason Lara was dead. And while they knew next to nothing about the details, which only served to piss them off more, they were right. It was his fault that she was gone.

No matter how long he lived, he would never be able to escape that fact. It was another link in the heavy chain of guilt he carried over women who had been killed or

575

injured because of who he was and what he did.

While meant as a slight, it was actually a blessing that Harvath wasn't invited to speak. Instead, he sat quietly with Lara's parents, holding Marco's hand when the little boy had reached out for his.

The Brits had a term for what he was feeling — gutted — but it didn't go far enough. Harvath was absolutely hollowed out.

The night before, he had stood outside the funeral home for hours in the rain. No matter how hard he tried, he couldn't summon the courage to go inside, not while the viewing was going on.

Lara's colleagues loved her dearly and he could tell by the amount of drinking that was going on in the parking lot that if he had shown his face inside, there would have been trouble. This was Boston after all. They were proud, profoundly decent people with a deep sense of right and wrong.

He didn't blame them. Each of them wanted to believe that had they been there, regardless of what had happened, they would have made a difference. That's who they were. They were cops, warriors. It was grossly unfair to them that Lara was gone and Harvath was still here. They couldn't willingly fathom a scenario in which he lived and she died. In their minds, it had to be a failing on his part. If only she hadn't left Boston. If only she had chosen a cop over whatever secret-squirrel bullshit Harvath did for a living.

Once all the cars had departed, once the funeral director and his staff had gone home for the evening, Harvath had disabled the alarm and had let himself inside.

They had done an amazing job. Lara looked beautiful. Pulling up a chair, he placed his hand atop hers.

For an hour, all he did was sit there. He didn't have the words, much less the breath, to speak.

This was the woman he was going to spend the rest of his life with. After putting off marriage for so long, he had finally taken the leap, only to have his bride ripped away from him.

The family he had put on hold so he could pursue his career had been within his grasp. He and Lara and Marco had been a perfect fit. She had lost her husband and Marco had lost his father. Harvath had arrived at the point where he was ready to take on both of those roles. But now it was all gone.

She was so smart, so beautiful, and so funny. What's more, she had understood him. More important, she had understood why he did what he did and why it was so important. In short, she not only loved him, but she allowed him to be who he was.

Gripping her hand, he let it all come out. He let her know how much he loved her, how much he missed her, and how sorry he was that she was gone and that he had not been able to save her.

And as he did, the iron door to the dark, cold place swung the rest of the way open.

Still exhausted, he fell asleep in the chair next to her.

It was just before dawn when her voice came to him, and told him that it was time to wake up.

He lingered for a moment in that halfway place between sleep and wakefulness, hoping she would say something more, that maybe she would tell him that everything was going to be okay, that she forgave him. He waited, but no further words came.

Looking at his watch, he saw that he would have barely enough time to make it back to his hotel to change before meeting up with Lara's parents at their apartment.

As he had been at the safe house in Maryland and wanted to catch the first available flight to Boston, Sloane had been kind enough to go to his house, pack him a bag, and bring it to him at the airport.

Though she had taken creative license on similar errands in the past, this time she was incredibly respectful — white shirt, black shoes, black tie, and black suit. She had even included a black overcoat, as well as a couple extra days' worth of subdued clothing.

She had also been thoughtful enough to include a heartfelt note of support. Everyone on the team, including Nicholas and even McGee, loved Lara. She was someone very special. All of them would have made the trip to Boston to be there for her funeral, but Harvath had asked them not to. Out of respect for him, they had all stayed back in D.C.

Upon arriving at Lara's parents' house, Marco had thrown his arms around Harvath and hadn't wanted to let go. There was a spark of his mother in him and it felt better than Harvath could have ever imagined to hold the little boy close.

After the burial, when they arrived at the hall where the wake was to take place, Harvath looked out the window of their limo at the steady stream of strangers parading in.

These were people Lara and her parents knew. None of them knew who he was. If the looks he had gotten at the mass and at the burial were any indication, he was not going to be very warmly received here either. On top of that, this was going to be wrenching for Marco.

Pulling his father-in-law aside, Harvath asked if he could take the little boy out to get something to eat and promised to bring him back to the apartment later. Lara's mother and father had both agreed.

After the grandparents had exited the limo, he had the driver take them to a little Boston breakfast place Lara had loved.

Seeing the pair dressed in dark suits and ties, the hostess must have intuited where they were coming from, because she waved them over and found them a table ahead of the other people who had already been waiting. Harvath tried to give her a tip for her kindness, but she refused to take it.

Looking at the children's menu, Marco had trouble deciding what to eat. Harvath told him that on a day like this pancakes were the right choice. He didn't know why, other than that when his father had died, one of his father's SEAL buddies had taken him for breakfast and had suggested the same.

After they had eaten, he asked Marco what he wanted to do. The little boy wanted ice cream, so that's what they did. They then went to the Lego store, a bookstore, and a spot on the banks of the Charles River where he liked to feed the ducks. All too soon, it was time to go home.

The limo had already gone back to the hall, so he and Marco had been walking and taking cabs. Instead of taking one all the way back to the apartment, he had them dropped off a few blocks away. He wanted to walk a little bit more.

Sensing that their time was growing short, Marco reached out and took his hand again as they made their way up the street.

Harvath, as tough as he wanted to be, was doing all he could to hold it together. He wasn't the only one who had lost the chance at a family — so had Marco. Both his mother and his father were gone.

Nearing the apartment, he dreaded saying good-bye. More to the point, he dreaded the question he knew was coming, "When will I see you again?" or worse, "Why can't you take me with you?"

But those weren't the words the little boy used. Instead, after squeezing his hand exactly as Lara always did, he looked at him and said, "I love you."

"I love you, too," replied Harvath as he kneeled down and gave the boy a long hug.

"Be good for your grandparents. I promise I will see you soon."

Marco smiled, gave Harvath one more hug around his neck, and then disappeared inside.

He was a good boy and Harvath meant what he had said. He loved him, just as much as he had loved Lara.

It took him several blocks to find a cab to take him to the cemetery. He wanted to spend time at Lara's grave before flying back to D.C.

Unlike at the funeral home where he had spent his time apologizing, this time, he remembered to be thankful.

In particular, he remembered to thank Lara for coming to him when he had been at his weakest in Russia. Whether he had imagined it, or whether it had actually been her, didn't matter. She had saved him and for that he was grateful.

After his time at her grave, he returned to the hotel to pick up his bag and then head out to the airport. He had two more funerals to attend in D.C.

Once those were over, the reckoning would begin.

CHAPTER 77

Washington, D.C.

With distinguished careers in the intelligence world, Lydia Ryan and Reed Carlton shared many of the same friends and colleagues.

In order to make it easier for those flying in from across the country and from around the world, it was decided to hold both services on the same weekend.

Lydia's would be on Friday and the Old Man's would take place on Sunday. Saturday was scheduled as a day off, so that people could rest their livers and recover from all the drinking.

The Ryan family organized a sedate viewing, followed by a tasteful Catholic mass and burial. That night, a block from Union Station, they rented out the entirety of the Dubliner for one of the most raucous Irish wakes Washington, D.C., had ever seen.

It was packed with personnel not only

from the CIA, but from allied intelligence agencies as well. As a courtesy, and as a precaution, Metro D.C. Police had closed down the street outside. They also brought out SWAT and K-9 units just to be safe. This kind of guest list was a terrorist's wet dream.

Poster-sized pictures of Lydia had been placed on easels around the bar. In every photo she was either laughing or flashing her bright, beautiful smile. The message from her mass was reinforced at the wake: *Life is short. Love who you are. Love what you do. Make every day count.*

Her family couldn't have picked a more perfect encapsulation of who she was. Still aching from his trip to Boston, Harvath was glad to be among his teammates — all of whom made sure he was not left alone.

Between the funeral and the wake, Harvath ended up seeing CIA personnel he hadn't seen in years. Among them were Rick Morrell and three of his teammates, De-Wolfe, Carlson, and Avigliano. Harvath had gone into Libya with them years ago hunting the heirs to Abu Nidal's terrorist organization.

They traded stories for a while until everyone drifted off in different directions to refresh their drinks and catch up with other long-lost friends.

It was after midnight when Harvath pulled Sloane aside and let her know he was going to leave.

"All right," she said, "I'll gather everybody else up."

"No. I'm good. I'm going back by myself."

"Are you sure?"

"I'm sure," he replied.

"How about I swing by tomorrow and just check in? Help you box stuff up?"

By "box stuff up" she meant boxing up Lara's things.

"Let's see how you feel in the morning," he said, nodding at the new drink she held in her hand. "Text me."

"You going to be okay to drive?"

Harvath nodded, "I'm fine. I'll talk to you tomorrow." And with that, he had quietly slipped out.

The next morning, Nicholas showed up at his place bright and early. Along with the dogs, he had brought with him the fixings for breakfast.

He had chosen to avoid the Dubliner for health reasons. A crowded room full of staggering drunks wasn't a good environment for a person his size. And the fact that he suffered from easily broken bones only compounded the potential risks.

Nicholas had, though, attended both the mass and the burial. His presence had sent whispers racing among the foreign intelligence operatives who had no idea that "The Troll" had received a full presidential pardon for his past deeds and had taken up residence in the United States.

Harvath was certain that while Nicholas couldn't be at the wake, he had raised a glass of good whiskey in Lydia Ryan's honor and had helped to send her off in style.

"You look better than I expected," the little man said, as he placed his shopping bags on the bench in the kitchen. "How late did you stay?"

"I slipped out sometime after midnight," he replied. "Coffee?"

"Tea, please," said Nicholas, nodding at Lara's tins.

"What kind?"

"What was her favorite?"

"Lapsang Souchong," he stated, pronouncing it proudly.

"That's what I'll have then."

After petting the dogs for several moments and putting down bowls of water for them, Harvath put a kettle on.

While he did, Nicholas clambered up onto one of the chairs at the dining table, opened his messenger bag, and laid out everything he had brought with him.

"Chase says you owe him 10 percent," said the little man.

"Ten percent of what?"

"Of whatever comes of this."

Harvath looked over as Nicholas held up the journal Harvath had taken from Teplov back in Russia.

When The Carlton Group jet had landed at Andrews, Harvath had slipped it to Chase with a request that he quietly pass it on to Nicholas.

Harvath had assumed, correctly, that he would be immediately taken into loose custody with an offer for medical attention, which he had declined, followed by transport to a secure location for his debriefing. Had he been carrying the journal, McGee and his people would have found it straightaway.

"I just want to say two things before we start," Nicholas declared. "First, I have a lot of respect for you and what you're planning to do. Second, I think you and your plan are fucking crazy."

"Good to know that I haven't lost my touch," Harvath replied as he prepared the cups and then brought everything over to the table when it was ready.

As he poured the hot water, Nicholas

explained what he had learned from the journal. Not only did they have a full name and background for Josef, they also learned who had selected him and had coordinated everything from the murders of Lara, Lydia, and Reed Carlton to the hiring of the Wagner mercenaries once the plane had gone down in Russia. It was a General out of the GRU named Minayev. And Minayev had been operating on direct orders from Russian President Peshkov.

When Sloane called early in the afternoon, sounding very hungover, Harvath told her everything was okay and that there was no need for her to drop by. Nevertheless, she insisted.

It wasn't until he put the call on speakerphone and she could hear Nicholas's voice that she believed he was there.

Nicholas seemed an odd choice to help box up Lara's things and decide what should go to her parents and what should go to charity, but if that's what Harvath wanted, she wasn't going to go against his wishes.

Telling Sloane that he would see her tomorrow at the Old Man's service, Harvath had disconnected the call and gotten back to his work with Nicholas.

They had a lot more to do before he

infiltrated back into Russia.

Technically, Reed Carlton's service hadn't
been a funeral. It had been a "memorial."

The Old Man's last will and testament
had been specific. And as executor, Harvath
had followed his wishes to the letter.

Cremation. Ashes to be placed into a cut-
down, silver-coated 75 mm artillery shell —
a crazy gift from some Raja whom Carlton
had befriended decades ago while working
at the CIA's station in New Delhi.

The memorial service at his local church
had been followed by a reception at Carlton's home, complete with a "well-stocked"
bar. Food had been permitted, "but don't
go overboard." And no "goddamn vegetables," he had instructed.

That had made Harvath smile. Even in
death, the Old Man had remained a detail
guy.

There had been a lot of particulars to go
over. Some were obvious, such as Harvath
being tasked with taking over the organization. Other details had been less obvious,
though a letter from Carlton explained that
in time, they would be.

His guest list was a who's who not only of
global intelligence personalities past and
present, but also of American politicians

and foreign leaders. The security alone was a sight to behold.

Though he didn't want to, Harvath worked all of the events, introducing himself and shaking hands. The Old Man had been very clear that he expected Harvath to assume control over his business, as well as his network of contacts.

Whether he ended up going the management route or staying in the field didn't matter. To have this many powerful, connected people in one place was an opportunity he needed to take advantage of.

Unlike Lydia's wake, the Old Man's wasn't one he could sneak out of. He was the heir apparent and everyone wanted time with him. So he had stayed till the end and till every last guest had left.

Wandering the empty house felt strange. It was hard to believe Carlton was gone. He had been a legend *and* an institution, someone people both turned to and aspired to. They had broken the mold when they had made him.

Harvath walked into the study. It was like a mini museum, filled with reminders of the Old Man's exploits, many of which most Americans would never be aware of. For a long, long time, he had been the person the nation had quietly turned to in order to solve its most pressing and dangerous problems.

That era, though, had passed. Many politicians, as well as many citizens, were willing to trade liberty in exchange for security. But as Ben Franklin was alleged to have said, *Those who would trade a little liberty for a little security deserved neither and would lose both.* The world was still a dangerous place, and it was growing more so.

The price of freedom had been and always would be *vigilance.* It required hard, nonstop, dangerous work. But the work was worth it.

And as long as there were men and women willing to give everything to preserve it, America could retain its freedom and continue to be the greatest beacon for hope and opportunity in the history of the world.

Deciding how to divvy up the Old Man's personal effects was going to take weeks. There were a handful of things he knew the CIA's historian would want to have, but there were others he felt should go to the International Spy Museum in D.C. It was important, in Harvath's opinion, that America be given a glimpse into what an amazing man Reed Carlton was and how much he had given his nation.

Of course, if the Old Man were still alive,

he'd resist such a thing and beat Harvath to within an inch of his life for suggesting it. That was simply who he was. He believed in America and what was required to protect it.

As executor, Harvath was responsible for the entirety of the Old Man's estate — a large part of which was his legacy. He was an inspirational figure and the good he had done could live well beyond his violent death at the safe house in New Hampshire. That was Harvath's plan. But it would have to wait.

Reed Carlton would have wanted him to do something else first. And, he would have been very specific about how he had wanted it done.

CHAPTER 78

Moscow

Two weeks later

Harvath had used a combination of intelligence assets to help him get all the way to, and into, Russia undetected.

A contact of his, Monika Jasinski at Polish Military Intelligence, had met him at the airport in Warsaw, then scrubbed clean all records of his arrival and transported him to the border with Belarus.

At the border, a team of smugglers loyal to the Old Man, who had also been handsomely rewarded on a recent operation by Chase and Sloane, picked him up and transported him across the country to the border with Russia.

There, he was met by an old acquaintance. Before the murders in New Hampshire, he had been developing her as an intelligence asset inside the FSB — Russia's equivalent of the CIA. She was a patriot who loved her country, but despised its system of government.

Bob McGee, Lydia Ryan, and even President Porter had all been aware that he had slowly been attempting to bring her over. This was the one part of the plan that Nicholas hated the most. He saw Alexandra Ivanova as its weakest link — an untested pillar they would be resting all of their weight upon.

Though she and Harvath had a long history, and despite the fact that he had even killed a major Russian mafia figure in the Caribbean the previous year to help advance her career, there was no telling how she would handle his request. He was putting his neck in a noose, handing her the other end, and closing his eyes.

The hardest part for Nicholas was that, while he loved the plan in general, there was no one he could go to help him push back on Harvath and the specifics. McGee and the CIA had no idea what they were doing. And that went double for the President. This was completely off-book, and therefore off anyone's radar.

The little man had argued as intensely as he could, but Harvath's mind had been made up. There was only one thing they had agreed with each other on — if Ivanova double-crossed them and Harvath ended up captured, the Russians would go to extraordinary lengths to guarantee there would be no rescue this time.

It was a risk that Harvath had been willing to take. In fact, "willingness" had nothing to do with it. After running it through his mind a thousand and one times, this had been the only path he could see available.

He knew it had to be the right course because the Russians wouldn't see it coming, and it was also exactly what the Old Man would have done. It was a plan that required a pair of the biggest balls anyone had ever seen.

Once he had the address he had been waiting on in Moscow, he prepped an envelope and sent it on its way. Inside was a letter to Russian president Fedor Peshkov. It was signed by Harvath and explained, in excruciating detail, everything he was going to do to him. It brought chilling new meaning to the words "hate mail."

Hiding in a farmhouse near the border between Belarus and Russia, Harvath had fieldstripped, cleaned, and reassembled Reed Carlton's 1911 pistol so many times that it gleamed in the darkness.

Putting together his kit for the operation, it had seemed appropriate to carry the legendary spymaster's favorite weapon. Even if Harvath never drew it, the mere fact that he had brought it along for protection would be a profound way of honoring him.

Of course, the greatest way to honor Carlton would be to avenge him, which was exactly why he was here.

When Alexandra Ivanova finally showed up, they had a brief exchange before he climbed into the cutout in her trunk. She covered him with a custom piece of carpeting, and shut the lid.

He felt every bump, jostle, and pothole in the road. The ride was absolutely brutal. But it was also absolutely necessary.

Ivanova was one of the smartest intelligence operatives Harvath had ever met. It was one of the reasons he had labored so hard to get her to come to work for him. She didn't have ice in her veins; what she had was molten steel.

She had agreed to the operation with one caveat: Everything that happened inside Russia was her call.

Naturally, Nicholas had balked at this condition and had told Harvath that he'd be better off cutting his own throat in D.C. At least then it would save SPEHA Rogers the trouble of negotiating the repatriation of his body.

Harvath, though, had agreed to all of her demands. He trusted Alexandra. If she had wanted to burn him, she could have done so long before now. As far as he was concerned, she was someone he could trust.

Riding in the secret compartment in the trunk, he expected to feel the car slow down at some point, if nothing else then for the border. The slowdown, though, never came. She kept the pedal to the metal.

Ivanova had assured him that as long as he could make it to the border, she could get him across. And apparently, she had been right.

When she pulled her less-than-new sedan off the highway, they were halfway to Moscow.

Opening the lid and pulling back the carpet, she let Harvath out of the back.

"Welcome to Russia," she joked.

Even though he wasn't in the mood, Harvath smiled. "Thank you," he said. "I ordered an in-flight meal, but never received it."

Without missing a beat, Alexandra responded, "I'll make sure to let my supervisor know. We value every passenger attempting to sneak into our country."

"Speaking of which," said Harvath, "how is it we didn't stop at a border checkpoint?"

"I bribed the guards. On the way out, I flashed my credentials and gave them all cartons of cigarettes. On the way back, I told them I'd be coming with live lobsters on melting ice destined for the Kremlin. None of them argued. They opened a lane for me and I drove straight through."

It was a good start. Harvath hoped it would last.

They spent the first night in a suburb on the outskirts of Moscow. Alexandra had done all of the advance work. She knew the routines of each target, where they would be and when. For the first one, though, Harvath wanted to see for himself.

The next morning, after a cold shower and a bad cup of coffee, she took him to the target's apartment building. Then they watched him emerge and followed him to work.

"Satisfied?" she asked.

Harvath nodded. The real satisfaction, though, would come the next morning. That's when the rubber would meet the road and Ivanova would have to prove her commitment to the operation.

Smuggling him across the border was a good start. But helping him to scratch the first name off his list was the real test. If she proved herself fully onboard tomorrow, it

would be one less thing he had to worry
about.

CHAPTER 79

They had spent the rest of that day checking in on the other targets and visiting the other locations. Everything was set, or at least as set as it was going to be.

That night, they stayed in and ate takeout that she had brought back to the apartment. She asked him what had happened, and he told her, *all* of it.

Alexandra's heart, which had always had a soft spot for him, broke. It was one of the worst stories of loss she had ever heard — possibly even worse than her own.

When the words stopped coming and he could no longer speak, she offered him the bed. Ever the gentleman, he took the couch.

She slept in her bedroom, the door open in case he changed his mind.

They rose well before dawn and made ready. He had brought money for Alexandra, which she tried to refuse, but he insisted. She was taking an enormous risk.

She deserved to be compensated.

There were four more envelopes, also filled with cash. She had promised that she would make sure they were quietly delivered to Sini and her husband Mokci, as well as the families of Jompá and Olá in Murmansk Oblast.

With everything cleaned up and put away, they went through the apartment once more, wiping it down for fingerprints. Harvath doubted the Russians would ever make the connection, but he didn't want to leave any proof that he and Alexandra knew each other and had ever been at the same location. She was too valuable an asset to lose.

Despite the cold, the car started right up. The moment it did, Harvath set the heater to High. He knew it wouldn't do any good until the engine had warmed up, but psychologically it made him feel better.

It was still dark as they made their way out onto the snow-covered suburban streets. Only a few cars were about, people getting a jump on the morning shift traffic.

Normally, Harvath wouldn't have involved Alexandra in this part of an operation, but he needed her language skills. It was critical that he extract absolutely unambiguous intelligence from their target. The less time he spent inside, the less chance of his getting caught.

Nicholas had been key to the entire operation. With only Teplov's journal, and what Harvath had been able to share with him, he had gone to work. It was astounding what he had been able to put together in just two weeks.

Pulling up behind the apartment building, Alexandra found a place to park and then, after she had killed the engine, they both exited the vehicle.

"Ready to go?" Harvath asked.

Alexandra pulled up the scarf, covering her face. "Ready to go," she replied.

They were using burner phones from Vladivostok. They might as well have been from Mars. Even if they were discovered, local police were never going to expend any manpower tracking down how they had come to Moscow.

Taking out his lock pick tools, Harvath unlocked the back door and waited for Alexandra to text that she was in place. Their target lived on the ground floor.

When the text came, he pressed his ear against the glass, waited until he heard the doorbell, and then let himself in.

The man lived alone and had no girlfriend that Nicholas had been able to ascertain based on his emails, texts, and social media pages. He also didn't have any pets. There was nothing else special about him other than he was about Harvath's height and weight and worked on the floor they needed.

As Alexandra fed him a line of bullshit at the front door, Harvath crept up silently on him from the back of the apartment. Once he was in range, he deployed his Taser and took him down.

Kicking his legs out of the way, Alexandra stepped inside and closed the front door.

The fluidity with which Harvath flex-cuffed him and threw a hood over his head demonstrated that he had done this before.

Grabbing a chair from the kitchen, Alexandra helped Harvath drag him into the bedroom and sit him down. There, as she pulled the barbed Taser probes out of him, Harvath tied him up.

The man couldn't see his attackers, but he could hear them. Harvath asked if he understood English. When the man claimed not to, everything else went through Alexandra.

They grilled him for over two hours until, looking at his watch, Harvath indicated that it was time to go.

After Alexandra had left the room, Harvath removed the man's hood, but only long enough to gag him and wrap several passes of duct tape around his mouth before replacing his hood.

Per Harvath's instructions, Alexandra returned with a gas can from the car and placed it beneath the chair. Even under the hood, the fumes were instantly recognizable. She explained in Russian that a bomb had been placed under him and that if he attempted to move, or made too much noise, it would explode.

She also relayed that as long as he cooperated, they would be back within twenty-four hours and would set him free. Who they were, where they were going, or why any of it involved him, they never revealed.

Going through his closet, Harvath found the clothes he needed and quickly got dressed. Then, in the living room, Alexandra handed over the man's ID badge and repeated how security at the entrance to the facility worked. Alexandra would go in first, and be nearby in case anything went wrong.

Harvath hoped that wouldn't be necessary. If there was one thing he knew, it was that nightshift workers were practically zombies once it was time to go home. The morning shift that replaced them was almost as bad, needing a lot of coffee — and most important, sunlight — before they were fully awake and functioning. It was the perfect time to make their move.

Leaving the man bound and gagged in the apartment, Harvath pocketed his cell phone and they headed out.

It was a short drive to their next stop and Alexandra parked out on the street, rather than in the employee parking lot, so that they wouldn't be impeded in making their escape.

By the time they got to the front entrance, there was already a line of employees slowly shuffling inside. Alexandra went first, followed by Harvath.

Completely wrapped up against the cold, all he was required to do was show an ID. The security guards never even asked him to show his face. Without looking at Alexandra, who had taken one of the public chairs just inside the entrance, he pressed on into the building.

Eschewing the employee locker room, he found a utility area where he dumped the man's coat, gloves, and scarf. From there, he was only one stairwell away from his target.

With his eyes downcast, he maintained the plodding, uninterested pace of the average Russian worker, while every cell inside him wanted to charge to his destination. He knew from experience, though, that sure and steady was what would win the race *and* get him what he wanted.

Because he moved the way that he did, no one gave him a second glance. He looked exactly as he had hoped he would. He looked as if he belonged there.

Arriving at the door, he took a deep breath and tried to steady his heart rate. *Breathe,* he reminded himself. So he did.

Reaching out for the cold, stainless steel handle, he opened the door and stepped inside.

The room was dark, its blinds closed. One of the things the man tied up back at the apartment had said was that upon entering, his job was to prep the room for the morning. So, that was exactly what Harvath did.

Opening the blinds, to allow the early rays of the sun to shine in, he heard something behind him. The patient was awake.

Turning, he smiled and said in English, "Good morning, Josef."

CHAPTER 80

Before the man could cry out, Harvath was on him.

Josef had been admitted to Moscow City Hospital Number 67 for a complicated spinal surgery due to injuries had had suffered in the crash. He was paralyzed from the waist down and could only move his upper body.

Stunning him with a blow to the head, Harvath disconnected his patient call button, slapped a piece of duct tape over his mouth, and then removed a syringe.

Reaching for Josef's IV, he injected it with succinylcholine and then, grabbing him by the throat, he pulled the piece of tape from his mouth.

"I told you back in New Hampshire I'd find you," said Harvath, "and that when I did, I'd kill you. So now, guess what?"

"Fuck you," gasped Josef.

"Don't talk," Harvath instructed. "Just

listen. You killed my wife and you also killed two of the most important people in the world to me. You dragged me all the way over here to your shithole country to interrogate and then kill me. It didn't work, though. You want to know why? Because you're a failure. You have always been a failure. And now you will die a failure."

"Fuck you, you —" Josef began again, but Harvath choked him quiet once more.

"I just injected you with suxamethonium chloride. Also known as sux. Right now, all of your muscles are starting to give up. In about sixty seconds you will be fully paralyzed and unable to breathe, but you'll still be fully conscious and aware of what's going on. Two minutes from now, when the nurses rush in to give you CPR, it'll be a lost cause. Before that happens, though, I'm going to make sure you die as painful a death as possible."

Withdrawing his hand from around the man's throat, he straightened up and struck the Russian brutally and repeatedly in and around his chest.

Josef tried to raise his arms to defend himself, but he could not. He tried to call out for help, but he was equally unable. He could do nothing but lie helplessly and watch it all happen, much the way Harvath had been forced to witness the murders of Lara, Lydia Ryan, and the Old Man.

When Harvath had finished pounding on him, he stood back. There was no doubt he had broken multiple ribs.

Josef was not only going to die of suffocation, but as the well-meaning medical staff pushed down on his chest in an effort to revive him, they were going to be exacerbating the pain of his broken ribs and helping to puncture his lungs.

It wasn't the slow death Harvath wanted to give him. That kind of pain would have taken weeks or months. But all things considered, it was a very nasty death he was all too happy to deliver.

Placing a bag-valve mask over the man's face, he pushed the emergency call button and shouted out instructions in perfect Russian, just as Christina had instructed him, for the local equivalent of a Code Blue.

Within moments, the room filled with medical personnel, all of whom were exclusively focused on the patient.

As they fought to revive Josef, Harvath slipped out the door, walked downstairs, and left the building without anyone noticing.

By the time he made it to the corner, Alexandra was already there, in the car, waiting for him. *One down, two to go.*

Their next target wouldn't be available for several hours. To her credit, Alexandra had taken that into consideration and had planned accordingly.

In an empty office across the street, she had placed a couple of cots, food, water, and even medical supplies in case the first hit had gone sideways.

Harvath had to hand it to her, she was very good at her job.

They passed the day and into the early evening in relative silence. Had he taken her up on her offer last night, they could have found a more enjoyable way to while away the hours, but it was what it was. As night fell and the city darkened, she brewed coffee and went over the next phase of the operation with him.

She knew General Minayev only by reputation. She had never met the GRU bigwig in person. And while she understood the reasoning behind the next phase of Harvath's operation, she found it particularly distasteful. Even so, she had agreed to go along with it.

Once more, Nicholas had been the key to their planning. Three times a week, Minayev rendezvoused with his mistress at a small apartment he owned not far from the cheese shop he so loved.

If the upper echelons of the FBI and CIA had as many men cheating on their wives as Russian Intelligence did, the American Congress would have been up in arms and rightly purging them left, right, and center. The fact that Russia condoned such behavior could only be added to the list of reasons they lagged behind the rest of the developed world when it came to law, order, and trust in government.

Corruption, sadly, wasn't something to be avoided in Russia, it was something to be studied and then expertly exploited.

Aside from the unseemliness of it all, what was particularly helpful was that the love-birds always ordered in. They did so via an app, which Nicholas had no trouble tapping into.

When the food arrived, Alexandra was standing on the chipped curb, waiting to receive it. As the driver sped off, she rang the bell, announced herself, and then sent Harvath up as the door buzzed open.

Reed Carlton's 1911 in his hand, he stepped out of the stairwell and into the hallway. Russian apartment buildings had always seemed to smell the same to him — fucking horrible. He didn't know what caused it. At its foundation, it had to be the cooking, but from there it was anybody's guess.

He waited for Alexandra to appear from the opposite stairwell and when she did, they approached the apartment door together.

After she rolled down her balaclava and took off her jacket to expose a Russian Security Services raid vest, Harvath knocked.

As they had anticipated, the mistress answered the door. There was no way Minayev was going to risk being seen here.

The woman was surprised to see a man standing at the door, when it had been a woman who had called up on the intercom from downstairs.

He put his index finger against his lips as if to say, "Shhh," and then pointed at Alexandra, who beckoned the young woman over to her.

Believing something official to be up, the mistress stepped into the hall and did as they instructed.

As she passed, Harvath slipped inside. He could smell Minayev before he even saw him.

The legend of the cheese the man ate smelling like a decomposing corpse didn't do it justice. It actually smelled *worse.* How his wife, much less his mistress, could stand to be with him was a total mystery. Both must have been suffering from anosmia.

Normally in a situation like this, Harvath would have felt comfortable drawing out the man's death. But the odor was so bad that he couldn't wait to get the hell out of the apartment.

Assuming his mistress was dealing with the delivery, Minayev sat in the living room, his back to the hall, watching TV.

Holstering his weapon, Harvath uncapped a new hypodermic needle and crept forward. With the television up so loud, Minayev never had a chance.

Harvath jammed the needle into the base of his neck, depressed the plunger, and held him down while he waited for the sux to do its work.

"Do you know who I am?" Harvath asked, as Minayev caught a glimpse of him out of the corner of his eye, before paralysis took hold.

The GRU man nodded.

"Josef killed my wife, my colleague, and my boss on your orders. Now, I'm here to kill you. But I'm not just going to kill you. I'm going to destroy your professional reputation as well. Even after your death, people will revile your name."

Harvath wanted to continue, but he could see that the man's breathing had slowed. Every muscle in his body had relaxed. He thirsted desperately for air, but lacked the ability to exercise his lungs and draw new oxygen in. Staring into his eyes, Harvath watched as he slowly asphyxiated.

Everything now came down to timing. Quickly, Harvath wrapped a cord around the man's neck, pulled it tight and dragged him with it into the bathroom.

There, he slung it up and over the door, attaching it to the doorknob on the other side.

Stripping off Minayev's clothing, he dressed him in the women's lingerie he had brought along and then scattered hard copies within reach of the child porn Nicholas had made sure would be discovered on all of his devices.

Out in the hallway, Alexandra didn't feel like talking. This was the part of it that she didn't like, the pornography. Her reaction was exactly what he was hoping other Russians would feel when the news broke.

As they left the building, he gave the okay for her anonymous source to contact the local paper.

It would not be a good day for the GRU. One of its most distinguished Generals

614

would be found hanged, by his own hand, via autoerotic asphyxiation and surrounded by child porn.

With two down, there was only one left to go.

CHAPTER 81

If you asked Muscovites who, on the social scene, they hated the most, privately, they would all give you the same answer. *Misha.*

Misha was the diminutive of Mikhail, and everyone knew who it referred to — Mikhail Peshkov, pride and joy of the Russian President, Fedor Peshkov.

It was said that the only thing the elder Peshkov loved more than his money and power was his son. He was his sole offspring, the only living memory of the President's deceased wife, who had also been his childhood sweetheart. The boy represented the continuation of the family bloodline, but like many only children, he had been recklessly spoiled by his over-adoring father.

The blinders the Russian President wore when it came to Misha had seen a spoiled child grow into a dangerous young adult.

Though barely into his twenties, the young man had become known not only for his gluttony and abandon, but also for his cruelty. Even the local Russian mafia despised him. Had it not been for his all-powerful father, he would have already been taken out.

But because of the elder Peshkov, he was free to run wild, free to terrorize businesses throughout Russia, legitimate and otherwise, with impunity.

He had caused grievous damage "bottling" prominent rich Russian nightclub goers by slamming their heads with champagne bottles, crippling and even killing prostitutes, and had pioneered a sick new form of polo that entailed running down stray dogs with cars.

Immediately after Harvath had read the dossier Nicholas had compiled, he couldn't wait to get his hands on him.

This target, though, was more difficult than the others. This one was a "twofer" and as such, it had to be executed flawlessly.

Even more than the son, Harvath wanted the Russian President to suffer. He wanted to grab the elder Peshkov by the throat, cut his eyes out with a penknife, and slowly lower him into a vat of acid, but that pain would have only been temporary. That wasn't good enough.

Harvath wanted Peshkov to suffer, as he

had suffered in losing Lara, Lydia, and the Old Man. He wanted the Russian President's pain to last for years. That was why he and Alexandra were here now.

The Federal Security Officers sitting in the cars outside Misha's loft hated the President's son as much as the rest of Moscow did. Harvath and Alexandra had no problem slipping past.

The officers posted inside the building were a different story.

Affixing a suppressor to the Old Man's 1911, Harvath had Alexandra in her short skirt, dark wig, and thigh-high boots come in the front door, while he entered from the back.

Having done presidential protective details, Harvath knew the extent to which the United States went to keep the children of prominent politicians safe. What he saw in the lobby was stunning.

There were two security agents in total. They were both focused on the front door, which allowed him to come in from the back unchallenged.

While Alexandra engaged Tweedledee and Tweedledum, telling them she was supposed to meet a girlfriend there for a party in one of the lofts, and they stared transfixed at the tops of her breasts in her low-cut top,

Harvath hit the stairs.

He had no idea if the twenty-six-year-old would be by himself or surrounded by some lowlife "posse." Either way, Harvath had a plan.

Creeping up to the top of the stairs, a pair of latex gloves on, he slowly pulled back the exit door and looked out.

For a moment, he couldn't believe it. Then he had to remind himself that he was in Russia. There were absolutely no guards on this floor.

That didn't mean there wasn't a guard inside the unit, but from what he had seen so far, he doubted it. The lazy perimeter security was an excellent indication of how little the guards thought of the President's son.

Walking over to the apartment door, Harvath pressed his pistol up against it and softly knocked.

Based on Nicholas's research, the man was a gamer. He spent up to sixteen hours some days on his Xbox. Harvath hoped that he was gaming now. The fact that no one had responded to his knock made him feel his hope wasn't without merit. It was also a pretty good indication that there was no guard waiting on the other side.

Removing his picks, he went to work. Like

everything else in Russia, the lock was a piece of shit. Within seconds, he was inside.

He crept forward into the loft until he heard someone cursing in Russian and froze.

With the 1911 against his chest in the Sul position, ready to be thrust out into the fight, he waited. The seconds passed interminably slowly. The pause felt like an eternity.

Finally he heard Misha howl with laughter and begin taunting some unseen person all over again. *The little motherfucker was definitely on his Xbox.*

This was Harvath's opportunity, and he moved cautiously forward.

In the large living room at the end of hall, Misha sat at a sleek glass and chrome desk, surrounded by empty bags of potato chips and energy drink cans.

With his eyes focused on the screen and headphones cutting off his hearing, he had no idea Harvath was right behind him until it was too late.

He felt the stab of the syringe as it was jabbed into the left side of his neck and the cold of the liquid content as it rushed into his body.

He reached for a panic button, but Harvath pulled his chair back before he could get to it.

The sux was fast acting. It was the last thing Peshkov's hideous son was able to do before paralysis overtook him. Death was not far behind.

Removing the vials of heroin, a dirty shoelace for a tourniquet, and a new needle, he got to work. The scene didn't have to be perfect, only believable.

When everything was complete, he texted Alexandra, and backed out of the apartment.

He took the stairs down to the ground floor, unscrewed the suppressor from his pistol, and put everything in his coat pockets. Then, he exited the building the same way he had come in. The security officers remained none the wiser.

They wouldn't roll back the CCTV footage until much later. And by then it would be too late.

Meeting Alexandra two blocks down, he climbed into her car and turned up the heater.

"How did it go?" she asked, as she put her car in gear and pulled out into traffic.

"Perfect," he replied. "There's only one thing left to do. Do you have the key for me?"

"Glove box," Alexandra said, nodding at it.

Harvath opened it and withdrew a small envelope with a post office box key inside. He was pleased. "Now all we have to do is decide on the best way to get it to him."

She looked at her watch and smiled. "I think I have an idea. How about a visit to the Ritz?"

Chapter 82

Getting anywhere near the Russian President was out of the question. The same was true for handing him any sort of a note or package. Felix Botnik, his Chief of Staff, though, was something else entirely.

A confirmed bachelor, Botnik was a renowned man about town. He was also a creature of habit, which drove the intelligence services crazy.

It was well known that he ate twice a week at one of Moscow's trendiest restaurants — the O2 Lounge on the twelfth floor of the Ritz Carlton Hotel.

Completely enclosed in glass, the rooftop establishment was popular for its stunning views of the Kremlin and of Red Square. The views inside, though, were said to be even better.

Every night, the O2 Lounge was packed with the city's richest, most powerful, and most beautiful people — making it the place to see and be seen.

It was always wall-to-wall, and if you weren't plugged in, you weren't going to ever find a seat as every table was marked with a "reserved" placard. As Chief of Staff to President Peshkov, Botnik didn't have that problem.

Arriving at O2, his table was already waiting for him. So was a crisp, off-white, Ritz Carlton envelope with his name neatly written across the front.

Opening it, he withdrew a small, flat key that looked as if it could have been to a safety deposit box. With it was a handwritten note on the hotel's stationery.

It simply said: *To President Fedor Peshkov. From Scot Harvath.* And it included an address.

Harvath had gotten the stationery at the front desk, written the note, and then carried the envelope upstairs, where he paid a waiter $100 to make sure it would be waiting for Botnik when he arrived.

The moment Botnik read Harvath's name on the note, he knew they were in trouble. His biggest concern was that the President might be at risk. Pulling out his cell phone, he had dialed Peshkov's Chief of Security and had headed quickly for the elevator.

By the time his driver had pulled up

downstairs, a plan had already been formulated and put in motion.

The drive to the main post office on Myasnitskaya took almost twenty minutes in Moscow traffic. By the time he arrived, the police had already closed off the street and an evacuation was under way. If Harvath had placed a bomb, they wanted to make sure that they kept the loss of life to a minimum.

It took an additional forty-five minutes before the bomb disposal team was on scene and could send their robot in. Opening the post office box, though, proved impossible. They needed a human for the job and suiting up one of the technicians took an additional twenty minutes. Shortly thereafter, they finally retrieved the letter.

After X-raying and testing it for hazardous materials, it was handed over to Botnik. Per its postmarks, the letter had been sent more than two weeks ago from the United States — Washington, D.C., to be specific. The sender was listed as Scot Harvath, and the return address Botnik had to look up on his phone. It turned out to belong not to Harvath, but rather to the International Spy Museum. If he was trying to be funny, the Chief of Staff didn't find it amusing.

Knowing that the President was waiting

on what they had found, he returned to his car to make the call. He had his driver remain outside the vehicle.

As Botnik read the letter, his heart froze in his chest. The things Harvath was threatening to do to Josef Kozak, General Minayev, and the President's son were horrifying.

On the other end of the line, he could hear Peshkov shouting directions to his security people to check on Misha, as well as to warn Minayev, and to alert the hospital Josef Kozak was being treated at.

Botnik's eyes scanned the rest of the letter. It ended with a final warning from Harvath. The only reason he had spared the Russian President was so that he would spend the rest of his life grieving his son — just as Harvath would grieve his wife and two dear friends. If Peshkov took any steps to retaliate, Harvath promised to find him and kill him in the most horrific way imaginable.

As the Chief of Staff finished reading, he heard the President cry out in anguish.

"Misha," Peshkov wailed. "No!"

CHAPTER 83

Little Torch Key
Florida

Harvath had been tempted to park himself near the Moscow post office to watch the fireworks, but Alexandra had warned him about pushing their luck. She had been right, of course.

She had also been right about getting the PO box key to Botnik at the Ritz. It had worked perfectly. As soon as he had left the envelope with the waiter in the O2 Lounge, he had exited the hotel, and met back up with her a couple of blocks away for the six-hour drive back to the border with Belarus. Though he would have liked to have gotten some sleep, he kept his eyes open and his head on a swivel the entire way.

When they met up with the Old Man's smugglers and said their good-byes, he thanked her. She had taken a lot of risks on his behalf and he wanted her to know how much he appreciated it. Without her, this could have very well turned into a suicide operation.

Climbing into the smuggler's truck, he made himself comfortable for his next six hours of driving to the border with Poland. There, he'd at least be back in NATO territory, though he couldn't let his guard down. At least not fully.

It wasn't until he was back on The Carlton Group jet and in the air that the weight of everything he had been under started to lift. Once he was in international airspace, he got up and poured himself a drink.

Returning to his seat, he raised the glass and toasted the Old Man. He hoped that somewhere, up there, Reed was proud of him.

As he sat there, sipping his bourbon, Harvath conducted a mental after-action report. He went over every single detail, contemplating what he could have done differently, and where appropriate, what he could have done better.

Once his review was complete, he went through all of it again, looking for anything that might identify Alexandra, or tie her directly to him. Fortunately, there was nothing he could come up with to be worried about.

From Josef's hospital where she had avoided the cameras and had stayed bundled up, to the interaction with Minayev's mistress where she had worn the balaclava, and finally to the security guards at Misha's loft where she had been wearing a dark wig and heavy makeup while making sure to never face the cameras, she had been the perfect partner. Even outside on Moscow's streets, she had made sure they stayed in the shadows.

Alexandra, thinking of everything, had taken down the telephone number of the management company for the building where they had left the hospital worker tied up. She had promised to phone in either a noise complaint or some sort of anonymous tip, so that the man would be found and cut loose.

He didn't know how she planned to get the envelopes full of cash up to Sini and everyone else, but he assumed that would be done anonymously as well. The less she showed her face, the better. There was no reason, especially after the fact, for her to be tied to any of that. Peshkov, eventually, was going to sift through everything that had happened, looking for someone to punish.

Harvath, though, would be far outside his

grasp, and he'd be insane to come after him again. The Russian President had gotten what was coming to him.

That left Harvath with only one loose end: Artur Kopec, whom Nicholas had gone to bat for.

While Kopec had admitted sharing information about his pending visit at the New Hampshire safe house, he claimed to have had no idea that an assault had been planned. Nicholas, who was famous for his shockproof bullshit detector, had believed him. It was why he had gone to bat for him and had asked Harvath to spare his life. He was also still an incredibly valuable asset and had played a minor role in getting Harvath out of Russia.

Harvath would need to speak with the Polish Intelligence officer himself before he would be satisfied. For the moment, he was content, albeit grudgingly, to let him live.

After a second drink and some hot food, Harvath had stretched out on the couch and closed his eyes.

He had felt sure that he'd fall asleep instantly. Sleep, though, didn't come. Instead, his thoughts had turned to Lara.

He went through all the recriminations — all the things he could have and should have done differently, all the things he wanted to tell her but never did, all of the time he had wasted taking extra assignments downrange because the jobs had sounded exciting, he went through all of it.

And then once he had steeped in it good and long, when the plane was getting ready to land, he put it all away. He packed it up in that iron box inside his mind and forced himself to look forward.

What was he going to do next? That was the question he needed most to answer, and the answer wasn't going to be easy. He hoped that taking some time off would help focus his mind.

When the jet touched down at Naval Air Station Key West, he was beyond ready to be done traveling. All he wanted to do was sit in one warm place and not move.

As the plane came to a stop and the pilot shut down the engines, the copilot opened the forward door and dropped the air stairs. Harvath thanked them for the ride and stepped outside.

He saw rustling palm trees and could smell the salt of the ocean. The balmy, humid air was nothing like what he had experienced in Russia. Closing his eyes, he stood there for a moment, feeling the sun on his skin and soaking it all in.

Soon enough, the roar from a pair of

F/A-18 Hornets shook him from his reverie. There'd be plenty of time for kicking back once he got to the resort.

Nicholas had arranged for a car, which was parked just outside the base commander's office. The keys had been left inside the gas cap as promised. It had that new car smell, overheated by being left in the sun, that reminded him of vacations he had taken as a kid.

Driving out through the main gate, he headed north twenty-five miles up US-1 to Little Torch Key. At Pirates Road, he pulled into the parking lot for Little Palm Island Resort. He checked in at the thatch-roofed welcome station and was put on the next motor launch for the island. He was the only guest aboard.

He had always loved Little Palm Island, because the only way to get there was by boat or seaplane. Sitting on the rear deck of the launch, he once again closed his eyes.

Suddenly, he felt a lot more charitable toward those SEALs who had foresworn cold winters for more tropical climes. Cutting through the open water, sea spray on his face, this was something he could see himself getting used to.

A pretty young crew member, tan, blonde, and in her twenties, appeared from the wheelhouse and brought him a freshly made rum concoction on a silver tray.

Thanking her and settling back with his cocktail, he looked out at the setting sun as it began its slow descent toward the horizon. This was definitely something he could get used to.

When the boat pulled up to the dock at Little Palm Island, he was met by one of the staff, who welcomed him back and led him to his West Indies–style bungalow, all of its doors and windows open wide to the breeze. Harvath recognized it immediately. It was the same room he had stayed in last time.

An ice bucket with a bottle of champagne had been placed on the coffee table. And even though his reservation had been for one, there were two glasses.

It seemed sad being in such a beautiful spot all alone. That must have been what the waiter had thought as he or she was setting everything up. One glass was sad, final. A second glass offered promise, possibility.

Removing the foil and unwinding the cage, he opened the champagne and poured himself a glass.

Sitting upon the luggage rack at the foot of the bed was the suitcase Sloane had been kind enough to pack for him and ship down.

He opened it, interested to see what she had packed, but it was empty. The staff had already hung his clothes and put everything away.

Crossing to the closet, he opened the doors and looked inside. As with his clothes for the funeral, she had been kind, packing good, conservative staples. She had also packed his running shoes, and in the dresser, he saw that she had included his workout clothes.

He was about to take his champagne out to the terrace when he noticed a large padded envelope sitting on the desk. There was nothing written on it, but he assumed that it had been among the items the staff had unpacked for him from his suitcase. Setting his glass down, he opened it.

For a moment, he couldn't believe what he was seeing. Inside was the framed, silver picture of Lara from his bedroom back in Virginia.

There she stood, on his dock, in her sundress, with a glass of white wine in her hand.

It was the same image of her that had come to him after he had fallen through the ice in Russia. Lara, in that same sundress, with that same glass of wine, had beckoned him to the safety and life-saving warmth of the trapper's cabin.

Looking at it now, he couldn't help but wonder if she was once again trying to save his life.

Whatever it was that she was trying to tell him, he now had plenty of time to listen.

Picking up the picture, and his glass, he headed outside. The sun was almost low enough to touch the water. He wanted to watch it disappear. Then he wanted to start thinking about what he was going to do next.

ACKNOWLEDGMENTS

I want to start out by thanking the most wonderful people in the writing process — you, the **readers**. You make all of the hard work worth it. Thank you for reading my books and for telling people about them.

Next, I want to thank the exceptional **booksellers**, who not only ignite passion for reading, but also fan the flames. You are gateways to incredible adventures, and I thank you for bringing my books and readers together.

As with every novel, I save this space to thank the courageous men and women who protect and defend our way of life. They work in intelligence, in the military, and in law enforcement. Several assisted with *Backlash,* and while I cannot openly name them, I want them to know how deeply grateful I am. Any and all mistakes herein are mine and mine alone.

Robert C. O'Brien (to whom this book

is dedicated) is an exceedingly good man who has given much to the country. You couldn't ask for a better neighbor or friend. I am honored to know him and deeply appreciate all that he has done for me and our nation.

James Ryan, **Sean Fontaine**, and **Chad Norberg** are three of my dearest friends. They are always there for me, especially when I need to kick ideas around. I thank them not only for their help with the book, but also for their continued dedication to doing what is right, no matter how hard, nor how dangerous.

Rob Saale, FBI (ret.) provided some incredibly helpful background for the book. Thank you for everything, but especially for your service to our great nation.

Michael Maness, CIA (ret.) was very generous with his time as I assembled the research for the book. Hopefully, by the time this goes to print, I will have taken him for a proper steak dinner and thanked him face-to-face.

Kristian J. Kelley, Deputy Chief, Gilford Police Department, could not have been kinder or more professional. As he is a graduate of the FBI's National Academy, I was impressed both with his experience and his commitment to his community. Thank you for your help.

U.S. Navy SEAL **Jack Carr** (ret.) was once again incredibly helpful with details for this book. He also continues to be one hell of a thriller author. If you haven't checked out his books yet, do it. You'll love his writing. Thank you, Jack.

U.S. Navy SEALs **Pete Scobell** (ret.), **Marcus Luttrell** (ret.), and **Paul Craig** (ret.) were also very kind with their time. Getting the details right is important to me, and I appreciate their help. Thank you, gentlemen.

John Barklow, U.S. Navy (ret.) has trained some of the most elite warriors on the planet in cold-weather survival. His discussions with me early on helped frame what Harvath would be facing and what he'd need to do to get out alive. I really appreciate all of his insight and exceptional expertise. Thanks, John.

Carey Lohrenz, U.S. Navy (ret.) and **Kenneth Johnson** are two impressive aviators who were incredibly helpful with all things airplane-related. Thank you.

My thanks as well go to my longtime friend **Patrick Ahern** for his digging into foreign snowmobiles for me. Hopefully, sometime soon, we'll get the chance to retrace some of our favorite routes via sled.

I have been with the outstanding people at **Simon & Schuster** since my very first thriller and want each and every one of them to know how much I value what they do for me, and how much I enjoy working with them.

Captaining the ship is the incomparable **Carolyn Reidy**. An author couldn't ask to work with a more respected, talented, and committed pro. Thank you for everything.

My magnificent publisher and editor, **Emily Bestler**, is what an author dreams about when they imagine a career as a writer. She is not only an incredible editor, but also an unfailing champion of her authors and a stellar publisher. She and her team at **Emily Bestler Books** blow me away with each book we do together. Thank you, all!

Atria publisher **Libby McGuire** and Associate publisher **Suzanne Donahue**, thank you for all of your incredible support!

Kristin Fassler and **Dana Trocker** in marketing, your enthusiasm, hard work, and fresh ideas are so appreciated.

Tons of work goes on behind the scenes in order to bring a book to market. To that end, I want to also call out and thank the amazing **Gary Urda**, the remarkable **Jonathan Karp**, and the unparalleled **John Hardy**. I couldn't do it without you.

Jen Long and the entire crew at **Pocket Books** are nothing short of fantastic. Thank you for your continued commitment to excellence and going the extra mile. I deeply appreciate all of you.

The **Simon & Schuster audio division** is composed of some of the coolest, most creative people you will ever meet. I extend my deepest thanks for another record-setting year to the phenomenal **Chris Lynch, Tom Spain, Sarah Lieberman, Desiree Vecchio, Karen Pearlman**, and **Armand Schultz**. You all are the best.

Speaking of the best, I want to give a BIG thank-you to the outstanding **Atria, Emily Bestler Books**, and **Pocket Books sales teams**. They knock it out of the park every single day. Without you, nothing else would be possible. Thank you a million times over.

David Brown, my sensational publicist, continues to crush it. From planning my elaborate tours, to handling all the wonderful media requests that come in, he tackles everything with exuberance and style. It is a pleasure to work with someone who is so good at what he does and takes such joy in doing it. Thank you, David.

Cindi Berger and the **team at PMK-BNC** are absolutely stupendous. The added PR wizardry they bring each year is simply incredible. Thank you for continuing to knock it out of the park.

One of my greatest joys of being at Simon & Schuster is being able to work with some amazingly talented people. These astonishing folks work tirelessly, and I want to express to them how grateful I am for everything they do for me. My thanks to the remarkable **Colin Shields, Paula Amendolara, Janice Fryer, Adene Corns, Liz Perl,** and **Lisa Keim**. In addition, I have to thank the exceptional **Gregory Hruska, Mark Speer,** and **Stuart Smith**. Thank you, all.

While I'm calling out stellar members of the Simon & Schuster family, I also want to recognize the fantastic **Lara Jones** at Emily Bestler Books. You do tons for me all year through. Thank you. I really appreciate you.

One of my favorite people at Simon & Schuster is also one of its hardest working, the unparalleled **Al Madocs** of the Atria/Emily Bestler Books Production Department. Al, I value your eagle eye more than you will ever know. Thank you for everything.

Thank you to the out-of-this-world talents, especially **Jimmy Iacobelli**, at the Atria/Emily Bestler Books and Pocket Books Art Departments. The stunning visuals you help to create truly set us apart.

Once again, I'd like to thank the fabulous **Saimah Haque, Sienna Farris, Whitney McNamara**, and **David Krivda** for another amazing year. Thank you for all that you do for me.

My beloved agent **Heide Lange** of **Sanford J. Greenburger Associates** is simply spectacular. Our partnership, as well as our friendship, continue to be two of my proudest accomplishments. My gratitude for everything that she has done for me knows no bounds. Thank you, Heide, from the bottom of my heart.

Heide is assisted by her world-class team, including **Samantha Isman** and **Iwalani Kim**. All of you at **Sanford J. Greenburger Associates** are like family to me, and I cannot thank you enough for another fantastic year!

Yvonne Ralsky — you are nothing short of superb. Every year, we set the bar higher and you keep coming up with new ways to leap over it. You know how much I value you, but I always enjoy putting it down in writing for everyone else to see. Thank you for everything.

They don't get any better than my marvelous entertainment attorney, **Scott Schwimer**. Handsome, humble, and wicked smart, I could neither have written a truer a friend, nor a fiercer advocate into my life. Thank you, Scottie, for being you.

Finally, I get to say my biggest thanks of all. To **my absolutely fantastic family** — thank you. Thank you for all of your love, your support, and the never-ending joy you bring me. Writing novels is a deeply satisfying career, but it would mean nothing without all of you. I love you more than I can ever put into words.

ABOUT THE AUTHOR

Brad Thor is the #1 *New York Times* bestselling author of eighteen thrillers, including *Spymaster, Use of Force, The Last Patriot* (nominated best thriller of the year by the International Thriller Writers Association), *Blowback* (recognized as one of the "Top 100 Killer Thrillers of All Time" by NPR), *The Athena Project,* and *Foreign Influence* (one of *Suspense Magazine*'s best political thrillers of the year). Visit his website at BradThor.com and follow Brad on Facebook at Facebook.com/BradThorOfficial and on Twitter @BradThor.

MAJOR EUROPEAN GOVERNMENTS

The Dorsey Series in Political Science

Consulting Editor   SAMUEL PATTERSON   *University of Iowa*

MAJOR EUROPEAN GOVERNMENTS

ALEX N. DRAGNICH, Ph.D.
Professor of Political Science
Vanderbilt University

JORGEN RASMUSSEN, Ph.D.
Professor of Political Science
Iowa State University

Fifth Edition

1978

 The Dorsey Press   Homewood, Illinois   60430

Irwin-Dorsey Limited   Georgetown, Ontario   L7G 4B3

ISBN 0-256-02054-X
Library of Congress Catalog Card No. 77–088311

Printed in the United States of America

3 4 5 6 7 8 9 0 MP 5 4 3 2 1 0

Preface

This fifth edition continues the collaboration which began in the fourth edition. Alex Dragnich is responsible primarily for the section on the Soviet Union, while Jorgen Rasmussen is responsible for the other sections. Nonetheless, this edition continues to be a collaborative work which has developed out of and built upon the original single-author book. Those familiar with previous editions will find much that they are used to—particularly in the basic organization—but they also will note changes, based on some of the newer developments in the study of politics.

Four of the six main sections of the book deal with single major political systems. Although we do compare these systems to others, including the United States, basically we examine each system separately. These sections have been revised and updated. The amount of change has depended upon events in each country since the previous edition and the availability of new analyses of their politics. This edition contains more illustrative material and graphics where these help to clarify or emphasize a particular point being made in the text.

The Introduction discusses the study of comparative politics without detailed reference to a particular political system. This section seeks to provide a general guide to the study of political systems. It introduces topics that will be the main focal points in the sections dealing with a single country and seeks to explain why these particular themes deserve study. Thus it provides an outline that can be used to study countries not included in this book.

Part V is new to this edition. The first portion of this section, dealing with Eurocommunism, covers a subject not considered in any systematic way in the previous edition. By the late 1970s this topic clearly had attained such importance to European politics that it merits consideration. Furthermore, this could adequately be done only in a comparative context and not as part of a section devoted to a single country. The latter portion of Part V combines topics previously covered in the final chapters of the British, French, and German sections. We decided we could assess the strengths and weaknesses of these political systems more effectively when they were compared and contrasted directly with each other rather than against some abstract standard. Evaluating these three democracies comparatively also enabled us to clarify the circumstances within which Eurocommunism has come to be a significant political development. Finally, the themes and organization of Part V provide the transition from European democracy to Soviet dictatorship. This was missing in the previous edition. Part V thus deals with recent significant political developments and also serves to integrate the book more effectively than in previous editions.

Studying a new subject usually requires learning a new vocabulary and becoming familiar with new concepts. We have tried to keep unfamiliar terms to a minimum and to avoid needless jargon. We seek to write clear, relatively untechnical prose. We introduce only those terms and concepts that aid fuller understanding of a subject and those that need to be known for further study in comparative politics.

We hope that students and faculty will find this edition to be useful and interesting. We are happy that some people appreciate our approach to the introductory study of comparative politics and we are happy to serve that clientele with this book.

In previous editions we have expressed our thanks to readers who have provided us with helpful comments. We are particularly pleased, in connection with this edition, to acknowledge the detailed and insightful observations of Peter B. Heller of Manhattan College and Robert C. Davey of Jackson Community College. Understandably, final responsibility for what is in this book must remain our own.

January 1978   ALEX N. DRAGNICH
                                        JORGEN RASMUSSEN

Contents

part IV
THE FEDERAL REPUBLIC OF GERMANY

Part I
INTRODUCTION

Introduction

THE ESSENCE OF POLITICS

Politics is, as one eminent political scientist has said, about "who gets what, when, how." In other words, politics is about conflict—its nature and the methods designed to cope with it. Some view the main function of organized government to be that of channeling conflict, that is, keeping it from erupting into violence. To be sure, politics is also concerned with wars, riots, and other disruptive acts, but in the main it deals with how society organizes to resolve conflicting and competing interests in ways that will not tear that society apart.

This book deals with the politics of four large, Western nations, each of which in the last century has known violent, as well as peaceful, political conflict. Britain has been the most stable, the least turbulent of the four. Domestic violence had been of little consequence in Britain during the 20th century until the late 1960s, when the dormant virus of religious discrimination and bigotry erupted anew in Northern Ireland. Thus in the 1970s snipings, fire bombings, and street fighting became common occurrences and a Catholic young lady even was tarred and feathered because she planned to marry a non-Catholic British soldier who was part of the peace-keeping force in Northern Ireland. In France the serious danger of an invasion of Paris by French paratroopers to seize control of the government brought one constitutional system to an end in 1958 and started the process for a new regime. Ten years later this regime found itself besieged by students and workers, who battled police in the streets and from behind barricades, events which contributed significantly to the process of driving the President from office the following year despite the fact

3

that he had served little more than half his term. Disruptive student demonstrations in the late 1960s in Germany made many wonder whether the
country was returning to the street fighting and political assassinations
that were rife during the Weimar Republic after World War I. That German experience with democracy ended when the Nazis came to power.
Through their secret police and concentration camps they practiced terror
and violence on a scale so vast as to be unbelievable. In Russia the
autocratic rule of the Tsar was terminated at the time of World War I by a
revolution and civil war, only to be replaced by an even more coercive
and repressive regime. The Communists engaged in systematic execution
of countless opponents and even purged hundreds of thousands of members of their own party. The millions of people sent to forced labor camps
exceeded even the number confined by the Nazis. In the quarter of a
century since the death of Stalin in 1953 the level of violence in Soviet
politics has declined markedly, although dissidents and various minority
groups are still subjected to persecution.

Violence is to be found in all societies, including the American. Sometimes it comes in cycles, alternating between adjustment or compromise
and a lashing out in destructive acts. Also, the level of violence clearly
differs from one society to another. Why should this be? Is it just that
there are more bad people in the Soviet Union than in Britain? Is it
because the Soviet leaders believe in "godless Communism" while the
British are thought to believe in socialism, which, perhaps, is not quite so
"godless?" And what about history? What difference does it make that
France has had over a dozen different regimes in the last 200 years while
Britain has had only one?

THE SCIENTIFIC METHOD AND THE
COMPARATIVE STUDY OF POLITICS

These comments provide concrete examples of the fundamental problem of politics—how to maintain social order while processing conflict
demands—and suggest why comparative study of politics is useful. As
people begin to acquire some knowledge of government and politics in
other countries, they are struck by the differences in political life. They
investigate further to obtain additional information. Then they seek to
account for the differences they have found: how can they explain the fact
that things are one way in one country and another in another? Is life to
remain a mystery—one surprise after another when things are pleasant
and one frustration after another when they are not? Or can some pattern
of events be discovered, an association or link among them which might
suggest a causal relation? Such a necessary relation would explain the
differences originally noted. But the explanation can be only a tentative

one until it is determined whether it is supported by the available evidence.

This is the process of making scientific discoveries, which are no more than new ways of thinking about familiar things. Such discoveries are desirable either for their practical utility or because their ability to explain why things happen as they do satisfies our curiosity. The familiar things explained are observed regularities—whenever it gets sufficiently cold outside, puddles of water freeze. These observed regularities are only descriptive reports, which do not explain anything. The mere fact that two things always have occurred together or in sequence is no guarantee that they will continue to do so. Thus the process of scientific discovery requires going beyond description to analysis.

The process of analysis separates an event into its component parts to help reveal relations, especially those which might not be readily apparent. This procedure helps to generate hypotheses—tentative solutions to problems, suggestions for interpreting data so that they make sense. The usefulness of these tentative solutions is tested through experimentation or observation. The experimental approach is preferable, since it tends to minimize the errors or distracting factors that are inherent in unplanned or unmanipulatable observations. By this process of verification, hypotheses are either rejected or transformed into laws.

A scientific law states the form and scope of a regularity. It tells how things known to be connected are related, whether, for example, they increase in size together or whether the one gets larger as the other gets smaller. It tells the circumstances in which the law applies, whether, for instance, it is true only when the temperature is above freezing. The significance of a law is that it implies that the stated relation is a necessary one, thus going beyond the mere report of an observed regularity.

When a number of laws whose scope has been established can be interrelated, the resulting system of knowledge is a theory. A theory's validity depends upon its ability to account for many diverse data simply and economically. The geocentric theory of the universe, for example, was abandoned not because it was disproven—it was not certain that the sun did not revolve around the earth—but because increasingly complex and elaborate explanations were required to make this theory conform with newly acquired information about the movement of heavenly bodies. As the explanations became more cumbersome the utility of continuing to cling to the theory decreased greatly and created pressures for a theory that could explain the available data more simply and would be more productive of useful subsidiary laws.

It is at this point that we come full circle in describing the process of scientific investigation. A theory helps to make a generalization into a law by providing reasons for the regularities observed. Furthermore, one can deduce from a theory what relations should prevail if the theory is correct and thus search for regularities not previously discovered. Should these regularities then be found, they can be established as laws, further buttressing the theory's validity.

As we noted, experimentation is a key method in the process of scientific discovery. Unfortunately, it rarely is possible in political science; people, unlike laboratory rats, are not expendable and do not tolerate being manipulated. Therefore, political scientists usually have to settle for observation, for gaining their data from uncontrolled situations and events. In an effort to avoid being misled by the presence of extraneous factors in the research sites they are forced to use, political scientists endeavor to compare political phenomena across national boundaries. If they can discover the same regularity in more than one country, they feel more certain that there is some link between the associated objects and that the relation is not a spurious one. Thus cross-national generalizations are essential for an empirically grounded theory of politics.

The idea of comparing political systems is by no means new. Hundreds of years ago Aristotle made a good beginning when he attempted to classify the constitutions of several Greek city states. Some critics feel in fact that political scientists have not advanced much in their study of politics since that time. They believe that students of politics have been content merely to observe political phenomena superficially or impressionistically and to describe laws, constitutions, and formal governmental structures without attempting to investigate political practice and the significant forces that move a particular political system. The result is to settle for, at best, comparative description, rather than analysis. To improve this condition they advocate more systematic and rigorous research with as great precision as existing research techniques will permit.

If one had an encyclopedic mind and a computer's ability to manipulate data, it would be possible to compare all of the world's nations, both past and present, at the same time. Lacking these capacities, one must restrict one's focus and select from among available alternatives. In this book we have chosen to discuss four countries that have some characteristics in common but which also exhibit many interesting contrasts—for example, levels of political violence. All four of these nations are major international powers. (Perhaps one should be called a superpower to distinguish its much greater strength internationally.) And three of them are European nations, while the Soviet Union is both European and Asian. Thus although these nations differ from the United States in many ways, Americans should find them more familiar than they would African, Asian, or, perhaps, even Latin-American countries. Study of them should be most useful in gaining perspective on American political practices. It also means that the three European ones are more likely to have some elements in their history and heritage in common than they would if we selected a country from each of the corners of the world. This should aid comparison, as should the fact that the Soviet Union's location and history have partially Westernized it.

The purpose of this book is to synthesize and report the results of previous investigation, thereby giving the reader a fuller knowledge of four important countries' political processes. This will be done from a comparative perspective so that the similarities and differences in these processes are emphasized. We will discuss some of the hypotheses and tentative explanations that seek to account for these differences and similarities. Our purpose is not so much to provide answers, however, as it is to raise questions and stimulate discussion, thereby encouraging further investigation. We hope that students will enter into a dialogue with the book. We wish to provide sufficient basic information to permit some generalization and to offer a few examples of useful generalizations based on this information. Thus it will be possible to move somewhat beyond the factual level toward abstraction and theoretical insight. This procedure should yield a fuller understanding of the process of governing.

DEMOCRATIC AND AUTOCRATIC POLITICAL SYSTEMS

We have observed that social conflict is common and the attempt to deal with it nonviolently a constantly pressing concern. Why should this be true? An ultimate answer would turn on one's conception of the nature of humans. Are people fundamentally good and simply corrupted by malignant social structures, as Communists assert? Or are they essentially and incorrigibly sinful, as Christians believe? We need not go this far, however, in answering the question. It is sufficient to observe that even in a prosperous country like the United States resources are scarce and, therefore, some people will not be satisfied with their allotment. If it is not to be everyone for themselves on the basis of whatever modes of conduct they choose to follow, if there is to be any kind of community, then there must be some rules, behavioral boundaries, accepted practices or procedures to structure action. Only if individual and group power is restrained can there be any kind of social order. Someone has to make the rules; someone has to assign the benefits; someone has to be able to apply any sanctions necessary to implement these decisions. A society's government is composed of whatever structures in that society are widely recognized as being properly engaged in these activities and as possessing as well the exclusive authority to set the limits within which force may be used legitimately. Political struggle between various segments of society involves their utilizing whatever power they may possess to try to control the government. Those segments that succeed will be able to make authoritative decisions—those that are binding throughout the society—or alter the procedures for making them.

Thus there are two basic political problems. First, given conflicting individual goals, wants, and needs, how is it possible to maintain social order? How is it possible to get people to obey authoritative decisions that they do not like? Especially, how is it possible to get them to do so voluntarily, assuming an ethical preference for a minimum of coercion? Second, how can the exercise of authoritative power be controlled to prevent the loss of freedom? In ancient Rome the question was put: *Quis custodiet ipsos custodes?* "Who will guard against those who themselves are guards?" How can we insure that those to whom we entrust the power to settle conflicts nonviolently do not abuse their power to tyrannize everyone? By what means can we call the wielders of political power to account to ensure that the use of authoritative power is responsible?

Whether political decision makers are accountable, whether political power is responsible—on such considerations turn one of the fundamental distinctions between types of political systems. Systems where these conditions prevail are democracies; those where on balance they do not are autocracies. Democracy is government by the people. But, since a nation obviously cannot be run by a mass town meeting, the ultimate test of democracy lies in whether those who govern can be removed peacefully when they no longer represent the majority will.

A democratic political system is built upon certain basic beliefs and principles. Although there is widespread agreement in non-Communist countries on these, the actual institutional arrangements of particular democracies vary considerably. At the center of the democratic faith is the belief that the individuals are important, that political institutions exist to serve them rather than the reverse, and that the government, therefore, exists by virtue of their consent. Closely related is the belief that individuals can manage their own affairs better than someone else can do it for them. This does not require assuming that people make no mistakes, that they do not at times misconceive their own best interests. It assumes only that in the long run people usually are good judges and can distinguish wise from unwise policies and capable from incompetent leaders. And it asserts that those mistakes which occur are preferable to paternalistic government, however efficient it might be, for without the opportunity to make mistakes and learn from them, human growth would be impossible. People who were not permitted to think and decide for themselves but were allowed to act only on command would no longer be human beings, but animals or robots.

Nevertheless, there must be some limits on individual behavior. In seeking to develop themselves, individuals cannot be permitted to infringe on the rights of others to attempt to realize their potential. This is why democratic government always is in a state of dynamic tension. The importance of the individual must be tempered perpetually by the need for authority to guard the rights of others. Thus a democratic society must be a flexible one rather than a fixed order, an open society allowing for change. To some this is an agreeable idea, for they believe that people can be the masters of their fate. But in others, constant change, even the prospect of such change, produces anxiety. They cannot readily adjust to new ideas and new ways of doing things and thus feel threatened by innovation. Taken to an extreme, such feelings are likely to culminate in an authoritarian personality, one which would be more at home in a dictatorial, rather than a democratic, system.

The emphasis on the worth of the individual is expressed politically in democracies through the principles of political equality, majority rule, toleration of opposition, and rule of law. Since it is impossible to insure that everyone has exactly the same amount of political influence, the effort to attain political equality normally is restricted to eliminating all extraneous obstacles, such as religion and occupation, to the right to vote and hold office, and to giving the same weight to each vote. Differences over who should hold government offices and what policies should be implemented are resolved in favor of persons and policies that gain the most votes in honest and frequent elections.

But while the majority is to prevail, it is expected to be tolerant of the minority. Minority opinion should not be dismissed cavalierly. Dissenting groups and parties should be free to organize, to assemble, and to speak and write freely as they seek to persuade people to support their programs and policies. At the next election they can offer an alternative set of leaders for approval by the voters. Thus systems in which only one political party can operate freely are not conducive to democracy. Not all one-party systems can be classified automatically as autocracies, however. In some nations, especially some of the developing ones, a fair degree of governmental accountability and of choice among alternative officeholders prevails even though the right to organize politically is circumscribed. The nature of parties, rather than their number, is the crucial aspect. Some single parties are much more open to an internal diversity of views than are other more monolithic ones.

While the channels for participation may vary from one democracy to another, it is essential that the rule of law prevail. Sanctions are not to be applied arbitrarily. The rules must be clear and known in advance. Convictions must conform with due process, that is, must be obtained fairly—confessions based on torture are not permitted, for example. Everyone must be subject equally to the law. And the government is not above the law, it must be able to cite authorization for all its actions.

The basic arrangements by which a particular country seeks to implement these beliefs and principles are set forth in its constitution. Constitutions are almost invariably written—Britain is the best-known exception—but commonly are augmented as well by certain traditionally established political practices known as usages or conventions which, although unmentioned in the written constitution, are nonetheless an essential part of the country's political system.

Although constitution writing was common in the ancient world, modern interest in it dates from the growth of the idea of limited government several centuries ago. The original justification for seeking to limit royal power through a document emphasized natural law—the need to make explicit certain precepts of justice and right which were thought to be divinely inspired and, therefore, eternal. Subsequently, the defense of constitutionalism became more pragmatic—the need to have an ordered political system in which stability, agreed-upon procedures, and specified individual rights would prevail, thus minimizing arbitrariness and the likelihood of revolutionary disruptions. Now even this defense is questioned, since it is recognized that merely committing words to paper does not guarantee anything if the ruling officials refuse to abide by it. In some ways, the Soviet Union has a model constitution, but little of it is operative. Nevertheless, constitutions should not be dismissed as unimportant; even nondemocratic countries feel that they must have constitutions which appear to be democratic, clearly recognizing the importance of symbols in politics. And in democratic countries constitutions can embody national ideals and thus influence political behavior.

The structures and procedures contained in the constitution vary considerably from one democracy to another. There is no single set of political institutions which a country must have to qualify as democratic. One of the objectives of this book is to indicate some of the contrasts among the three democracies included. Yet the consensus which is essential to a stable democracy is an agreement on procedures, on the fundamental rules. Democracy is regarded by many as a method of arriving at political decisions; it need not imply any commitment to particular policies or goals. Such a commitment is more characteristic of utopian or millenarian dictatorial systems. It should be clear, then, that democracy does not require any particular type of economic system. Some countries, like Britain and France, have instituted a considerable amount of government ownership of economic enterprises and along with other countries, like Sweden, have established an extensive system of social welfare benefits. This does not make them any the less democratic; in fact some would argue that they are more democratic as a result. But this requires talking of "social" or "economic" democracy and loses sight of the point made above that democracy is a method. Beyond defense of the basic principles outlined previously, it makes no substantive demands upon a nation and leaves the choice of particular political, social, and economic structures up to each nation. Some of these systems may, in fact, work better than others. But, as we have observed, one of the hallmarks of democracy is to allow people freedom to make their own decisions and then to assess the results of their choices.

Since most Americans have lived only under democratic government, they tend to believe that this is a natural or typical state of affairs. It should be emphasized, however, that for most of history (even for most people today) one form or another of autocracy has been most common. A brief discussion of the differences among these systems will help to place in perspective the one included in this book—the Soviet Union.

Perhaps the earliest form of autocratic rule was exemplified by the chief of a tribe or clan. Such rulers still are to be found in places where tradition-bound societies exist in relative isolation. Greater numbers of people were ruled over by potentates who assumed the title of king or emperor. Various of these rulers assumed an aura of holiness or divinity as a means of legitimating their power. The ruler of Tibet prior to its conquest by China is one of the best contemporary examples.

Autocratic rule in the form of monarchy has been important in the history of Europe for most of the past 2,000 years. But modern European monarchies have become constitutional, with real political power vested in popularly elected officials. Elsewhere, however, particularly in some of the countries of the Middle East, the monarch's power remains virtually unlimited.

The oldest formalized dictatorship, still another form of autocratic rule, was found in ancient Rome. A leader often would be given extensive and unchallenged powers to deal with a certain crisis. But unlike most modern dictators, he was elected rather than self-designated and served for only a limited time, never more than six months. Perhaps the best known of such dictators was Cincinnatus (fifth century B.C.), a farmer who went back to his plow after having dealt with the situation that brought about the emergency grant of power. Modern democracies frequently provide for special reserve powers to meet crises. Their granting extraordinary powers to the executive sometimes is labelled "constitutional dictatorship."

In the modern world there are several types of autocracies. Some, including the quasi-military strong man type found in some Latin-American countries, have only limited aims and can be labelled dictatorships. In such regimes the dictator has complete control of the political and military establishments, and censorship and the police are used to suppress internal opposition. The dictator may have little or no interest, however, in the operation of the economy or in other activities of the society. Thus people are left to pursue their own goals unhindered, so long as these do not constitute a threat to the dictatorship or encroach upon the economic interests of those backing the regime.

The fully developed modern autocracy, however, is totalitarian—a label that includes both Nazi-Fascist and Communist types. Such systems are characterized by an official ideology—a system of ideas about the nature, operation, and goals of society. Unlike the democratic faith, these beliefs reject the idea that people can govern themselves, even though the political leaders may claim to speak for the people and to govern in their interest. No other beliefs are permitted to compete for public support. The official ideology, proclaimed and interpreted by those who rule the system, is the sole one.

This ideology is the guide in an effort to remake people and society totally. Totalitarianism, as the word suggests, means that the autocracy concerns itself with everything in the society. Politics comes to include personal, social, and cultural behavior, and all other aspects of life. The rulers seek to eliminate all private spheres of activity concerning the individual alone.

If the ideology is the guide for the transformation of society, the instrument for this process is the single, elite party. It is to protect, propagate, and implement the ideology. Therefore, this form of government sometimes is called "party dictatorship." All other political groups are outlawed and the pronouncements of the party must be accepted unquestioningly. Assisting the party are a variety of auxiliary agencies such as youth groups, women's organizations, and sport clubs. Only those groups approved and controlled by the party may exist. Thus these groups help to ensure that the people are occupied with acceptable activities and can be kept track of easily and mobilized to carry out the will of the state.

To help discourage any opposition, the rulers use terror and repression widely. The way in which victims are selected at times seems irrational, for it often is not clear to them how they have offended the state. This irrationality of sanctions is calculated to sow anxiety among the population and to discourage people from trusting or depending upon anyone. Thus it helps to eliminate all alternative centers of loyalty in the society and makes at least the appearance, if not the fact, of fervent commitment to the party and service to it the only possible hope of safety.

Certain elements of modern totalitarian regimes can be found in earlier authoritarian or despotic systems, but that does not mean that those systems were totalitarian. Unlike modern totalitarian governments, they did not seek to destroy or completely dominate all existing political, economic, and social relationships. They were not bent on undertaking large-scale social engineering with the aim of building a new unity around one ideology—that of the rulers. Totalitarianism is a phenomenon associated with the 20th century's technological advance.

TYPOLOGIES AND TYPES OF VARIABLES

What we have been doing in these last few pages is to outline a simple classification scheme or typology whose main types or categories are democracy, monarchy, dictatorship, and totalitarianism. The criteria for distinguishing among these types were the extent of popular distribution of political power, the security of fundamental rights, and the scope of governmental penetration into the society. Classifying political systems according to basic type is a good way to begin a rigorous study of comparative politics. Any classification system admittedly sacrifices some detailed information by grouping together for the sake of generalization things that are not exactly the same. No two people are alike, and yet they clearly have enough in common to be grouped together and distinguished from horses. In fact it is only when we begin to group things according to one or more criteria that we can discover just how much those objects grouped together have in common, and in what regards they differ from each other and from other objects not grouped with them. In other words, similarities and differences spring to view and one begins the process of questioning and seeking answers outlined previously in this chapter.

In addition to the typology just discussed at length, others frequently used in comparative politics are one-, two-, or multi-party system; presidential or parliamentary system; and federal or unitary system. Applying these to the countries included in this book, Britain, for example, is a two-party parliamentary democracy with a unitary division of powers, while Germany is a multi-party parliamentary democracy with a federal division of powers. Britain has never had a dictatorial government in modern times, while France had some experience with it in the 19th century and in the 20th century endured dictatorial government during the Nazi occupation of France in World War II. On the other hand, Germany provided one of the modern classic examples of totalitarian government from 1933 to 1945, and the Soviet Union has been a totalitarian system since the close of World War I.

Once political systems have been grouped according to type, and differences and similarities begin to emerge, where does one begin the search for explanations or reasons? In trying to discover why a country's politics is as it is, both political and nonpolitical factors should be considered. For example, must a country attain a certain level of economic development before it can become a democracy? Or, turning to political factors, does a federal division of powers affect the political party system differently than does a unitary division?

If the basic research question in the study of politics is formulated as: Who governs by what means for what purpose? then we are placing least emphasis on the latter part of the question. We will not be discussing individual motivation to any great extent nor will we proceed very far in examining the impact of societal goals upon the quality of life, except where this has particular relevance for the maintenance of the political system. We focus primarily upon ascertaining what groups exercise political power in each system and upon discussing the way in which and the structures through which they do so. We examine, then, the channels, procedures, and structures for the adjustment of conflict within the bounds of the prevailing political system in each of the four nations we have selected. This does not mean that we regard the prevailing systems as immutable. A system too rigid to adapt to changing circumstances is apt to be highly brittle. Therefore, we cannot ignore a concern with the process of systemic change and this concern may require some assessment of societal goals.

ENVIRONMENTAL CONSIDERATIONS

One of the intellectual battles that long have raged in psychology is whether one should seek the primary factors helping to explain an individual's behavior in environment or heredity—nurture or nature, as the choice is starkly put. Is a personality most shaped by those abilities with which a person is born or by the situations experienced and the training received after birth? Most psychologists probably would argue now that neither can be ignored and that whichever of the two has the greater impact may vary with the individual. So also in political science, we must not overlook the impact of environment upon political systems.

This needs to be stressed because political science has tended to slight geographic factors, largely as a reaction against geopolitics. This late 19th and early 20th century approach to international relations argued that the country which controlled Eastern Europe would dominate the heartland—the Eurasian land mass—and, thereby, the world. The fact that now this approach is largely discredited and considered a pseudoscience should not be allowed to eliminate geographic considerations from politics. A country's location can affect its politics. Where its boundaries are natural ones—rivers, oceans, mountains—rather than an arbitrary line drawn across an open plain, it may feel less threatened by its neighbors and be less likely to build up a strong military establishment and to accept militaristic values. Geographic barriers within a nation's borders can hamper communication and thwart development of a sense of national unity. Finally, a country's location and geographical characteristics will determine its supply of natural resources, which will have a major impact on both its domestic and foreign politics.

The supply of natural resources is an element in a country's level of economic development—to broaden the idea of environment beyond physical geographic factors. This topic has received considerable attention from political scientists in recent years, as many efforts have been made to relate various measures of economic development to type of political system. Some have argued that a high level of prosperity in a nation affects its politics by making political conflict less ideological and more pragmatic, thus reducing the heat and fervor of political battle. When the great majority of the people are relatively well-off, the conflict over the allocation of resources is presumed to be less sharp, thus facilitating compromise. Level of economic development also affects the class structure in politically important ways. Industrialization requires a large class of manual, mass-production workers, whose values and behavior are likely to differ rather markedly from the rest of the population. But as industrialization becomes fully mature, the proportion of manual workers in the work force begins to decline and the share composed of service workers rises sharply. In both their life style and economic situation such workers are likely to have much more in common with the middle class than are manual workers. Thus the relative change in these two groups' sizes would seem likely to contribute to greater similarity of outlook in a society and help to reduce the sharpness of political conflict.

Technological advance both requires and contributes to the improvement of a nation's communications network. This creates an opportunity for wider circulation of more information about government actions and eases popular communication of political preferences to governmental officials. Improved communications also can help to unify a country through the nationalizing effects of mass media on public opinion. In a more prosperous nation more money can be spent to provide mass, public education. Raising the educational level makes possible an intelligent use of the greater volume of information supplied by the improved communications network. Mass public education can contribute significantly to a common socialization process in which the predominant values of the society—both political and nonpolitical—are inculcated.

An advanced level of economic development with its necessary concentration of workers in major urban areas also gives rise to a host of complex problems foreign to the simple society of a pastoral economy— problems of transportation, health care, pollution, crime. Many of these can be dealt with effectively only by collective action through government, thus expanding the load of demands and wants which the political structures must process. So complex does life become that it is necessary for individuals and social structures to specialize if they are to have the abilities and knowledge needed to cope with contemporary problems. Efficiency demands that personnel be recruited, retained, and promoted on the basis of merit, rather than kinship or caste. This need to bureaucratize structures is not confined to the economic sector of a society, but is present as well in the political. Not only do particular structures become more complex, but the entire group system becomes more elaborate as new occupational and economic groups are created and grow with economic development. Many of these groups will have political objectives and, therefore, obviously will affect the nature of a country's politics. The advance of technology, coupled with increasing attainment of bureaucratic structures of the ideal type, enhances the capabilities of governments to control their environments and thus to achieve their goals more readily. Depending upon the orientation of the government, this can mean either greater material prosperity and fuller social services for the population or more repressive totalitarian control of their lives.

Table I–1 is suggestive of the political implications of level of economic development. It relates the popular accountability of governmental power

TABLE I–1
Political Implications of Economic Development

Governmental Responsibility

Economic Condition	Democracy	Limited Democracy	Limited Autocracy	Autocracy
Strong	19	1	0	3
Good	7	5	1	7
Poor	5	4	2	9
Weak	4	5	17	14

in 103 of the world's nations to their economic circumstances.[1] A country's ratings on such characteristics as freedom of the press, constitutionalism, party competition, freedom of political association, and the political role of the police and military were combined to determine its placement in the governmental responsibility typology. It was assigned to one of the four economic condition categories on the basis of its combined ratings of GNP per capita, stage of economic development, literacy rate, and percentage of the work force engaged in agriculture. The result of assigning the 103 countries to one or another of the 16 cells in the typology is to demonstrate a relation between democracy and economic development so strong that it is extremely unlikely that this distribution of nations could have occurred by chance.

The other interesting aspect of Table I–1 can be revealed by a simple deviant case analysis. The upper right quadrant contains 11 countries and the lower left quadrant 18, which contradict the general finding of a

---

[1] The source of information for classifying nations was Arthur Banks' and Robert Textor's *A Cross-Polity Survey* (Cambridge, Mass.: M.I.T. Press, 1963), an ambitious attempt to collect data on 57 characteristics, most of them political, for all the independent countries of the world. Characteristics 13, 26, 28, 29, 30, 41, 54, and 55 were utilized to classify countries according to extent of governmental responsibility, and characteristics 7, 9, 11, and 12 to establish their economic condition. Each country was scored according to the ranking given them by Banks and Textor on each of the 12 characteristics. Since data were not always available for each country on every characteristic, even after "retrieving," the scores available for the eight political characteristics were averaged to obtain a single score, as were also the scores available for the four economic characteristics. On the basis of these two average scores each nation was assigned to a particular cell of the taxonomy.

relation between governmental responsibility and economic condition. In the one case economic conditions are good or better, and yet government tends to be more autocratic than democratic. In the other, the government is on balance democratic despite poor or worse economic conditions. Almost all of the first group—nine—are European nations. In most cases a Communist regime has given these countries a dictatorial or totalitarian government despite their economic strength. This is in part related to our earlier comment that totalitarianism is a phenomenon associated with 20th century technological advance. It counsels guarding against the too easy assumption that economic development alone automatically will make a political system more democratic. Two thirds of the group in the lower left quadrant—which contains no European nations—are Latin American and African nations. For a variety of reasons, which would have to be ascertained by more detailed studies, they were able, at the time the data were gathered, to operate relatively democratic political systems despite unfavorable economic circumstances. Whether they will continue to be able to do so remains to be seen. Thus good economic conditions are neither necessary nor sufficient for attaining a high level of governmental popular responsibility, although they would seem to facilitate it.

The interpretation of the data in Table I–1 must be qualified further because of its static nature. It simply presents the relation between two factors at a single point in time; it does not reveal anything about the dynamic effect of the *process* of development. While a high level of economic development may be favorable to a democratic political system, the process of attaining that level may give rise to such conflicts and dislocations and may require such tight social controls that governmental responsibility is lessened in the short run. The relation between political and economic factors clearly is complex, but obviously demonstrates the necessity of examining a political system's environment.

HISTORY AND POLITICAL CULTURE

The process of economic development is only one aspect of a country's history. Other aspects of its previous experiences must be considered as well, since they give rise to values, beliefs, and practices that have a major impact upon politics. Anyone who has lived for a time in a nation other than his or her own becomes aware of differences in outlook toward politics and government. In some countries government is regarded as a hostile force and contacts with it are to be avoided as much as possible, while in other countries it is seen as a beneficial agency of considerable use in improving the quality of life. In Britain the police are widely respected and generally thought to be incorruptible, while in much of the United States quite the reverse attitudes and beliefs prevail. In the United

States cheating on income tax, though often condoned, is not encouraged, while in France managing to trick the tax collector out of a sizable sum is thought to be very praiseworthy.

Over the years a people begins to build up out of its experiences a body of what may be called "folk wisdom" about government and politics. Political scientists refer to this as political culture, which may be defined more precisely as (1) the sum of individual evaluative attitudes and emotive feelings toward politics and the existing political system and (2) perceptions, feelings, and evaluations of the role of the individual in the political process.[2] These values and beliefs are handed down from one generation to another, often without any conscious effort to do so. This process is called political socialization; it helps to provide continuity in political values and attitudes from one generation to the next. The importance of the belief system into which individuals are socialized is that it disposes them to regard the political system in a particular way before they have had any firsthand contact with it and thus provides a frame of reference for interpreting their experiences when contact does occur.

The political culture into which individuals are socialized is significant as well because it affects the way in which they relate politically to others. The distribution of attitudes on fundamental political matters in a given society can take any one of a number of forms, three of which are illustrated in Figure I–1.[3] In the first case, consensus is widespread in the society and political conflict can be waged relatively peacefully, since the

FIGURE I–1
Patterns of Attitude Distribution

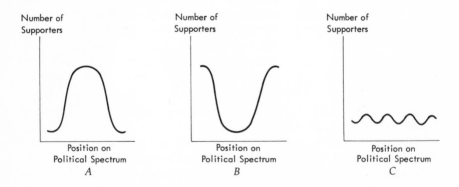

<hr />

[2] For more detailed discussion of the concept of political culture, see the best-known single book on this subject, Gabriel Almond and Sidney Verba, *The Civic Culture* (Boston: Little, Brown and Co., 1965), especially pp. 11–26.

[3] Anthony Downs discusses the effect of voter distribution upon party systems in *An Economic Theory of Democracy* (New York: Harper & Row, 1957), pp. 114–32.

opponents share the same basic values. In the second case, however, a sharp cleavage polarizes the society into two hostile camps and threatens a violent disruption of the system. In the final case the society is fractionalized into a number of competing sections. The inability of any of these to come even close to commanding majority support could stalemate the political system and produce political apathy and alienation among many of the citizens. Some factions may become so alienated and frustrated that they resort to extralegal tactics in an effort to galvanize the immobile political system into taking the actions which they feel to be essential, or to destroy it so that it can be replaced with what they believe will be a more effective political system.

It is not just the distribution of attitudes, the cleavage patterns prevailing in a society, that are significant, but also how people conceive of the political process. When their views of the proper political structures, procedures, and policies not only differ, but are mutually exclusive as well, when they prefer a politics of redemption to one of convenience, then an explosive situation is the result.[4] The political style characteristic of those who regard politics as the procedure for establishing the true faith is exhortation as they seek to convert the lost souls. Those who see politics as an instrumental process are more likely to employ a political style of bargaining and negotiation as they seek to adjust conflicting desires by a compromise that will satisfy most people at least temporarily.

The effect which attitude distribution and a population's view of politics have on each other is unclear. It may be that a distribution like that of *A* in Figure I–1 helps to encourage an instrumental view of politics, since the participants know that the stakes are relatively limited; losing the political struggle will not be a catastrophe and there will be further contests in which one's side may prevail. But a distribution like *B* turns the political process into a holy war in which the stakes become survival, not just temporary setback and thus encourages dogmatism and distrust. On the other hand it may be the fact that much of the population conceives of the political process instrumentally that helps to distribute most opinions around a single mode, as in *A*, and the inclination to see politics as a battle for Truth that polarizes society into the bimodal distribution of *B*. And

---

[4] The distinction between the politics of redemption and of convenience comes from Glenn Tinder, *Political Thinking: The Perennial Questions* (Boston: Little, Brown and Co., 1970), pp. 108–11. The former is characterized by a belief that politics seeks "a life on earth that is altogether good. . . . Felicity is not a gift of God, and it is not reserved for a heavenly existence or a time after death. It can be attained through human planning and can be attained here on earth." The mood of those who view politics this way is "the impatience and disgust of those who feel that men have betrayed their potentialities. Finding themselves in hell, they have called for the creation of heaven." The mood of those who reject this conception of politics is one "of low expectations and low demands since the world either cannot, or need not, be much improved. Government is not expected to bring salvation but only to enhance the convenience of life."

whatever the direction of the causal link, the question of whether an opinion distribution like C results in stalemated or effective government is determined largely by whether the participants regard politics instrumentally or redemptively.

The cleavage patterns and political culture of a nation are shaped to a considerable extent by the order and nature of major political or social crises or conflicts. Some of the fundamental historical divisions which have affected the shape of politics in Western Europe today are the conflicts between the church and the state, between primary and secondary producers, and between workers and employers. Whether these crises could be faced one at a time or whether all required action at the same time made a considerable amount of difference. This is not just a matter of their historical order of occurrence, for, even if one crisis did arise at a period subsequent to another, if the former one had not been solved the two would have become intermingled in the political process. Thus the political "load" to be carried by the political system—the magnitude and complexity of the issues to be processed—would be likely to exceed the capacity of the system. Not only that but the newer issues seldom would be considered on their own merits, since the interjection of the still unsolved older issues into the debate would produce an unthinking conditioned response pro or con. For much of the 20th century one had only to raise the question of the Church on any issue in French politics and most of the political participants, like Pavlov's dogs, would froth at the mouth. The result of such intermingling of crises is that nothing is accomplished very well.

These are some of the considerations that make it desirable to examine a country's history to see what cleavage patterns and political culture it has produced. This study is essential if one is to discover why one people holds one type of political values and another, another; why one type of political structure is viable and effective in one nation and another type in another or why the same type of structure is functional in one system and not in another.

PARTICIPATORY STRUCTURES

Cleavage patterns and political culture affect the way in which political organizations fit together in a nation's political system. To label the political elements of a society a "system" implies that they can be distinguished analytically from the other parts of the society and that they are interrelated with each other.[5] The term political system is broader than

---

[5] For a discussion of the use of systems theory in political science, see Oran Young, *Systems of Political Science* (Englewood Cliffs, N.J.: Prentice-Hall, Inc., 1968), especially chap. 2.

government, since the former includes attitudes and behavior patterns rather than just formal organizations. Popular participation is a good starting point for analysis of the political system; if no one wanted anything done, but could meet their needs unassisted, there would be no need for a political process.

To start with needs and wants—inputs, as they are termed by some political scientists—is not to argue that people constantly are clamoring for action. In any political system relatively few people make specific demands upon the government. Typically, most people do not want to be bothered by political matters; they prefer to turn over to someone else the job of seeking general social conditions that make life liveable. Yet *some* people do wish to be involved actively in political decision-making and many of the rest wish to be heard on a few occasions when they feel particularly strongly about a matter. The type and amount of political participation which people feel is proper for them is influenced, of course, by a society's political culture and by the subculture within the groups to which an individual belongs. But also important is whether the political structures and practices themselves encourage or discourage participation, whether obstacles exist which make access to decision makers difficult.

Making demands, however, is only one of the two types of political participation; the other is expressing support for the system and its agents. Such expressions may be positive endorsements of particular leaders or policies. Or they may be expressed indirectly. For example, when people vote in an election they not only are expressing their preferences among the contending candidates, but also, unless they vote for anti-system candidates, are supporting the existing political system. Just as there would be no need for a political system were there no demand inputs, so a political system could not exist unless there were support inputs.

Demands and supports may originate with the public or be stimulated by governmental agencies or by political structures whose apparent primary purpose is simply to communicate public opinion. But almost never is public opinion transmitted in its original form to decision makers; instead, as demand and support inputs travel through the channels for political communications, they are altered. The extent to which they are distorted, and public influence upon government thereby lessened, is a key question in the analysis of a country's political process.

Three subsystems of a nation's political system are concerned primarily with participation—the electoral system, the group system, and the party system. Starting with the one not composed of group structures, the electoral system must be studied both in terms of its regulations and the behaviors and practices associated with it. In seeking to discover the extent of access in a political system, for example, it matters little that legally everyone may vote, if blacks who do are visited by night riders. Similarly, access is affected if a large number of people feel compelled to vote as the parish priest tells them to do.

The way in which the votes are counted and the winners determined is of paramount importance. The same number of votes can yield a considerably different share of the seats in a legislature depending upon whether a country employs a single member/simple plurality system, as do the United States and Britain, or a proportional representation system, as does Germany. Still another result would be possible by employing the double ballot system now used in France. So decisive do some political scientists feel the impact of the electoral system to be that they argue that it is the major determinant of the type of party system existing in a country, and that the entire quality of a country's politics revolves around its electoral arrangements. Some even go so far as to maintain that the wrong electoral system can seriously weaken democracy and encourage the rise of dictatorship. The essence of the argument is that proportional representation makes it much easier than does the single member/simple plurality system for small political factions to win a share of power. This tends to encourage a distribution of opinion like that of C in Figure I–1 above. And, since there is no incentive, as there is under the single member/simple plurality system, to combine with others to increase voting support, a redemptive perception of the political process may develop. The result is an embittered and ineffective politics with the democratic system likely to be replaced with a dictatorial one. It will be important to note the extent to which the three democratic nations discussed in this book provide evidence to support or challenge this argument.

Although groups are active politically in almost all societies, the type predominating varies a good deal, with important implications for the political process. Groups can be distinguished as being associational, nonassociational, or institutional.[6] The first term refers to groups formed voluntarily by people who may not have much more in common than a shared interest, the advancement of which is the purpose for forming the group, such as the PTA. Membership in nonassociational groups is not by conscious choice but by virtue of what one is. Such groups exist totally apart from any desire to exert political influence or to advance any particular interest. An example of such a group would be one based on ethnic or racial distinctions where membership in the group is so automatic as to be unquestioned, as in a tribe. Institutional groups do not have as their primary or original purpose the expressing of interests. They are bodies formally established as part of the government, but which, nonetheless, are very active in the political process in arguing the merits of a narrow range

---

[6] Types of interest groups and their impact on the political process are discussed by Gabriel Almond and G. Bingham Powell, Jr., in *Comparative Politics: A Developmental Approach* (Boston: Little, Brown and Co., 1966), chap. 4.

of interests. In so doing they may establish close ties with associational or nonassociational groups, thereby giving the institutional group an aura of popular support that it otherwise might not appear to have and the other groups an apparent official endorsement. The Army Corps of Engineers in the United States is an example.

Where associational interest groups are weak, popular access and, hence, governmental accountability tend to be limited. An instrumental view of politics and the ability to devise acceptable compromises may be jeopardized in systems where nonassociational groups are strong, since the continued existence of such groups may be at stake when interests important to them are challenged. Where institutional interest groups are so strong that they dominate or displace associational groups, decision making tends to be more concentrated within the political elite. Furthermore, while all groups are structured hierarchically to some extent, associational groups, given their voluntary origin and membership, have a greater potential for democratic organization and thus are potentially better vehicles for popular control of the government.

Whether groups are largely autonomous or dependent on other political or governmental structures affects their role in and impact on the political process. Where a particular set of groups and a political party share the same members to a considerable extent, their stands and outlooks tend to reinforce each other and thus contribute to a sharpening of partisanship. On the other hand, where groups are independent for the most part, overlapping or partially shared memberships are more common. This has the effect of exposing people to a greater diversity of views and helps to reduce dogmatism. Also, where groups are tied to political parties, fragmentation of a particular interest is likely; each party, for example, may sponsor its own trade union group. This makes cooperation difficult between those who otherwise would be allied. Their working at cross-purposes will reduce the effectiveness of whatever access they are able to obtain for presenting their members' views—if the workers seem to be speaking with three or four conflicting voices, governmental officials will not know to which to respond and so may decide to ignore them all.

As we indicated in our discussion of typologies, one distinction between political systems which often has been employed turns on the number of parties. Clearly the nature of the political process is different in a country where only one party may legally offer candidates and communicate with the citizens from what it is in a country where two or more parties compete for support. The reason for separating two-party from multi-party systems is related to the basic function of parties. A democratic society has so many groups voicing their views and interests that voters cannot possibly examine the merits of all their proposals and decide which of them are preferable. The purpose of parties is to filter or weed out these proposals and then consider the interrelations of those remaining so that a coherent set of policy proposals emerges rather than a jumbled collection of proposals, each of which may be sound and desirable but which, taken together, are so contradictory that they cancel each other out.

Parties simplify and focus policy issues so that voters are presented with a clear choice of alternative programs. A two-party system is presumed to be able to do this more effectively than is a multi-party system, because in the former, one party of necessity must have a legislative majority, while in the latter coalitions are likely. A coalition combines the legislative representatives of two or more parties in support of an executive, termed a cabinet, which is composed of a prime minister and important department heads. In parliamentary systems the terms *Cabinet* and *Government* are used interchangeably, just as in the United States we refer to the President and other top officials collectively as the Administration.

Policy conflicts among coalition partners may make cabinets unstable and short-lived. Thus they are unlikely to be effective in dealing with a nation's problems and hardly can be expected to implement any program requiring a continuing commitment. Even should these difficulties not arise, the need for compromise among coalition partners may destroy all coherence in policy. Such a cabinet may implement a series of unrelated measures as it satisfies the desires of first one party and then another of those included in the coalition. Thus, although each party may have presented the electorate with a set of integrated proposals, only bits of each are enacted and no party is able to carry out its program. The voters' opportunity for a clear choice among alternatives is reduced; they are denied the chance of getting the governmental action they prefer even when they give the most votes to the party advocating their preferences.

Despite these difficulties associated with coalitions, arguing that a multi-party system necessarily lessens governmental accountability is questionable. Coalition governments sometimes can avoid these impediments to effective government. The leading party, for example, may so dominate its coalition associates as to permit them little influence over policy, and thus the coherence of the Government's program would not be lessened greatly. Furthermore, the performance of coalition governments is affected at least as much by the type of parties operating in a nation as by the type of party system.

Parties may be pragmatic and work together well in devising a coherent compromise program or they may be rigidly dogmatic and refuse to cooperate with each other at all. This produces weak and ineffective minority Governments, ones that are supported in the legislature by fewer than half of the members. Parties may be highly unified or simply loose collections of individuals and local or regional political machines. When parties are organized in this latter way—as the Democratic and Republican parties are—then it is hard to argue that a clear choice has been presented to the voters simply because they have the alternative of voting for one label or another. A multi-party system in which each party was relatively non-ideological and highly unified would simplify and focus the policy issues at least as well, if not better than a system involving two loosely cohering parties.

In the study of parties four main foci are especially important—doctrines and policies, supporters, strength, and organization. The initial question is: For what does this party stand—what views and actions does it want to make authoritatively binding on the entire population by having them sanctioned by government? Does it have a vision of totally transforming society and human nature, or simply a list of preferred policies over which it is willing to bargain and compromise? Is it simply a personal following of an attractive leader and dedicated to attaining power largely for its own sake with little concern for one set of policies or another?

Having ascertained a party's basic purposes, one wants to know to whom this type of party appeals. From what groups, segments of society, kinds of individuals does it get most of its support? Is it able, for example, to cut across the main political divisions of a society and thus help to moderate political conflict or does it tend to reinforce and perpetuate existing divisions by drawing support from only one narrow segment? Are most of its adherents so bound to it by socioeconomic factors that they will continue to support it come what may? If this should be the case the party may not be very responsive, since it would feel that it could count on continued support regardless of whether it attempted to ascertain or even listen to the policy preferences of its supporters.

Constancy of support raises the matter of party strength. To how many of whatever type of people does a party with these policies appeal? A political system in which a Communist party can win a quarter or a third of the vote is forced to function very differently from one in which that party's support is negligible. In the former case parties some considerable distance apart on the political spectrum are forced into a coalition if there is to be a majority Cabinet, yet precisely because of the parties' distance, the majority is likely to exist in name only, especially if the parties are loosely organized rather than tightly unified.

Party organization is a crucial factor in governmental accountability in another way as well. The distribution of power within a party determines whether it can serve as a channel for communicating the views of political activists to the government, or whether the leaders so dominate the party that communication is almost entirely from the top down, with party members serving simply to implement the leaders' views. Roberto Michels's Iron Law of Oligarchy maintains that the latter situation must necessarily prevail in all parties however democratic they claim to be.

Should this be true, the policy-making process would be even more elite-dominated than it otherwise would be.

Whether one would choose to call such a system democratic turns upon whether one conceives of democracy as requiring participation in the policy-making process or only in the leadership recruitment process. Some are willing to argue that a system is democratic if the political elite are selected and removable by the people. In this view the function of political parties is not policy making but maintaining competition between sets of leaders who have been tested, apprenticed, and provided with political experience through the parties. The parties thus cultivate the conditions that make democratic politics possible.

It must be questioned, however, whether this conception so restricts the role of popular participation as to lose one of its principal benefits. Participation is one means of trying to answer the question we raised above: How do you get people to follow authoritative decisions voluntarily? If people have participated in the making of a decision, they may be more willing to accept the result even if they do not like the substance. They may feel that they had a fair hearing and since they were unable to convince enough others to support them, they should gracefully accept defeat for the time being. Also while participating they may have come to understand better the alternatives to their view and find that these and those who hold them are not so bad after all. Whether these benefits can be obtained when participation is restricted largely to the leadership recruitment process is by no means certain. On the other hand, involving millions of people meaningfully in the policy-making process is a formidable task. No country yet has been able to devise political structures capable of doing this satisfactorily. Even in democracies popular participation in policy making is limited.

Nonetheless, a society's arrangements for popular participation have a fundamental impact upon the nature of its politics. Questions of the type raised in this discussion must be investigated if one is to gain an adequate understanding of the extent of governmental accountability in any nation.

GOVERNMENTAL STRUCTURES AND PROCESSES

As we have suggested, the purpose of participatory structures is to provide a means through which people can express support of the governmental system and its agents and make demands upon them. Governmental organs process these inputs, converting them into authoritative rules binding on the entire society. It sometimes is thought that there are three main stages or subroutines to this process: the making of the rules by legislatures and executives; the implementing of the rules by the bureaucracy; the adjudicating of conflicts that arise under the law by the judiciary. Reality, however, is not this simple. It is important to understand that, once law properly is conceived of as not just formal statutes but as the entire body of binding rules for a society, administrators and judges make law just as surely as do legislators. Legislatures often draft statutes in general language, leaving administrators to fill in detailed provisions, thereby expanding the latters' rule-making authority. Furthermore, the vast expansion of governmental activities over the past several decades has required that in a wide variety of areas administrators must decide to whom and in what circumstances laws shall apply, since statutes often are not unambiguous and degrees of leniency or severity of enforcement are not uncommon. The power of courts to formulate authoritative rules is most obvious in a country such as the United States, where they have the power to void a rule made by the legislature by declaring it unconstitutional. But even in countries where courts lack this power, as in Britain, the fact that they must interpret the law to apply it to particular cases means that they constantly are deciding the specific details of the law.

Such specific or de facto delegation of legislative authority poses problems for democracy, for few judges and administrators are elected and most have permanent tenure except for malfeasance. How are these wielders of political power to be made accountable so as to attain responsible government? The elected and accountable legislature and executive have the job of surveillance and control of the administrators. The arrangements in any particular system for carrying out this responsibility must be examined to see whether there is power adequate for control without its being so intrusive upon the administrative process that efficiency is destroyed. In the case of the courts the matter is further complicated by the fact that no one in a democratic system wants to see the courts become partisan organs. Yet does not the strict independence of the judiciary threaten so to insulate the judges from popular preferences that all accountability is destroyed? Although right is not necessarily what the majority wants, yet a strong argument can be made that to a considerable extent the courts should "follow the election returns."

Some countries use courts or quasi-judicial officials and procedures to try to control administrators. France, for example, in addition to the regular court system has a separate system of courts for the adjudication of conflicts arising from challenges to administrative action. Britain and a few other countries have established an ombudsman—an official to whom complaints about administrative action can be referred—to investigate whether citizens have been treated improperly in their contact with governmental officials. In either case the objective is to provide the individual with an opportunity for redress or appeal in situations where administrative power may have been abused.

The use of one governmental organ to control another calls to mind the distinction sometimes made between separation of power systems and fusion of power systems. In the former, also known as a presidential system, the executive and legislative branches are independent of each other, while in the latter, also called a parliamentary system, the members of the executive are members of the legislature as well. In the presidential system the legislature may refuse to enact the program requested by the executive, but they are not empowered to remove the executive from office because of this political clash. In the parliamentary system, however, the legislature can eject the executive and then proceed to select a new one from among its members.

Which of these two types of systems offers the greater accountability to the people is difficult to say and turns in part upon how parties operate in the legislature. Another important factor is the distribution of power between the executive and the legislature, regardless of whether they are fused or separated. And related to this is the perception prevailing in a society of where the main political leadership should be exerted. What role is the legislature to play? Is it to be a partner with the executive in policy making or is it to perform primarily the function of criticizing and controlling the executive in its direction of the government and formulation of policy? The answer seems to be affected more by political culture or prevailing practices than by whether the constitutional structure provides for separation or fusion of powers. Through most of the 19th century in the United States political leadership resided in the Congress rather than the President, while in the 20th century this largely has reversed. Similarly, in Britain the present model of dominant Cabinet leadership did not emerge until about the latter third of the 19th century.

Just as so common a matter as the internal structure of political parties has significant implications for responsible government, so also the organization of the legislature needs to be examined. Legislative procedure can be drawn up in such a way as to facilitate the passage of laws and create few, if any, obstacles to enacting the executive's legislative program. Alternatively there may be, as in the United States Congress, a number of roadblocks providing ample opportunity for ambushing proposed policy. Legislatures may have extensive information-gathering facilities which enable them to examine executive actions knowledgeably or they may be dependent upon the executive structures for expert knowledge with a consequent lessening of accountability. Whatever the organizational details, however, it must be borne in mind that the actual operation will be influenced considerably by the nature of the parties in the system. The personal characteristics and political style of leaders are important factors as well. Charles de Gaulle was able to dominate the French legislature for many years not so much because of the power vested in the office of President of France as because of his personality, background, and operating procedures. No other political figure in France would have dared to decide on his or her own authority the major issues de Gaulle often did.

The distribution of power between the executive and the legislature is not the only one which needs to be examined. In addition to the separation of powers the division of powers is significant—the allocation of responsibilities between the central and subnational units of government. Systems which are federal, where the distribution of power is established in the constitution and cannot be changed without the consent of both the central and the subnational governments, can be distinguished from those which are unitary, where the subnational governments are created by the central government and exercise only whatever powers the central government chooses to grant them for only so long as it wishes to do so. This is not, however, a particularly useful contrast to make in most cases. Some systems which have a federal constitution, do not operate that way in practice, such as the Soviet Union. And there is considerable difference in the degree of decentralization among unitary systems. In France and Italy, for example, the powers of local government are much more restricted and the functions much more centrally directed than they are in Britain, despite the fact that all three countries are unitary systems. Thus one cannot rely upon labels in seeking to ascertain the division of powers in a political system, but must study its operation to discover the actual distribution.

Some would argue that the greater the extent of decentralization the greater the degree of self-government. Allowing many decisions to be made by governmental units other than the central ones increases the number of access points and thus should aid in securing accountability. Decentralization also permits greater variety in authoritative policy, thus making it possible to accommodate regional differences. On the other hand, if this is carried to an extreme the result could be the breakup of a single nation into two or more countries or a civil war to prevent such an event. Then, too, little evidence exists to suggest that most people take a greater interest in local and regional government than in central government or are better informed concerning the former. Thus policy making may be even more elite-dominated at the subnational level than it is at the central level. So bringing government closer to the people by decentralizing may not increase the level of democracy. Instead, it may be a slogan utilized by groups insufficiently strong to win nationally to get the locus of decision shifted to the subnational level where they may be able to control at least some of the subnational units of government.

SYSTEM INSTITUTIONALIZATION AND DURABILITY

The fundamental purpose of the political system as it performs its basic function of making authoritative rules is to enable a society to adapt to, and thus cope successfully with, changes in its environment. The first essential is that the political system become institutionalized, that its structures become valued for themselves rather than for the popularity of those who hold positions in them. It then acquires some durability so that it can adapt to changing circumstances without disintegrating. When structures are institutionalized there can be some regularity in the way in which a society grapples with the problems that face it. The importance of this regularity should not be slighted, for it must be remembered that a major element in individual freedom is a lack of arbitrariness in one's environment. Where life is chaos—one damn thing after another, in Aldous Huxley's words—there can be no freedom. Yet because a society's environment is not frozen, its political system must be sufficiently flexible to adapt to new situations. Thus the question becomes one of dynamic stability—the ability of the system to maintain itself by changing in accordance with established procedures. Change in any other way becomes merely a contest of brute force and defeats the whole object of creating a political system, which is to try to make it possible for people to govern themselves in a civilized fashion rather than living like animals.

A system which is malfunctioning, which is failing to gratify the demands made upon it and to meet the challenge of its environment, may be able to endure for some time, despite the dissatisfaction which it produces, if it has built up sufficient legitimacy, that is, if most people feel that it is a morally sound system that conforms to the basic values of the prevailing political culture. But persistent severe malfunctioning can exhaust the supply of legitimacy, thus forcing a major overhaul of the system and threatening violence. In seeking to evaluate the durability of any political system, therefore, one needs to examine the extent to which the political system is institutionalized, the degree of legitimacy accorded it, and the way in which the basic political functions are being performed with what impact upon political behavior and culture. For despite the contrasts between political systems which this chapter has pointed out, such systems are basically alike in having to perform the same functions. Regardless of whether input channels are opened widely for the people at large or restricted to a ruling elite, inputs must be processed efficiently and the society enabled to deal with an everchanging environment. Even a well-armed dictatorship cannot maintain itself for long if it fails to meet these requirements.

In fact one might speculate that autocracies may be more fragile than democracies because their constant use of repression alienates much of the population, thus destroying the legitimacy of the system and encouraging attempts to overthrow it. If we use as an index of system durability a nation's rating on four measures—age of current governmental structure, governmental stability, sharpness of conflict, and existence of alienated groups—then there is some evidence, as Table I–2

TABLE I–2
System Durability Related to Type of Government

| System Durability | Governmental Responsibility | |
	Democracy and Limited Democracy	Limited Autocracy and Autocracy
Good	34	15
Poor	14	28

indicates, to suggest that our expectation is correct.[7] The durability of most democratic systems is good, while that of most autocratic systems is poor. Nonetheless, several autocratic systems do rate "good" as regards system durability. They appear to be capable of sustaining sufficient repression to thwart any challenge to the regime while delivering sufficient benefits to win some voluntary support. Technological advance can increase a government's capabilities in both cases.

Of the 14 nations whose durability is poor despite their being democratic, seven are in Latin America. This is an evidence of the troubled politics of that area, where, as is well known, coups and countercoups are frequent and the life of many governments is brief. Thus, while several of these countries may be democratic currently, there can be little assurance that they will continue to remain so during the next ten years. The apparent crumbling of the political order in Uruguay in the early 1970s is an example of the dangers to democracy.

It is interesting to note, however, that the relation between durability and economic condition is even stronger than that between durability and governmental responsibility. As Table I–3 indicates, most systems where economic conditions are good or better are durable, while the great majority of those whose economic condition is poor or worse are not. Economic condition might be taken as evidence of a system's ability to cope successfully with its environment and thus as a measure of its success in performing the functions necessary to maintaining the system. Thus it is not surprising that those systems which would seem unable to do this do not enjoy very good prospects for continued existence. Of the six whose

---

[7] The main source of data for these measures was again Banks's and Textor's *A Cross-Polity Survey.* The first measure uses somewhat different categories than Banks and Textor employed for characteristic 19. Thus their classifications were supplemented by reference to standard yearbooks and almanacs. The latter three measures are derived from their characteristics 27, 31, and 36. The difficulty which they had in classifying countries on these three characteristics requires reducing the total number of countries included in Table I–2 to 91 compared with the 103 included in Table I–1. Several of the nations excluded were Communist systems. The four measures were combined into a single score as explained in the note dealing with Table I–1. The four governmental responsibility categories of that table have been collapsed to form the two categories employed in Table I–2.

TABLE I–3
System Durability Related to Economic Condition

System Durability	Economic Condition	
	Strong and Good	Poor and Weak
Good	32	17
Poor	6	45

endurance is tenuous despite an ability to perform economic tasks well, two thirds are Latin American nations, again evidence of the lack of political institutionalization in this area.

Economic condition and governmental responsibility are not, of course, the only factors related to system durability. Also likely to have a significar.t impact are type of political culture, level of social trust, and extent of international conflict. The point here has been simply to indicate the association of a few factors in order to suggest what is unusual and, therefore, especially needs explanation. Neither the Weimar Republic in Germany nor the Fourth Republic in France was durable, although both were democratic and, in the latter case, the country's economic condition was good as well. And currently, political observers still have some question about the durability of the republics of Germany and France. Tables I–2 and I–3 help to indicate the extent to which this is an untypical situation, requiring further investigation. Thus classification schemes or typologies can be used to stimulate research.

In summary, then, in this chapter we have discussed some of the main foci for the comparative study of political systems. We have raised a number of basic questions and indicated their implications in general terms. Thus this chapter provides a loose outline around which the material in each of the specific country sections contained in this book will be organized. In most instances the issues raised here are as significant for a totalitarian system—the Soviet Union—as they are for democratic systems—Britain, France, and Germany. The following detailed examinations of each of these four systems will refer to these issues explicitly or implicitly to indicate concretely how they and the responses each nation has made to them have shaped their political systems and affected their operation.

BIBLIOGRAPHICAL NOTE

In addition to the books mentioned in the footnotes, the following are suggested as beginning reading for those who wish to pursue further the topics discussed in this section.

For a general discussion of scientific method and scientific entities see Stephen Toulmin, *The Philosophy of Science: An Introduction* (New York: Harper & Row, 1960). Basic concepts and methods in the study of political phenomena are examined in Robert Dahl, *Modern Political Analysis,* 2d ed. (Englewood Cliffs, N.J.: Prentice-Hall, Inc., 1970). The aims and procedures of rigorous investigation in comparative politics are succinctly discussed by Harrow Scarrow in *Comparative Political Analysis: An Introduction* (New York: Harper & Row, 1969).

The basic characteristics of democracy and autocracy are examined in Robert Dahl, *A Preface to Democratic Theory* (Chicago: University of Chicago Press, 1956), and Carl Friedrich and Zbigniew Brzezinski, *Totalitarian Dictatorship and Autocracy,* 2d ed. rev. by Friedrich (Cambridge, Mass.: Harvard University Press, 1965). The relation between various types of government and economic conditions are investigated in Robert Holt and John Turner, *The Political Basis of Economic Development* (Princeton, N.J.: D. Van Nostrand & Co., Inc., 1966), which, contrary to usual practice, makes politics the independent variable. For a discussion of the issues raised by the related topic of political change, see Samuel Huntington, *Political Order in Changing Society* (New Haven, Conn.: Yale University Press, 1968).

The values and structures affecting political behavior are the concern of Richard Dawson and Kenneth Pewitt, *Political Socialization* (Boston: Little, Brown and Co., 1969), and Lester Milbrath, *Political Participation* (Chicago: Rand McNally, 1965). The latter book makes a special effort to synthesize the results of previous research into a series of basic propositions. While difficult reading, the long introductory essay by the editors in Seymour Lipset and Stein Rokkan, eds., *Party Systems and Voter Alignments* (New York: Free Press, 1967), is a starting point for study of cleavage patterns and societal response to historical crises.

One of the best-known efforts to provide a framework for the comparative analysis of political parties is Maurice Duverger, *Political Parties,* trans. Barbara and Robert North, 2d ed. rev. (London: Methuen, 1959). Some of the basic issues in party structures and party systems are discussed in Leon Epstein, *Political Parties in Western Democracies* (New York: Frederick A. Praeger, Inc., 1967). A concise, clearly written, and rigorous study of the relation between party systems and electoral systems is Douglas Rae, *The Political Consequences of Electoral Laws,* rev. ed. (New Haven, Conn.: Yale University Press, 1971).

Some of the basic reading on governmental structures includes Douglas Verney, *The Analysis of Political Systems* (London: Routledge and Kegan Paul, 1959); Ferrel Heady, *Public Administration: A Comparative Perspective* (Englewood Cliffs, N.J.: Prentice-Hall, Inc., 1966); Ivo Duchacek, *Comparative Federalism* (New York: Holt, Rinehart and Winston, 1970); and Henry Abraham, *Courts and Judges* (Oxford: Oxford University Press, 1959). Gerhard Loewenberg, ed., *Modern Parliaments: Change or Decline?* (Chicago: Aldine-Atherton, 1971), is a judiciously selected collection of seven essays presenting a variety of viewpoints on the basic problems and controversies affecting legislatures in Western democracies.

Part II

THE UNITED KINGDOM OF GREAT BRITAIN AND NORTHERN IRELAND

Atlantic

Ocean

North

Sea

SCOTLAND

NORTHERN
IRELAND

IRELAND

Irish Sea

St. George's Channel

WALES

ENGLAND

London

English Channel

Tho' much is taken, much abides; and tho'
We are not now that strength which in old days
Moved earth and heaven; that which we are, we are;
One equal temper of heroic hearts,
Make weak by time and fate, but strong in will
To strive, to seek, to find, and not to yield.

Tennyson

1

The Context of British Politics

PHYSICAL SETTING

Perhaps it is the influence of Arthurian romance that once led someone to liken the British Isles to a castle surrounded by a moat. The image serves to emphasize three characteristics of Britain's geographical setting which are of basic importance to its politics—Britain is a small, maritime nation which clearly is separated from its most immediate political neighbors.

With a total area somewhat in excess of 94,000 square miles the country is smaller than ten American states, Oregon being the most comparable in size. From the northern tip of Scotland to the southern coast of England is just under 600 miles; California is one third again as long. Given an island of this relatively limited area, it is not surprising to learn that one is never farther than 75 miles from tidal water anywhere in Britain or 110 miles from the ocean proper. Birmingham, located in what the British refer to as the Midlands, is only 95 miles from the sea.

Despite its small geographical size, Britain has a large population. Only ten nations exceed its total of 56 million. Most of the population—46 million—live in England, with 5.2 million residing in Scotland, 2.8 million in Wales, and 1.5 million in Northern Ireland.[1] Combining small geo-

[1] The United Kingdom of Great Britain and Northern Ireland is composed of four countries or, some would say, nations. England occupies the bulk of the main island with Wales in the west central portion and Scotland in the north. Northern Ireland is composed of the six counties located in the northeastern tip of the island across the Irish Sea from Great Britain, the term used to refer to England, Wales, and Scotland as a group. The remainder of that island is the Republic of Eire or Ireland, which is completely independent from Britain. Although the United Kingdom of Great Britain and Northern Ireland is the official name of the country with which this section deals, the term Britain is accepted as correct for semi-official purposes and will be employed in this book to refer to the entire political entity. We will refer to the people of the country as British or Britons. One needs only to remember not to call a Scotsman or a Welshman, English.

graphical size with a large population makes Britain one of the most densely populated countries in the world. It is considerably more densely populated than India and well over ten times more densely populated than the United States. Furthermore, if England alone is considered—ignoring the more sparsely populated areas of Scotland—the population density exceeds 900 per square mile, by far greater than that of Japan.

Associated with the density of population is high urbanization. More than four times as many people in England and Wales live in urban districts (one of the subdivisions of local government) as in rural districts. Much more so than Americans, Britons are city dwellers. Yet curiously a single city is preeminent and dominates all the rest. London is the political, cultural, and commercial hub of the country; the center for these various activities is not split among a number of cities as it is in the United States. London is preeminent in size as well; over one eighth of the entire British population lives in London, which with a population of 7.3 million is the fourth largest city in the world. The second largest city in Britain—Birmingham—lags far behind with only slightly over 1 million population.

High urbanization places a special strain on governmental capabilities because of increased demands for services. Matters of crime control, transportation, health and sanitation, food distribution, recreational facilities, and the like, which can be handled on a private basis when most people live in rural areas, become pressing public concerns when most people dwell in urban settings. Thus, whatever the political philosophy of the party in power, government must play a more activist, interventionist role in a highly urbanized society than it does in one that is more rural.

The smallness of Britain and the concentration of population in urban areas are a great aid to ease of communication, especially given the excellent rail network which has existed for many decades. A train ride of only an hour and a half takes one to Birmingham. A journey of two and a half hours is sufficient to reach most of the principal English cities, including Exeter in the West Country (the penninsula which juts out into the Atlantic Ocean) and Manchester and Leeds to the north. Even Newcastle, about 45 miles from the Scottish border, can be reached in three and a half hours.

The rail network enables England to have a national press, something which really has not developed in the United States. People who live in the north or west can read at breakfast the same newspaper, albeit an earlier edition, as do Londoners with their breakfasts. Thus the papers published in the capital city circulate widely throughout the country and help to nationalize opinion. Unlike the situation in the United States, there are no important English regional news media centers. As a result people are more likely to react to political events similarly throughout the

FIGURE 1-1
Travel Times by Rail from London to Other Cities

country and not to vary considerably in attitudes from one region to
another. Furthermore, the smaller a country's geographical area the less
likely are there to be variations in geography, climate, life style, principal
occupations, social relations, and similar matters which can have a considerable impact upon politics, as Americans well know.

So great is the contrast with the American political setting in this regard that American students of British politics long have stressed the great homogeneity of Britain and the British people. Although true, compared to the United States, this point has been overemphasized. Customs, food preferences, speech patterns, and the like vary considerably even within England alone, and when Northern Ireland, Scotland, and Wales are considered as well, the contrasts are marked. While many of these regional differences may have little or no political impact, others are significant.

Events in the late 1960s and early 1970s, such as political assassinations, bombings, riots, armed conflict between Protestants and Catholics, and extended use of troops to maintain order, amply demonstrated that sectarian factors play a much greater role in politics in Northern Ireland than they do in the rest of the United Kingdom. In the rural parts of Wales printing election material in Welsh is not uncommon nor is conducting campaign rallies in Welsh. Over a decade ago a thorough examination of Scottish political behavior concluded that Scotland had to be considered a separate political region in Britain, in part because class affected party preference less and religion affected it considerably more than was true in England.[2] During the 1970s the growing support for the Welsh and, especially, the Scottish nationalist movements, which want Wales and Scotland to separate from Britain and become independent countries, clearly has demonstrated the diversity of political patterns in Britain.

We must stress that our comments above about the rail network and a national press referred only to England. Not without significance for the rise of nationalist (separatist) feeling is the fact that Scotland is sufficiently far from London to have its own press. Most London-published papers can be obtained in Scotland, but their circulation is quite limited. The typical Glaswegian of whatever social class does not read the same paper as does his or her London counterpart.

Thus although the British in terms of their political attitudes and behavior are more alike than are Americans, they are far from being homogeneous nationally. Despite the smallness of the country and the existence of an English national press, political patterns vary at times not only between London and Cardiff, Belfast, and Edinburgh, but also between London and the West Country and Yorkshire.

Britain appears more homogeneous than it is because there is no sizable minority group. Catholics make up about 8 percent of the population and Jews less than 1 percent, each being less than one third of their proportion in the population of the United States. The number of nonwhites is difficult to determine exactly, but the proportion cannot be much greater than 3 percent of the population. Nonetheless, racial relations have come

---

[2] Ian Budge and D. W. Urwin, *Scottish Political Behavior: A Case Study in British Homogeneity* (London: Longmans, Green, 1966).

to be a major issue in British politics in the last decade, as is discussed more fully in the next chapter.

Another factor which makes the British appear homogeneous is a highly developed sense of national identity. This in turn is related to Britain's clear separation from the continent. Except for the issue of the relation between North Ireland and the Republic of Ireland there has been no question about the location of the boundaries of Britain since the union with Scotland well over three and one-half centuries ago. The 20-mile-wide English Channel has been a geographical feature of major importance. It has enabled Britain to escape complete involvement in many European wars and has saved it from invasion since the Norman Conquest of 1066. France and Poland, to mention only two examples, doubtless often have wished that 20 miles of water separated them from their neighbors.

The absence of land frontiers has meant that Britain usually has not sought to maintain a large standing army and has preferred instead to develop its navy (referred to in Britain as the Senior Service). In 1832, not many years after the Napoleonic Wars, Britain had only 11,000 troops, an army smaller than the Chicago police force in 1968. Consequently, through most of Britain's history, royal absolutism has been easier to combat than on the continent, for, although a navy is an important weapon in international relations, it is not much assistance in combating domestic challenges to governmental power. The deemphasis of the army also has helped to keep Britain free of the effect of militarism, which often has bedeviled continental politics.

Britain's maritime geographic position also was in large measure responsible for its commercial and military position. The discovery of the New World and the establishment of new trade routes via the Atlantic made Britain the center of world commerce. Industry, cities, and commerce grew apace. Trade and the need to control the waters around the British Isles for defense purposes went hand in hand. At the same time, Britain's dependence on sea power encouraged the growth of the empire. In short, the seas not only became commercial highways but also avenues which led to discovery, exploration, empire, and naval supremacy.

Given Britain's world role, isolationism has not been an important political position in modern British politics. Britain frequently intervened on the continent to maintain a balance of power which would not threaten it. Nonetheless, the British have remained aloof from the continent in some ways. When in the 1960s President Charles de Gaulle of France barred Britain from the European Economic Community (Common Market) with the observation that the British really were not European, there was an element of truth in his position. The British have not traditionally thought of themselves as being an integral part of Europe; they have felt that their history of stable government and gradually expanding liberties has demonstrated a political tradition and competence different from and superior to those of most continental nations. This is one of the reasons why British membership in the Common Market has been such a divisive issue in recent politics. Had it not been for 20 miles of water, and the history associated with it, almost certainly Britain would have been a charter member.

The factor which drove Britain to seek membership in the Common Market despite its traditional aloofness from the continent was the importance of international trade to its economy. Moderate climate together with sizable acreages of good agricultural land enabled the British to produce a large part of their foodstuffs until about a century and a half ago. But as the country industrialized and its population grew, it began to import large quantities of food. Because of advances in ocean transportation and the unsuitability of much of the land for wheat in any case, many food products could be imported more economically than they could be produced domestically. Furthermore, as the doctrine of Free Trade prevailed, tariffs were eliminated and by the middle of the 19th century agriculture was little protected or encouraged. Only between World Wars I and II did British farmers again receive some tariff protection and only during World War II was an elaborate farm subsidy system developed. As a result of these factors Britain is not self-sufficient in food production and must engage in international trade to feed its population. In addition, since it does not possess many natural resources other than coal and iron, it has to import raw materials for its industries.

Thus Britain's balance of payments is a crucial economic consideration. Selling sufficient manufactured goods to obtain the foreign currencies needed to pay for necessary foodstuffs and raw materials is essential to national survival. Again the point is that whatever the political philosophy of the party in power, considerable intervention in economic affairs is likely to be necessary. Aside from any domestic problems that it might create, continued inflation always carries the danger that Britain will price itself out of its international markets. Thus British Governments make frequent use of taxation, currency controls, export/import regulations, and similar devices to affect the domestic economy and alter consumption patterns.

Paradoxically, Britain's international trade position has been weakened in part by having been the pioneer of the Industrial Revolution. Coal, iron, good harbors, and urbanized population all helped to make Britain the first industrial nation. This was a major source of world power in the 19th and early 20th centuries. But it also has meant that British industry has hesitated to modernize manufacturing methods. Consequently much industrial equipment suffers from obsolescence, and modern management techniques have been little utilized. In 1966, for example, two to four times as many men were required to produce the same output of steel, chemicals, metal products, transport equipment, and machinery as in the United States. In fact, except for metal products Britain was less efficient in its use of manpower in all of these industries than were West Germany,

FIGURE 1–2
Productive Efficiency in Selected Industries in Selected Countries

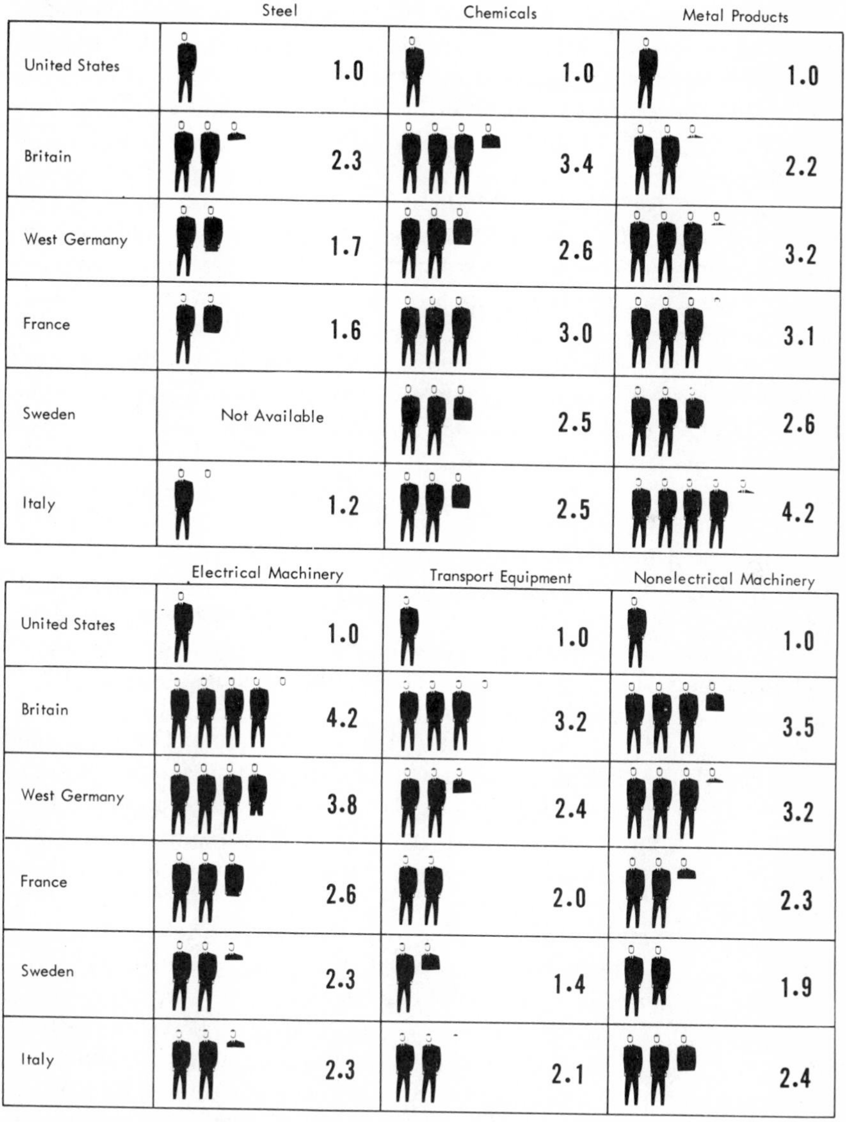

	Steel	Chemicals	Metal Products
United States	1.0	1.0	1.0
Britain	2.3	3.4	2.2
West Germany	1.7	2.6	3.2
France	1.6	3.0	3.1
Sweden	Not Available	2.5	2.6
Italy	1.2	2.5	4.2

	Electrical Machinery	Transport Equipment	Nonelectrical Machinery
United States	1.0	1.0	1.0
Britain	4.2	3.2	3.5
West Germany	3.8	2.4	3.2
France	2.6	2.0	2.3
Sweden	2.3	1.4	1.9
Italy	2.3	2.1	2.4

Key: Number of men required to produce same output as one man in the United States (1966).
Source: *The Economist,* October 1, 1966, p. 63.

Sweden, France, or Italy (see Figure 1–2). Many hope that the economies of producing for a larger market and the heightened competitive challenge which are offered by membership in the Common Market will help to strengthen British industry.

Double digit inflation and balance of payments deficits have made the economy Britain's most pressing problem of the 1970s. In 1967 British currency (the pound sterling) had to be devalued by more than 14 percent to the rate of £ = $2.40. In the mid-1970s the pound began an alarmingly rapid drop in value and by 1976 was worth only about two thirds as much as it had been a decade earlier. Adding to Britain's woes was the recognition that it was being passed by economically by some surprising countries. Not only had West Germany and France long ago moved ahead of Britain with per capita incomes 75 percent and 55 percent greater, so that within the EEC only Italy and Ireland had lower figures than did Britain, but in the mid-1970s East Germany also moved ahead of Britain in per capita income and Czechoslovakia was only $140 per person behind.

Clearly the problems and demands which confront the British political system and the way in which it responds to these are greatly influenced by the country's physical setting. Whereas in the past this setting has been a considerable asset in the political development of the country, it is by no means certain that this continues to be the case.

HISTORICAL BACKGROUND

The original population of the British Isles was not, as most people would think, Anglo-Saxon, but rather Iberian, a people widespread in Western Europe as far as the Caucasus. At an early date various Celtic groups invaded Britain; one was the forerunner of the Scots, another of the Welsh, and a third of the Irish. This was the population mixture which the Romans found when they invaded in A.D. 43.

Although the Roman occupation of Britain lasted about 400 years it had surprisingly little long-range effect upon British political institutions. The rugged Welsh and Scottish countryside prevented the Romans from dominating the entire island. In northern England they simply built a wall across the country to keep the barbarians out. While they did occupy Wales, they did little more than establish a system of forts, and their control in the mountainous areas was tenuous. These differences in Roman control contribute to the regional differences already noted.

As the Romans withdrew with the collapse of their Empire, the Celts surged back from the fringe areas into which they had been driven. Even before this had occurred the Norsemen had begun raiding Britain. These attacks by Jutes, Anglo-Saxons, and Danes lasted from around 300 to 1000 and destroyed virtually all remnants of Roman civilization. The area dominated by the Norsemen largely coincided, for similar reasons, with that controlled by the Romans. Thus the English legal system did not develop in a Roman law tradition as is true of continental political systems. About the only lasting contribution of the Romans to Britain's development was their system of roads; few others were built in Britain during the 13 centuries following the Romans' departure.

The Norsemen were not just raiders, but rather began to settle and intermix with the native population. Eventually this resulted in the formation of a Saxon kingdom, which was instrumental in driving the Danes from Britain and establishing an English nation. But at this point a threat from a new direction proved successful. The Normans, invading from across the Channel in France, conquered England in 1066 under William I.

The importance of the Conquest lies first in the fact that it unified the country by eliminating the several different dukedoms into which it formerly had been divided. Thus a major step in the essential process of nation building was taken under William's centralized rule. The other important result of the Conquest was to introduce the feudal system into England. Under the feudal system the rights, as well as the duties, of the nobility were specified. Although obligated to render certain services in exchange for the lands they were granted by the King, nobles also were to enjoy certain rights so long as they remained loyal. Should disputes arise concerning these rights and duties, they were to be settled in a council of the King and his leading lords. Thus were laid the foundations which eventually supported constitutionalism and parliamentary government.

The gains made under William's rule were almost lost in a period of virtual anarchy following his death. Eventually, however, central control was reexerted. Perhaps the most important fact of English history for several centuries was the country's ability to maintain a balance between feudal anarchy and tyrannical kingship. At any given moment one or the other might be ascendant, but equilibrium was achieved much more consistently than in any other European country.

This was not so much the product of wise rulers' policies purposefully directed toward such an end, as it was the serendipitous outcome of variously motivated actions. For example, in the 12th century the Crown developed a policy of sending judges throughout the kingdom to settle disputes other than by resort to arms. The aim was to help unify the country and to increase central revenues by collecting legal fees. But the result was to lay the foundation for the common law, one of Britain's major contributions to constitutional government. In deciding the controversies presented to them, the itinerent judges tended to rely more on tradition, the customs of the local people, and precedent than upon formal edicts or statutes. This practice gave rise to the idea that the judges were bit by bit elaborating a "higher law" more valid than that embodied in any written legal code. This in turn suggested that The Law was above the king and that any rules which he made which clashed with it were unjust and invalid. The concept of limited government developed from such thinking.

One of the leading governmental structures in controlling royal power was Parliament. Lacking sufficient revenue to finance his policies, King John decided in 1213 to extend taxation to the lower nobility. Since they were too numerous all to be summoned to the Great Council to pass the tax, John ordered that representative knights be chosen to attend. This was the initial step in representative government, since until that time those who participated in the decision-making process were included simply because of their personal eminence and spoke only for themselves. Later in the same century the brief parliament of the rebel Simon de Montfort called representatives of the townspeople as well as of the knights. This practice was legitimated in 1295 when a recognized ruler, Edward I, repeated it.

From these feeble beginnings a collective body of representatives came into being and acquired the name Parliament. It had very little authority of its own, was not popularly elected, and met only at the king's discretion. Sometimes several years separated its meetings. Moreover, it was not so much a legislative body as a kind of high court of justice concerned with judicial and administrative matters. And even in these matters, the commoners from the counties and the boroughs did not sit with the king and his lords to take part in their decisions. In time, the commoners developed into a gathering which could present grievances to the monarch. But not until the 14th century were they told to elect a speaker (to speak for them), and not until the reign of Henry V (1413–22) did they begin putting their petitions in the form in which they wished them enacted, thus initiating what could be called a legislative process.

Parliament was not intended to be an instrument for controlling the king's government. Gradually, however, this gathering of feudal representatives came to control the monarch and later its descendant came to be controlled itself by a popular electorate. The growing power of Parliament was made evident as the House of Commons gradually acquired the right of originating all bills for raising or disbursing revenue. As a result, the support of the Commons became essential to the Crown.

Nonetheless, Charles I attempted to rule without Parliamentary support and declined to call Parliament into session from 1629 to 1640. Such high-handed government, which was characterized by illegal taxation, martial law, and arbitrary imprisonment, combined with religious conflict between Protestants and Anglicans to culminate in a civil war during the 1640s. The king was executed and the monarchy was replaced by a republic, which tended to be an autocracy under General Oliver Cromwell. With Cromwell's death the regime disintegrated, because of factional conflict within the army, and the monarchy was restored. This period of little over a decade more than three centuries ago is the only experience England has had with republican government. The dearth of achievements during that time is one reason why few people in Britain today favor abolishing the monarchy.

The rule of James II raised again the questions of whether Britain was to be a Catholic or a Protestant country and whether ultimate power was to reside with the monarchy or with Parliament. In 1688 James was driven from the throne in a bloodless revolution and Parliament invited his Protestant daughter Mary and her husband William to become monarchs. Since Mary was not the immediate heir to the throne, Parliament had demonstrated its power to determine who would wear the Crown. By their acceptance of the throne, William and Mary acknowledged the supremacy of Parliament. At a time when continental European feudal kingdoms were turning into absolute monarchies, feudal limitations on the royal prerogative in England were developing into parliamentary restrictions on the exercise of Crown powers. The crucial question was whether the king could make laws outside of Parliament. The Civil War confirmed that the king was not above the law and that the common law could be amended only in Parliament. Since 1689 no monarch has ever challenged the supremacy of Parliament.

This is not to suggest that after 1689 monarchs lacked influence in government. On the contrary, many of them exercised great influence, but they had to depend upon Parliament for funds and for the laws they administered. Moreover, in the long, peaceful evolution of British political institutions since that time the power and influence of the monarch have steadily declined.

As the influence of the monarchs declined, the real work of Parliament came to be done in the two Houses sitting separately. Parliamentary supremacy, therefore, meant that the monarch would have to govern through ministers who were acceptable to Parliament. During his wars with France, for example, William III experienced difficulties with the House of Commons. Hitherto his ministers had been chosen from both political parties. Between 1693 and 1696, however, he dismissed the Tories and allotted all the great offices to the Whigs, who had a majority in the House of Commons. Heretofore turbulent, the House now became docile. For the monarch this was a matter of convenience, for political circumstances forced him to make use of ministers who could manage the House.

Out of these circumstances grew the practice of selecting the chief ministers exclusively from the party or faction that had effective control of the House of Commons. Since the views and policies of the Crown were determined by the party with a majority in the House of Commons, the ministers of necessity became, in effect, a committee of that party. By countersigning the king's acts, the ministers thereby assumed responsibility for them. Although they were the king's advisers, they were limited in the advice they could give by the political complexion of the party they represented. Until political parties became strong the king could play one group off against another, but he could not prevail against a united party commanding a majority in the House of Commons.

The king's advisers, who became known collectively as the Cabinet, began meeting without him in the 18th century to decide what advice they were going to give him. As political parties developed, the Cabinet came to give the monarch only such advice as its party was willing to have translated into public policy. Indeed, it could give no other advice, unless it wished to risk being removed from office by adverse votes in Parliament. In the end, the Cabinet's policies could only be those which could command the support of its party, as represented in Parliament. Furthermore, as the power of the House of Lords declined in the second half of the 19th century and on into the 20th, it was the political situation in the House of Commons which became of chief importance.

Coinciding with this shift in power was the growing democratization of the House of Commons. At the start of the 19th century the House of Commons was by no means a democratic body. Beginning in 1832, in a process that extended for almost a century, Britain broadened the franchise, thereby making the country's political leadership more accountable to the people.

Associated with expanded suffrage was the development of political parties. The Whigs and Tories of the 17th century, although in some ways scarcely more than factions, can be said to be the earliest British political parties. They developed more or less definite principles and the concept of a unified leadership, which was to characterize their successors. Not until the 19th century, however, did a modern party system, not resting on personal loyalty and patronage, appear.

The growth of political parties went hand in hand with the evolution of the cabinet system. That the two should be closely connected is understandable, for the existence of at least two parties means that there is always an alternative to the Government in power, a vital prerequisite to the cabinet system of government. This alternative is now officially recognized under the name of Her Majesty's Loyal Opposition.

At several points in this brief summary of British political history we have had occasion to note that a certain basic change occurred gradually and in stages. The evolutionary nature of British political development and the continuity which such a process provides need to be stressed. Perhaps the sharpest break in this history was the English Civil War and the republican form of government which resulted from it. But this proved to be only a brief hiatus with little lasting effect. The point is that in Britain, unlike many other nations, reforms have been neither sharp nor sudden. As a result they have won acceptance more readily and seldom have produced enduring extreme political cleavages.

In recent years, however, British historians have tended to emphasize the discontinuities, the breaks in British historical development. While it cannot be argued that British history can be graphed as an ascending straight line, yet its development has been smoother than French or American history. British history is not characterized by major watershed events like the French Revolution. And although there were at times reversals or periods of stagnation, it is possible to trace through British history a long-term trend toward greater control over governmental power, a trend toward increased responsibility or accountability to the people.

This trend continued until about the half century from 1870 to 1920. During that period several events occurred which suggest that this long-term development may not just have taken a temporary downturn, but may have been reversed. The period of greatest accountability in British politics may be past. Ironically this reversal occurred during the period in which, in terms of extension of the franchise, democracy was most fully realized. The factors involved in this seeming paradox will be a major focus in the following chapters.

BIBLIOGRAPHICAL NOTE

For a compendium of information on a wide variety of aspects of British life see either *Britain* [*year*]: *An Official Handbook* (London: HMSO, published annually) or Anthony Sampson, *The New Anatomy of Britain* (London: Hodder & Stoughton, 1971). Detailed economic and social information is available in B. E. Coates and E. M. Rawstron, *Regional Variations in Britain* (London: Batsford, 1971).

The standard source for British history are the various titles in the Oxford History of England series. For more recent surveys of British history see the works of T. L. Jarman and David Thomson. Modern British history is covered in Kingsley Smellie, *Great Britain Since 1688* (Ann Arbor: University of Michigan Press, 1964), and R. K. Webb, *Modern Britain* (New York: Dodd, Mead and Co., 1969).

2

The Foundations of
British Politics

CONSTITUTIONAL ELEMENTS AND PRINCIPLES

As the discussion in the previous chapter has shown, restraints or limitations on government power have been a feature of British politics for some time. Effective restraints on political power are synonymous with the concept of constitutionalism. The term also has come to mean that the powers conferred on government will not be exercised arbitrarily but in conformity with certain rules or principles. Thus, libertarian constitutions not only limit the powers of governments but also obligate them to adhere to definite procedural safeguards in the performance of their functions. In addition, constitutions allocate power among the various levels and branches of government.

Constitutionalism should not be confused with democracy. It is possible for a country to have limited, constitutional government without being very democratic in the sense of popular accountability of government—Britain in the first half of the 19th century, for example. Thus at this point we are more concerned with the formal, legal restraints on government than with the political limitations involved in popular accountability.

This distinction is very difficult to maintain in the case of Britain, however, for there limitations on governmental power are not the product of constitutional guarantees in the way they are in many other free nations. Britain does not have a single group of Founding Fathers; it did not have an original constitutional convention (or, alternatively, it has a permanent one). For Britain long has been said to have an unwritten constitution. This means simply that it does not have a single framework document to allocate, restrain, and channel political power for the system.

Instead the British constitution is composed of four basic elements: historical documents, acts of Parliament, judicial decisions, and conventions of the constitution. Of these four it is only the latter that in fact usually is not written down. The first three sometimes are referred to as the "Law of the Constitution."

Heading the list of the historic documents is Magna Carta (1215). It did not result from popular revolution and it contained little that was new. Intended primarily as a statement of existing feudal law, it was secured by a handful of barons who insisted on redress from the rule of autocratic kings. It is a constitutional landmark, first, because it reinforced the notion that the king was not above certain principles of law, and that should he refuse to obey them, the nation had the right to force him to do so. Second, the Great Charter embodied provisions that were in the interest of persons other than the barons. Although the clauses which sought to protect baronial privilege have never been repealed, they fell into disuse. The clauses which breathed the spirit of benevolent reform, however, have survived. Finally, Magna Carta achieved importance as a touchstone or bulwark of the nation's liberties. Britons invoked its principles whenever they felt that the monarch was exceeding his or her authority.

Not every act of Parliament is considered a part of the constitution. The criterion for inclusion is whether a statute deals with fundamental political questions like the distribution of power among various governmental organs, the procedures for making authoritative decisions, or the basic rights of the people. Such statutes sometimes are referred to informally as organic laws to distinguish them from ordinary legislation. Among the acts of Parliament normally considered part of the British constitution are the several Reform Acts, which extended the franchise, and the Parliament Acts of 1911 and 1949, which reduced the powers of the House of Lords.

While enacted statutes did not, by and large, produce constitutional changes until after 1832, the body of legal rules known as the common law, which grew up apart from any action by Parliament, has helped to shape British political institutions over the centuries. The sources of the common law must be sought in the customs and mores of English communities and the application of these by the judges in cases which came before them. With the passage of time, a whole body of legal rules was thus developed. As these became fairly uniform throughout the country, common to the whole realm, they acquired the designation the common law. Most guarantees of civil rights under the British constitution, for example, are rooted in the common law.

More recently the courts have contributed to constitutional growth through their interpretation of the great charters, the organic acts, and the common law itself. These judicial decisions, like the common law, although not set down in the precise form of a legislative act or a formal constitutional document, are nevertheless written and may be found in various legal and judicial collections or commentaries. It must be noted, however, that, although important judicial decisions are an element of the British constitution, no British court has the judicial review power of American courts to declare laws unconstitutional. This point is discussed more fully in Chapters 5 and 8.

Conventions of the constitution—the fourth element—are constitutional practices which in the United States would be referred to as custom and usage. While most of these are not written, this is not their distinguishing characteristic. Rather the basic question is whether a particular practice is enforceable, whether it can be the basis for a legal judgment. If so, then the practice is common law rather than a convention. Conventions are not legally enforceable, although they may be maintained by strong political sanctions.

This comment helps to suggest what is required to establish a convention. Precedent or tradition is not sufficient by itself to make a practice a convention. There must be as well logical and normative support for the practice. It is not just that something has been done a certain way in the past but that it makes sense to continue doing it that way and people feel bound to continue the practice. If the monarch refused to accept as Prime Minister the person preferred by a majority of the House of Commons, the government could not function, since no other person would have the support necessary to get any legislation approved by the Commons. Thus it is logical and sensible for the monarch to accept the Commons' choice. The Prime Minister must have a seat in the House of Commons not because the law says so, but because it is felt in the 20th century that it would be wrong for him or her to be in the nonelective House of Lords. The prevailing democratic political values provide normative support for this practice and help to make it a convention.

To Americans used to having a formal constitution with a Bill of Rights, the British constitution may not seem to offer much protection for basic liberties. Particularly may this seem to be true when one grasps the fact that the second of the four elements of the British constitution means that Parliament can amend the constitution at will the same way as it passes any regular legislation. No extraordinary majorities or referenda are required. Nonetheless, liberties are at least as firmly grounded in Britain as in the United States. As will be noted in the section on the Soviet Union, written catalogues of rights are no guarantee of freedom. The U.S. Constitution could not prevent a determined group from establishing a dictatorship in this country. The crucial consideration would be popular response to this attempt. This is to say that ultimately constitutions, even written ones, are, like conventions, politically enforceable. In Britain the political culture long has provided support for limiting the government and favoring fair play and justice. Nonetheless, in recent years possible passage of a bill of rights has received considerable discussion in Britain. That this might occur is no longer inconceivable, especially should the House of Lords be abolished to make Parliament a unicameral legislature.

Given the nature of the British constitution, it is impossible to draw up a comprehensive list of basic constitutional principles that would be acceptable to all experts. We can, however, mention several of the leading ones.

1. Liberty of the Citizen. The rule of law prevails in Britain. This means, among other things, that the government is not above the law; it cannot do whatever it pleases but must be able to cite legal authorization for its actions. All citizens are equal before the law. Convictions for breaking the law must conform with due process; torture, for example, may not be used to secure confessions. The law must be publicly known in advance before it is enforced.

2. Democracy. As previously noted this principle is distinguishable from liberty. It is concerned not so much with seeing that citizens' right to fair treatment is not transgressed, as it is with providing an opportunity for them to participate in authoritative decision making. The government is to do what the majority, not the minority, desire. In Britain, as in most mass democracies, this means primarily universal suffrage supported by the ability to form parties and pressure groups and to communicate with one's representatives.

3. Parliamentary Supremacy. The ultimate legal authority in Britain is Parliament. Since Parliament can alter the constitution at will, its actions never can be declared unconstitutional by any court in the land. All Acts of Parliament are legally valid.

4. Constitutional Monarchy. It follows from principles 1 and 3 that the British monarchy must be a constitutional, limited one rather than an arbitrary or autocratic one. Since the rule of law prevails and Parliament holds final power, the monarch is restrained. Thus, although an hereditary monarch continues to reign over Britain, the occupant of this position does not rule, as we will discuss more fully in a later chapter.

5. Unitary Government. Unlike the United States and Germany, Britain is not a federal system. In Britain the local governmental units owe their power and existence to Parliament, which can alter them at will. This relation clearly is associated with principle 3, that Parliament is the final authority. Unitary government in Britain was qualified slightly until 1972 by the existence of a separate parliament in Northern Ireland. This body passed domestic legislation for Northern Ireland, although its actions could be supplemented or overridden by the national Parliament meeting in London. In 1972 the Northern Ireland parliament was suspended because of sharp religious conflict between Catholics and Protestants there and London assumed direct rule.

The increasing strength of the Scottish and Welsh nationalist parties in the 1970s motivated the Labour Government to introduce devolution legislation in Parliament late in 1976. Directly elected assemblies were proposed to be created for both Scotland and Wales. The Welsh assembly was to be limited mainly to supervising administration in Wales, but the Scottish assembly was to be empowered to legislate for Scotland on a wide variety of subjects. Even should this reform be enacted, however, the British Parliament still would be able to reject any Scottish legislation it found unacceptable. Therefore, although the plan is to delegate some central power to the subnational level, Britain will remain an unitary system and not become a federal one.

6. *Parliamentary Government/Cabinet Government.*   Again in contrast to the United States, Britain has a fusion, rather than a separation, of powers. The executive structures are not separated from the legislature, but in their origin and maintenance are intertwined with it. Parliamentary supremacy—principle 3—clearly implies the existence of a dependent, rather than an autonomous, executive. The principle of constitutional monarchy is relevant as well, since the Cabinet system has helped to avoid conflict between the monarch and the Parliament. The Cabinet has served as something of a buffer or mediator between the ruler and those political leaders empowered to make authoritative rules for the society. Britain's system is characterized as Cabinet Government also because in the 20th century the Cabinet has become the most powerful element in the British political system.

7. *Party Government.*   If parliamentary government is to produce stable Cabinets, well-organized, disciplined parties are essential. The life of British Cabinets was much more tenuous when political groups were based on personal attachments rather than party loyalty. Furthermore, it is difficult to conceive of a political process in a mass democracy—principle 2—which would not give rise to a fairly well-developed party system to channel and stimulate demands for governmental action.

POLITICAL CULTURE AND CLEAVAGES

The study of national character is recognized as a very dubious approach to understanding a country's politics. This method lent itself too easily to stereotypes and prejudices. Yet few would deny that the examination of aggregate behavior patterns can be quite revealing about a people and their political system. Thus political scientists have come to concentrate more on the political culture approach. They have been less concerned to describe the typical person of a given country and more interested in seeking to isolate the values and attitudes that characterize the society.[1] So we wish to summarize some of the main themes of British political culture as exemplified by the collective behavior of the population.

Aside from Northern Ireland, British society is remarkably less violent than American. The number of murders in New York City in a year is well over one and a half times the number in all of the British Isles. Furthermore, since guns are tightly controlled, less than 10 percent of all murders were shootings and only about 7 percent of all robberies involved guns. This is despite the fact, or perhaps because of it, that the British police, except for rare, specially authorized circumstances, do not carry guns. Nonetheless, in the decade ending in 1974 only 11 policemen were killed throughout all England and Wales.

Although some recent cases of policy corruption and abuse of authority have come to light, the British police retain a level of respect remarkably high by American standards. A recent survey found that 90 percent or more of the adult London public respected, trusted, and liked the police.[2]

This low level of violence carries on over into the sociopolitical sphere also. Since 1842 only nine people have died in political demonstrations, riots, or industrial confrontations in Britain. No one has died in an industrial confrontation since 1911 and not a single person was killed in a riot from 1919 to 1974.[3]

The British political culture is characterized by a rather conservative attitude toward political change. Tradition is very important in British politics, and frequently the fact that something has been done a certain way for some period of time is accepted as sufficient reason for continuing to do it that way.[4] At the very least it is a strong argument for regarding proposed changes warily and examining them thoroughly. Furthermore, when change does occur, the British prefer for it to come about gradually, bit by bit over a period of some time.

Related to this preference for evolutionary development is the fact that the British political culture is a pragmatic, relatively nonideological one.

---

[1] Gabriel Almond and Sidney Verba, *The Civic Culture* (Boston: Little, Brown and Co., 1965), especially Chap. 1.

[2] William Belson, *The Public and the Police* (London: Harper and Row, 1975), cited in Richard Clutterbuck, "Threats to Public Order in Britain," paper presented at the 1977 meetings of the Political Studies Association of the United Kingdom, p. 6.

[3] Clutterbuck, p. 15.

[4] The political correspondent for *The Guardian,* one of Britain's leading papers, has commented: "Ask the British why they go about things in a certain way and they will examine themselves in great detail, search down into the roots of their long modern experience, and arrive at the conclusion that they do things a certain way because they have always done them that way. The tried is nearly always preferred to the untried, time is much honored; the British pay visits to the past and discover that it works. . . . change, even when, as recently, it may be quite rapid and radical, is usually accomplished by sleight of hand. Tradition is viewed not as inimical to change but as the sound basis for change." Peter Jenkins, *The Battle of Downing Street* (London: Charles Knight, 1970), p. 15.

Grand abstract social theories do not impress the British much. This is one of the reasons why Marxism has had so little impact in Britain. The British prefer a practical, functional approach to politics. It matters little to them that a system may have some illogical aspects so long as it works. Thus they have piled new political institutions on old and altered the original purpose of others all very untidily, but nonetheless effectively. They have been able to maintain continuity of political development by retaining old institutions while shifting power around.

The practical, empirical approach which prevails in Britain is reflected in that school of philosophy known as British empiricism. This group of thinkers, including Locke, Berkeley, and Hume, rejected the rationalism of the Frenchman Descartes in favor of a philosophy grounded in experience. This tradition has helped to make it possible in Britain to discuss political issues on their concrete merits rather than on their supposed logical virtues.

This fact in turn helps to support another element in British political culture—tolerance and the spirit of compromise. When one's opponents simply are urging the value of limited, practical reform rather than advocating the virtues of transforming the entire system, then one feels less threatened by their possible victory. As a result one is more willing to tolerate their views and to attempt to work out some course of action that will be mutually agreeable.

Of course, the British have not always been tolerant, as the religious conflicts of the 17th century demonstrate. This illustrates one of the pitfalls of the national character approach; there is not some inherent characteristic of the British people which makes them tolerant. It simply is the case that the British have for some time been willing to allow unpopular minority views to be expressed freely in their country. They have not sought to outlaw the Communist party nor have they felt the need to create an un-British Activities Committee.

In the 1960s and 1970s, however, it became clear that this toleration of diversity in political matters did not extend as readily into racial relations. Although the nonwhite population of Britain is only about 3 percent, its rapid growth during the 1960s and its concentration in a relative few areas has produced many sharp reactions. Some "coloureds" (the British lump Indians, Pakistanis, and West Indians together under this label) have been forced to move from their homes because of pressure from their white neighbors, and others have been discriminated against in employment. Some politicians, the best known of them the right-wing Conservative Enoch Powell, have linked nonwhites with crime, disease, and the destruction of British culture. They have favored sharply curtailing or even eliminating further nonwhite immigration into Britain and have suggested that the government pay the immigrants to return to their native countries.

During the past decade legislative action on race relations has moved in two directions, which some might regard as contradictory, but which the British hope are complementary. Immigration into Britain now is much more tightly restricted than formerly, but racial discrimination against nonwhite residents in Britain is more widely prohibited than it had been. It is hoped that the nonwhites can be more easily assimilated and their rights protected if their number in Britain is kept relatively low. The leaders of Britain's three main parties generally agree on this approach, but many average Britons want stronger actions against nonwhites. This emotional issue continues to be an important one in British politics and illustrates the limits of tolerance in Britain.

Despite the success of some politicians in stirring up the racial issue in Britain, the British political culture is correctly regarded as one character- ized by a considerable amount of personal emotional stability. Although the British have had charismatic leaders, like Winston Churchill, dem- agogues are rare. Mass enthusiasms bordering on hysteria seldom are a factor in British politics. This is not to say that the British lack commit- ment, but that even intense support tends to be more of the staid, than the emotional, type. The image of bulldog determination is an accurate one. The chief exception to this in the British Isles are the Welsh, who tend to favor a more florid and rhetorical political style. Most English people are uncomfortable with such profuseness and suspicious of it.

A final element of British political culture is individualism. Britons are not just free; they are truculently free. At times this results in trivial concerns; many more Britons than Americans see the census as an inva- sion of privacy and object to cooperating with the process. More impor- tantly, the stress on individual values means that a Briton is determined not to be put upon, is determined to resist all tyranny. As with toleration, this value is more prevalent in political than in social or economic matters. Feelings both of social solidarity and of social deference are prevalent in Britain and must be discussed in the remaining part of this chapter.

As we noted in the first chapter, Britons tend to be more homogeneous than Americans. There is one characteristic, however, in which Ameri- cans differ less from each other than do Britons. This is the most impor- tant political cleavage in Britain—social class.

Class differences have long been a part of British life, although in some significant respects these have varied from class divisions elsewhere in Europe. First of all, the British nobility have always remained a relatively small group, since only the oldest person in the family inherits the title while the other members continue as commoners. Secondly, because the barrier between classes has not been rigid, and because there have been manifold differences within classes, it has been possible for persons to move up the social ladder. Thirdly, class divisions have only partially been based on economic differences. Moreover, although titled personages have occupied, until recent times, a large share of the privileged positions, no class or group has stood in any privileged legal relationship to the state since the first part of the 16th century. Also, many of the peerages created in the last century constituted rewards for achieving eminence in the arts, science, or government service (diplomacy, military service, and politics).

The British population can be grouped into classes in a number of different ways. Whatever the categories used, two important points must be made. First, political power is exercised primarily not by the hereditary aristocracy but by the upper middle class. The latter is to a considerable extent a leisured class. In contrast with the United States, politics is seen as being a much more suitable and honorable career than business for someone of this social standing. Second, the sharpest break, the greatest gulf between classes, occurs between the manual workers and all those above them. In terms of values and behavior these two segments of society differ markedly from each other.

Class distinctions in Britain are not blurred to the extent that they are in the United States. People are typed according to social status, and the treatment which they receive depends upon whether they are above or below the social position of those with whom they happen to be dealing. A Briton can tell within a few minutes of beginning to talk with strangers what their social position is, since their speech patterns and accent identify them.

One of the key elements in maintaining a fairly sharply stratified society in Britain is the educational system. Whereas in the United States education and occupation tend to determine social status, in Britain social status tends to determine education and occupation. Although students may remain in the state-supported school system until they are 18, very few choose to linger beyond the compulsory schooling age of 16; especially is this true in secondary modern and comprehensive schools. About a quarter of the students in the state-supported school system attend secondary modern schools. These schools provide a general education with some vocational emphasis and are intended for average and weaker students. As a result, a middle-class child who is assigned to such a school is regarded by his or her family as an academic failure. The more capable students, about 10 percent of the total, are assigned to grammar schools to receive a more academic, college-preparatory education.

The comprehensive school, now attended by about 60 percent of the students, was devised in an effort to eliminate the distinction between the elite education of the grammar school and the mediocre education of the secondary modern. In support of its egalitarian principles, the Labour party has favored requiring local school boards to establish comprehensive schools, while the Conservatives have opposed this, arguing that to abandon the grammar schools would dilute the quality of education. Although the comprehensives are intended for both those students planning to go on to college and those ending their education with secondary school, they distinguish between their two types of students. Thus, even in the most egalitarian type of school, the college-bound stream receives different training. As noted above, few students in the comprehensive schools choose to remain on until they are 18. The grammar school remains, then, the chief entry route from the state-supported school system to higher education. While nearly half of the students in grammar schools go on to further education, less than a quarter of the students in comprehensive and secondary modern schools do. Thus the debate over elite education versus popular education continues in Britain.

Although the controversy over the form of state-supported education remains an important political issue in Britain, even more significant as a basis for social cleavage are the so-called public schools. These schools actually are privately operated and available only to those who can afford to pay sizable tuition fees or can win scholarships. Although only one sixteenth as many students attend these schools as are in the state-operated schools, the public schools are of immense political and social significance. In fact, attendance at the proper public school for one's secondary education is much more important for one's social status than is attendance at Oxford or Cambridge University.

The most famous of all British public schools is Eton, founded in 1441. Although it has a student body of little more than 1,000, Eton has produced 18 British Prime Ministers over the years. Furthermore, of all Conservative Cabinet ministers from 1918 to 1955 well over half (57 percent) had been to Eton and about one quarter of all Conservative members of Parliament during this time were Old Etonians.[5] The tie which men who attended the same public school, however many years apart, feel for each other is a significant factor in relations among the British political elite.

The British educational system has emphasized the training of an elite. Even the Labour party has not objected very strenuously to this approach; what it has sought is an equal opportunity for the talented from the lower classes to rise along with the wealthy. Thus, for example, approximately three fourths of the students in British universities now receive some financial support from government. Yet students from a working class background make up only 20 percent of those in higher education. It generally is believed that the public schools provide a surer avenue for university entrance. And, in any event, they reinforce the exalted social status even of those not attending universities.

Although many people in Britain regard social class distinctions as invidious and needlessly divisive, yet the fact of social stratification is widely accepted even by those who do not benefit from it. Many members

---

[5] W. P. Buck, *Amateurs and Professionals in British Politics* (Chicago: University of Chicago Press, 1963).

of the working class will freely admit that they lack the breeding and training of the upper classes. Rather than protesting against the power and prestige of those in these classes, many workers defer to them and do not question their superior social position. The existence of such a deferential attitude is relevant to voting behavior and will be examined in more detail in Chapter 4.

It must be reemphasized that class differences are not solely or even primarily matters of economic disparities. A skilled worker, for example, may think of him or herself as working class while a clerk or teacher may prefer the designation middle class; yet the best-paid skilled workers earn considerably more than the lowest-paid teachers and clerks and do not have the burden of trying to maintain a middle class life style. Increased income cannot readily be translated, however, into the manners, speech, social habits, and other class attributes essential for winning acceptance as an equal by the upper classes. Feelings of working class solidarity, which tend to reinforce existing behavioral differences, are reinforced by the fact that 40 percent of the British labor force is unionized compared to only 25 percent in the United States.

Income is not a major factor in class distinctions, in part because the extremes in distribution of income typical in the United States are relatively unknown in Britain. In 1973, 30 percent of all incomes were less than $2,300 before taxes. The next 30 percent ranged from $2,300 to $4,500, while the next 30 percent picked up at that point and rose to $7,800. Only 4 percent of all incomes exceeded $9,500 before taxes. Anyone whose take-home pay exceeded $125 a week would have found him or herself among the richest 10 percent of all income earners.

Perhaps more significant, because more unequal, is the distribution of wealth. The top 1 percent of the population over 18 owns a quarter of all personal wealth in Britain, while the bottom 80 percent owns little more than one fifth. Thus the disparity in resources with its resultant impact upon quality of life is sufficiently great that inequalities in distribution of financial resources remains an important political issue.

Although social stratification remains significant in Britain, a levelling process has been under way for some time, especially since the end of World War II. A large proportion of Britons tend now to think of themselves as lower middle class. This is in large measure due to post-World-War-II prosperity, high taxes on the wealthy, and expanded social services for the rest of the population. Something of a social and economic revolution has been effected which has had the net effect of improving the living standard of the working classes and of lowering it for many of the wealthy. Some of the aristocracy, for example, can afford to maintain their landed estates and lavish homes only by operating them as tourist attractions. As the physical conditions of life have become less disparate and the lot of the lowest classes more tolerable, attention has begun to shift in Britain toward the inequalities in the human quality of life. Whatever happens economically, class barriers will continue to exist in Britain until one can relate comfortably to someone from another class as a fellow human being. That point has yet to be reached in Britain.

BIBLIOGRAPHICAL NOTE

Albert Dicey, *Introduction to the Study of the Law of the Constitution,* 10th ed. (New York: Macmillan Co., 1961), and Frederic W. Maitland, *The Constitutional History of England* (Cambridge: Macmillan Co., 1908) are considered among the classics of British political literature. Equally perceptive contemporary works are Leopold Amery, *Thoughts on the Constitution* (London: Oxford University Press, 1953), and Harold Laski, *Reflections on the Constitution* (New York: The Viking Press, 1951). Perhaps the most cited work on the British political system is Walter Bagehot, *The English Constitution,* first published in 1867. See the 1963 Fontana edition for an interesting commentary on Bagehot's contemporary relevance by R. H. S. Crossman. Also useful are Sir Ivor Jennings, *The British Constitution,* 5th rev. ed. (Cambridge: Cambridge University Press, 1966), and Geoffrey Marshall and Graeme Moodie, *Some Problems of the Constitution,* rev. ed. (London: Hutchinson, 1961).

The following books provide additional information on social class in Britain: Wilhelm Guttsman, *The British Political Elite* (New York: Basic Books, 1964), and Brian Jackson, *Working Class Community* (London: Routledge and Kegan Paul, 1968). The importance of education in social stratification is made clear in Rupert Wilkinson, *The Prefects: British Leadership and the Public School Tradition* (Oxford: Oxford University Press, 1963).

The role of race in British politics is discussed in Paul Foot, *Immigration and Race in Britain Politics* (Harmondsworth, England: Penguin, 1965). The most detailed study of race relations is E. J. B. Rose, et al., *Colour and Citizenship* (London: Oxford University Press, 1969).

3

Expression of Individual and Collective Interest

THE ELECTORAL SYSTEM

As recently as the 1950s Britain was more democratic than the United States as regards the extent of the franchise. Virtually no legal bars to voting existed. No literacy test had to be passed; no poll tax had to be paid; no period of local residency had to be served. Furthermore, social and racial pressures against voting were unknown and legislative districts were much more fairly and equally drawn than was true in the United States. Yet during the 19th century the United States was considerably more democratic than Britain concerning the extent of the franchise. To explain this we briefly discuss the development of the British electoral system.

By the beginning of the 19th century, suffrage rules had become confused and chaotic in Britain. In some towns many adult males could vote, whereas in others not even 1 percent could do so. In some towns property determined eligibility; in others, it was membership in the municipal corporation—membership acquired by birth, marriage, or purchase. Moreover, representation in the Commons was not according to population. Each county and each borough, irrespective of its size, was entitled to two members in the Commons.

The inequities of this situation were worsened by the Industrial Revolution. Despite a rapid growth in population, many of the newer factory towns, like Manchester and Birmingham, were unrepresented in Parliament, while many previously thriving rural towns which were virtually deserted continued to send two Members each to the House of Commons. Although it had slid into the sea, Dunwich retained two Members in

Parliament. The fish at Dunwich were better represented than the people of Manchester. The Members from these rotten boroughs often were selected by no more than a handful of freemen, usually nonresidents, who owned a few dilapidated buildings. In such circumstances membership in the House of Commons frequently was bought and sold with a few men able to swing the balance of power.

The first step in altering this situation to produce greater democratic accountability was the Reform Act of 1832. It redistributed the seats in the Commons and broadened the suffrage. Representation still was not proportional to population, but many rotten boroughs were eliminated and the more populous towns gained some 150 seats. By providing for uniform suffrage requirements in the towns and by extending the suffrage to certain classes of tenants in the counties, the Act added more than 200,000 voters to the electorate, thereby increasing it by about 50 percent. In the United States, by way of contrast, this was the period of Jacksonian democracy, when universal manhood suffrage for whites was widely established. In Britain, even after the Reform Act only about 7 percent of the total adult population could vote (see Figure 3–1).

Although the franchise was broadened further in 1867, it was not until the reform of 1884 that most men could vote. Only in 1918 did Britain finally enact universal manhood suffrage. At the same time the vote was extended to women over 30. Only then could a majority of the adult population vote. Finally, in 1928, women between 21 and 30 were enfranchised as well. Thus, electoral reform required five installments (six if one counts the introduction of the secret ballot in 1872) over a period of a century. This is a classic example of the typical British approach to political reform. Nor was the process of extending the franchise ended in 1928, for in 1969 the voting age was lowered to 18.

In Britain, government officials assume the responsibility of registering voters. This is done once a year, usually in a house-to-house canvass. The list of registered voters is posted on bulletin boards in public buildings or other public places. People not on the list, who believe they should be, may protest to the registration officer and, if the decision is unsatisfactory, may appeal to the county court. Similarly, any person may protest the inclusion of persons he or she considers ineligible. The British approach to registration produces a larger percentage of qualified voters than in the United States.

General elections, in which every Member of the Commons stands for reelection, must occur at least once every five years. But, since the date of elections is not fixed, they may occur much more frequently. In fact Britain held two general elections in a single year in both 1910 and 1974. On the other hand, even the five-year limit may be exceeded if both Houses of Parliament approve. This was done during both World Wars to avoid having an election when the country was fighting for survival.

FIGURE 3–1
Growth of the Franchise

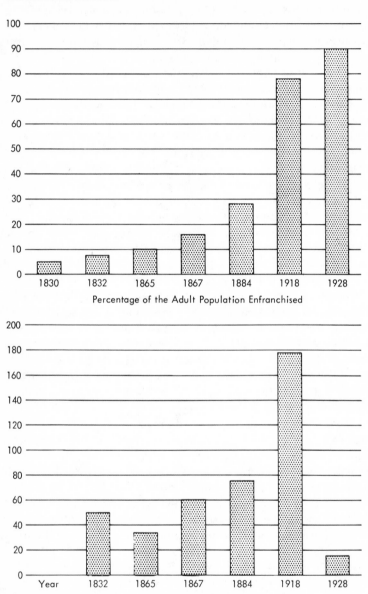

Despite this flexibility in the timing of elections, it is interesting to note that from 1900 through 1976 Britain has had almost the same number of general elections as the United States has had presidential elections—21 to 20. This does not mean that it makes no difference which practice is followed. Under the British system the scheduling of an election becomes an important consideration in the governing party's electoral strategy. They can wait until unemployment is low, prosperity is growing, or major new policies have been implemented successfully before calling an election in the hopes of capitalizing politically on these developments. Also, British electoral practice makes the mandate theory of elections a bit more plausible. According to this theory the electorate is given a choice between alternative courses of action and approves one or the other. The winning party then is said to have a mandate for its policy. Thus, an election comes to resemble a referendum. In 1972, for example, some people favored calling a general election on the question of whether Britain should enter the European Economic Community (EEC).

Eventually in early summer 1975, however, in a major political innovation a referendum was held on EEC membership. At the time, the Government maintained that never again would a referendum be used for any issue. Opponents of the referendum, who argued that once the first one was held there could be no way of preventing frequent resort to this device, did not have to wait long to have their fears substantiated. In December 1976 the Government conceded that referenda would be held in Scotland and Wales before any devolution proposals were implemented. Whether referenda will occur with such frequency and on such issues as to alter the nature of British general elections cannot yet be ascertained.

In addition to general elections, the only other elections for national political office in Britain are by-elections. Whenever a seat falls vacant through death or resignation of a Member, an election is called to fill it. Primary elections do not exist in Britain, since local political parties select candidates privately within their own organizations. Furthermore, the only office to be filled in any constituency in a British general election is representative for that district. Local elections never are held at the same time. And it is impossible to vote directly for the Prime Minister, unless one lives in the constituency he or she represents. Even then one votes for him or her only as a legislative representative and not as Prime Minister.

As a result the British ballot is extremely simple and straightforward. There are no referenda or bond issues to clutter the ballot. Typically, all that appear on the ballot are three to five names of candidates seeking election to Parliament from that constituency. Candidates' addresses and occupations are included on the ballot, but until 1969 that was all. Only then were party labels permitted. Now candidates may use up to six words to describe their party affiliation. Some independent candidates use the label to make a last-minute political statement. In 1970, one candidate styled herself on the ballot as "Stop the SE Asian War." A few prefer a lighter touch as did the candidate in a 1976 by-election who labelled himself "Lorimer Brizbeep, Science Fiction Loony Party." Naturally, the press referred to him for short as the Loony candidate.

Although nomination is a party rather than a public matter, various rules apply to getting one's name on the ballot. Certain classes of persons are not eligible for nomination. Among these are judges of the High Court and the Court of Appeal, ordained priests or deacons of the Church of England, ministers of the Church of Scotland, and priests of the Roman Catholic Church, persons holding an office of profit under or from the Crown, persons convicted of treason or felony, and those found guilty of corrupt or illegal practices in connection with elections. Candidates are not required, either by law or by custom, to live in the district they represent. This is evidence of the limited impact of local factors on national politics and of the existence of unitary, rather than federal, government in Britain. Nonetheless, some candidates will promise to move their home to a particular district, if they are elected as its representative. Those who have local connections will refer to opponents lacking these as "carpetbaggers." These strategies probably are not worth many votes.

To get one's name on the ballot, then, one needs only the signatures of ten qualified voters from that constituency. This is so incredibly easy compared to the United States that one would guess that there must be some catch. And there is, in the form of a £150 (about $275) deposit. Unless a candidate can win at least one eighth of the vote, he or she forfeits the deposit. Candidates not supported by one of the three main parties or by the nationalist movements have virtually no hope of meeting this requirement. Even Liberal party candidates find it difficult—182 of them, over half of all the party's candidates, lost their deposit in 1970. Nonetheless, as we have seen, the deposit requirement does not eliminate all Loony candidates.

In contrast with American campaigns, British elections are brief. The campaign legally does not begin until Parliament is dissolved, less than three weeks before the day of the election. Of course, political activity is not confined to this period; parties constantly oppose each other in Parliament and seek support among the electorate as a year-round activity. Furthermore, as it begins to appear likely that the ruling party will call an election, appeals to the voters through such means as extensive advertising campaigns are intensified.

The use of television during British campaigns is relatively limited. Parties and candidates are not permitted to buy time for special broadcasts or spot announcements. Instead the principal parties are officially allotted free time on television. The programs which they prepare are broadcast simultaneously over the government-owned BBC and the

FIGURE 3–2
Labour Party 1974 Election Poster

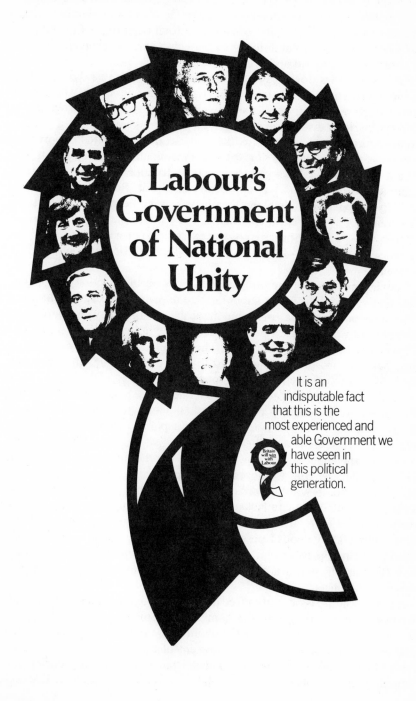

commercially operated ITV. Given the shortness of the formal election campaign in Britain, it perhaps is not too surprising that the time available to all parties for national television in the October 1974 election totaled less than two and a half hours. Most of this total went to the Conservative and Labour parties. In addition the nationalist parties received a total of 30 minutes in Scotland and Wales.

Television news does cover the elections, although this did not occur during a general election until 1959. Until then one never would have known from watching newscasts that an election was in progress. In addition, various discussion or interview programs give some of the less prominent candidates, as well as the party leaders, a limited opportunity to express their views. At times it is very difficult to accomplish this in Britain because the laws governing equal treatment by the broadcast media are so ambiguous, yet apparently stringent. Some candidates, by refusing to appear on television themselves, have been able to block the appearance of all their local opponents. The Labour party's unwillingness to appear on the same program as the extreme right-wing National Front caused several telecasts to be cancelled or altered during the October 1974 election.

Canvassing is one of the principal activities during election campaigns. The candidate and his or her supporters go door-to-door in a constituency seeking support from the voters and inquiring whether they have any questions about the candidate's policies. They hope in this fashion to discover who intends to vote for their party. Then on election day they can check the official record of who has voted to insure that those who said they would support them actually turn out to vote.

Candidates address voters at various meetings, sometimes during the course of a single evening presenting their views to three or four small groups meeting in schools or other public places. Particularly at large gatherings, heckling is a well-established British practice. The aim is not to disrupt the meeting by preventing the candidate from being heard. Rather the heckler tries to shout out some politically embarrassing charge that the candidate will find difficult to handle, thus presumably demonstrating that the candidate lacks a quick mind. Despite occasions of such lively give-and-take, attendance at campaign meetings has shown a long-term decline. Only about 5 percent of the electorate attends even a single meeting during the campaign. Meetings are more important in rural areas than they are in urban areas, but even there they rarely are a central activity any longer.

Each candidate is permitted free use of the mails to send one communication to the voters during the campaign. Typically this "election address" will be a four-page leaflet containing the candidate's picture, some biographical information, and a statement of the policies he or she supports. These addresses, like much else that occurs locally during the campaign, also emphasize the candidate's party and its leaders. The pic-

FIGURE 3–3
Conservative Party 1974 Election Poster

ture of the national Leader and a message of endorsement from him or her
may be included, for example. Great emphasis on national leaders is a
relatively recent development. The British are a bit uneasy with this and
tend to regard it as Americanization or Presidentialization of their electoral campaigns.

Each candidate must appoint an election agent (campaign manager) who is required by law to handle the account for *all* election campaign expenses, except the personal expenses of the candidate him or herself. No one except the candidate, the election agent, or persons authorized by the agent, in writing, can spend money in an effort to get a candidate elected or another one defeated. Any unauthorized expenditure on behalf of a particular candidate (or against an opponent) for a particular constituency is prohibited. Expenditures between elections are not covered by these regulations.

Furthermore, the amount of money which a candidate is permitted to spend is limited. He or she is restricted to a maximum of £1,075 plus a small allowance per voter. This produces a ceiling of around £1,600 in most constituencies. Few candidates spend this much; even Labour and Conservative candidates average only around £1,200. National party organizations are not limited in their expenditure, but they must not back individual candidates (including even their party Leader and potential Prime Minister) in their process of urging voters to support their party instead of the opposing party. Were they to do so, the cost would have to be included in the individual candidate's official statement of expenses.

To avoid this problem it had been the custom for parties to refrain from advertising in the national press during the campaign. In February 1974, however, the Liberal party did run newspaper ads and was not taken to court over individual candidates' official statements of expenses. Thus in the October 1974 election the major parties followed suit with national press advertising campaigns of their own.

Given the briefness of election campaigns, the national parties spend more money on advertising during the preelection period than they do during the campaign itself. Compared to the vast sums spent during American Presidential elections, expenditure in Britain is miniscule, even if the preelection period is considered. Prior to the 1964 election the Conservatives spent $2.8 million, while the Labour party could manage only $0.9 million. Although prior to the 1970 election the Conservatives had to reduce spending to $1.2 million, Labour had to cut back to $0.5 million. Furthermore, the Labour party has to contend with hostile advertising campaigns of various business groups. In 1964, for example, business groups spent $5.3 million in opposing government ownership of industry, a policy firmly connected in the public's mind with the Labour party. This sum was about half again as much as both major political parties combined spent on advertising during the same period. Campaign expenditures in 1974 obviously were larger than usual since two general elections were held in a single year. Each of the two major parties spent a total of well over $2 million, while the Liberals limited themselves to little more than $0.5 million.

Important as national political activities are, ultimately general elections are 635 separate local contests. As in the United States, each constituency returns only one representative—that candidate who wins more votes than anyone else—regardless of whether this constitutes a majority of the votes cast. Because of Britain's smaller population and the larger size of the House of Commons, the ratio of voters to representatives is considerably smaller in Britain than it is in the United States. Most constituencies have from 50,000 to 70,000 voters with few being greater than 80,000 or less than 40,000.

The British have made greater efforts since World War II than have Americans to maintain relatively equal constituencies. Extensive boundary changes were implemented in 1950 and further changes were carried out in 1955. The law was amended to avoid such frequent changes and now requires a review of boundaries no oftener than every 10 years and at least every 15. Thus, constituency boundaries should have been altered for the 1970 election. This did not occur because the Labour Government feared that implementing the changes proposed by the permanent boundary commissions might cost their party 25 to 30 seats in the upcoming election. With the return to power of the Conservatives in the 1970 election, the boundary changes were accepted. Thus, for the 1974 elections 5 new constituencies were created and the boundaries of 429 existing ones were changed; in 182 of these instances the change was extensive.

Despite all the national and local campaign activity, few people—only 11 percent in 1970—decide during the campaign period how they will vote. But perhaps such activity helps to keep turnout relatively high by American standards. Only once in the 20th century—the first election in which women could vote—has turnout fallen below 70 percent. In one post–World War II election it reached 84 percent. High rates of electoral participation cannot be attributed in most cases to doubts about the local results. From 1955 to 1970, for example, 75 percent of the seats in the House of Commons always were won by the same party. The limited number of seats lost by one party to another at each postwar general election can be seen from Figure 3–4. (The 1950 and February 1974 elections are omitted because of the extensive boundary changes.)

The simple ballot and the absence of pressures against voting doubtless help to maintain a high turnout. The smaller size of constituencies facilitates contact with the candidates, which also may aid participation. Furthermore, legislative elections usually occur less frequently than in the United States; therefore, voters need not go to the polls as often. Party organization in general tends to be more efficient; as much as half of the electorate in a constituency may be canvassed. Even more significant is the fact that more people in Britain than in the United States feel a strong tie to a political party. Electors tend strongly to vote for the party, not the candidate. A candidate's personal vote is estimated to be no more than about 3,000 votes, with rare exceptions. As one voter told a pollster, "I'd

FIGURE 3–4
Percentage of Seats Changing Hands at General Election

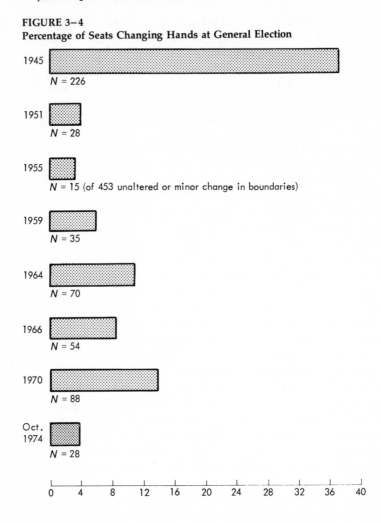

vote for a pig if my party put one up." This sentiment is related to the class feelings which are so much a part of British politics. A number of people feel that they would be "letting our side down" if they did not turn out to vote against the party identified with the other class. We discuss the bases of party support more fully in the following chapter.

THE INTEREST GROUP SYSTEM

Political interest groups are actively involved in the process of making governmental decisions in Britain. To Americans this statement will seem unexceptional. Britons have been slow to admit the existence of interest groups in their country, however, and rather unwilling to recognize their importance in the political process. Interest group activity has carried the negative connotation of special pleading or shady pressures aimed at perverting the common good in the service of a narrow segment of society. While the British were prepared to agree that such things happened in the United States, they believed that British politics functioned on a loftier plane. Nonetheless, interest groups long have existed in Britain. In fact one can argue that they are more intimately involved in the decision-making process in Britain than in the United States.

The conflict-of-interest laws force most members of Congress to be very discreet in their relations with interest groups. In Britain, however, it is perfectly acceptable for a Member of Parliament to have a direct financial relation with an interest group. Well over 40 percent of the Labour MPs are sponsored, primarily by trade unions, while on the Conservative side many MPs are company directors. Sponsored MPs may simply have some or all of their electoral expenses paid by an interest group; this frees their local parties from having to bear the cost and makes them more attractive candidates to them. Frequently, sponsored MPs also are provided with some financial assistance in meeting their expenses as MPs and even may receive a supplement to their salaries.

One of the few limits on sponsoring organizations is that they cannot order an MP to vote a certain way on particular legislation. Nevertheless, some Labour MPs have gotten into trouble with sponsoring unions because of the way they have voted in the Commons, and unions have withdrawn sponsorship from MPs who were not felt to be sufficiently loyal to the policies favored by the unions. Certainly a sponsoring organization may legitimately expect ''its'' MPs to express its views in Parliament whenever matters in which it is interested come up.

Although individual MPs can be useful to interest groups, they really cannot be very important. This is because committees of the Commons do not possess powers comparable to those exercised by Congressional committees. Also, the strong discipline exerted over British parliamentary parties means that MPs really are not free to change their votes in response to interest group activity, as is discussed more fully in Chapter 6.

If they are to be effective, therefore, British pressure groups must seek to exert their influence on those who have the power of making decisions—the Government, or the Administration as we would say in the United States. Since only the Government has a majority, special interests seek to persuade it that what is desired is not contrary to the national interest. Their approach is twofold. If new legislation is the object, they will attempt to convince the minister of the appropriate department. If money is involved, it is imperative that the Chancellor of the Exchequer also be convinced, for proposals to spend money require recommendations from the Crown.

Interest groups are not just concerned with obtaining new laws. Particularly in a welfare state they are more likely to be concerned with the administration of existing laws. Administration is a part of policy making, since the way in which a law is implemented can alter its impact considerably. Furthermore, a good deal of contemporary legislation takes the form of rather general framework laws, leaving the issuing of detailed regulations to the administrators. Thus, interest groups cannot confine themselves solely to events in Parliament.

So closely intertwined with the decision-making process in Britain are interest groups that they frequently do not even have to take the initiative. Prior consultation with interests is an accepted procedure. Before a bill is introduced into Parliament, the governmental department working on it will discuss it with relevant groups. This discussion concerns only the general principles of the bill; to examine a draft bill would infringe Parliament's rights.

Nonetheless, this procedure is important, because at this point, before it has committed itself publicly to all the details of the legislation, the Government is more willing to accept proposals to change some aspect of its plans. The significance of these contacts can be seen also in the fact that many groups view Parliamentary action as a last resort to be tried only when all else has failed. Of course, not every interest group has these valuable contacts with governmental departments. But the major groups do. Those groups which have not yet been able to win such recognition may be forced to utilize only Parliamentary activities and contacts. Although more visible, such methods are more likely to be a sign of weakness than of strength.

Thus, instead of dealing with a legislator, the agent of a British pressure group is more concerned to maintain close contacts with civil servants. The scope and frequency of these contacts were accelerated greatly in Britain by World War II. Many private groups—for example, producers' associations—became quasi-governmental then in an effort to ensure the most efficient use of resources. The aim was to integrate the productive capacity of the country as tightly as possible into the Government's war plans without having to expand public ownership. The extensive consultation to which both government and interests became accustomed carried on over into the postwar period.

The government recognizes that many of an interest group's staff are experts in a particular field and thus can provide valuable opinions on what measures are practicable. Furthermore, in some cases interest groups will possess much more detailed information about a topic or enterprise than is available to the government. Finally, if compliance is to be voluntary rather than coerced, the government is well advised to consult closely with those who are most likely to be affected directly by its actions. Thus, the government recognizes liaison with interest groups as an essential component of the governmental process. Departments may send draft regulations to interest groups before these orders are issued in their official form. Moreover, some departments have permanent advisory committees, where special interests are represented on a continuing basis.

The basic point is that interest groups in any system naturally focus their efforts at the point where power resides. In part in Britain this is with the electorate. So, like American interest groups, British ones spend some time trying to influence public opinion. But, unlike the situation in the United States, the legislature has only a limited role in initiating and shaping legislation, so that interest groups are not very active in this sphere. They tend to function more behind the scenes, which helps to explain why their activities were overlooked for so long in Britain. In fact, in Britain one can argue that the visibility of an interest group's activity is inversely related to its strength and effectiveness. Thus, although the role of interests in the British political process seems different, it is basically the same.

The differences lie simply in the fact that British interests concentrate more of their efforts at a different level in the governmental system. Furthermore, because authoritative power is highly concentrated in Britain, not diffuse as it is in the United States, interests focus on fewer points. This fact in turn affects the structure of interests. If they are to relate effectively to this concentration of power, they too must be highly centralized. Thus, in Britain, unions, farmers, veterans, and business are each represented primarily by one major interest group, which includes a greater percentage of the relevant population than do the several groups functioning in each interest area in the United States. The Trades Union Congress, for example, encompasses 85 percent of all trade unionists in Britain, while in the United States union members are split chiefly among the AFL-CIO, the Auto Workers, and the Teamsters.

Interest groups, then, are highly active and effective in Britain. Contrary to the attitude still frequently encountered in Britain, this is not a fact in itself to be viewed with alarm, for the interest group system provides citizens with a valuable means of making their views known to those holding authoritative power. And because these views are the product of collective action, they cannot be ignored as easily as can those of a large number of people functioning individually. A problem arises only when some group becomes so powerful that it can dominate the political process and proceeds to exert its strength primarily for the benefit of its members. In Britain many people now feel that the trade unions have reached this point. That is one of the issues dividing the two major parties. In the following chapter we explore the differences between the parties in detail.

BIBLIOGRAPHICAL NOTE

Campaign procedures, issues, and events for each general election since 1945 are discussed in the Nuffield College series of election studies, *The British General Election of* [*year*]. Since 1951 these books have been authored either individually or jointly by David Butler. On the role of television in politics, see Joseph Trenaman and Denis McQuail, *Television and the Political Image* (London: Methuen, 1961). For campaign techniques see Richard Rose, *Influencing Voters* (London: Faber, 1967).

General works on interest groups include: S. E. Finer, *Anonymous Empire*, 2d rev. ed. (London, Pall Mall, 1966); A. M. Potter, *Organized Groups in British National Politics* (London: Faber, 1961); and J. D. Stewart, *British Pressure Groups* (Oxford: Oxford University Press, 1958). Among the works on particular groups that are especially interesting are Harry Eckstein, *Pressure Group Politics: The Case of the British Medical Association* (London: Allen & Unwin, 1960), and Peter Self and Herbert J. Storing, *The State and the Farmer* (London: Allen & Unwin, 1962).

4

Political Parties

THE PARTY SYSTEM

A country's electoral system to some extent shapes the form of popular participation in the policy-making process. The interest group system channels and focuses the expression of demands and supports even more. Yet, if there were no political structures beyond these, inputs would enter governmental structures in extremely diffuse form and the process of sorting them out so that effective and acceptable governmental action could be taken would be virtually impossible.

It is difficult, therefore, to visualize modern democratic government's functioning without political parties. Where representatives are chosen by a broad electorate, the problem of ascertaining the will of the people and translating it into effective action requires organization. That organization is provided by political parties. They develop programs and select leaders to present to the electorate. They seek to persuade voters to support them at the polls. Between elections, the party in power, by defending the policies and actions of its leaders, seeks to create and to maintain the impression that the country is being governed in a desirable way and that the opposition could not do so well. The party out of power, by criticizing the policies and actions (or lack thereof) of the Government, desires to promote the opposite impression. Democratic government today is party government.

Although the rudimentary origins of British political parties can be traced back several centuries, many writers prefer to date their origin about 1700, when the two major political groupings were called the Tories and the Whigs. But it was not until well into the next century that a modern party system began to emerge. Only then did loyalty to party doctrine begin to replace personal connections as the basis of party organization. To a considerable extent this was brought about by the parties' need to organize the new electorate as the franchise was extended. Membership in Parliamentary factions became more stable and party organization outside of Parliament began to develop. This led in turn to a broadening of party membership beyond a handful of elected officials and party workers, a trend accelerated by the appearance of the Labour party in 1900. Thus at the beginning of the 20th century Britain had a fully developed modern party system.

Britain's party system usually has been labelled a two-party one, with the Conservatives opposing first the Liberals, in the 19th and early 20th centuries, and then the Labour party, in recent years. To conclude, therefore, that it is the same as the American system would be a mistake, however. In the ten general elections which Britain has held from 1945 through 1974, 29 percent of all the candidates for the House of Commons have been neither Labour nor Conservative. Nearly two thirds (64 percent) of all the electoral contests in individual constituencies have involved candidates from parties other than Labour and Conservative. And well over a quarter (29 percent) of all the candidates elected have received less than a majority of the vote in their individual district, which obviously means that more than two candidates were standing for election.

Only when party strengths in the House of Commons are considered does Britain resemble a two-party system. Since 1945 the Labour and Conservative parties always have held between them at least 94 percent of the seats. (see Figure 4–1) Not only have they been the only parties that have had any prospect of forming a Government, but they have not been forced by limited Parliamentary strength to form a coalition by including another party in the Government.

Until recently Britain deviated from a strict two-party system primarily because of the continued survival of the Liberal party. In the first quarter of the 20th century the Liberals rapidly lost votes to the newly formed Labour party. But the Liberals did not disappear, as happened when the Republicans displaced the Whig party in the American two-party system. They have continued to contest elections and maintain as extensive a party organization as their finances permit. Although since 1945 their strength in Parliament has been limited, they have had some impact on the policies of the major parties and the political attitudes of the public.

Sectarian conflict in Northern Ireland and the rise of nationalism in Wales and Scotland have combined in the 1970s to produce even greater departures from the ideal two-party system. Prior to then the Northern Ireland MPs usually were integrated into the Conservative party and the nationalists were unable to win any representation. Thus, in six elections, from 1950 through 1966, only ten MPs not associated with one of the three leading parties were elected. In February 1974, however, the figure jumped to 24 for a single election and in October rose to 27, both figures

FIGURE 4–1

The Two Leading Parties' Percentage of the Seats in Parliament at 20th Century
General Elections

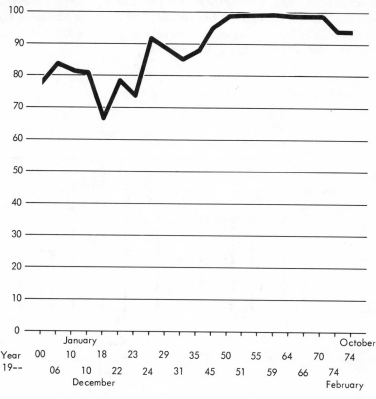

larger than the number of such MPs elected at any election for over half a
century.

The electoral system has been one of the factors that in the past has
helped to maintain a two-party system in Britain. As the Labour party
developed, Britain became a three-party system for a time. By the middle
of this century, if not before, it had returned to the two-party form. Under
the single member, simple plurality system, the share of seats in Parliament which a party wins is not related to the proportion of the popular
vote which it receives. Unless a party can concentrate its support in a
number of constituencies, it can gain a substantial share of the popular
vote without winning any seats.

To a considerable extent this has been the Liberals' problem. Their
difficulties have been compounded by the pragmatic nature of the British
electorate. Voters who might be favorable to many of the Liberals'
policies assume correctly that the party has no chance of gaining substan-

tial representation in Parliament. Not wanting to "waste" their vote and feeling no compulsion to demonstrate their ideological stance, as might a French voter, they choose between the Labour and Conservative parties. Figure 4–2 provides a pre–World War II instance and a more recent example of how the electoral system works to the Liberals' disadvantage and the benefit of the major parties.

FIGURE 4–2
Relation between Share of Vote and Seats in Parliament

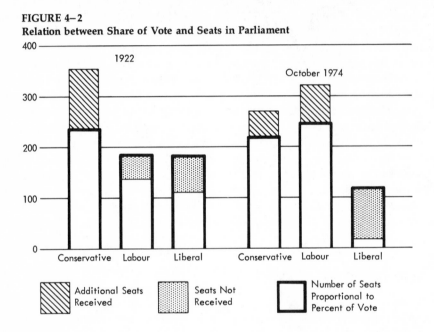

This aspect of the electoral system has not been a major handicap to the nationalist parties, however, precisely because, as we noted above is essential under the British electoral system, they have been able to concentrate their support. In October 1974 the Liberals, with 619 candidates and more than 18 percent of the popular vote, won only 13 seats in the House of Commons. The Scottish Nationalists, contesting only the 71 seats in Scotland, obtained less than 3 percent of the total national vote, but won 11 seats. The crucial difference was that within Scotland the Nationalists received more than 30 percent of the vote, a regional concentration of support nowhere approached by the Liberals.

Third parties, especially nation-wide ones, also encounter problems in breaking the strength of the two main parties because of the electoral deposit. Totally apart from campaign expenses, a party must risk about $175,000 in deposits to contest every constituency. Minor parties would have to expect to lose most of this sum. For a small party, whose income is likely to be limited, this presents a major financial burden.

Also relevant is the limited allocation of radio and television time. Minor parties are not given the opportunity which major parties have of utilizing these powerful mass media channels to win supporters. The amount of time granted the Liberals clearly tells the electorate that this party is not as important as are Labour and the Conservatives.

Nonetheless, one should not conclude that such legal regulations are all that are necessary to produce a two-party system. As noted in Part I, the distribution of political attitudes in a society is a major factor in shaping the party system. The functioning of the entire British governmental system tends to encourage the electorate to think in terms of supporting either the party controlling the Government or their chief opponents, who really provide the only viable alternative. Given the prevalence of such attitudes the Liberals would have a difficult task even were the electoral system altered as they wish to a system which would give them a share of Parliamentary strength more proportional to their popular support. Devolution to Wales and Scotland may cause the nationalist parties to shift their focus from the House of Commons to their regional assemblies, thus moderating their impact on the party system. Thus, on balance there is reason to think that the current departures from the two-party system in Britain are likely to be temporary. In the meantime, however, these departures continue to affect significantly the political process in Britain.

THE LEADING PARTIES

Having examined the British party system, we turn to an analysis of the parties themselves, with major emphasis on the Conservative and Labour parties but with some reference to the Liberals and the nationalists. We will discuss first what the leading parties stand for and then who it is in the population that supports one policy mix or the other. Who is it that finds a party of a particular type attractive? From there we move on to examining the parties' strength. How widespread is the support which a party receives and what are its prospects? This consideration in turn raises questions about the effectiveness of a party's organization. We broaden this fourth consideration to discuss as well the distribution of power within a party in order to assess its role as a participatory channel in a democracy.

Party Programs and Policies

Discussing the Conservatives' program is difficult because many Conservatives would question whether such a thing exists. Certainly they would object to anyone's presuming to study Conservative ideology, for they charge that being doctrinaire is a Socialist defect, from which they are free. They would contend that Conservatism is more an attitude toward society than it is a coherent set of doctrines. The Conservatives present themselves as the party of governmental experience, the party composed of the traditional ruling class, obviously best suited by heredity and tradition to run the country. At times their appeal to the electorate almost seems to be: Never mind our policies, simply trust our capable leaders, who will be able to take the proper action whatever the circumstances may be.

The Conservatives have been identified with support for the traditional elements of British society—the monarchy, the established church, the military, the existing social structure, the public school system. They have been a party of the elite, of the status quo. Yet they have not been reactionary nor even conservative, in American terms. They have demonstrated adaptability. While they have opposed some of their opponents' welfare measures, they have accepted socialized medicine and have introduced some welfare measures of their own. The Conservatives have acted similarly with respect to public ownership. Although they are opposed to it in principle, they have reversed very little of what Labour has implemented. And in fact some government-owned concerns were nationalized under Conservative Governments.

Thus the Conservatives seek a middle way between the excesses of both individualism and collectivism. They prefer individual freedom to bureaucratic direction and believe that widespread ownership of property is essential to a healthy democracy. Yet they recognize that social considerations may override these views. The party never has supported laissez faire, but has accepted the idea that governmental action may be necessary to correct economic abuses and stimulate the economy.

The important point is that usually the Conservatives do not feel that there is much either that needs to be reformed or that can be. They do not believe that social inequality is bad or can be eliminated. Different people contribute differently to society, so it is only natural that their rewards and political influence should vary as well.

At the same time, however, the Conservatives stress the idea of national unity; they appeal to feelings of community. Despite their association with the elite social and political groups, they see themselves as the only truly national party, representative of all interests rather than just a single section, as they charge Labour is. The Conservatives' ability to win the votes of many workers can be cited in support of this claim. The Conservatives berate Socialists for emphasizing class divisions and thus needlessly stirring up ill feelings. This desire for national unity is related to the Conservatives' concern with national honor. They see their party as the repository of the national interest and at times seem to believe that they are the only true patriots. The British flag almost invariably is displayed prominently at Conservative party meetings. For a British party to criticize the country's foreign or colonial policy is reprehensible in their view.

Thus, it seems ironic that it was the Conservative party which arranged for British entry into the Common Market, while the Labour party became increasingly hostile to this step. Labour has been more concerned than have the Conservatives about what would happen to the Commonwealth, the contemporary descendant of the British Empire, which always made Conservative hearts quicken with pride. The Conservative leaders have had to cope with some internal party opposition on this issue, but they have been able to win the support of the bulk of the party.

To a considerable extent the Conservatives fought the February 1974 election on the question, "Who governs?" The Conservative Government of Edward Heath felt that its efforts to combat inflation were being undermined by excessive wage demands on the part of some unions. They argued that the Government, not the coal miners, had been elected to determine economic policy. This analysis of the proper distribution of power in Britain did not particularly recommend itself to the electorate, who proceeded to vote the Conservatives out of office. As a result the party has backed off somewhat from its position, but still feels that much of what it said during the campaign has been borne out by subsequent events.

In addition to keeping wage claims from being irresponsible, the Conservatives seek to fight inflation by reducing government spending and, therefore, cutting back in some public services. The party seeks to devise policies that will facilitate home ownership rather than continuing to expand public housing. Conservatives wish to maintain the elite or, as they would say, the quality segment of the school system. They also are promising greater response to the public's desire for further limitations of "coloured" immigration. The current party leadership desires little, if any, devolution to Scotland and Wales. Since a significant minority of the party, including some former leaders, favors creation of a Scottish assembly, the party's policy statements on this subject have been rather ambiguous.

The basic doctrine of the Labour party is democratic socialism. It has been little influenced by Marxism; rather its intellectual heritage derives from Christian socialists of the social gospel school and the Fabian Society. In addition the party is greatly influenced, as its name suggests, by being based on the trades unions. Hugh Gaitskell, a former Leader of the party, once said of the Independent Labour party, a forerunner of the Labour party, that its "socialism was derived far more from the Methodist Church and a Christian approach than from Continental revolutionaries."[1] Similarly the Fabian Society would have nothing to do with

---

[1] Hugh Gaitskell, *Recent Developments in British Socialist Thinking* (London: Co-operative Union, n.d. [circa 1960]), p. 4.

Marxist revolutionaries. In an 1896 statement of purpose the Fabians begged "those socialists who are looking forward to a sensational historical crisis, to join some other society."[2]

Sidney Webb, one of the most influential leaders of the Fabians and the Labour party around the turn of the century, once explained the conditions which were essential if political and social reform were to occur in Britain. For change to occur it must (1) come democratically; (2) be gradual, causing no dislocation; (3) not be regarded as immoral; (4) be achieved constitutionally and peacefully.[3] Hardly a cry to man the barricades against the capitalist oppressors! The Fabians believed that sound factual research would be sufficient to establish the case for socialism in the minds of all reasonable people.

The influence of the Fabians has been of great significance in the development of the Labour party's orientation toward politics. The Fabians demonstrated that it was possible to be a socialist without having to use Marxist jargon or swallow an abstract, elaborate theory of history. They made advocacy of moderate reform respectable by showing that one could be for widespread change without having to be a revolutionary.

For about the last two decades the Labour party has been torn between two contrasting views of socialism. The left wing of the party, which believes that it alone is remaining true to the party's basic principles, sees the essence of socialism as nationalization—government ownership of "the commanding heights of the economy." The party has been committed formally to such a policy since 1918. The left has felt that in a democracy large concentrations of economic power must be publicly controlled to ensure that they will serve social ends rather than the benefit of a few. The object is to ensure that the working class, through its representatives, exercises power.

But to the bulk of the party and its leaders, nationalization no longer seems a panacea for social ills. They feel that the fairly extensive program of nationalization which Labour implemented in Britain from 1945 to 1951 did little to promote greater equality by redistributing the wealth. In their view socialism is not so much a matter of government ownership of the means of production, distribution, and exchange as it is a quest for social justice, not that the left wing is not also concerned with social justice. To obtain this goal the government should maintain a floor of basic benefits and services available to all as of right and to ensure that everyone truly has an equal opportunity to rise above that floor to the maximum of his or her ability.

Labour's concern with equality is not limited simply to correcting dis-

---

[2] Quoted in Margaret Cole, *The Story of Fabian Socialism* (London: Mercury Books, 1963), p. 92.

[3] *Fabian Essays in Socialism,* ed. G. Bernard Shaw (Garden City, New York: Doubleday, n.d.), p. 51.

parities in wealth and income. They seek as well to transform the values of British society so as to eliminate snobbery and privilege. They want to destroy the class barriers and social inequalities which now are obstacles to free social intercourse between people of differing status. British socialism is not just an economic doctrine. The founder of the Labour party, Keir Hardie, observed, "Socialism is at bottom a question of ethics or morals. It has to do mainly with the relationships which should exist between a man and his fellows."[4]

In international affairs the party has opposed colonialism and has been less nationalistic than the Conservatives. Nonetheless, the Labour party has been much less supportive of British membership in the Common Market than have been Conservatives; thus, on this question they have shown much more concern about maintaining Britain's national autonomy. Labourites opposed to British membership in the EEC argued that membership would undermine Britain's ties with the Commonwealth by redirecting its trade patterns toward Europe. Probably more important, particularly to the left wing of the Labour party which is where opposition to the EEC primarily was concentrated, was the fear that membership would deny Britain the power to control fully her own economy and thereby prevent socialistic reforms. The fact that socialist parties in Europe have been among the strongest supporters of the EEC did little to dissuade the Labour left from its belief that the EEC is an alliance of capitalists designed to protect the economic interests of the elite. The overwhelming two-to-one vote in favor of EEC membership in the referendum of June 1975 appeared to have settled the issue, but the left wing of the party continues to agitate for Britain's withdrawal.

Although never a majority position, pacifism traditionally has been strong in the Labour party. This belief has combined at times with the left wing's considerable distrust of the United States as a capitalist power, to produce neutralist sentiments. On occasion the party has favored withdrawal of American bases from Britain and unilateral nuclear disarmament by Britain. Usually the party leaders have been able to reverse or ignore such resolutions.

Immediately after World War II the policy differences between the Labour and Conservative parties seemed to be clear-cut; the choice offered the voters appeared much sharper than that provided in the United States by American parties. During the 1950s and 1960s, however, the two main British parties seemed to converge on policies. The word "Butskellism," a combination of the names of Richard Butler, the number two man in the Conservative party, and of Hugh Gaitskell, the Leader of the Labour party, was coined to suggest how little difference there was between what the parties advocated. Two polls in the mid-1960s found that

---

[4] Quoted in Socialist Union, *Twentieth Century Socialism* (Harmondsworth, England: Penguin, 1956).

40 to 50 percent of the electorate failed to see any important difference between the parties.

The election of the Conservatives under Edward Heath in 1970 reversed this trend, however. Labour charged Heath's Government with being the most right-wing Conservative Government since World War II, feeling that policies on unions, wages, social services, and education were a step back toward the 1930s. The confrontation between the Heath Government and the miners in the winter of 1973–74 thus was for Labour merely the ultimate evidence that all their accusations were true. Political conflict in Britain, at least in its rhetoric, has sharpened considerably and the alternatives presented by the two main parties may be as distinct as they were in 1945. Certainly the new Leader of the Conservatives, Margaret Thatcher, is widely regarded as being considerably more right-wing than Heath. At the same time, however, the pressure of economic problems has forced the Labour Government to reduce or forego many of its plans for government action; for the time being, then, the difference in practice between the two parties is not huge.

The Liberal party's response to "Butskellism" was to attempt to provide the voters the choice which the main parties no longer seemed to do. The Liberals offer social reform without socialism. Instead of public ownership of industry, for example, they have advocated co-ownership. A firm's workers would share in the profits and be represented both at the management and governing board levels. This would ensure that workers would share in deciding how the business would be run and, presumably, make them feel more a part of the business. The Liberals believe that such reforms would help to eliminate class bitterness in Britain and improve productive efficiency.

Another distinctive Liberal policy has been decentralization of government. They want to establish regional governments to move Britain toward a federal system, a step regarded as making government more efficient and closer to the people. The rise of nationalism and the main parties' response to this has made Liberal policy seem less unique. The ultimate aim of the nationalist parties is complete independence from the United Kingdom. Since they know that the majority of the population in neither Wales or Scotland favors this, they sometimes try to make the break seem less drastic by describing their goal as Commonwealth status. Only when one bothers to reflect that this is the position of fully independent nations such as Canada and Australia and that the nationalists also talk of control over foreign affairs and defense and of obtaining seats in the United Nations does one understand that what they seek goes far beyond the Liberals' federal proposals, to say nothing of the Labour Government's devolution plans.

The nationalists do present policies on other issues. Plaid Cymru, the

Welsh nationalists, are especially concerned with defending Welsh language and culture. Issues of this type are much less important to the Scot Nats, who emphasize more economic policy, particularly measures to fight the poverty that exists in many parts of Scotland. Nonetheless, both parties are primarily one-issue parties; independence overshadows all else that they might propose.

The Bases of Party Support

Except for inner London and the urban industrial areas, the Conservatives dominate England from somewhat south of Manchester to the southern coast. (The results for October 1974, appearing in Figure 4–3, provide a roughly accurate example of the situation.) Until recently Northern Ireland has been an almost exclusive Conservative preserve. Of the 96 electoral contests from 1945 through 1970 for Northern Ireland's 12 seats, the Conservatives have won 80. (Recent sectarian conflict in Northern Ireland has so changed the political situation that since 1974 none of its MPs can be considered part of either major party.) Labour's dominance in Wales has been almost as great; it has won about three fourths of all the contests there (267 of 359). Party strengths are a bit more balanced, although hardly equal, in Scotland. Labour has won 395 seats and the Conservatives 267 since 1945. In England, Labour's strength is the mirror image of the Conservatives'; it does best in nonsuburban London and the north. Labour polls best in city centers, especially in the old industrial towns, and in mining areas. The Liberals' greatest electoral success has been in the Celtic Fringe—Scotland, Wales, Devon, and Cornwall. These regional variations in party strength are another evidence that Britain is not politically homogeneous.

The recent rise of the nationalists has made these contrasts even sharper. In the October 1974 election, the Scottish Nationalists became the second strongest party in Scotland, gaining 25 percent more votes than did the Conservatives and trailing Labour by only 6 percentage points. The support for Plaid Cymru, while significant, was not nearly so great, as it polled little more than a tenth of the vote in Wales.

The political challenge of the nationalists is a worrying threat to the major parties, especially Labour. Were it not for the seats which it won in Scotland and Wales, Labour would not have returned to power in February 1974, since it trailed the Conservatives by 30 seats in England. Of the seats which the Scottish Nationalists had the best chance of gaining in the next election, 11 were won by Labour in October 1974 and only 4 by the Conservatives.

Traditionally, the Conservatives drew their chief support from the

FIGURE 4–3
Distribution of Parliamentary Seats in October 1974 Election

Key:
Conservatives
Labour
Liberals
Others

landed element in British society. Around the turn of the century, however, many industrialists left the Liberals for the Conservatives. Now the
party is strongly supported by business and professional people—
including the military—and farmers. Labour's main strength is with the
workers and some elements of the lower middle class like teachers. About

one fourth of the middle class usually votes Labour, but this does not offset the fact that one fourth to one third of the numerically larger working class usually votes Conservative.

A good deal of research has been directed toward endeavoring to find out why so many workers do not choose to vote for a party which in its name and policies clearly claims to represent their interests. One widely accepted theory has stressed the importance of feelings of deference.[5] This view argues that those of lower social status in Britain believe that intelligence and ability are inherent and unique to those above them, that such qualities are not attainable through education or by wealth. Therefore, those of higher social status should be selected to run the government, since they clearly are the most able. Some evidence suggests that the political importance of deference is declining. Only among those aged 45 and older do feelings of deference seem strongly to encourage support for the Conservatives.

Evidence of this type has led to detailed study sharply questioning the deference theory of British voting behavior.[6] This approach emphasizes the importance of historical changes in the party system. Some time had to pass from the founding of the Labour party around the turn of the century until most voters would first come to political awareness in a system in which Labour, rather than the Liberals, were seen as the normal alternative to the Conservatives. Until then, working-class Liberals who recognized that continued voting for the party they most preferred had become futile would be more likely to switch to the Conservatives than to Labour.

Regardless of the relative validity of these theories, the potential threat to the Conservatives is obvious. One should not conclude, however, that the Conservatives necessarily will lose the important support which they have gained in the past from the working class. The point is that the reason for this support may change from deference or family tradition to more pragmatic assessment of Conservative accomplishments. Thus this group might be more open to persuasion to change their vote, but Labour still would have to convince them that it could run the government more effectively.

Labour's concern in recent years has been whether increased prosperity in Britain would produce middle class attitudes among even manual workers and thus shift their allegiance away from Labour to the Conservatives. This topic also has attracted much research; the conclusion seems

---

[5] See especially Robert McKenzie and Allan Silver, *Angels in Marble* (Chicago: University of Chicago Press, 1968).

[6] David Butler and Donald Stokes, *Political Change in Britain*, 2d college ed. (New York: St. Martin's Press, 1976), especially pp. 117–38.

to be that Labour need not feel threatened by growing prosperity.[7] As with the question of deference, it is more a matter of a change in the motives for support than one of substantial realignments of voting blocks. Prosperous workers would be more likely to vote Labour on the basis of pragmatic assessment of its performance rather than because of feelings of class solidarity.

Insofar as deference, family tradition, and social class decline and pragmatic evaluations of party performance increase as the bases for the electorate's choice among the parties, fairly substantial, short-term shifts in electoral support can be anticipated. The figures in Table 4–1 for the popular vote do indeed demonstrate that British politics have become considerably more fluid in the 1970s. At the same time, as we noted above, the contrast in the political orientations of the Labour and Conservative parties has become sharper than it was during the period of "Butskellism." The heightened temperature of partisan conflict may convince the voters that social class cleavages should be as important as they used to be in voting choice.

Party Strengths

The results of all general elections since 1945 in Britain appear in Table 4–1. After winning an overwhelming victory in 1945, the Labour party just managed to retain power in 1950 and the next year lost control of the Government. This was despite the fact that in 1951 Labour polled more votes than did the Conservatives, more in fact than any party before or since. From 1951 through 1959 the Conservatives won three consecutive general elections, an unprecedented accomplishment. Returned to power by a narrow margin in 1964, Labour won a substantial victory in 1966 but surprisingly was defeated by an unusually large shift of seats to the Conservatives in 1970. Although they received more votes than did Labour in February 1974, the Conservatives did not win quite as many seats and, thus, were driven from office. Labour, although the largest party in the House of Commons, had to form a minority Government since it was several seats short of an absolute majority. Several months later Labour called another election in hopes of winning firm control of Parliament. They were successful, but just barely, gaining only one seat more than an absolute majority.

Even this tenuous hold soon disappeared, erased by conflicts within Labour over devolution and defeats in by-elections. By the close of 1976 Labour had been reduced to winning crucial divisions in the House of

---

[7] See especially John Goldthorpe et al., *The Affluent Worker: Political Attitudes and Behaviour* (Cambridge: Cambridge University Press, 1968).

TABLE 4-1
Party Strengths Since World War II in General Elections

	1945	1950	1951	1955	1959	1964	1966	1970	Feb. 1974	Oct. 1974
Seats in the House of Commons										
Conservative	213	299	321	345	365	304	253	330	296	276
Labour	393	315	295	277	258	317	363	287	301	319
Liberal..............	12	9	6	6	6	9	12	6	14	13
Others	22	2	3.	2	1	0	2	7	24	27
Percentage of the Popular Vote										
Conservative	40	44	48	50	49	43	42	46	38	36
Labour	48	46	49	46	44	44	48	43	37	39
Liberal..............	9	9	3	3	6	11	9	7	19	18
Others	3	1	1	1	1	1	2	3	5	7

Commons on the basis of the vote of an obscure independent MP who owned a tavern in Northern Ireland.[8]

The results of both 1974 general elections departed significantly from those of the ten previous post–World War II elections. For the first time, neither major party was able to win as much as 40 percent of the popular vote. Not since 1929, when the Liberal party still was a major force, had this occurred. This low share of the popular vote for both major parties has been interpreted as evidence of public disenchantment with both contrasting sets of remedies for Britain's ills. Clearly, the Liberals were a principal beneficiary of this dissatisfaction. On the other hand, public opinion polls since the 1974 elections suggest that support for the Liberals is extremely soft. They will be fortunate to retain what they won in 1974; to expect further gains is a delusion. Only the Scottish Nationalists and, perhaps, Plaid Cymru reasonably can hope for solid electoral gains. For the immediate future the major parties' search for a working Parliamentary majority offers as much promise of success as did the quest for the Holy Grail. This fact of necessity will have a major impact upon the relations between the House of Commons and the Cabinet and, conceivably, also upon the power structure and Parliamentary behavior of British parties.

Another element in a party's strength, because it presumably affects a

[8] In Britain taverns are known as "pubs," short for public house, and those who run them are called publicans. The MP involved is sympathetic to removing Northern Ireland from the United Kingdom and merging it with the Republic of Ireland. Given the combination of his political views and his occupation, the press dubbed him "the republican publican."

party's attractiveness to the electorate and the degree of confidence they are willing to place in it, is internal factionalism. The Conservative party has done rather better than Labour in containing internal party disputes. It is not so much that disagreements do not occur in the Conservative party as it is the party's ability usually to keep them out of the public eye. The Labour party maintains that this is evidence that the Conservatives conduct their operations less democratically. In part the difference is due to the parties' contrasting views on leadership. The Conservatives in general have great confidence in their leaders and feel that they should be supported loyally. A considerable portion of the Labour party, however, distrusts its leaders and suspects them of not really being full-blooded socialists. Thus while the rank and file in the Conservative party are disposed to follow, many Labourites are inclined to criticize and berate.

Furthermore, when divisions do occur within the Conservative party, the factional groupings to which they give rise tend to be temporary, ad hoc alliances.[9] Those who were opponents on one issue are likely to be working together on another. In the Labour party, factions are more like permanent blocs which retain a fairly constant membership over time. Those who are on the left remain there from one issue to another in constant opposition to those in other factions, a situation that makes it fairly easy for the Conservatives to tell the electorate that Labour cannot even run its own affairs, much less govern the country.

Although much smaller than the major parties, the Liberals have been even more debilitated by internal conflict. Suspicion of the party leaders is strong among Liberals also. And even the party's top leaders frequently have been unable to take a common position on public issues, a situation much less usual and acceptable in Britain than in the United States.

The financial resources of the Conservatives are substantially greater than those of Labour. The Conservatives maintain that this is essential to offset the free assistance which Labour receives from the unions. They contended that a public statement of their finances would be misleading and refused to publish their accounts as Labour did. But in 1967 Labour passed legislation compelling businesses to publish their contributions to political parties. Therefore, the Conservatives decided to begin publishing their accounts.

The great cost of the Conservatives' pre-election campaign in 1963–64 substantially cut their financial reserves. Furthermore, the party was beginning to run an annual deficit in its regular budget. If the deficit had been continued at its prevailing rate, the reserves which the party had in October 1967 would have been wiped out in two years. Consequently the party launched a special fund drive in the fall of 1967, which raised £2.25

---

[9] S. E. Finer, H. B. Berrington, and D. J. Bartholomew, *Backbench Opinion in the House of Commons 1955–59* (New York: Pergamon Press, Inc., 1961).

million ($5.4 million) in the next year and a half. This, combined with some economies, strengthened the party's finances so that by 1970 its reserves were around £900,000. Having to fight two general elections in one year, however, meant that 1974 proved to be a considerable financial drain. Thus by the spring of 1975 reserves had dropped to £585,000. The party could be encouraged nonetheless by the fact that their accounts for fiscal 1975–76 showed a small surplus of income over expenditure.

The Labour party also was running increasing deficits in its regular budget during the late 1960s despite its financial connection with the trade union movement. Its reserves have been roughly about half those available to the Conservatives and its regular income only one half to one third that of the Conservatives. By 1975 Labour had an accumulated deficit in its general fund of over £200,000 and anticipated that this would grow to £750,000 by the end of 1977.

Even Labour's financial situation has seemed great riches in the eyes of the Liberals, who during the late 1950s were trying to operate their national party machinery on an annual budget of $50,000. While the party's financial situation improved substantially during the 1960s, the Liberals still are forced to make do on an annual income of only about one ninth to one tenth that of Labour. In 1976, not for the first time, they had to reduce the national headquarters staff to meet expenses. Running the Liberal party requires a constant search for financial angels to save the party from the pit of bankruptcy.

Party Organization and Power Structure

The modern British party system is the product of the gradual expansion of the electorate since 1832. Before that date, parties were groups of men in Parliament who, on great issues, thought, talked, and, for the most part, voted alike. But even inside Parliament there was no party organization in the modern sense.

Prior to 1832 there was little or no need for party organization. The franchise was so limited and parliamentary seats were controlled by so few people that there was no need for an organized effort to persuade the public and to seek its votes. With the Great Reform Act of 1832, however, the electorate was enlarged, necessitating the compilation of lists of qualified electors. Consequently, each party sought to insure that all its qualified supporters were registered and that the names of all unqualified opponents were removed from the voting lists. For this purpose, registration societies were formed; these groups constituted the beginning of party organization at the constituency level.

Not until 1867, however, was a national grouping of constituency associations begun. The passage of the Second Reform Act, further extending the suffrage, in effect made the national organization of parties a necessity. In that year was formed the first of the great party organizations, the National Union of Conservative and Unionist Associations. Thus, more than a third of a century elapsed between the initial founding of the registration societies and the effective mobilization of national party organizations in support of party candidates.

Both major parties in Britain are highly centralized organizations, sharply contrasting with the rather loose structure of American parties. Although both Labour and Conservatives concentrate considerable power in the hands of their national leaders, the former operates somewhat more democratically than the latter.

While cognizant of the need for a national party organization, Conservative leaders intended from the beginning that the voluntary, mass party organization outside of Parliament should be the servant of the Parliamentary party. The National Union was not to usurp any of the functions of the Parliamentary leadership. Thus, although there are other national party organs of importance—committees dealing with policy, finance, and selection of candidates, for example—none of these are responsible to the mass party organization. The policy committee reports to the Leader, who appoints its chairman and vice-chairman. Half of its other members are selected by the Parliamentary party, thus leaving the mass party a minor share in its operations.

From time to time, ways of keeping the Parliamentary leaders more intimately in touch with the rank and file of the party have been explored, but the leaders have fought persistently every suggestion that the National Union should be accorded effective control over the party in Parliament or over the party's central office, which is under the control of the Leader. He or she appoints the party chairman, two vice-chairmen, and two treasurers, who are responsible for directing the activities of the central headquarters' professional staff. Thus the National Union is limited to being an educative political force and an aid to the winning of elections. It serves as a channel for communication between the party's Parliamentary leaders and the rank and file party members in the country and provides the most active of the latter with some limited opportunity for involvement in the formulation of party policies.

The basic organizational unit of the Conservative mass party is the local constituency association. To be a party member in Britain one cannot just declare a party preference, as is true most places in the United States, but must formally join a local association and annually pay the small sum required as dues. The Conservatives have been one of the most successful parties in the democratic world in recruiting regular members. During the 1950s their membership rose to around 2.75 million and even now, at about half that, still is quite substantial.

Although the primary function of the local association is to conduct publicity and raise money with the view to securing the election of Conservatives to Parliament, its most significant role is the selection of candidates. For this purpose the executive council of the local association appoints a selection committee. The committee may invite seven or eight would-be candidates for interviews but ultimately will recommend two or three. These are invited to a special meeting of the council, where they make speeches and answer questions. The council then selects one to recommend to a general meeting of the local party. Approval of the council's choice by this meeting is virtually automatic.

Early in the selection process the chairman of the local association usually will have requested the party's national headquarters to suggest names of potential candidates. Names which the local selection committee receives by other means are supposed to be cleared with national headquarters. Nonetheless, this does not always occur. The local associations are very jealous of their power to choose whomever they wish as their candidate. If the local party feels that the national headquarters is trying to impose a particular person upon them as their candidate, that is the last person they would select. Thus, although the national headquarters formally has the power to veto a local association's choice for candidate, this never happens. Given the number of safe seats (those consistently won by the same party) as noted in the previous chapter, the small group of people composing the local executive and the selection committee wield considerable power in determining who shall occupy the chief positions of governmental power in Britain.

The various local associations are joined together in the National Union of Conservative and Unionist Associations. The principal organs of the National Union are the annual Conference, the Central Council, and the Executive Committee.

The Conference is a yearly meeting which lasts three and one-half days. Each local association, irrespective of its size, has the right to send seven members (exclusive of MP or prospective MP, certified agent, and certified organizer) to the Conference. More than 5,000 persons have the right to attend, but since 1945 attendance has averaged between 3,000 and 4,000. Although the first Conference was held in 1867, nearly 20 years passed before current political questions were debated and resolutions regarding them adopted. Although the Conference has continued to pass such resolutions, it has no power to formulate party policy. In the main, it has tended to serve as a demonstration of party unity and support for the leaders. But, while leaders cannot be bound by Conference decisions, they can be politically embarrassed by them. Conservative Conferences regularly pass resolutions urging the reintroduction of capital punishment in Britain, although the party leaders make no efforts, when they are in power, to comply.

The Conference, besides being unable to formulate policy, lacks the power to act as the party's governing body. This authority is vested in the

Central Council, which normally meets once a year and is, in effect, a briefer and smaller version of the annual Conference. It consists of the party Leader, all Conservative members of Parliament (including peers), prospective Conservative candidates, members of the executive committee of the National Union, representatives of the National Advisory Committee of the National Union, and four representatives of each constituency organization. Meetings of the Central Council afford constituency representatives an opportunity to express their opinions on any matter that especially concerns them and to get firsthand reports from the leaders.

The executive committee of the National Union, with a membership approximating 150, normally meets every other month. It consists of the Leader and other principal officers of the party, together with representatives of the areas, each of which encompasses several constituencies. It concerns itself, in the intervals between the meetings of the Central Council, with matters under the jurisdiction of the Council. Much of the detailed work is performed by the General Purposes Subcommittee. This subcommittee also prepares the agenda for the annual Conference as well as for the Central Council.

Most of the Conservative Parliamentary party's organizational structure has been created in the half century since 1922. In that year an intraparty revolution which drove the Leader from his position led to the creation of the Conservative Private Members Committee (popularly known as the 1922 Committee). This committee is primarily an organization of Conservative backbenchers, the less prominent Members of Parliament not part of the top leadership group. The chairman of the 1922 Committee has direct access to the leaders, to whom he or she conveys the views of the backbenchers. Since votes are not normally taken in the Committee, it becomes the duty of the chairman to interpret the "sense of the meeting." Although the 1922 Committee is not authorized to formulate policy for the party, rank and file MPs speak their minds freely.

Moreover, through the 1922 Committee Conservative MPs are organized into functional committees. These party committees are not to be confused with the committees of the House of Commons. The scope of these various party committees corresponds to governmental ministries and departments. In these committees Conservative MPs discuss in detail current political issues and Government policies and help to crystalize the party's attitude on them. In this way the party also can attempt to hammer out differences in private in an endeavor to maintain a united front in public.

Although the views of the backbenchers are kept constantly in mind by the Leader, the closest advisors are his or her Cabinet colleagues when the party is in power. When the party is out of power the same group is formally known as the Consultative Committee (popularly as the Shadow

Cabinet). The Conservative Leader has complete power to designate whomever he or she wishes to this group of advisors regardless of whether the party is in or out of power.

Active and important as all these previously mentioned party structures are, it is the Leader who is preeminent, heading the party in a fashion surpassing that of any American politician. He or she is the one person to whom party adherents, both in and out of Parliament, look for day-to-day leadership. Being either an actual or a potential Prime Minister, he or she has enormous authority over other MPs. While remaining party Leader, he or she is the authoritative voice of the party. National Headquarters is the Leader's personal party machine. He or she appoints the Chief Whip of the Parliamentary party and selects the Shadow Cabinet. The Leader is not bound by any policy resolution of the mass party and, instead, is recognized to have exclusive responsibility for party policy. None of these things is true of the Labour Leader.

Nonetheless, the Conservative Leader is accountable. Prior to 1965 the Leader was said to "emerge." That is to say that, when the position became vacant, its new occupant was chosen in behind-the-scene negotiations before the formal party meeting was called to officially elect him. The selection of Lord Home as Leader in 1963 by this process dissatisfied many prominent Conservatives. While Home was the second choice of many, they preferred someone before him. Their lack of consensus on a first preference helped to put Home into the post of Leader.

As a result, the selection process was altered to one of explicit election by Conservative MPs. Special majorities and multiple ballots are provided for to help insure that the person selected has broad support. The choice of the MPs must be confirmed by a meeting of about 1,000 people—all Conservatives in both Houses of Parliament, Conservative prospective candidates, and members of the Executive Committee. This meeting is unlikely to be anything other than a rubber stamp.

Although the first use of the new procedures merely confirmed the existing Leader in office, the next occasion produced surprising results. Having led the party to two electoral defeats in 1974, Edward Heath's position as Leader had been seriously weakened. Few anticipated, however, that Margaret Thatcher, a not especially prominent member of the Shadow Cabinet, would be able to gain more votes than Heath, as in fact occurred. That a party as supportive of tradition as the Conservatives should become the first British party to choose a woman as Leader was amazing.

In summary, the Conservative party is very hierarchically structured, and at the apex of the party is the Leader. Yet, despite possessing great strength even when the party is out of office, the Leader can be driven from his or her position by strong opposition from Parliamentary colleagues or the mass party. In fact, in the 20th century Conservative Leaders have suffered this fate more frequently than have Labour Leaders. Although one hardly can characterize the Conservative party as democratic, the Leader is responsible to the followers. His or her power is checked by the constant need to win acceptance for the actions he or she wishes the party to take.

Unlike the Conservative party, which was organized from inside Parliament, the Labour party was organized from the outside. That is to say that the party grew up first in the country and then got representatives elected to Parliament. This has made a profound difference in structure of the Labour party and its organizational values. The Labour party has regarded itself as a *movement* aimed at voicing the people's interest in the political process. Many Labour members view the Parliamentary Labour Party simply as the instrument through which this objective is to be accomplished. Thus the Parliamentary Labour Party is to serve the mass party by seeing that its principles are carried into law. This is precisely the reverse of the Conservative party's organizational ethos. In that party the mass party is to serve the Parliamentary party by providing money and personnel to win elections.

The Labour party was founded in 1900 when representatives of the Independent Labour Party, the Fabian Society, various socialist groups, and several of the trades unions met to form the Labour Representation Committee. The key decision was that MPs elected with its support should be totally independent of either the Conservative or the Liberal parties. In 1903 the unions took the crucial step of increasing their nominal financial support of the LRC to a substantial regular levy. In 1906 the LRC changed its name to the present one of Labour party. Within 22 years of its founding it had driven the Liberal party (with the aid of factional feuds within the Liberals) into third place in the House of Commons; within 24 years it provided the country's Prime Minister; within 45 years it won an absolute majority of the seats in the Commons at a general election.

Labour's organizational structure is more complex than that of the Conservatives. The mass organization not only coordinates the activities of the local constituency associations but includes as well various related organizations, primarily unions and cooperative societies. Organizations of this type affiliate with the Labour party at both the national and the local level. It is the semifederated nature of the party's organization that accounts for its having two types of membership—direct and indirect.

One may join the Labour party directly by paying dues to a local association, just as is done in the Conservative party. But of the party's more than 6 million members, fewer than half a million are direct members. The great bulk of the members are indirect, are members simply because the union to which they belong has affiliated with the Labour party and has paid a political levy for each of its members. Thus many indirect members may not really favor the Labour party at all. Should they strongly oppose Labour, as those workers who vote Conservative must obviously do, they can "contract out"—sign a formal statement that they do not wish to have any of their union dues paid to Labour. Since the sum per individual is so small, however—typically less than $1 a year— and since there usually is strong pressure from one's fellow workers to pay the levy, few union members contract out regardless of their attitude toward Labour.

The governing body of the local constituency association is the General Management Committee, composed of delegates from ward committees and the affiliated organizations. Since the GMC meets only annually, effective power is wielded by the executive committee, which is chosen by the GMC and meets monthly.

As in the Conservative party, one of the most important powers of the local Labour association is to select the party's parliamentary candidate in that constituency. The Labour party's national headquarters, however, tends to be more actively involved in the selection process. The local executive will prepare a short list of candidates for the GMC to select from among. The National Executive Committee must have an opportunity to comment upon the candidates before a choice is made. Furthermore, the decision of the GMC is not official until it has been endorsed by the NEC. And in by-elections the local association must share with the NEC the power to select the candidate. Nonetheless, most of the power of selection remains with the local party. Given the number of safe seats in Britain, this means that the local parties can shape the nature of the Labour party in the long run by choosing candidates sympathetic with either the right wing or the left wing of the party. It also is relevant to note that trade union nominees often have an advantage in the selection process because their unions may pay as much as 80 percent of the election expenses. Forty percent of the Labour MPs elected in October 1974 were sponsored by trade unions.

The governing body of the mass party is the annual Conference. Well over 1,000 delegates from local associations and affiliated organizations attend these gatherings, whose principal business is to discuss and vote upon the various policy resolutions which these groups have submitted. When formal votes, called card votes, are taken on these resolutions, heads of the various delegations hold up cards indicating how many members their organization has in the party. Thus, regardless of the number of delegates present in the hall at the time of the decision, votes totalling 5 or 6 million are not uncommon.

The policy-making power of Conference is a matter of some dispute and considerable importance. Varous party documents and leaders have said from time to time that Conference is the ultimate authority in the entire party and thus controls the PLP. Were this true, it would mean that

Labour MPs were accountable not to their constituents but to Conference, a fact which would raise a basic constitutional issue of short-circuiting democracy. MPs are protected from such control first of all by the general admission that Conference can not dictate to the PLP how it should vote on a particular issue. Furthermore, although the principles endorsed by Conference are to be carried out as soon as practicable, the party's constitution does not say who is to determine this practicability. Thus, while Labour leaders cannot defy Conference, they have some discretion about when and how its decisions are to be implemented and in some instances they may decide that the time never is suitable.

Such procrastination may be risky, however, for the Leader must report annually to Conference on the work of the PLP during the preceding year. This report then is debated by the delegates, who may wish to know why their previous resolutions have not been heeded.

Whatever the power of Conference over the PLP, it is clear that it directs the National Executive Committee, which is responsible for the work of the mass party when Conference is not in session. It sees to the enforcement of the party's constitution, rules, and standing orders. It has the power to expel a Labour MP from party membership and, should the local association stand by their excommunicated MP, it has the power to disaffiliate it from the national party.

The party's professional staff operates under the NEC and its subcommittees. The Labour head office, popularly known as Transport House, is not the personal machine of the party Leader. It is the servant of the Conference and of the NEC.

Except for the Leader, Deputy Leader, and the Young Socialist delegate, who are ex-officio members, the 29 members of the NEC are chosen by Conference. Actually, 12 members are nominated by the trade unions and elected by their delegations to Conference. Socialist and cooperative organizations affiliated with the party select one member. Seven members are nominated and elected by the constituency and other local subdivisions of the party. Five women members are elected by the whole Conference from among those nominated by affiliated organizations; the trade unions have sufficient Conference votes to choose all five of these. The same is true of the treasurer of the party, who is nominated by affiliated organizations and elected by the whole Conference. The trade unions are therefore in a position to select 18 of the 29 members on the National Executive Committee. Add to this the fact that the card vote system means that six large unions hold a majority of the votes at Conference and one easily can see the great potential power which unions have in the Labour party.

During the 1940s and 1950s this situation did not produce any difficulty. The union leaders normally were moderates, who were happy to accept the policies of the Parliamentary leaders. In fact the Parliamentary leaders found the union leaders useful allies in fending off attacks from extremist delegates from the local associations. Furthermore, regardless of how the NEC was selected, the majority of its members usually came from the Parliamentary Labour Party. This was true in part because the more powerful union leaders preferred to serve on the General Council of the Trades Union Congress, rather than on the NEC. Thus those union leaders who did serve on the NEC tended to be the less important ones and could be influenced relatively easily by the Parliamentary leaders.

Increasingly during the 1950s, however, struggles over policy so divided the PLP that the mere fact that a majority of the NEC were MPs could not guarantee control to the Parliamentary leaders. More importantly, the rise to power of a new generation of union leaders in Britain led to policy conflict between them and the Parliamentary leaders. In part this is because Britain's economic situation has forced Labour Governments to take action that the unions do not like. But it also is due to the fact that some of the more recent leaders of Britain's largest unions are more militant than their predecessors were on foreign affairs as well as domestic policy. Thus, whereas in the past the Parliamentary leaders could count on the power of the unions to save them at Conference from the left-wing enthusiasms of the local associations, now the unions frequently are allied with the left. This has made the task of leading the Labour party, difficult at best, an even more onerous job.

The Leader's task of party management also is complicated by the fact that the Parliamentary Labour Party can make binding policy decisions when Labour is out of power. Thus, unlike the situation in the Conservative party, the Leader regularly attends meetings of the PLP and until 1970 presided over them. In 1970 the offices of Leader and Chairman of the PLP were separated, however, with the holder of the latter position presiding. When Labour controls the Government it always has sought to maintain close communication between those in the Government and its backbenchers by creating a special committee, known in recent years as the Liaison Committee. The chairman of this committee has occupied a position similar to that of the chairman of the 1922 Committee in the Conservative party. It was this position which in effect was perpetuated, when Labour went into opposition in 1970, by separating the offices of Leader and Chairman.

When Labour is out of office it selects annually a Parliamentary Committee to direct the PLP's activities. To those 12 MPs receiving the most votes from their colleagues are added the Leader, the Deputy Leader, the Chairman, and the Chief Whip. The Labour party in the House of Lords also has three representatives on the Committee. This committee is in effect the party's Shadow Cabinet, although the Leader may find it necessary to include a few more MPs in order to insure that someone will be responsible for keeping a close watch over all important areas of Government policy.

The PLP is organized into two sets of overlapping committees—11 area groups and 13 subject groups. The former are used in party management to help insure that Labour MPs attend important debates in the Commons and vote as the party wishes. The latter are similar to the Conservatives' functional committees. They provide some opportunity for MPs of little prominence to have some input into the party's policy-making process. The committees are less important when the party is in power—when the Cabinet makes party policy—and even when the party is out of power the committees' influence is limited and depends to a considerable extent upon the amount of status within the party which a particular committee chairman possesses.

Given its conception of itself as a democratic movement of the people, the Labour party was slow to designate someone Leader. The PLP had a chairman in its early years, but this was simply because of functional necessity—someone had to preside over PLP meetings. Certainly the position was not intended to carry any special authority or power. During the first two decades of the party's existence, six men held the post and four years was the longest unbroken term. When the party finally reconciled itself to having a Leader, it had the misfortune of a traumatic experience in 1931 with the first man to hold that title—Ramsay Mac Donald. Without going into the historical details, suffice it to say that the Labour party believes that MacDonald betrayed the movement by forming a coalition government which, although he was its Prime Minister, was dominated by the Conservatives.

While the party office of Leader survived this experience, it reinforced the suspicions already widespread in the party that a taste of power was sufficient to make those at the top of the party sell out party interests and personal principle for personal gain and glory. One of the ways in which a Labour Leader can attempt to counteract these suspicions is to reassure the party that he or she is a true socialist. Someone has observed that the Labour party can be led only from the left of center. This is why Harold Wilson and Clement Attlee were more successful as Leaders than Hugh Gaitskell.

The PLP annually elects the Leader. Most of these elections are not real contests, since a Leader rarely is opposed when he or she stands for reelection. Contrasts in the power of the Labour and the Conservative Leaders have been mentioned already. To summarize them: (1) the Labour Leader does not choose the bulk of the Shadow Cabinet or appoint the Chief Whip, but the PLP does; (2) Labour headquarters is not the personal machine of the Leader, but is directed by the NEC; (3) the Labour Leader is not empowered to make policy on his or her own authority;

(4) the Conservative Leader is not required to report to the party's Conference annually on the work of the Parliamentary party.

Despite these restraints and the complications which they produce in the process of party leadership for the Labour Leader, the fact remains that he or she is the most powerful figure in the party just as the Conservative Leader is. And when Labour is in power, the Leader, who then becomes Prime Minister, functions basically as the Conservative counterpart does when that party controls the Government. The Labour Prime Minister can pick a Cabinet as he or she chooses, and the Cabinet runs the Government with little interference from the rest of the party. Of course, a Labour Prime Minister cannot afford to ignore strongly held views in the party, but no Conservative Leader, for all his or her power, can do that either. And if the most important evidence of power is the ability to retain one's office, then the Labour Leader is stronger than the Conservative. For, as previously noted, in the 20th century intraparty revolts have driven Leaders from power more often in the Conservative than in the Labour party.

Regardless, then, of the contrasts in party rhetoric and accusation, regardless of the contrasting intentions of those who founded the parties and the parties' reversed pattern of development, one of the leading experts on British parties has argued that the two major parties have fundamentally the same power structure.[10] He contend that the structure of British government requires that this be true. The Leader of a British party either is Prime Minister or is the alternative candidate for the post; thus he or she either has immense power or potentially has it. Parliamentary democracy requires that Governments and MPs be responsible to the electorate rather than to some limited section of the society; thus they must be free from party control external to Parliament. And this, he feels, has been true of the way in which the Labour party has operated in practice. Thus the structural differences of the parties have been a matter of nuances and atmosphere. While these are important, they are not perhaps, fundamental.

As we have noted already, the parties' policy differences certainly are not fundamental. Their greatest contrast, then, may be in their clientele. And if, as suggested in the first part of this chapter, a change in voter motivation results in a more fluid electorate, this contrast may be blurred as well. The major British parties offer a choice of alternatives sufficient to maintain popular interest, commitment, and even (of a limited few) zeal. Yet the alternatives are not so stark, the stakes of electoral competition so high, that the political game is transformed into a struggle for survival. Politics in Britain is characterized by some excitement, not by anxiety.

---

[10] Robert McKenzie, *British Political Parties,* 2d ed. (London: Mercury Books, 1963).

BIBLIOGRAPHICAL NOTE

The basic contemporary work on British parties is the McKenzie book mentioned in Footnote 10. For the Liberal party, which McKenzie ignores, see Jorgen Rasmussen, *The Liberal Party* (London: Constable, 1965). McKenzie and Silver, cited in Footnote 5, contains an excellent summary of Conservative beliefs. For a discussion of party development in terms of British political values and social development see, Samuel Beer, *British Politics in the Collectivist Age* (New York: Alfred A. Knopf, (Inc., 1965). Two basic works on the Fabians are the Cole book cited in Footnote 2 and A. M. McBriar, *Fabian Socialism and English Politics, 1884–1918* (Cambridge: Cambridge University Press, 1966).

The best studies of the process of candidate selection are Austin Ranney, *Pathways to Parliament* (London: Macmillan, 1965), and Michael Rush, *The Selection of Parliamentary Candidates* (London: Nelson, 1969).

A good source for election results and a great deal of other political and social information is David Butler and Anne Sloman, *British Political Facts, 1900–1975,* 4th ed. (London: Macmillan, 1975). After each general election *The Times* publishes a Guide to the House of Commons with all the election results plus brief biographical notes of all the candidates.

A study of voting behavior of fundamental importance is the Butler and Stokes book cited in Footnote 6.

5

The Structure
for Securing
Accountability

Having examined the leading political parties, we turn now to the governmental structures through which they operate. This chapter discusses the structure which for years has been regarded as being at the heart of British government. By providing a forum for debate among the leading politicians, Parliament has been the focal point of the political process. We confine ourselves in this chapter primarily to describing Parliament and its procedures, along with conveying something of its atmosphere. Similarly, the following chapter begins by describing the executive. Then in the latter part of that chapter we take a more dynamic and analytical approach in discussing how Parliament and the executive interact.

THE HOUSE OF COMMONS

The Chamber and Its Members

The chamber in which the House of Commons meets is a small, rectangular room. Although the membership of the Commons is about half again as large as the U.S. House of Representatives, its meeting room is only about one fourth as large. The Commons' chamber is far too small to seat all its members; less than two thirds can squeeze into its green leather-covered benches at any one time. There are no desks to be assigned to individual members. Instead the Members sit on tiers of benches with the two main parties facing each other across a wide aisle running lengthwise down the center of the chamber. The detailed arrangements can be seen from Figure 5–1, which presents an aerial view of the main floor of the Commons and its balcony.

After its destruction by a Nazi bomb in World War II, the chamber was rebuilt along its old lines, except for more modern lighting, a voice-amplification system, air conditioning, leather-covered foam rubber on the benches, and a less ornate design of interior decoration. Winston Churchill, supported by his colleagues (including the Labour leader, Clement Attlee), wanted the House rebuilt along the old lines for two reasons. First, he was convinced that an oblong chamber facilitated the preservation of a two-party system. Crossing the floor (that is, changing parties), which he had done twice, was, in his opinion, difficult and required serious consideration, whereas a semicircular arrangement permitted members to move easily from left to right, or vice versa, in varying shades of political opinion. Second, he believed that a chamber which could not seat all its members would be better suited to the conversational style of speaking which had prevailed in the House. If it were large enough to accommodate all its members, he argued, "nine tenths of its debates will be conducted in the depressing atmosphere of an almost empty or half-empty chamber."[1]

The presiding officer of the Commons, the Speaker, dressed in the traditional garb of knee breeches, wig, and long black gown, sits in a canopied chair at the head of the chamber. At the long table in front of him sit the clerks of the House, also in wig and gown, recording its proceedings. On the table rest two dispatch boxes and the receptacles for the Mace, the symbol of the monarch's authority.

The House of Commons currently consists of 635 elected members. Almost every British subject who is 21 years old or over is legally qualified for a seat in the Commons. Among those specifically excluded are members of the peerage (except Irish nobility), clergymen, and persons holding offices of profit under the Crown (ministers of the Crown excepted). In practice, however, the Members usually are well into middle age.[2] The median age of MPs is around 50, with the Labour Members tending to be slightly older. Most MPs are experienced legislators; little more than one fifth of those elected in October 1974 first entered the House of Commons during that year.

The occupational background of the Members differs considerably between the major parties. Among the Conservatives the largest single group is company officials (about one fifth of all Conservative MPs), with barristers (trial lawyers) close behind. Farmers and journalists are other

---

[1] Winston Churchill, *The Second World War: Closing the Ring* (Boston: Houghton Mifflin, 1951), p. 169.

[2] David Butler and Dennis Kavanagh, *The British General Election of October 1974* (London: Macmillan, 1975), chap. 9. This is also the source for the information in the following two paragraphs.

FIGURE 5-1
Arrangement of Seating in the House of Commons

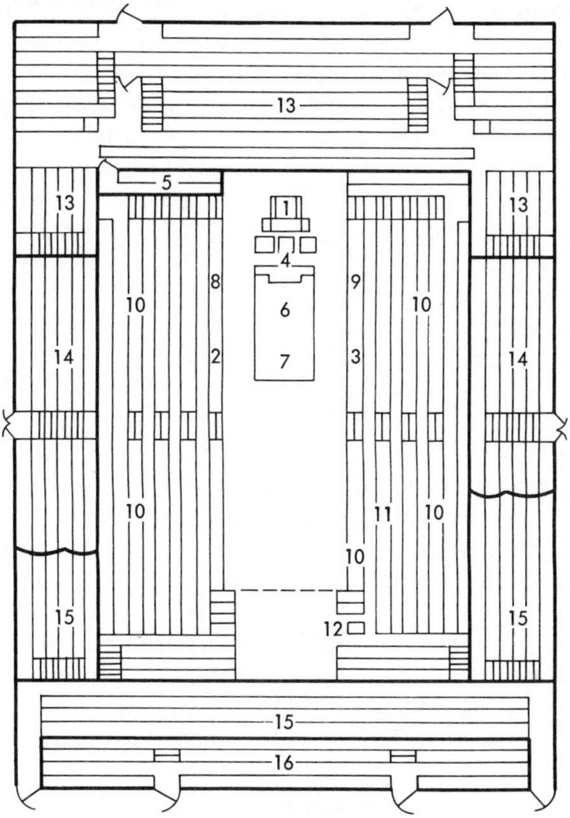

1. The Speaker.
2. Prime Minister or Government spokesman.
3. Leader of the Opposition or Opposition spokesman.
4. Clerks at the Table.
5. Civil Servants in attendance.
6. The Table.
7. The Mace.
8. Government front bench, occupied by Ministers.
9. Opposition front bench.
10. Back benches.
11. Other opposition parties.
12. Serjeant-at-Arms.
13. Hansard and press gallery.
14. Members' side galleries.
15. Special galleries, including Peers', "Distinguished Strangers,"
    Diplomatic and Commonwealth galleries.
16. The Public gallery.

sizable groups. In the Labour party the largest occupational groups—each including about a quarter of the party's MPs—are manual workers of all types and teachers at whatever level of education. Also important, although less so than in the Conservative party, are barristers and journalists. Since 1951 the percentage of Conservative MPs from business backgrounds has tended to drop and the proportion of those from professions to increase. During the same period the percentage of working-class MPs in the Labour party has dropped while that of Members from professional backgrounds has increased. Thus both parties have been moving away from their class base as regards the occupations of their MPs and are becoming more like each other. Both parties have been choosing professional types as candidates.

Educational contrasts are even more marked. Half of the Conservative MPs went to Oxford or Cambridge, while only a quarter of the Labour MPs did. In keeping with the comments on education and the class system in Chapter 2, the differences in secondary schooling are more striking still. Three fourths of all Conservative MPs attended public schools, while only one fifth of Labour MPs did so. Furthermore, fully a quarter of Conservative MPs attended either Eton, Harrow, or Winchester. Only four Labour MPs attended one of these schools. Even among what could be called the political elite, social class differences between the two parties are sharply etched.

Prior to 1911 Members received no compensation. Then a salary of £400 a year was instituted, which has been increased over the years. Until a few years ago little was done beyond this to help MPs meet the expense of public service. This was attributable largely to the fear that if Britain paid her MPs a decent salary some rotter would try to make a good thing of it and stand for Parliament just for the money. The basic salary now is £6,270 (about $11,500) to which is added a subsistence allowance of £1,350 (about $2,500) for MPs not regularly living in London. Not until 1969 was an MP allowed to use the mails for constituency business without having to pay postage. And not until then was any provision made for secretarial assistance. Now an MP is reimbursed up to £3,687 a year for secretarial assistance. Expenses of traveling to and in the local constituency also are covered.

Lack of office space still prevents each MP from having a permanent individual office. It is not uncommon to see an MP sitting on a stone bench in one of the hallways near the Commons chamber dictating to a secretary. Members are immune from arrest arising from civil suit and exempt from jury duty. And they have no legal responsibility—cannot be sued for slander—for statements made during debates in the Commons. All in all, however, the material returns for being an MP hardly are great. One must either have a high sense of public service or a strong desire to be near the seat of power to undertake this career.

Powers and Procedures

The powers of the House of Commons can be stated briefly: Parliament is supreme. This means that the Commons—given the concurrence of the Lords or an overriding of their opposition—literally can do whatever its Members want. No matter how outrageous it may be, any law passed by Parliament is valid.

The procedures through which the Commons exercises this power deserve some comment. Each fall the Parliamentary session is opened with the Speech from the Throne. The monarch delivers this speech from a throne in the House of Lords with Members of the Commons packed together at the foot of the chamber. While the Speech is addressed to the Lords, the monarch turns to the Commons alone when reference is made to the financial requests which will be presented to them. Although the monarch delivers the speech, it is drafted by the Cabinet and is a statement of the Government's legislative plans for the coming Parliamentary session. Thus it is the equivalent of the President's State of the Union Message in the United States.

The Commons spends about the next week discussing the Speech in general. Then it begins to consider specific bills that the Government has submitted to it. The House of Commons devotes more floor time to its business than any other legislative body in the world. In a typical year it meets for 150 to 180 days and averages well over 1,500 hours of sittings. This is almost five times as many hours as that spent by the German Bundestag and one-third longer than the United States Senate. Except on Fridays the Commons meets at 2:30 in the afternoon and normally adjourns at 10:30 in the evening. Friday sessions run from 11:00 to 4:30 to enable MPs to get away for weekend visits to their constituencies.

The atmosphere inside the House is conditioned by the Speaker. He or she presides over its proceedings and acts as its ceremonial head. The Speaker has no gavel or bell, but merely rises and, if need be, says, "Order, Order." He or she is accorded great respect, and the Speaker's moral and psychological authority is far greater than any written rules would imply.

Unlike the Speaker of the United States House of Representatives, the Speaker of the House of Commons is nonpartisan. Speakers are selected by the Prime Minister and colleagues and then formally elected by the House, usually without dissent by the opposition parties. As a rule, Speakers are backbenchers, or at least have not been prominent in their party's affairs. In addition to possessing such personal traits as tact, patience, and judicial temperament, Speakers must be thoroughly versed in the rules and procedures of the Commons. Once elected, Speakers divorce themselves from their party's activities. Since this prohibits any sort of partisan campaign speech, the custom had been not to oppose

Speakers when they stood for reelection in a general election. Since the mid-1960s, however, first independent and then partisan candidates have contested Speakers' constituencies.

Since the daily sittings of the Commons run without break for at least eight hours and frequently longer, the Speaker obviously needs assistance in presiding over the meetings. Furthermore, the Speaker does not preside over the Commons when it meets in Committee of the Whole. When the Speaker is absent, the Commons is presided over by either the chairman or one of the two deputy chairmen (despite the title, women have held one of these positions) of the Ways and Means Committee. Although these three officers of the House, unlike the Speaker, do not sever their ties with their parties, they are expected to be just as impartial as is the Speaker. To help insure this, they do not vote in any of the divisions of the House of Commons. Since everyone understands that those who preside over the House must be absolutely impartial and fair to all, it is not surprising that the Speaker and the other three officers are selected from the opposition parties as frequently as from the Government party, a practice which would be totally unheard of in the United States.

The legislative process begins when a member of the Government (the typical way) or an ordinary MP introduces a bill. In the latter case this is referred to as a private member's bill. Bills of limited application relevant only to specific localities are known as private bills, while those of general application and public importance are termed public bills. We will be concerned only with the procedure for passing public bills; the procedure for private bills differs in some ways.

All bills must go through three readings plus consideration by a committee and usually a report stage as well. The first reading is merely a formality to get the bill into the legislative process; no debate occurs at this time. The second reading is unquestionably the most crucial stage for any bill. The essence of this stage is a debate on the main principles of the bill. Amendments are not in order; the Commons must either kill the bill or continue it on its way.

If a bill passes second reading, its final passage is virtually assured. Nonetheless, it must now go to committee for detailed consideration and amendment in light of the views expressed in the Commons during the second reading debate. It is important to note that the committee stage in Britain comes later in the legislative process than is true in the United States. In the Congress bills are sent to committee immediately after first reading and before the legislature as a whole has had an opportunity to express its views on the subject in the bill. In Britain, when a committee receives a bill, the House of Commons already has voted that it approves of the bill in general. Thus a Congressional Committee may spend weeks on a bill only to see it killed on the floor when finally it is reported out of committee. This virtually never occurs in Britain, where committees can carry out their work guided by general approval and suggestions for alteration already voiced by the Commons.

The most controversial bills, as a rule, go to the Committee of the Whole—that is, to the House sitting as a committee. This makes the rules of procedure more informal and permits many more Members to participate. Obviously, however, it is much more time-consuming than is the standing committee route. Thus at times, especially in the 1970s, taking a bill in Committee of the Whole has been a means of forcing the Government to make significant concessions in the content of legislation or to abandon a bill entirely.

If a bill has not been amended in Committee of the Whole, it goes directly to third reading. When, more typically, it has been amended or has been considered by one of the standing committees, then it returns to the Commons for report stage before going on to third reading. Report stage offers a last opportunity for amendments of substance, since the vote on third reading, except for possible minor technical changes, is on the entire bill.

Except for the Scottish committee and the Welsh committee, the standing committees of the Commons have no specified subject matter; they are designated simply by letters of the alphabet. In fact, the standing committees do not even have any permanent existence. When a bill is sent to committee, the Committee on Selection appoints 16 to 30 MPs to serve on that committee. The Committee on Selection is chosen annually by the Commons to staff the standing committees. The chairman of a standing committee is selected by the Speaker of the House. Since the chairman, like the Speaker in the Commons, is to be completely impartial in presiding over the committee, a member of the Opposition may be appointed.

Since the standing committees are not permanent and have no functional specialization and since they do not have the power to kill legislation, MPs do not compete for membership on committees. There is no seniority system in the House of Commons. The Committee on Selection tries, of course, to appoint to the committees MPs with knowledge relevant to the bills being considered. Yet it is crucial to note that the British system does not provide for constant surveillance by small groups of expert legislators over the actions and the proposals of the executive.

Commons standing committees do not hold formal public hearings on the bills sent to them. They call no expert witnesses to testify for or against a bill. If some expert feels he or she has some information which the committee would find useful, that individual must communicate it to one of the committee members. This does not mean, as our discussion in Chapter 3 made clear, that interest groups have no role in the legislative process. But it helps to explain why they use different tactics in Britain. Since the Commons already has accepted the bill in principle, the standing committee to which it is sent cannot kill it or mutilate it out of recognition. Its job simply is to give the bill the detailed consideration for which the Commons did not have time and to make those changes which second reading debate indicated that the Commons desired.

The absence in Britain of permanent subject matter legislative committees has led many people to conclude that the Commons is at a severe disadvantage in its relations with the Government, which has at its disposal the expertise of the entire civil service. Thus the Commons frequently is not well informed on the subjects with which it must deal and is forced to yield to the Government's plans because they are based on superior knowledge. In an effort to rectify this situation, the Commons in the late 1960s began experimenting with specialist select committees. Of the six that were created, three focused on particular executive departments—for example, Agriculture—and three on broader subject matter cutting across more than one department—for example, Race Relations and Immigration. These committees did have the power to call witnesses and to hold readily accessible public sessions, some of which even took place outside of London. Their function, however, was rather more informative than legislative. No bills were sent to them. Rather, they simply collected information on which they could base a report to the Commons in order to expand its knowledge on certain topics. Thus, these specialist select committees had only one of the functions of Congressional committees.

In general the specialist select committees were felt to be useful. Yet any strengthening or further development of them raises a fundamental issue concerning the ultimate location of power in the British system. The Commons wants to be better informed, so that it can exert greater control over the Government; the Government does not want to give up any of its power and wants to avoid any reform that would make it beholden to the Commons. And since the Government currently controls the Commons, with rare exceptions, fundamental reform of the Commons committee system is unlikely.

When the Conservatives returned to power in 1970, they continued until the next general election the three specialist select committees dealing with broad subjects. They created also a Select Committee on Public Expenditure to consider the implications of the Government's policy objectives. In addition to a steering group, this committee is divided into six subcommittees to focus on particular topics, such as defense and external affairs. This reform, which was continued by the Labour Government, may help to enhance the Commons' collective expertise to some extent. The Government, whatever its party composition, clearly does not intend to relinquish any of its power. Therefore, until a major change occurs in party discipline in the Commons (a topic we discuss in the next chapter) or the party system is transformed from a two-party to a multi-party one, such tinkering with the committee system will not fundamentally reform the governmental system.

Every democratic legislature must face the problem of how debate can be limited to avoid dogmatic obstruction without trampling on the rights of those favoring unpopular views to gain a full hearing for their position. In Britain closure, the proposal to end debate and take a vote on an issue, requires only a simple majority vote of the Commons provided that at least 100 Members vote to end debate. The Speaker may refuse a motion for closure, however, if he or she feels that some significant views have not yet been adequately heard. The Speaker's impartiality and considerateness, mentioned above, are essential to insuring that neither the will of the majority nor the rights of the minority are violated in the legislative process.

To insure that the business of the Commons is processed promptly, the Speaker, on his or her own initiative, may ignore amendments proposed by small, atypical segments of the Commons. This power is referred to as the "kangaroo" closure. During the report stage of a bill he or she, in effect, hops over insignificant amendments, calling for action on only those amendments that he or she thinks are supported by substantial sections of the Members. The chairmen of Ways and Means and of the standing committees possess this power as well.

Another form of closure utilized in the Commons is the "guillotine." Officially it is referred to as "allocation of time orders." It is most often employed when a bill is likely to arouse lengthy and fierce opposition. The guillotine sets time limits for each stage (committee, report stage, and third reading) in the consideration of a bill. Moreover, it makes dilatory and adjournment motions out of order, and it removes other impediments (such as time regularly set aside for the consideration of certain subjects) to a speedy consideration of a legislative matter. Through the employment of the guillotine, the opposition's great weapon of delay is nullified before the debate begins. The kangaroo is particularly significant when a measure is being considered under allocation of time orders, for it enables the House to concentrate on the most important amendments in the time allotted.

In addition to these collective limits on debate, individual MPs are slightly restrained as well. Except when the Commons is in Committee of the Whole, MPs may speak only once on any motion. Furthermore, they must be relevant or the Speaker can order them to stop speaking. Beyond this, there is no time limit on speeches. Since reading prepared speeches is prohibited, the difficulty of speaking for very long without violating the requirement of relevancy is something of a limit. Although some speeches in the Commons may be lengthy, the American type of filibuster is unknown.

Some votes in the House of Commons simply are by voice. When the results are in doubt or when a formal record of each Member's voting is desired—as on major legislation—the Speaker calls for a division of the

House. Members then have six minutes to enter one or the other of the two "division lobbies" around the Commons' chamber. Each party's whips make certain that late-arriving MPs enter the proper lobby. As Members file out of the division lobbies, they give their names to clerks, who check them off the list of Members, and are counted by tellers. After all the Members have left the lobbies, the tellers and the clerks make certain that their total for the ayes (and in the other lobby, the noes) agree and the results are reported back in the chamber to the Speaker.

Calling a division may seem, on first thought, like a cumbersome and time-consuming method of providing a recorded vote. It also gives rise to snide comments about Members being herded through the lobbies like sheep. Actually, a division takes only about 10 minutes, compared with something like 45 minutes for a roll call vote in the U.S. House of Representatives, which has only two thirds as many members as does the Commons. In fact, the only speedier method of taking a recorded vote would be to use one of the systems of electronic voting employed in some American state legislatures. Since MPs do not have assigned desks, however, this device would be difficult to use in the Commons.

Function in the Policy Process

Not counting the time spent in discussing financial matters, the Commons devotes only about two fifths of its time to the debating and passing of legislation. Furthermore, strong party discipline (which we discuss in the next chapter) has moved the center of decision making from the Commons to the Cabinet. The Cabinet is the policy maker, while the Commons does little more than ratify. The most important function of the Commons, then, is to call the Government to account. It is in the House that the Government is forced to defend and justify its actions and proposals. The Commons serves as an arena for debate, criticism, and the ventilation of grievances.

Since the real function of the House is to question and to debate the policies and the actions of the Government, it seems pertinent to ask, To what purpose? In normal circumstances, the Opposition does not expect to defeat the Government in the Commons. Nor, indeed, does it hope to modify the Government's policy in any important respect. Therefore, its main aim is to utilize its position in the House to persuade enough people in the country to give it a majority at the next election. The Opposition seeks to convert the electorate and not the Government's party. Nevertheless, Governments at times have modified or even withdrawn proposals which met with criticism in the House. The attitude of the House is often a reflection of electoral dislikes, and this is what makes debate important.

By criticizing the Government, the Opposition sets before the electorate the major conflicts of policy. The duty of Her Majesty's Opposition is to oppose, but there is mutual forbearance, for the minority knows that the majority's duty is to govern. The Opposition is aware, moreover, that it must be ready to accept office should it succeed in defeating the Government in an election.

While being challenged is not especially pleasant, the Government may well benefit from the debate of its legislative proposals and governing record. By being forced to explain and defend its actions, the Majority contributes its share to the shaping of public opinion. Having to respond to criticism helps to attune the Government to public opinion and may enable it to cope with discontent before being engulfed by it in a general election. Furthermore, debate may reveal minor complaints and doubts among the Government's supporters; astute party managers recognize the need to respond promptly to these evidences of discontent before they grow into major dissatisfaction. A Government with a solid working majority in the Commons is little influenced by criticism from opposition parties since this is only to be expected; growing dissent among the Government's followers, however, is certain to produce concern and, usually, response.

Traditionally one of the best known means of calling the Government to account has been ''question hour.'' Four days a week (no question hour on Fridays) the first order of business in the Commons consists of replies by Cabinet ministers to questions that have been submitted at least two days in advance by nonministerial Members of the House. Each Member may submit two questions addressed to those ministers in whose sphere of responsibility the matter inquired about falls. The Prime Minister is required to reply to questions twice each week. Questions may be designed to embarrass a minister, call attention to minor injustices in the bureaucracy, or simply obtain information. In the hands of skilled MPs this procedure has been a potent weapon in the past. More recently, however, a number of people have begun to be skeptical about the power of question time to control the Government.

Ministers have experts in their departments to prepare answers to questions. Once an answer is made to a question, however, any Member may ask a supplementary question, provided it is related (the Speaker will not permit unrelated ones), and the supplementaries must be answered at once. At this point the minister is on his or her own, although civil servants may be in the box (a row of seats at the end of the House to the right and behind the Speaker). The box is separated from the House chamber by a low partition and technically is not a part of it. Because no messengers are used, conversation and notes pass over the partition if the minister needs help. The minister's Parliamentary Private Secretary, a Member of the House, is present also to assist, if necessary. If the minister is a member of the House of Lords, questions in the Commons relative to his or her department are handled by the Parliamentary Secretary of the department, who is a Member of the Commons.

A minister may refuse to answer a question on the ground that to do so would be injurious to the national interest—for example, questions about delicate foreign negotiations in progress. The Government usually seeks to avoid such a course if possible, for the impression may quickly spread that the question has embarrassed it or that it has something to hide. A minister who does not know the department's subject well and who cannot think on his or her feet will be a liability to the Government. Careers may be jeopardized and reputations broken by consistently poor performances during question hour.

On occasion the Government itself makes use of the question hour by getting its supporters to ask questions, thereby enabling it to correct false or misleading information or to quell rumors. An abuse of question hour was discovered in 1971. Some ministers were asking their civil servants to prepare innocuous questions which would be submitted by Government supporters. This would so clog up the Commons question agenda that questions submitted by the Opposition would not have to be answered orally. Question hour ends at 3:30 P.M. and all of the questions scheduled for that day which have not been answered receive only a written reply. If the Member submitting a question wants an oral reply—which is the only way that supplementaries are possible—then he or she must have the question rescheduled for another time, perhaps a week or two later when its significance may be greatly reduced.

Although this abuse is not to be continued, the additional problem remains that ministers are very skilled in not telling the Commons anything that they do not wish it to know. Thus, although question hour is a worthwhile procedure, many wonder whether it is as effective a device for controlling the Government as usually is thought. Some would argue that creating a full system of specialist committees would breathe new life into question hour by enabling MPs to ask more searching questions which the Government could not evade as easily.

In addition to question hour, MPs have an opportunity to criticize the Government and call it to account at the end of each day, except Friday. At 10 P.M. the Commons' regular business is halted for an adjournment debate. During the next half hour before the House automatically adjourns, MPs can discuss a particular grievance or aspect of Government policy. At times an MP who feels that he or she did not receive a satisfactory reply from a minister during question hour will have an opportunity to pursue the matter further during this period.

Longer adjournment debates on matters of special urgency are possible as well. After question hour an MP may move that the Commons adjourn on "a specific and important matter that should have urgent consideration." If the Speaker agrees that the subject meets these criteria and the request, if opposed, is supported by 40 MPs, a special three-hour debate is scheduled the following day immediately after questions. Alternatively, if the Speaker feels that it is necessary, he or she can schedule the debate for 7 P.M. on the day of the request. The House does not argue the merits of whether it should go home, but rather discusses the urgent topic which the MP had raised.

On other occasions the Government itself may move that the House adjourn immediately after questions. Since anything is relevant on a motion to adjourn, this step permits a wide-ranging debate on some topic of current interest. The Government arranges in consultation with the Opposition for the scheduling of such debates. Alternatively, the Opposition may submit a motion of censure against or lack of confidence in the Government. While such motions normally are focused on a particular alleged failing of the Government, the resultant debates have a broad scope.

The point of all these procedures is that in Britain it is possible to have public, face-to-face discussions by the top political figures of current political issues precisely at the time they are of greatest prominence. The fact that the Government cooperates with the Opposition in arranging these debates is evidence of the great importance attached in Britain to fair play, free speech, and responsible government. For those in power to help provide their opponents with opportunities to drive them from power is a remarkable rarity among the world's nations. The concern is whether heightened party discipline and growing executive expertise in an era of increasingly complex governmental policies are robbing the Commons of the ability to take full advantage of these procedures for controlling the Government. In so far as that is true, the accountability of the Government may have declined in Britain in the second half of the 20th century. To the extent that it has, democracy will have been attenuated.

THE HOUSE OF LORDS

Turning now to the upper house of Parliament—the House of Lords—we examine briefly a huge legislative body with a potential membership of over 1,000. None of them is elected and most of them are entitled to membership simply because they have inherited a title from their forebearer. Those who have not inherited membership have been appointed because of their eminence in various fields. In addition the Lords includes 26 bishops of the Church of England and nine Lords of Appeal in Ordinary, who are the leading judges of the land.

Granting excuses to those Lords who indicate they do not care to attend reduces the body's effective size to 750. Its working size of active members is smaller still—about 200. To help improve the quality of the

Lords' active members by recruiting capable people who objected to an hereditary aristocracy, Parliament passed a Life Peerages Act in 1958. This made it possible to appoint people to the Lords for their lifetime only. When they die their title and membership in the Lords do not pass on to their oldest son.

The Lords meet less frequently than the Commons and their meetings are shorter. Procedure is more informal than in the Commons; there are no standing committees and no closure. The Lord Chancellor, a member of the Government, presides over the Lords. Unlike the Speaker in the Commons, he takes an active part in debate. Many members of the Lords are not active in any political party, but enough of them are to give the Conservatives a permanent majority in that House.

Given this political situation the powers of the Lords are of some importance. A major constitutional crisis resulted in limitation of the Lords' powers in 1911. These were reduced further by the Parliament Act of 1949. For a bill to become law it must pass both Houses of Parliament. If they disagree, the bill can be shuttled back and forth in an effort to gain a consensus. Should the Lords ultimately object, this can be no more than a suspensive veto, for if the Commons reintroduces the bill the following year and passes it in its original form, it becomes law regardless of the Lords' opposition. Furthermore, financial legislation becomes law 30 days after passage by the Commons despite even initial opposition from the Lords.

In 1968 the Labour Government proposed a major reform of the powers and membership of the Lords. The Lords' delaying power was to be reduced to six months at most, and only life peers would be allowed to vote in the upper chamber's divisions. A strange coalition of the left wing of the Labour party and the right wing of the Conservative party objected so vigorously that the Government had to abandon its plans. The Conservatives feared that reducing the delaying power would rob the Lords of any effective power, while the Labourites were concerned that limiting voting rights might make the Lords too credible. This not only would increase the Lords' influence, but also would help to perpetuate what the Labour left regards as a symbol of the social inequality they believe is inappropriate to a democratic polity. This incident at least demonstrated that the Government cannot always get the Commons to accept its plans.

While the Lords' limited power of delay may not be viewed as a significant legislative function, the more careful consideration which measures receive as a result of this power ought not to be underestimated. The Lords can consider amendments for which the Commons did not have time and play a useful role in technical revision and wording. Also, the body's membership enables it to hold useful debates by nonpartisan experts on topics of public interest.

With the increasing use of delegated legislation by ministries, the

House of Lords is in a far better position than the House of Commons to look for probable abuses resulting from delegated legislation, provisional orders, and so on. The Lords have the time, they have people of experience, they have the legal talent, and some can usually be found who are interested in matters regarded as dull or unspectacular by others. Even if interest in these matters were more rewarding, the rules of the Commons so rigidly ration its time that a private Member has little chance of doing much about statutory instruments.

Perhaps the best brief assessment of the Lords is that offered by Herbert Morrison, a prominent figure in Labour's 1945–51 Government, who wrote, "The fact that the House of Lords has many irrational features is not in itself fatal in British eyes, for we have a considerable capacity for making the irrational work; and if a thing works we tend rather to like it, or at any rate to put up with it."[3] A more quintessentially British comment would be hard to find, and it explains well why prospects for the continued existence of an anachronism like the Lords are favorable.

BIBLIOGRAPHICAL NOTE

As an active Labour politician for many years Herbert Morrison provides many useful insights in his book, mentioned in Footnote 3. Although a bit out of date, Eric Taylor, *The House of Commons at Work,* 7th ed. (Harmondsworth, England: Penguin, 1967), remains useful on procedure in the Commons. This can be supplemented with S. A. Walkland, *The Legislative Process in Great Britain* (London: Allen & Unwin, 1968). For interesting comparisons with the United States, see Kenneth Bradshaw and David Pring, *Parliament and Congress* (London: Constable, 1972).

For discussion of the reform of Parliament, see Andrew Hill and Anthony Wichelow, *What's Wrong with Parliament?* (Harmondsworth, England: Penguin, 1964), and Bernard Crick, *The Reform of Parliament,* rev. ed. (London: Weidenfeld & Nicolson, 1968). The work of the specialist select committees is discussed in Alfred Morris, ed., *The Growth of Parliamentary Scrutiny by Committee* (London: Pergamon Press, Inc., 1970).

---

[3] Lord Morrison of Lambet, *Government and Parliament,* 3d ed. (London: Oxford University Press, 1964), p. 205.

6

Policy-Making Structures

When Political power slipped from the king's hands, the Cabinet fell heir to the Crown powers. The concept of Crown powers remained, and it became well established that the decision to exercise these powers was made by ministers and not by the king. Subsequently, the ministers were made answerable to Parliament for their acts. In the 20th century, political scientists began generally to use the term "cabinet government" as descriptive of the British form of government, thereby recognizing the predominant role of the Cabinet. The aptness of this term will become evident as we look at the elements of the cabinet system, its operation, and its relationships to other political institutions. To understand the British system of government, therefore, is in large measure to appreciate the central role of the Cabinet and how that role is played. But first we need to examine the monarchy to see the limited role and powers to which that institution has been reduced.

THE ROLE OF THE MONARCHY

So far as British law is concerned Queen Elizabeth II can veto legislation, designate whomever she chooses as Prime Minister and make other key Governmental appointments, summon and dissolve Parliament at will, and, having received advice from her ministers, decide what her Government's policy and actions will be. In actual practice none of this is true, for the British, in typical fashion, have shifted power around within the governmental system by custom rather than by statute. Thus, while dissolution of Parliament, for example, remains a Crown power, the current sovereign exercises this power by convention only when told to do so by the Prime Minister.

A British monarch has not vetoed a bill for well over two and a half centuries. A monarch has not dismissed a Government because he or she disliked their policies for almost a century and a half. And it has been over a century since a monarch refused to dissolve Parliament when the Government desired this. For a monarch to do any of these things would violate conventions of the constitution and involve the ruler personally in partisan policies—the actions could not fail to aid one party and injure the other—something which the monarch must avoid at all costs.

Furthermore, the monarch has no discretion in designating the Prime Minister. General elections determine who will be Prime Minister; the Leader of the party with the largest number of seats in the House of Commons is entitled to that office. Each party, as we have seen in Chapter 4, has a formal procedure for choosing a new Leader should their current one die or resign. And should they be in power, it would be that new Leader who would become the Prime Minister. The parties would not permit the monarch to select their Leader for them by picking a Prime Minister.

Should a Government be defeated in Parliament and resign instead of dissolving the Commons, the monarch must call the Leader of the Opposition to let that person attempt to become Prime Minister by forming a Government. This must be done without seeking anyone's advice, for not to do so could only be interpreted as an effort to keep the recognized Leader of the Opposition out of office. Once again this clearly would be a partisan political act, which a monarch must shun.

Nor does the monarch have any greater power in selecting other members of the Government. The Prime Minister assigns Government offices without any assistance from the monarch. And as for the Government's policies, these are decided by the Cabinet. The Cabinet does not advise the monarch what to do; the monarch, at best, can only suggest to the Cabinet what it might do.

But although Queen Elizabeth now has little real power, she can retain some influence. The extent to which a British monarch can influence political policy is greatly circumscribed by the ability, the capacity for hard work, and the personality of the occupant of the throne, as well as the political climate of the times. Given perceptiveness, the monarch can, over the years, accumulate much information and experience. Cabinet minutes and papers, Foreign Office telegrams, and other official papers are sent to the palace daily. In addition, the Queen may ask for information and she may talk with distinguished persons. If she is willing to read, to study, and to ponder questions of public policy, she can be very well informed.

Outside opinions not clouded by political partisanship often are useful to a Prime Minister, especially when they come from one with long experience. Queen Elizabeth, in her early 50s, already has been served by seven different occupants of the office of Prime Minister. Thus she can provide a continuity in government and an active recollection of previous decisions not available from anyone in the Cabinet.

The value and impact of the Queen's opinions, however, should not be exaggerated. She tends to lead an insulated life with little personal contact with the people. Moreover, regardless of the quality of her insights, the policies of the Government cannot, in the main, diverge too much from the political program of the party on whose support the Government depends. The Queen can influence her ministers only to the extent that her views are considered sound, and provided that they do not go contrary to important party aims and programs.

The monarchy has survived in Britain, and indeed has become a respected institution, because of its successful transition from a position of virtually absolute authority to that of political neutrality. This political neutrality of the monarch is but one phase in the evolution of the British system. In no small measure it stemmed from changes that followed the Reform Act of 1832, which made Cabinets dependent on the vote of the people and not on the favor of the monarch. The practice of collective responsibility (to be discussed below) made it possible for the people's representatives in the Commons to hold the Government accountable for the way in which it governed. The throne thus was spared from having to involve itself in the political struggles of the country.

It can readily be appreciated that if the Queen were to identify herself with a particular group of party politicians or a specific political program she would become a politician, subject to criticism and attack like all other politicians. She could not appeal to the people against the Cabinet without expecting the Cabinet to appeal to the people against her. Moreover, she not only is impartial but, what is perhaps more important, she is believed by the public at large to be impartial. This position was not attained until relatively recent times. Queen Victoria, for example, was a political partisan during many years of her reign.

Thus, while the Prime Minister is the political head of government, the monarch is the ceremonial or symbolic head of state. In this capacity the monarch provides an apolitical focus for national loyalty. Queen Elizabeth personifies the state; she is a *living* symbol of the nation and thus is able to stir patriotic feelings more successfully than a flag or a song. In addition, by devoting much time and energy to ceremonial functions, such as meeting arriving foreign dignitaries, the monarch relieves the Prime Minister and his colleagues of many time-consuming duties.

Over a century ago in a classic study of British government, Walter Bagehot argued that the Head of State—the monarch—played a dignified role, while the Head of Government—the Prime Minister and his Cabinet colleagues—performed an efficient function. The Cabinet was to run the Government behind the scenes, while public ceremony suggested that the monarch actually was in charge. In his view monarchial pomp so awed the public that it would accept laws and regulations; if people were to discover that politicians made the decisions they would be less willing to obey. Many Britons today may have an excessively exalted view of the monarch's powers, but few cannot know that politicians hold the real power. Nonetheless, it remains useful to distinguish between a Head of State and a Head of Government. In the United States, where the President combines both roles, it frequently is quite difficult to criticize the President as a partisan Head of Government without appearing to be attacking him as the symbolic Head of State. And while criticizing the former is legitimate, criticizing the latter clearly is not.

Finally, it can be argued that the monarch serves something of a lightning rod function. People frequently desire a certain amount of charisma in their politics. If an unscrupulous politician with such an attribute were to gain power, he or she would pose a serious threat to democracy. Rather than try to banish charisma from government, the British allow for its channeling through the monarchy. This presents no danger because the monarch's powers have been reduced to virtually nothing. Thus the monarchy can help to discharge popular passions which otherwise might be used to jeopardize the system. The role of the monarchy in system maintenance should not be ignored.

THE CABINET AND THE PRIME MINISTER

The essence of British Cabinet Government is a fusion of legislative and executive powers. The electorate decides only what the party strengths are to be in the House of Commons. The leaders of the majority—or largest—party, while retaining their seats in the Commons, are joined by the leaders of the same party from the Lords to form the Government, a group of 80 to 100 ministers. The Government is responsible for governing the country, for making all the basic policy and administrative decisions. But it exercises this responsibility only so long as its leaders—the Prime Minister and the Cabinet—maintain the support and confidence of the House of Commons. The Commons can at any time vote the Cabinet out of office or force it to resign by defeating it on a major policy issue. In such circumstances a Government could call for a general election in an effort to regain its strength in the Commons or it could allow its opponents to endeavor to form a Government able to obtain the support of the Commons.

At the heart of the Government is the Cabinet, the group of top party leaders most of whom head particular administrative departments or ministries. British law makes little reference to the Cabinet. Its powers, functions, and composition are almost wholly a matter of custom. The Cabinet has no set size nor is there any list of governmental positions whose holders must be included in the Cabinet. In fact the law does not even require that a member have a seat in Parliament.

In recent years the Cabinet has numbered from 17 to 24, depending entirely on the Prime Minister's wishes. Those political leaders holding key positions, like Foreign Secretary (the equivalent of the American Secretary of State), invariably are included in the Cabinet. Not since before World War II has someone not having a seat in Parliament been a member of the Cabinet, apart from one brief interim exception. And those in charge of the most important ministries usually will be in the Commons rather than the Lords.

In choosing the Cabinet the Prime Minister will be influenced by certain political considerations. Several of his or her party colleagues, because of their experience and accomplishments, will have to be included. They will have had Parliamentary experience in the shadow cabinet, a term used to designate the Parliamentary leaders of the opposition party, and, perhaps, will have had some experience in office when their party formed a previous Government. The Prime Minister will seek to build a coherent Cabinet, as free as possible from personal antagonisms. On the other hand, the Cabinet must be able to command respect and exercise authority among a broad range of party followers in Parliament. To do so often requires including people of varying political orientations within the leading party. A Cabinet all of whose members think alike is unlikely to remain in office long or be very effective.

Including the heads of ministries in the Cabinet is desirable because it helps to bring to Cabinet decisions the administrative knowledge and experience essential to formulating workable policies. Having some members with little or no departmental responsibilities also is important so that greater thought can be given to long-range policy or special ad hoc problems that cut across departmental lines. The number of ministers without portfolio (lacking specific departmental assignments) is not large, but several other posts require little administrative time, thus leaving their holders to work on matters that the Prime Minister considers important.

The Prime Minister is further limited in the appointment of ministers by the Ministers of the Crown Act (1937), which requires that a minimum number be from the House of Lords. The act establishes two lists of ministers and provides the maximum number of House of Commons' members on each. In effect, this means that at least a small number of ministers will be members of the upper house. But this limitation is not really a serious one, for the Prime Minister would, in any event, want to have persons in the Lords who could act as spokespersons for the Government. When a minister is in the Lords, the undersecretary or secretary must be in the Commons (although the reverse is not necessarily true), where the crucial defense of the Government's policies takes place.

The Cabinet has no statutory power. Rather it makes decisions which are implemented, because of custom and party discipline, by those with legal authority. The job of the Cabinet is to lead. It is responsible for the final determination of what programs and policies are to be submitted to Parliament. But it must also lay down the main principles, in accordance with policies prescribed by Parliament, that guide the administration of various government departments. And it must be ever ready to defend, before Parliament, its policies as well as the manner in which they are being implemented. Indeed, it must account to the House of Commons for everything that goes on in the day-to-day workings of a far-flung bureaucracy.

Traditionally, the Cabinet operated very informally; there were no agendas, no minutes, no record of decisions other than a letter sent to the monarch by the Prime Minister reporting on meetings. The result, as one would expect, frequently was confusion. While tolerable in peacetime, such a system would not be permitted to endure during World War I. A Cabinet secretariat was created in 1916 and now is firmly institutionalized in the Cabinet Office. The secretariat issues notices of Cabinet meetings and Cabinet committee meetings, prepares the Cabinet agenda (under the direction of the Prime Minister), circulates memoranda and documents relevant to items on the agenda, and records Cabinet discussions and decisions. This latter record is called Cabinet Conclusions. Initially these provided a full summary of each Cabinet meeting. Now they offer only a general outline of the main points made in the meeting without attributing these to any particular minister. The Conclusions state all the points agreed upon by the Cabinet. They are circulated to all ministers regardless of whether they are in the Cabinet. Ministers are expected to implement any decision relevant to their administrative responsibilities. The Cabinet Office is responsible for verifying that the respective departments act in accord with the Cabinet Conclusions.

The Cabinet meets regularly for about two to three hours each Thursday morning, although it can be summoned whenever the Prime Minister chooses, and additional meetings on Tuesday mornings and even other times are not uncommon. Since the relevant ministers or a Cabinet committee are expected to have discussed an issue in some detail before it comes to the Cabinet, lengthy debates on a single topic are unusual. Thus the Cabinet can cover a good number of matters in a typical meeting.

Formal voting in the Cabinet is extremely rare. Instead when the Prime Minister feels a subject has been discussed adequately he or she will "collect the voices." This procedure involves having Cabinet members in turn briefly state their final views on the subject. The Prime Minister sums up by stating what he or she takes to be the sense of the meeting, which then becomes Government policy.

While they may differ in the secret confines of the Cabinet room, members of the Cabinet are obligated to tell the same story in public. Any one of them who does not resign is responsible for all aspects of the Government's policies. Similarly, those ministers outside of the Cabinet, who have had no direct voice in making most of the Government's policies, must be prepared to defend all Cabinet decisions or else resign from the Government. No member of the Government can reject criticism at a later time on the ground that he or she had not originally agreed with the decision. This is the doctrine of collective responsibility. Thus when Parliament challenges a minister on the policies implemented by his or her department, it is attacking the entire Government. To censure the minister would be to drive the entire Government from office.

At the same time, the Cabinet need not defend a minister's errors of judgment of faulty administration. Collective responsibility extends only to matters of policy. Each minister is responsible individually for the proper operation of his or her department. Should he or she be forced to resign for mistakes of this type, the Cabinet would remain in office.

The load the Cabinet must carry has increased considerably in recent years because of the large number and complexity of matters with which government has become occupied. To help ease this load, a system of Cabinet committees has been created. Nonetheless, the Cabinet must spend so much time on departmental business or particular items of legislation that it has only limited opportunity for general discussion of policy.

In an effort to alleviate this problem, Prime Minister Harold Wilson sought to restructure the executive in the late 1960s. He wanted to upgrade the Cabinet committees and govern more through them, thereby reducing the number of Cabinet meetings. With the exception of a few key ministers, those who dissented from the decisions taken in Cabinet committees would not be allowed to reopen the issue in a Cabinet meeting unless the Prime Minister or the chairman of the Cabinet committee involved agreed. He subsequently appointed a Parliamentary Committee of ten (later reduced to seven) leading members of the Cabinet to examine long-range political strategy. In this way he hoped to avoid the tendency prevalent in the Cabinet of thinking only in departmental terms. In the year or two that this system operated before Labour's defeat in the 1970 General Election, it did not prove to be very useful. When the Conservatives returned to power, Prime Minister Heath did not continue it.

Instead, in a potentially significant restructuring of the executive, Heath established in the autumn of 1970 a Central Policy Review Staff in the Cabinet Office. This group is composed of about 18 experts on a variety of subjects, who are drawn from both within and outside the bureaucracy. These experts can be called upon for assistance when policy is being formed in Cabinet committees. They are to suggest alternative means of achieving the Government's goals and to help insure that current departmental policies are assessed in terms of the Government's long-range objectives taken as a whole.

Whether the creation of the CPRS will result in strengthening the Cabinet as a whole or only the Prime Minister cannot yet be determined. Thus far it does not appear to have had as much impact on policy-making as might have been anticipated. Nonetheless, the CPRS, along with the ad hoc Cabinet Office Units dealing with specific policy areas, are the closest that Britain has come yet to creating something equivalent to the American Executive Office of the President.

As should be obvious from much of the preceding discussion, the Prime Minister is the apex of the Cabinet, the axis around which the British Cabinet system revolves. Interestingly, the office does not even exist in British law. There are no qualifications which one must possess to be eligible for the office. In fact a salary was not even provided for the Prime Minister until 1937.

In practice one becomes a potential Prime Minister by being chosen Leader of a party. When that party holds the largest number of seats in the House of Commons, the Leader is summoned by the monarch to become Prime Minister and form a Government. Constitutional practice has firmly established that the Prime Minister must have a seat in the House of Commons. There has not been a Prime Minister from the House of Lords since Lord Salisbury left office in 1902.[1]

Given the fusion of executive and legislative branches in Britain, it is not surprising that British Prime Ministers have considerable legislative experience before attaining that office. Of the 16 men who have become Prime Minister in this century, the least that anyone had served in Parliament prior to becoming Prime Minister was 14 years, and the mean length of prior service was 25 years. Winston Churchill had been in Parliament 38 years before he became Prime Minister. By way of contrast, 8 of the 14 men who have become President of the United States in the 20th century have had no prior Congressional experience at all. The mean period of service for the 6 having had this experience was only 14 years.

The route to the top political post in Britain is much narrower than it is in the United States. One must work one's way up in the party through service in the legislature. There are no alternative routes such as being governor of a large state, war hero, or prominent in business, which have been among the means to Presidential nomination in the United States. Thus one's political future in Britain would seem to be much more depen-

---

[1] In 1963, the Earl of Home was made Prime Minister, but this was after the passage of the Peerage Act, 1963, which permits a peer to give up a title. Lord Home promptly gave up his title, became Sir Alec Douglas-Home, and was elected to the House of Commons, where he had served for a number of years before he had become a peer.

dent upon the favor of party leaders. If one rebels against the leaders, one is not likely to receive appointment to the subsidiary offices in which one can demonstrate having the abilities necessary for top political office. Yet it must also be admitted that four of the eight men who have served as Prime Minister since the end of World War II had been party rebels at earlier stages in their careers. Despite stepping out of line, they were able, for a variety of reasons, to survive and advance.

Given the length of legislative service that most Prime Ministers have, it is clear that a person cannot be particularly young when reaching the post. The mean age on first becoming Prime Minister of the 20 men who held the post from 1868 to 1976 was 58. Harold Wilson, in becoming Prime Minister in 1964 when he was 48, was one of only two men in the past century to reach the post before their 50th birthday. Of 21 U.S. Presidents from 1869 to 1977, the mean age on first becoming President was 53.

The Prime Minister's functions are varied. He or she presides over meetings of the Cabinet, in this role giving advice and engaging in preliminary consideration of plans long before these can be brought before the Cabinet. In addition, he or she must be aware of what goes on in the various departments, for failure to do so risks possible embarrassment. Furthermore, he or she advises in the appointment of bishops, superior judges, permanent secretaries, and others, and, last, but not least, must manage the party majority in Parliament and in the country. He or she also must pay attention to the moods of public opinion which affect the popularity of his or her Government and which will affect the political life of his or her party at the next election. At election time he or she stands for election to the House of Commons in a single constituency, but as Prime Minister goes to the country as Leader of his or her party.

A Prime Minister owes much to his or her party, for by choosing someone to be its Leader it in effect decides that that person shall be Prime Minister when it wins an election. A Leader does well not to lose sight of this indebtedness for, as noted in Chapter 4, a Leader who persistently fails to consult with colleagues and alienates the party's MPs can be driven from power. This remains true even when the Leader has become Prime Minister.

A Prime Minister, however, is not just the puppet of a party. The Leader of a party is by definition preeminent. With British elections increasingly seeming to turn on the issue of who will become Prime Minister, the Leader's standing in the party is enhanced further. Typically he or she should be an electoral asset which the party hardly can afford to lose. Certainly leaders who are electoral liabilities cannot expect to remain at the head of a party for long. So long as one leads the party, the ability to direct the party machine is a considerable power which in turn strengthens one's position as Prime Minister.

The Prime Minister dominates the Government because he or she directs the Cabinet and is far more than merely first among Cabinet equals. A Prime Minister can appoint, dismiss, or reshuffle Cabinet colleagues and can commit the Cabinet to new policies by announcing them publicly, without having first consulted the Cabinet members. Individual ministers, on the other hand, may find themselves disowned by the Cabinet should they make basic decisions without first consulting the Cabinet or the Prime Minister.

Control over the civil service also is a significant power; the Prime Minister appoints the civil servants to the top positions in each department. On the other hand, a Prime Minister does not have the huge staff of an American President. In 1974 the total number of employees in the Prime Minister's private office, counting not only clerks and typists, but messengers and cleaners as well, was under 100. Including those in the noncivil service political office also would add only a handful more.

The power, prestige, and authority of the office of Prime Minister are such that some experts have argued that just as power earlier passed from Parliament to the Cabinet, it now has continued on into the Prime Minister's hands. The correct label for the British system, according to them, is not Parliamentary Supremacy, or even Cabinet Supremacy, but Prime Ministerial Government.[2]

With power in the Government, the bureaucracy, and the party, the Prime Minister obviously plays a leading role in directing the country. Yet the Prime Minister does not have the constitutional powers of an American President and does not dominate the governmental process to the same extent. A Prime Minister is not elected for a fixed term. He or she must retain the support of his or her followers and cannot ignore the views of the Cabinet the way an American President can. Since 1895 the terms of office of British Prime Ministers have ranged from ½ year to 8½ years, with the median 3½ years. During roughly the same period American Presidents have served from 2½ years to 12 years, with the median 5¼ years. Thus, a British Prime Minister has less time than does an American President to have some impact upon the political process by implementing his or her program fairly fully.

The absence in Britain, however, of a separation of powers system with checks and balances greatly strengthens the executive as a whole vis-à-vis the legislature. Thus, although within the executive branch the American President is more powerful than the British Prime Minister, the British executive as a whole is more powerful than the American executive. The following section's discussion of executive-legislative relations in Britain will make this clear.

---

[2] For a brief statement of these views see Richard Crossman, *The Myths of Cabinet Government* (Cambridge, Mass.: Harvard University Press, 1972), especially Lecture II.

LEGISLATIVE-EXECUTIVE RELATIONS

The first principle to note is that in the legislative process the Government plays the dominant role. In general, the Cabinet determines what matters are to be considered and how much time is to be allotted to each. It decides what legislative program will be presented to Parliament and how its time will be apportioned to this and other matters which demand Parliamentary action. In collaboration with the leaders of Her Majesty's Opposition, the Cabinet decides how much time and what days the Opposition may have to discuss what it wants to discuss.

Prior to each legislative session, the Cabinet decides what legislative proposals, taken to a considerable extent from the party's platform, should be introduced and passed in the time available. This requires some selectivity, since the demands on Parliament's time are such that considerably less than half of the available days can be assigned to Government legislation. Usually each ministry has bills it wants passed. Moreover, a number of matters require enactment each year and consume a great deal of time. Those items which the Cabinet chooses for action always receive first priority.

Unlike American practice, the raising and spending of money in Britain can be proposed only by ministers of the Crown. A bill which authorizes expenditure, although it does not appropriate the money, also requires a recommendation from the Crown at some point. Motions to increase expenditures are contrary to standing orders (rules of the House), a circumstance that prevents pork-barrel legislation. Motions to reduce expenditures are in order, but would no doubt be regarded as questions of confidence by the Government, whose responsibility it is to exercise initiative in the raising and spending of money. Since ministers of the Crown play such an important role in money matters, it is obvious that the voice of the Treasury would be significant. All departmental requests for money must undergo scrutiny in the Treasury. In the end, however, the position of the Treasury is only as strong as the influence of the Chancellor of the Exchequer on Cabinet colleagues, for the Cabinet is collectively responsible for all policy, including fiscal.

Subject to Cabinet direction, the leader of the House of Commons, who is designated by the Prime Minister, is responsible for the business of the House and the Government's program. His or her responsibilities, however, are not to the Cabinet alone. He or she must also guard the legitimate rights of the Opposition, as well as the rights of the House as a whole, including those of the backbenchers.

Under the supervision of the leader, the Government chief whip manages things and makes the detailed day-to-day arrangements. This is done in consultation with the chief whip of the Opposition, who receives advance notice of the matters the Government intends to submit to the

House during the following week. The two chief whips are known as the "usual channels."

The Government chief whip is assisted by a deputy chief whip and by a varying number of junior whips. All the whips are members of Parliament, and most of the Government whips are ministers and, as such, receive salaries. The chief whip has an office at 12 Downing Street (No. 10 is the residence of the Prime Minister), where there are accommodations also for the junior whips. The main Opposition party has several whips as well. The Government even pays an official salary to three of them. This is further evidence of the importance attached in Britain to having a loyal Opposition prepared to challenge the Government and offer an alternative set of leaders.

Government whips must see to it that Government business is not hindered by procedural failures. It is their duty to see that the Members of the Government party attend House sittings and that they vote "right" when votes are taken. In dealing with their party colleagues, whips employ persuasion rather than bullying. Such tasks require people of tact, patience, restraint, and a willingness to be self-effacing.

Whips convey to ministers the worries, the anxieties, and the complaints of the backbenchers. It is imperative that leaders know the mood of their followers in order to judge the impact of proposed or pending Government measures. For this purpose, there is a close and systematic contact between the whips and the party's rank and file in the House. This is usually the duty of the junior whips rather than the chief whip.

Formal communications to the respective party members are issued in the form of written messages, also known as whips. On Thursday of each week, the leader of the House announces the business that is to be brought before the Commons during the following week (beginning the following Tuesday and ending the Monday thereafter). On Friday, whips are mailed to all party members, although there are occasions when special whips are circulated. The whip informs party members of the various matters to come before the House each day of the following week, and it may indicate who the main speakers will be. The relative importance of each subject is indicated by underlining it once, twice, or three times. If underlined only once, the matter is not considered of great importance. Items underlined twice are fairly important, and may indicate a possible vote. A three-line whip suggests that a vote is almost certain, and every member is expected to be present, unless ill or unavoidably absent. A debate or a vote on a motion of censure is always three-line business.

All MPs are expected to vote the way that their party instructs them to regardless of their personal attitudes on the issue or any comments that they may have made during the course of the debate in the Commons. Abstaining is about as far as an MP can go in refusing to support the party's line and even that can get him or her in trouble at times. The only exception is when a party decides to permit a free vote. In that case no party position is announced and MPs are free to vote as they wish. But when, as usually is the case, a party takes a stand, an MP must fall in line and obey or suffer the consequences.

If an MP rebels on an issue of sufficient importance or frequently enough, he or she may have the whip withdrawn. In the Conservative party this is vested in the Leader, while in the Labour party it requires a majority vote of the Parliamentary Labour Party. The result is to expel an MP from the party in Parliament. In the Labour party the action is reported to the National Executive Committee, which may decide to expel the offender from membership in the Labour party entirely. Thus rebels risk ending their political careers.

Given this situation it is understandable that party cohesion—the disciplined voting of all Parliamentary members of the same party in the same way—is extremely high in Britain. Revolts within the major parties occur only infrequently and normally are confined to relatively small groups. The American situation of a coalition of Democrats and Republicans passing legislation in opposition to another grouping of other Democrats and Republicans is unknown in Britain.

To conclude, however, that British MPs are simply a group of cowardly sheep terrorized by their leaders through their brutal whips would be a mistake. The matter of party cohesion is more complex than this and involves more than simple threats and coercion. In certain circumstances—for example, when dissent does not move one nearer to the opposing party—an MP can depart from the party's line without suffering punishment.

More important is the fact that for a variety of reasons MPs want to vote consistently with their party. In the first place, if enough MPs vote against their party when it is in office, this will force it to resign. Then the opposing party will come to power, and clearly they must regard that as a worse alternative or they would be members of that other party. Furthermore, British MPs perceive the role of legislator differently than do members of the American Congress. The typical MP recognizes that he or she has not been elected because of any personal abilities or magnetism, but rather because of the party label. People vote for an individual in order to give a particular party the majority in Parliament which its leaders need to carry out its policies.

To the extent that Britain is more homogeneous than the United States, political issues are more national instead of regional. Thus, unlike a member of Congress, an MP has neither the opportunity nor the necessity to deviate from the party line. Being less likely to be subject to regional pressures, an MP is less likely to need to disagree with national leaders. For the most part his or her constituents will not be clamouring for stands at variance with the national leaders. And precisely because this is likely to be true, an MP will have little opportunity to win local popularity by defying the national leaders.

Finally, it must be remembered that back-bench party committees are able to have some influence on proposed legislation before it is submitted to the Commons. Furthermore, since the executive has worked out the details of a bill, it has been in close contact with the relevant interest groups. Thus when a bill arrives in the Commons it is likely to be an elaborately worked out set of compromises which does not permit any extensive alteration if it is to be widely acceptable. Combine this with the fact that no person can be an expert on more than a few matters; on any given issue most MPs will be uninformed or uninterested. Why in such circumstances should they be expected to do anything other than vote as their leaders tell them to, especially since frequent caucuses of the Parliamentary Labour Party help to set the party line, particularly when Labour is in opposition?

Thus, with rare exceptions British Parliamentary parties are highly cohesive. The Commons can vote the Government out of office at any time, but this simply does not occur. The last time that a Government resigned because of a vote in the House of Commons was in 1940 and even then the Government had won the division by 81 votes. In the mid 1970s the Labour Government did have difficulty in controlling the Commons and came close to losing some divisions which would have forced it to resign. But this was a situation in which by-election losses had cost the Government its majority in the Commons.

When, as usually has been the case, a party wins a working majority of seats in a general election, it normally can count on getting its legislative program through the Parliament. Its proposals do not have to hurdle a number of obstacles or fear being ambushed by a hostile committee chairperson. The Government knows that it has the votes to pass the bills. And though its term in office may not be fixed, it can pick the time that it wishes to call for a new election.

To say this is to raise the question of whether Parliament has become of no importance, a mere rubber stamp. Some observers have gone so far as to employ the term "Cabinet dictatorship" in referring to the British system. Obviously this is extreme terminology, since the Government's authority rests not upon such weapons of dictatorship as a secret police force but upon majority Parliamentary support, which can be withdrawn.

Furthermore, it must be recognized that a good deal can be said for concentrating power as the British system does. Such a system concentrates responsibility as well. A British Government never can argue that its program was thwarted by the perversity of a handful of strategically placed legislators. Under the British system not only does the same party control the executive as controls the legislature, but the same section of a party controls both. Unlike the situation in the United States, there are not Congressional Democrats and Presidential Democrats responsible to contrasting constituencies and thus perpetually at odds with each other despite nominally belonging to the same party. Thus when things do not get done or when that which does get done is objectionable, the voters know whom to blame. And at the next election they can remove from power those who are blameworthy and install their opponents.

Nonetheless, such a system does mean that the legislature and individual members of it cannot wield the power possessed by the American Congress or virtually exercise a legislative veto as do some of its key members. Granting that the power distribution in the British system must differ from that in the American, some observers maintain that Parliament played a more significant role in the governmental process a century ago than it does now. Thus, in the last decade a number of proposals for the reform of the House of Commons have been debated. We have referred already in Chapter 5 to the experiments with the committee system and the concern to revitalize question hour. Changing the procedure for discussing financial matters to permit the Commons to consider long-range, rather than year-to-year, commitments in a systematic fashion has been proposed, as has providing the Commons with a greatly enlarged research staff so that it could fully capitalize on such an opportunity. Televising the Commons' debates has been suggested as a means both of improving communication with the electorate and of modernizing outworn procedures of the Commons. These and other proposals, such as the Cabinet's ceasing to regard every division of the House as a vote of confidence, probably would enhance the reputation, if not necessarily the power, of the Commons.

Even should these reforms not materialize, the House of Commons is not the Government's poodle. Governments can be influenced without having to be defeated. The purpose of debate in the Commons is not to defeat the Government, but to force it to defend its actions. This is not an inconsequential requirement, for this necessity means that the Government runs a great risk in committing itself to a policy without adequately examining its implications or in implementing a policy that appears to treat some segment of society unjustly. If it does so the Commons will demand a public accounting and defense. The issues will be debated in the Commons and the alternatives aired. And the Government that consistently appears to be incompetent, ham-fisted, and callous will find its support dwindling not only among the electorate, but among its Parliamentary followers as well. The Government may not appear to be influenced much in the Commons debates precisely because it already has been influenced so much in seeking to draw up proposals that can be defended as logical and generally fair.

Nor is the impact of the Commons limited to minor matters or questions of detail. In the summer of 1969 the Labour Government was forced to abandon both its labor legislation and its proposed reform of the House of Lords because of the strength of opposition to these measures in the Commons. Admittedly, it is fairly unusual to be able to pin down the influence of the Commons this clearly, although other examples could be added. Nonetheless, even when the Commons' impact is not dramatic, it is still true to say that it is pervasive; the Commons' role in the governmental process remains significant. The Commons' influence does vary considerably, however, from one subject to another. Despite the existence in the past of the Estimates Committee and currently of the Select Committee on Expenditure, the Commons has not been able to develop sufficient expertise to exert much control over financial and budgetary matters. Its influence in defense and foreign affairs has tended to be weak also. Yet on occasion crucial debates occur even in these areas. The Heath Government was especially concerned about the debate in October 1971 on British membership in the Common Market and exerted considerable effort to insure winning the vote in the Commons. The opposition of Labour to membership, and serious defections within the Conservative party were the cause of the Government's anxiety. Although the Government won 356 to 244, the uncertainty it had felt concerning the results suggests the influence which the Commons can have.

BIBLIOGRAPHICAL NOTE

The following are useful sources on the monarchy: Frank Hardie, *The Political Influence of the British Monarchy*, 1868–1952 (London: Batsford, 1970); Kingsley Martin, *The Crown and the Establishment*, rev. ed. (Harmondsworth, England: Penguin, 1965); and Sir Charles Petrie, *The Modern British Monarchy* (London: Eyre & Spottiswoode, 1961).

The standard work on the Cabinet is John Mackintosh, *The British Cabinet*, 2d ed. (London: Stevens, 1968). For an inside view by a former Labour minister, see Patrick Gordon Walker, *The Cabinet*, rev. ed. (London: Cape, 1972). For a critical comparison of the Cabinet system in foreign affairs to that of the Presidential system, see Kenneth Waltz, *Foreign Policy and Democratic Politics* (Boston: Little, Brown and Co. 1967). Ronald Butt strongly defends Parliament from charges of lack of significant political impact in *The Power of Parliament* (London: Constable, 1967).

Two detailed studies of party cohesion are Leon Epstein, *British Politics in the Suez Crisis* (London: Pall Mall, 1964), and Robert Jackson, *Rebels and Whips* (London: Macmillan, 1968).

Many of the studies included in Richard Rose, ed., *Policy-Making in Britain* (London: Macmillan, 1969), are relevant to the topics covered in this chapter.

7

Policy-Implementing
Structures

THE CIVIL SERVICE AND ITS POLITICAL SUPERVISORS

The enactment of a statute by a legislature by no means adequately solves a pressing public problem. In some ways the conclusion of what may have been a long and laborious legislative struggle is no more than the beginning of a search for a solution, for once a law is passed it must be implemented; its provisions must be applied to the relevant people or circumstances. This is by no means an automatic process. Some laws may be ignored generally by those entrusted with their implementation and become a dead letter. And even when an effort is made to implement the law fully, those whose task this is find that the intent of the legislature is by no means completely clear and that many specific cases do not quite fit the general provisions of the law. Thus it is that administrators become policy makers to some extent. Their day-to-day decisions concerning how a law will be implemented determine the real content or provisions of the law.

Administrative positions, then, are posts of some power and importance. The contact that most citizens have with government is not with legislators or top executive leaders, but with low- or medium-level administrators—bureaucrats. This is the point at which government touches one personally. Given this situation, the central problem of administration is to attain both efficiency and responsibility. One wants to avoid the waste and frustration of incompetence and one wants to ensure that no locus of power is uncontrolled so that democracy is abridged.

The difficulty is that efficiency and responsibility or accountability are

136

to some extent mutually exclusive. The well-known bureaucratic red tape, for example, is nothing other than the detailed records that must be kept to justify administrative action should the legislators—representing the people—call the bureaucrats to account for particular actions. The endless forms that governmental agencies fill out and file could be disposed of almost totally if there never would be a need to justify an action. On the other hand, one could attain a high level of responsibility if the bureaucracy was totally replaced each time a new party came to power. But the prospects for efficient, experienced administration would not be bright in such circumstances.

Staffing the Bureaucracy

Although the British never had to contend with such Jacksonian ideas of rotation in office as bedeviled American politics in the 19th century, they still had a patronage system well into that century. Merit or ability had nothing to do with appointment to governmental administrative positions. Government employment was something in the nature of unemployment relief for otherwise unoccupied aristocrats. So far were the British from notions of rotation in office that the holder of a government position acquired property rights to his job. He could sell it; he could will it; if it were abolished, he was entitled to compensation.

While this situation was an obstacle to the establishment of a civil service system, it was not as difficult to overcome as were the combined impediments of patronage *and* rotation in office, which prevailed in the United States. Once people could be convinced in Britain that administrators should be an aristocracy of talent rather than of inherited title, values supportive of a professional civil service system would exist. Thus, it was in 1870, 13 years prior to similar action in the United States, that the principle of open competition for governmental jobs was established and the various governmental departments were unified into a single civil service system.

The British civil service system was created by an Order in Council under the prerogative powers of the Crown. These powers are the residue discretionary authority legally remaining to the Crown. As the previous chapter noted, the exercise of Crown powers rests with the Cabinet; despite their name they are not subject to the personal decision of the current sovereign. The significant point rather is that the operation of the civil service still is governed chiefly by various Orders in Council and the regulations made under their authorization. Parliament could act, but it has passed little legislation regulating the internal organization of the civil service.

Approximately 700,000 people are employed by the national government in Britain, but 200,000 of these are industrial workers not normally considered to be civil servants. These industrial workers are not those employed by nationalized industry, but rather include those working for such governmental enterprises as the Royal Ordnance factories and the Royal Naval docks. About 40 percent of the half million true civil servants constitute the basic skeleton of the civil service. These are the general administrators of varying levels of abilities who fill each department's basic positions. Such specialists as are needed—for example, statisticians and chemists—are fitted into this basic structure at appropriate points.

Until 1971 these general administrators were divided into three main classes, based on the importance of the work entrusted to them and their abilities and education. These distinctions were abolished on the recommendation in 1968 of a special committee headed by Lord Fulton and charged with making a fundamental review and assessment of the civil service. The charge was that these class distinctions had become too rigid and stood in the way of recruiting or promoting the best persons for responsible positions. Since, as noted above, the civil service is governed largely by Orders in Council, once the Government decided to accept the recommendations of the Fulton Report, they could be implemented as soon as practicable.

The former three basic civil service classes have been replaced by a single integrated administrative group, which reaches from lowly clerical assistants up into the top levels of bureaucracy. To some extent recruitment into the civil service at various levels continues to be geared to the school system, with certain jobs open to those of the age at which one can leave school, finish school, or graduate from college. But the key point is that the various positions now have been combined into a single hierarchy running continuously from bottom to top. Even if one has entered at the bottom with limited education, with suitable abilities he or she can progress up the ladder. Those who have entered the civil service instead of going to college can compete with the college graduates for posts around middle level. Exact placement in the hierarchy is determined by one's examination grade.

Most examinations are written, although interviews have become more important in recent years. The written examination tests general knowledge, proficiency in English, and knowledge of two or three academic subjects chosen from a large number of alternatives. As this suggests, the British have sought to recruit civil servants on the basis of general ability and not on the basis of preparation and training for a specific job. The British feel that top minds can quickly learn specific job requirements after they have been appointed to their position. In any event, they remain convinced that a knowledge of classical Greek is excellent preparation for life and admirable training for being in charge of public affairs. This stress upon the amateur was criticized by the Fulton Report, which favored a greater effort to recruit people for specific jobs. On the recommendation of the Fulton Report, a new Civil Service Department was created in 1968, which, by absorbing the Civil Service Commission, became responsible for recruitment. Also in accord with the Fulton Report, in 1970 a new civil service college was opened. This school provides technical and managerial training for civil servants to enhance their administrative skills, instead of relying merely on experience and trial and error.

Given the reforms discussed in the two previous paragraphs, recruitment procedures currently are in a state of some flux. It is doubtful, however, that any changes will do much to alter the situation which continues to be a problem for the civil service—the class bias of its recruits. A disproportionately low number of people of working-class background enter the civil service. As a result it is dominated by the middle class and seems, particularly to Labour supporters, to embody middle-class values. Despite post-World-War-II efforts to broaden recruitment into the civil service and expanded educational opportunity, the class composition of the civil service remains largely the same as it was prior to World War II. Only 11 percent of the top administrators in the civil service come from a manual-working-class background. And educationally the typical civil servant has gone from public school to Oxford or Cambridge.

Organizing the Bureaucracy

The principal activities in implementing the Governments' policies are carried out by some two dozen departments and ministries, whose political heads are responsible to the House of Commons. Each ministry and department is staffed by permanent civil servants headed by the permanent secretary. (See Figure 7–1.) Above this hierarchy are a handful of political appointees—typically the minister and two to four associates—to give political direction to the department. The minister serves at the pleasure of the Prime Minister, as do the minister's associates, whom the Prime Minister has picked in consultation with the minister.

Policy and administration fuse at the ministerial level. Ministers, as Members of Parliament and of the Government, are both policy makers and administrators. Clearly, they can devote only part time to the latter job, even though they are responsible to the Commons for it. Ministers must spend much time in the Commons for its debates, must keep in touch with constituents, and must be involved in party activities. Much time is required also for meetings of the Cabinet and its committees.

Ministers can delegate some tasks to the political appointees who assist them—variously titled Minister of State, Undersecretary of State, and Parliamentary Secretary. These persons also are members of the Government party and have seats in either the House of Commons or the House of Lords. When a minister is in the Lords, it is imperative that his or her immediate assistant be in the Commons to defend the department's

FIGURE 7–1
Typical Administrative Structure of a British Ministry

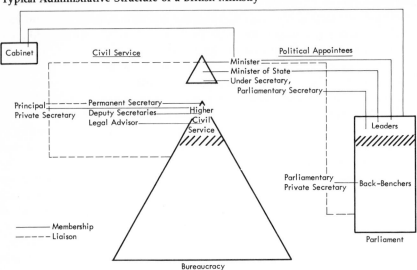

policies in the legislative body which has the power to censure the Government. Ministers of State rank above secretaries and undersecretaries in that they have some discretionary powers. The secretaries relieve ministers of less important duties. By learning the business of administrative departments, secretaries qualify themselves for eventual promotion to ministerial rank. Secretaries cannot determine policy on their own; they cannot override the opinions of permanent civil servants, but must refer these views to their minister.

A minister is assisted as well by a Parliamentary Private Secretary (PPS). A PPS, also a Member of Parliament, is not technically part of the Government; he or she receives no administrative salary, as do the others we have mentioned, in addition to MP's pay. PPSs perform a variety of tasks for their ministers. They are expected to know the temper of the House so that a minister does not encounter an unexpected revolt against a ministry's policies. They convey both the ministers' views to the party's back-bench supporters and the back-benchers' grievances to the ministers.

The minister alone is responsible to the House of Commons for what happens in a department; he or she takes the credit as well as the blame. The British operate on the principle of protecting the civil servants, for, if they should be subject to questioning by committees of the Commons or other bodies, the minister could not expect faithful service and absolute loyalty from them. The British do not believe that civil servants should be dragged into the political arena, nor do they believe that their prestige and influence should be subjected to the hazards of popular prejudice. These are the occupational risks of the politician and not of the expert administrative official, for to subject the latter to this is to jeopardize effective performance of administrative duties.

Thus, when a department is guilty of maladministration, the minister will criticize privately those civil servants responsible for the failure, but publicly he or she personally must accept the blame. If the failure is sufficiently bad, the minister may be forced to resign. Instead, however, he or she may apologize to Parliament, indicate that there was no way of knowing about the action in advance, and guarantee that he or she has taken steps to ensure that it cannot happen again.

Several observers of British government have argued that this practice of individual ministerial responsibility no longer operates. A Cabinet may decide to treat a colleague's poor administration as a matter of collective responsibility and thus spare him or her the embarrassment of resigning. Such a development lessens control over the administration of Government policy and weakens the accountability of administrative power, for if the minister is not really responsible and the civil servants are kept from being publicly responsible so as to guard their efficiency, no one is responsible. Thus, abandoning the doctrine of ministerial responsibility destroys the effective solution which the British had found to what we noted at the beginning of this chapter is the basic problem of public administration—the reconciliation of efficiency with accountability.

Treasury Control

Although until 1968 the Civil Service Commission was responsible for recruitment of administrators, the civil service was controlled for a half century by the Treasury, under the direction of the Prime Minister, who also has the title of First Lord of the Treasury. A 1920 Order in Council gave the Treasury power to supervise the standards and conditions of work in the civil service. The permanent secretary of the Treasury was the permanent head of the civil service.

This meant that the Treasury had two important links with other departments and ministries. One link, a financial officer, was responsible for regularity in accounting and in scrutinizing proposals for new expenditures. The other, the principal establishment officer, was responsible for office organization and for matters affecting the staff, which might develop anywhere in the ministry. Most other departments stood in a somewhat inferior position to the Treasury. While the control over finance was the most effective power exercised by the Treasury over other departments, its predominance was also psychological.

The Fulton Report objected to management of the civil service being dominated by a department whose main functions concerned other matters. Thus, when Prime Minister Wilson, acting on the Report's recommendations, in 1968 created a Civil Service Department, he not only put it in charge of recruitment, but gave it as well the managerial functions previously exercised by the Treasury. The permanent head of the civil service now is the permanent secretary of this new department rather than an official in the Treasury. The department is nominally under the Prime Minister, but its actual day-to-day operations are directed by a Cabinet minister he appoints for that purpose.

Thus Treasury control now is a matter of accounting control. The Treasury designates an accounting officer in each department, usually the chief financial officer of the permanent secretary. This officer is responsible, through the minister, to Parliament for departmental expenditures. Moreover, he or she is personally and pecuniarily liable to the Treasury for unauthorized or irregular expenditures unless he or she has protested to the minister in writing and has received authority from the minister to incur such expenditures.

The Policy Role of the Civil Service

While the minister is the political head of a department or ministry, the nonpolitical head is the permanent secretary—a career civil servant who is the true administrative chief of the agency (see Figure 7–1). He or she is responsible for the general organization and efficiency of the agency and for the advice given to the minister on behalf of its permanent civil service. Staff are not to deal directly with the minister without the knowledge and approval of the permanent secretary. Given the fact that in most cases he or she will have been at the top of the department much longer than the minister has been, the permanent secretary is in an excellent position to have considerable influence on policy formation. The contrast, then, with the American administrative structure is that in Britain the top positions in the civil service reach much higher up into the policy process. The British view is that it is not possible to recruit and retain really capable people in the civil service unless they have the prospect of attaining eventually a position of some real significance. The position of permanent secretary clearly meets this requirement.

In most cases a minister works most closely with the permanent secretary and a principal private secretary. The latter is a promising young civil servant in the department whom the minister has chosen as a special assistant. The principal private secretary shields the minister from unnecessary engagements and needless paper work. Simultaneously, he or she should be close to the permanent secretary and see that a continuous link is maintained between the minister and the permanent secretary.

A minister also has some contact with the department's or ministry's legal advisor and a few deputy secretaries. Only the civil servants in this top group, usually referred to as the higher civil service, are in a position to exercise real and direct influence on important policy matters. They are trusted advisors to and loyal servants of each succeeding minister. It is only by keeping them out of the political arena and making them rather faceless mandarins that they are able to play this role. This is in sharp contrast to American and French practice; in the United States there is a large turnover in top posts, while in France the minister brings in a personal cabinet of trusted advisors to protect him or her from the civil servants.

When the Labour party came to power in 1945, many of its adherents were fearful lest an unsympathetic civil service sabotage the party's nationalization program. This did not occur; the civil servants loyally assisted their political supervisors in implementing Labour's economic and industrial policies. One of the Labour ministers of that day wrote later that his general experience led him to conclude that if the minister "knows what he wants and is intelligent in going about it, he can command the understanding cooperation and support of his civil servants. [Moreover,] in my experience our civil service generally prefers a minister with a mind of his own to a mere rubber stamp."[1] Perhaps the most graphic illustration of the political neutrality of the civil service concerns nationalization of iron and steel. The civil servants who after the Conservative victory in 1951 helped the party to denationalize iron and steel were precisely the same ones who only a few years earlier aided Labour in working out the details of nationalization and then implementing it.

The Royal Commission on the Civil Service in 1929 merely stated what long had been understood: "determination of policy is the function of ministers," while the "business of the civil servant [is] to strive to carry out that policy with precisely the same good will whether he agrees with it or not."[2] At the same time, the higher civil servants clearly are in a position to exercise considerable direct influence on policy decisions. "The most important function of the great permanent official is not to carry out decisions already taken by ministers, but to advise them what decisions they should take. . . ."[3]

Since top civil servants serve on the basis of merit while their political supervisors hold their position on the basis of electoral fortunes and other political considerations, the civil servants are likely to have greater sub-

---

[1] Lord Morrison of Lambeth, *Government and Parliament*, 3rd ed. (London: Oxford University Press, 1964), pp. 320, 326. See also former Prime Minister Attlee's chapter in William A. Robson, *The Civil Service in Britain and France* (New York: Macmillan Co., 1956).

[2] Royal Commission on the Civil Service (1929–31), *Minutes of Evidence*, p. 1268.

[3] H. E. Dale, *The Higher Civil Service of Great Britain* (London: Oxford University Press, 1941), p. 46.

stantive knowledge concerning the policy decisions which a ministry must make. Furthermore, since the top civil servants, again unlike the ministers, remain at their posts typically for 10 to 15 years, they will have to cope with the long-range consequences of today's decisions. Thus any responsible top civil servant must be certain that the minister understands fully the difficulties associated with any particular course of action.

The issue is whether they dwell excessively on such concerns. The top civil service has been criticized frequently for being too cautious, too suspicious of innovation, too willing to argue that something cannot be done simply because it never has been done. Some members of the Labour party feel that this orientation hampers them, as the party more dedicated to social reform, more than it does the Conservatives. They accept that the top civil servants are neutral, nonpartisan. But they feel that the higher civil service is more concerned to tell them why certain policies cannot be implemented than it is to find ways of carrying out reform. A determined minister will not have a program sabotaged, but any signs of indecision may result in the higher civil servants managing the minister rather than the reverse.

Thus for probity, loyalty, discretion, and intelligence the British civil service probably is unsurpassed. Whether it is the ideal instrument for social reform is another matter.

CONTROL OF ADMINISTRATIVE DISCRETION

Although administrators in the normal performance of their duties are involved necessarily in rule making to some extent, the expansion of governmental activities in the economic and social realms has increased greatly these kinds of activities. Parliament has tended to pass laws in a skeletal form, entrusting to administrators the authority to fill in the details. Two major problems have arisen as a result: (1) providing adequate safeguards so that rule-making authority will be exercised in conformity with the basic statute, and (2) insuring that citizen's rights will not be violated by administrative boards or tribunals, many of whose decisions are judicial in nature, without recourse to appeal in the courts.

The reasons for delegation of rule-making authority are compelling. Parliament cannot set out in an act all the details of administration. The pressure upon Parliamentary time does not permit adequate consideration. The subject matter of much modern legislation is often of a technical nature, which cannot be effectively debated. Moreover, in large and complex schemes of reform it is impossible to foresee all contingencies which may arise; it cannot be known whether conditions will change, requiring modifications in detailed statutory provisions. Flexibility is essential, for it permits experimentation and makes possible adaptations in accordance with actual practice. Finally, statutory rules can be prepared in greater leisure and with more care, minimizing the possibility of serious errors.

The fear that administrative rule making may go beyond the intent of the original legislative enactment is increased by the absence in Britain of constitutional limitations on the legislature. Moreover, the role of the courts is far more modest than in the United States. British courts cannot ask whether Parliament had the right to legislate and, consequently, to bestow rule-making power. They merely can ask: Is the rule-making body acting in accordance with the procedural framework prescribed by law?

Given such considerations, the British have attempted to establish certain safeguards in the exercise of rule-making authority. First of all, ministers are able to make rules and regulations that have the effect of law only when authorized to do so by statute. Secondly, all rules made in a department must be confirmed by a minister. Thirdly, an increasing number of statutes are requiring consultation with advisory committees prior to the making of regulations. All departments in the economic and social sphere use advisory committees. The effectiveness of consultation, however, depends upon how the minister conceives his or her duty to consult and the extent to which advisory bodies are representative of the interests affected.

As a further safeguard, Parliament is empowered, by passing an adverse resolution, to nullify regulations laid before it. Typically, Parliament is given 40 days in which to act. In practice, however, neither House exerts much control in this way. Parliament tends to lack both the time and the expert knowledge to supervise effectively the full range of administrative decisions. The House of Commons Select Committee on Statutory Instruments serves a useful purpose in calling attention to unusual rules or those involving an unexpected use of powers. Although the Committee itself cannot void the rule, it can bring the matter to the Commons' attention and help it to make a more competent decision. Administrative agencies know this and try to avoid action that would lead to Parliamentary criticism.

The increasing number of rules made by administrators has provoked concern for individual rights. To resolve conflicts between governmental agencies seeking to implement a policy and citizens alleging that their rights have been invaded, various ministries have established administrative tribunals. These tribunals are staffed by experts possessing the special experience or training related to the relevant field. Because the tribunals operate less formally than the regular courts, they tend to be speedier and cheaper.

Nonetheless, the tribunals have drawn criticism precisely because they do not follow all the rules that would apply in a court of law. For example, the lack of an opportunity to cross-examine those who testify at a tribunal may make it difficult to refute their comments and to establish the validity of one's own case. Furthermore, since the head of a department appoints the members of the administrative tribunal that will deal with questions arising out of that department's actions, it almost appears that the department is being permitted to be a judge in its own case.

To meet some of the criticism of administrative tribunals, Parliament passed the Tribunals and Inquiries Act in 1958. The purpose was to provide for some measure of appeal from the tribunals to the courts. In addition to certain procedural reforms, the Act established the principle of judicial scrutiny on points of law. Moreover, it set up a council to review and report on the workings of some 30 designated administrative tribunals.

Despite these reforms, some people continued to be dissatisfied with the tribunal system. They even charged that Britain's ancient liberties were being snuffed out by a powerful bureaucracy hiding behind weak and overworked ministers. Therefore, in 1967 Britain decided to try an approach similar to that utilized by Scandinavia and New Zealand and create an ombudsman, or Parliamentary Commissioner for Administration.

The Commissioner's powers are more limited, however, than those usually associated with an ombudsman. He or she is an officer of Parliament and is permitted to consider only those complaints that come through its members. His or her authority is also restricted to investigating and reporting to Parliament. The actions of local governmental units and nationalized industries are among the matters excluded from his or her jurisdiction, as are matters of overriding national interest and foreign relations.

Initially the Commissioner was limited to examining only matters of maladministration and was not permitted to question any discretionary decision which was made in accord with proper procedures. A Select Committee was created in the House of Commons to supervise the Commissioner's work and to follow up on any reforms which his or her reports showed were needed. In accord with the suggestion of this committee, in 1968 the Commissioner extended the scope of his jurisdiction somewhat. He would now examine as well cases where administrative action was so "thoroughly bad in quality" that it suggested the existence of bias or perversity. And he would accept cases where, despite correct application of the rules, considerable hardship and injustice had been visited upon a person. In such cases the Commissioner would investigate whether the department concerned had reviewed adequately the applicable rule to see what changes needed to be made to prevent such results in the future.

Even with this expanded scope, most complaints referred to the Commissioner have proven to be outside the established jurisdiction. Of those with which the Commissioner is authorized to deal, about 10 to 13 percent have revealed instances of maladministration. In the first four years of the Commissioner's operations his investigations and reports resulted in over

60 persons' receiving a total of more than a quarter of a million dollars in compensation for administrative mistreatment.

Given the limitations on the British ombudsman, he or she clearly cannot defend Britons fully from abuse of administrative discretion. Expansion of the Commissioner's powers or additional machinery clearly are needed to solve the problem. Nonetheless, the reform has met with limited success and does provide a useful supplementary safeguard to administrative tribunals for obtaining a responsible bureaucracy.

ACCOUNTABILITY IN THE NATIONALIZED INDUSTRIES

Increasingly in the 20th century administrators have become involved in implementing social and economic policies. Yet control of the economy and regulation of business can be distinguished from the direct management and ownership of specific enterprises. In this sense nationalized industries—government-owned concerns—are not a part of the regular administrative structure. Yet they must be administered by governmental agents. Thus, this chapter on the structures for implementing governmental policies cannot close without some attention to the public corporation—the device used in Britain for managing nationalized, or publicly owned, industries.

Although the Labour party is closely identified with nationalization, it did not originate public ownership in Britain. London Passenger Transport, domestic telegraph, telephones, transmission of electricity, foreign air service, and radio all were taken into public ownership by non-Labour Governments. Nonetheless, there remained considerable scope for further public ownership when Labour first won an absolute majority in the House of Commons in 1945. From 1945 to 1951 Labour extended nationalization in aviation, electricity, and communication and introduced it in the financial system, coal, transportation, gas, and iron and steel. Despite this expansion, publicly owned firms employ only 8 percent of the total work force in Britain, produce only 11 percent of the gross domestic product, and account for only 19 percent of the fixed investment; contrary to widespread misconception in the United States, Britain remains largely a private enterprise economy.[4] The Labour party never has intended to collectivize all commercial activity down to the corner fish and chips shop. They felt it sufficient for the government to acquire only the essential industries, the so-called commanding heights of the economy.

---

[4] *The Economist,* 27 November 1976, p. 15.

In deciding what type of administrative structure was to be employed in running the nationalized industries, the Government was influenced by the fact that these industries, unlike such governmental functions as defense and foreign relations, clearly were commercial undertakings. A clearly identifiable service was being rendered directly to specific people who were paying for it. Efficient management of such an operation seemed to require greater flexibility in day-to-day operations than is possible in a government department that must keep a record of all decisions to reply to any inquiries to justify its actions. On the other hand, the principle of responsibility to Parliament had to be preserved. The organizational form chosen to attempt to comply with these conflicting demands was the public corporation. Organizationally these corporations were under the jurisdictions of ministers who would be responsible to Parliament for their work. But the corporations were given considerable latitude in making many decisions without reference to ministers. Hence ministers would not be responsible for all of the corporations' decisions.

Although nationalized industries do vary in the details of their structures, public corporations share five basic features. Their finances are self-contained, that is, their accounts are kept separate from those of the regular government. They are run by specially appointed boards, whose members normally serve for fixed terms. Neither the members of the boards nor those who work in nationalized industry are civil servants. The boards governing the industries do not seek to make a profit, but to provide the best service; a nationalized industry is supposed to break even over a period of years. No political figure exercises day-to-day control over the managerial activity of the board. The following paragraphs discuss in greater detail the implications of these principles and the general operation of the public corporations.

The board of a public corporation is appointed by the appropriate minister, who has power to remove members and is responsible to Parliament for the appointments. He or she also determines the salaries and conditions of service of the board members. While the minister is given certain powers of control and direction, the board has the duty of operating and managing the industry in the public interest. The minister is required, however, to approve the borrowing and the capital investments the board wishes to undertake. Also, he or she has to approve programs of research and development. In addition, the minister has control over the consumer councils. Finally, the minister is required to lay before Parliament the annual report and statement of accounts of the corporation.

To help make public corporations responsive to their customers, consumer councils were established. Through this machinery the views of consumers are to be brought systematically to the boards and the relevant ministers. The consumer councils are appointed by the minister. As a general rule, he or she is obligated to consult representative consumer groups often specified by statute, before making the appointments. In practice, the minister asks for a panel of nominees from which most of the members are chosen, although some (for example, civic leaders) are his or her personal appointees. Most councils have representatives from the board or corporation governing the industry. The size of the councils varies from 3 to 30. Some councils exist on the national level only, while some are regional and local only. None exists on all three levels. On the average, they meet about six to eight times a year; the national councils meet less often than regional or local ones.

The duties of the councils are to consider and to make recommendations in matters of consumer interest raised by actual or potential consumers, initiated by the councils, or referred to them by the minister. The implementation of recommendations depends in large part upon the minister. There is reason to believe, however, that councils in many instances do not even have the opportunity of making recommendations.

On the other hand, councils are sometimes informed of general plans, and can make representations on the basis of these, which gives them some share in policy formulation. Some councils are tied closely enough to industry, through direct representation, to have a voice in policy, while others have no direct relation to their industries.

The most obvious defect in the consumer councils is that they are too little known and too little used. One reason is consumer indifference. Another is to be found in the fact that there are no effective organizations to represent general consumer interests. Moreover, competing channels exist: advisory committees in government departments and the continued practice of ministers of meeting directly with representatives of the leading interest groups. Often the councils find themselves in a dilemma. They must depend on the agency for information and remedial action, but at the same time they must be independent of the agency to assure the consumer a vigorous voice. They must, at one and the same time, have the confidence of both the minister and the consumers.

In creating the public corporation and in vesting it with what seemed to be the necessary authority, the British were aware that situations would probably arise which would make it impossible to assess responsibility. The older concept that ministers were responsible for every administrative act in their departments had to be modified significantly. Ministers cannot be held accountable for the actions of the boards of public corporations unless these actions required their consent or could have been overruled by them. Examples of these are borrowing and capital investment.

Ministers can issue general instructions or policy directives to boards. This occurs rarely, however, because such action is regarded as reflecting on a board's competence. Thus a board may try to comply with a minister's informally expressed wishes so as to avoid receiving a directive. If no directive is issued, then, obviously, the minister cannot be questioned in Parliament about it and the board's annual report has nothing to disclose on the matter.

Ministers have ample opportunity to influence and direct boards other than by directives. They frequently discuss relevant business informally with the heads of boards. Thus they can raise questions about those aspects of policy or management on which they feel strongly.

Boards are controlled as well to a considerable extent by the Treasury through its inquiries concerning income and expenditures.

Thus the basic problem is not so much that the public corporations are autonomous—a power unto themselves—as it is that they are subject to Government direction without the Government's having to answer fully for the policies which they are pursuing.

The Commons' Public Accounts Committee devotes some time to examining the finances of the public corporations. Since 1956 the Select Committee on Nationalized Industry has scrutinized the reports and accounts of the nationalized industries in order to inform the Commons about the aims, activities, and problems of the boards operating them. Some critics insist that the Committee does not probe deeply enough. Other observers contend that to do so would be to interfere in the industries' day-to-day operations and thereby lower their efficiency. Still others maintain that although the Committee does an excellent job, no one pays much attention to its reports. Here again more adequate research staff and secretarial service would be of considerable help. But MPs will have to devote greater time and effort to controlling the nationalized industries than most of them have been willing to do so far, if the situation really is to be changed.

Parliament does find some time to debate the annual reports of the boards of the nationalized industries. Given the shortage of Parliamentary time, only about two or three reports can be debated fully each year. Thus, given the large number of nationalized industries, a considerable time usually elapses between major Parliamentary examination of any particular industry.

A satisfactory solution to the problem of attaining both commercial flexibility and political accountability has yet to be worked out. The nationalized industries undoubtedly are more subject to governmental control than they were before they were taken into public ownership. Yet, despite their being owned by the public and operated in its name, it clearly is questionable to maintain that they are responsible to the electorate even in the limited sense that the Government and MPs are. This short-circuiting of accountability is made more unpalatable by a growing feeling that government could exercise just as much control over industry through legislation as it does through outright ownership.

BIBLIOGRAPHICAL NOTE

Detailed studies of various government departments are found in the New Whitehall series published by Allen & Unwin at various times under various titles. For a detailed, formalistic study of the entire administrative structure see W. J. M. MacKenzie and J. W. Grove, *Central Administration in Britain* (London: Longmans, Green, 1957). See also D. N. Chester and F. M. G. Willson, eds., *The Organization of British Central Government 1914–1964*, 2d rev. ed. (London: Allen & Unwin, 1968).

Relations with outside interests are discussed in Political and Economic Planning, *Advisory Committees in British Government* (London: Allen & Unwin, 1960). The role of the Treasury is covered in Samuel Brittan, *Steering the Economy: The Role of the Treasury* (London: Secker & Warburg, 1969).

Useful works on the civil service include: R. A. Chapman, *The Higher Civil Service in Britain* (London: Constable, 1970); Geoffrey Fry, *Statesmen in Disguise* (London: Macmillan, 1969); and Edgar Gladden, *Civil Services in the United Kingdom, 1853–1970*, 3d rev. ed. (London: Cass, 1967).

For a discussion from an insider's viewpoint of the difficulties in utilizing technological innovation in government decision making and policy, see Jeremy Bray, *Decision in Government* (London: Gollancz, 1970).

Sir Carleton Allen examines administrative law and justice in *Law and Orders*, 3rd ed. (London: Stevens, 1965).

On nationalized industry see A. H. Hanson, *Parliament and Public Ownership*, 2d ed. (London: Cassell, 1962), and William Robson, *Nationalized Industry and Public Ownership*, rev. ed. (London: Allen & Unwin, 1962).

8

The Legal Resolution of Conflicts

THE ORGANIZATION OF THE JUDICIARY

The problem of responsibility or accountability mentioned in the last chapter in connection with administration is relevant as well to the judicial system. Insofar as judges exercise political power, they should be subject to popular control in order to maintain democracy. Thus at the state level in the United States it is not unusual for judges to be elected and to serve only short terms before they must stand for reelection. Yet at the same time most people feel that judges should be objective, that they should not be swayed by political considerations in reaching their rulings. The law should not be just a matter of transient majority opinion. Paradoxically, then, people want judges to be both above and subject to politics.

Although British judges are not elected, it might appear at first glance that they are to some extent involved in politics. The head of the legal system, the Lord Chancellor, is a member of the Cabinet, appointed by the Prime Minister. He or she has no fixed term and always is replaced immediately when the Opposition forms a new Government. Most British judges are appointed on the advice of the Lord Chancellor. A few of the top judicial appointments are even made by the Prime Minister, usually after consulting with the Lord Chancellor. Unlike the situation in the United States, no legislative approval for these appointments is required.

Nonetheless, the British judiciary is independent of rather than subservient to the political interests of the Government. In order to keep the monarch from controlling the judiciary, the Act of Settlement of 1701 provided that judges serve not "at the pleasure of the Crown," but "during good behavior." In effect this means permanent tenure. A judge can be removed from office only by vote of both House of Parliament. This occurred only in 1830, when a judge had misappropriated funds.

Judges are appointed because of their professional competence and not for their political opinions or activities. Until 1972 appointments were made from that portion of the legal profession which principally is engaged in court work, the barristers, as distinguished from the soliciters, who deal directly with the client, prepare the case outside of court, and brief the barristers to present the case. Before a person can practice law before the courts, he or she must be "called to the Bar" by one of the four Inns of Court—incorporated associations of lawyers not subject to government control—which will admit only those who possess the high qualities of education and discipline that will help to perpetuate the long tradition of professional independence built up by the Inns. Under the Courts Acts of 1971, which went into effect at the start of 1972, soliciters also now may become judges. They are eligible, just as barristers are, for appointment as part-time lower level judges known as recorders. After five years' experience in this position, they are eligible for appointment to the circuit bench of full-time judges.

Since judges are not subject to popular control, the British solution to the problem of accountability is to curtail the amount of power exercised by judges. As we explained in Chapter 5, Parliament is supreme; there are no constitutional limitations on its power. Thus no British judge ever has the task of checking a statute against a constitution to see whether the former is a valid exercise of authorized power. Obviously, judges must interpret the law in applying it to particular cases. Their interpretations are not final, however; Parliament can reverse them by passing a new law. Until the law is amended, its provisions are what the judges say they are. To this extent they can check arbitrary government action.

Like so many other institutions of British government, the court system was shaped and altered by usage over a period of years. One-time itinerant royal commissioners, who were concerned mainly with looking after the king's financial affairs, eventually became itinerant judges. As royal commissioners, they had little judicial authority; as itinerant judges their main function became judicial. These itinerant judges visited each county three or four times a year to determine whether charges of serious crimes—the lesser offenses were handled by the sheriff and, later, by justices of the peace—were accurate.

Consequently, the practice of hearing almost all criminal cases in the county where the crime was committed became well established. In civil cases of any importance, however, the proceedings were held at Westminster, which meant that participants, witnesses, and others with an interest in the case had to travel to London for the trial. Because of the hardship imposed by such travel in those days, some decentralization became necessary. Justices of the Assize Courts, who were the best available justices, were sent to the counties to hear cases. The points of law, however, were argued mainly at Westminster and the formal judgment was rendered there.

Perhaps the greatest strides in the systematization of the British judicial system were made during the reign of Henry II. At that time the system of royal writs, which are the root of common law procedure, was inaugurated. These writs required that disputes be brought before royal authorities for settlement. Moreover, Henry II adopted and perfected the system of itinerant judges. In addition, he established the principle of the king's peace—that is, a crime should no longer be considered a wrong against the individual but rather a wrong against the state. Finally, he asserted the exclusive jurisdiction of the Curia Regis in the case of all serious crimes, and he hastened the demise of the older methods of trial (such as ordeal or battle), which led to the development of trial by jury.

Although the British legal system was unified into a national system both in its structure and its appointment procedures, it remains divided to some extent into separate judicial hierarchies. The rules which courts apply can be placed in two categories: those that set up standards governing the relationship between individuals and government and those which regulate the relationships between individuals and other individuals. The former is usually called public law and the latter private law. Public law includes three types of law: constitutional, administrative, and criminal. Court actions under criminal law are referred to as criminal cases, whereas most other legal actions, notably those between individuals, are designated as civil cases.

The criminal law embraces offenses against the state and those offenses against individuals which are judged sufficiently grave (such as murder and arson) to be offenses against society as a whole. Related to this difference is a contrast in sanctions. The sanction of criminal law is punitive; the object is to punish the guilty. Civil law cases seek to compensate an injured party, force those who have entered into legal obligations to fulfill them, or prevent people from so acting as to damage the interests or property of others.

In Britain, unlike the situation in the United States, the courts dealing with criminal cases are to a considerable extent distinct from those having civil jurisdiction. (refer to Figure 8–1 for the following discussion of the structure of the court system.) Minor criminal cases are dealt with in Britain by justices of the peace (unpaid) or by magistrates. Summary offenses (those not requiring an indictment) also are tried at this level, as are indictable offenses which are triable summarily when the accused consents and the court thinks this expedient. Juries are not used in any of these cases. The magistrates' courts also examine evidence in the case of indictable offenses to decide whether there should be a trial in a higher court.

FIGURE 8–1
The British Court System

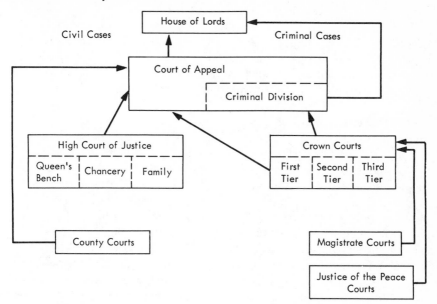

Appeals from this level go to a Crown Court, where juries are used. Serious crimes, such as murder, start in a Crown Court. These courts, created by the Courts Act of 1971, are divided into three tiers. The first-tier courts, sitting in 24 of the largest cities, are staffed by judges from the High Court and from the circuit bench. While the Crown Courts' primary function at this tier is to deal with the most important criminal cases and hear appeals from the magistrates' courts, they also handle some of the civil cases formerly heard by the High Court. The second tier sits in another 19 cities of smaller size. Jurisdiction at this level is confined to criminal cases. Third-tier Crown Courts are located in another 46 towns. At this level not only is the jurisdiction limited to criminal cases, but the judges all are drawn from the circuit bench—no judges from the High Court participate. Only the less serious criminal cases can originate at this level. Examples are assault with intent to rob, wounding, and forgeries. Any crime more serious than this must start at the first or second tier. Appeals from the Crown Courts go to the Court of Appeal, in most instances to the Criminal Division of that court.

Civil cases involving damages no greater than £750 (about $1,300) usually originate in county courts, which sit at frequent intervals. Appeals may be taken from them to the Court of Appeal. More important cases, such as those relating to civil liberties or cases which are or are likely to become test cases, are first brought to the appropriate division of the High Court. Similarly, cases involving large sums of money also come to the High Court in the first instance.

The High Court of Justice is divided into three divisions: (1) Queen's bench; (2) chancery (equity); and (3) family (divorce and probate). The Queen's bench division assigns justices to both civil and criminal courts. These three divisions of the high court, along with the Court of Appeal, are sometimes referred to as the Supreme Court of Judicature, as if it were one court.

In a few cases a further appeal may be taken to the House of Lords. Since the Lords is also the court of last resort for criminal appeals, the two judicial hierarchies finally are joined in a common body. Appeals to the Lords never are automatic, never are a matter of right. Rather they require the approval of either the Lords or the Court of Appeal, regardless of whether they are criminal or civil cases. The House of Lords considers only questions of law and not of fact. Actually it is not the entire House that hears appeals, although technically all peers are eligible to do so. By custom the judicial business of the Lords is left to the nine Lords of Appeal in Ordinary, plus, on occasion, the Lord Chancellor, former Lord Chancellors, and peers who have held high judicial office. The Lords of Appeal, usually known as law lords, are appointed to the Lords for life by the Prime Minister, after having shown outstanding legal ability.

Since the House of Lords itself technically is the highest court of appeal, the law lords cannot sit as a court when the Lords is in session. Therefore, in order not to interrupt their work, the device of appellate committees of three or five law lords was inaugurated in 1948. The other law lords accept the decision of each committee as though it were made by the entire group, just as the House of Lords accepts the decisions of the law lords as though it had been made by the entire House. A majority vote is sufficient to decide a case in an appellate committee. In addition to the majority opinion explaining the reasons for the decision, there may be concurring and dissenting opinions published.

THE ROLE OF COMMON LAW IN BRITISH JUSTICE

In Chapter 1 we referred briefly to the early development of the English judicial system and the evolution of common law. We touched on the common law again in the discussion in Chapter 2 of the constitutional foundations of British politics. Thus, concluding the British section of this book by returning to this topic is appropriate.

The common law is one of the three great systems of law existing in the world. It and the Roman law system are the best known, partly because they have been copied extensively. The common law system spread to most areas which came under British influence, including the United States. Roman law prevails on the European continent and in Japan and Turkey. Interestingly Scottish law is in the Roman tradition and thus Scotland has a system of courts separate from those for England and Wales.

One of the main distinctions between common law and Roman law is that while the former is based on judicial decisions the latter is founded on legal codes. These codes may be legislative reactions to litigation, and yet it is statutes rather than judicial decisions that are at the heart of the system. Similarly, in common law systems the fact that legislatures pass many statutes does not alter the fact that judicial decisions are the backbone of the system. Thus, in some senses, judges in a Roman law system turn to the legal code to ascertain how to decide cases, while judges in a common law system seek to find the law by examining previous judicial decisions.

The importance attached to judicial decisions in a common law system can be seen also in *stare decisis,* the principle that the rulings made in previous similar cases should decide current cases. Precedent is important and generally binding. Until 1966 the House of Lords could not reverse its decisions in previous cases. Now it may do so, but only providing that there is a good reason for departing from earlier rulings. Under Roman law systems, while attention is paid to previous cases, there generally is no rule that they are to be considered binding on subsequent cases.

Another difference in the two systems concerns the personnel of the judiciary. In the Roman law tradition, a lawyer must choose at an early age whether to go into the judiciary or into practice before the courts. In the Roman law system, the judiciary is a part of the administrative hierarchy and is a separate profession from that of the practicing lawyer. The justices are trained for the courts through the ministries of justice. In common law systems, on the other hand, judges are drawn from the legal profession.

In the early history of British courts there were, in addition to the king's courts, several other types, including private feudal courts. In the long run the king's courts superseded the others, however, simply because the former provided better justice. Royal justice became the most popular justice. By the end of the 14th century, the central courts were staffed by professional judges appointed by the king from among the practicing barristers. These courts were known as the common law courts, as a way of distinguishing them from the ecclesiastical courts and other special tribunals.

The common law has its origin in judicial decisions, which were initially based on the customs or usages of various English communities where the traveling justices held court. Since earlier decisions tended to set the pattern for deciding subsequent cases, this developing body of regulations sometimes was referred to as "case law." In time the king's judges applied the same body of legal rules to the entire nation, hence, the term "common,"—that is, common to the whole realm. Note that law made in this fashion left many topics untouched and did not seek to cover them until specific cases arose which required decision.

The common law was aided in its development by the medieval notion that law existed (divinely ordained) and that the problem was to find it; it was not conceived that the state could alter the law. Moreover, in administering the "law and custom of the realm," the courts had in large measure to rely on custom simply because there was little formal law to administer.

Initially, reported cases served as precedents, first simply as evidence of the law or some principle, and later as a rule that became binding upon future cases and lower courts. After a time, noted jurists, such as Glanville, Coke, and Blackstone, made an attempt to bring together (1) decisions which had been made with respect to certain subjects (for example, marriage, inheritance) and (2) decisions made at various places but essentially based on the same or a similar set of facts. These collections or commentaries served in effect to "codify" much of the common law.

The process of bringing the rules of the common law together revealed some obvious defects. In some areas the relevant cases needed to be distinguished more sharply by new rules; in other areas the need for new laws was plain. And even before the great jurists wrote their commentaries the need to modify or supplement the common law—because its rules could not promote justice or prevent injustice in all types of cases—was becoming obvious.

Under the common law, certain types of disputes were not covered or were covered only imperfectly. In some cases real injustices resulted. Under the common law, for example, contracts made under threat of life or limb were invalid, but contracts facilitated by the more subtle influences, such as alcoholic drinks, were valid. In another type of case (tort as well as contract), the only remedy known to the common law was damages. In many instances the remedy was akin to bolting the barn door after the horse had been stolen. Money damages, for example, could not replace a large shade tree which had been cut down or irreparably damaged. All legal systems confront at times the question of how to preserve the regularity and certainty of the law while avoiding a rigidity that would cause suffering in individual cases. In England the Lord Chancellor acted, in effect, as the king's conscience in such instances. Gradually a whole system of legal rules known as equity (or chancery) grew out of the Lord Chancellor's decisions in cases appealed to the king in an effort to gain relief from common law decisions that seemed unjust. By the early part of the 19th century a whole series of equity cases had established "a set of rules which could be invoked to supplement the deficiencies of common law or to ease the clumsy working of common law actions and remedies."[1] Equity dealt with civil controversies, not criminal cases, and established the practice of issuing an injunction to prevent threatened injury or nuisance.

Until late in the 19th century, the equity courts were separate from the regular law courts. The Judicature Acts of 1873–75, however, ended the separation of law and equity, and provision was made that *all* courts should apply and use both sets of rules. In case of conflict between them, equity was to prevail. Where statutes are applicable, however, they supersede both the common law and equity.

Prior to 1832 the typical court case did not involve any laws passed by Parliament. Increasingly Parliament has legislated in areas governed previously by common law or equity. The purpose has not been to repeal case law, but to provide rules to cover expanding governmental activities. Although both criminal and civil law have been modified extensively by statute, judge-made law still is basic in most areas of British jurisprudence.

Since the American legal system is a common law system, it is not surprising that judicial procedure in Britain and the United States is similar. The rules of evidence are designed to protect the accused and place the burden of proof on the prosecution. Nonetheless, some significant differences exist in the two countries' legal procedures.

One significant difference is that in Britain the legal profession is divided into solicitors and barristers. The solicitors usually do not try cases in court, while the barristers do virtually nothing else. The solicitors advise clients, engage barristers to try cases, and prepare such cases for trial. One cannot be both a solicitor and a barrister. Nor may a solicitor and a barrister enter into partnership. Standards of professional ethics are set for solicitors by the Law Society, while the Inns of Court have this responsibility for barristers. One interesting and significant result of this division in the legal profession is that the total number of barristers is relatively small, which enables judges to better assess their strengths and weaknesses.

Another significant difference between the British and American legal systems is the contrasting approach to criminal prosecutions. Britain does not have a system of public prosecutors comparable to our district attorneys, although the office of public prosecutor does exist. Criminal prosecution may be undertaken as well, however, by the police and private individuals. In certain lesser crimes a private person employs a solicitor,

---

[1] R. M. Jackson, *The Machinery of Justice in England*, 4th ed. (Cambridge: Cambridge University Press, 1964), p. 7.

with whom the police cooperate fully, and is reimbursed for prosecution costs out of public funds. In the great bulk of criminal cases, especially those involving professional crimes, the police prosecute. When an offense is punishable by death and for certain other categories of offenses, the office of the public prosecutor brings the case.

That British judges play a more active role in the course of the trial is yet another difference. They may, for example, comment on the evidence presented as well as on the failure of the defendant to testify. Moreover, news media may not report on a case prior to its being tried. In this way the British hope to insure a fair trial uninfluenced by popular passions which sometimes can be stirred up by the pretrial reporting of information concerning cases of heinous crimes.

The atmosphere of British courts is much more formal and sedate than often is the case in the United States. While the Perry Mason stereotype has little validity in the American court room, it is even less applicable in Britain. There is little blustering or hectoring; quiet questioning prevails. Both judges and barristers are attired not only in robes but in wigs as well to help lend dignity to the proceedings.

British courts and judges command widespread respect. Earlier in the century British justice was criticized for favoring the rich. Shortly after World War II a system of legal aid and advice was established to help solve this problem. This enables those who are unable to meet the costs of litigation to obtain legal aid and advice free or to pay for it according to a scale adapted to their means. Although the government finances the program, it is administered by the legal profession. Judicial decisions rarely produce political controversy, largely because they seldom involve political issues. By reducing the political power of the courts and by appointing as judges only those who have demonstrated outstanding legal abilities, the British have created a court system known for its incorruptibility, objectivity, and devotion to individual rights.

BIBLIOGRAPHICAL NOTE

For a shorter treatment of the structure of the court system than the Jackson book cited in Footnote 2, see H. G. Hanbury, *English Courts of Law*, 4th ed., prepared by D. Yardley (London: Oxford University Press, 1967). Judicial personnel are studied in Brian Abel-Smith, *Lawyers and Courts* (London: Heinemann, 1967). See also Harry Street, *Freedom, the Individual and the Law*, 2d ed. (Harmondsworth: Penguin, 1967).

The bibliographical suggestions for Chapter 2 contain several titles that discuss the nature of English law. Also useful is Sir Allen Kemp, *Common and Statute Law in the Making*, 7th ed. (London: Oxford University Press, 1964).

Part III

FRANCE

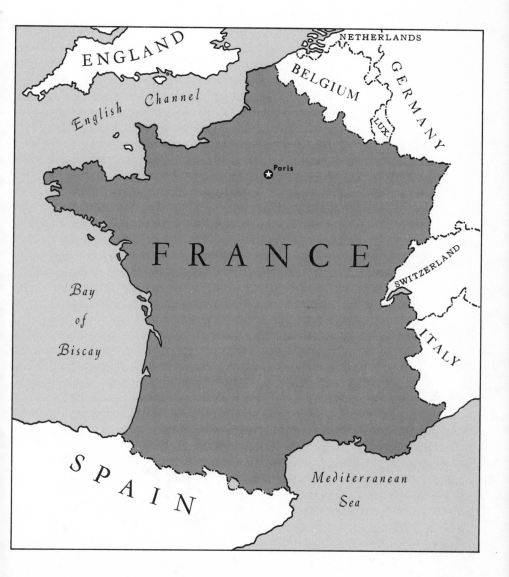

9

The Context of French Politics

GEOPHYSICAL AND SOCIOECONOMIC DIVERSITIES

Although France is geographically the largest country in Western Europe, it is considerably smaller than the state of Texas. Thus the area is compact, and there are no formidable mountain barriers inside the country. Navigable rivers, an extensive network of canals, and a railway system provided the country with a superb system of internal communication long before the coming of the airplane. On the north, west, and south, France is surrounded by water, while the Alps and the Pyrenees offer partial protection to the southeast and southwest. The Rhine River and the open country of the northeast constitute the one break in the natural protection pattern.

While this geophysical configuration has helped to give French people a very highly developed sense of national identity, ease in communication has not produced as great homogeneity nor nationalized opinion to the same extent as in Great Britain. Significant regional differences are common. One of the principal ones is the contrast between north and south, which some people trace back to the effect of the Romans in the south contrasted with the influence of Germanic tribes in the north. Instead of contrasting the France north of the Loire River (which enters the Atlantic Ocean at Nantes) with that south of the Loire, some experts contend that the contrasts between "two nations" can be sharpened by dividing the country east and west of a line running from Caen on the English Channel to Marseilles on the Mediterranean Sea. However the line is drawn, the point is that the south/west portion is largely a rural area of conservative

163

farmers and population decline, while the north/east section is an area of large factories, modern farms, and dynamic growth.

Another frequently cited contrast is that between Paris and the provinces. The city of Paris has played a unique role in the history of modern France, sometimes identified with France itself, while on other occasions considered something other than an integral part of the nation. Irrespective of how one looks upon the city, it cannot be denied that Paris has influenced the destiny of France. The phenomenal population growth of the city (one Parisian for every 50 French people less than 200 years ago as compared with one for every eight today) enable it to monopolize many facets of French life—national administration, banking, industry, and intellectual and artistic life. More than one third of all industrial and commercial profits are earned in the Parisian area, while more than half of the turnover of French businesses takes place in the same area. While a moderate trend toward dispersal seems to be in progress, Paris still employs the vast majority of French workers in several important industrial and commercial sectors of the economy. It clearly is the model for contemporary urban life, since only three other cities in France exceed a population of 350,000. France is not nearly as highly urbanized as is Britain. Despite the growth of urban areas in France in recent years, the typical community remains the small market town. The hectic, hurried life of Paris differs from the more deliberate, less hustled, and philosophical attitude in the provinces.

An important element in the provincial mind is a feeling of attachment to the soil. The average French peasant's (the term usually used for farmers) particular piece of land has been in the family for generations. Thus it is a family heirloom, not just a piece of ground. This strong family tradition has been an obstacle to improving the productivity of the land. The desire to farm in the same way as previous generations did has meant resistance to modern agricultural techniques. By the 1960s some of this was beginning to change. Especially important was the merging of about one fifth of the land previously in small, less efficient farms into larger, more productive units.

Despite French slowness in modernizing agriculture, the country's abundance of fertile soil, variety of climates, and adequate rainfall have combined to yield a productive and diversified agricultural sector. A good supply of natural resources has helped to balance the total economy. A base for industry was provided by the abundance of iron ore, bauxite, and potash.

Nonetheless, France long remained a nation of small farmers, artisans, and shopkeepers. While Britain led the Industrial Revolution, France was slow to follow. Change was hampered by the attachment to the soil already mentioned, the artisan or hand-crafting conception of manufacturing, and the achievement of a balanced and prosperous economic order prior to the Industrial Revolution.

The French were slow to adopt power-driven machinery in many industries. As artisans they took great pride in conceiving and creating quality individual products. They abhorred the idea of mass producing the exact same item over and over again with machines. Quality and craftsmanship were preferred over quantity and standardization.

Having achieved a prosperous and balanced economy, the French saw little reason for change. During the 17th and 18th centuries, agriculture, commerce, and handicraft production were the dominant features of economic life in France. Soil, climate, and industrious peasants made France relatively self-sufficient. Manufacturing was limited to a few people and tended to emphasize luxury goods. But this balance was to be upset in the 19th century, which became the century of coal, iron, and applied science, with an emphasis on mass-produced consumer goods. Large-scale enterprises left the craftspeople behind. The French economy resisted change at the time that technical advances were enabling foreign agriculture and foreign industry to compete successfully with its own counterparts.

France entered the 20th century a comparatively rich nation, largely self-sufficient, and still maintaining a nice balance between agriculture and industry. Instead of responding to competition, both at home and abroad, with more effective production, however, the policy followed was one of cartels, tariffs, and subsidies. While the French pay lip service to individualism and the profit motive, the basic characteristic of their economy has been corporate or collective. Individual enterprise has been curtailed considerably. Cartels have protected industrialists from domestic competition, while high tariffs and restrictive quotas have shielded them from foreign competition. Peasants have demanded subsidies so they can buy the expensive French-produced goods, while workers have sought wage supplements and other benefits. Prior to the formation of the de Gaulle Republic, which reduced subsidies, approximately one third of the French national budget went for direct or indirect subsidies.

French business tended to take an uncapitalistic view of commercial enterprise.[1] Most businesses were relatively small, family enterprises which aimed rather more at perpetuating the family name than at making profits. Competition was the reverse of cutthroat, since to drive a competitor from business was to ruin a family, a result desired by no responsible person of principle. Similarly, there was little willingness to risk capital in some new venture, since this was to risk ruining the family's status. Profits tended to be small and merely withdrawn rather than reinvested. Little money was spent to replace obsolete machinery. Limited production runs resulted in high unit cost because of a lack of economies of scale. The multiplicity of small businesses meant that capital was not effectively

---

[1] These comments are based on Jesse Pitts, "Continuity and Change in Bourgeois France," in Stanley Hoffman et al., *In Search of France* (New York: Harper & Row, 1963), pp. 244–54. But see also the qualifications and more extensive discussion of the French economy by Charles Kindleberger in the same volume.

concentrated to support innovative production methods requiring sizable initial expenditure.

The result was economic stagnation despite France's great potential for balanced economic strength. In 1938 France's gross national product was only slightly higher than it had been just prior to World War I; the country had grown hardly at all in a quarter of century. It had sought to maintain itself as a nation of villagers in a world of cities. It had been unable or unwilling to submit unproductive ideas and institutions to external competition, from which they long had been protected. Modern industry, as well as industrial workers, had been regarded as foreign intruders. In brief, France tried to remain aloof from the real world of the 20th century.

France's lagging economic development can be seen in its distribution of the labor force. While industrial workers account for about 55 percent of the British work force, they are only about 40 percent of the French one. Given the limited size of many manufacturing concerns, mass unionization has not progressed as far in France as in many other Western democracies. Only 16 percent of the French workers are unionized, compared to 22 percent in the United States, 40 percent in Germany, and 45 percent in Sweden. In the United States and Britain only 5 percent and 3 percent, respectively, of the work force is engaged in agriculture, while in France it is 12 percent. Furthermore, France has a greater percentage of economic units involved in distribution than does any other industrialized nation. This means a large number of middlemen, each of whom receives only a small profit. This, combined with high unit costs for many manufacturers, has helped to produce a large number of marginal and disaffected business people.

Developments in the late 1950s and in the 1960s, however, seemed to reverse these conditions. The economy grew rapidly, assisted to a considerable extent by various governmental policies. The government promoted scientific research and technical education, improved rural public utilities and trade and distribution channels, and reformed tax and investment laws. New resources were developed, particularly oil, electricity, and nuclear energy. Industrial enterprises were merged to produce more efficient units and became less reluctant to employ modern technology. By 1963 industrial production was double what it had been in 1952 and in 1972 was 70 percent greater than it had been in 1962. During this latter period France's growth surpassed even that of Germany. In agriculture, too, more advanced methods and techniques were introduced. In the late 1960s and early 1970s the value of agricultural production increased 40 percent in only five years. By 1974 France, with a per capita personal consumption of $3,119, was almost as prosperous as Germany ($3,312) and far ahead of Britain ($2,142).[2]

---

[2] For an excellent social and economic study of contemporary France, see John Ardagh, *The New French Revolution* (New York: Harper & Row, 1969). Also see Jean-Jacques Servan-Schreiber, *The American Challenge* (New York: Atheneum Publishers, 1968).

Changes have occurred as well in the French population. With something over 52 million people, France is somewhat smaller than Britain and considerably smaller than Germany. This was not true in the past, for in 1800 France was the most populous country in Europe, well over twice as large as Britain. Just as the economy stagnated, so population growth lagged behind that of other European countries. In 1940 France had only a couple of million more people than it had had in 1860. From 1930 to 1940 the total population (not the growth *rate*, but the absolute numbers) actually declined.

A major explanation for these figures is the great number of Frenchmen killed in World War I—1.5 million. The United States, which then was twice as populous as France, lost only 115,000 in World War I. And in World War II, when the U.S. population was 3.5 times as great as France's had been in 1914, we lost only 400,000. One of the effects of this human disaster was that, while France had as many men of military age as did Germany in 1870, in 1940 it had only half as many. This helps to explain why the overt, regular French military resistance to Germany collapsed so early in World War II. Another effect concerns the quality of political leadership in France between World Wars I and II. In many cases France had to rely disproportionately upon the old or second-raters for leaders; many of the middle-aged men of quality who would have led the nation were dead.

Because of the declining birth rate and the war losses France was seen three decades ago as a country of old people. But after World War II the birth rate began to climb, a trend that lasted through the 1950s. After a slight decline, the birth rate leveled off in the 1960s at a figure considerably higher than prior to World War II. This change is partially regional, more true of the dynamic north/east than of the static south/west. The migration of population from the static to the dynamic areas also is a factor. The total population of some areas in the south of France has declined by as much as 50 percent.

Whatever the regional disparities, France overall is becoming a younger nation and thus rather more youth-oriented. Figure 9–1 illustrates the age distribution of the French population. That young people can be a significant political force was demonstrated in May 1968 when student demonstrations initiated a process which ultimately led to the President's resignation. The large concentration of students in the Paris area—well over 100,000, more than in all France in 1945—enhances the potential political impact of students. Nonetheless, or perhaps precisely because of this power, the gap in communication between generations is especially marked in France.

> A relatively active population supports both the great new wave of the not yet productive young and the growing numbers of longer-lived unproductive old people . . . for [this middle-aged] generation which has a practical monopoly of the French Establishment, and which has known depression,

FIGURE 9–1

Pyramid of Age Groups of the Total Population and of the Working Population as of January 1, 1968

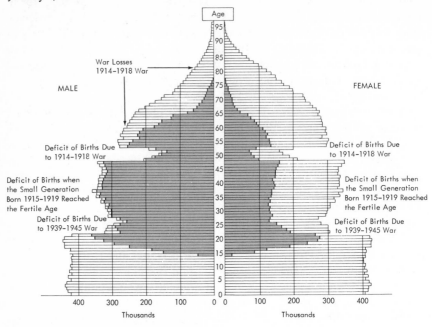

The shaded area represents the working population.
Source: *INSEE* and *Documentation Française.*

defeat, occupation, and the disappointed hopes of the Liberation, the abstract student complaints of the oppressive and repressive nature of French society and the evils of more widespread prosperity, seem even more incredible, incomprehensible and insane than they do to the middle-aged in countries with less tortured histories.[3]

In religion, France is nominally Catholic. About 40 million of the population have been baptized, and these are overwhelmingly Catholic. The active Protestants and Jews constitute no more than a million. The great mass of Catholics are not practicing Catholics in the American sense, because they are, in the main, Catholics only at four moments of their lives—birth, first communion, marriage, and death.

Furthermore, despite the large number of nominal Catholics in France, anticlericalism is widespread. The *ancien regime* was founded on a double absolutism, king *and* church, while the republican tradition has been characterized by a double revolt. Largely because the church opposed republican institutions throughout the 19th century, church and state were

---

[3] David Goldey in Philip Williams, *French Politicians and Elections 1951–1969* (Cambridge: Cambridge University Press, 1970), p. 227.

separated formally in 1904. Most Frenchmen, and a considerable number of Frenchwomen as well, while willing to allow the church to operate freely within its limited sphere, are concerned to see that it does not overstep its boundaries. The French are determined not to sacrifice the freedom of mind and spirit and of intellectual inquiry which they value so highly.

HISTORICAL BACKGROUND

France was one of the first countries in Europe to develop a sense of national unity, symbolized by the monarchy. Unlike Britain, however, France did not make steady strides toward stable and effective political democracy. Progress of this type came later than in Britain and was characterized by a number of interruptions and reversals. Moreover, the transitions—notably the Revolution of 1789—were more violent and more disruptive of political unity than those experienced by the British. In brief, a sense of national unity was not accompanied by an evolving agreement concerning the nature of the nation's political institutions. Evidence of this lack of agreement is the fact that in less than 200 years the basic form or type of government in France has been altered over a dozen times. This lack of continuity in regime means that it is very unlikely that many people will feel any sense of traditional attachment to the existing governmental system.

France of the *ancien régime* (from about 1000 to 1789) was governed by the King, who wielded his powers through secretaries of state personally selected and directed by him. They, in turn, exercised their authority through a centralized bureaucratic machine, which was several centuries in the making and which was perfected under King Louis XIV. After Louis XIV, however, the political structure lacked cohesion, being characterized by weakness and division.

A type of representative assembly, called the Estates General, had come into being in France in the 14th century. It was to represent the three estates (classes). The first two, the clergy and the nobility, were by far the most powerful, although they represented only about 5 percent of the population. The third estate was a catchall in which the middle class (bourgeoisie) was the most important. The feeble attempts of the Estates General to limit the monarchy were singularly unsuccessful. The irrelevance of the Estates General to the political system is clear from the fact that it did not even meet from 1614 to 1789. Obviously, this body could not evolve into an effective check on the monarch in the way that the British Parliament was doing at that time.

What the Estates General did not do in the way of limiting royal authority, was attempted, to a degree, by the *parlements,* of which France had a number, the most important being the *Parlement* of Paris. *Parlements* were primarily law courts which had exercised some advisory powers in the medieval period. Because royal decrees were promulgated by registering them with *parlement,* the *parlement* became able to criticize and even refuse to register them. For strong monarchs this was merely a nuisance, since they could overrule such refusals. Under weaker rulers, however, *parlements* became centers of opposition and were regarded by many as guardians of liberties. Ironically, *parlements* often opposed needed reforms and thus contributed in part to the ineffectiveness and stagnation of the political system.

The king's decision in 1788 to suspend *parlements* and to call a meeting of the Estates General for May 1789 was a confession of defeat, signifying the end of absolute monarchy. But the privileged classes, which had sided with the *parlements,* had not counted on the possibility of the Third Estate's taking over the revolt and turning it to its own ends. Similarly, the Third Estate set in motion certain forces it could not control. Within a brief span of time, the constitutional struggle turned to civil war and a profound social revolution.

The French Revoluation had a tremendous impact, especially in Europe, raising the hopes of peoples in the struggle against monarchical regimes. On the other hand, it disappointed many of its supporters, not only because of the excesses (such as arbitrary executions) but also because it seemed unable to produce a stable political order. For France it ushered in a century of political turmoil, which culminated in the establishment in 1875 of the Third Republic, a tentative compromise which few expected to last, but which proved to be the most durable political system which France has tried from the Revolution down to today.

The revolutionaries at first attempted to establish a constitutional monarchy. But Louis XVI was unwilling to accommodate himself to reality in the fashion of British monarchs and refused to accept a new status of limited power. His constant intrigues against the constitutional government's officials soon led to the creation of a republic and to his execution. So great were the social and political dislocations of this period that France had to endure virtual anarchy. The Convention—the legislative body which was the supreme governmental organ—proved too weak and inexperienced to govern the country effectively. The system rapidly moved toward increasing executive dominance, especially as Napoleon Bonaparte gained prominence. Finally, in 1804, Napoleon was able to have himself declared emperor, thus ending the First Republic and replacing it with the First Empire.

This development was not a triumph of the old order. Napoleon had perverted the revolution, but he had not destroyed it. He was not from an aristocratic background and his opportunity to rise to political power would not have occurred had it not been for the Revolution. Furthermore, he did not abolish all the Revolution's institutional reforms. While he did effect a reconciliation with church, its leaders did not return to the positions of political dominance they formerly had occupied. Nor did the nobility recoup its losses. And Napoleon did at least pretend to consult the citizens through the frequent use of plebiscites. So thorough and valuable were his modifications of the bureaucracy that the Napoleonic system still provides the basic structure for French administration.

Military defeat ended Napoleon's rule and brought the old Bourbon ruling house back to the throne. In a classic phrase it is said that the Bourbons had learned nothing and forgotten nothing. They governed entirely as though the Revolution never had occurred. Once again they demonstrated their inability to adapt to changed conditions. Their high-handed rule produced another revolution—this one more moderate—in 1830. A new king, one willing to accept the position of a constitutional monarch, was placed on the throne.

By now, however, revolution had come to be seen as virtually a regular part of the political process. Thus in 1848 unemployment and discontent in Paris combined with conflict over extension of the franchise to topple the monarchy and create the Second Republic. Napoleon's nephew Louis was elected President. He quickly parodied his uncle by making himself emperor in 1852, a move sanctioned by 97 percent of the voters in a plebiscite.

As with his uncle before him, Louis Napoleon's rule was ended by military defeat—in the Franco-Prussian War in 1870. Thus the Third Republic was proclaimed to replace the Second Empire. A sizable majority of those elected to the National Assembly in 1871, however, were monarchists. Reacting against this and the ending of the war, Paris set up its own government—the Commune. Putting down this attempted secession produced the bloodiest civil war in French history, with 20,000 people killed during the last week of fighting. Marxists subsequently developed the myth that the Commune was a self-conscious proletarian uprising. And a century later they continue to honor the Communards as martyrs.

The National Assembly elected in 1871 governed France for the next five years, even though this went beyond the stated purpose for which it was convened. Before it dissolved it formulated the constitutional instruments that were to govern France for the next 65 years.

Thus a century of political turmoil came to an uneasy and perhaps uncertain end. Unlike the English Revolution of 1688, which established (without bloodshed) the supremacy of Parliament, the French Revolution succeeded only in asserting the democratic ideal of popular sovereignty. It produced no lasting agreement, at least prior to 1875, on how this ideal was to be embodied in governmental institutions. The question of where responsibility for political acts was to rest was not adequately answered (or at best, was answered only provisionally) by any of the attempts at political organization from 1789 to 1875.

Much to everyone's surprise the Third Republic did not prove to be a stopgap political system. Instead of soon being replaced by a restored monarchy, as many anticipated, it became the longest-lived of any French political system since the Revolution, surviving World War I and the depression, to be ended by France's defeat by Germany in 1940. Although the Third Republic as a system or regime was quite stable, its executive was very unstable. Premiers frequently fell from power and Cabinets often were reconstituted, since an effective majority for any one political position rarely existed in the legislature.

During World War II the part of France not occupied by the Germans was governed by a puppet government located in Vichy. After the Liberation the population voted overwhelmingly to have a new constitution rather than return to the Third Republic. When the constituent assembly submitted its proposed constitution to the people, the nation, which consistently and frequently had given virtual unanimous approval to anything the two Napoleons had proposed, rejected it. A revised constitution subsequently was approved—but only barely. While it was bad enough that the vote was only 9 million for to 8 million against, the result was made disastrous by the fact that another 8 million abstained. Thus throughout the Fourth Republic the supporters of Charles de Gaulle, who adamantly opposed the constitution as providing for too weak a government, taunted those in power with the fact that their political system had the approval of only 37 percent of the population. Crippled by such a birth defect, the Fourth Republic was unlikely to enjoy a long life.

The Fourth Republic's life expectancy deteriorated further because it came to resemble the Third Republic, only more so. The same executive instability, the same governmental ineffectiveness, the same dissatisfaction soon were rampant. The average life of a Cabinet was even shorter in the Fourth Republic than it had been in the Third—now less than six months. During 1951 and 1958 the average length of government crises, the time from the resignation of one government to the agreement upon its successor, was two and one half weeks.

In January 1958 a public opinion poll asked a sample of the population, "What would you do if there were a coup?" Only 4 percent said that they would actively oppose it and the majority responded that they would do nothing. Not surprisingly, four months later the Fourth Republic collapsed under a virtual coup. The system would probably have survived if it had not been for the government's inability to maintain the French colonial empire. Economic conditions at home had improved greatly in 1953–57. Paradoxically, the increasing prosperity seemed to magnify the reverses in the foreign field, which were pulling France's international prestige downhill, and which had consumed much of her material and human resources.

The immediate circumstances leading to the downfall of the Fourth Republic can be summed up in one word—Algeria. The French settlers there, numbering at least 1,500,000, were determined to resort to violence, if need be, against what appeared to be the helplessness of the government in Paris to cope with the Moslem nationalist movement in Algeria. In this attitude they were supported by professional army officers, partly because of the humiliating defeat in Indochina and a no less humiliating withdrawal from Suez in 1956. Moreover, it was apparent that certain army units in Algeria and in France meant business. The threat of a military revolution was real.

The government was undercut further by the fact that many people in France itself sympathized with the Algerian settlers and the army. Furthermore, while many other people, particularly the younger generations, cared little about Algeria, they were equally apathetic about defending the established political system, given its general aura of ineffectiveness.

The French Government concluded that the only acceptable way of avoiding an almost certain military dictatorship was to call upon the country's World War II hero, General Charles de Gaulle, to form a government. On June 1, 1958, he was made Premier—the last one of the Fourth Republic—and was empowered, as he had insisted upon, to rule by decree for six months and to revise the constitution drastically.

Instead of summoning a constituent assembly, de Gaulle turned the task of drafting a new constitution over to a handful of his supporters who could be trusted to devise a document embodying his views on the proper form of government, in particular the need for a strong executive. When the proposed constitution was submitted to a referendum, the population reverted to their voting patterns under the Napoleons. Eighty percent voted in favor of it, with only 15 percent abstaining. Thus, unlike the Fourth Republic, the Fifth began life with the approval of two thirds of the electorate, apparently vindicating the Gaullists' jeers at the Fourth.

During the next ten years de Gaulle's actions amply demonstrated his predominance within the French political process. He extracted France from the Algerian dilemma, illustrated French domination of the Common Market by vetoing British membership, and gained an enhanced international prominence for France through the development of a nuclear force and closer relations with the Soviet Union. Then in May 1968, the arrest of an extremist student leader mushroomed without warning into a confrontation between the government and the students, which eventually included the workers. While de Gaulle was able to ride out this storm, it becomes clear in retrospect that his authority had been weakened fatally.

The following April a referendum was held on the question of reorganizing the government so as to strengthen regional structures and to transform the Senate and further reduce its powers. As he had done for previous referenda during his decade of power, de Gaulle threatened that were his proposals for reform not approved by a substantial margin he would resign. The technique which in the past had worked so well now backfired; 53 percent of those voting said no. Some analysts have argued that the negative vote represented not so much a rejection of the substance of the reforms as it did a refusal to allow de Gaulle to continue to govern in a high-handed fashion. Unbending as ever, de Gaulle resigned as President.

The years that have passed since his resignation have provided a partial answer to the question asked almost from the inception of the Fifth Republic: *Après* de Gaulle? Contrary to what he sometimes had predictated, de Gaulle's departure was not followed by chaos. The system that was drawn up to his specifications has endured even beyond his death in 1970. This is not to claim that it has established itself among the French people. Given France's history since the Revolution few would be willing to speculate on how many more years the Fifth Republic will endure.

BIBLIOGRAPHICAL NOTE

The Ardagh book cited in Footnote 2 is very informative on a wide variety of aspects of contemporary French life. A valuable essay on social change in France since World War II is Laurence Wylie's contribution to the Hoffman book mentioned in Footnote 1.

A great number of French histories are readily available. Gordon Wright, *France in Modern Times* (New York: Rand McNally, 1960), is reliable and comprehensive. A standard, relatively brief source is David Thomson, *Democracy in France since 1870,* 4th ed. (London: Oxford University Press, 1964). Philip Williams is a leading authority on the Fourth and Fifth Republics. His study of the Fourth is *Crisis and Compromise* (Garden City, New York: Doubleday, 1966). For the Fifth he has collaborated with Martin Harrison on *Politics and Society in de Gaulle's Republic* (Garden City, New York: Doubleday, 1973).

10

The Foundations of
French Politics

THE REPUBLICS' CONSTITUTIONAL TRADITIONS

Given the great variety of governmental systems that France has had
since the Revolution, it is difficult to speak of a single constitutional tradition. Between the Revolution and the establishment of the Third Republic
the French experimented with about a dozen constitutions. The relative
durability of various French political systems is indicated in Figure 10–1.
Although the average lifespan of each was brief, these constitutions usually were elaborate, long, and detailed documents. But, as history has
demonstrated, the care and precision with which a constitution is drawn
has no relation to its survival. Nor does practice in drafting constitutions
guarantee their workability.

The most durable of French constitutions was that of the Third Republic. Since it, along with the Fourth Republic, which, contrary to the intentions of its founders, came to resemble its predecessor so closely, spanned
a total of 77 years (two fifths of France's history since the Revolution),
discussion of their basic constitutional principles is necessary. This also
will help to clarify how greatly the Fifth Republic's basic provisions depart from previous tradition.

The constitution of the Third Republic consisted of three laws drawn
up in 1875 as a temporary expedient by a monarchist assembly which
could not decide which of two royal families should rule France. This was
a compromise which neither faction wanted and neither side believed
would endure. The three laws do not resemble a constitutional document.
The Law on the Organization of the Public Powers vests legislative power
in a Chamber of Deputies and a Senate, provides for a formal executive

FIGURE 10–1
Regime Instability

France 1789–1978

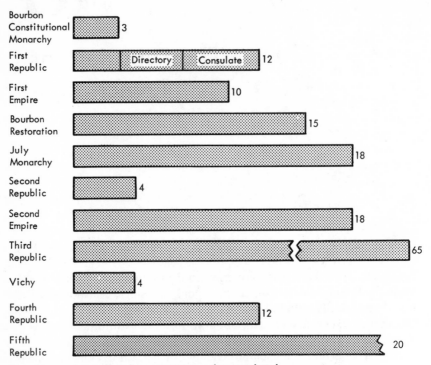

Bourbon
Constitutional   3
Monarchy

First   Directory   Consulate   12
Republic

First   10
Empire

Bourbon   15
Restoration

July   18
Monarchy

Second   4
Republic

Second   18
Empire

Third   65
Republic

Vichy   4

Fourth   12
Republic

Fifth   20
Republic

Note: The numbers indicate how many years each system lasted.

(president), prescribes that ministers are responsible to both houses of the legislature, and provides for a method of amending these arrangements. The Law on the Organization of the Senate prescribes in more detail the organization and the powers of that body. The Law on the Relations of the Public Powers, passed several months after the other two, seeks to regulate more precisely governmental procedures involving the legislature and the executive.

The essential point to remember is that these three laws provided a mere structural framework, with the actual operation of the system to be worked out in practice. These laws did not place any limitations on the powers of government, except that the republican form of government would not be subject to amendment. The two houses, acting together, could presumably legislate about anything when and as they wished. And since there was no judicial review in the American sense, they had no fear of being overruled. Furthermore, this meant that formally amending the constitution was unnecessary.

More in accord with French tradition, the constitution of the Fourth Republic was detailed and logical, but, in the main, it ratified the political practices that had evolved under the Third. Some efforts were made to remedy the most serious shortcomings, primarily the relatively rapid turnover of Cabinets. Spur-of-the-moment votes of confidence, which had brought down so many Governments in the prewar period, were eliminated. A cooling-off period of 24 hours was required and only the Premier (prime minister) was permitted to ask for a vote of confidence. The Cabinet was required to retain the support of only the lower house. Furthermore, it was not forced to resign on either a vote of confidence or a motion of censure unless an absolute majority voted against it. And to give the Cabinet a weapon against the legislature, it was empowered to dissolve Parliament and call for new elections.

In practice, all of this made little difference. Governments resigned when they could not get their legislative proposals passed, regardless of whether an absolute majority had voted against them. And the power of dissolution was hemmed in with sufficient limitations as to be meaningless.

The French political system under the Third and Fourth Republics was essentially parliamentary. France was governed by ministers responsible to an elected legislature; the head of state was more a symbol than an effective political power; and there was no judicial review in the American sense. The system also was unitary, as contrasted with federal. While both these features characterize the British system as well, the French Republics differed from it in several significant aspects.

Although Britain also is a unitary political system, its local units of government have more power than do corresponding units in France. Political authority is much more centralized in France. British local government, although limited in discretionary powers, is not just a sub-unit in the national administrative structure, as is largely the case in France.

As for contrasts in the parliamentary structure, France, instead of a monarch, had a President, elected for seven years by the two houses of Parliament meeting as one body. This President was, however, the ceremonial head of state just as is the British monarch. The President's political acts were the acts of ministers who were politically responsible to the legislature. Since no political party had a majority in Parliament, the President had some influence in deciding who would form the Cabinet.

The main contrast with Britain appeared in the nature of the Cabinet. Instead of two major parties, the Third and Fourth Republics had several major ones plus a number of smaller ones, all electing some members to the legislature. A Cabinet could obtain the support of a majority in Parliament only by including members from a number of parties. Every Cabinet, therefore, was a coalition of divergent views. While the coalition parties usually could agree on minor matters, they rarely favored the same action on the crucial issues. Consequently, French Cabinets could not implement decisive party pledges and did all they could to avoid having to act on anything of real importance. When the evil day could no longer be postponed and something had to be done, the typical result was the breakup of the coalition and the fall of the Government.

Although Cabinets were short-lived, instability was not as pronounced as it appeared on the surface, because a number of members of an outgoing Cabinet would always be found in the succeeding one. Certain men served in Cabinet after Cabinet, in the same or different posts, which meant that there was a great deal more continuity and experience in Cabinets than surface impressions indicated. This does not detract, however, from the fact that most major problems could not be dealt with in a forthright manner.

The Cabinet was weak, partly because the Premier could not be a strong unifying party leader as in Britain. His task was more that of a broker or compromiser seeking to get divergent groups to work together. Often one or more of these groups saw more advantage in voting against the Cabinet than in supporting it. The advantage lay, first, in avoiding responsibility for decisions that might prove to be politically unpopular. In addition, some parties at times had reason to believe that they would gain greater influence in the new Cabinet which would be formed following the breakup of the present one. They could play this game of political musical chairs with impunity because they did not need to anticipate a new election, which might have cost them seats in the legislature.

The Premier was empowered legally to dissolve the lower house, acting in the name of the President, but the consent of the Senate was required. This provision was a dead letter, however, because in the early years of the Third Republic President MacMahon had misused it. In an effort to obtain a more conservative Government personally acceptable to him, he dissolved the Chamber of Deputies and called for new elections despite the fact that the existing Premier and Cabinet had effective Parliamentary support. Supporters of Parliamentary democracy considered MacMahon's action a virtual coup d'état and raised a storm of protest. The power of dissolution thus came to be held in such ill repute that it was not used again until late in the Fourth Republic, some 80 years later.

French Cabinets were weakened also by certain practices that had developed in Parliamentary procedure. The Cabinet could not determine, as in Britain, the way Parliament's time would be spent. More than that, it could not even insist on priority for its own measures. Nor could it control financial matters. Parliament could increase expenditures without providing the new funds to cover it; such legislative irresponsibility was prohibited in Britain. Parliamentary Cabinets that lack control over finance and legislative agendas hardly can be effective.

The practice of proxy voting—the casting of all of a party's Parliamentary votes by a single person regardless of whether all the members are present—further undermined the Cabinets. This practice assured a sizable bloc of votes against the Cabinet on any issue. The parties supporting the Cabinet never were so united and were unwilling to give it unqualified support in advance. The Cabinet, therefore, had to canvas its supposed supporters constantly to ascertain whether and in what numbers they intended to defect. In brief, French coalitions had little political cohesion.

Finally, the Cabinet was at the mercy of Parliamentary committees. Instead of being able to guide and shape the work of committees, as in Britain, Cabinet members often were treated hostilely. Cabinet measures often were buried or so rewritten as to constitute but a faint resemblance to the original. It was not unusual for committees to report measures that could be described, at best, as undesirable by the Government.

During the Third Republic, the Cabinet had to please both houses of Parliament, although adverse votes in the Senate came to mean less and less in terms of the Cabinet's political survival. The lower house increased its power and influence. During the Fourth Republic, France had essentially a one-house legislature, called the National Assembly, although an upper house, the Council of the Republic, was retained. The upper house could, at best, merely delay measures for a brief time.

Because of the weakness of the Cabinet, particularly in its relationship to Parliament, French parliamentarism came generally to be known as assembly government, signifying the predominant power of the legislature. This contrasts with the term cabinet government, which is often used for the British parliamentary system signifying the predominant power of the Cabinet.

The main aim of the drafters of the Fifth Republic's constitution was to get away from a system in which Parliament predominated—one that had failed to provide effective leadership. Their answer was to strengthen the executive in its relations with the legislature. This was done in two ways: first by giving substantive powers, especially in times of crisis, to the formerly powerless chief of state, the President; second by conferring greater powers on the Premier by limiting the Parliament's policy making powers and its powers to vote Governments out of office.

On paper, the new constitution established the essential features of a traditional parliamentary government, but modified it to give the executive (President and Premier) the real power in policy making. Correspondingly, the powers of Parliament were reduced or circumscribed. This in itself would appear to be a move in the direction of British practice. In actuality, however, the French Parliament has been shorn of its power to hold the executive politically accountable. To be sure, the Cabinet is said to be responsible to the popularly elected lower house, the National Assembly, but the Assembly is severely hampered in the methods it can employ in seeking to hold the Cabinet accountable.

An innovation for France in the Fifth Republic constitution is the creation of a Constitutional Council. To some extent it functions to keep Parliament within the bounds of the power granted it in the constitution. To this end it has been given a very limited form of judicial review. The details of these provisions are discussed in a subsequent chapter.

The procedure for altering the constitution is much more formal under the Fifth Republic than it was in the Third. Amendments may be proposed by the President, by the Premier, or by members of Parliament. In each case a proposed amendment must obtain a majority in each house of Parliament. After passage by the two houses, the proposed amendment, if initiated by members of Parliament, must be submitted for ratification by the people in a referendum. If the proposed amendment is initiated by the President or the Premier, however, ratification (after passage by the two houses) may, at the discretion of the President, be achieved by either popular referendum or a three-fifths majority vote in a specially called joint meeting of the two houses of Parliament.

Despite these detailed provisions, in 1962 the constitution was amended by a different procedure. It is illustrative of de Gaulle's conception of his role and authority that, when he found it inconvenient to follow the rules set forth in the constitution drawn up to his instructions, he employed other means that he found more congenial. De Gaulle had his Premier propose amending the constitution to provide for direct election of the President. Instead of sending this proposal to Parliament, since there was some doubt whether it would pass, it was submitted directly to a referendum. Popular approval was deemed to be sufficient to implement the proposal. Thus, strange as it sounds, the French constitution was amended unconstitutionally. This simply is one evidence of the fact that in France, as on the continent generally, constitutionalism—the idea that certain rules of the game must be observed and can be altered only by special procedures—is not firmly established.

PARADOXES OF A FRAGMENTED CULTURE

As this comment concerning the status of constitutionalism suggests, French political culture differs markedly from that of Britain and the United States. The consensus taken for granted in these two countries is absent. Continental political cultures are fragmented; the populace differs not just on short-range policy preferences, but on basic fundamentals.[1] In the United States and Britain the expression of political desires is largely institutionalized, channeled within existing political structures. The polit-

---

[1] This discussion draws upon Gabriel Almond, "Comparative Political Systems," *Journal of Politics* 18 (August 1956), pp. 391–409.

ical process, then, is a pragmatic conflict over securing immediate goals. On the continent a political battle has raged over the basic form of the governmental system and the survival of the various subcultures supporting one alternative or another. In such a situation political leaders come to the political arena not with policy options to bargain over, but with exclusive and conflicting views of the proper political culture and system. Politics involves basic clashes with high ideological tone. Politics becomes a matter of faith rather than of instrumentality or effectiveness.

Historically, political culture has clashed with the political system in France. The parliamentary system common on the continent is a form of government requiring bargaining. The culture prevailing has encouraged not 'compromise but exhortation and attempts at conversion of the benighted. Since fundamentals instead of policy alternatives have been at stake, dogmatism and hostility have been encouraged. Furthermore, an ultimate resort to violence has seemed justifiable. Especially has this been true in France, since often in the last two centuries reforming the governmental system along more democratic lines or protecting what democracy existed often has required armed domestic conflict. France seems to have been engaged in constant domestic strife which often has erupted into civil conflict.

Such conflict helped during the Third and Fourth Republics to produce immobilism—ineffective government unable to cope with the needs and problems of its society. This created a threat of what has been termed a Caesaristic breakthrough, which is a movement of charismatic nationalism that breaks the boundaries of the political subcultures. It is able temporarily to unify the fragmented culture, thus overcoming immobilism in a coercive fashion. Fragmented political cultures, then, have a potential or tendency toward totalitarian or authoritarian regimes. In France the rule of two Napoleons and of de Gaulle illustrate this tendency to varying degrees.

The fundamental issue of French politics since the Revolution has been the clash between the desire for democracy and the desire for stable, effective government. Stated another way, French politics for the last two centuries has been a constant, and as yet unsuccessful, attempt to reconcile the principle of aristocratic command with the principle of democratic consent. As regards governmental organs, this polarity is institutionalized as a conflict between the executive and the legislature.

The conflict between the two stated principles remains unresolved because of a basic paradox in French political culture. On the one hand many people dislike assembly government, one in which the legislature is the dominant power, because during the times it has existed the government usually has been weak and ineffective—immobile. One might think that it would be only the reform elements that would object to this situation. But conservatives dislike it as well. For the pervasive theme of

France's past is that of national greatness. In the 17th and 18th centuries, and during most of the 19th, France was undisputedly the leading nation on the Continent politically, economically, culturally, and intellectually. The French people have not forgotten the era of grandeur when French alliances controlled Europe and the French Empire extended over six continents. This cannot but be a factor in the nation's political subconscious, in the concept that the French have of themselves and their role among the nations.

Yet French political institutions in the age of greatness were absolutist—monarchical and clerical. They had bestowed on France a certain unity, an organic conception of the state. The French Revolution swept away these political institutions, although it took another 100 years for republican institutions to gain a relatively firm, if not always decisive, foothold. For some, the absolutist institutions continued to be the ideal, although supported by a decreasing number of people. Yet the impact of the Revolution was unsettling; the greater part of French political history since then has been characterized as a period in which the French have been searching for a new political consensus.

Thus, one might conclude that there would be general agreement in France on strengthening the executive to retain international prominence and to take effective domestic action. That this is not true brings up the other element of the paradox. The progressive political elements in France fear that strengthening the executive will be the first step toward destroying the Republic and replacing it with an authoritarian regime. They are haunted by the spectre of the man on horseback, by the threat of a Caesaristic breakthrough. Napoleon, Marshall MacMahon, General de Gaulle all are leaders who rose to prominence because of their military exploits and whose democratic credentials were nonexistent, bogus, or tattered.

The attitudes of the French democrats contain still a further paradox. On the one hand they would contend that the popular will always is right. In fact, in France there is some question whether democratic thought makes any provision for minority right; the democratic tradition tends to be one of unlimited majority rule. French democrats oppose checks on the legislature because it is the instrument of the popular majority. Curiously, they feel that it is only through the legislature that popular sovereignty can be expressed. They refuse to concede that a popularly elected chief executive can represent the popular will as well as a group of individual legislative representatives can, or, for that matter, even can represent the popular will at all. For popularly elected executives, they feel, are not democrats; they cannot be trusted, but will attempt to subvert the democratic system as both the Napoleons did. Thus the people, whose will is always right, cannot be trusted to vote for a chief executive. They will fail to perceive the dangerous characteristics of a charismatic leader; they will be taken in by the glamour of a famous name and will elect a man who will destroy the Republic.

So it follows that the executive must be beholden to the legislature, if the Republic is to survive. But a weakened executive combined with the multi-party system prevailing in France inevitably produces executive instability and immobile government. The democrats' fears produce the type of system which is unable to produce the reform policy outputs they most desire. Any proposal for changing the system toward one which might be sufficiently effective to implement their policy goals, they regard with suspicion and hostility as a threat to the Republic.

Suspicion of the political motives of others is worsened in France by conflict over the role of the church. Many identify the church with reaction and view it as an obstacle to liberty. Thus it follows that those who support the views of the church must also be suspect. However desirable their policy suggestions may appear to be on the surface, there must be something wrong with them.

Another object of suspicion is the state itself. Since the state possesses power, it is a potential tyrant. Consequently, one needs to be constantly on guard lest freedom be lost. It follows, therefore, that grants of authority must be limited and surrounded with safeguards. It is in this psychology—pessimism about human nature and the distrust of people— that the French belief in written law is rooted.

An outgrowth of this attitude is the view that the state is something apart from and above the individual, and not necessarily benevolent. In contrast to the British idea that the state exists to protect and serve the people, the French view the state as a would-be master, an intruder, threatening to the individual. The French suspect that if they join an association (state or other) they will have to give more than they will receive. This belief gives rise to the tendency on the part of citizens to get as much as possible from the state while at the same time contributing as little as possible. It is this attitude that has caused many observers of the French political scene to conclude that there is an absence of civic spirit in France.

The fear and distrust of the state has made it difficult for the French to organize a workable political authority. They have not wanted a system of government that vests significant authority in anyone, least of all in a strong executive. They have tried different forms of government, but none has been completely satisfactory. For the vast majority, the least unsatisfactory has been the republican form, provided it did not attempt to grapple with problems over which the country is divided seriously.

Given the high level of suspicion in French society, it is not surprising that the French tend to be isolated from one another, to be strong individualists. One specialist has suggested that they fear face-to-face relations.[2] This in turn may help to explain their great interest in abstract matters of principle. Moreover, the French are proud of their individualism and independence of mind. They do not want ready opinions; theirs is the critical approach. They want to discuss, to think, to analyze, and to reach conclusions on their own. They seek to inject intelligence and reasoning into everything. They resist advertising, and inquiries into their personal life are resented.

French individuality has no doubt made for high cultural achievements, but it has also led to frustrations. For example, the analytical approach made it difficult to determine the final resting place of France's Unknown Soldier. A location associated with the Revolution would be offensive to those who had never accepted it. A similar difficulty was encountered when a chapel was suggested, because there was no proof that the Unknown Soldier was even a Christian, let alone a Catholic—hence the risk of blasphemy. By contrast, no one in England considered the theological implication of the decision to bury that country's Unknown Soldier in Westminster Abbey.

Paradoxically, the French practical bent is no handicap to a discussion of abstract ideas and high principles. Then they become idealists, internationalists, humanists. While accepting tolerance as an intellectual necessity, their skepticism makes them wary of compromise. Although having a vigorous interest in the ideas that underlie politics, they are cynical toward those who practice politics. This attitude, coupled with French reluctance to forget injury, even if by doing so the common interest would be served, has made for anything but efficiency in government.

Moreover, French political life has been characterized by an emphasis on ideology and principle. This has meant that the various political factions could not be counted on to embrace compromise as a workable system on a continuing basis. Certain factions might compromise on certain issues and, therefore, constitute a majority in the resolution of those issues, but on other issues they might be determined to force the Government out of office, rejecting all compromise proposals no matter how reasonable. In other words, the Government of the day was forced, as a price of staying in office, to seek a new majority combination on each basic problem that it was compelled to tackle.

Inability to resolve political problems effectively has made it more difficult for French Governments to cope with the social and economic trends of this century. Industrialization and large-scale trade unionism brought in their wake social and economic problems whose solutions could hardly wait until the French had reached agreement on basic politi-

---

[2] Michel Crozier, *The Bureaucratic Phenomenon* (Chicago: University of Chicago Press, 1964).

cal questions. While the moderate political groups managed to retain control (often precarious), many French people were expressing their exasperation by voting for extremist political parties of the left or right. The Communists, for example, have managed to poll over 20 percent of the popular vote in most elections since World War II. While polling a considerably smaller percentage of the vote, groups on the far right have served to augment the size of antidemocratic blocs in the legislature and in a number of municipal councils. Fortunately for France, the extremist groups have been in a minority, but that minority has been large enough to constitute an ever-present danger to French democracy.

In brief, France has lacked the type of practical political consensus that exists in Britain. Whatever consensus has existed has been of a somewhat abstract nature, typified by the rallying cry of the Revolution—liberty, equality, fraternity. But many of the issues raised by that very Revolution have made practical political agreements difficult. More recently, the unsettling experience of defeat and occupation in World War II, including the experience of a collaborationist regime (Vichy) under Nazi auspices, has led to a more profound search for the source of France's difficulties. Or perhaps it was more of a search for a scapegoat—a search that did not leave the system of government and its leaders unscathed. Moreover, the costly, desperate, and largely unsuccessful battle to save the empire after World War II also contributed to France's difficulty in seeking to find a unifying political consensus.

Thus the viability of democratic government in France remains something of a question mark. France clearly has a strong democratic tradition. And when, between World Wars I and II, European problems and turmoil drove Germany and Italy from democracy to authoritarian systems, France managed to survive as a democracy. But democratic values are not firmly established in France because it also has a competing tradition. Not sufficiently repressive to be termed authoritarian, this value system has been labelled the administrative tradition—government "through an elite, supported by a powerful and centralized bureaucracy."[3] It is this tradition which the Fifth Republic embodies. This is not to deny that the Fifth Republic is a democracy, but rather to emphasize that some democratic procedures and principles are unattenuated. And it is this, combined with a past history and future possibility of a Caesaristic breakthrough, that prevent one from being certain of the prospects of French democracy.

This discussion of French values should not close without noting that the French are agreed on one thing—the value of the French way of life, particularly as embodied in French culture and language. The French have felt something of a mission to civilize the rest of the world by as-

---

[3] Nicholas Wahl, *The Fifth Republic* (New York: Random House, Inc., 1959), p. 28.

similating it into French culture. This belief in the superiority of their culture has made the French at times appear intolerant of other nations and cultures. The important point is that the French are intensely loyal to their nation. The unfortunate problem is that this loyalty fails to carry over, not only to the parties in power at any given time, but even to the governmental system itself. It is this lack of commitment which so distinguishes French politics from British or American.

BIBLIOGRAPHICAL NOTE

Two very insightful discussions of French political cultures are the essays by Hoffman and Goguel in the Hoffman book cited in Footnote 1 in the previous chapter. The principles in accord with which French politicians appeared to operate in the Fourth Republic are discussed in Nathan Leites, *On the Game of Politics in France* (Stanford: Stanford University Press, 1959). For an interesting effort to assess the impact upon political culture of socioeconomic change in Fifth Republic France, see Harvey Waterman, *Political Change in Contemporary France* (Columbus, Ohio: Charles Merrill, 1969).

Contemporary discussions of the launching of the Fourth and Fifth Republics and some examination of the essence of each system and its relation to French political tradition are Gordon Wright, *The Reshaping of French Democracy* (New York: Reynal & Hitchcock, 1948), and the Wahl book cited in Footnote 3.

11

Expression of Individual and Collective Interest

RECENT ELECTORAL SYSTEMS

Difficult as it may be to believe, it nonetheless is true that the French have altered their electoral system even more frequently than they have changed their form of government. Rarely does a French electoral system endure beyond two elections without some significant alteration in procedures. This constant tinkering with the system has not been motivated by a desire to satisfy some idealistic abstract conception of electoral justice. Instead the changes have been partisan attempts by those in power to strengthen their own position and weaken their major challengers.

Many people mistakenly believe that the typical French electoral system provides for proportional representation—an effort to make the partisan distribution of the seats in the legislature correspond closely to each party's share of the popular vote. Actually France rarely used proportional representation (PR) prior to the Fourth Republic and never in a pure form. This is an important fact, because it sometimes has been argued that PR helps to produce a multi-party system. Yet France had several competing parties long before it adopted PR. This clearly weakens the argument concerning the effect of PR and requires searching for less mechanical explanations for the existence of a multi-party system in France.

PR may be employed in a variety of forms, some of which favor large parties and others, small parties. At the start of the Fourth Republic the French used the highest average method. An illustration of how this might work in a hypothetical constituency appears in part A of the example given below. This method is more favorable to large parties, but produces a fairly close correspondence between share of votes and share of seats.

Example of Operation of Proportional Representation

A constituency returning 5 members to the legislature casts its votes thus:

Party	Numbers	Percent
Communists	52,000	26
RPF	36,000	18
Socialists	34,000	17
MRP	32,000	16
Independents	24,000	12
Radicals	22,000	11
	200,000	

A.   Highest average method
   1.   On each round divide a party's total vote by the number of seats it
        would have if it were given that round's seat.
   2.   The figure obtained is that party's average vote per seat.
   3.   The party with the highest average on that round wins the seat.

1st Round	2d Round	3d Round	4th Round	5th Round
Com ... 52,000	RPF 36,000	Soc 34,000	MRP ... 32,000	Com ... 26,000
RPF 36,000	Soc 34,000	MRP ... 32,000	Com ... 26,000	Ind 24,000
Soc 34,000	MRP ... 32,000	Com ... 26,000	Ind 24,000	Rad 22,000
MRP ... 32,000	Com ... 26,000	Ind 24,000	Rad 22,000	RPF 18,000
Ind 24,000	Ind 24,000	Rad 22,000	RPF 18,000	Soc 17,000
Rad 22,000	Rad 22,000	RPF 18,000	Soc 17,000	MRP ... 16,000
Com win 1	RPF wins 1	Soc win 1	MRP wins 1	Com win 1

As the 1951 election approached, however, the parties in power feared that the Communists and the supporters of de Gaulle would gain a majority of the seats and thus paralyze the government by combined opposition from the Left and the Right. So they rigged the electoral system. Parties were permitted to declare that they were allied in any particular constituency and, if combining the votes which the candidate slates of these parties received gave the alliance more than 50 percent of the vote, it would receive all of the seats in that constituency instead of just its proportional share. The allies were not compelled to agree on a common set of candidates, but could simply declare formally that they were allied. The al-

B. Highest remainder method
   1. Divide the total vote by the number of seats to get the electoral quotient.
   2. Any party gaining this many votes gets a seat.
   3. For each seat the party wins, deduct the quotient from its total vote.
   4. On each round the party with the highest remainder of votes wins the seats.

Electoral quotient = 40,000 (200,000 divided by 5)

1st round—Communists win a seat since they are over 40,000

2d Round		*3d Round*		*4th Round*		*5th Round*	
RPF	36,000	Soc	34,000	MRP	32,000	Ind	24,000
Soc	34,000	MRP	32,000	Ind	24,000	Rad	22,000
MRP	32,000	Ind	24,000	Rad	22,000	Com	12,000
Ind	24,000	Rad	22,000	Com	12,000	RPF	0
Rad	22,000	Com	12,000	RPF	0	Soc	0
Com	12,000	RPF	0	Soc	0	MRP	0
RPF wins 1		Soc win 1		MRP wins 1		Ind win 1	

liance clearly was in name only. Furthermore, the PR system was altered to the highest remainder method (illustrated in Example B) in a few areas where the Communists and the Gaullists were known to be strongest, since this form of PR works against large parties and benefits smaller ones. The results of this manipulation were to give the Gaullists 26 seats fewer than they otherwise would have received and the Communists 71 seats fewer. The strategy was successful in that it did prevent the Left and the Right from getting a majority between them, but the questionable morality of such action hardly could have strengthened peoples' respect for the governmental system.

When de Gaulle returned to power in 1958, he decided to change the electoral system to the double ballot system that had prevailed in one form or another for much of the Third Republic. Interestingly, the leaders of the party organized to support de Gaulle, the Union for the New Republic, did not favor this system. They felt it would be difficult for the new political faces in the Union for the New Republic to defeat the better-known candidates of the old parties. De Gaulle did not want the Union to achieve a majority victory, since he did not want to be beholden to any political group.

Under the current electoral system, France is divided into single-member districts, unlike the multi-member constituencies used for PR in the Fourth Republic. There are, in effect, two elections, or ballots, held one week apart on Sundays. Candidates who receive a majority in the first election are elected. In the districts where no one receives a majority, there is a runoff, or second ballot, in which the winner is determined by a mere plurality. In the interval between the two ballots, candidates may drop out (those who receive less than 10 percent of the electorate must do so), and several parties may seek to combine their support in favor of a single candidate. No new candidate may appear, however, on the second ballot. In 1968 one third of all constituencies were won on the first ballot. This was a major increase over the three previous elections in the Fifth Republic; prior to 1968 the proportion had never exceeded one fifth. In 1973 only 12 percent of the contests were won on the first ballot. Only in the first Fifth Republic election in 1958 was the proportion lower.

Except for minor differences, such as the injunction against new candidates on the second ballot, this system was employed in 12 out of 16 elections between 1875 and 1940 inclusive, and is by far the simplest of the systems that have been used.

It should be emphasized that there is nothing even remotely proportional about the double ballot system. In 1958, for example, about 7 million Communist and Socialist voters elected 54 members of the National Assembly, while about 4 million voters for the Union for the New Republic returned 212 members. In 1968 the Left political parties got the same share of the vote as did the Gaullists, but received less than one third as many seats.

Early in 1977 the followers of President Giscard d'Estaing began to think about switching the electoral system back to PR prior to the 1978 elections. They hoped in this way to damp down the growing strength of the Left. They feared that the double ballot system would magnify a small Communist and Socialist popular vote majority into a landslide of Parliamentary seats. The Gaullists remain adamantly opposed to PR, however, since, as the largest single party, they believe they can obtain the greatest Parliamentary mileage from their popular vote under the double ballot system. Thus it appears that the electoral system will continue in basically its present form for at least a bit longer.

To be a candidate for the National Assembly, one must be a French citizen and at least 23 years old. One need not reside in the constituency where one is running. Candidates must deposit 1,000 francs (approximately $200), which is forfeited by those who do not receive at least 5 percent of the votes cast. Those who do poll that much are reimbursed for certain portions of their campaign costs, such as posters, printing, and mailing. These are supposed to be the only cost, but unofficial posters and circulars are not illegal. Since there is no maximum on campaign costs, candidates even may put out a newspaper which will support their candidacy. On the other hand, the government does limit the size and number of the posters for which it will pay. Furthermore, these may appear only on officially designated sites, which are allocated to the candidates by the government.

Political campaigns are brief (about three weeks), as in Britain. The electoral lists are revised annually and the burden of registration is on the government instead of the individual voter, as in the United States. Women have been enfranchised only since World War II, but now universal suffrage prevails at age 18.

As in Britain, Parliamentary elections occur at irregular intervals. The National Assembly has a term of five years, but may be dissolved for new elections at any time the President chooses. The only limitation is that elections must be at least 12 months apart. Unlike the British, the French usually do not hold by-elections to fill vacancies in the National Assembly. Instead a candidate must, when nominated, designate a substitute, whose name appears on the ballot along with the candidate's. Thus, should a member of the National Assembly die or resign because of joining the Cabinet (as required by the constitution), the remainder of the term is served by the substitute. Nor are there primary elections in France, since candidates are nominated by decisions of political parties.

Radio and television are of limited importance during election campaigns. Parties which contest at least 75 seats—about 15 percent of the total—qualify for a limited amount of free time. But this hardly makes up for the fact that, during the time between elections, Government spokespeople are covered in detail by the government-owned radio and television, while opposition political leaders' speeches and activities hardly are reported at all. Even the allocation of the limited free time during campaigns is inequitable. In 1967 the Government got a total of three hours' time before the first ballot and the same amount was given to all the opposition parties combined to divide among themselves. A similar procedure was followed in 1973.

The electoral procedures discussed to this point pertain only to the lower house of the legislature; the upper house, the Senate, is elected indirectly. Members of local and regional legislative bodies along with members of the National Assembly—a total group of about 100,000—are the only people who may vote for Senators. Over half of those eligible to vote come from rural communities of less than 1,500 population. This helps to make the Senate a more conservative body than the National Assembly. Also relevant is the fact that Senators must be at least 35 years old. Furthermore, the Senate can never entirely respond to current political attitudes since, like the American Senate, it is a continuing body and has only one third of its membership replenished at any one election. This process is even slower in France, since Senators have nine-year terms.

The third type of national election in France is that for President. At the start of the Fifth Republic the President was chosen by an electoral college very similar in composition to the group which continues to elect

Senators. But in 1962, as the previous chapter noted, the constitution was unconstitutionally amended to provide for direct election of the President. De Gaulle was insistent on this change because of the attempts on his life.[1] He felt that while he had sufficient personal magnetism to make the office a strong one, no one else did. Thus, were he to be assassinated, his successor would have great difficulty in preventing a return to the tradition of weak executives of the Third and Fourth Republics. A President who had won the direct support of a majority of the electorate might, however, be in a sufficiently strong position to be able to resist the encroachments of the legislature. This is to say that while de Gaulle felt no need of a popular mandate to legitimate his rule, he believed that the mere mortals who would come after him would need this to be effective.

Presidential elections are to occur every seven years and there is no limit on the number of terms a President may serve. Nominations are made by petitions signed by at least 100 members of Parliament, members of the Economic and Social Council, general councilors, or elected mayors, provided that such signatures include citizens from at least 10 of the 95 departments into which the country is divided. Election is by a majority of the votes cast; if no candidate obtains a majority there is a runoff election on the second Sunday following. The runoff is between the two candidates who have obtained the highest number of votes on the first ballot.

Each Presidential candidate is required to deposit the equivalent of $2,000 which is forfeited if the candidate receives less than 5 percent of the total vote cast. Those who receive 5 percent or more not only get back their deposits, but in addition receive the equivalent of $20,000 to help defray campaign expenses. Also, each candidate gets two hours of television time and a like amount of radio time without cost (first ballot as well as runoff). The broadcast time must be used by the candidate personally, although others designated by him or her take part also. As is true of Parliamentary elections, the campaign is quite brief by American standards—only two or three weeks.

The first election under the amended system occurred in 1965, when de Gaulle's first term expired. In this first popular election of a French President since 1848, turnout was high—85 percent of the electorate voted. To almost everyone's surprise, de Gaulle did not win on the first ballot, receiving only 44 percent of the vote. His main challenger was François Mitterand, head of a rather small left-center group which had been created during World War II, who polled 32 percent of the vote. On the second ballot de Gaulle received 55 percent to Mitterand's 45.

Although the next election should not have occurred until 1972, de

---

[1] There is no vice president in France. If the President is incapacitated temporarily, the president of the Senate acts as President. If the President dies, resigns, or is incapacitated permanently, a new election is held within 50 days.

Gaulle's resignation in 1969 forced an early election. The leading candidate was Georges Pompidou, who had served de Gaulle as Premier for some years before falling into his disfavor in 1968. The election suggested that de Gaulle's personal charisma was not as great as he himself and many others had thought. Pompidou did as well as de Gaulle had done in 1965, polling 44 percent of the vote, although the turnout was down slightly to 78 percent. Pompidou's main challenger was Alain Poher, a little known Senator, who had suddenly won prominence simply because he happened to be president of the Senate when de Gaulle resigned. Thus he became acting President of France briefly. Poher received 23 percent of the vote, the Communist candidate, Jacques Duclos, was close behind with 21 percent. Mitterand did not choose to run. On the second ballot Pompidou won 58 percent of the vote, better than de Gaulle had in 1965, although the turnout was 15 percentage points lower than it had been then, so that he received fewer votes than de Gaulle had.

Poher again became acting President briefly in April 1974 when Pompidou died. Although Pompidou had been in ill health for some time, his death was unexpected and he had no opportunity to indicate whom he preferred as his successor. Twelve candidates were nominated, but only three were able to gain more than 4 percent of the vote. François Mitterand, supported by the Socialists, Communists, and other Left groups, won more than 43 percent of the vote. Valéry Giscard d'Estaing of the Independent Republicans, who had been Minister of Finance and Economic Affairs under Presidents de Gaulle and Pompidou, was second with almost 33 percent. Giscard had taken an ambiguous stance toward the Gaullists for several years. In general he supported them, but without enthusiasm and only with qualifications. His position was well summed up by the 1967 election slogan of his Independent Republicans, "Yes, but . . .." A surprisingly distant third—due largely to factionalism within the movement—was the Gaullist candidate, former Premier Jacques Chaban-Delmas with 15 percent.

Since no candidate had won an absolute majority, a runoff election between Mitterand and Giscard occurred. The latter obtained sufficient support from Gaullists to gain 50.8 percent of the vote—a majority of only 425,000 votes. The turnout rate—88 percent—was the highest ever recorded.

THE ROLE OF INTEREST GROUPS

The very idea of interest or pressure groups is, at least in theory, repugnant to the French. Influenced by Rousseau's concept of the general will, they like to maintain that no one should stand between the citizen and the government. In practice, however, pressure groups have been important and active in France. The traditional attitude seemed to be that if pressure groups are to win favors they should do so unseen via the back door. To some extent this attitude has changed in recent times. The constitution of the Fourth Republic officially recognized pressure groups when it set up an economic council whose members were chosen by trade unions, business associations, and agricultural organizations. A similar institution, the Economic and Social Council, is provided for by the constitution of the Fifth Republic. In both instances, however, the powers of the council were advisory.

Among the multitude of organizations that lobby for favors, the most effective have been the agricultural associations (especially the alcohol lobby), the veterans, and those championing the interests of small (usually inefficient) business. Organized labor is split into several federations, often hostile to one another, and has been weakened thereby. Moreover, the large Communist-controlled trade unions often have been more concerned with throwing their strength against the political system than to seek modest improvements in pay and working conditions.

The methods pressure groups have employed have varied, although the groups usually have sought to keep in close touch with political parties in Parliament, particularly on the committees. In election campaigns they have supported some candidates financially.

The large number of parties and political groupings in France has meant that a number of them have resembled interest groups, or at least have spoken for such groups. Perhaps the best example of a party cum pressure group was the Poujadists. This movement was organized in 1953 by Pierre Poujade to defend the interests of small, marginal businesses which were being injured by economic change as France sought to modernize the economy. The first chapter in this section indicated some of the structural impediments to economic growth in France. While removing these impediments would strengthen the entire economy, many individual businesses would be adversely affected by these measures. The most dramatic of the Poujadists' activities involved their conflict with tax officials. The Poujadists opposed permitting government agents to inspect shopkeepers' books in order to assess their taxes; they wanted the government simply to accept the shopkeepers' word, which by long tradition greatly understates their amount of tax liability. So the Poujadists physically barred tax agents from shops and assulted tax offices.

When the 1956 election was called, the Poujadists decided to expand their activities by running a number of candidates for Parliament. Despite their political inexperience and short existence, they managed to poll 2.5 million votes—12 percent of the total cast—and win 52 seats in Parliament. Rapidly changing economic and political conditions soon made the issue for which the Poujadists had organized less important and the group rapidly disappeared as a political force. Although it has had no importance during the Fifth Republic, it illustrates the difficulty of drawing a sharp distinction between pressures groups and political parties.

In the Fifth Republic, because of the shift of power from Parliament to the executive, interest groups have altered their focus of action. They have been paying less attention to Parliament than in the past. At the same time, they have been more active in the executive branch of government. However, their task has not been made easy by General de Gaulle's known hostility to pressure groups.

In Part I one of the three types of interest groups mentioned was institutional groups. These were defined as groups which, although they had not been formed primarily to express interests, had become heavily engaged in such activities, despite being a part of the formal governmental system. One such institutional interest group of particular importance in recent French politics is the army. As suggested in Chapter 9, the army played a decisive role in the overthrow of the Fourth Republic. This was contrary to the well-established principle that in a democracy the civil power must be supreme. The events leading to the overthrow of the Fourth Republic raise a serious doubt about the durability of democratic institutions in France. Furthermore, the army's rationale in acting against the Fourth Republic conceivably could be used, given the relevant changes in specific details, to justify similar subverting of the Fifth Republic. Therefore, the army's position should be summarized briefly.

The army reasoned that since a modernized fighting force could not cope with a guerrilla force having strong indigenous ties, the only way to end conflict in Algeria was to exterminate the rebel organization by whatever means, however extreme, and replace it with a new political structure. Since the nation's political leaders did not seem to the army to grasp the necessity of this strategy, they had to be educated. At first, the army sought merely to ensure that its views were heard adequately. While the government conceded some of the action the army sought, it did not embrace fully a military solution. The army responded by arguing that while the civil and military authorities should work together, in a subversive war the army had to be the final judge of what policies were essential.

Soon the army went even further. Some army officers declared that the civil administration was swayed by partisan political considerations, thus so weakening the government's resolve to act effectively that the rebels would be encouraged to hold out until France capitulated. Only the army, which was above political influences, could act fully in the national interest. Thus the army, in effect, was seeking to *be* the government.

Although the army was instrumental in bringing de Gaulle back to power, he did not implement—to many people's surprise and the army's disillusionment—their ideas. When in 1959 de Gaulle proposed self-determination for Algeria, a number of French army officers (some active and some retired) and their sympathizers made several desperate bids to prevent Algerian independence. These involved forthright efforts to defeat referendums, open rebellion in Algeria (and the seizure of power there in some areas for a brief period), as well as the creation of the Secret Army Organization (OAS), whose aim was to overthrow de Gaulle. These actions, as well as the attempt to assassinate President de Gaulle, ended in failure.

Currently the army's activities are not so visible or dramatic. Nonetheless, it should be obvious that there remain in the military a number of officers who believe that their forces should play an active political role, especially when the regularly elected officials seem to be ineffective or misguided. How the army would respond were the Left to win control of Parliament and then manage to get President Giscard to resign, forcing an early Presidential election, remains an open question.

BIBLIOGRAPHICAL NOTE

For a fairly comprehensive, yet brief discussion of French electoral laws (and election results), Peter Campbell, *French Electoral System and Elections since 1789*, 2d ed. (London: Faber, 1965) is very useful. Philip Williams, *French Politicians and Elections 1951–1969* (Cambridge: Cambridge University Press, 1970), discusses the campaign and the results of each of the elections of the Fifth Republic, except for 1973.

For a detailed discussion of the impact of Algeria on French politics, as well as of de Gaulle's various maneuvers to keep the army in line, see Roy C. Macridis and Bernard E. Brown, *The De Gaulle Republic: Quest for Unity* (Homewood, Ill.: Dorsey Press, 1960), as well as their *Supplement to the De Gaulle Republic* (1963). Also see William G. Andrews, *French Politics and Algeria: The Process of Policy Formation, 1954–1962* (New York: Appleton-Century-Crofts, 1962). Two works concerned with the role of the army in French politics are John Ambler, *Soldiers Against the State* (Garden City, New York: Doubleday, 1968), and George Kelly, *Lost Soldiers* (Cambridge, Mass.: M.I.T. Press, 1965).

Other works examining interest groups include Henry Ehrmann, *French Labor from Popular Front to Liberation* (New York: Oxford University Press, 1947), and *Organized Business in France* (Princeton, N.J.: Princeton University Press, 1957); V. Lorwin, *The French Labor Movement* (Cambridge, Mass.: Harvard University Press, 1954); J. Meynaud, *Les Groupes de pression en France* (Paris: Armand Colin, 1958); James M. Clark, *Teachers and Politics in France: A Pressure Group Study of the Federation de l'Education Nationale* (Syracuse, N.Y.: Syracuse University Press, 1967); and John Sheahan, *Promotion and Control of Industry in Post-War France* (Cambridge, Mass.: Harvard University Press, 1963). Three shorter studies of particular value are Bernard E. Brown, "Pressure Politics in France," *The Journal of Politics* 18 (November 1956), pp. 702–19; "Alcohol and Politics in France," *American Political Science Review* 51 (December 1957), pp. 976–94; and "Pressure Politics in the Fifth Republic," *Journal of Politics* 25 (November 1963), pp. 509–25.

12

Political Parties

A MULTI-PARTY SYSTEM

Traditionally, European political parties have been much more ideologically oriented than have American and British parties. This is less true now in France than earlier in the century. Furthermore, the extent of emphasis on ideology varies considerably from one French party to another. Nonetheless, the lack of political consensus and the existence of sharp cleavages over basic issues such as the role of the church have encouraged French parties to appeal to the electorate in a style more ideological than that of American parties.

The greater a party's emphasis on ideology, the narrower its appeal is likely to be. When a party merely stands for a particular mix of policy positions on short-range issues, people who like most of what it offers usually will be willing to accept some objectionable policy stands. But when the appeal is more doctrinal, support requires a greater degree of commitment, which is unlikely to be forthcoming unless the entire program is acceptable. The more ideological a party's appeal, the more it attempts to present an integrated series of doctrines relevant to many aspects of life, the more difficult it is to secure the agreement of a large number of people.

Add to this ideological approach the tendency mentioned in the previous chapter of pressure groups to convert themselves into parties, plus the existence of a fairly rigid class structure, and one begins to expect the French party system to be a multi-party one. This clearly has been the case. (see Figure 12–1) In past elections national parties sometimes have numbered between 10 to 20, in addition to a number of purely local or regional parties. For example, in 1958, 12 parties qualified for free radio and television time by running at least 75 candidates each.

The number of parties and the diverse political approaches in France cannot be explained simply. In part, the reason can be traced to an absence of consensus or a common understanding concerning the basis and form of government. At the time when political parties were forming in the United States and in Britain, the nature of the form of government in those two countries was not really in question. The differences that divided people into parties were primarily over the policies which government should follow. In France, on the other hand, the formation of political parties preceded agreement on the nature of the system of government. Differences over the question of how the state should be organized could not help but creep into party positions. Moreover, by the time the Third Republic was organized and a certain consensus achieved (1875–85), parties organized along class lines had appeared (first the Socialists and, in this century, the Communists). In other words, just when Republicanism had become respectable, a new source of division had arisen to perpetuate the multi-party system.

French governmental practices helped to perpetuate these divisions and maintain a variety of parties. Under Assembly government little Parliamentary discipline existed; deputies could do as they pleased politically and be secure for at least the full term of Parliament. The electoral system, whether PR or not, did not encourage any merger of political groupings, at least not on the first ballot and, therefore, not between elections.

The development of only two or three broadly based catchall parties also was hindered by the fact that at the base of much French political thinking is an idealism that rejects compromise and halfway measures— hence the striving for a politically pure, ideologically committed party, unlikely to gain support from more than a narrow segment of the electorate. General distrust of others and suspicion of their motives made relinquishing some of one's goals for the sake of common pursuit of other objectives difficult. This distrust tended to give people qualms that their own parties might become too effectively organized. Should this happen, they feared that those in charge of the party would use it to serve their own ends. Thus, better to have a small, poorly organized party that one could be certain of controlling, than a large, efficient party that would be less amenable to internal democratic control.

France's current move toward a more widely shared prosperity seems to be accompanied by some decline in the importance of ideology in the political process. Perhaps, then, some restructuring of the party system so as to reduce the number of parties is likely. Nonetheless, since political habits and practices seldom change rapidly, such a development is by no means certain.

Given the multiplicity of parties which has prevailed, fractionalization

FIGURE 12-1
The Two Leading Parties' Percentage of the Vote in Elections in the Fourth and Fifth Republics

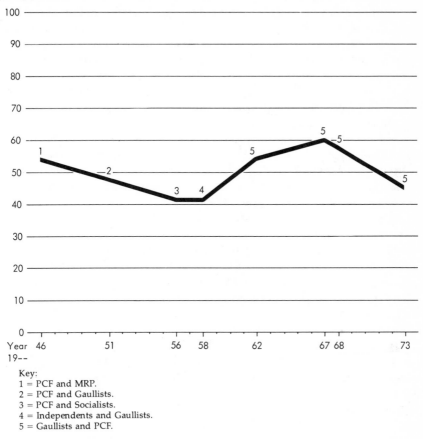

Key:
1 = PCF and MRP.
2 = PCF and Gaullists.
3 = PCF and Socialists.
4 = Independents and Gaullists.
5 = Gaullists and PCF.

of the vote is only to be expected. The Gaullists far outstripped the success of any other political party since the end of World War II by gaining almost two fifths of the vote in the late 1960s. Thus, even the most successful party has not begun to approach a majority of the vote. The political composition of Parliament has reflected this situation with no single party usually being able to control a majority of the seats. In the United States diverse interests compete for influence within institutionalized parties prior to elections as two broad, opposing coalitions are built up. In France this process occurs later in another arena; coalitions are constructed *in the legislature between* parties *after* the election. This coalition process tends to compound the apparent confusion of the French party system. Candidates who have been elected under a variety of labels may join together after the election to form a group in Parliament under still another label.

The multiplicity of French parties is matched by their diversity in organization and politics. Politically, they range from parties that emphasize rigid adherence to principle, such as the Communist party, to parties that espouse no principle and are the personal followers of one individual. Organizationally, they vary from the tight discipline that the Communists and Socialists have imposed to the largely unorganized groups on the far right. And, as the close of the previous paragraph indicated, some Parliamentary groupings have little or no organization in the country other than a number of personal electoral machines.

Another characteristic of French parties is their fluidity. New parties skyrocket into prominence, bursting on the political scene in a dazzling display of pyrotechnics only to shimmer rapidly out of sight, leaving not a trace. Usually these parties do not embody significant shifts in political opinions and tendencies. Studies of French voting behavior indicate a fairly steady and consistent pattern. To be sure, Gaullism is new, but even it possesses characteristics that are an inheritance from the past. What change, in the main, are the party labels. There has always been a large protest vote, for example, but from election it may be recorded under differing party labels. A large portion of the vote cast in 1958 for the party that supported de Gaulle was a protest vote.

The French constitution says that "political parties and groups may compete for votes. They may form and carry on their activities freely. They must respect the principles of national sovereignty and of democracy." It is obvious that the last sentence lays the foundation for possible action against antidemocratic parties of the right or left. No action has been taken, however, against the Communist party or its principal publications. But in 1959 the government did dissolve the small Nationalist party, an extreme rightist group formed with the avowed aim of fighting against French democracy. Subsequently, the Cabinet has banned certain protest meetings scheduled by Communists or their sympathizers, as well as similar meetings by rightist groups. Moreover, the government has banned about 150 newspapers at both ends of the political spectrum. Obviously, this proviso of the constitution gives the government of the day a considerable latitude in acting against extremist political groups.

THE LEADING PARTIES

Since the end of World War II the six principal political forces in France have been the Communists, the Socialists, the Radicals, the Christian Democrats, the Gaullists, and the Republicans. Together these six never have polled less than 85 percent of the popular vote and usually have gained over 90. The remainder of this chapter will be devoted to these most prominent groups.

Doctrines and Politics

The French Communist party (PCF) clings closely to basic Marxist doctrine. The nature of this ideology is examined fully in Part V on the Soviet Union, and thus is not elaborated here. Suffice it to say that the PCF has been perhaps the most hard-line Communist party operating in a democratic, Western political system. This does not mean that it is a highly subversive, revolutionary force. The student and worker street demonstrations in 1968, for example, were organized almost totally apart from the Communist party, which became involved only at a relatively late date and after considerable doubt and hesitation. The point rather is that the PCF has been extremely dogmatic in its policies and rigid in its rhetoric. Furthermore, the PCF has been the Western party most loyal to Moscow.

Recently, however, the party has begun to alter its stance. Many in the party criticized the Russian invasion of Czechoslovakia in 1968, and in 1972 formally condemned the political trials being carried out in that Communist country. A few years later the PCF even went so far as to criticize the Soviet Union for the way it was treating its dissident citizens. In the 1973 elections the PCF endeavored to project the image of a reasonable reform party. The PCF no longer is as willing as it once was to continue mouthing the same old Marxist cliches and has begun to question, or at least qualify, some basic Marxist concepts such as the dictatorship of the proletariat.

The Socialist party also has been doctrinally dogmatic and inflexible. As recently as 1946 it refused to revise its 1905 statement of principles which declared that it was a party of class warfare aiming at constructing a communistic society. In 1962 the party finally did alter its position by labeling itself both "reformist and revolutionary" instead of just "essentially revolutionary." And it did qualify its stand on collective ownership of the means of production and exchange by saying that this remedy did not extend to those who were not exploiting their workers.

All this is largely a semantic game, for most Socialists would be frightened to death by a revolution. But in France it often is electorally wise to sound more militant or extreme than one in fact is. In practice the Socialists have been flexible, even opportunistic. The party long has been social democratic rather than Marxist. It accepts a mixed economy and is concerned mainly to ensure that sufficient social welfare programs are available along with some redistribution of wealth to aid the lower middle class and the workers.

The Socialists participated in several post-war Governments, including the interim de Gaulle Government (1958). After the inauguration of the Fifth Republic, however, the Socialists formed a "constructive opposition" to de Gaulle. They supported his foreign policies, including his efforts to bring peace to Algeria, but they opposed some of his domestic policies, including aid to Catholic schools and those social and fiscal policies whose costs they believed would be borne disproportionately by the working class. And they were critical of what they regarded as a lack of respect for the constitution shown by both the President and the Cabinet.

In 1972 the Communists and the Socialists, who had talked about cooperation on the Left for some time, finally agreed to a Common Program. One of the key elements was a pledge to nationalize banking, insurance and credit, and nine of France's largest private companies. Following the Left's success in the 1977 local elections, the party leaders have been working on updating the Common Program as they prepare for the next Parliamentary elections, in which they anticipate impressive gains. The Communists wish to add to the list of companies to be nationalized, while the Socialists do not. This is one of the key differences between the parties, since the Communists now have accepted the Socialists' support for direct elections for the Common Market Parliament.

The center of the political spectrum in France has been fractionalized and amorphous. Here are located the Radical Socialists and the Christian Democrats. The Radicals always have been associated with support for the republican political system—favoring universal suffrage, civil liberties, and Parliamentary preeminence and opposing the church. Despite their name, they long have been conservative in economic matters, regarding with suspicion any extensive government economic planning. In the early years of the Fifth Republic the Radicals supported General de Gaulle but were increasingly suspicious of the new political institutions. They were particularly unhappy about the failure of the system to provide effective Parliamentary control of the Cabinet. They opposed de Gaulle's efforts to develop an independent atomic striking force and criticized his position on NATO. In the mid 1970s the left-wing Radicals, led by Robert Fabre, cooperated with the Socialists and Communists in the Common Program.

During the Fourth Republic and the early years of the Fifth, France's Christian Democrats were organized in the Popular Republican Movement (MRP). The MRP grew out of the World War II resistance movement against the Nazis. It was essentially a party of Christian socialism; anti-Marxist and against class war, it was also critical of free enterprise. Aside from supporting liberal social and economic policies, however, the MRP favored basically conservative policies. It was strongly influenced by Catholicism and supported aid to Catholic schools. Because of this support, it parted company with the Socialists, with whom it otherwise had much in common.

The MRP for several years cautiously supported de Gaulle, and a number of its leaders held cabinet posts. Although anxious to assist de Gaulle in finding a solution to the Algerian question, the party was from the outset uneasy about several developments in the Fifth Republic. It opposed some of the economic policies of the Government, as well as the Government's inclination to rely too much on technocrats. And it was anxious about the role of the army in the new regime. Nevertheless, its ministers stayed in the Cabinet until May 1962.

The MRP ministers' departure from the Government was precipitated by de Gaulle's ridiculing (at a press conference) the idea of European political integration. The party had, for some time prior to May 1962, been unhappy with de Gaulle's nationalistic defense policies. And as the party that had in the postwar period been the strongest proponent of European unity and European integration, it could not tolerate de Gaulle's attack on its cherished program. The party's departure from the cabinet was also aided by the fact that its leaders did not like the trend toward a presidential system in France.

When Pompidou replaced de Gaulle as President, he managed to win back some of the Christian Democrats who felt he was more supportive of European political unity. Thus the movement split into pro- and anti-Government wings. President Giscard, on the other hand, proved acceptable to both wings, so few policy differences stood in the way of the two factions merging. This they did in 1976 to form the Center for Social Democracy (CDS), selecting Jean Lecanuet as president of the party.

The Gaullist movement has changed its name many times over the last three decades. Its origin goes back to 1947, when de Gaulle and his followers founded the Rally of the French People (RPF). The RPF was said to be not a party but a movement or rally that advocated a reform of the constitution. Initially, the RPF had considerable success, but after 1954 its strength diminished and eventually it disappeared. By refusing to accept the responsibility of governing, although it had the largest number of deputies at one time, it constituted an essentially antidemocratic bloc in the National Assembly. After de Gaulle's return to power in 1958, however, his followers founded the Union for the New Republic (UNR). Although de Gaulle refused to be a member or even a patron of the UNR, so great was his antipathy to political parties, this did not stop the party from proclaiming its loyalty to him. Nor did his resignation as President and subsequent death destroy the movement. Late in 1976 the movement changed its name yet again to the Rally for the Republic (RPR) with Jacques Chirac the inheritor of the General's mantle.

The Gaullists have stood more for loyalty to a person than for particular policies. Although they agreed on the need for de Gaulle's leadership, they were divided on exactly what role he should play. Furthermore, while they believed that France needed a national renewal, they were vague regarding what specific goals this involved and divided on the means of achieving them. They were, however, clearly opposed to the existing political system and desired reform of the constitution to provide for stronger executive leadership.

Perhaps the Gaullists are best characterized as nationalistic rather than conservative. Traditionally these two positions have been distinct in France. Nationalists frequently have been willing for a strong executive to act to improve workers' living standards. This has been seen as a means of cementing together the various classes of the nation and thus strengthening it. The Conservative party in Britain has a similar tradition stretching back to Disraeli in the latter part of the 19th century. Thus the Gaullists have supported some economic and social reform. They have continued the French governmental economic planning system and substantial public investment. In addition they have favored a profit-sharing system for industrial workers, despite the opposition of the Communists, among others.

Some UNR followers fell by the wayside because of what they regarded as a sellout in Algeria, and some even sought to overthrow the regime by unconstitutional means. But settlement of the Algerian question made the party more homogeneous and perhaps more inclined to develop long-range programs for the problems France faced.

The RPR under Chirac continues to stress the national unity theme, but also advocates decisive government to combat the growing strength of the Left. Chirac presents himself as the one leader who can save France from a Communist takeover. A key element in his strategy is reduction of unemployment and reform of the tax laws so that those with greater wealth would pay more. He believes that such action would convince workers to vote for France (that is, the RPR) rather than for the Left.

The true conservatives in France, in a right-wing economic sense, are in the Republican party. (The Republicans also have changed their name frequently. Prior to 1977 they most frequently were known as the Independent Republicans or, simply, Independents.) The Republicans generally have opposed economic and social reform and have rejected state interference in economic affairs, except for subsidies to farmers and protective tariffs for business. Thus, on economic issues they have much in common with right-wing Radical Socialists. But they part company with them on the clerical issue, for, in conformity with traditional conservative opinion, the Republicans strongly favor state aid to Catholic schools and generally support the position of the church.

Although having some doubts about de Gaulle, the Republicans initially supported him. What divided the party more than anything else was de Gaulle's Algerian policy and his granting of independence to France's former African colonies. Some of their Parliamentary leaders remained cautious and noncommittal, but many of them became increasingly hostile, with some demonstrating sympathy for the Secret Army Organization

(OAS) that was seeking to overthrow de Gaulle by force. Moreover, in the domestic field, the party was never happy about de Gaulle's desires for modernization of the economy, national planning, and increased taxes.

The 1962 Parliamentary elections split the party, with the smaller faction making common cause for a time with the remnants of the MRP before dwindling to insignificance. The larger, pro-Gaullist segment was organized into an effective grouping by Valéry Giscard d'Estaing. The Republicans under Giscard managed to give general support to the Gaullist Government, while at the same time keeping it at arm's length. Thus they managed to avoid any blame for the student and worker demonstrations of 1968, a fact that was one element in Giscard's successful contest for the Presidency in 1974. Despite the Republicans' traditional political position, Giscard, both during his campaign and subsequently as President, has tried to project a liberal reform image on social issues such as easier abortions.

Party Appeals and Supporters

A number of factors help to explain Communist strength in France. There is a tradition of voting for the revolutionary Left in France, partly because the Left was the historical defender of republican institutions, and partly because it was the antirepublican forces that brutally suppressed the workers' uprisings in 1848 and 1871. The Communist party, more or less fortuitously, inherited the leftist position and thereby became the beneficiary of the leftist voting tradition. In addition, the Communist party devotes a great deal of time and effort to its organizational and propaganda drives. It sponsors youth groups and discussion and protest meetings, and it puts out numerous publications. Moreover, it controls a large part of the trade union movement. It has convinced many workers that the Communist party is *the* working-class party. These workers are not really interested in the Soviet Union; they are disturbed by the real or fancied injustices of French society. In control of the largest trade unions, the Communist party has been able to mobilize workers to vote, to contribute to the party treasury, and to participate in Communist-organized demonstrations.

Aside from the workers, the Communist party has found some support among lower-class peasants. To them the party does not talk of collectivization. Rather, the party has systematically attempted to place one person in each village who knows the peasants and their problems. His or her main job is to help the peasants in their problems with the local bureaucracy. And the peasants have demonstrated their gratitude with votes for the party.

The Communist party in large measure has been the recipient of support from the discontented in various social and economic groups. In-

206 Major European Governments

cluded here are some intellectuals—particularly elementary school teachers and some civil servants—and persons with no party allegiance who are anxious to cast a protest vote. They are not necessarily convinced that the Communists would straighten out "the mess"; they are just voting against conditions as they are.

Despite having been out of the Government for four decades, the Communist party has been able to demonstrate that it is a party of action and not just of words. It has organized cooperatives to sell goods cheaply to members and has provided poor tenants with legal aid against landlords. Furthermore, its extensive organization permits it to offer posts of responsibility and power to a number of people. It thus can provide an opportunity of gaining a sense of personal accomplishment for those whose social origins might otherwise deny them this chance.

It must be emphasized that the French are not as fearful of Communism as are Americans. Half of those questioned in a 1965 poll said that the Communists had been very or fairly useful in French politics during the previous 20 years, and 40 percent were willing to accept Communist ministers in the Government.

While the Communists have been particularly strong around Paris and France's northern industrial area, the party's support has been geographically well distributed. Its ability to gain support from poor farmers and farm workers in the south helps to give it a balanced pattern of support. Only the Gaullists can rival its ability to draw well throught the nation. The main areas of Communist strength can be seen in Figure 12–2.

While still seeking working class support, the Socialists have lost ground among the workers. This was almost inevitable, for the Socialists, when in power during the Fourth Republic, were forced to be reasonable and hence compromised on trade union claims. In doing so, they were forfeiting some worker support to the Communists. Similarly, in seeking long overdue reforms, the Socialists were frustrated by peasant and petty bourgeois opposition, which could only result in a net gain for the Communists.

The Socialists cannot really be considered a working-class party, as they were earlier in the century. About a quarter of the party's members are miners or workers in small factories. But the bulk of the working class, especially those in large, modern industry, support the Communists. About another quarter of the Socialists' members are civil servants. The Socialists have become a middle-class party, appealing mainly to white-collar workers, teachers, and some shopkeepers. The party's support is geographically concentrated in the north and along the southern coast. It gets some support in the south from wine growers and other farmers. The party has lost ground in central France and is especially weak around Paris.

The Radicals traditionally have been the party of the little man. They

FIGURE 12–2
Communist Strength in Fourth and Fifth Republics

over 25% Communist in
Elections from 1951–1968

over 25% Communist in
1951, 1956 and at Least
20% in 1968

have appealed most to small businesspeople, shopkeepers, and farmers along with country doctors and lawyers. The largest single occupational group is farmers, accounting for about one third of the party's support: The party is closely identified with static southern agricultural interests. In some ways it appeals to those who are not yet fully reconciled to 20th-century society. The party's leaders frequently have been more progressive, but they have been unable to alter the party's basic orientation. The geographical distribution of Socialist and Radical strength appears in Figure 12–3.

The MRP, although determined to be a party of the Left, as shown by its backing of progressive economic and social policies, found its most effective support coming from traditionally conservative areas—areas in which the church had always been strongest. Thus the enthusiasm of the party militants for social reform was not shared by the vast bulk of the party's electoral supporters, the principal exception being its supporters among the workers.

Increasingly the party became a regional political force, doing best in the Catholic east and west. It was in the more industrial east that it was able to win some working-class support, about one fifth of its total support. But the party's main appeal was to the lower middle class—salaried workers, civil servants, less prosperous professional people, lower level business executives, shopkeepers. That is to say that occupationally the pattern of support was similar to that of the Socialists. The important difference, of course, is religion, with those who were active Catholics supporting the Christian Democrats.

The Gaullists appeal to all those who were opposed to the Fourth Republic because of its Algerian policy or for other reasons. They also gained the support of "apolitical" voters for whom stability and prosperity were uppermost. The Gaullists have demonstrated considerable appeal among the younger generation of industrialists, engineers, and professional people. They also have received support from the lower middle class, such as the salaried elements in plants and industrial firms. Finally, they have received some working-class support as well. Almost from the beginning of the Fifth Republic, a number of UNR deputies understood the importance of working-class support to the movement's future and sought it through autonomous workers' syndicates and worker representation on the central committee of the party.

The Gaullists have had strong support from women and Catholics. Its charismatic nationalism even has enabled it to win a sizable number of adherents away from the Communists. In the Fourth Republic Gaullist support was concentrated in the industrial north and in urban areas. While retaining these bases of strength, the movement in the Fifth Republic has expanded into the south to gain rural support as well as can be seen from

FIGURE 12-3
Democratic Left Strength in Fourth and Fifth Republics

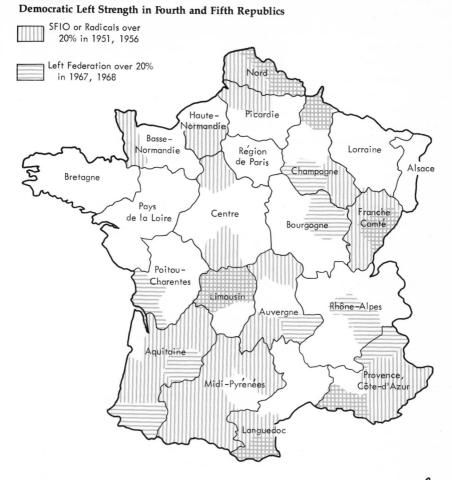

SFIO or Radicals over
20% in 1951, 1956

Left Federation over 20%
in 1967, 1968

Figure 12–4. Thus, in terms of its pattern of support it truly can claim to be a national party.

The supporters of the Republicans have included both the relatively wealthy and the lower middle class. Conservative industrialists and businesspeople (including shopkeepers) along with bankers and managers have joined with conservative farmers and some civil servants to back the party. Having strong Catholic support, the Republicans polled well in the traditionally conservative Catholic east and west. This is to say that the liberal Catholics preferred the MRP, while the conservative ones favored the Independents. The other area of geographical strength for the Independents was the rural south-central section.

Party Strengths

The Communist party, after its founding in France in 1920, gradually gained strength to emerge after World War II as the largest single party in the country. During the Fourth Republic it always polled more than a quarter of the popular vote and had at least one sixth, and usually more, of the seats in the lower house of Parliament. In the first election of the Fifth Republic in 1958, however, the Communists lost considerable support, especially to the Gaullists, and fell below one fifth of the vote. Furthermore, since no other party would cooperate with them, the revised electoral system worked against them to cut their strength in Parliament even more drastically—they received only ten seats. This was far too few to be recognized as an official group. Thus they were deprived of committee assignments and could not introduce censure motions by themselves.

In subsequent elections during de Gaulle's presidency, the Communists recovered slightly and increased their share of the vote by 2 to 4 percentage points over what it had been in 1958. More important was their greater representation in Parliament. Depending upon what cooperative arrangements the party was able to make with other parties, it won from 34 to 73 seats. Although the party had recovered, it clearly was not the major political force in Parliament that it had been during the Fourth Republic. But it must be emphasized that this was not because its appeal to French voters had declined sharply. Except for 1958, its share of the vote was only a few percentage points lower than it had been.

In 1973, although the party increased its share of the vote slightly, basically it remained stable at about one fifth. Cooperation with the Socialists paid greater dividends in seats, however. The French Communist party more than doubled in strength in the National Assembly to return to its 1967 position of 73 seats. The areas where gains were made can be seen in Figure 12–5. Thus it is the third largest group in Parliament.

Like all other French parties, the Communists have had difficulty in retaining members. Immediately after Word War II the party expanded rapidly to over a million members. Now it claims to have only about

FIGURE 12–4
Gaullist Strength in Fourth and Fifth Republics

at Least 25% in 1951 and
at Least 20% in 1958

at Least 30% in 1962

at Least 40% in 1967, 1968

at Least 40% in 1968, but
None of the Above

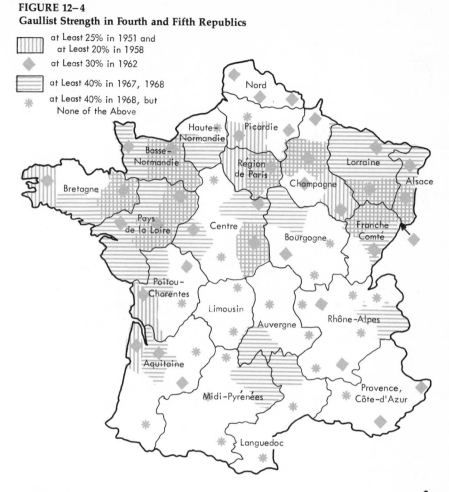

Paris

Corse

FIGURE 12–5
Party Strength Shifts in 1973 Parliamentary Elections

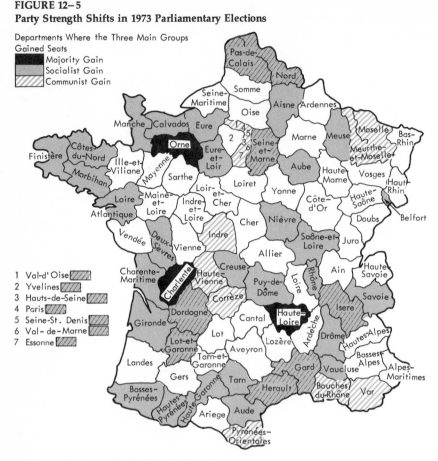

Departments Where the Three Main Groups
Gained Seats
■ Majority Gain
▨ Socialist Gain
▨ Communist Gain

1 Val-d'Oise
2 Yvelines
3 Hauts-de-Seine
4 Paris
5 Seine-St. Denis
6 Val-de-Marne
7 Essonne

Source: *The Economist*, March 17, 1973, p. 32.

400,000 and many experts feel that the true figure may be only about 150,000.

The party has been troubled also by internal conflict. The Soviet invasion of Czechoslovakia in 1968 made many leaders question the party's traditional support for the Soviet Union. Others have been bothered by the leaders' unwillingness to modernize party doctrine in the way that the Italian Communists have. The Italian Communists' willingness to permit more open debate in the party also has been attractive. The French Communists, however, in 1972 expelled their most vocal dissident from the party, despite his long years of service. Since one of the leaders in this step was the party's new general secretary, Georges Marchais, there is some question whether his effort to project a moderate image in the 1973 elections was anything other than an electoral strategy. Unless the party really is willing to depart from its rigid positions on doctrine and organization, there will continue to be internal unrest.

This would weaken the party precisely at the point that traditionally has been its source of greatest strength. The party has been highly organized from its basic local unit, the cell, up through the governing secretariat. Tight central control over this machinery has meant that a highly disciplined force was available to carry out the decisions of the party leaders. The party's members in Parliament were not free to vote however they might have wished, but were required to vote in a single bloc according to the orders of the leading party bureaucrats. While this hardly made for free representation, it did produce an extremely strong Parliamentary group. This cohesive behavior in Parliament has not been altered, but dissension in the party could lead to purges and splintering which would weaken its electoral strength.

Immediately after World War II the Socialists were able to poll a quarter of the vote. They soon declined, however, and by the latter stages of the Fourth Republic were gaining less than one sixth of the vote. This decline in popular support continued into the Fifth Republic. Thus, in the late 1960s the party entered the Federation of the Democratic and Socialist Left—an electoral alliance with some Radicals and other political groups which was intended to grow into a new political party. In 1967 the Left Federation was able to gain a fifth of the vote and a quarter of the seats in Parliament. But the following year, although its support fell only a couple of percentage points, its representation in Parliament was cut in half. The Socialists themselves held only about 43 seats.

Comparison of the 1973 election results with those of the late 1960s is somewhat difficult. Given the formation of the Left Federation, there is some problem in separating out the strength of the Socialists from that of their allies. Furthermore, since the 1968 elections took place at a time of considerable tension and anxiety due to the student and worker demonstrations, its results were especially disadvantageous to the Left. Thus, the elections of the previous year may be the better benchmark.

Given these qualifications, the following are the most important features of the 1973 results for the Socialists. In winning 89 seats they doubled their representation in the National Assembly and attained their greatest Parliamentary strength of the Fifth Republic. The diversified geographic nature of these gains can be seen in Figure 12–5. With more than 19 percent of the popular vote, they gained their greatest support since 1946. Yet the Socialists were not euphoric; the 1973 elections were a classic illustration of how one can make great gains and yet lose while opponents suffer disastrous losses and yet are victorious. Although the Socialists had more seats in Parliament than the Communists, the Communists continued to be the more popular party in terms of share of vote. The polls prior to the elections had given the Socialists some hope that this might change, but it did not. Furthermore, the Socialists and Communists seriously had hoped to deny the Gaullists and their allies a majority in the National Assembly. They had even anticipated being sufficiently strong to force President Pompidou to make a Socialist the Premier. This, too, proved to be a vain hope.

The 1974 Presidential elections frustrated the Socialists further. Their candidate, François Mitterand, who unexpectedly had run de Gaulle such a close race in 1965, this time had a lead of ten percentage points on the first ballot. Yet on the second and deciding ballot he lost by under half a million votes. The party's bid for governmental power had been thwarted yet again.

Although the Socialists were the party which introduced to France the idea of dues-paying, card-carrying mass membership, at the party's high point in 1946 it had only 350,000 members. Now it has declined to less than 80,000. This has had serious financial implications for the party and has made it very difficult to maintain an adequate national party organization.

Socialist party rules have tended to discourage young people. A person must be a party member for five years to be eligible to be a delegate to the party congress, a member of the executive committee, an editor of a party paper, or a candidate for Parliament. It is no accident that the average age of Socialist deputies in the Assembly, as well as their delegates at party conferences, is higher than that of any other party.

An apparent gap between leaders and followers has produced dissatisfied rumblings. Some Socialists feel that the party's doctrinal foundations need to be reexamined seriously. The old slogans and oft-repeated remedies do not seem to make sense in the light of the new problems of an increasingly industrialized society. Yet throughout the 1960s the leadership refused to consider revising the party's doctrine in the way that the German Social Democrats had. One of the principal obstacles to reform was Guy Mollet, who had dominated the party from the post of secretary general since the end of World War II. When he finally relinquished his post in 1970, the reform elements began to refurbish the party under Mitterand.

The restructuring of the Socialist party did not result, however, in moving them toward the center of the political spectrum, as their Common Program with the Communists indicates. Although this Program supports expanded government ownership of industry, Mitterand, in keeping with a general commitment to participatory democracy, seems to be thinking of some form of syndicalism for these industries in order to increase the influence of the workers.

Recent public opinion polls and the local elections of 1977 indicate not only considerable gains for the Left in general, but for the Socialists in particular. They clearly have moved ahead of the Communists in popular support. Thus they look forward confidently to providing the Premier after the 1978 elections. Whether these hopes will be disappointed as were similar ones in the early 1970s remains to be seen.

The Radicals were the leading party for most of the Third Republic, falling behind the Socialists only in the 1930s. During the early years of the Fourth Republic, the Radicals and their allies were able to poll only about one tenth of the vote, a figure which they increased slightly in 1956. Always a party of personalities, the Radicals and their allies provided 8 of 17 Premiers of the Fourth Republic. Their central position in the political spectrum meant that despite their small size they were well placed to be the party around which coalitions could form.

The party always has been very loosely organized both inside and outside of Parliament. Its external organization has consisted largely of a network of committees usually headed by *notables*—politicians of local prominence and status. The party was little more than an alliance of personal political machines. It is almost impossible for such a party to be cohesive in Parliament. On almost any key issue the Radicals would be divided into three groups—yes, no, and abstain. Some Radicals members of Parliament did not even hesitate to vote against a Premier who belonged to their own party.

During the 1950s Pierre Mendès-France, one of the most dynamic of the Fourth Republic Premiers, tried to revise the party's organizational structure to make it more unified and attempted to move its economic policies to the left-center. He succeeded only in splitting the party. Then in the late 1960s Jean-Jacques Servan-Schreiber, a flashy magazine publisher and the author of *The American Challenge*, also sought to modernize the party. His rather domineering and self-serving tactics again split the party.

Early in the Fifth Republic the Radicals were able to win only 8 percent of the vote and only few more seats than the 30 required to be recognized as an official group. During the late 1960s most of the Radicals were junior partners with the Socialists in the Left Federation.

For the 1973 election, however, most of the Radicals—those following Servan-Schreiber—cooperated with the Christian Democrats in a new center group known as the Reformists. The rest of the party continued in alliance with the Socialists. These left Radicals won only about a dozen seats in 1973 with less than 2 percent of the vote. Poor as this result was, it surpassed that of the Servan-Schreiber Radicals, who returned only 7 of their number to the National Assembly. The Radicals' future looks very dim.

For a party less than two years old, the MRP made a tremendous impact at the start of the Fourth Republic. In one of the 1946 elections it polled almost 30 percent of the vote, more than any other party including the Communists. In part this was because the MRP was widely thought to be de Gaulle's favorite, since no Gaullist party then existed. The formation of a Gaullist party in the late 1940s hurt the MRP considerably; for the remainder of Fourth Republic it obtained less than half as much support as it initially had, eventually dropping to little more than one tenth of the vote.

In the early years of the Fifth Republic the MRP's support remained at about this level. Then in the late 1960s part of the group defected to join the Gaullists. The rest of party allied with the anti-Gaullist Independents and some others. As a result of these shifts the MRP was formally dissolved in 1968 to be replaced by the Democratic Center under Jean Lecanuet, who had been a candidate for President in 1965. The 1969 Presidential election split the Christian Democrats again. Thus in the 1973 legislative elections the smaller segment under Jacques Duhamel cooperated with the Gaullists while the larger portion under Lecanuet was allied with Servan-Schreiber's Radicals in the Reformists.

The two factions emerged from the 1973 elections with virtually equal Parliamentary strength—each winning about two dozen seats. Dwindling support meant that when the two groups recombined to form the Center for Social Democracy in 1977 its Parliamentary strength was only 25. Thus the fate of the Christian Democrats is not greatly different from that of the other center party, the Radicals.

The Gaullists did not exist as a party at the start of the Fourth Republic. But they did fight the 1951 election, winning over one fifth of the vote and gaining more seats in the lower house of Parliament than any other party. But the party's strength rapidly dissipated, especially after de Gaulle disowned it in 1953 as a failure. Although the Gaullists had to start from scratch at the beginning of the Fifth Republic, they again polled one fifth of the vote and gained well over two fifths of the seats. Throughout the remainder of de Gaulle's presidency, the Gaullists continued to increase their share of the vote and their strength in Parliament.

In the elections of 1962, the UNR polled 32 percent on the first ballot and 40.5 percent on the second. It elected 233 members out of a total of 482, but when 41 other pro-Gaullist deputies were added, the total was 274, a clear majority. Some observers were prone to look upon the election as a second referendum in which the voters had reasserted their support of General de Gaulle—a victory for him rather than for the party. But a majority for one political group for the first time in the history of Republican France cannot be minimized.

By 1968 the party by itself was able to poll almost two fifths of the vote and win over three fifths of the seats in the lower house. Thus a single party controlled a firm working majority in Parliament—an unprecedented situation in French politics. By 1973, however, scandals in the government and other embarrassments—such as the Gaullist Premier's using loopholes in the law to avoid paying income tax—began to erode its support. Furthermore, de Gaulle's personal magnetism no longer was available to attract people to the party. Thus many voters felt that it was time to end the party's 15-year domination of the government.

Despite the party's efforts to win support by frightening the electorate with visions of Communist-Socialist rape and pillage, it lost considerable ground. The Gaullists share of the popular vote declined by one third compared with 1968, and their total number of seats was the lowest of the Fifth Republic. Yet, with almost one quarter of the vote, they remained the most popular single party and their 184 seats were more than double the seats held by the number two party—the Socialists. Furthermore, in conjunction with their allies they continued to control Parliament, having 30 seats more than a bare majority. Thus the specter of a non-Gaullist Premier for the Fifth Republic was laid to rest for another five years.

Despite its preeminence during the Fifth Republic, the durability of the Gaullist movement as a political force remains somewhat uncertain. Unlike its Fourth Republic forerunner, the RPF, the movement has not been organized as a mass party. That is to say that it has been based primarily on Parliament rather than on an integrated grass-roots organization like the Socialists. In the late 1960s the movement did change its structure somewhat in the direction of a mass party. Nonetheless, it remained basically a cadre party with fewer than 200,000 members, compared to the 1.5 million the movement had had in the Fourth Republic. Chirac's reorganization of the movement into the Rally for the Republic could develop as easily into a personal machine as into a mass party.

The movement has managed at least to survive de Gaulle's passing from the political scene, unlike its experience in the Fourth Republic. But without him the movement at times has been weakened by factionalism, as happened in the 1974 Presidential election. If Chirac's Rally can manage to prevent the victory of the Left in 1978 elections, the triumph would enhance its status considerably and help to secure Chirac's election as President in 1981. In those circumstances the Gaullist heritage and movement would have considerable life left to it. But if the 1978 elections turn the Gaullists out of power, then the RPR seems likely to dissipate just as the RPF did in the Fourth Republic. Gaullism can continue without de Gaulle, but not without governmental power.

The French right never has been organized effectively into a single major party. Following World War II a small number of right-wing deputies, mainly from poor, strongly Catholic areas, formed a Parliamentary group which became the nucleus of the Independents and Peasants party. Other small conservative parties joined and eventually the Independents surpassed the strength of the MRP and equalled that of the Socialists with about one seventh of the vote.

In the first election in the Fifth Republic, the Independents surprisingly gained over one fifth of the vote, the largest vote cast for any party. In fact, it was the only party closely associated with the previous regime to make such gains. This is all the more remarkable because the conservative tide behind the Gaullists could have been expected to decrease their strength. The only explanation seems to be that the Independents made their gains at the expense of the Radicals and the MRP. With 120 seats they were the second largest group in the National Assembly and the largest party in the Senate. Since they were far from being a cohesive Parliamentary force, however, their effective power was less than these figures would suggest.

If the Independents hoped to build a strong, effective party on their strengthened Parliamentary base, they soon were disappointed. In many areas the continued growth of the Gaullists was at the expense of the Independents. Furthermore, the party split in 1962 over the question of support for de Gaulle. The anti-Gaullist group was left with only a handful of seats and has ceased to be an effective Parliamentary force.

The majority faction, led by Giscard d'Estaing, continued, however, to increase its Parliamentary strength. After the 1968 elections the Giscardiens were second only to the Gaullists, but a very distant second, with 62 seats. Most of these seats were won because of the Giscardiens' alliance with the Gaullists; the group polled only 8 percent of the vote—less than the Communists, Left Federation, or Christian Democrats. The Giscardiens did all they could to get the maximum mileage out of association with the Gaullists without being so closely identified with them that they would have to share the blame for the Government's shortcomings. This fence straddling tactic was succinctly summarized by Giscard's 1967 slogan, "Yes, but . . .

Giscard's Independent Republicans fared relatively well in the 1973 elections. Their 7 percent of the vote was only slightly lower than what they had received in 1968; they did not suffer the dramatic losses of the Gaullists. While they lost some of their strength in the National Assembly, with 54 seats they were about one-quarter larger than they were after the 1967 elections.

Giscard's victory in the 1974 Presidential election has not proven to be of any great advantage to the Republicans. On the one hand, it is clear that they are not the center of power, since Chirac and the Gaullists control Parliament. On the other hand, it is difficult to disclaim all responsibility for economic conditions when the head of your party is the country's President and has appointed a Premier belonging to no party so that the President's policies will be carried out without question. Thus the Republicans hardly can expect significant gains in strength.

In summary, the French party system of the late 1970s is dominated by four principal groups—the Gaullists and the Republicans on the right and the Communists and Socialists on the left. The system is somewhat less fractionalized than it was during the Fourth Republic, but clearly remains a multi-party system. While some of the actors have been changed (or at least acquired new stage names), the basic nature of the system has not been altered. The Left is more united than it has been for well over a generation, yet internal conflicts and suspicions remain; the Center is more divided and ineffective than ever; the Right is effectively unified, but its durability is uncertain.

Some people have argued that one of the reasons the United States has a two-party system is because of the Presidency. This is, given the power of the office, the supreme political prize in American politics. Therefore considerable party activity is directed toward attempting to win this office. Since only a broadly based national party can have any hope of success in this contest, American parties are forced to be coalitions of diverse, even discordant, interests united primarily by their desire to win the ultimate victory. This quest for a winning coalition prohibits the luxury of small, programmatic parties, each appealing to a narrow segment of the electorate.

In France also the Presidency clearly is the supreme prize. As will become clear in the following two chapters, the French President dominates the policy process even more than does the American President. Yet there is little evidence that the quest for this office has altered the basic nature of the French party system. Of course, it is naive to think that a single institutional feature can by itself transform a nation's political traditions and life immediately. Yet it is proper to note that thus far one looks in vain for any significant change in this direction.

BIBLIOGRAPHICAL NOTE

Among the best sources on parties and politics in the Fourth Republic are the Williams book mentioned in the Bibliographical Note for Chapter 9 and Duncan MacRae, Jr., *Parliament, Parties, and Society in France, 1946–1958* (New York: St. Martin's Press, 1967). See also the various essays covering the Fifth as well as the Fourth Republic in the Williams book mentioned in the Note for Chapter 11. Although Maurice Duverger's *Political Parties*, translated by Barbara and Robert North, 2d ed. rev. (London: Methuen, 1959), covers political parties generally, much of his material deals with French parties. Jean Laponce, *The Government of the Fifth Republic: French Parties and the Constitution* (Berkeley: University of California Press, 1961), focuses solely on French parties and discusses, among other topics, party organizational structure.

A number of studies of particular French parties have been written. Especially useful is Jean Charlot, *The Gaullist Phenomenon*, translated by Monica Charlot and Marianne Neighbour (London: Allen & Unwin, 1971), which includes the Giscardiens as well as the regular Gaullists. Frank Wilson, *The French Democratic Left, 1963–1969* (Stanford: Stanford University Press, 1971), examines the problems of trying to reform the Socialist party into an effective Left political force. Other interesting studies are Charles Micaud, *Communism and the French Left* (New York: Frederick A. Praeger, Inc., 1963), and François de Tarr, *The French Radical Party from Herriot to Mendes-France* (New York: Oxford University Press, 1961).

13

The Legislative System

THE COMPOSITION OF THE HOUSES OF PARLIAMENT

The French Parliament is divided into two houses. The popularly elected National Assembly consists of 490 members—473 from France proper, 10 from overseas departments, and 7 from overseas territories. The Senate's 283 members are elected indirectly. Election procedures, qualifications for office, and term of service were discussed in Chapter 11.

The physical arrangement of each house is much more like that of the United States Congress than of the British Parliament. Members sit in a semicircular scheme, but because of the many parties it is difficult to have a clear-cut dividing line between Government and Opposition. Deputies are grouped according to political coloration, from the far left (presiding officer's left) to the extreme right.

Seating arrangements have at times caused some controversy. At the beginning of the Fifth Republic the Gaullists favored an arrangement like that of the British House of Commons. But they were unable to win the support of any other political group for this and were not sufficiently strong themselves to carry it. Nonetheless, they won their demand that they be allowed to occupy the central seats, thus demonstrating to the electorate that they were not a reactionary party of the right.[1]

The reduction of Communist strength in the National Assembly in the Fifth Republic has had a significant impact on the social composition of

---

[1] Philip Williams, *The French Parliament* (New York: Frederick A. Praeger, Inc., 1968) p. 36. This is source for some of the other information in these paragraphs.

the chamber. Whereas in the Fourth Republic workers had made up 13 percent of the lower house or more, during de Gaulle's Presidency the proportion of workers was only half this great for just a brief period and usually was much lower than even that. Teachers have become the largest single occupational group in the lower house, with lawyers, doctors, and civil servants the other principal groups. In keeping with its more rural and conservative electorate, the Senate has contained even fewer workers but has a sizable portion of farmers. The latter's share of seats in the upper house has been two to three times greater than in the lower house—normally making it the largest single occupational group in the upper house.

The first Parliament of the Fifth Republic saw a considerable number of new faces in the lower house. Less than 30 percent of those deputies who stood for reelection were successful. While it would not be quite true to conclude that most of the deputies elected were inexperienced—most of them either had been active in local politics or unsuccessful candidates for Parliament in previous elections—yet this is evidence of the extent to which the electorate was turning its back on the national politicians of the Fourth Republic. Even after the next elections in 1962 almost half—45 percent—of the members of the lower house had never served in that body before. One thing that did remain the same about recruitment patterns was local government experience. As had been true in both the Third and Fourth Republics, well over a majority—three fourths in 1958—had been members of local government councils previously. Many deputies continue to serve in such an office, in fact, since in France there is no bar to being a member of the national legislature and of a local legislature simultaneously.

The situation in the Senate differed considerably, however, with regard to turnover. The results of the first election were a virtual return to the Fourth Republic. Of those members of the upper house who stood for reelection, 84 percent were reelected. And many of those who were new to the Senate simply were experienced national politicians who had been unable to retain their seats in the earlier election for the lower house.

The new Senate was almost a duplicate of the old Council of the Republic of the Fourth Republic. This was reflected in the election of a Radical as president of the Senate—the same man who had held the position since 1947. Subsequent elections have altered the composition only slightly. In almost every case, especially when one allows for party splits, party strengths in the upper house have fluctuated only a few percentage points over the entire period of the Fifth Republic. Even after the 1971 Senate elections, the Gaullists were only the fifth largest party in the Senate. Thus, during most of the Fifth Republic the Senate has been a much sharper critic of the Government than has the National Assembly. The Government has been helped by the fact that its allies, the Giscardiens, are the largest group in the Senate—one fifth or more of the seats in recent years—and by the upper house's limited powers, as will be discussed subsequently.

POWERS AND PROCEDURES

Unlike the basic law of the Third and Fourth Republics, the constitution of the Fifth seeks to spell out the powers of Parliament and, by stating that in other areas the Government can legislate by decree, it seeks to limit them. One of the first limitations is on the length of legislative sessions, of which there are two annually; each session is limited to three months. Special sessions, not to exceed 12 days in length and to deal with a specific agenda, can be called at the request of the Premier or a majority of the Assembly. In 1961, however, during a period of emergency rule, President de Gaulle refused to summon a special session of Parliament even though the members of Parliament wishing one had complied with all the required procedures. Although his action seemed clearly to violate the constitution, there was nothing the Parliament could do about it. It simply was another illustration of de Gaulle's refusal to abide by the rules, even those drawn up under his guidance, whenever it was inconvenient for him to do so.

Within the sphere of power granted to the legislature, a distinction is made between those areas in which it is to make the regulations and those in which it is only to lay down the general or basic principles. Parliament can legislate in detail on the following matters: civil rights and obligations; nationality, contracts, gifts, and inheritance; crimes and criminal procedures, taxation and currency, electoral systems; public institutions; economic plans, including nationalization and denationalization of enterprises. But Parliament can establish only the policy outlines and must leave to the executive the filling in of details in the following areas: general organization of national defense; education; property rights; employment, unions, and social security; administration of local government units. In all other areas, except for declaring war, ratifying treaties, and voting the budget, the constitution says that the Government may legislate by decree. Furthermore, the Government may ask the legislature to delegate to it even those powers specifically given to the legislature.

Since the Parliament's enumerated powers appear quite broad, this statement of its sphere may not seem to be a serious limitation. And as for legislation by executive decree, this long has been a French tradition. The difference is that in the past such *cadre* laws always were based on grants of authority to the executive from the legislature, grants which could be revoked at any time. This now is only partially true. Most of the executive's decree power now comes from the constitution, and thus is not subject to control or alteration by the Parliament. In addition, the new step of limiting the Parliament's competency to only those areas specified is part of a deliberate effort to restrict it and make it subject to the executive.

In addition to its legislative function, Parliament is supposed to have a role in the amendment of the constitution. But, as discussed previously in Chapter 10, this has been circumvented on one occasion. Thus Parliament's power and status in that area has been jeopardized as well.

The upper chamber of the legislature was a weak body during the Fourth Republic, quite in contrast to the Senate of the Third Republic. In returning in the Fifth Republic to the old name for the upper house, an effort was made to restore that chamber to much of its former power. This was a deliberate political tactic. The Gaullists were uncertain of their ability to control the lower house, but were confident that they would have an ally in the conservative upper house. Therefore they sought to give it considerably more power than that possessed by the Council of the Republic in the Fourth Republic.

With a few exceptions the formal powers of the Senate equal those of the National Assembly. Finance bills must be submitted to the National Assembly first. But should the lower house fail to act within 40 days, then the Government can introduce the bill in the upper house. If the two houses cannot agree on a bill, it dies, unless the Government intervenes to call for a conference committee composed of members chosen from each house. Even if this committee formulates a compromise acceptable to the representatives from both houses, its agreed draft can be submitted to both houses only if the Government approves and only with those amendments that the Government favors. If the committee fails to secure agreement, then the Government has the option of asking the National Assembly to act. Its decision is final regardless of the views of the Senate.

Presumably, if the Cabinet and Senate were of like mind and the Assembly hostile, the Senate could be employed to exercise a veto power in legislation. On the other hand, the Senate can be overruled only if the Cabinet and the Assembly agree. Thus, the Senate can serve as a check upon the Assembly but not upon the Government. This means that the different political composition of the Senate, mentioned above, has posed no problem for the Government. Furthermore, since the Senate lacks the power to censure the Government and remove it from office, opposition control of the upper house is of little consequence. The Government simply has lacked an ally that it expected to have. But, since for most of the Fifth Republic the Government has had a solid majority in the National Assembly, it has not needed any ally to help control that body.

The present constitution deals with legislative procedure in greater detail than have past ones. The constitution now gives the Cabinet such control over Parliamentary time and over finance that the interminable debates that used to take place on the budget and other bills, often designed to embarrass and defeat the Government, are no more. Moreover, the constitution stipulates that the legislature's standing orders cannot go into effect until they have been examined by the Constitutional Council to make sure that they conform with the constitution.

Each chamber is presided over by a president. French presiding officers remain members of their respective political parties, unlike the Speaker of the House of Commons, and do not have the Speaker's unchallenged authority. In the past, they were elected to their posts annually, but the constitution now provides that the president of the Assembly is elected for its duration, while the president of the Senate is elected every three years—that is, after each partial renewal of its membership. Moreover, the standing orders now give the presiding officer more authority in controlling debate and in calling members to order than his or her predecessors had. Each of the two presiding officers holds a position of great prestige; the president of the Senate replaces the President of the Republic if the latter is incapacitated.

In order to be represented on committees in the National Assembly, according to standing orders, a parliamentary group must have at least 30 members. It is partially because of this requirement that certain party representatives in the Assembly have affiliated with others. This provision was the means by which the Communists were denied any formal role in the National Assembly's procedures during the first four years of the Fifth Republic despite their having received one fifth of the popular vote. The leaders of the various political groups in the National Assembly are required to submit an official declaration of their group's policy. All members and affiliates of a group are required to sign this statement, but usually it is so vague as to be virtually meaningless. Special debating privileges are granted to the leaders of recognized groups. In recent years four to six groups have been entitled formally to committee assignments, with each group receiving appointments in proportion to its strength. Nonetheless, party strengths are not the same on each committee. The groups trade seats with each other so as to maximize their strength on those committees dealing with subjects of special interest to them. Once its allocation for a particular committee finally is determined, each party decides which of its members shall fill the seats.

The number of committees has been reduced from 19 in the Fourth Republic to 6 for two reasons: to reduce the authority of committees and to avoid the time-wasting practice of submitting identical matters to several committees. Under the Fourth Republic committees were independent centers of power, just as they are in the United States Congress. The committees were numerous enough so that each could build up a fund of expertise in a specialized area. The chairpersons of committees became virtual shadow ministers, able to keep a close watch and considerable control over the members of the Cabinet. In a multi-party system having no single party as the Opposition, this was an important element in legislative dominance of the executive.

The smaller number of committees in the Fifth Republic means that committees are larger and less specialized. For most of the time two committees have had 60 members each and the other four 90 each. These committees are prevented from being unwieldy largely by absenteeism. Only those members particularly interested in the bill being discussed are likely to attend a given session. Nonetheless, the larger size of the committees has meant that it is more difficult than it had been in the Fourth Republic for a pressure group to secure a majority in a committee and thus get it to recommend legislation which it favors.

Special committees consisting of not more than 30 members with no more than 15 from any single permanent committee may be created on an ad hoc basis to deal with a particular bill. These have not been used to any great extent, particularly in recent years. Also possible are committees of inquiry, comparable to select committees in the House of Commons.

Another innovation in legislative procedure concerns proxy voting. In the past, French legislators quite frequently gave to one of their colleagues, usually the leader of their party bloc in Parliament, the right to cast their votes when they were away. This practice of proxy voting grew up rather than the practice of pairing, with the result that often one person could cast a sizable number of votes. The new constitution, in theory, abolishes this practice. Proxy voting is still possible, but only in case of a specific reason (for example, illness or being away on Government business), and no member may cast more than one proxy vote.

In practice, however, proxy voting continues to a considerable degree. This is made possible because of the installation of electronic voting in the National Assembly. A member who plans to be away simply gives the key to the voting instrument on his or her desk to a colleague who votes for the absent member. In this fashion members avoid the loss of salary intended to penalize those who fail to vote regularly.

Although the Government has ultimate control of the Parliament's timetable, the National Assembly does have a committee that deals with these matters. The Conference of Presidents, composed of the leaders of all recognized groups, the chairpersons of the committees, the six vice presidents of the National Assembly, and its president, sets the agenda and allots the amount of time to be spent in debating each item. Voting in the Conference is on the basis of formal group strength in the National Assembly. Given the power of the Government in these matters, however, the Conference votes only infrequently. It serves more as a channel for communicating the views of the various formal groups to the Government and a means of negotiating with the Government and, at times, persuading it to change its mind on matters of legislative priorities.

The Conference plays a more powerful role in the matter of Parliamentary questions. Question time occurs only once a week in the Fifth Republic. Questions to Governmental ministers may be either of two types. On those without debate, following the minister's answer to the question the member of Parliament who asked the question may comment for no more than five minutes. The minister may reply briefly and then the next question is taken. Questions with debate permit the member to make a 30-minute speech in response to the minister's answer. And following the minister's reply to this speech there is general debate. The Conference decides which questions shall be scheduled and whether they shall be with or without debate.

Question time is not nearly as effective or important in France as it is in Britain. In part this is because it occurs only once a week. Another factor is the Government's disdainful attitude toward this portion of Parliamentary activity. Instead of having ministers respond to questions directed toward their particular areas of responsibility, a single minister is designated to answer all questions of whatever subject on a given day. Thus the whole idea of question time as a period in which those directly responsible for a particular portion of the Government's policy and activities could be called to account was defeated.

LEGISLATIVE-EXECUTIVE RELATIONS

Some of the information already covered in this chapter has touched at various points on executive-legislative relations. We have noted the limiting of the Parliament's sphere of competence and the corresponding expansion of the Cabinet's, the ability of the Cabinet to play one house off against the other, the reduction of Parliament's surveillance of the executive through committees and questions, and the Cabinet's greatly enhanced control of the Parliament's timetable. For a cabinet to exercise powers of this type in a parliamentary system is not unusual, provided, of course, that it is responsible to a popularly elected legislature for the way in which it exercises its authority. (The exercise of substantive powers by the French President, who is accountable to no one, constitutes a serious modification of the parliamentary system. This point is discussed in more detail in the next chapter.) This is the essence of the parliamentary system—the ability of the legislature to replace the executive whenever the former loses confidence in the latter. The constitution of the Fifth Republic does provide that the Cabinet is responsible for the powers exercised by it to the National Assembly.

The methods for exacting ministerial responsibility are not always precise. Article 49 states: "The Premier, after deliberation in the Council of Ministers, may pledge the responsibility of his Government to the National Assembly with regard to the program of the Government, or with regard to a declaration of general policy, as the case may be." In the early years of the Fifth Republic this was interpreted to mean that when a Premier formed a Cabinet he would make a general statement of policy to the National Assembly, which could reject the Cabinet by a simple majority, and thus force it to resign. In the latter years of de Gaulle's Presidency and all through Pompidou's, however, Premiers ceased to ask the National Assembly for a vote of confidence when they formed a Government, although they usually did make a statement of what their policy would be. Apparently, French Presidents were trying to make clear that Cabinets were responsible more to them than to Parliament. President Giscard appeared to revive the original practice when in 1974 he had his first Premier, Jacques Chirac, ask the National Assembly for a vote of confidence on the new Government's policy. With his second Premier, Raymond Barre, however, he did not do this.

When the Government wishes to insure that some particularly essential legislation is passed, the Premier can stake the life of the Cabinet on a specific bill. The Cabinet is presumed to have the confidence of the National Assembly unless a censure motion is filed within the following 24 hours. Filing such a motion requires the support of at least one tenth of the members of the National Assembly. Once a motion is filed there must be a delay of at least 48 hours before the vote—thus giving the Government an opportunity to mobilize its maximum support. If the motion receives the votes of a majority of the total membership of the National Assembly (not just of those voting), then the Cabinet is forced to resign. If the motion fails to obtain this absolute majority, then the bill to which the Government has committed itself is considered approved.

Under this procedure a bill can become law even though *a majority of those present* have expressed their disapproval, because a censure motion fails unless it receives *a majority of the total membership.* In fact, unless a motion of censure is moved, a bill can become law without ever having been voted upon at all. The general effect of this procedure is that the Cabinet can go on with its program unless the Assembly is willing to turn it out of office. The Government has pledged its life on a particular legislative text a dozen times during the Fifth Republic. On all but two occasions its opponents responded with a censure motion. None of these motions, however, passed.

The Cabinet's Parliamentary opponents need not wait for it to raise the question of confidence. A motion of censure may be moved whenever at least one tenth of the members of the Assembly so desire. The founders of the Fifth Republic did not intend to permit a faction in the National Assembly to make life unpleasant for the Cabinet by constantly moving censure, thus employing the censure motion as a propaganda or obstructionist device. Therefore, they provided that if a motion of censure fails to pass, then none of those (at least one tenth of the total membership) who signed the motion in order to get it on the agenda may sign another such motion for the remainder of the session of Parliament. (This limit on the signing of censure motions does not apply in those cases when the Cabinet has initiated the process by staking its life on a bill.) During the Fifth Republic about a dozen and a half motions of censure have been moved in these circumstances. Only one of these—objecting to de Gaulle's attempt to circumvent the procedure for amending the constitution—passed. Instead of having the Government resign, de Gaulle dissolved Parliament, held new elections, and used a referendum to amend the constitution precisely as he had intended. Both the elections and the referendum were substantial victories for de Gaulle. Thus, censure motions have proven completely ineffective in controlling the Government.

In the Third Republic and, to a lesser extent, the Fourth, Cabinets were called to account also in another way—by means of interpellations. These were like questions except that at the end of the debate following a minister's response a vote was held. Often during the Third Republic, Governments considered an adverse vote on an interpellation to be evidence that they had lost the confidence of Parliament and would resign from office. At the beginning of the Fifth Republic the rules of procedure which the National Assembly formulated for itself permitted interpellations. The Government opposed continuing this practice and referred the matter to the Constitutional Council, which, as we noted previously, is the final authority of the constitutional validity of Parliament's rules. The Council agreed with the Government and decided that all votes and resolutions on questions were unconstitutional. Thus, once again Parliament was shorn of a previously exercised power.

The Fifth Republic deliberately seeks to break with the past tradition of Assembly dominance. In the two previous republics, deputies ousted Cabinets with impunity and with no fear of dissolution, which might jeopardize their seats in the Assembly. The resulting instability was further complicated after World War II by the presence in the Assembly of a large antidemocratic bloc—the Communists on the far left and the ultraconservatives on the far right. Both the Government and the democratic opposition had to contend with this political fact of life. This is one reason why each Cabinet was in large measure a reshuffle of the previous one.

To avoid Assembly pressure and harassment, the Cabinet now is provided with certain procedural safeguards, as we have discussed. In turn, the Assembly's powers have been reduced correspondingly. Aside from the successful censure motion mentioned above, the Cabinet has experienced no serious difficulty with Parliament. In part this has been because in the Fifth Republic the real locus of policy-making power has been not the Cabinet but the President; the National Assembly has no way of calling the President to account. Also significant has been the changed political composition of the National Assembly. In sharp contrast to the Third and Fourth Republics, the Cabinet has not had to worry about maintaining a supportive coalition in the legislature. Only during the first four years of the Fifth Republic did the Gaullist Government lack an assured working majority in the National Assembly.

During the early years of the Fifth Republic, relations between the legislature and the Cabinet were poor. In part this was due to a difference in background between many ministers and the legislators. Since the constitution prohibits ministers from serving simultaneously in Parliament, many ministers were recruited from the civil service. Thus they frequently tended to be somewhat isolated from public opinion and rather unsympathetic to the concerns of legislators who had to face the electorate periodically. Although Cabinets continue to include some former civil servants, this is less common since de Gaulle no longer is President. Furthermore, the increased strength of the Gaullists in the National Assembly also helped improve executive-legislative relations.

The combined impact of constitutional reform and party system change appears to have remedied the long-standing problem of executive instability. In 12 years the Fourth Republic had 22 Premiers; in its first 12 years the Fifth had only 4 and even after more than 17 years had had only 7. While Premiers in the Fourth Republic averaged only six months in office, in the Fifth they have averaged almost three years. The contrasting patterns of Government durability can be seen from Figure 13–1.

Thus far in the Fifth Republic the President has wielded the real executive power, with the Premier and the Cabinet reduced to little more than the President's agents. Some thought that this relationship might change once de Gaulle departed from the Presidency. But Presidents Pompidou and Giscard have played essentially the role even though their styles have varied. Of course, some future President might conceive of the office as that of ceremonial head of state and thus allow the Premier and the Cabinet to exercise real executive power. And since they are responsible to the National Assembly, this development might well increase the power and status of the legislature. The precedents do seem to be hardening, however, against such a development.

In the meantime the Parliament not only exercises little control over the executive, but also is ineffective as a critic of the key policy makers. Philip Williams, one of the foremost students of French politics, grants that Parliament performs its legislative function more efficiently than ever before. But he also concludes:

Parliament is sadly inefficient as a forum for popular grievances, as a check on the administration, as a defender of the liberties of the subject, or as a political sounding-board for the opposition (or indeed government) to appeal

FIGURE 13–1
Number of Years Served in Office by Each Premier, 1946–1976

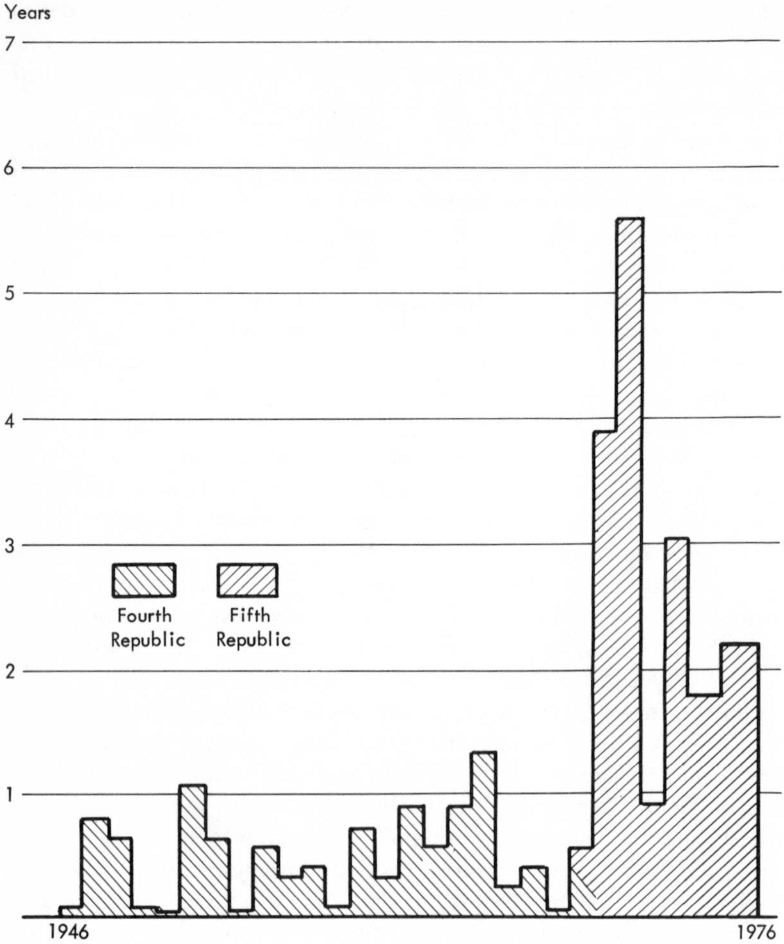

Years

to the electorate . . . In the old regime Parliament dominated the Government and denied itself effective leadership. In the new regime the Government dominates Parliament and denies itself effective criticism.[2]

Thus the fundamental problem of French politics—establishment of a balanced relation between the executive and the legislature—remains unsolved.

---

[2] Philip Williams, *The French Parliament,* p. 118, and "Parliament under the Fifth French Republic: Patterns of Executive Domination," in Gerhard Loewenberg, ed., *Modern Parliaments: Change or Decline?* (Chicago: Aldine-Atherton, 1971), p. 109.

BIBLIOGRAPHICAL NOTE

The Williams book cited in Footnote 1, despite its brevity, contains much useful information on both the law and practice concerning the National Assembly in the Fifth Republic. The Loewenberg book mentioned in Footnote 2 contains, in addition to the essay by Williams, an article on Parliament by François Goguel. Portions of the Laponce book, noted in the suggestions for Chapter 12 deal with Parliament. And a particularly useful study of Parliament under the Fourth Republic is D. W. S. Lidderdale, *The Parliament of France* (London: Hansard Society, 1951).

14

Policy-Making Structures

The constitution of the Fifth Republic provides for a dual executive—President and a Cabinet—not too much unlike that existing in the Fourth Republic. The constitution does strengthen the position of the President, but political policy making is clearly vested in the Cabinet, which is responsible to the popularly elected National Assembly. In practice, however, de Gaulle so interpreted the constitution—an interpretation acquiesced in at a time of crisis by the Cabinet, Parliament, and the country generally—as to make the President's role predominant in the determination of national policy. With de Gaulle no longer on the scene, questions have arisen as to the workability of this system, particularly in the matter of the relationship between the President and the Cabinet and of these two to Parliament. The ability to find answers to such questions will in large part determine whether the Fifth Republic's structure will be modified.

FORMAL POWERS AND DUTIES OF THE PRESIDENT

The French President is designated the head of state, while the Premier is to be the head of the Government. This does not mean that the President is to be simply a ceremonial figure like the British monarch. He or she is to be the guarantor of national independence, of the integrity of the territory, of respect for international treaties and agreements. He or she is entrusted with the task of protecting the constitution and to this end is to use his or her power to "arbitrate" among political forces and governmental bodies to insure the regular functioning of the state and its continuity. This responsibility is so vague that it is hard to know precisely what action it authorizes; at times de Gaulle seemed to feel that it justified his taking whatever action he felt necessary.

The President's powers are impressive. Some of them, such as the power to pardon, the appointment of ambassadors, and nominations to civil, army, and judicial posts, require the signature of the Premier (and possibly another minister), in true parliamentary form. But a number of substantive powers are exercised by the President alone, without any reference to advice from those who can be held politically accountable in Parliament.

The President designates the Premier, although this choice must be approved by the National Assembly. The President has a major, at times even dominant, voice in the Premier's selection of the Cabinet. The President may send messages to Parliament, but they cannot be the subject of debate. He or she may dissolve the National Assembly, although not more often than once a year. The only requirement is to consult the Premier and the presidents of the two assemblies. On the other hand, the President may refuse to grant the Premier's request for a dissolution. The President cannot hold a referendum unless the Premier proposes one; alternatively, the President can refuse the request of either the Premier or the Parliament for a referendum. Thus the constitution does create a system of some checks and balances. The actual operation of the system turns to a considerable extent upon the personalities of the two main political executives. On the other hand, the fact that thus far the President has been the dominant figure for all of the Fifth Republic is building up certain traditional conceptions of the two top executive offices.

Despite the power and importance of the French President, it is noteworthy that he or she lacks the veto power of the American President. The President may ask the Constitutional Council (three of whose members he or she appoints and whose president he or she designates) to rule on the constitutionality of Parliamentary bills and laws. And the President may, if the Premier agrees, ask Parliament to reconsider a bill that they have passed. While Parliament must then vote on the bill again, no special majority is required to repass it, so this cannot be considered a veto power.

The most impressive of the President's powers and the area where he or she clearly rises above the Premier are the emergency powers. ''When the institutions of the Republic, the independence of the nation, the integrity of its territory, or the fulfillment of its international commitments are threatened in a grave and immediate manner,'' says Article 16 of the constitution, ''and the regular functioning of the constitutional governmental authorities is interrupted, the President of the Republic shall take the measures required by these circumstances.'' It is necessary only to consult the Premier, the presidents of the assemblies, and the Constitutional Council, and to inform the nation of the measures being taken. While so ruling, however, the President may not dissolve or adjourn Parliament. The constitution stipulates that the measures taken "must be prompted by the desire to ensure to the constitutional governmental authorities, in the shortest possible time, the means of fulfilling their assigned functions." But since no formal time limit is specified, the duration of the emergency powers is in fact unlimited and depends only on the will of the President.

While Parliament does meet when the emergency powers are in effect, it apparently is prevented from censuring the Government. At any rate, no censure motions were allowed during the five months during 1961, which is the only period in which Article 16 has been invoked. The supporting reasoning was that were the Government to be censured, it might be deemed desirable to dissolve Parliament and call for new elections in an effort to determine whether the public supported the Government or the Parliament. But, since Article 16 prohibits dissolution of the Parliament during the use of emergency powers, it would be impossible to call an election. Therefore a motion to censure should not be allowed to create such an impasse. Thus in yet another way the powers of Parliament were restricted.

DE GAULLE'S CONCEPTUALIZATION AND SHAPING OF THE OFFICE

During the first dozen years of the Fifth Republic the system was dominated by Charles de Gaulle from the office of President. So much was this the case that some observers referred to France during this period as the de Gaulle Republic. While de Gaulle no longer is President, his actions during the formative years of the system had considerable impact in fleshing out the bare bones of the constitution; he created expectations and established precedents which continue to influence the operation of the system. Thus it is necessary to consider the period of his Presidency in some detail.

Although often seeking to convey the impression that he stood above the partisan battles of the political arena, de Gaulle was the prime mover in the politics of the Fifth Republic during his Presidency. In exercising personal leadership he often violated both the spirit and the letter of the constitution. But since he arrogated to himself the power to interpret the meaning of the constitution whenever he believed it important or necessary to do so, no serious challenge to his personal rule arose prior to the crisis of 1968. His actions, however, evoked criticism and thereby made him the subject of political controversy.

De Gaulle exercised his personal leadership in several ways. First of all, through visits to foreign heads of states and their visits to him, and through declarations of foreign and domestic policy, he became the spokesman for the nation. His insistence on pomp and ceremony caused the limelight to focus on him. Secondly, through his employment of the referendum, he sought to buttress his authority by demonstrations of popular approval. It should be noted in this connection that the constitution does not give the President the right to initiate referendums, only to refuse to call for them when asked to do so by the Cabinet or by Parliament. Yet it is evident that those which were held came as a result of his initiative. The one which amended the constitution to provide for popular election of the President was opposed by the National Assembly, but this was to no avail. Even the Constitutional Council was powerless to stand in the way.

Many of the French were most disturbed, given the past abuse of plebiscites discussed in Chapter 9, to be told by the President that the referendum had become a normal feature of government—a way, in effect, of circumventing Parliament. Although in the early years of his tenure de Gaulle used the referendum effectively (in disposing of the Algerian question), demonstrating that a vocal opposition often constituted but a minority, an unsuccessful referendum led to his downfall in 1969.

Thirdly, de Gaulle actively sought to determine Cabinet policy in fields he considered vital, and he was instrumental in the dismissal of certain ministers and the appointment of their successors. At times he made policy and simply communicated it to the Cabinet without the benefit of discussion or deliberation in the Cabinet. Often, by consulting technical committees or his personal adivsers, he bypassed the ministers. Sometimes he contradicted previous statements of his Premier, who was forced to ''change his mind'' publicly.

Some students of the French system developed the doctrine of reserve powers and open areas to explain de Gaulle's conception of the office of President. Under this interpretation the subjects of defense and foreign policy were reserved for Presidential action, despite the constitution's making the Premier responsible for defense. The argument was that defense and foreign policy clearly affect the whole nation, so they must be the concern of the President, given the duties placed upon him as already described. Domestic policy was an open area where discussion of policy alternatives could be carried on more freely by the rest of the executive. These matters were likely to lack the exalted importance of defense and foreign policy and thus be beneath the President's dignity; they were, as de Gaulle once contemptuously dismissed them, ''decisions concerning the price of milk.'' Yet even in domestic matters it was to be recognized that the President's views would be decisive should he care to intervene. Despite this qualification, de Gaulle himself never accepted the doctrine or reserve powers and open areas. He felt that such a conceptualization was too restrictive—his policy area should be unlimited.

Finally, in the exercise of the President's emergency powers, de Gaulle insisted that he was the sole judge of the propriety of all Governmental actions for the duration of the emergency. He thus refused to permit the convocation of a special session of the National Assembly during such a period, even though a majority of the deputies demanded one in accordance with constitutional provisions. The manner in which the President conducted himself during the five months of emergency rule in 1961 at the time of the military insurrection in Algeria was in many ways reassuring. But whether the situation in Algeria met the constitutional requirements for emergency rule was questionable. So also was his refusal to permit the special session of Parliament, particularly since the constitution explicitly states that during a period of emergency rule the President may not dissolve Parliament.

De Gaulle was able to exert personal leadership in these various ways because of his success in appealing to French national pride. On matters such as the future of NATO, the development of the Common Market, and relations with the Soviet Union, de Gaulle forced other countries to recognize that France's views must be given considerable weight. Domestically, he was willing to attack any and all established institutions if he felt it necessary. He did do something about housing. He did do something about university reforms, particularly in the establishment of new technical universities. He successfully fought the Catholic hierarchy in the matter of adoption and child care laws. He acted on the problem of high school dropouts. And he instituted the equivalent of the U.S. Securities and Exchange Commission.

Most experts on French politics have been inclined to regard the Presidency of de Gaulle as unique. He truly was larger than life; no one else even approaches his prominence and importance in French politics during the last third of a century. In fact, one might conclude that no French person since the first Napoleon had such personal attraction and significance for his compatriots. Yet also becoming increasingly clear is the extent to which the governmental structures and political forces which de Gaulle's rule created have a vitality of their own beyond that which his personality gave to them. Were they to prove viable in the long run, this probably would be the memorial which de Gaulle would find most satisfying, since, despite his arrogance, he sought not his own glory but the revitalizing of his nation. The elections of 1973 demonstrated that the Gaullists and their allies could win majority support even when de Gaulle no longer was alive to appeal to the electorate on a personal basis. And, while President Pompidou hardly had de Gaulle's personal magnetism, he certainly was not a weak President. In fact, some argued that governmental power was concentrated even more in the hands of the President under him than it had been under de Gaulle. The beginnings of Giscard's Presidency did not suggest that he planned to diminish his role in the policy process. Thus, de Gaulle may have succeeded in bequeathing to his nation stronger executive rule and a more effective political system.

Whatever the uniqueness of de Gaulle's Presidency, his exit from power certainly was singular—although quite characteristic of him. In his 1968 New Year's address, de Gaulle confidently predicted that while other countries were beset with confusion, France would continue to be an example of order. Less than six months later, France was shaken by a severe economic, social, and political crisis. The upheaval began with student protests at the University of Naterre, but quickly spread to the Sorbonne. The destructiveness of the students and the excessively brutal police response focused most of the attention on the Paris protests. Student demonstrations occurred, however, at most French universities and even at some high schools.

The student demonstrations triggered worker protests. Within a few days more than half of France's industrial work force was out on strike and workers had occupied hundreds of factories. When the Government promised university reforms, the workers demanded greater economic benefits, and were not in a mood to accept partial concessions by the Government and the management. Virtually everything came to a standstill. The economy seemed to be approaching a state of paralysis.

Both student and worker actions were symptomatic of a desire for change and modernization, and a reaction against a regime that had seemingly lost interest in reform. The problem of the centralized and outmoded operation of the universities was compounded by an increase in enrollment from 170,000 to 602,000 students in less than ten years. The general prosperity of the 1960s had benefited the workers but little, particularly in the light of the spiraling inflation. An important aspect of the crisis was the threat of repolarization at a time when the political feuds of the earlier regimes seemed to be passing away.

The French Government seemed helpless to deal with the crisis. De Gaulle waited, then announced plans for a referendum in June that would empower him to deal with economic and university reforms, presenting the whole matter as a choice between him and chaos. It soon became apparent that the chances of a successful referendum were dim. De Gaulle temporized further and, amid rumors that he would resign, having assured himself of army support he dissolved the National Assembly, calling for new elections.

This proved to be a brilliant political stroke, for in June it led to a landslide victory for the Gaullists. The people were tired of disorder. In part, the vote was one of disgust against the rioters, many of them nonstudents who had taken over after the initial demonstrations. The ordinary French person did not take kindly to words such as "serves you right" being scribbled on memorial plaques honoring students and professors who had fallen in wars in defense of France.

Moreover, de Gaulle and his Premier, Georges Pompidou (the principal architect of the electoral victory), succeeded in pinning much of the blame on the Communists. In point of fact, the Communist party demonstrated no leadership in the crisis and had in no way sought to seize power. Some of its spokesmen had even accused the students of anarchism and disorderly radicalism. In the electoral campaign, they sought to dissociate themselves (and the workers) from the excesses committed by the students, but to no avail.

The landslide victory, even though President de Gaulle refused to reappoint Pompidou as Premier, seemed to provide smoother sailing for the Gaullists and the Fifth Republic. In early 1969, however, de Gaulle again sought to amend the constitution by way of the referendum. One proposal was to make the French Senate an advisory body. Another proposed change was to strengthen regionalism by replacing the 95 departments with 21 regions. These regions were to be governed by locally elected assemblies with significant powers, including taxation. De Gaulle had sketched out these ideas for regional reform prior to the 1968 crisis.

Although de Gaulle stated clearly that he would not remain in office if the referendum failed, the electorate rejected his proposals, 10.5 million yes to 11.9 million no. De Gaulle promptly declared that he was ceasing to exercise his functions as President of the Republic. In the Presidential elections held in June 1969, Georges Pompidou, who had been de Gaulle's Premier between 1962 and 1968, was elected.

De Gaulle had not needed to make the threat of resignation nor was he obligated to carry it out once the referendum was lost. But clearly, for a man as concerned with honor as he was, there was no alternative. He felt repudiated by the French people and, as he had done 23 years earlier when they had rejected his advice, he turned his back on them and left them to work out their destiny by themselves. No one can say whether the French really did intend to reject de Gaulle or whether they really believed he would carry out his threat if the referendum failed. Perhaps the best interpretation is that they had grown weary of his high-handed style of government and, just as adolescents seek to establish themselves as people not subject completely to their parents' values and plans for them, rebelled. The other relevant factor was that for the first time in the Fifth Republic many of the French felt that an alternative was available. Whereas in the past the choice, as de Gaulle himself often had posed it, was either de Gaulle or chaos, in 1969 a competent replacement for de Gaulle was available—Pompidou. Had de Gaulle not made the mistake of dismissing Pompidou as Premier, despite his importance in helping the Gaullists to win the 1968 elections, Pompidou might not have made it so clear that he was quite prepared to succeed de Gaulle in the President's office. Pompidou had demonstrated in May 1968 that he could act coolly and effectively. Thus, the French decided to defy their guardian's instructions, relatively secure in the knowledge that the bogeyman really would not get them for their transgression.

PRESIDENTIAL RELATIONS WITH THE REST OF THE EXECUTIVE

During the Third and Fourth Republics, the Premier and his colleagues usually were referred to as the Cabinet, although their official name was the Council of Ministers. The bulk of their deliberations were held in an informal atmosphere under the chairmanship of the Premier. In such a capacity they were known as the Cabinet Council. In order for their acts to be valid, however, they had to meet as the Council of Ministers, over which the President of the Republic presided. These were brief meetings to give legal form to what had been hammered out at length in the Cabinet. Under the Fifth Republic, on the other hand, meetings of the Cabinet have been infrequent. All major discussions have taken place in meetings of the Council of Ministers, with the President presiding.

The Council is composed of the Premier, appointed by the President, and an indefinite number of ministers (about 30) whom the Premier is supposed to nominate. During the Third and Fourth Republics, ministers were usually members of Parliament, although practice did not dictate that they must be, as in Great Britain. The present constitution makes this impossible. Article 23 states that "the office of members of the Government shall be incompatible with the exercise of any parliamentary mandate, with the holding of any office at the national level, in business, professional or labor organizations, and with any public employment or professional activity." Members of Parliament can, and have, become ministers, but when doing so they resign from the house to which they had been elected. Nonetheless, they are permitted to speak in Parliament and, in practice, engage freely in the debates; they are not permitted, however, to vote.

The Premier and the Council, according to the constitution, "determine and direct" the policies of the nation. Moreover, the Premier directs the Government and is responsible for national defense. In practice, however, these powers have, in the main, been exercised by the President and his close advisers. The Council ministers have not protested this transfer of authority; indeed they seem to have acquiesced willingly, being content with implementing the President's policies. In other circumstances with different personalities, practice might very well differ significantly. Had de Gaulle chosen in 1958 to be Premier rather than President, the balance of power between the two offices clearly would have been reversed.

The broad constitutional grant of authority to the Council is augmented by Article 38 of the constitution, which says: "The Government may, in order to carry out its program, ask Parliament to authorize it, for a limited period, to take through ordinances measures that are normally within the domain of law." In February 1960 the Premier, pursuant to this article, demanded and received a broad delegation of authority to govern by decree for a period of 14 months. This grant of power was ostensibly made "for the maintenance of law and order, the safeguarding of the State and the Constitution, and the pacification and administration of Algeria." The sole limitation on this grant of authority was the express proviso that Parliament could not be dissolved during this period. Article 41, however, prevents Parliament from seeking to legislate in areas where it has delegated decree powers to the Council.

In two areas where French Councils were notoriously weak in the past—areas where British Governments are strong—the constitution clearly strengthens them. Concerning control of fiscal matters, Article 40 states, "Bills and amendments introduced by members of Parliament shall not be considered when their adoption would have as a consequence either a diminution of public financial resources, or the creation or increase of public expenditures." And concerning Council proposals, Article 48 states, "the discussion of bills filed or agreed upon by the Government shall have priority on the agenda of the Assemblies in the order set by the Government." Other articles give the Government sufficient power to speed the passage of finance bills, and, in the event Parliament fails to act within a specified time (70 days), the budget bill can be put into effect by decree (a power that the Government thus far has not needed to use).

Furthermore, the Government has the power to structure the debate and decisions on legislation in its favor. Legislative committees are not permitted to bury Government bills; if they take too long the Government can recall the bill to the legislature. Nor can the committees amend Government bills; all they can do is to suggest to the house how the Government's text should be changed, and this only after the Government has presented its case for the bill as it stands. Thus the bill emerges intact from the committee and the Government needs only to beat off attacks rather than being faced with the problem of piecing together a coalition willing to restore a mutilated bill to its previous form. Furthermore, the Government can refuse to allow any amendment to be presented in the legislature itself which had not been proposed during the time a bill was in committee. Thus it is safeguarded from being caught unaware by a proposal not as innocuous as it might seem on the surface. Finally, the Government can determine how the bill will be voted upon. It can select only certain subsections of the bill for a vote, ignoring others, or it can simply require a single vote on an entire bill. This would rule out the chance for any amendments and force the members of the legislature to accept or reject the bill as a whole. In this way opponents of certain provisions of a bill may be forced to swallow their dislike for these portions for the sake of getting the entire bill.

French Councils in the Third and Fourth Republics were weak, resulting in general Governmental instability. What is the Fifth Republic's answer to Assembly government? Is it the establishment of a strong Council along British lines, or is it the foresaking of parliamentary traditions and the inauguration of presidential government along American lines? The aim of the framers of the new constitution was to strengthen the executive and to produce greater stability, but, as the preceding discussion has indicated, the government of France is neither presidential nor cabinet, as these terms are generally understood in Great Britain and in the United States.

Possibilities for conflict, not only between the legislature and the executive, but also between the President and the Premier, have been built into the Fifth Republic. The constitution grants the Premier a share of the executive power and provides him or her with some checks upon the President. On paper the Premier would appear to be a more important figure in the Fifth Republic than was the case in the Fourth. At that time the Premier was by no means necessarily the most important person in the Council. He might simply be one of a number of leaders of a small center party which was well placed on the political spectrum to serve as the focal point for a coalition. Thus, he frequently had to compromise on policy and even was limited in his ability to appoint his Council members. Certain parties were recognized to have claims on particular posts and the Premier would have to accept whomever they designated for the job. However much the Premier's position in the Fifth Republic might appear to be enhanced over this, in fact he has not been a significant figure because he has been willing to defer to the directions of the President. But this situation could change with different personalities in the two top executive posts. As we noted previously, the chief constitutional edge of the President over the Premier is the former's possession of the emergency powers. To this can be added the fact that the President is assured of a seven-year term, while the Premier could be voted out of office by the National Assembly at any time. Thus the President is less accountable and more secure.

In examining the shift in power between the executive and the legislature we observed that, extensive as the constitutional reforms are, the shift in power that has occurred between these two branches is as much the result of the emergence in the National Assembly of a firm majority coalition centered on a single large party. So also the conclusion regarding the shift in power within the executive must be that constitutional alterations are not the sole cause. What the alterations have done is to create, in the Presidency, an office which, in the hands of a skillful and dynamic leader, can become the focus of the political process. But it would be premature to conclude that a similar observation is inappropriate for the office of Premier. That post, occupied by an astute political leader and faced by a mediocre President, could develop a new prominence. Had Poher, instead of Pompidou, won the 1969 Presidential election we would be writing of how the Presidency had lost its importance once de Gaulle relinquished office. As the Fifth Republic has operated thus far it has been more a presidential than a parliamentary system even though the Council is responsible to the National Assembly. But that is only the prevailing practice, not the constitutional necessity.

An important change does seem to have occurred, however, in political values. De Gaulle's rule and heritage seem to have weakened considerably the traditional French hostility to a strong executive. The development of a French consensus around a more workable party and cabinet system seems much more possible than in the past.

BIBLIOGRAPHICAL NOTE

Malcolm Anderson's *Government in France: An Introduction to the Executive Power* (Oxford: Pergamon Press, Inc., 1970) is best described by the subtitle and serves as the most useful book focusing mainly on the executive. Chapters 1 and 3 of F. Ridley and J. Blondel's *Public Administration in France* (London: Routledge & Kegan Paul, 1964), deal with the President, the Prime Minister, and the Cabinet. Beyond this, almost any book on the Fifth Republic will contain portions on the President, given the dominant role of this office. And given the significance of de Gaulle in shaping the Presidency, almost any book on him will deal in part with the executive. Among the many biographies of de Gaulle, one especially worthy of mention is Alexander Werth, *De Gaulle: A Political Biography* (New York: Simon and Schuster, 1966).

15

Policy-Implementing Structures

The outstanding characteristic of French public administration is its centralization. Like Britain, France is a unitary state; yet French administration, which retains a great deal of the absolutist tradition, is more centralized. What the British call local government is more appropriately referred to in France as administration. The centralized bureaucracy of Napoleon's time has survived and has played an important role in French public life largely because of the weakness and instability of the political executive. Stability in administration in the midst of political instability was no doubt recognized and appreciated by the French people. Some political parties sought, however, to combat the autocratic aspects of the bureaucracy. But, since the average tenure of a minister was approximately six months (Third and Fourth Republics), little could be done to carry through with reform measures. Under the Fifth Republic, important reforms have been made.

Paradoxically, administration in France also can be characterized as dispersed or loosely integrated. At the national level (as distinguished from the national-local relation mentioned in the first paragraph), departmental integration tends to be less advanced than in Britain.

Another important feature of French public administration is the system of administrative law. This system, operating through an independent structure of courts, provides for an efficient, easy, and inexpensive method of testing the validity of governmental actions, as well as providing for adequate restitution to injured parties.

A more recent attribute of French administration is its deep involvement in the national economy. Economic planning, national and regional, designed to eliminate glaring contrasts between "private wealth and public poverty," has required both new authority to administrative subdivisions and machinery for coordinating the efforts of the private and public sectors of the economy.

STAFFING THE BUREAUCRACY

Not until the Fourth Republic did France establish a single, unified civil service system. The principle of selection of civil servants by merit had been instituted prior to that time, but individual government departments had a relatively free hand to recruit staff by their own procedures. As a result, personnel seldom moved from one ministry to another. Civil servants acquired a highly specialized knowledge of their own ministry but lacked a broad view of government operation. Recruitment was unified by law after World War II, with general conditions established to govern promotion and discipline. But even then some areas remained outside the civil service code (for example, nationalized enterprises and technical branches such as mining and engineering).

Another aim of the post-World-War-II reforms was to provide for the recruitment and training of persons for the higher civil service. For this purpose, the National School of Administration (ENA) was created. Admission to the school is through keen competition from two groups: (1) persons not older than 26 who hold degrees or diplomas from universities or technical schools, and (2) bureaucrats between the ages of 26 and 30 who have had at least five years of service. From those admitted are recruited the "superior" functionaries and civil administrators.

Two means of entry into the ENA were provided in an attempt to reduce the traditional class bias of the civil service—a problem in France just as in Britain. The second means mentioned would permit those from lower economic levels to rise to positions of responsibility, if they were capable, even if they lacked a university education. But the intended result has not been achieved; there has been no great change in the class composition of the French civil service. The lower civil servants have not scored as well on the entrance exam as have the university graduates.

The school course lasts for two years, with a third year possible. In the first year, the student serves as an intern with some high functionary, but away from Paris. At the end of the year, he or she is required to submit an original study (at least 50 pages) on some phase of administration. The second year is spent in Paris, interning in one of the central ministries acquiring experience in general administration, economic and fiscal administration, social administration, and the foreign service. At the end of the year, the student takes an examination in each of these areas, and on the basis of his or her rank in each, makes a choice of career among the positions available. For those who are selected to participate in the third year, there are specialized studies and other internships. During one's attendance at the ENA, one not only pays no fees, but receives a salary as well, since one clearly is being trained for a government position.

While the post-World-War-II recruitment procedures have not resulted in dramatic changes in the class composition of the civil service, they have produced greater uniformity in the training of personnel. This in turn helps to facilitate transferrability of staff.

For a long time the pay of French civil servants was regarded as very low, but the situation has improved. In the lower and middle grades, civil servants are better off than their counterparts in private business. At higher levels, however, the position of the civil servant is relatively poorer, particularly in such technical areas as scientific research.

Paradoxically, although the bureaucracy is distrusted widely, being a part of it is prestigeous. Many apply for civil service positions. Furthermore, morale is high, particularly among those in the upper ranks. Personal ties are especially close between influential public servants. Given the brief tenure of ministers in the Third and Fourth Republics, civil servants have a tradition of being able to play an influential role in policymaking.

THE IMPACT OF BUREAUCRATIC STRUCTURE UPON PUBLIC POLICY

National Administration

As in Britain, the administrative system is directed by the political ministers. As a rule there is a secretary and/or an undersecretary, who is supposed to assist the minister. Below them are the directors, who are the equivalent of assistant secretaries and who head *directions*, or divisions. Their immediate subordinates are the bureau chiefs. All these people, together with the rank and file civil servants, are permanent appointees and usually not subject to removal by the minister.

In the past, all ministers designated to head departments came to their posts distrusting the bureaucracy of their respective departments. Their distrust usually was well founded, not so much because they could not remove the permanent officials, but mainly because the brief tenure of ministers created an attitude among the civil servants that any radical departures or innovations desired by an incoming minister should not be taken too seriously because his or her place would be taken soon by another person. This was true of some departments, notably foreign affairs, and particularly when the same person held the same ministerial post in several succeeding Cabinets.

Because of this distrust of the permanent officials, French ministers appoint a small group of people who enjoy their absolute confidence and who share their ideas. These people, who advise and assist the ministers and who act as intermediaries between them and the permanent staff, are known collectively as the cabinet. Sometimes they are referred to as ministerial cabinets. Each such cabinet has a chief, an assistant chief, a secretary, and several attachés. Ministers are in no way limited by civil service regulations in the choice of these people. The more important ones are usually mature and experienced, but the attachés are bright young people who have just completed their education in law or politics. The attachés work without a salary. They are anxious to make government a career and are glad to get the experience. Moreover, their positions carry prestige. Before leaving office, ministers usually find places for their cabinets in the permanent service.

Several important consequences result from this structure and its associated practices. As in the United States, but not as in Britain, French administrative departments lack a career civil servant serving as permanent secretary. Thus, coordination of internal department affairs must be accomplished by the minister's cabinet, rather than by a civil servant. This means that, contrary to what some have argued, Government crises in France were important. Some have suggested that although ministers came and went with great rapidity, this made little difference, since the civil service could keep government operating efficiently. But the lack of a permanent secretary on the British model made coordination and continuity of policy more difficult to maintain during crises and thus resulted in a less coherent or integrated output than otherwise would have been the case.

The civil service did provide an element of continuity in the unstable political situation of the Third and Fourth Republics and did have considerable impact on government policy. Civil servants always could drag their feet on any distasteful policy, hoping that the new minister, who in most cases was certain to arrive in a few months, would reverse previous decisions. Had ministries been structured as in Britain, the civil service would have been even more powerful. And the problem of securing the accountability of the policy makers to the electorate would have been increased as well.

In the Fifth Republic the political executive exerts more control over administration than it did in the Third and Fourth Republics. More stable Governments have meant greater life expectancy in office for ministers. Furthermore, in the early years of the Fifth Republic, as noted in Chapter 13, many members of the Council were chosen from the top level of the civil service. Since they were familiar with the values and modes of operation of the civil service, they were better able to communicate with bureaucrats and thus were more likely to be able to secure the compliance of their subordinates than were the politicians of the Third and Fourth Republics.

In summary, then, structural reforms have been carried out in France since the end of World War II which have helped to produce greater interdepartmental integration. Intradepartmental centralization has not proceeded as far. It has been strengthened during the Fifth Republic, but only on the basis of behavior patterns rather than by structural alteration.

The Prefectorial System

Turning now to national-local relations, we examine that aspect of French administration that has been centralized since at least the days of Napoleon and in some ways since the heyday of the Bourbon monarchs.

Below the national level, for purposes of administration, France is divided into some 95 principal areas, called departments (not to be confused with the departments or ministries of the national government). Although each department is subdivided into about 35 cantons and although in each canton there are a number of communes, the really important administrative unit is the department. Each department has a general council, which is a type of departmental assembly, although general councils do not possess powers usually associated with local government. Members of general councils are popularly elected for six-year terms, and although they receive no pay, the quality of the people who serve is high. Many of them are members of the National Assembly or the Senate. General councilors are members of the electoral colleges which elect members of the Senate. In general, it may be said that departments serve the interests of national administration rather than those of local autonomy.

All subnational units of government in France are dependent completely upon the national government for their power and existence. The national government, quite in contrast with the situation in the United States, can reorganize or abolish the subnational units at will. There are no states' rights in France. The local units of government, then, simply are one branch of a single, unified state. This is not just a matter of some subnational units of government serving as administrative agents for some national programs, as can happen in the United States. Instead, in France, there exists a direct line of administrative responsibility from the national to the local level. Embodying this responsibility at the department level is the prefect. The prefect, the chief executive officer of the department, is appointed by the national government.

Characteristic of the centralization of French public administration is the fact that one ministry, the Ministry of Interior, supervises the carrying out of all national laws throughout France. This is done through the prefect, who is appointed by the Minister of Interior and may be removed by him or her at will. Thus there is direct and centralized control of the administration of public affairs. To appreciate the far-ranging powers of the Minister of Interior, one must visualize the central control of everything from the police to the supervision of elections.

As the foregoing suggests, prefects exercise extensive powers, although usually limited by detailed instructions from the Minister of Interior. In some instances, however, they are permitted a free hand. In addition to transmitting information and implementing ministerial instructions, prefects direct all the state services within a department. In addition to directing a considerable staff, they control both subprefects and mayors. They also appoint many officials, such as schoolteachers, letter carriers, and tax collectors. Moreover, in addition to administering a department, they are expected to perform political tasks at that level.

Like other effective administrators, prefects rely more on persuasion than on dictation. They must anticipate conflicts and seek to compromise differences. While serving their national political chief, they must seek also to be impartial in local matters, show discretion, and be accessible. Extensive experience as a subprefect is essential to sound performance of the prefect's duties.

Associated with the prefect in administering the affairs of the department is the general council. Compared to the prefect's powers, those of the general council are meager. It may not make political representation to the central government and can consider only those matters referred to it by the prefect. While in some matters its decision is final, in many others it can be revoked within three months. Similarly, municipal councils cannot make final decisions on a long list of subjects without the prefect's prior approval.

In dealing with departmental political units, therefore, prefects really are masters rather than servants. If a commune does not balance its budget, the prefect can raise taxes to do so. If a commune does not provide various mandatory services which the national government requires, the prefect includes these services in the budget and raises taxes to cover them.

In France this system of controls is referred to as tutelage. This aptly describes the relation between the national and subnational levels of government. Such tight control is understandable when one recalls that the Revolution and the Republic have had to battle for acceptance for years in France. Such a centralized system of administration helps to ensure unified Republicanism throughout the country. Local control of education, for example, might have allowed too great a clerical influence in some areas. More recently, local control of the police might have raised problems of potential Communist subversion in the late 1940s in those areas where the Communists were the strongest party.

Because administration is so centralized, political party activity tends to be greatest at focal points in the administrative hierarchy, which means principally in Paris and at the department prefectures. It is interesting to note that while the newer parties, notably the Gaullists, have gained ascendancy in Paris, the older parties continue to dominate in the departmental administration.

In the early years of the Fifth Republic several steps were taken to improve the administrative system. Should these also have had the effect of breaking up the power of the older parties at the departmental level, the Gaullists hardly would have been unhappy. To facilitate cooperation among the 95 departments and, in particular, to promote the central government's plans for economic growth, the departments were grouped into 21 economic regions. For the most part these groupings conform to the historic regional areas (for example, Normandy, Burgundy, Brittany). The Government designates superprefects to act as coordinators, mainly for the regional economic programs. Moreover, the prefects have increased responsibility for management, arbitration, and coordination of economic activities in their respective departments.

To facilitate cooperation among communes and among departments, the old regulation prohibiting lateral communication—intercommunal or interdepartmental—has been modified. The prohibition was motivated initially by the desire to avoid any danger of concerted opposition to the central government. Now two or more communes can associate more easily to establish joint services or to plan and implement joint public works programs. In large population areas, urban districts that involve several communities may be created to perform necessary services that the localities may not be able to perform individually. This may be done by local initiative or by request of the central government. Also, the consolidation of small communes has been made easier.

In addition, the Government undertook a number of reforms designed to improve local administration. One of these was the creation of the Paris Area Authority, which seeks to deal more effectively with the enormous problems of this vast concentration of people, comprising one fifth of the population of France and affecting several units of administration. The Central Markets *(Les Halles)*, which were inefficient, unhygienic, and monopolistic, constituted one of the most serious problems of the Paris area. The Paris Area Authority decentralized and reorganized many of the Central Markets' operations, and subsequently moved them from the center of the city. Similarly, the acute problem of the operating deficits of the public transportation system, due in part to conflicting jurisdictions and in part to the refusal of the communities to invest in necessary modifications, has now been faced and solutions worked out.

Another effort to improve local administration was a series of measures designed to give local areas more freedom by lessening state supervision, rendering local taxation more flexible, and broadening the scope of local administration. Departmental budgets no longer need central approval if they are balanced and the interest due on loans does not exceed 10 percent of the departmental tax revenues. Similarly, financial supervision of communes with populations exceeding 9,000 has been reduced and other activities affecting even those with fewer than 9,000 are supervised less than formerly by central government.

Moreover, the local tax structure has been reformed. A number of taxes which have yielded inconsequential returns have been abolished and replaced by taxes which are more flexible and better adapted to present economic conditions. At the same time, a complete revision of land assessments has been undertaken and the local system of business turnover taxes has been modified. Moreover, the maintenance of highways within communes is now the responsibility of the communes rather than of the departments.

While some of these efforts to improve local administration are couched in terms of greater local autonomy, and in some areas more local independence will no doubt result, the basic aim is to improve a highly centralized administration and not to decentralize it. In the referendum of 1969, de Gaulle seemed to be aiming at genuine regional autonomy, but the voters rejected it, in part because it was coupled with the proposal to make the Senate an advisory body.

From what has been said in the preceding pages, it can be seen that coordination and control of administration is in the hands of the Minister of Interior and the prefects, as well as in the hands of such control bodies as the Court of Accounts and the administrative courts (discussed below). Parliament does have committees of inquiry, but these are less effective than the select committees in Britain. And insofar as Parliamentary control over the political executive is ineffective, popular accountability to the electorate is attenuated. Thus the tightening of executive control over administration as a result of increased Government stability in the Fifth Republic has not produced automatically more responsible and responsive government.

PROTECTION AGAINST MALADMINISTRATION

One way of attempting to secure administrative accountability is through a system of administrative law and courts. It must be emphasized, however, that this approach seeks to prevent or rectify abuse of administrative power or maladministration rather than to control the policy-formation aspect of administration. That is to say, it deals more with individual cases than with general matters of policy alternatives.

The French have a separate body of law, called administrative law, which determines the rights and liabilities of the servants of the state as well as the rights and liabilities of citizens in their relations with these agents of the state. The basic philosophy embodied in such a system is contrary to the notion that the "king can do no wrong." In the French view, the state is a responsible person and its administrators are agents or instruments, and hence cannot be held personally liable for wrongful acts. Consequently, special courts, called administrative courts, have been established to hear administrative law cases.

This system seems to have originated in the French Revolution and the events that preceded it. Even the *ancien régime* had been subjected to intolerable restraints by the law courts. With the coming of the Revolution, all parties were agreed that the courts would be a stumbling block to the new order, and all were determined to change things. A revolutionary law of 1790 declared that judicial functions must remain distinct from the administrative ones, while the constitution of 1791 forbade the courts from engaging in actions that would infringe upon the administrative field.

These actions were in line with Montesquieu's interpretation of the separation of powers as understood by Frenchmen—that is, the courts must not interfere with the freedom of administrative action. Theoretically, under this philosophy, the government can do anything it pleases without any fear from the ordinary courts. But, over the decades, safeguards evolved in the form of administrative courts with definite procedures and a coherent body of law to guide them. The result is a system which makes government responsible for its acts and protects the individual citizen from administrative excesses.

Administrative courts do not function like regular courts. When one feels wronged by administrative action, he or she files a petition indicating the objectionable action and specifying the remedy sought. The court then functions like an investigating committee to ascertain the facts of the matter. The petitioner does not need to hire a lawyer, since it is up to the court to be certain that all relevant points of law are brought out. After all the relevant information is gathered, the court announces its findings. Then in closed session it decides whether there is a basis for voiding the action taken by administrators in this particular case.

One advantage of this system is that costs are extremely low even if one loses a complaint. Thus, even those with little money are not prevented from seeking redress from maladministration. The administrative courts have a high reputation for fairness; many, in fact, feel that justice is more likely to be done here than in the regular court system. The administrative courts have been losing, however, one of their former advantages—that of speedy disposition of cases. Delays—as much as two years between petition and decision—are no longer uncommon, especially in important cases.

The impact of the system is limited by the fact that only administrative acts, and not other governmental actions, are subject to control by administrative courts. Actions by administrative agencies may be nullified only if the agency or administrators in question were not empowered to do what they did or sought to do, if prescribed forms of procedure were not observed, if power was abused (that is, legal acts performed for purposes not contemplated by the law), or if there was an error in the law. In short, an administrative court may not challenge the right of a law to exist, but only the way it is being implemented. In recent years, however, decisions have tended to expand the scope of review, to emphasize merit instead of merely technicalities in deciding cases. Nonetheless, the system's ability to protect civil liberties is restricted because action by judges and the police cannot be challenged in administrative courts. Arrests and searches, for example, are not under the administrative courts' jurisdiction. Because government has in recent years gone into areas where the ordinary law already applied (such as nationalization and the protection of property rights), the line of demarcation between private law and administrative law has become less clear. If government does violence to the right of property or public freedom, it may be subject to the jurisdiction of the ordinary courts. In cases of disagreement as to jurisdiction, the Court of Conflicts decides.

At the top of the administrative hierarchy is the Council of State. Its membership is approximately 180, divided into five bodies or sections. Only one of the five sections is concerned with judicial business; the other four act in a consultative capacity to the Government on administrative questions. The advice rendered does not bind, however, the judicial section in litigation that may come before it. The public prestige the Council enjoys stems from its judicial section. In all its work, despite the fact that its members are appointed and may be removed by the Cabinet (upon recommendation of the Minister of Justice), the Council seems relatively free from subservience to the executive, and some observers believe that if it has a bias it is in favor of the citizen.

There is no specified term for membership on the Council of State. It is expected that those who are appointed to it will make it a life career. The leading graduates of the National School of Administration provide the main source of appointees. In addition a small number of members can be appointed for one-year terms because of their expertise in special areas which may have come to occupy the Council's attention. As a way of protecting its interests, each ministry designates an official of high rank who participates in all meetings of the Council of State when matters of concern to the ministry are being considered.

If the administrative exercise of discretionary power is challenged, the Council of State will require the ministry concerned to state its reasons for its actions. The Council is empowered to call for documents and files relevant to the case. The Council endeavors to insure that administrative actions are reasonable, while preserving to administrators the discretion of action which properly belongs to them. The Council is the ultimate umpire to determine whether administrators exceeded the power vested in them. Despite its difficult task, the Council has struck a balance which has gained the confidence of both the administrators and the citizens. The existence of such a body empowered to redress grievances helps to make administrators act more responsibly.

Prior to 1954, the Council of State heard the majority of claims in administrative matters, although claims in minor matters were heard in prefectural councils. In that year, a radical change in jurisdiction was introduced. The prefectural councils of the Seine (Paris) and Alsace and Lorraine (Strasbourg), together with 21 interdepartmental prefectural councils, were transformed into 23 administrative tribunals. The majority of claims now are channeled to these administrative tribunals, but the Council of State still retains control, mostly through appeals, which it must hear. Also, the Council may exercise original jurisdiction in matters that affect several administrative tribunals. Similarly, the Council still acts as the court of first instance in disputes that concern the rights of civil servants.

The four nonjudicial sections of the Council of State give opinions to the Cabinet on all matters on which it seeks advice. In some areas the Cabinet is obligated to ask for advice—for example, on Cabinet measures submitted to Parliament, on its decree laws, and on all its nonlegislative decrees. Since 1945, the Council has been empowered to take the initiative in directing the Cabinet's attention to areas where it believes legislative or administrative reforms are needed. As suggested above, advisory opinions of the Council are not binding upon the Cabinet or the Council's judicial section. On the other hand, the Council's prestige is such that the Government frequently does follow its advice. Thus, the Council is regarded by many as a check upon the abuse of the decree power.

Only recently and with considerable hesitation have the French decided to create an ombudsman—called in France the *Médiateur*. One might argue that the need for such an official was less pressing in France than in Britain, given the administrative law system which we have been discussing. Nonetheless, the French now have the opportunity to seek redress from maladministration in some cases without having to go through even the quasi-judicial procedures of the administrative courts. Like Britain, France has been more cautious than Sweden in creating this new position. A French person with a complaint against an administrator cannot go directly to the *Médiateur*. Instead he or she must communicate with a member of Parliament, who will decide whether the complaint has sufficient merit to be passed on for action by the *Médiateur*.

The first *Médiateur*, Antoine Pinay, was appointed in January 1973, and so it is too early to see how successful this reform will prove to be. Pinay served both as Premier and Minister of Finance during the Fourth Republic and was the first Minister of Finance in the Fifth Republic. His success during the Fourth Republic in combating inflation made him widely respected. Since he has the confidence of so many French people, he would seem to be an ideal choice to shape the office of *Médiateur* during its formative years. The only problem is that since Pinay was 81 when appointed there is some question whether he retains sufficient vigor for the post. Whatever the result, he or his successors provide the French people with one more potential safeguard against administrative abuse.

BIBLIOGRAPHICAL NOTE

The most thorough study of French administration is the Ridley and Blondel book mentioned in the Bibliographical Note for the previous chapter. Two works by Brian Chapman, *Introduction to French Local Government* (London: Allen and Unwin, 1953), and *The Prefects and Provincial France* (London: Allen and Unwin, 1955), are penetrating studies of local government and administration in France. Other useful specialized studies are Roger Gregoire, *The French Civil Service* (Brussels: Int. Inst. Administrative Services, 1965), and Margherita Rindel, *The Administrative Functions of the French Conseil d'Etat* (London: Weidenfeld & Nicolson, 1970). A study more concerned with the politics than the structure of local government is Mark Kesselman, *The Ambiguous Consensus: A Study of Local Government in France* (New York: Alfred A. Knopf, Inc., 1967). Finally, an interesting analytical study from the point of view of organizational theory is Michel Crozier, *The Bureaucratic Phenomenon* (Chicago: University of Chicago Press, 1964). For a comparative view of the administrative law system, see Bernard Schwartz, *French Administrative Law and the Common-Law World* (New York: New York University Press, 1954).

16

Judicial Structures

The French judicial system is based on Roman law. Because of its systematic codification under Napoleon, French law is often referred to as the Napoleonic Code. In our treatment of Britain, we noted that common law is largely case law as modified by legislative enactments. Roman law, on the other hand, is primarily code law. Carefully drawn statutes enable the Roman law judge to turn to the law for every case, instead of seeking to find it in the decisions of previous cases, as is often the case in common law. Interpretation of previous cases can be used to provide some flexibility in Roman law systems, but this practice is not as essential as in common law systems. The trademark of the common law is *stare decisis* (adherence to decided cases); in other words, previous cases decide present ones. Roman law systems have in recent decades made some use of precedent, especially in France, but there is no acceptance of the principle that precedent is binding in future cases.

The constitution of the Third Republic made no reference to the judiciary or a judicial system. In practice, as already indicated in the preceding chapter, a dual system of courts developed—ordinary courts and administrative courts. Our discussion of administrative courts pointed out that any conflict of jurisdiction between the two court systems is resolved by the Court of Conflicts. This judicial system, as it evolved, received general acceptance and was virtually untouched by the constitution of the Fourth Republic. In the early years of the Fifth Republic, however, a number of changes were made. These sought: (1) to modernize a court system which originated at a time when 75 percent of the population was rural; (2) to improve rules of procedure and to clarify jurisdictions; (3) to improve the training of judges; and (4) to establish the Constitutional Council, mainly as a check on Parliament.

ORGANIZATION AND STAFFING OF THE COURTS

The independence of the judiciary is well recognized in France. Judges hold office during good behavior and are not subject to removal by the executive. Instead of recruiting judges from the legal profession, as is done in the United States and Britain, the French view the judiciary as part of the administrative hierarchy and a separate profession from the practice of law. Hence French legal graduates must choose at an early age whether they are going into the judiciary or whether they are going to practice before the courts. In France, the bench is a career.

Judges are recruited from law graduates under 27 years old who have passed a competitive examination and who then spend four years in the newly established National Center of Judicial Studies. The center is designed to do for the judiciary what the National School of Administration is supposed to do for the civil service—namely, produce a judiciary of competence and high standing. In the past, would-be magistrates were recruited in a similar way, but after their successful admission they usually learned the practical aspects of judicial business by spending a year or two in subordinate positions while awaiting appointments to judicial posts. Presumably, the Center of Judicial Studies will now prepare a person for appointment to a judicial post without his or her serving what in the past amounted to a type of apprenticeship.

Other changes in recent years have simplified judicial procedures and have altered the rules governing the classification and promotion of judges. There is now only one corps of judges for all courts, except for the Court of Cassation, which is considered outside the hierarchy. Moreover, there are only two main ranks: judges of lower courts and judges of the courts of appeal. Promotions are based on seniority and merit. Unlike the past, judges now can be promoted without having to move to a new court.

The general supervision of the judiciary is in the hands of the High Council of the Judiciary. It is presided over by the President of the Republic and the Minister of Justice. There are nine members appointed by the President for four-year terms. The Council presents names for appointments to the Court of Cassation and for first presidents of the courts of appeal. Actual appointment is by the President. The Council advises on the appointment of other judges, whose names are proposed by the Minister of Justice. The Council also acts as a disciplinary council for judges. Finally, the President must consult the Council before pardoning persons sentenced to capital punishment and may consult it in cases of petition for reprieve of sentence.

At the bottom of the court hierarchy are the minor (local) courts of first instance *(Tribunaux d'Instance)*, which replace the justices of the peace. Each of these courts may have several judges, who are required to reside in the place where the court is situated. Each case, however, is heard by a single judge, who has more power than did the justice of the peace. These courts are intended to be the most important units in the judicial system—courts that will ensure prompt and inexpensive settlement of the most common types of civil cases.

Above these courts are the major courts of first instance *(Tribunaux de Grande Instance)*. These courts have jurisdiction throughout a department, although the larger departments may have two or more of them. These courts try the more important civil cases and hear some appeals, such as those from the special technical labor and commercial courts. Each case is heard by an uneven number of judges who render a verdict by majority vote.

Criminal cases are heard by police courts or correctional courts, depending upon the seriousness of the offense. Criminal cases of the utmost seriousness, such as murder, are tried in the assize courts. These usually convene quarterly in each department. They are composed of 3 judges and 9 jurors (the only jurors used in any French court), who make up a jury of 12. Eight votes are necessary for conviction.

There are 27 courts of appeal, one for each of the existing judicial districts. They were untouched by the recent reforms except that their jurisdiction has been extended, particularly to cases arising from the field of social legislation. The decisions of the children's courts, commercial courts, farm lease courts, labor conciliation boards, and social security commissions may now be appealed to the courts of appeal.

At the top of the judicial hierarchy is the Court of Cassation. It has three sections: the criminal chamber, the civil chamber, and the chamber of requests. Each section has a president and 15 judges. Criminal appeals go directly to the criminal chamber, but civil appeals are funneled through the chamber of requests, which forwards only those appeals that it believes contain substantial grounds for reversal. Like the American highest courts, the Court of Cassation does not finally dispose of an appealed case. A reversal of a lower court decision—that is, a successful appeal— merely means that the case is sent back for retrial. In retrying the case the lower court is to act in accord with the reasoning of the higher court in sending the case back.

Finally, there is a High Court of Justice to try the President or other members of the Government for high crimes and misdemeanors. Before they can be tried, however, the National Assembly and the Senate must vote indictments, which require an absolute majority of the membership of each body.

In 1963, the Government succeeded in getting Parliament to establish a special Court for the Security of the State as a means of combating subversion. This action stemmed mainly from the various terrorist acts of civil and military elements who sought to impede de Gaulle's efforts to settle the Algerian problem. The new court is composed of civilian magistrates and high military officers. There is no jury, and appeals may be made to the Court of Cassation.

French judicial procedure is sometimes said to be characterized by the *inquisitorial* system, as opposed to the *accusatorial* system, which characterizes British and American judicial practice. The principal difference is that the inquisitorial emphasizes the rights of society and seeks a prompt repression of crime, while the accusatorial places emphasis on the rights of the accused and attempts to safeguard him or her from possible injustice.

After an arrest has been made, the examining magistrate *(juge d'instruction)* must decide if there is a prima facie case. He or she examines witnesses, including the arrested person (but in the presence of his or her lawyer), and studies other pertinent information. Neither the accused nor his or her counsel is present at the examination of witnesses, although a confrontation in court subsequently is a fairly regular practice. However, the defense counsel has access at all times to the dossier the examining magistrate is compiling. The record compiled mixes facts and rumors which may tend to incriminate the accused, and may include a survey of the accused's past. If the examining magistrate decides that there is a case, the accused is committed for trial; otherwise he or she goes free.

Under this system, despite the declaration of the Rights of Man, which asserts that a person is "considered innocent until he had been found guilty," the accused is not presumed to be innocent. If the examining magistrate decides that the accused is to be tried, he or she is, in effect, saying: "After a careful examination of witnesses, including yourself and anyone else who knows anything about the case, we believe you are guilty. But if you can explain your conduct to the satisfaction of the majority of the jury, they have the power to free you if they wish." The French are apt to observe, however, that this is not far different from what happens in Britain or the United States, except that the French are less hypocritical about it. It may be significant, however, that in the Anglo-American system the accused does not have to take the witness stand—something he or she cannot escape doing in France.

At the trial, the presiding judge does not act as an umpire of a duel between two opposing sets of lawyers. Rather, the judge conducts the trial from beginning to end. He or she has the complete dossier and is familiar with it. He or she interrogates the witnesses, beginning with the accused. The sole aim is to discover the truth. During the trial, witnesses are able to talk at length and there is no rule of evidence which excludes irrelevant eloquence on their part. Lawyers do not directly cross-examine witnesses; they only suggest questions to the judge, who propounds them. There is no summing up of a case in the British-American manner.

It is of interest that in addition to the criminal action the injured party may seek damages. This action may be taken separately, or the injured party may join the criminal prosecution, being represented by counsel. Strangely enough, it is possible for a person to be ordered to pay damages for the murder of someone whom, according to the jury, he or she was not guilty of killing.

On the whole, French courts are free from technicalities, they are trusted to do substantial justice, and the law is less likely to be tortured out of its obvious meaning than is true in the United States or Britain. Justice in France is also more accessible and cheaper. Just as France considers crime an offense against society, and therefore engages actively in the prosecution of the accused, it also provides legal aid to those who cannot afford it.

THE STATUS OF JUDICIAL REVIEW

Traditionally, France, like most other European countries, has not had the American equivalent of judicial review. Courts could not question the right of the legislature to legislate on anything it wished. This was due, perhaps, to the fact that French constitutions have been unlike the American. They did not impose specific limits on what the legislature could do; there were no prohibitions, and no powers reserved to subordinate units such as the states. The very concept of judicial review did not arouse much enthusiasm or support.

The constitution of the Fourth Republic established a Constitutional Committee to determine whether the laws passed by the National Assembly implied amendment of the constitution. The Committee could not nullify acts of the legislature, and yet the constitution gave it power to send measures back to the legislature for reconsideration if in its opinion they implied amendment of the constitution. Should Parliament persist, the law could not be promulgated until the constitution was amended in ways prescribed by the constitution itself. Since the constitution could be amended by the legislature, however, no one regarded the Constitutional Committee as a judicial hurdle to the aims and desires of the legislature.

As we indicated in Chapter 13, the constitution of the Fifth Republic departs from French tradition in seeking to specify, and thereby limit, the powers of Parliament. Since Parliament no longer is completely free to legislate as it chooses, a need for some form of judicial review arises. The question now can be raised whether Parliament has overstepped the bounds of its power. The principal mechanism for making this determination is a new Fifth Republic institution, the Constitutional Council, although the Council of State also is involved to some extent.

The basic membership of the Constitutional Council is nine people appointed for nine-year terms. Three of these are chosen by the President of the Republic, another three by the president of the National Assembly, and the final three by the president of the Senate. Former Presidents of the Republic also are members. The Council has a number of functions. For example, it is in charge of supervising elections. If the Government asks it to do so, it decides whether the President is so incapacitated that his or her powers should be exercised by the president of the Senate. But its main concern is with questions of constitutional interpretation.

As you may have concluded from Chapters 13 and 14, there easily can be some confusion under the Fifth Republic's constitution concerning the boundary line between the executive's and the legislature's policy-forming power. This is compounded by the fact that the laws of the Fourth Republic, passed under a different constitutional distribution of power, did not cease to exist simply because a new constitution went into effect. If the laws of the Fourth Republic still on the books are to be modified, who has the power to alter them now? If they are in the legislature's field, then they can be amended by a new law. But should they now be in the executive's field, they can be altered by decree. Where assignment of a law to one branch's field or the other's is in doubt, the matter is referred to the Council of State. Like other decisions of the Council of State, its opinion is only advisory, although usually followed.

The Constitutional Council is entrusted with making a similar decision in the case of laws passed since the beginning of the Fifth Republic in 1958. The Government can challenge a law by contending that the subject with which it deals falls within the executive's decree power and thus cannot be dealt with by Parliament. Should the Council agree with this contention, the Government is permitted to alter the law by decree. No provision is made for Parliament to object, however, should it feel that the executive has issued a decree in an area that seems to have been reserved to Parliament. As noted in previous chapters, the Fifth Republic tilts the power balance decisively in the executive's direction.

The Constitutional Council is not really declaring a law unconstitutional in these circumstances. Instead it simply is relieving the Government, if it agrees with it, of having to alter a disagreeable law by having new legislation passed and permitting it to make the changes itself. In another type of situation, however, the Constitutional Council can void a law as unconstitutional. The Premier, the President of the Republic, or the president of either house of Parliament can question the constitutionality of a law during the 15-day period between final passage and promulgation. If the Council agrees with the challenge, the law cannot go into effect. But if one of these four people does not raise the issue within the specified time and the law is promulgated, it remains valid regardless of whether it seems to violate the constitution. Its constitutionality cannot be challenged thereafter. These procedures were liberalized slightly in 1974 to permit 60 members of Parliament similarly to question the constitutionality of a newly passed law.

While this is a form of judicial review, it is very different from procedures in the United States. In the first place the Constitutional Council is not the final appellate court for the regular court system as is true of the American Supreme Court. Secondly, the decision in France on constitutionality is being made in abstract. In contrast with American law, there is no case or controversy involved; no effort has been made to apply the law. Thus the Constitutional Council is giving something like what is called in American law an advisory opinion. This the U.S. Supreme Court will not do. In its view one must have an actual legal conflict between opposed parties to be able to ascertain the full ramifications of a law; rights cannot be specified in the abstract. Given the Anglo-American emphasis on the case law approach, this position is understandable. Similarly, given the French preference for the Roman or code law system, it is understandable that the French feel that issues of constitutionality are best decided in the abstract when a general, rather than a specific rule, can be laid down and when the details of a particular case are not allowed to get in the way of deciding issues of basic principle. Somewhat less easy to understand is why the power to challenge a law's constitutionality should be prohibited to the average citizen. To this extent American citizens have a much stronger defense of their basic rights than do French citizens.

In practice the Constitutional Council has not proven to be the powerful institution that the U.S. Supreme Court is. In the early years of the Fifth Republic the Council tended to support the Government's effort to obtain interpretations of the constitution which would expand the executive's power at the expense of Parliament. The Council avoided a direct confrontation with the President in 1962 over the question of amendment of the constitution. As mentioned in a previous chapter, de Gaulle resorted to a referendum to change the constitution to provide for direct election of the President instead of using the procedures for amendment set forth in the constitution. When the matter was referred to the Council after the referendum, the Council held that it lacked jurisdiction. It interpreted its powers to apply only to laws passed by Parliament and not to what the people had done in a referendum. Had they decided otherwise, the result would have been a major constitutional crisis. Yet the decision also demonstrated the unwillingness of any governmental organ to attempt to thwart de Gaulle in the pursuit of his goals. To say that the Council is simply the Government's puppet, however, would not be fair. Increasingly during the 1960s the Council refused to uphold the Government's challenging of Parliamentary action. Nonetheless, it clearly is

not the potential check upon executive action that the U.S. Supreme
Court is.

BIBLIOGRAPHICAL NOTE

Discussions of French law and legal philosophy may be found in René David
and Henry DeVries, *The French Legal System: An Introduction to Civil Law
Systems* (New York: Oceana Publications, Inc., 1958), and Sir Maurice Sheldon
Amos and F. P. Walton, *Introduction to French Law*, 3d ed. (Oxford: Oxford
University Press, 1967).

Part IV

THE FEDERAL
REPUBLIC OF
GERMANY

17

The Context of German Politics

PHYSICAL SETTING

Germany's geographic position places it astride the center of the European continent. The Federal Republic of Germany (to give it its official name) lies to the east and north of France and stretches from the northern boundary of Switzerland to the North Sea and the southern boundary of Denmark. About half the size of pre–World War II Germany, the area of the Federal Republic is comparable to that of Britain, or about half the area of France.

Germany does not have well-defined geographic frontiers except perhaps for the seacoast in the north, which is interrupted by the Jutland peninsula. This is especially a problem in the east, given the delicate relations between East and West Germany. All the main rivers, except for the Weser and the Ems, either rise on foreign soil or leave Germany for other countries. Its greatest river is the Rhine, which originates in Switzerland and flows into the sea in Holland. Germany's North Sea boundary made possible the emergence of great ports, such as Bremen and Hamburg, and the development of sea trade.

Climate and topography vary considerably. In the north are the lowlands and river valleys, while much of the center is uplands, with moderate mountain ranges rising to the west and east. In the south the river valleys are low, while the mountains rise to greater heights, especially as one approaches the Alps. Rainfall is usually ample, particularly in the north, and the soil is fertile.

Germany is a rich nation, particularly in those things that are necessary to a modern industrialized society. It has been particularly well endowed in coal and iron, as well as in many industrial chemicals. Its traditional agricultural areas, however, were in the eastern part of the nation, which are now within the boundaries of Poland or the German Democratic Republic (East Germany).

One of the really important keys to the growth of Germany as a power was its rapid transformation in the latter half of the 19th century from a primarily agrarian country to a modern industrial nation. Economic growth was particularly phenomenal after unification. German coal production jumped from about 30 million metric tons in 1871 to more than 190 million tons in 1914. Similarly, from a low of a few hundred thousand tons in 1850, Germany forged ahead in iron extraction to more than 8 million tons in 1900, equaling that of Britain, and, then, more than doubling the output of Britain before World War I. By 1913, Germany had also become Britain's rival in merchant shipping. Considerable progress was made in organic chemistry and the consequent development of such products as synthetic drugs and dyes. Moreover, Germany developed a sizable electric power industry.

In the late 19th century, then, Germany jumped from a precapitalist economy to a mature capitalistic one with heavy corporate concentrations and cartels. The result has been the traditional absence in Germany of a sizable small business middle class. About three fourths of the German working population work for salaries and wages—roughly one half being workers and one fourth occupying white collar positions. About a third of the remaining 25 percent of the working force are farmers. Thus the urban self-employed number only slightly more than 14 percent of the working population.

Despite the numerical prominence of the workers, class distinctions have been sharp and significant in German politics. As in France, income distribution has been less equal than in either Britain or Scandinavia. Furthermore, educational opportunity has not been widespread. Thus it has been difficult for people from a working class background to rise to a new status or more prestigious occupation. These factors have produced some class conflict and bitterness.

Germany's rapid industrial and commercial expansion was facilitated by a banking system purposely designed to promote economic growth. This enabled the country to build an economic empire that extended far beyond its borders. Large enterprises evolved into cartels (monopolies), which were successful in fixing prices, regulating markets, and avoiding competition at home and abroad. The name I. G. Farben came to symbolize this economic giant, which was to become a tool of the state in two world wars.

Germany's position as the industrial leader of Europe was not greatly affected by World War I. This was because the war did not damage Germany physically, since the fighting did not take place on German soil.

World War II inflicted heavy damage and destruction, but, paradoxically, Germany made a more rapid and a substantially sounder recovery than after World War I. To some extent, this recovery was accelerated by American aid, but the Germans deserve the primary credit. Some have argued, also, that German recovery could not have been nearly so rapid if it had not been for the giant stream of refugees and expellees from the east, who represented almost insuperable problems in the immediate postwar years but whose human energy contributed greatly to the extent and speed of economic reconstruction.

The widespread destruction of World War II proved ultimately to be something of an asset; it forced the adoption of new productive techniques and equipment. These in turn helped to reduce the unit cost of production. Thus, while Britain was continuing to produce with increasingly obsolete machinery, German industry of necessity was introducing more efficient methods. Furthermore, during the early years of German recovery the fact that German military expenditures were severely limited by the Allies meant that scarce capital was not drained off in that direction and thus could be devoted to industrial recovery. Nor did Germany spend money on aid to underdeveloped countries to the extent that Britain and France, for example, did.

In any event, the recovery was phenomenal. By 1953, Germany had achieved an industrial output that was 59 percent larger than in 1936. By 1956, its gold and dollar reserves were larger than Britain's. Its exports quadrupled between 1952 and 1961, in part because of the heavy investment in the production of goods for export. In many areas, Germany's share of the export market exceeded that of Britain or the United States. Twenty percent of the world's manufactured exports come from German shops and factories. By 1965, Germany was producing every 12th ton of steel and every 14th ton of coal of the world's output. Germany's total national income surpassed that of France in 1960. And its GNP rose to third largest in the world until Japan overtook it in 1968.

Just as it is for Britain, foreign trade remains crucial for Germany. The country is not able to produce enough food to feed its population, especially now that its traditional agricultural areas lie in East Germany. Farm output has increased at a steady rate, but more slowly than has industrial growth. Thus trade remains essential.

With a population of around 62 million, Germany is about 20 percent larger than France. Prior to World War II the portion of Germany which now is the Federal Republic had a population of less than 40 million. The increase is accounted for largely by the 10 million refugees and expellees who have come from the Soviet zone and from areas taken over by other Communist-controlled governments. The population density in the Federal Republic exceeds that of the United Kingdom (646 per square mile compared to 594) but is far less dense than in England alone.

Most of the refugees were similar to the rest of the population in being of a Germanic background. But they clearly differed in feeling dispossessed and disaffected. Nonetheless, these refugees and expellees have, for the most part, been integrated, and most of them regard the Federal Republic as their home (they do not even use the term "new home"). This integration was facilitated by a number of government measures, only some of which were of an economic nature. One economic measure was the law on the "equalization of the burden," passed in 1952 and designed to help others in addition to the refugees. Under this law, all able people were to contribute half of what they possessed for redistribution and equalization. Certain public organizations, such as the central banks and religious and charitable institutions, were exempt. The tax base of the lean year 1948–49 was used to determine a person's worth, and individuals and companies were given the opportunity of spreading their payments over 30 years. Out of the fund thus created, the refugees, as well as other Germans who had suffered war damages or who were wiped out by the currency reform, were assisted (according to a complex formula) through grants or loans for housing, furniture, and pension payments.

Despite the successful integration of the refugees into the rest of the population, Germany remains a country of considerable ethnic diversity. A related factor is the relatively late unification of Germany as a single nation. This permitted the growth of differing customs and dialects in the area now covered by Germany.

The German Federal Republic is divided almost equally along religious lines, the Protestants having a slight majority over the Roman Catholics. Prior to World War II Protestants had outnumbered Catholics two to one. The balance was shifted because the areas now under Communist control were overwhelmingly Protestant. The influx of refugees has resulted in the establishment of large Protestant communities in former Catholic areas, such as Bavaria.

As one would expect, these several diversities are reflected in Germany's politics. We will see examples of this in subsequent chapters in examining the party system and the federal system.

HISTORICAL BACKGROUND

Germany is a prosperous, well-educated, Western nation—all characteristics that various studies have found to be associated with democratic political systems. Yet some lingering doubt remains whether democracy is established firmly in Germany. The problem is not like that of France, where other political traditions challenge the democratic tradition. Instead it is the lack in Germany of any democratic tradition at all. Since the formation of the present political system in 1949, Germany has experienced almost twice as many years of parliamentary democracy as in the whole of its previous history.

During the period when Britain and France were strong nations, the area of Germany was occupied by a group of weak and divided states. There had once been the Holy Roman Empire (German), but from the 13th century to the Napoleonic era there was no Germany in a political sense. The Reformation and the religious wars of the 16th century had split the Protestant north and the Catholic south. The Thirty Years' War of the 17th century left much devastation and a greatly reduced population. As a consequence, after the Peace of Westphalia (1648) separate states grew apace. In 1800 there were 314 different states, some large, but most of them small.

Napoleon, more than any other person, was responsible for smashing this conglomeration of small states, which was to lead to their ultimate unification. The struggle as to who should unify Germany was, in the end, between Austria and Prussia. Prussia had been rising in power. Its rulers built up the country's strength by a combination of ruthless military power and the modernization of the economy. Frederick the Great (1740–86) raised Prussia from a weak principality to one of the strongest military states in Europe. But the real regeneration of Prussia came after its disastrous defeat by Napoleon in 1806. Military conscription was introduced, certain feudal institutions were swept away, and the bureaucracy was modernized.

Under the impact of revolutionary France and the consequent developments in the Germanies themselves, the number of German states was sharply reduced. After Napoleon's fall from power, consolidation of the German states continued. At the Congress of Vienna (1815), the German Confederation, a loose combination of 38 states, was established. The most influential of the German states were Austria and Prussia, with Austria predominating. In the end, however, it was Prussia that was to unify Germany.

This fact was immensely significant for Germany's political development, for Prussia was not a liberal monarchy, but a militaristic society. There was nothing remotely democratic about the political system. The democratic revolution of 1848 was repressed, which drove many of the democratic middle class to migrate, especially to the United States. Unlike the situation in Britain, there was no hope that the political system could be liberalized from within. Thus, political leadership among the middle class, those who in many countries played a key role in the movement toward democracy, was greatly weakened. Yet certain virtues must be conceded to the Prussian system. The rulers did not live in the luxury of the French Bourbons, but preferred a rather austere or Spartan existence. Administration was scrupulously honest; there was not a hint of corruption. And the system's legal codes were adhered to rigidly, which meant that arbitrary governmental action was extremely rare. Thus, for all its lack of democracy the system was attractive to many.

The person who capped the unification efforts, and who, in a real sense, was the unifier of Germany, was Otto von Bismarck (1815–98). At the age of 47, he was made minister-president of Prussia. He was to guide the nation's destinies, and to a large extent Europe's destiny as well, for three decades. From the outset, he made it clear that he was no democrat. His method would be force, "blood and iron." In two quick wars, against Denmark in 1864 and against Austria in 1866, he established Prussia's dominance, after which he set up the North German Confederation (1867), a union of 22 states and principalities. The unification was made complete after the rapid defeat of France in 1870 and the subsequent ceding to Germany of Alsace and a part of Lorraine. In January 1871, the North German Confederation was abolished and a German empire, consisting of Prussia and the North and South German states, was proclaimed. By "blood and iron" Germany had been unified.

The unified Germany was called the Empire or the Second Reich (the Holy Roman Empire being considered the first one). The Empire lasted half again as long as any German political system since then has. (See Figure 17–1). Although the Empire supposedly was organized as a federal union of 25 states, one of these, Prussia, held a predominant position in the federation, being able to veto any amendment of the constitution. Moreover, although powers not delegated to the central government were in theory retained by the states, more and more powers were transferred to the central authorities. State authorities were also made less meaningful by the fact that the central government made almost exclusive use of local administration for the implementation of imperial legislation, although

FIGURE 17–1
German Regimes Since Unification, 1871–1978

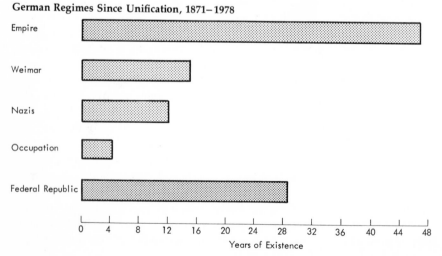

scholars differ on this point. The principal civil servants of the nation were in and around the capital, Berlin.

Bismarck did more than unify the nation. For the next 20 years (1871–90), he manipulated and guided the social forces in the Empire and made Imperial Germany a power among the nations of Europe. In domestic policy, he is best known for his actions against, first, the Catholic Church and, then, the Social Democrats. The first, known as the *Kulturkampf* ("fight for civilization"), was not so much an antireligious campaign as it was an effort to undermine the moral and intellectual authority of the Church. Bismarck's memory of his conflicts with Catholic France and Catholic Austria were still fresh, and he suspected the political loyalties of German Catholics in a possible war of revenge. His actions against priests, nuns, and monks, and his expulsion of the Jesuits, together with the confiscation of Catholic Church property, no doubt contributed significantly to the formation of the Catholic Center party. But when this party became reconciled to the German Empire in its existing form and when its political demands turned out to be exceedingly moderate, Bismarck readily repealed the anti-Catholic laws. More than that, he sought to enlist the Catholics in what he had come to regard as a more important struggle—his campaign against the Social Democrats.

Bismarck apparently feared that the Paris Commune of 1871 could be repeated in Germany. He seemingly did not seek or desire the cooperation of the workers. His laws against the Socialist press and Socialist associations also hurt the liberals. But the Social Democrats continued to take part in electoral campaigns and to increase their strength, suggesting that the anti-Socialist laws were merely a propaganda move, or were ineffective, or both. Whether Bismarck would have pursued more repressive measures is a matter for conjecture, for he was dismissed by the new monarch (William II) in 1890, the year that the Social Democratic vote jumped from 0.75 million to 1.5 million.

Bismarck wanted a strong and united Germany. He believed that this could best be achieved by a certain balance of social forces, notably through a compromise between the middle class, too weak to achieve power on its own, and the military aristocracy of Prussia. The king of Prussia and the military aristocracy were all-powerful politically, and Bismarck did not really change this. In the light of the existing international situation, he did not believe that he could weaken the military. And he did not think that the weak middle class could manage the domestic political disagreements in a defenseless Germany. At the same time, it would have been difficult, perhaps impossible, to extract concessions from the military or to expect the king to renounce important powers.

Bismarck introduced a program of state welfare that was very extensive for that time and got certain concessions for the middle class, such as the appointment of liberals to important administrative posts and to certain posts in the Prussian Cabinet. At the same time, he tried to show the members of the Prussian aristocracy that they must learn to live with liberal ministers and must reconcile themselves to the growing wealth and power of the cities. Similarly, he attempted to induce the middle class to accept the modest concessions simply because the international situation did not permit a significant weakening of the military or of the Emperor. The result was a type of unstable equilibrium which was to collapse after the departure of Bismarck in 1890.

In the remaining years of the Empire (after 1890), real power was in the hands of William II. Prior to Germany's entrance in World War I, he had several Chancellors, and neither he nor they sought to make meaningful concessions to the middle class or to come to terms with the working class. The workers, it might be added parenthetically, increased their voting strength during his reign from 1.5 to 4.25 million ballots cast for the Social Democratic party. There was no real move to establish parliamentary government. On occasion, certain political groups were consulted before the introduction of measures in the Reichstag, but the Reichstag was never taken into confidence on really important matters, and it apparently did not dare to challenge the authority of the Emperor. It is true that the Reichstag did condemn the Government in the handling of certain affairs, but the outbreak of the war prevented any meaningful developments therefrom.

In view of the past failures to achieve parliamentary government in Germany, it seems ironic that it was handed to the Reichstag by General Ludendorff without a struggle in October 1918, when he admitted that the war was lost. With the appointment of Prince Max of Baden as Chancellor (prime minister), parliamentary government was established in Germany. The Imperial constitution was revised quickly to provide that the Imperial Chancellor must possess the confidence of the Reichstag in order to remain in office, and that he was responsible for all political acts of the Emperor. By the end of October, Germany was a constitutional monarchy, but this escaped general notice. With the end of World War I, the political system of the Empire also came to an end, and Germany embarked on its first real experiment in democracy.

In January 1919, the Germans elected a constituent assembly, which met the following month in the city of Weimar. It immediately set about drafting a new constitution for the nation. The delegates approached their work systematically; among them were some of the best constitutional experts in Germany. They knew that they wanted to provide for a democratic form of government. Consequently, they gave serious thought to the parliamentary system, the Swiss type, and the American presidential form (the last mainly because of the influence of Max Weber). Ultimately, they decided on the parliamentary system.

Germany was organized on a federal basis, with 17 states (Länder).

Remembering Prussia's dominance of the previous federation, the framers made sure that its position would be weak in the new organization. The central government, however, was vested with strong authority, considerably stronger than that of the American national government at the time. Moreover, its powers could be augmented by amendment, which could be brought into force by a two-thirds vote in each of the two houses of Parliament. In this way, even the boundaries of the member states could be altered, even against their wishes.

Unfortunately, democratic parliamentary government lasted little more than a decade. Like the Third Republic in France, the Weimar Republic experienced considerable cabinet instability. In 14 years there were 20 different Cabinets, which made difficult effective government action to deal with the problems facing Germany. Thus, to many Germans the government looked rather weak and indecisive compared with what they had been used to under the Empire. And at the time of the Weimar Republic weak government was a particular liability.

The old order seemed to be crumbling in Germany. In a country where the family traditionally had been a very hierarchical, even authoritarian structure, children no longer respected their parents. The father's generation was seen as having brought defeat in the war. Furthermore, with the economic collapse of 1929 many fathers were unable to support their families. By 1932 almost one third of the working force was unemployed. Another pillar of the old order—the monetary system—was falling apart. After World War I the mark finally stabilized at a rate of 4.2 trillion to the dollar. This wiped out pensions and savings and hit hardest at the middle class—the segment of the population often regarded as the foundation of a democratic political system. In 1929 economic collapse made it appear to Germans that they would have to experience this financial chaos yet once again. Anyone who has collected German postage stamps of the Weimar period is familiar with this financial turmoil. Stamps constantly were being surcharged—reissued with new higher values printed over them—as the value of the mark plummeted.

Thus, to many Germans life came to appear meaningless, to be without order. Sociologists term this mental state anomie. And they suggest that the behavior typically associated with anomie is to seek a saviour. One searches for someone who can eliminate the aimlessness of existence by stating rules and guides for life authoritatively. No democratic politician or structure was able to satisfy this felt need.

Into this vacuum stepped the perfect charismatic leader—Adolf Hitler, who spoke as one having authority. Hitler told the Germans exactly what they wished to hear at that point: that it was not their fault that they had lost the war, for the democrats, particularly the Jews, had betrayed the army. He denounced the Treaty of Versailles, hated by all Germans for the harsh terms it imposed on Germany in ending World War I, and promised that he would make Germany strong enough to ignore its terms. Germans were a superior people, he proclaimed, and must be restored to their former greatness. He used the business interests' fears of Communism and their hostility to the trade unions to get financial support from the pillars of society. Thus he was able to create a political organization and make an electoral appeal equal, if not superior, to that of the other parties.

In general, the Weimar Republic never succeeded in creating a political consensus. The country was torn ideologically between the far right and the far left, which represented sizable elements of the population that did not believe in a democratic order. The country was also torn economically and politically; to many, Weimar became synonymous with poverty, national humiliation, and fruitless debate in the Reichstag. The climate of fear and frustration which Hitler sought to dramatize and exacerbate was, in the end, to help him get to power. But before the existing discontents could be shaped into a political force, it was necessary to have a leader and an efficient organization. These Hitler and the Nazis provided.

Given the rising tide of nationalism in Germany in reaction to the harshness of the peace treaty and the general dissatisfaction on economic and other matters, it is not surprising that by 1930 about one third of the electorate was voting for extremist parties. And then in 1932 Hitler's Nazi party polled 14 million votes, leading all other parties and winning almost 40 percent of the seats in the legislature. Originally attracting demobilized soldiers who could not adjust to civilian life, the party soon had gathered a motley crew of social misfits, cranks, political adventurers, criminals, and some idealists. By 1930, it drew strong support from the lower middle classes, from the youth, and from the militarists. It also received the support of significant financial and business circles. Organized along military lines, the Nazi party stirred up delirious demonstrations and carried violence into the streets and into the gatherings of the other parties. In the midst of the chaos, President Hindenburg asked Hitler to form a Cabinet of "national concentration" in which the Nazis and the Nationalists were to share power. Although initially keeping only three Cabinet posts for themselves, the Nazis made sure that they were the key ones, which gave them control from the beginning.

Hitler's entry into the Government was completely legal. When he was called in January 1933 to form a government, the only possible majority in the Parliament included his Nazi party. The only alternative to Hitler would have been for some one to rule without regard to Parliament. Since the army feared that this step might produce civil war, the governmental officials decided to call Hitler. Thus, ironically, Hitler came to power as part of an attempt to avoid civil war and illegality.

In March 1933 new elections were held in which the Nazis curbed their opponents' use of radio, press, and assembly and looted and destroyed the offices and organizations of other parties. In the end they and their allies, the Nationalists, won over half of the seats in the legislature. On March 24, 1933, in an atmosphere of indescribable frenzy, coercion, and terror, an Enabling Act was passed which became the "constitution" of Nazi totalitarianism in a system called the Third Reich. This title recalled the international prowess of Germany under the Empire and the grandeur of the Holy Roman Empire. The consolidation of the dictatorship was rapid. A secret police organization rooted out opponents, real or imagined. Other political parties were abolished and suspect newspapers shut down. Concentration camps were established and new recruits brought in continually. Controls on business and labor were soon invoked to preserve the totalitarian pattern. When President Hindenburg died in 1934, Hitler conveniently merged the two offices, making himself the unquestioned ruler of Germany.

The domestic record of the dictatorship—from the harnessing of German industrial might to the military and the development of an aggressive foreign policy, to the horrors of the gas chambers and mass exterminations—is a matter of historical record. The ruthlessness of the Nazi leaders, the techniques of Nazi party control of the masses, the launching of World War II, and, finally, the end of the dictatorship are also a matter of record, but not really within the scope of this book.

After its defeat in World War II, Germany was, by prearrangement, divided into four occupation zones—one each for the major allied powers which had fought against her. Berlin, located inside the Soviet zone, was similarly divided into four sectors. Although designed as temporary transition measures, the occupation zones took on an air of permanence once it became clear that the Soviet Union was interested in the reconstruction and unification of the country only on its own terms. Thereupon, the three Western powers decided to permit the unification of their three zones, in order that the Germans could begin governing themselves. To this end, the Germans drafted a constitution (technically the Basic Law) with the advice and assistance of Allied experts. On May 23, 1949, it went into effect and the Germans began their second experiment in self-government. Although the Basic Law provides that it will cease to exist as soon as Germany is reunited and a new constitution drafted, it appears to have achieved a type of permanence.

The Federal Republic created by the Basic Law has lasted for over a quarter of a century; soon it will be twice as old as the total life span of the Weimar Republic. The great prosperity of Germany, the stability of Cabinets under the Basic Law, and the decline of ideology in politics (to be discussed in the chapter dealing with political parties) all make it clear that "Bonn is not Weimar." A tradition of democratic parliamentary government is developing in Germany, and it is only the past history of the country that makes one hesitate to affirm that democracy is firmly established there.

BIBLIOGRAPHICAL NOTE

Studies useful as introductions to Germany are: Michael Balfour, *West Germany* (New York: Frederick A. Praeger, Inc., 1968); Ralf Dahrendorf, *Society and Democracy in Germany* (Garden City, N.Y.: Doubleday, 1967); and Robert E. Dickinson, *Germany, A General and Regional Geography* (New York: E. P. Dutton, 1953).

A standard history is Marshall Dill, *Germany: A Modern History* (Ann Arbor: University of Michigan Press, 1961). More specialized studies of particular periods include John Conway, ed., *The Path to Dictatorship 1918–1933: Ten Essays by German Scholars* (Garden City, N.Y.: Doubleday, 1966); Franz L. Neumann, *Behemoth, The Structure and Practice of National Socialism 1933–1944*, 2d ed. (New York: Oxford University Press, 1944); Alan Bullock, *Hitler: A Study in Tyranny*, rev. ed. (New York: Harper & Row, 1970); Peter Merkl, *The Origin of the West German Republic* (New York: Oxford University Press, 1963); Richard Hiscocks, *The Adenauer Era* (Philadelphia: Lippincott, 1966); and Alfred Grosser, *Germany in Our Time: A Political History of the Postwar Years* (New York: Frederick A. Praeger, Inc., 1971).

18

The Foundations of
German Politics

CONSTITUTIONAL HERITAGE

Since the constitution of the Empire remains the longest-lived of all constitutions of modern Germany, any discussion of German constitutional traditions must consider it in some detail. The system could claim some elements of democracy. In addition to extensive social legislation like old age pensions and national health insurance, it enfranchised all men 25 or older. Britain, long considered a model democracy, did not make the right to vote this extensive until 1918, nearly a half century later. Yet the Empire was not a parliamentary democracy because the powers of the legislature (Reichstag) were so insignificant that it was unable to develop into a genuine instrument of the popular will and served mainly as a debating society. The center of political gravity was the Bundesrat, whose members were controlled by the separate states. Since Prussia had 17 votes out of a total of 48 (no other state had more than 6), it needs to be reemphasized that the King of Prussia exercised firm, if indirect, control. The power of Prussia was further enhanced by virtue of the fact that the Prime Minister of Prussia was also the German Chancellor.

The executive power was wielded by the Emperor and by the Chancellor (Prime Minister). The monarch occupied a dual position as King of Prussia and German Emperor. Although he could not veto laws passed by the legislature, they were rarely passed except on the initiative of the Chancellor, whom the Emperor could appoint and dismiss. Bismarck, for many years kingpin of the whole system as Chancellor, never really formed an Imperial Cabinet but governed Germany from his position as Prime Minister of Prussia. Prussia, or more appropriately, the Emperor and his Chancellor, ruled Germany.

The position of the Chancellor vis-à-vis the legislature was strong, for the Parliament could not compel him to resign. Other ministers, chosen from members of the high bureaucracy rather than from Parliamentarians or party leaders, were only assistants to the Chancellor and personally responsible to him. Because the Reichstag was more openly critical of certain governmental policies in the post-Bismarck period, and because it insisted on more budgetary powers, Bismarck's successors thought it desirable to make political bargains to get their budgets adopted, while at the same time not acknowledging responsibility to the Reichstag.

Since World War I supposedly had been fought to make the world safe for democracy, the victors decided that Germany must have a democratic constitution and war hysteria against the German Emperor meant that the system would have to be a republic. The constitution for the Weimar Republic was regarded as a very progressive document for its time. The legislature was made up of two houses, the Reichstag, which was elected by universal, equal, direct, and secret suffrage, and the Reichsrat, whose members were appointed by the governments of the member states. While the Reichsrat possessed legislative powers, it had in fact only a qualified veto, for its actions could be nullified by a two-thirds vote in the lower house. Thus the popularly elected house in fact had the bulk of legislative power.

Even the public at large was given a role in the legislative process. Deadlocks between the two houses were to be resolved by referendum. Furthermore, legislation could be launched by popular initiative, a novel procedure which had been pioneered at the state level in the Western United States by the Progressive movement. This was thought to make the greatest possible provision for popular participation in the governmental process. Furthermore, the electoral system was felt to be quite democratic and just. It was a form of proportional representation in which the number of seats in the legislature was not predetermined. A party would receive one seat for every 60,000 votes it gained. Thus all interests and opinions would be represented in the legislative process.

A new office of President was created, which would be filled by popular election. The President was not just a figurehead like the British monarch or the President of France in the Third Republic. Instead, he wielded real power, being able, among other things, to dissolve the Reichstag and dismiss the Cabinet. The office of Chancellor was retained. Despite the legislature's delegating considerable authority to the executive in the postwar crisis years (1919–23) and during the years of economic depression (1930–33), the Chancellor's position never was very strong. In part this was because as in Third Republic France there was no majority party in Parliament. All Cabinets were coalitions, usually short-lived, representing varying political views. This circumstance also afforded the President greater flexibility in the choice of a Chancellor.

Perhaps the President's most important single power was contained in Article 48. This provision had been intended to provide the government with extraordinary powers to defend itself in a constitutional crisis. When the President felt that such a situation had arisen he could permit the Cabinet to do whatever was necessary to restore order. This sounds rather similar to Article 16 of the present French constitution. Unlike the French situation, however, the Germans did attempt to include some safeguards on these emergency powers. The grant of power to the Cabinet was to lapse as soon as the emergency was over. All actions taken under this power had to be submitted to Parliament and it could void them. Furthermore, the constitution was not to be infringed. The importance of this limitation was compromised, however, by the fact that some basic rights—for example, free speech, free assembly, and the right to habeas corpus—could be suspended under the emergency powers.

Some observers have blamed Article 48 for the downfall of the Weimar Republic. By 1930, ten parties were able to gain over a million votes each and the electoral system insured that each received substantial representation in Parliament. As a result it became impossible to construct a majority coalition. The inability of the Government to get its budget passed was declared an emergency within the terms of Article 48. And from 1930 on, this provision was used to make up for the lack of a Parliamentary majority. Government in Germany came to be largely rule by decree, so that Hitler's initial actions did not seem so different from those already being engaged in under a democratic system.

Regardless of whether Article 48 and proportional representation contributed materially to the collapse of democracy in Germany in the 1930s, both the Western Allies and the Germans themselves were very conscious of such elements in Germany's previous constitutional history. Thus, when it came time after World War II to draw up a new constitution which was to seek once again to bring democracy to Germany, deliberate efforts were made to rectify the supposed shortcomings and loopholes of the Weimar constitution. The drafters of the Basic Law sought to make the position of Chancellor more secure, for example, with the result that he or she now occupies a strong position vis-à-vis the legislature. And a complicated form of proportional representation was devised in an effort to retain the element of electoral justice, while avoiding the supposed defects of proportional representation. The details of these and other such provisions will be examined more fully in subsequent chapters. The point here simply is that the present German constitution is influenced very much by the German past.

In addition to the provisions already mentioned, the constitution organizes the country along federal lines. The central government is given the exclusive right to legislate in such fields as foreign affairs, citizenship, currency and coinage, railways, posts and telecommunications, and copyrights. It is supposed to have concurrent power with the Länder (the states) in civil and criminal law, laws relating to the economy, labor, agriculture, public welfare, ocean and coastal shipping, and in "the prevention of the abuse of economic power" (antitrust actions). In other areas, notably education and cultural affairs, the Länder are supposed to exercise primary responsibility. In case of conflict between laws of the central government and those of the states, the national laws are to prevail. And the central government is vested with sufficient authority to force states to fulfill their duties as prescribed by the Basic Law.

In at least two areas—taxation and education—the trend has been toward strengthening the powers of the central government. In the matter of taxes, the states (especially the richer ones) wanted as much independence as possible, while the central government desired to equalize the distribution of major tax revenues between the rich and poor states. After much opposition and delay, the central government in 1969 finally won. The Basic Law was amended so as to give the national government increased powers in the finance field and authority that would ease the redistribution of tax revenues among the states. At the same time, amendments were adopted which gave the central government increased responsibilities in the area of educational planning. The purpose was to improve education, as well as to introduce a degree of uniformity, so that citizens moving from one state to another would not be handicapped by the hitherto existing differences in educational requirements.

The Basic Law may be amended by a two-thirds vote of the members of each house of Parliament. Some provisions, however, are unamendable. These include those portions of the Basic Law which affect the organization of the Republic into Länder, as well as those sections which provide the basic form of democratic organization, including the protection of fundamental civil liberties.

Under American influence, the Basic Law sets up a Federal Constitutional Court, with powers to annul acts of the legislature or the administration if they violate the Basic Law. The Court is also authorized to forbid unconstitutional parties if such action is recommended by the Cabinet. On the basis of such requests, it banned a neo-Nazi party in 1952 and the Communist party in 1956.

The most significant amendment to the Basic Law thus far came two decades after the start of the present system and dealt with the touchy and hitherto unresolved question of emergency powers. This amendment, consisting of 17 articles, is commonly called the emergency constitution. Ten years of discussion and debate preceded its adoption. Because the emergency powers of the Weimar constitution had been used to bypass Parliament and ultimately to destroy democracy, the Germans were wary of any emergency powers. Yet they realized that a need might arise for them. Consequently, the major concern in drafting the amendment was the protection and survival of the democratic order in times of crisis.

The existence of any emergency must be recognized by the Bundestag (lower house) with the approval of the Bundesrat (upper house). In both cases a two-thirds vote is required and in the Bundestag this two thirds must include at least a majority of its total members.

In the event that insuperable obstacles prevent the Bundestag from meeting, or if the situation demands immediate action, an emergency parliament, called a Joint Committee, will act. The Joint Committee, by a two-thirds vote consisting of at least a majority of its members, decides if the conditions are such that it should act. The Joint Committee is made up of 33 members, two thirds of whom are Bundestag deputies and one third Bundesrat members (one from each of the states). The 22 members from the Bundestag are selected so as to represent the political parties in proportion to their Parliamentary strength, but members of the Cabinet may not be included.

The emergency constitution specifies in considerable detail various procedural and substantive safeguards. Among other things, the dissolution of the Bundestag during a period of emergency is forbidden. The Constitutional Court cannot be tampered with. Moreover, the Bundestag, with the approval of the Bundesrat, can repeal laws of the Joint Committee and can declare an emergency at an end at any time.[1]

POLITICAL CULTURE

German political life until the end of World War I was characterized by autocracy. The lack of progress in the adoption of democratic institutions was in sharp contrast with the rapid strides Germany was making in the material realm (rapid industrialization, and so forth). It also contrasted sharply with the liberal political developments that were taking place in other Western European countries.

In 1848 the revolutionary tide swept across Europe, leaving many monarchs shaking in their boots. This was true also in Germany. Yet even more than in other European countries, efforts to secure reform were abortive.

As one historian has observed,

> 1848 was, indeed, a tragic year in German history. On the surface, it seemed that the streams of rationalism—liberalism, democracy, social contract, egalitarianism, tolerance, constitutionalism—were converging in a common stream at last in the Germanies . . . German intellectuals suddenly found themselves the spokesmen for their people at a critical moment in their

---

[1] For a text of the amendments to the Basic Law and statements by Kurt Kiesinger and Willy Brandt, see "Special Report," *Inter Nationes* (Bad Godesberg, 1968). The amendments were approved in the Bundestag by a vote of 384 to 100, and unanimously in the Bundesrat.

history. . . . [They] sought unity through persuasion, progress through moderation, and a better world through the practice of tolerance and good-will. They failed.[2]

In the years after 1848, German political developments continued along the authoritarian path, especially after Bismarck came to office in 1862. However, some gains for popular democracy were registered in that Bismarck, avowedly no democrat, was forced to accept some of its trappings, such as a moderately free press, political parties, elections, and a legislature. Although Bismarck openly denounced parliamentarism, and although the legislature was, in the main, powerless, the German people were learning some of the rudiments of the democratic process. But the struggle against liberalism in all its forms continued, with no prospect for the realization of a responsible form of government.

Since Bismarck opposed the establishment of parliamentary govern-ment, the net effect of his policies was to strengthen the forces of Prussian conservatism. At the same time, these policies were to result in an inten-sification of the internal political struggle. Under Bismarck the Reichstag was, on the whole, powerless. It could refuse to pass the budget, but such actions could be and were circumvented. The Reichstag could debate, but it had no influence on military or foreign policy. In short, the authority of the Emperor was not limited during Bismarck's long tenure as Chancellor.

The position of parliamentary democracy was subverted in yet another way. Parliament had contributed nothing to German unity; in fact, it had seemed to stand in the way by seeking to hamper the strengthening of the Prussian army. It was Prussian conquest that had unified Germany. The apparent lesson was that might makes right. In German politics personal morality came to be divorced from reasons of state. That is to say that behavior such as duplicity and ruthlessness, which would not have been contenanced by political leaders in their social relations with others was utilized by these same leaders in their political and governmental actions. Success was the only criterion for judging political actions. Power politics was the order of the day. And this approach would yield its greatest dividends when supported by a military spirit which valued order, author-ity, and unquestioning obedience to one's superiors.

Yet all this is not to say that the German political tradition is one of arbitrary government. For another fundamental German value is legalism. There is a firm conviction in Germany that order requires an all-encompassing set of rules. These rules are not to be the product of exten-sive popular discussion, but are to be the result of detailed study by experts. And since these rules are formulated by those who have the knowledge and training necessary for this task, naturally the rules should

---

[2] Louis L. Snyder, *Basic History of Modern Germany* (New York: D. Van Nostrand Co., Inc., 1957), p. 38.

be followed. Thus the good citizen does not seek to participate in the process of making the rules but wants only to be told what the rules are so that he or she can observe them.[3]

Thus it was that the democratic political process had little prestige or attraction for most Germans. The ideal rather was the hierarchical, orderly system of the Empire. Bureaucrats were seen as the true superiors of society, in part because of their education and honesty, in part because the government bureaucracy historically had been staffed in Germany by the nobility. As late as 1951 almost a majority—45 percent—of those polled in Germany said that the time of the Empire was the best period in recent German history.

Germany, as we have seen then, entered the third decade of the 20th century with a political legacy that did not augur well for the orderly establishment of a democratic form of government. The war had destroyed the autocratic system and ushered in Germany's first real experiment in democracy. The Weimar Republic, however, was not created because Germans suddenly had changed their political values, but because the victors insisted that Germany must be a democratic republic. And Weimar hardly was sufficiently long-lived or satisfying enough to be a very effective means of developing support for democratic values. Within little more than a decade, Germany reverted under Hitler to a political pattern even more thoroughly authoritarian than that of the Empire.

Nazism was more than just exaggerated nationalism or anti-Semitism or a reaction to defeat and to Weimar. These were a part of the picture, to be sure, but only a part of it. Some of the ideas on which the Nazi movement was built went back at least 100 years. They depicted a past golden age when the German people (the mystical *Volk*) lived in harmony and happiness, partly because they were superior to other people and partly because they were close to the soil. The Industrial Revolution and its consequences—big cities, modern ways, and those who had brought this about (Jews)—uprooted the *Volk* and corrupted many of them. The doctrines associated with this point of view were formulated and propagated by several generations of teachers and students.

In promising Germany a new glory and telling Germans that they were a superior people, Hitler was arguing that Germany had a destiny, a *Kultur* mission. *Kultur* could be advanced, he proclaimed, only by superior races subjugating inferior ones. Much of this was not new, for German thinkers long had talked of the importance of a *Kulturstaat*. In their view democracies were concerned with mediocrity, not greatness. Emphasizing popular participation and politics was dealing with the trivial; philosophy, *Kultur*—these were the truly profound matters. *Kultur* was not the same as

---

[3] See the discussion in Gabriel Almond and Sidney Verba, *The Civic Culture* (Boston: Little, Brown and Co., 1965), pp. 126–35, 321–23.

civilization; it did not involve the sophistication of degenerate French society. Instead it expressed primitive, pure *Volk* mores. These mores attained their validity by conforming to and expressing the forces of nature, the vital life forces. These subconscious, mystical forces can be felt in the blood by all those who are racially pure. (So, if all this does not make much sense to you, you know what your problem is.)

The stereotypical German is a very rational, calculating, unemotional person. He or she is seen as being very methodical and disciplined. What is not so widely understood is that this is only one stream or theme in German culture. There is as well a wild, romantic, undisciplined strain in the German tradition. And it was to this tradition that Hitler and the Nazis were returning.

In yet another way Nazi ideology drew upon a traditional theme in German thought. German political thinking long had tended to personify the state, to make it of considerably greater importance than the individual. Hegel, for example, one of Germany's foremost political philosophers from the early 19th century, had interpreted the course of history as the progressive revelation of the *Weltgeist* ("World Spirit"). This revelation, he maintained, was made visible not in individuals but in nations. And, of course, the highest revelation of the World Spirit was in the Prussian state.

Because the Nazi ideas were often set forth in philosophical and quasi-scientific language, they gained a certain amount of acceptance in respectable academic circles and were embraced by right-wing political groups. But it seems significant to note that these ideas did not become a serious political force until they were wedded with the genius of Adolf Hitler and the disciplined organization of the Nazi party. Even then they might not have become a powerful political force if it had not been for the combination of other circumstances (the economic crisis, the legacy of defeat, the ex-army officers unable to adjust to civilian life, the debt-ridden peasants, and the alleged Communist threat), which Hitler could and did exploit to the fullest.

Given that Nazi values did draw upon the German past in a way which the democratic values of Weimar did not, many people were concerned after World War II that there would be no democratic value consensus to support and make viable the present democratic system in Germany. Because democratic institutions failed to take root in Germany, and particularly because autocratic rulers took the country to war twice in the first half of this century, many observers had sought the answer in traits of national character.

National character is a very unreliable topic. Nonetheless, it certainly is a fact that liberal institutions, which emphasized the dignity of the individual and popular control of government, simply did not take hold in Germany. Perhaps the speed with which it became a powerful industrial nation simply precluded that. Industrialization was slower in Britain and in other Western European countries, and it was largely the work of private entrepreneurs. In Germany, on the other hand, liberal institutions not only did not have the time to take root but they also had to struggle against an industrialization tide spurred by government action.

Moreover, it should also be noted that when industrialization came, feudalism had not yet been swept aside. The aristocracy was still a power in the 19th century. The bourgeoisie had gained little headway and was excluded from public life. All this began to change, but the middle class was becoming influential long before it had learned to shoulder any political or social responsibilities. This subject is far too complex to be explained away by the phrase "national character."

Some writers have pointed to the divergent behavior of Germans as individuals and as a group. One of the best known of their writers, Goethe, once remarked: "The Germans—so worthy as individuals, and so miserable in the mass!" The Germans are well known for their hard work. They have demonstrated their ability in science and technology. They have produced great masterpieces in music, art, and literature. And yet, collectively, they seem to have shown little resistance to authority and dictatorship.

Out of this tortured political past a new political consensus seems to be emerging. A new democratic system is taking shape. Given the past, however, most observers are tempering their optimism with caution. Yet there is evidence that democracy is putting down solid roots. First of all, while differences of opinion exist about many matters, no political party of any importance questions the present democratic constitutional structure. The ideological quarrels that dogged Germany's first experiment in democracy seem to be totally absent. Second, political or civic education seems to be accepted as a fact of life. The press is interested in political questions and comments freely on them. Ordinary citizens write letters to the newspapers on burning issues of the day. Political lectures and discussions draw good audiences. Television programs dealing with topics of current interest seem to be popular. Third, there is a growing awareness of the power of public opinion. Finally, there are indications that young people are forming their own views. They do not seem to want much guidance from a generation that has been identified with the horrors of the past or with a narrow nationalism. This is not to suggest that most of the young people are militant democrats, but they are under no illusions about Germany's past. In general, therefore, it can be said that a democratic political consensus is well on the way to being established in Germany.

This democratic revival was one of the objectives of Allied occupation policies, but it is by no means clear how much they contributed. These policies were, in the main, associated with the words "denazification" and "demilitarization." Denazification, as originally conceived, turned out to be impossible, and demilitarization had to be revised once the conclusion was reached that Germany was needed to buttress the Western defense against the growing Communist threat.

The denazification program had two related objectives: (1) to acquaint the Germans with the horrors of the Nazi era, thereby also inculcating the moral values of a free way of life; and (2) to remove from positions in public and semipublic office, as well as from positions of responsibility in important private undertakings, all persons who had been more than nominal participants in Nazi party activities. The latter objective could be attained only partially. Examining millions of dossiers was not an easy task. Moreover, the conclusion was reached soon that most cases demanded individual consideration. Most important, perhaps, too many Germans who had had Nazi connections were simply indispensable to the running of the country, with the frequent consequence that punishment was meted out to lesser offenders while some who had been more closely associated with Nazism were rewarded with jobs. In the initial period, however, denazification did remove a number of persons with Nazi connections from the judiciary, the communications media, teaching, and the civil service. In addition, many of the pre-Hitler trade union leaders were reinstated in their jobs.

The first objective, however, seems to have been achieved in considerable measure. Allied effort contributed significantly in assisting the Germans to revamp their educational system, and thereby to present to future German citizens a more objective view of their history and the world about them.

While it would be erroneous to contend that today's Germany is a totally different Germany, it would be equally erroneous to assert that Germany has not changed significantly. Change in any society rarely is rapid; yet great strides are evident in Germany. Most Germans are aware of the evils of their past, notably the Nazi era, but they do not like to talk about them. They have not come to terms fully with their recent past. It is disquieting that polls in the latter part of the 1960s found that one third of those questioned believed that Hitler would have been one of the greatest German statesmen had it not been for the war and that only one third would do anything to prevent a new Nazi party from coming to power.

There has been a reluctance to root out and to punish former Nazis. Yet many judges have been fair and courageous in seeing that justice is done eventually. And most people—83 percent—think that those engaging in anti-Semitic activity should be punished by the courts. The radical right exists, but it is small, lacks money, and has no support from any significant quarter. The number of militant democrats may not be large, which is true of most democratic societies, but the Germans have come to realize what is and what is not a democratic order. And there are signs that the citizens have become more vigilant in guarding against those who would subvert the democratic system.

Furthermore, 62 percent have come to feel that the current period is the best years of Germany's history, while three quarters say that democracy is the best form of government. Nonetheless, it is clear from Almond and Verba's *The Civic Culture* data presented in Figure 18–1 that Germans do not have the same high regard for their political system, either absolutely or relatively, that Americans do. And Figure 18–2 suggests that Germans continue to regard the role of the individual in the political process in a different way than do Americans.

FIGURE 18–1
Aspects of Nation of Which One Is Proud

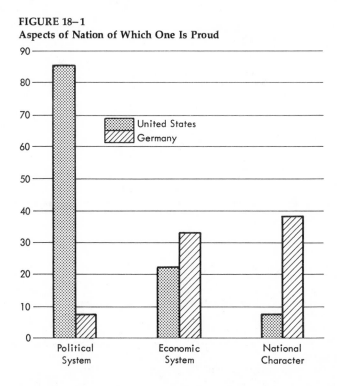

It is important to note, however, that there seem to be significant differences in values between younger and older Germans. Younger Germans, especially those below 35, attach considerably greater importance to free speech and political participation and less importance to economic security and domestic order than do older Germans. Democratic values seem to have a firmer hold on the younger generations.[4] While this may produce some intergenerational tensions in the short run, in the long run it should be supportive of a democratic system. Despite these prospects and the fact that limited, responsible government is established in Germany now more firmly than ever before in the country's history, it must be remem-

---

[4] Ronald Inglehart, "The Silent Revolution in Europe: Intergenerational Change in Post-Industrial Societies," *American Political Science Review* 65 (December 1971): 991–1017.

FIGURE 18–2
Perception of Citizen's Role

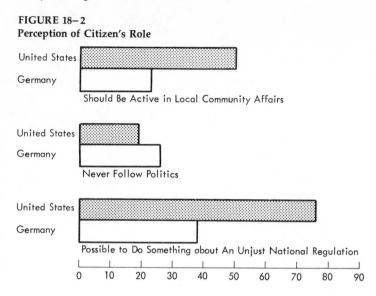

bered that this is a German version of democracy. Therefore, it can be expected to differ from the American and British systems in several ways.

BIBLIOGRAPHICAL NOTE

Parts of Edward McWhinney, *Constitutionalism in Germany and the Federal Constitutional Court* (Leyden: Sythoff, 1962), and S. Rosenne, *Constitutionalism in Germany and the Federal Constitutional Court* (New York: Oceana Publications, 1962), deal with German constitutionalism. For background on the provisions of the present Basic Law, see John Golay, *The Founding of the Federal Republic of Germany* (Chicago: University of Chicago Press, 1958).

Important studies of German political values include Fritz Stern, *The Politics of Cultural Despair: A Study in the Rise of the Germanic Ideology* (Berkeley: University of California Press, 1961), and two books by George Mosse, *The Crisis of German Ideology: Intellectual Origins of the Third Reich* (New York: Grosset & Dunlap, 1964), and *Nazi Culture: Intellectual, Cultural and Social Life in the Third Reich* (New York: Grosset & Dunlap, 1966). Also interesting are Peter Viereck, *Metapolitics: The Roots of the Nazi Mind* (New York: Capricorn 1961), and Peter Gay, *Weimar Culture: The Outsider as Insider* (New York: Harper & Row, 1968). See also the sections dealing with Germany in the Almond and Verba study cited in Footnote 3. On political socialization through the schools, the collection of materials edited by Walter Stahl, *Education for Democracy in West Germany* (New York: Frederick A. Praeger, Inc., 1961), is valuable. Finally, an excellent novel by Richard Hughes, *The Fox in the Attic* (New York: New American Library, 1961), skillfully captures the feeling and values of the Weimar period and compares and contrasts these with life in Britain in the same period.

19

Expression of Individual and Collective Interest

THE ELECTORAL SYSTEM

In devising their present electoral system, the Germans were of two minds. On the one hand, like many other Europeans, they were attracted by the seeming justice or fairness of proportional representation. It somehow seems only proper that a party's share of the seats in the legislature should correspond closely to its share of the popular vote—a result that occurs only by accident under the Anglo-American single member, simple plurality system. Yet they also were aware that proportional representation (PR) is widely thought to have significant defects. And for the Germans this was not just a matter of abstract belief, since the experience of the Weimar Republic was taken by many as clear proof that PR affects the party system quite negatively. And so the Germans endeavored to devise a hybrid system as a compromise. This is why the electoral system we are about to examine is so complex. The Germans wanted a system that would secure electoral justice but would not fractionalize the party system, that would avoid the depersonalization of representation—the lack of contact between legislator and voter—involved in pure PR, and would provide some obstacle to the development of extreme, antidemocratic parties.

As we explained in discussing PR in the French Fourth Republic, under this electoral system each constituency returns several members to the legislature. This means that any given voter is not represented by a single legislator. This might sound like an improvement on the American system. But it means that no one legislator is responsible for a given constituency and thus the several representatives for a constituency can pass the

buck among themselves. No single representative need feel a special responsibility for the area. Nor need he or she make much effort to respond
to the needs and views of the constituents. So long as a representative
satisfies the local party leaders, he or she can be certain that his or her
name will continue to be placed near the top of the party's slate of candidates. And under PR that is sufficient to ensure election, if the party is of
any size at all. Thus, there is little incentive to be a good constituency
person, circulating widely in the district and seeking to serve the voters.

To avoid this defect, the German electoral system has an element of the
single member, simple plurality system. The country is divided into 248
constituencies, each of which returns one representative.[1] The boundary
lines are drawn on the basis of the number of qualified electors in each
constituency, with the requirement that no constituency's electorate may
be more than one third above or below the national average. The candidate in each district receiving the greatest number of votes—regardless of
whether this is a majority—is elected, just as in the United States.

This part of the electoral system applies to only half of the members of
the Bundestag, or lower house of Parliament. The other half are elected
from state party lists and represent an entire state rather than a single
member constituency. Thus each German elector is entitled to vote
twice—once for a specific candidate to represent the local district and
once for a party from whose list of candidates the top ones will represent
the entire state. A sample ballot for a German election appears in Figure
19–1.

The complicated part of the system is that the votes cast on the party
list side of the ballot determine the party strengths for the entire Parliament and not just for half the membership. Despite the single member,
simple plurality element, the entire system is proportional representation.
All the votes cast for the Social Democratic party list (to use that party as
an example) in each of the ten German states are added together to produce a national total vote. Highest average PR is used to determine how
many of the total 496 seats in Parliament the Social Democrats are entitled
to, given their vote. These seats must in turn be allocated to the various
states. This is done by having the various Social Democratic state parties,
in effect, run against each other. Thus if 20 percent of the Social Democrats' total national vote was cast in Lower Saxony, then 20 percent of the
number of seats in Parliament to which the Social Democrats were entitled would be allocated to Lower Saxony. In this way the number of
Social Democrats elected in each state is determined.

Once this has been done, the number of single member seats that the
Social Democrats already have won in a particular state is subtracted
from the number to which they are entitled in that state under PR. The

---

[1] The best explanation of the electoral law is Uwe Kitzinger, "The West German Electoral Law," *Parliamentary Affairs* 11 (Spring 1958), pp. 220–37.

FIGURE 19–1
Sample Ballot

Stimmzettel

für die Bundestagswahl im Wahlkreis 63 Bonn am 28. September 1969

Sie haben 2 Stimmen

(X) (X)

hier Erststimme
für die Wahl
eines Wahlkreisabgeordneten

hier Zweitstimme
für die Wahl
einer Landesliste (Partei)

#	Erststimme		#	Zweitstimme
1	**Hauser, Johannes Aloisius** (gen. Alo) Rechtsanwalt Bonn-Bad Godesberg, Horionstr. 16 **CDU** Christlich Demokratische Union Deutschlands	◯	◯ **CDU** Christlich Demokratische Union Deutschlands — Dr. Schröder, Dr. Barzel, Katzer, Bewerunge, Frau Brauksiepe	1
2	**Freiherr Ostman v. d. Leye, Wilderich** Verleger Bonn, Stiftsplatz 2 **SPD** Sozialdemo-kratische Partei Deutschlands	◯	◯ **SPD** Sozialdemokratische Partei Deutschlands — Brandt, Prof. Dr. Schiller, Arendt, Neemann, Wienand	2
3	**Dr. Schäfer, Hans** Staatssekretär a. D. Bonn-Bad Godesberg, Gotenstr. 56 **FDP** Freie Demokratische Partei	◯	◯ **FDP** Freie Demokratische Partei — Scheel, Dr. Mende, Genscher, Frau Funcke, Zoglmann	3
4	**Kampkötter, Günter** Amtmann Bonn, Weberstr. 2 a **ADF** Aktion Demokratischer Fortschritt	◯	◯ **ADF** Aktion Demokratischer Fortschritt — Behrisch, Bachmann, Sanß, Selberg, Frau Thiele	4
5		◯	◯ **Zen-trum** Deutsche Zentrumspartei — Ribbeheger, Dr. Reismann, Rölle, Hellenthal, Averhoff	5
6		◯	◯ **EP** Europa Partei — Ruban, Hüttmann, Wigger, Kayser, Heering	6
7		◯	◯ **FSU** Freisoziale Union - Demokratische Mitte - Dr. Keßler, Wandel, Schacht, Triebler, Schmülling	7
8		◯	◯ **GPD** Gesamtdeutsche Partei — Wollner, Otto, Petersen, Broschell, Frau Ivenhof	8
9	**von Thadden, Adolf** Schriftleiter Benthe, Lärchenweg 6 **NPD** Nationaldemo-kratische Partei Deutschlands	◯	◯ **NPD** Nationaldemokratische Partei Deutschlands — von Thadden, Dr. Kather, Dr. Lamker, Mörs, Dr. Schwartländer	9
10		◯	◯ **UAP** Unabhängige Arbeiter-Partei (Deutsche Sozialisten) — Drees, Villmow, Kliese, Daumann, Schlichting	10
11	**Dr. Daniels, Wilhelm** Notar Bonn, Poppelsdorfer Allee 36 Aktionskomitee „Daniels in den Bundestag" **Parteilos**	◯	◯	11
12	**Dr. Bursche, Herbert** Ministerialrat Bonn, Am Römerkastell 7 **DV** Deutsche Volkspartei	◯	◯	12

Druck: J. F. Carthaus, Bonn

difference is the number of candidates from the top of the Social Democrats' state party list who will be declared elected. Thus, if it is determined that the Social Democrats are entitled under PR to 27 seats from Hesse and they have won 15 single member seats there, then the first 12 names on their party list for Hesse would be elected also (unless some of this group had won single member constituencies, in which case their names would be skipped over on the party list). This means that although in the whole nation half of the members of the Bundestag are elected in single member, simple plurality districts, in any given state such representatives may be more or less than half of the total state delegation in the Bundestag.

Should a party win more single member seats than the total number of seats to which it is entitled in a given state, it is permitted to keep the extra seats. This is an unusual event, but it has occurred a few times with the result that the total number of seats in the Bundestag may vary slightly from one election to the next.

In order to avoid the splintering effects of PR, minor parties are hampered. A party must win 5 percent of the total national vote or three of the single member constituencies to be allowed to participate in the proportional sharing of seats. This means that it either must have generalized support throughout the country at something more than a minimal level or must have concentrated strength in some region sufficient to outpoll other parties.

The result is that, if a party wins two single member seats and 4.9 percent of the vote nationally, it gets only the two single member seats in the Bundestag. Whereas, if it wins three constituencies and 4.9 percent of the vote, it obtains 24 seats (4.9 percent of 496). Should it win no single member seats, but gain 5 percent of the national vote, then it gains 25 seats. Thus at this marginal point winning an additional constituency or another .1 percent of the national vote is worth about two dozen additional seats.

An unintended result of this system is that voting for a minor party that fails to qualify for participation in the proportional sharing of seats is, in effect, voting to reduce your state's representation in Parliament. Only the number of single member seats is predetermined for each state. As we have noted, a state's total representation is not necessarily exactly twice the number of its constituencies. Given that a state's representation is a function of the share of the total national party vote each state party receives, anything which reduces a state's total vote—as excluding the votes cast for minor parties does—tends to reduce its strength in Parliament. Furthermore, abstention clearly has the same effect.

This detailed discussion of the electoral system is intended to clarify our initial statement of Germany's goals. Since the electoral system allocates to parties a share of the total seats in Parliament roughly equal to their share of the popular vote, the system is deemed fair. Since it allows each elector to vote for a single candidate to be the district's representative, it contains an element of personal representation and concern. And insofar as it establishes a hurdle which minor parties must clear before they are represented in Parliament, it avoids the fractionalization of the party system frequently associated with PR. The system is complex, but it has done a good job in achieving the conflicting goals sought of it.

The effect of the system is that parties that have concentrated support in many areas will win most of their seats by electing representatives from the single member constituencies. Parties with a considerable national following which do not concentrate their vote sufficiently to emerge ahead in very many constituencies still will win a considerable number of representatives, with most of them coming from the state party lists. The success of Germany's two main parties along these lines in the last five elections reveals an interesting pattern, as shown in Table 19–1. Initially the Christian Democrats won the great bulk of their seats in the single member districts, doing considerably better in this regard than did the Social Democrats. At the end of the 1960s this pattern reversed and by 1972 was almost exactly the opposite of what it had been ten years earlier. The most recent election produced another change, with each party faring the same.

TABLE 19–1
Percent of Each Party's Total Representation Won in Single Member Constituencies

	1957	1961	1965	1969	1972	1976
Christian Democrats	72	64	63	50	43	55
Social Democrats	27	48	46	57	66	53

In addition to examining the way in which the parties gain their seats, it is important to consider the impact of the electoral system on party strengths. If the Bundestag had been composed only of the single member constituency representatives in 1972, then the Social Democrats would have dominated it by holding 61 percent of the total membership instead of having only 46 percent as actually was the case. With an electoral system of only single member constituencies, the Christian Democrats in 1976 would have had 54 percent of the seats; instead they just failed to get a majority with 49 percent. The electoral system permitted the Social Democrats and the Free Democrats to remain in power with a coalition government and prevented the Christian Democrats' return to office. The Free Democrats have a strong stake in the present electoral system. Were the PR aspect of the electoral system to be eliminated, the Free Democrats would be banished totally from the Bundestag, since they are unable to elect anyone in a single member district and gained all of their current 39 seats through PR.

Given relative stability of public opinion, PR tends to stabilize party strengths in the legislature. The Social Democrats' share of the popular vote dropped only three percentage points from 1972 to 1976, and thus, under the German electoral system their share of the seats in the Bundestag dropped by only three percentage points. Had there been only single member districts, however, their legislative strength would have fallen by 15 percentage points from 61 percent of the seats to 46 percent. Thus to some extent PR makes elections a bit less of a gamble for parties.

In addition to the PR hurdle, newly formed small parties face another obstacle. A party which has not previously been represented in either the national legislature or any state legislature must obtain 200 signatures in each one of the 248 single member constituencies before the party can put its party list candidates on the ballot. Should someone wish to run as an independent, he or she needs only to get 200 signatures in his or her electoral district. Nonetheless, independent candidates are relatively unusual in German elections.

Since there are no primary elections in Germany, nomination is by parties. Candidates for single member districts are selected either by all the party members in that district or by a special nominating committee. The state party lists are drawn up by regular state party organs. While national party leaders have some influence in this process, they are not permitted to draw up the lists themselves to avoid giving them too much power within the party. Placement on the list is crucial, since those near the top are certain to be elected, while those far down the list have little hope. Thus, one's political career could be terminated by adverse position on the list. Were national leaders able to prepare all the state lists, they would have immense power over their followers by being able to penalize intraparty opponents by putting them low on the list. But, although the process of candidate selection is decentralized, this is not to say that it involves extensive popular participation. The size of the group making the selections varies from about 25 to about 250, quite small compared with the number of people voting in American primaries even when turnout is very low.

Candidates must be at least 18 years old. They are not required to live in the state they represent, as is the case in the United States, but in point of fact most of them do.

Suffrage is universal at age 18, except for the usual disqualifications, such as insanity. The burden of registration is on the government, rather than the individual. Lists of eligible voters are posted well in advance of an election, affording ample opportunity for corrections of errors. Voter turnout is quite good in Germany—there seems to be a high sense of civic duty—usually running between 86 and 88 percent of those eligible. Only in the first postwar election of 1949 did turnout fall below 80 percent. In the 1972 election 91 percent of those eligible voted, the highest turnout in German history, and this level was maintained in 1976. High participation can be attributed to the fact that, like the French, the Germans vote on Sunday. Moreover, there are voting facilities at railway stations and at hospitals and sanatoria, enabling persons to vote who otherwise might find it difficult to get to the polls.

Since, as we have seen, under the German electoral system each voter can vote twice—once for a candidate and once for a party—there is a unique opportunity to study whether voters are influenced by candidates' personality. For example, a person might not be a supporter of a particular party, but might find that party's candidate in a particular election an especially capable and attractive person. Such a voter might decide to depart from his or her usual party loyalty to vote for such an appealing candidate. During the 1950s in the United States many people who normally thought of themselves as Democrats nonetheless voted for the Republican Presidential candidate, Eisenhower, because they agreed with millions of others, "I Like Ike." Unlike American voters, German voters are not faced with having to choose between their party and an especially attractive opposition party candidate. They can vote for such a candidate on one side of ballot and still vote for their party on the other half. Furthermore, since it is the party list vote and not the candidate vote that determines partisan strength in the Bundestag, they can split their vote in this sense without helping the opposition party at all. Their vote for the individual candidate will aid only him or her and not that party.

Despite this opportunity German voters do not seem to cast their two ballots in contrasting ways. In 1976 individual Social Democratic candidates won 43.7 percent of the vote, while their party lists obtained 42.6 percent. The difference was even less in the case of the Christian Democrats with their individual candidates gaining only 0.3 of a percentage point more than did their party lists. The greatest difference, although still not large, occurred in the case of the Free Democrats, where the gap was 1.5 percentage points. Interestingly, in the case of the Free Democrats the gain was in the opposite direction; their party lists won a greater share of the vote than did their individual candidates. At least a few German voters seem to be saying that although the Free Democrats may lack outstanding, personally magnetic candidates, the party deserves some support as a small counterweight and control on the major Social Democrats and Christian Democrats.

Political campaigns are relatively long in Germany, running two or three months instead of the approximately three-week period utilized in Britain and France. Free radio and television time is given to the main parties, with the two leading ones getting approximately equal time. In any given area of the country the total time available to a major party is only about two hours. Most of this is used in several five-minute broadcasts. Parties other than the two main ones receive considerably less time, and some of the tiny ones get nothing at all.

The electoral law does not impose limitations on campaign spending, which has increased with each election. In the 1957 electoral campaign, for example, it was estimated that the three major parties spent upward of $12 million, or four to five times the total spent by the three political parties in the previous general election in Britain.[2] In the 1961 electoral campaign, the amount spent increased by at least one third. Partly as a result of these rising expenditures, the three major parties reached an agreement in January 1965 not only to limit the amounts of money to be spent in that year's campaign but also to impose other rules governing the nature of the election battle.

Under this agreement, the CDU and its Bavarian affilate (CSU) were limited to slightly over $4 million, while the Social Democrats and the Free Democrats were limited to $3.75 million each. Moreover, the parties agreed to have their books audited by a certified accountant, who was to make a public finding by mid-1966. Alleged violations of the agreement were to be brought before a special court. Nonfinancial aspects of the agreement included a prohibition on campaign posters prior to 30 days preceding the election, and their posting only in designated areas; a ban on newspaper or magazine advertising until eight weeks before the election; a prohibition against skywriting; and a limitation on the number of leaflets (two per party) that may be sent to German households.

A similar agreement was reached to govern the 1969 election. It even banned personal attacks on political opponents (not always honored in the final days of the campaign) and reduced the limit on the display of campaign posters to the 20-day period prior to election day.

The Christian Democrats had been spending what were, by European standards, enormous sums on electioneering. They were mounting massive advertising campaigns and employing survey and public relations techniques. This was facilitated by the 1954 income tax law, which had permitted taxpayers to deduct political contributions. Then in 1958 the Federal Constitutional Court declared this law unconstitutional, which severely limited the Christian Democrats' income.

As a result Germany began an interesting experiment in governmental subsidies to parties. Parties were given grants by the national government in proportion to their number of seats in the Bundestag. These grants totaled $1.25 million a year initially, but by 1964 had reached $9.5 million. Furthermore, other levels of government also were contributing to parties so that such subsidies accounted for about 60 percent of total party income.

---

[2] Uwe Kitzinger, *German Electoral Politics: A Study of the 1957 Campaign* (London: Oxford University Press, 1960), p. 202.

Then in July 1966 the Court restricted this law. The Court held that the government could not finance party activities designed to mold public opinion but could help only in "necessary expenses of a reasonable election campaign." Furthermore, this help had to be extended even to those parties which did not have seats in the Bundestag. As a result of this decision the Christian Democrats had to release 40 percent of the salaried staff at central headquarters. The decision was less of a blow to the Social Democrats, since their large number of dues-paying members gave them an annual income of $4.25 million. On the other hand, the Social Democrats hardly were living in luxury. So they, as well as the Christian Democrats, felt a need to devise a party subsidy law which would meet all constitutional tests.

The result was the Political Parties Act of 1967, which provided that all parties that polled 2.5 percent of the total vote or more in the previous election would be paid at the rate of 2.5 DM (somewhat less than 90 cents) per vote. This involved a total cost to the national government of about $25 million. Even these measures did not satisfy the Court; it ruled that parties getting as little as 0.5 percent of the vote must receive payment. The result of this decision was that in the 1969 election the neo-Nazi party received $400,000 from the national government to help pay its campaign expenses.

Currently, then, German parties receive a sizable portion of their income from the government. No strings are attached to the use of this money and the government must provide it to supporters and opponents alike. During the 1972–76 Parliamentary session, campaign subsidies from the national government to all parties totalled about $56 million. Some people are bothered to see parties so dependent financially on the government and they worry that the situation might lend itself to abuse. And some wonder whether even the present law puts newly created minor parties in an impossible situation. The major parties are so much more rewarded financially that it would seem to freeze the party system. Minor parties simply cannot hope to compete.

Defenders of the German measures can respond by questioning whether it is a healthy political situation to have parties dependent on wealthy special interest for financial support. Clearly they expect parties to support those measures of special interest to them in return for the money they give. And if, as in the United States, giving seems to be disproportionally great to one party, then party competition may be greatly weakened. The United States is making the first tentative efforts to cope with this problem. Governmental grants to parties have been instituted in this country, also. The difference is that in the United States these grants make up a much smaller portion of total party income and that the allocation of the funds is not determined by party strength, but by the preferences of individual taxpayers. Despite the differences between the

German and American systems of party subsidies, it will be interesting to watch developments in Germany to see whether the United States can learn anything which will help to improve the American procedures.

THE ROLE OF INTEREST GROUPS

As in other democracies, interest groups are very much a part of the political process in Germany. Initially the public tended to distrust them. Nevertheless, interest groups developed rapidly and sought to exert their influence on political parties both in and out of Government.

The principal categories of interest groups are religious, business, and labor. The church groups were particularly important at the outset because, in the chaos of 1945, they appeared to be the only solid institutions left. Allied occupation authorities often asked church leaders to take jobs in local government. Subsequently, many of them became influential in party circles, especially in the CDU. The activities of Roman Catholic groups and organizations are usually to be found on the side of the CDU. From their point of view, the SPD is suspect, because in its origins it was Marxist, materialist, and godless. The FDP, because of its secular attitude, was not much better. Some CDU supporters have been unhappy about Catholic activity on behalf of the CDU, fearing that the CDU would become solely a Catholic party. Moreover, many liberals in the CDU pointed out that the SPD had changed its outlook considerably and that Christians should be able to find a home in the SPD.

There is no established church in Germany, but there never has been any formal separation of church and state, either. Consequently, the state collects religious taxes and pays the clergy and church educators. In theory, each baptized German belongs to some church and unless he or she officially declares to have left it, is taxed for its support.

Labor is active primarily through the German Federation of Trade Unions, which has a membership of approximately 7.5 million. About 40 percent of the German workers are organized, about the same as in Britain. Most trade union officials (certainly a large majority), are card-carrying Social Democrats. In the immediate postwar years, labor union sympathy for the SPD was open. Since 1957, however, a formal neutrality in politics has been the rule. While the preponderant majority of labor votes is cast for the SPD, labor demands generally are made in nonpolitical terms. German trade unions are owners or part owners of a number of businesses, including banks, cooperatives, breweries, hotels, insurance companies, and publishing houses. The fourth largest bank in Germany is owned by the unions as is a large construction company that has been active in building low-cost and middle-income housing throughout Germany.

The Federation of German Industry is the most powerful organization in the business field. Nearly 90 percent of all industrial and commercial firms belong to it. In politics it has been openly pro-CDU. It has promoted some business leaders for elective office.

The German Farmers' Association has been the principal spokesgroup for the farmers. It generally has favored the CDU, but it often has provided a forum for members of other parties to present their views. Because the CDU has polled large majorities in the rural areas, and because the organization has on occasion indicated that it might not go on supporting CDU candidates, the Farmers' Association is listened to by CDU leaders and its demands are considered carefully.

All the major interest groups have been successful in getting people elected to the Bundestag who are favorable to them. In the Bundestag elected in 1961, for example, the number of CDU deputies known to be favorable to various interests were: farmers, 47; industry and commerce, 32; labor, 29; retail merchants and tradespeople, 20; leading business employees, 9. Among the SPD deputies, 47 represented labor, while 9 were associated with business groups, 5 were leading business employees, 8 represented retail merchants and tradespeople, and only 3 the farmers. In the FDP, industry and commerce elected 18, the farmers elected 12, while leading business employees and retail merchants and tradespeople had 3 and 4, respectively. The workers could count only 2 supporters among the FDP deputies.[3] There were many more deputies in each of the categories, particularly in the CDU and SPD, who leaned toward a particular interest group, although not necessarily openly identified with it.

The techniques and methods which interest groups utilize are varied. Since ministerial officials draft legislation, interest groups have tended to go to them more often than to Bundestag members or to the ministers. In this respect, their work has been facilitated by the fact that advisory bodies of experts have been set up in a number of ministries. In these advisory bodies are to be found representatives of interest groups, providing a natural point of contact with officials of the ministries. Moreover, at times ministers have been unsure about proposed legislation, and hence have not wanted to take the responsibility of advocating it without knowing what the public reaction would be. Consequently, they have authorized their associates to try out the proposed legislation on the interest groups concerned. In this way, interest groups often have been able to act as a more effective check on the government than have the members of Parliament.

Although individual members of the legislature cannot be the source of legislation, interest groups do not ignore Parliament. In the Bundestag the interest groups have concentrated on committees; they have sought to increase the number of committees so as to permit greater specializa-

---

[3] The foregoing figures are taken from Walter Stahl, *Politics of Postwar Germany* (New York: Frederick A. Praeger, Inc., 1964), p. 29.

tion and in this way be certain to be represented by their friends on issues of importance to them. Members of the Bundestag usually are assigned to committees on the basis of special competence in the topic with which the committee is dealing. More often than not these expert legislators have, or have had, some association with an interest group. Thus an interest group, in some senses, is represented by its own people. This provides a channel for focusing influence upon the bureaucracy should it prove to be unresponsive.

Finally, interest groups have sought the paid services of civil servants for periods of time. German law permits civil servants to take leave and return to their posts at a later time. Consequently, interest groups have been able to prevail upon civil servants to take leave from their jobs and to join them in a full-time paid capacity. One does not need much imagination to visualize the value of a qualified civil servant who knows the inside of the regulatory process which happens to affect some interest group.

The political parties, of course, seek to harmonize group interests with party principles. Where this can be done, no serious problem arises. Where this cannot be done, parties seek to play off one interest against another. Sometimes, however, the result is division in party ranks. The most important struggle takes place not when votes are taken in the Bundestag but, rather, when new proposals are being debated in the ministries and existing measures are being implemented, as well as when legislation is being hammered out in committees.

BIBLIOGRAPHICAL NOTE

Discussions of the German electoral system with reference to particular elections include the Kitzinger book cited in Footnote 2, James Pollock et al., *German Democracy at Work* (Ann Arbor: University of Michigan Press, 1955), and the July 1970 issue of *Comparative Politics*, which analyzes the 1969 elections. On governmental campaign subsidies and other aspects of electoral expenditure and party finance, see Uwe Schleth and Michael Pinto-Duschinsky, "Why Public Subsidies Have Become the Major Sources of Party Funds in West Germany, but Not in Great Britain," in Arnold Heidenheimer, *Comparative Political Finance* (Lexington, Mass.: Heath, 1970). Although mainly concerned with state elections, portions of R. J. C. Preece, *"Land" Elections in the German Federal Republic* (London: Longmans, Green, 1968), are relevant to national elections.

For studies of interest groups, see the following: Gerard Braunthal, *The Federation of German Industry in Politics* (Ithaca, N.Y.: Cornell University Press, 1965); Karl Deutsch and Lewis Edinger, *Germany Rejoins the Powers: Mass Opinion, Interest Groups and Elites in Contemporary German Foreign Policy* (Stanford, Cal.: Stanford University Press, 1959); and William Safran, *Veto Group Politics: the Case of Health Insurance Reform in West Germany* (San Francisco: Chandler, 1967).

20

Political Parties

AN EVOLVING PARTY SYSTEM

Traditionally German parties have stressed ideology and doctrine. In part this is because, as explained in Chapter 17, during the Empire under the virtually personal rule of the Kaiser and his Chancellor, parties had little influence on government policy. Taking a moderate stand in an attempt to gain increased popular support was largely pointless; the Chancellor ran the country as he wished regardless of party strengths in the Parliament. Parties had little opportunity to attempt to put their policies into effect; they could not be distinguished on the grounds of what they had done. Thus, they developed very rigid, unrealistic doctrines which served to distinguish them sharply from each other.

Parties of this type were termed *Weltanschauung* parties. Literally translated this means "world view." This is to say that these parties presented all-embracing philosophical outlooks; they offered the voters not just alternative sets of policies, as do American parties, but a comprehensive political faith. When any new issue arose, this faith would determine the party's position on that question. Thus, its policies and doctrines were to be an integrated whole, intellectually satisfying to its supporters.

Weltanschauung parties tended to be totalitarian in a special sense. It was not that they were against liberty or supported dictatorship. Instead it was that they failed to recognize any distinction between public life and private life; everything was party life. Parties formed a wide variety of auxiliary groups dealing with sports, hobbies, adult education, and the like, so that a connection between a party and its supporters could be maintained even during social and recreational time.

The impact of these factors on the party system should be obvious—they helped to fractionalize the party system. A party that stresses ideology and doctrine is likely to have a rather narrow appeal. The more comprehensive a faith it presents, the fewer will be the number of people willing to accept all its views. And insofar as it is a faith and not just a set of policies that is being presented, one is forced to accept everything or seek another party. Only true believers are welcomed into *Weltanschauung* parties. Thus, each party appeals to only a limited segment of the electorate and a multi-party system prevails.

During the Empire, German parties ranged from the Conservative party on the right, which was mainly interested in protecting Prussia's privileged position and the welfare of the great landowners, to the Social Democratic party on the left, which espoused a radical reconstruction of the economic system and the establishment of political democracy. In between were the Center party, which was really a conservative Catholic party, often cooperating with the Conservatives; the National Liberals, a party of industrial leaders with a sizable middle-class following and a program of political reform that would alter Prussia's favored position; and the Progressives, a free trade party which emphasized the desirability of inaugurating a genuine parliamentary system.

As already noted, these parties could talk but did not have real control over policy. And even in the case of a veritable political vacuum in 1916, they were unable to grasp power. By 1912 the Social Democrats were the largest party in the Reichstag; yet they seemed ill suited to govern. They refused to enter any Cabinet unless the whole political system were changed. Because of this stance, they were regarded in some circles as unpatriotic. In 1914, however, the Social Democratic deputies in the Reichstag voted to support war credits and entered into an agreement not to oppose the Government.

By the end of 1915 the Social Democrats faced another dilemma. By that time it was evident that Germany was engaged in a war of conquest, and some Social Democratic deputies refused to support further war credits, thus splitting the party. The majority, however, believed they were bound by the 1914 commitments. They argued, further, that if a reversal of their earlier position served to disunite the nation and Germany were to lose the war, the Social Democrats would be blamed for the defeat. This was not an enviable position for the strongest party in the Reichstag, particularly a party that was dedicated to democracy and opposed to the whole Imperial system.

With the formation of the Weimar Republic, parties had a greater opportunity to play a role in the policy process. But the political party configuration in the Reichstag never was propitious for the success of German democracy. No party could command a majority. Secondly, the antidemocratic parties represented a stumbling block. On the far right were the German National People's party and the Nazi party (National Socialist German Workers party or NSDAP). Although the former was more important in the early years as a focus of reaction and opposition to Weimar, the latter was to become the effective enemy of the Republic. On the far left was the Communist party, patterned after the Russian model and exhibiting a consistently negative attitude toward the Republic.

The center of political power during Weimar was to be found largely in the Catholic Center party and the German Democratic party, with the aid of the Social Democratic party. The Center party was the most influential and the most stable, its membership cutting across all social strata. As a real party of the center, it could lean either way, and did at various times, participating in all Cabinets. The Democratic party, a continuation of the former Progressives, gave strong support to the Republic but, as did many other liberal parties in Europe, it declined gradually. The Social Democrats fought against the extreme right as well as the extreme left (Communists), and helped to shape the Weimar constitution, although in the end few of their principles were adopted. Although Marxist in theory, the Social Democratic party was much more like the British Labour party in practice. Its membership in the Reichstag rose steadily and, although it never gained majority support, its leaders headed coalition Cabinets for approximately three years and participated in several Cabinets headed by leaders of other parties.

Had the Weimar Republic endured longer, the party system might well have evolved into a more effective structure. But democracy was too short-lived for any fundamental transformation of parties or the party system. The Nazis, of course, did transform the party system, but in a negative way by outlawing all parties but their own to produce a totalitarian one-party system.

With the defeat of Nazi Germany, the Western occupation authorities wished to reestablish democracy in Germany. Recognizing the essential role of parties in a democratic system, they began authorizing political party activities on the local level as early as August 1945; by 1946 the right was extended to the state level. At the same time, parties suspected of having Nazi leanings were not permitted to operate. It was not until 1948 that the United States relinquished all control over the regulation of German political parties in its zone of occupation. The British and the French finally relinquished control in their zones in early 1950.

While the occupation authorities sought to prevent the formation of antidemocratic parties, they did not attempt to shape the form of the party system. When the procedure of licensing parties was abandoned, 31 had been approved. Thus it appeared that the German party system would take on its traditional multi-party form with doctrinaire, limited-appeal parties.

The German Basic Law, which went into effect in 1949, took a similar approach to the party system. Parties are free to organize, but those which, "according to their aims and the conduct of their members, seek to impair or abolish the libertarian democratic basic order or to jeopardize the existence of the Federal Republic of Germany are unconstitutional." The Constitutional Court, upon petition of the Cabinet or of either house of the legislature, is empowered to rule on this question. Pursuant to this power, it banned a neo-Nazi party and the Communist party. Both subsequently reappeared under new names. These parties have had such limited support, however, that taking them to the Court again hardly seemed worthwhile. Thus it would be hard to argue that the constitution is responsible for any fundamental change in the party system.

Nonetheless, the German party system clearly has been in the process of a fundamental change in the last quarter of a century. (See Figure 20–1.) In the first postwar election, 1949, 11 parties elected deputies to the Bundestag with no one party approaching a majority of the popular vote or seats. The two leading parties, the Social Democrats and the Christian Democrats, received 60 percent of the vote and two thirds of the seats. Four years later the Christian Democrats, with 45 percent of the vote, got half of the seats, and the number of parties with seats in the Bundestag was halved. In the next election the Christian Democrats gained further support to win half of the popular vote. This unprecedented accomplishment had been totally unexpected less than a decade before.

At the same time as this advance of the Christian Democrats, the Social Democrats were making steady, although less spectacular gains. Thus, in the 1976 election the Christian Democrats and the Social Democrats received 92 percent of the votes and seats. And only one other party, the Free Democrats, was able to elect anyone to the Bundestag.

The trend toward a two-party system has been unmistakable, but the reasons for it are less evident. The electoral system alone does not account for it, although the 5 percent barrier has served to discourage small splinter parties. Some observers have suggested that Konrad Adenauer's domineering role in his long tenure as Chancellor encouraged his opponents to support the only significant opposition party, the Social Democrats. His success, at the same time, brought additional supporters to the Christian Democrats. Other analysts have pointed out that the old causes of faction—class lines and a dominant Prussia—were no longer a fact of political life in Germany. And a potential new source of faction—the refugees and expellees—quickly disappeared with the successful integration of these elements in German society. It has also been suggested that the actions of political leaders and interest groups tended to stress the importance of the two major political formations in postwar Germany.

Compared to Weimar *Weltanschauungen* parties, both leading parties in the Bonn Republic have been moderate, less dogmatic, and more willing to compromise on demands and policies. The Christian Democrats' doctrines have been vague, while the Social Democrats have shown them-

FIGURE 20–1
Two Leading Parties' Share of the Vote in Post-World War II German Elections

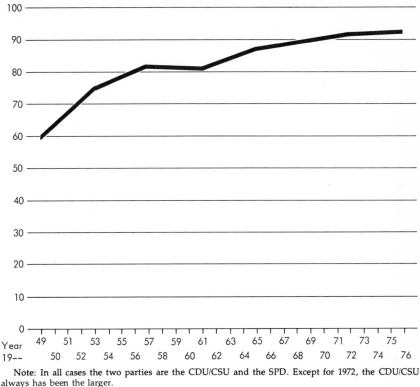

Note: In all cases the two parties are the CDU/CSU and the SPD. Except for 1972, the CDU/CSU always has been the larger.

selves willing to make substantial revisions in their basic policies. As a result, both parties have achieved much greater success than Weimar parties in constructing a coalition of diverse supporters. The sectional, limited appeal party, typical of Weimar, is not the norm in the Bonn Republic.

While it is difficult to assign specific weight to the various factors and developments mentioned, they clearly have combined to simplify the German party system and alter the nature of German politics. The more moderate and pragmatic nature of political conflict in Germany is a very favorable development for the future of a viable democratic system there.

THE LEADING PARTIES

The oldest party in Germany, in existence for over a century, is the SPD or Social Democratic party. During the 1930s, when the party was suppressed by the Nazis, its leaders went underground or into exile. In

1945 the party was revived to become first the major opposition party and then, in 1969, the major governing party.

In contrast to the SPD, the Christian Democratic Union/Christian Social Union (CDU/CSU) is a postwar product. A Catholic Center party had been active in German politics down through the Weimar Republic, but the Christian Democrats are not direct descendants of that party. The CDU/CSU was intended to be a union of all Christians, not just Catholics, since Protestants as well had suffered under the Nazis, and Christians of both types were opposed to Communist advance after World War II. The party's first leader, Konrad Adenauer, although a Catholic, opposed clericalism. The fact that his successor, Ludwig Erhard, was a Protestant helped to further the party's nondenominational image. As we will clarify when we discuss party organization, the Christian Democrats are something of an alliance between the CSU, which operates only in Bavaria, and the CDU, which exists in the rest of the country. Nonetheless, we will use the initials CDU to refer to the entire organization, except in those instances in which we need to distinguish between the main party and its southern affiliate.

The other party represented in the Bundestag, the Free Democrats (FDP), also is a postwar creation. Although, like the CDU, something of an heir to an earlier political tradition, the party was formed in 1948 by the merger of four separate regional parties sharing similar liberal views.

Doctrines and Policies

Although one might expect the CDU to have a religious *Weltanschauung,* the party has not developed a well-thought-out and unified program. A community of religious views does not guarantee agreement on political issues and the CDU, appealing to both Catholics and Protestants, lacks even religious consensus. Thus, its Christian orientation has amounted to little more than acceptance of the traditional values of Western civilization and vague references to the dignity of humans and divine moral law.

Just as compromise of contrasting religious views has produced a vague policy, so also compromise between different economic groups has resulted in ambiguous stands. Since the party offers a political home to Christian trade unionists as well as to big industry and finance, it has been forced to favor policies attractive to both. In the immediate postwar years, the CDU advocated, especially in industrial areas, nationalization of basic industries. But as the German recovery progressed, this part of the program was toned down or dropped altogether. In areas where the working class vote was inconsequential, the party was more a free enterprise party from the beginning. In general the party's goal is a "socially minded market economy," that is, free enterprise tempered by social conscience. The CDU was successful in the early and mid-1960s in getting laws enacted which were designed to promote widespread ownership of stocks and securities, particularly among lower- and middle-income groups. Tax and other inducements were offered to both employers and employees as a means of encouraging more and more people to invest in the economy.

For the first 20 years of the CDU's existence one person, Adenauer, was the party leader, and for 14 of those years he also served as Chancellor of Germany. Thus, to a considerable extent he came to embody the CDU's policy. Its objectives did not need to be elaborated any further than to urge continued support for Adenauer's direction of Germany's affairs. A graphic example of this is the party's appeal in the 1957 election. Their posters were pictures of Adenauer's head with the simple exhortation "No Experiments."

In foreign policy Adenauer sought to make Germany once again an acceptable member of the international community and an influential member of the Western alliance. Although he negotiated with the Soviet Union, he took a hard and, some thought, excessively inflexible line on relations with Communist countries. In keeping with this tradition the CDU has been quite skeptical of the *Ostpolitik* policy launched under SPD Chancellor Willy Brandt. It fears that too much has been conceded to the Russians, East Germans, and Poles for too little or too uncertain returns.

Although emphasizing its doubts about *Ostpolitik*, the CDU put its principal stress in the 1972 election upon the economic issue. It blamed Germany's high rate of inflation upon Socialist mismanagement of the economy. But it failed to offer any plan to correct the problem other than to advocate a return to the social market economy. During its short period in opposition it had done no more than it had when it was in power to develop a set of alternative policies. Its appeal to the voters was not so much a positive one as it was to warn that the left wing of the SPD was gaining control and would damage the country with wild schemes.

CDU tactics changed little for the 1976 election. The party continued to attack the SPD for mismanaging the economy and for running up a large budget deficit. Opposition to *Ostpolitik* was given a bit more prominence. The effort to paint the SPD as dangerous radicals was carried further by telling the electorate that the choice was between "Freedom or Socialism."

Although the SPD originated in the 19th century as a Marxist party, it already had begun to lose some of its extreme views around the turn of the century. The party came to accept parliamentary democracy and gradual, evolutionary reform. When its left wing split off to form the Communist party after World War I, the party became still more moderate. The party's transformation into a contemporary social democratic party was not completed, however, until well into the Bonn Republic. In large measure this delay was due to the influence of Kurt Schumacher, the party's first leader after World War II. Schumacher had been a socialist for too long to be willing to consider any revision of basic party doctrine. Thus, for example, in keeping with traditional party policy the SPD opposed German rearmament and membership in NATO. Schumacher scorned Adenauer as "the Chancellor of the Allies" for advocating these measures.

Schumacher's death in 1952, combined with the failure of the SPD to expand its electoral support as rapidly as the CDU, encouraged a reassessment of party policy during the 1950s. This process culminated in a major revision of party policy in 1959. This new basic program of the SPD usually is referred to as the Bad Godesberg Program after the name of the town where the party meet to approve the program.[1]

The Bad Godesberg Program reverses the three main policy themes or doctrines that traditionally were associated with the SPD—socialism, pacifism, and anticlericalism. The aim was to project an image of a moderate, nondogmatic party. Thus, in economic matters the Program does not talk of such traditional socialist policies as total state planning or class struggle. Instead, free competition was, incredibly, said to be one of the "essential conditions of a social democratic economic policy." The SPD explained that it favored "a free market wherever free competition really exists." "Efficient small and medium-sized enterprises are to be strengthened to enable them to prevail in competition with large-scale enterprises." This is about as socialist as Teddy Roosevelt's trust busting was.

The traditional remedy of public ownership was not ignored entirely. Where there were natural monopolies, as in the supply of electricity, public ownership would be necessary. And government-owned industries might be useful competitors to keep private concerns from so dominating the economy as to abridge freedom. But the Program went on to warn that "every concentration of economic power, even in the hands of the state, harbours dangers." While conservatives might observe that concentrated economic power would be a danger especially, rather than even, in the hands of the state, yet they would agree that this represents a new attitude by socialists toward government economic action. To guard against the danger, the SPD indicated that it wanted to avoid a centralized bureaucracy. Thus any government-owned business should be run by governing boards representing workers and consumers. In any event, government ownership was viewed as a last resort which, apparently unfortunately, might be required in some cases, but which the true socialist would resist with great effort. The aim should be not to abolish the capitalist system

---

[1] The text of the Bad Godesberg Program appears in William Andrews, ed., *European Political Institutions*, 2d ed. (Princeton: D. Van Nostrand Co., Inc., 1966), pp. 187–98.

but to correct its abuses—a goal that perhaps even the head of General Motors might be willing to accept. The party's slogan in the 1960s was the innocuous: "As much competition as possible—as much planning as necessary."

Given Marx's view on religion—the opiate of the people—it hardly is surprising that socialist parties traditionally have been anticlerical. This disposition has been reinforced in Europe by the highly conservative social and economic stance of the Church at most times and its active involvement in politics. In Germany this hostility has been directed at least as much against the Lutheran Church, which as the dominant Protestant faith almost has been an established church, as against the Catholic Church.

Reversing all this, the Bad Godesberg Program revealed that socialism was "rooted in Christian ethics, humanism, and classical philosophy." Had there been many Moslems in Germany, that religion probably would have been included as a source as well. Contrary to what some may have thought, the SPD emphasized that it "does not proclaim ultimate truths . . . out of respect for the individual's choice in these matters of conscience." And just in case someone still had not gotten the point, the Program proclaimed that "freedom to preach the gospel must be protected." The party did stop short of changing its name to Christian Socialists.

Finally, the party changed its stance on military matters. It gave firm support to military preparations essential for national defense. The year after the Bad Godesberg conference, the SPD defense spokesman in the Bundestag carried this reversal in policy to the next stage by formally announcing the party's acceptance of German membership in NATO.

Thus the SPD became more of a social democratic or social welfare party than a socialist party. It is concerned about those members of society whom the CDU's social market economy policies have not cared for adequately. The SPD clearly is the more reform-minded party. Yet the policy differences between the two leading parties have narrowed significantly. The alternatives now are social welfare or welfare capitalism instead of Marxist socialism and laissez faire capitalism.

For the 1976 campaign the SPD produced a virtual remake of the CDU's 1957 Adenauer poster. A picture of Chancellor Helmut Schmidt carried the caption, "Experience is What Counts." The SPD countered the CDU charge that their *Ostpolitik* was soft on Communism by asserting that the Christian Democrats were warmongers. They told the electorate that to vote for the SPD was to "Vote for Peace."

The convergence of the two main parties' policies has made staking out a distinctive position very difficult for the other party represented in the Bundestag, the Free Democrats. The FDP's shifts in orientation also have blurred its image. The FDP's original aim was to appeal to those who disliked socialism but also opposed religious values in politics. It emphasized the need for political, religious, and economic freedom. Gradually by the early 1960s it had come to stress the last of these most and had moved to the right on the political spectrum. This shift halted in 1966 when the party withdrew from its coalition with the CDU. Since then, the FDP has sought to present a more liberal and reform-minded image. As the only party in the Bundestag in opposition to the Grand Coalition of the CDU and the SPD in the late 1960s, the FDP offered energetic and constructive criticism of the Government. After the 1969 elections it joined the SPD in a coalition government.

Despite these developments, policy strains exist between the FDP and SPD. The FDP tends to be rather unsympathetic to the demands and power of the trade unions. And it also is very dubious about SPD plans for extending the system of worker participation in the management of private industry. In fact, some observers have commented that the main reason why the coalition between the SPD and the FDP worked successfully from 1969 to 1972 was the fact that the Government's main concern during this period was foreign policy. In these matters the coalition partners were in considerable agreement, especially given that the FDP leader, Walter Scheel, was the Foreign Secretary. But in domestic policy, toward which the Government began to turn its attention in 1973, the two parties differ more.

Nonetheless, the coalition between the FDP and the SPD not only continued during the early 1970s, but was renewed following the 1976 election despite the efforts of the CDU to woo the FDP over to them. It must be stressed, however, that this was at the national level only. On the state level some coalitions between the SPD and the FDP have crumbled and have been replaced by CDU coalitions with the FDP. Some observers believe that these developments foretell what will happen on the national level in a few years.

Prior to the 1976 election, however, the FDP and SPD did manage to work out a compromise on the domestic issue which had been causing the greatest contention between them—the extent of worker participation in the management of industry. Although legislation was passed expanding this arrangement—a victory for the SPD—the FDP was able to force a significant concession which resulted in the trade unions gaining less power than they had wanted on the managing boards of German industry. While hardly satisfied, the unions are willing to accept the result, at least for the present.

Thus, despite their differences, the SPD and the FDP have managed to maintain a working partnership. The Christian Democrats are divided sharply on their strategy toward the FDP. Some of them, for example party Leader Helmut Kohl, want to project a moderate image to win over the FDP, while others like the head of the CSU, Franz Josef Strauss, want to write off the FDP as a lost cause and have the Christian Democrats take a strongly conservative line in both domestic and foreign policy.

Supporters and Strengths

As we noted, the religious component of the CDU's policy has not been especially marked. Nonetheless, at the start of the Bonn Republic its Christian aspect did have a particular appeal to some. Christian precepts afforded a rallying symbol for many who had been guilty of blindness toward the Hitler regime. This aspect of the party seems, however, to have been more attractive to Catholics than to Protestants, for the CDU has succeeded only partially in its effort not to be a denominational party. Although slightly less than half the population of Germany is Catholic, 60 percent of the CDU's voters are and 75 percent of its members are. Thus, while the CDU clearly is a secular party, religion is an important factor in its electoral support.

The religious aspect helps to account for the class diversity of the CDU electorate. To be sure, the percentage of support for the CDU does increase as you go up the income scale. But backing from Christian trade unionists gives the party sizable support among the working class as well. In addition, the party always has had strong support from the middle class. Increasingly over the years it has gained supporters among industrialists and farmers. The party's supposed religious stance usually is cited as the reason that it is able to win more support among women than is the SPD.

Those Länder, or states, where the CDU is strong can be seen from Figure 20–2. Combining this map with the one in Figure 20–3 helps to indicate the importance of religion in support for the CDU. The CDU has done well in some states where Catholics are in a minority, and so clearly matters other than religion are important in German voting behavior. On the other hand, however, in every Land 45 percent or more Catholic, the CDU has been strong. The religious composition of Bavaria and Rhineland-Palatainate is an important factor in explaining why these two states, both among the less prosperous areas of Germany, vote consistently for the Christian Democrats instead of for the more welfare-, reform-minded SPD. The Christian Democrats' strength in Bavaria is especially important, since it is the second largest German Land and returns almost one fifth of the members of the Bundestag.

For most of the Bonn Republic, the CDU was the dominant Government party. Although, as Table 20–1 shows, it won only eight seats more than the SPD in the first election, it formed the Government and the SPD became the Opposition. During the next two elections the CDU gained considerable ground, mainly at the expense of the minor parties. The

FIGURE 20–2
Major Party Strengths and Prosperity

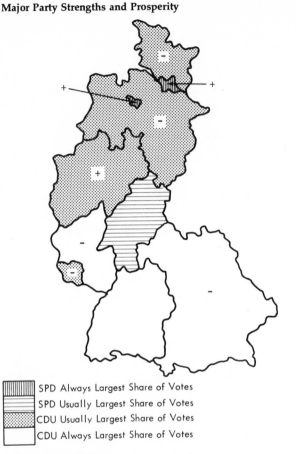

SPD Always Largest Share of Votes
SPD Usually Largest Share of Votes
CDU Usually Largest Share of Votes
CDU Always Largest Share of Votes

Per capita taxable income:
+ above national average
national average
− below national average

vagueness of the party's doctrines and the appeal of Adenauer enabled the CDU to construct a broad coalition of diverse supporters. This culminated in the party's winning half of the popular vote in 1957, an event unique in German political history. Then, during the 1960s, the party lost a little ground, dropping back to about where it had been in 1953. From 1966 to 1969 the Christian Democrats had to share power in the Grand Coalition with their chief rivals, the SPD. And since 1969 the CDU has had to watch the SPD run the country, since it now has become the Opposition.

Having held power for 20 years, the CDU has not adjusted very well to the role of the Opposition party. Internal conflicts and disagreements,

FIGURE 20–3
Percent Catholic of Population, by Land

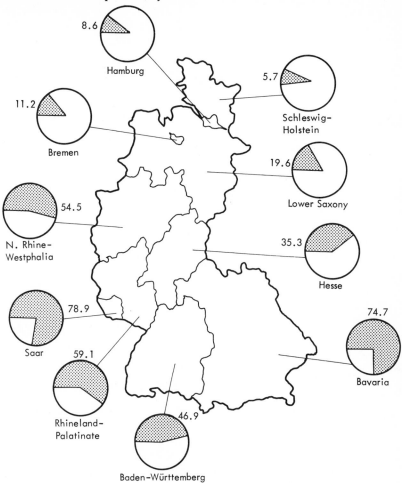

especially between the CDU and the CSU, have hampered the party. No longer having the power of a Government position to strengthen themselves, the party's leaders have appeared weak and unable to repel challengers to their authority. Nonetheless, the Christian Democrats did make substantial electoral gains in the 1976 elections, falling only 6 seats short of an absolute majority. Furthermore, as Figure 20–4 indicates, the Christian Democrats' gains were not confined to their areas of traditionally greatest strength. Although Figure 20–4 does not indicate it, the Christian Democrats made even greater gains in a number of cities, which normally have been the backbone of SPD strength.

TABLE 20–1
Election Results in the Bonn Republic

	1949		1953		1957		1961		1965		1969		1972		1976	
	%	Seats	%	Seats	%	Seats	%	Seats	%	Seats	%	Seats	%	Seats	%	Seats
CDU/CSU	31	139	45	243	50	270	45	242	48	245	46	242	45	225	49	243
SPD	29	131	29	151	32	169	36	190	39	202	43	224	46	230	43	214
FDP	12	52	10	48	8	41	13	67	10	49	6	30	8	41	8	39
Others	28	80	17	45	10	17	6	0	4	0	5	0	1	0	1	0

FIGURE 20–4
Shift in Popular Vote to Christian Democrats in 1976
Compared with 1972

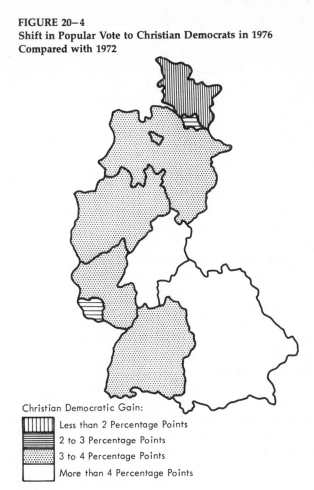

Christian Democratic Gain:

|||||| Less than 2 Percentage Points
≡ 2 to 3 Percentage Points
░ 3 to 4 Percentage Points
☐ More than 4 Percentage Points

Given the absence in Germany of a strong Communist party, the SPD gains the bulk of the working-class vote. Almost three fourths of the SPD vote comes from this source. White collar workers, intellectuals, and pensioners are the other main supporting groups. As Figure 20–2 shows, the SPD is strongest in the "city-states" of Hamburg and Bremen. The large number of workers in these urban, industrialized states helps to account for this strength. And as Figure 20–3 shows, the proportion of Catholics in these two Länder is quite low. Germany has other industrial areas. But except for the Saar, the Länder are sufficiently large to encompass rural areas as well, which tends to dilute the impact of the working-class vote. Even the Saar is not totally industrial and in any event has the highest proportion of Catholics of any German Land.

As already noted, the SPD did nearly as well as the CDU in the first election. The SPD was hurt by the division of Germany into two countries. What is now East Germany includes many areas that formerly were SPD strongholds, in part because that section of Germany was much more heavily Protestant than what is now West Germany. Had East Germany been part of the Bonn Republic the SPD almost certainly would have been the largest party, as it had been at various times in both Imperial and Weimar Germany. As it was, had the Russians not objected to considering West Berlin a part of West Germany, the SPD would have been the strongest party in the Bundestag in 1949, since the delegation from West Berlin was overwhelmingly Socialist.

The SPD's failure to expand its support at the same rate as the CDU appeared to condemn it perpetually to the role of Opposition party. By the late 1950s the party almost had convinced itself that it never could hope to win more than a third of the popular vote. This mood of resignation or futility helped those who wanted to modernized the party's doctrines to carry out the revisions of the Bad Godesberg Program. Since all else apparently had failed to bring success, party members were more willing to consider changing the party's image.

One hesitates to argue that a single factor could be the cause of a major change in party fortunes, for, after all, in any democracy the voters eventually become dissatisfied with the party in power and decide that it is time for a change. And it was highly unlikely, as indeed has proven to be the case, that once Adenauer had passed from the scene the CDU would be able to find another leader of his abilities and electoral appeal. In any event, in the ten years leading up to the Bad Godesberg Program the SPD vote increased by only 3 percentage points, while the following decade saw a gain of 11 percentage points. By the early 1970s the SPD not only had become the dominant party in the Government coalition, but had managed to win a slightly greater share of the popular vote than did the Christian Democrats. Such results have convinced many SPD members that the party owes its success to the Bad Godesberg Program and Willy Brandt, the party chairman since 1964. Despite some loss of support in the 1976 election, the SPD remains substantially stronger than it was prior to Bad Godesberg.

The Free Democrats' main source of support has been the urban, Protestant middle class. It has appealed to professional and business people who feel that the CDU is too dominated by big business. Yet given the fact, as we have noted, that the FDP in the 1960s seemed to be moving to the right, the party also has gained support from large conservative industrialists who believe the CDU is too welfare minded. These diverse perceptions are indicative of the general ambiguity of party platforms in Germany. The FDP also has received some support from large farmers. With its shift back toward the center of the political spectrum and its coalition with the SPD, it has become more attractive to liberals, intellectuals, and students. Over the years the heart of the FDP's support has tended to shift from the self-employed middle class to white-collar workers and civil servants.

The electoral success of the FDP has been rather limited, as can be seen from Table 20–1. During the 1950s the party seemed to be heading for elimination from the Bundestag, as had occurred to all other minor parties. In the 1961 election, however, the FDP enjoyed its greatest electoral success. Most observers believed that the FDP had gained CDU voters who had defected from their own party as a form of protest against the refusal of Adenauer to retire, despite being 85 years old. The fact that the party began slipping once again in the next election tends to support this view.

The decline progressed so far that by the 1972 election some people were speculating that the FDP might not be able to clear the 5 percent barrier of the electoral system and would be eliminated from the Bundestag. The party did rather better, however, than had been expected. But some have argued that this was due to the votes of those who did not want the CDU to return to office and yet could not bring themselves to vote for the SPD. Therefore they supported the FDP, knowing that it would continue the coalition with the SPD, which would keep the CDU out of power.

Recent elections appear to have stabilized electoral support for the FDP. The fact that Germany has PR means that the FDP can convert its electoral support into enough seats in the legislature to influence policy significantly as a junior partner in a coalition Government. Recall that in both 1974 elections in Britain the Liberal party won well over twice as great a share of popular vote as did the FDP in Germany in 1976. Yet under the British electoral system the Liberals gained hardly more than a dozen seats, only about one third as many as the FDP, and thus have not been given Cabinet seats in a coalition Government.

As Table 20–1 shows, support for parties other than the three just discussed has dwindled to almost nothing. Nonetheless, two additional parties—one at each end of the political spectrum—deserve comment. An attempt to revive a Nazi-type party, under the label of Socialist Reich party, was unsuccessful. The party received some support in state elections in northern Germany in the early 1950s but was banned by the Federal Constitutional Court in 1952. A new right-wing party, mainly a coalition of three small parties, was formed in late 1964 to contest the election of September 1965. Calling itself the National Democratic party, the group succeeded in polling only 2 percent of the popular vote and failed to elect any deputies to the Bundestag. By 1968, however, it had elected 62 members in seven of the ten state legislatures. In the 1969 national elections, the NPD nominated more than 400 candidates but succeeded in polling only 4 percent of the total vote. Thus the 5 percent barrier of the electoral law kept the NPD out of Parliament. By 1972 the party had lost even what little support it previously had held. Thus the brief scare that a new Nazi party had started on the route to power in Germany was seen as having been an unnecessary concern.

The Communists' position had been roughly similar. In 1949 they polled 6 percent of the vote and won 15 seats in the Bundestag. But, when their support dropped to only 2 percent in 1953, they were eliminated from Parliament. In 1956 the Constitutional Court ruled favorably on the Cabinet's petition that the party be banned, in accordance with the constitutional injunction against antidemocratic parties. Many Germans doubted the political wisdom of this action, although legally sound, because it gave the Communists an opportunity to say that the government feared the victory of its ideas.

In late 1968 a new Communist party (a direct heir of the one banned in 1956) was organized. Many members of the former party rallied to the new group, now seeking to present the image of a reformist but nonradical party. Perhaps fearing that it might be banned, the party's chairman was careful to state publicly that the goals of the party conformed to the tenets of the Basic Law. Although now free to appeal to the voters, the Communists, like the neo-Nazis, have had virtually no success. This can be attributed to several factors. Many German soldiers saw something of Communism in Russia during the war. More important is the experience of those who have escaped from East Germany or who are refugees from other Communist controlled countries in Eastern Europe. The Berlin wall and the heavily patrolled boundary between East and West Germany hardly are good advertisements for Communism either. Finally the rapid economic recovery of West Germany and its continued prosperity make consideration of any extreme political doctrines unnecessary.

Party Organization and Power Structure

Despite the constitutional stipulation that parties participate in the formation of the political will of the people, the Germans have held aloof from party activities. Although earlier in the century party membership was relatively common in Germany, in 1953, when 32 million Germans were participating in a national election, less than 1.5 million of them were party members. The Nazi experience and its aftermath of denazification may well have made people cautious about joining parties and suggested that politics is best left alone. The German tradition of respect for authority and suspicion of a government based on debate and controversy seems as well to encourage some distrust of parties. Moreover, the exclusive and at times, autocratic attitude of party officials has discouraged potential recruits. In keeping with its working-class tradition, the SPD is the party that has placed the greatest emphasis on recruiting party members, in the sense of dues-paying, card-carrying adherents as distinct from verbal supporters.

Although the Basic Law says that political parties must account for the sources of their income, this requirement was not implemented by appropriate legislation until 1967. The Social Democrats had voluntarily published figures on income and expenditure, but the CDU and the FDP had not. The SPD therefore pushed for the enactment of legislation that would force a public accounting, a move that was successfully resisted for a long time by the other two parties.

The 1967 legislation stipulates that donations to a political party, or to one or more of its regional associations, which exceed the equivalent of $8,500 annually by an individual must be reported. Similarly, legally constituted bodies which contribute the equivalent of $85,000 or more must also be included in the party's report. Parties must publish the names and addresses of such donors. Personal donations up to about $200 per year are tax-exempt.

The major sources of party funds are three: membership dues, contributions from individuals and groups, and allocations from public funds. The SPD is the only party that receives substantial income from dues, which are graduated according to the income of members. In addition, the SPD asks its Bundestag deputies to contribute 20 percent of their salaries. The CDU also expects its Bundestag and Landtag deputies to make yearly contributions, although these are considerably smaller than those of the SPD.

An important source of funds for the CDU and the FDP is the so-called sponsors' associations, which really are intermediaries between these parties and business firms. The firms were induced to contribute, because in this way they could fight "the socialists," and also because the law permitted certain tax exemptions to firms making such contributions. The sponsors' associations have received support from a majority of all employers (more from large corporations). The contributors could indicate to which party they wanted the funds to go, but actual distribution was roughly in proportion to the relative strength of the two parties. Some small parties also have received help, but this has been relatively insignificant.

The SPD, through the state government of Hesse acting as the petitioner, challenged the constitutionality of the tax exemption granted to a sponsor group that was formed to collect money from a restricted number of large firms in industry, banking, trade, and insurance. In 1958 the Constitutional Court nullified the law granting the exemption. It held that a law which accords financially well-to-do citizens a privileged status violates "the basic right of citizens to equality." Since this decision was handed down, the contributions to sponsors' associations have declined, and the CDU and FDP have turned more to trade associations for direct support.

Even before the decision, however, those administering the political funds were dissatisfied about the way the system was working. Once a party received support from a sponsor association, its partners in the coalition also demanded funds. Moreover, nearly half of the business community was uncooperative. Many businessmen were doubtful about the results, because they found Bundestag members more interested in their party's popularity than in the contributors of funds. Yet the desire to keep the Social Democrats out kept the checks coming in.

The SPD cannot expect contributions from large corporations, but it has managed to sell expensive advertising space in its publications to certain businesses, notably breweries and department stores. Public relations contributions come from the party's own business firms, primarily newspapers and newsprint importers.

As we noted in the previous chapter, all German parties now are dependant to a considerable extent upon governmental subsidies.

The CDU party constitution designates the organizational levels (national, state, district, and local) and provides for party governing bodies.[2] Among the governing bodies is the annual party convention, which elects a party chairman (two-year term) and supposedly determines the basic outlines of policy. The Federal Committee, selected in a complicated manner, concerns itself with political and organizational matters; chooses the Election Commission, which participates with the CDU Land associations in the nomination of candidates to the Bundestag; and elects a treasurer and 15 members of the Federal Executive Committee, whose job it is to carry out party decisions. Since the Federal Executive Committee meets only every three months, it elects the Managing Executive Committee to direct day-to-day operations.

This brief organizational outline suggests that the CDU is a hierarchical and centralized organization. Adenauer's long tenure as leader and his patriarchial attitude toward his party associates heightened this impression. In actual practice, however, party organization at the Land level tends to have a fair amount of autonomy from central control. Furthermore, most of the paid party workers are at the Land level rather than at national party headquarters. On the other hand, although welcoming dues-paying members, the CDU never has succeeded in boosting membership much beyond 300,000. Thus, the result of party decentralization is not to give great influence in party matters to the rank and file, but rather to strengthen the power of regional party leaders.

---

[2] For a copy of the statute of the CDU, see John C. Lane and James K. Pollock, *Source Materials on the Government and Politics of Germany* (Ann Arbor, Mich.: George Wahr, 1964), pp. 187–91.

The importance of regional leaders is most pronounced in Bavaria. In this state the Christian Democrats are known as the Christian Social Union. The CDU does not run any candidates in Bavaria, while the CSU contests elections only there, leaving the rest of Germany to the CDU. The CSU is a separate party organization. Under the electoral law, for example, the votes received by the CSU are not combined with those for the CDU to determine a single total of Christian Democratic seats in the Bundestag. Although the CSU and CDU work together closely in the Bundestag, yet the CSU has its own set of party officers and frequently caucuses separately from the rest of the Christian Democrats, who have been elected under the CDU label.

Perhaps even more important in emphasizing the autonomy of the CSU from the CDU is the Bavarian affiliate's leader—Franz Josef Strauss. So long as Adenauer was leader of the CDU, Strauss was overshadowed by the national party leader. But since subsequent CDU leaders have lacked Adenauer's strength, Strauss has tended to overshadow them. Many Germans, both without and within the CDU, are highly suspicious of Strauss.

Comparing Strauss with Winston Churchill is, perhaps, not too far-fetched. Like Churchill, Strauss has great personal magnetism for many. Yet he also is extremely erratic, often given to great errors of judgement. In 1962, for example, while serving as Minister of Defense, Strauss ordered the police to raid the offices of the newsmagazine *Der Spiegel* ostensibly to search for improperly obtained classified military information, but really to silence its criticisms of the Government's defense policies. For many people this incident was evidence of Strauss' lack of commitment to democratic values. The fear was not that he was a potential dictator, but that were he to become Chancellor he would govern even more high-handedly than did de Gaulle in France.

Precisely because Strauss arouses such fears and anxieties, it is unlikely that he ever will become the national leader of the Christian Democrats or Chancellor. Yet the fact that his CSU group usually makes up one fifth of the total Christian Democratic strength in the Bundestag gives him considerable influence within the party. In five out of the eight national elections, the CSU, running candidates only in Bavaria, has polled more votes than has the FDP, operating on a national basis. In the 1976 elections the greatest Christian Democratic gains were in Bavaria, where the CSU increased its vote by almost 5 percentage points (see Figure 20–4). With 60 percent of the vote in Bavaria, the CSU had won a level of support greater than that of any other party in any other German state. Furthermore, the CSU share (22 percent) of the total Christian Democratic representation now is the largest it ever has been.

Strauss' capacity for mischief seems unlimited. In 1972 on the vote to ratify the treaties with the Soviet Union and Poland, which were part of the SPD's *Ostpolitik,* the national Christian Democrat leader, Rainer Barzel, wanted his party to vote in favor to demonstrate that Germany was united in trying to close the books on the past and establish normal relations with countries that had suffered Nazi aggression in World War II. Strong opposition from Strauss, however, forced Barzel to instruct the Christian Democrat members of the Bundestag to abstain on the vote.

For some time Strauss has toyed with the idea of expanding the CSU beyond the borders of Bavaria to organize the party and run candidates in the rest of Germany. He has seen this strategy as a means of driving the SPD from power. He argues that CSU candidates would gain the support of those who now vote for minor parties or abstain because they are not offered sufficiently conservative candidates. Thus the total Christian Democratic vote and its strength in the legislature would be increased. (Strauss' strategy is similar to that of the Goldwater-Reagan wing of the Republican party in the United States.) The national Christian Democratic leaders see things differently; they feel that the CSU candidates would take votes away from the CDU candidates without tapping any significant new sources of support. Thus, the result would be merely to strengthen the CSU at the expense of the CDU.

Whatever the probable outcome, the breaking point appeared to have been reached late in 1976. Strauss indicated that the CSU would not form a joint group with the CDU in the Bundestag, as it always had done in the past, and that he would move ahead with plans for expanding the CSU to all of Germany because Helmut Kohl, the national CDU leader had cost the Christian Democrats the 1976 elections by not taking a sufficiently hard line against socialism. Kohl responded that the CDU was beginning plans to establish itself in Bavaria, thus challenging the CSU for the Christian Democratic vote there. Perhaps it was this threat that drove Strauss back into line. At the last minute Strauss changed his mind and the CSU and CDU formed their usual joint legislative group. Nonetheless, it would be a mistake to believe that Strauss has given up his desire to be the top Christian Democratic leader by one means or another.

Although Helmut Kohl won the immediate battle, most people felt that over-all the controversy further weakened his position as national party leader. Strauss and others in the CDU continue to criticize both his tactics and his policies. Thus Kohl has not projected clearly the image of being in charge of the party. As a result the Christian Democrats remain in disarray despite their recent electoral gains.

Highly organized and having a strong hierarchy, the SPD is much more centralized than is the CDU.[3] Yet, paradoxically, it also has more of a tradition of rank-and-file participation. The SPD has tended to regard

---

[3] For the organization statute of the SPD, see Lane and Pollock, *Source Materials on the Government and Politics of Germany,* pp. 192–96.

itself as more of a working-class movement than a political party. It has sought a large membership, which was to be given an extensive voice in party decisions. Although the party claims to have over a million members, the stress on intraparty democracy has been more talk than reality. The leadership usually dominates party elections sufficiently to perpetuate itself in power and controls the party decision-making process so as to get its policies endorsed. In fact one of the classic studies of party organization, which concluded that all parties were oligarchies, was based to a considerable extent upon the way in which the SPD operated in the early part of the 20th century.[4]

The SPD holds a rank-and-file party conference every two years plus extraordinary conferences as needed. The conference elects the Executive, which wields the real power over party affairs. On policy matters, fundamental questions of organization, and election strategy, the Executive must consult with the Party Council before acting. Nonetheless, as the party rules make clear, the Executive is responsible for "the control of the party," for "conducting the party's business," and for guiding "the fundamental attitude of the party organs." Since the Executive meets only once a month, the day-to-day business of the party is conducted by the Managing Committee, composed of the two party chairmen and four or five paid party officials from the Executive. Given its function, the Managing Committee also exercises considerable influence on party policy.

The left wing of the SPD and the party's youth organization (the Jusos) have criticized the leadership for being too moderate and failing to implement more radical measures on government ownership of industry and redistribution of wealth. Although Willy Brandt is felt to be a bit more sympathetic to, or at least tolerant of such dissent, both he and Chancellor Helmut Schmidt have resisted any effort to shift the party away from the fundamental orientation of the Bad Godesberg Program.

Although in general the structure and operation of the SPD remain largely as they have been in the past, one significant change has occurred. The party no longer is connected officially with the trade unions. In order to get a united union movement, trade union leaders decided to avoid any party affiliations such as had been the practice in Germany and still exist in Britain. Thus, both Christian and socialist trade unionists could belong to the same organization. Nonetheless, many trade union leaders favor the SPD and actively assist the party even though their unions are not associated formally with it. This probably is one of the reasons why a separate Federation of Christian Trade Unions was formed in 1955. Despite this division of the unions on religious lines the German Federation of Trade Unions remains formally unconnected with the SPD.

[4] Robert Michels, *Political Parties,* translated by Eden and Cedar Paul (New York: Dover, 1959); first published in 1915.

The FDP is really a loose federation of Land parties, although the standing orders adopted in 1960 seek to impose more control from the center.[5] Despite its support of the unitary principle of governmental organization, its own organization is federal. The chairman of the party has less authority over its members than is true in the two major parties. Moreover, the party has prided itself on the lack of strict party discipline. Its members in the Bundestag and in the Land legislatures have been a great deal more independent than have the deputies of other parties. The defection of some FDP members of the Bundestag from support for the Government in 1972 produced the first attempt to use the constructive vote of no confidence procedure (explained more fully in Chapter 22) and resulted in calling elections a year early.

While more cohesive than the FDP, the major parties are not rigid blocks. The Christian Democrats are a diverse group, including businesspeople, farmers, and workers; conservatives as well as liberals. Added to these tensions are the regional fissures typified by Strauss and CSU. As for the SPD, abandoning Marxist ideology, which for a long time was the distinctive feature of the party, has made some adherents unhappy, despite the obvious electoral success of this step. The SPD's expanded electoral appeal means that it, like the Christian Democrats, has become a coalition of diverse interests and groups with all the potential internal conflicts that such a development implies. Nonetheless, the leading German parties have avoided splintering into a number of minor parties. And this is despite Germany's having a proportional representation electoral system, which is alleged by some political scientists to fractionalize the party system by encouraging disgruntled factions to split off from their party to form a new organization.

While the SPD has enjoyed some success in obtaining a mass party membership, it remains true that the great bulk of Germans are aloof from party activities. This, coupled with the main parties' vague doctrines and broadened appeal, suggests that German parties are becoming electoral machines, just as American parties are. They no longer are ideological or sectional group movements. Their purpose is not so much to serve as a vehicle for popular participation in the policy-making process as it is to support alternative teams of leaders who periodically appeal to the total electorate for power to run the government. While such a reorientation may reduce the opportunity for the rank and file to influence policy, it is likely to encourage more flexibility and compromise in politics. It must be emphasized that, instead of being a betrayal of principle, this is an important ingredient in the successful operation of a viable democratic system. To this extent the development of German parties and of the party system enhances the prospects for stable democracy.

---

[5] For standing orders of the FDP, see Lane and Pollock, *Source Materials on the Government and Politics of Germany*, pp. 197–99.

BIBLIOGRAPHICAL NOTE

Although a comprehensive study of German political parties has not yet appeared in English, Arnold J. Heidenheimer's *Adenauer and the CDU: The Rise of the Leader and the Integration of the Party* (The Hague: Martinus Nijhoff, 1960) constitutes an excellent first step. Three useful works on the SPD are: Douglas A. Chalmers, *The Social Democratic Party of Germany* (New Haven, Conn.: Yale University Press, 1964); Richard N. Hunt, *German Social Democracy, 1918–1933* (New Haven, Conn.: Yale University Press, 1964); and Harold K. Schellenger, Jr., *The SPD in the Bonn Republic: A Socialist Party Modernizes* (The Hague: Martinus Nijhoff, 1968).

21

The Legislative System

THE COMPOSITION OF THE HOUSES OF PARLIAMENT

Like virtually every other country, Germany has a bicameral legislature, although the composition of the upper house is relatively unusual. The lower house, the Bundestag, is composed of 496 members, elected by the procedures discussed in Chapter 19. Their term of office is four years, unless the Bundestag is dissolved early, which has occurred only in 1972. In addition 22 delegates are chosen from West Berlin. Instead of being popularly elected by the West Berliners, they are selected by the legislature for West Berlin. They are not permitted to vote in regular sessions of the Bundestag on legislative matters or in the election of the Chancellor. They can participate fully in debates on bills, however, and do have a vote in the Bundestag's committees. This peculiar situation is due to the fact that the Soviet Union refuses to recognize West Berlin as a part of the Federal Republic of Germany.

The upper house, the Bundesrat, is to provide a federal component in the legislature, just as the American Senate is. In implementing the federal principle Germany has gone beyond even the United States. American Senators do represent their respective states, but, since 1913, have been elected by the people of those states. Thus, they do not really represent the constituent governmental units of the federal system. They did so more nearly prior to 1913, when they were selected by state legislatures. In Germany members of the Bundesrat clearly represent the state governments, since they are chosen by the executive branch of those governments. A comparable practice in the United States would be for the governor of a state, in consultation with his or her executive associates, to appoint the two United States Senators from that state. Such a procedure insures that the views of the state governments are considered in the national legislative process. Thus it can be argued that "states' opinions," if not "states' rights," has been carried a step farther in Germany than in the United States.

The Bundesrat members usually are members of the cabinet of their state government and hence play a dual national and local role. The Bundesrat has no set term and its members continue to serve so long as their state governments send them to the national legislature. Each German state has from three to five members in the Bundesrat depending upon the state's population. West Berlin is permitted to send four "observers" to the Bundesrat. Although they are allowed to vote in the chamber's regular sessions, this is only advisory, since the votes are not counted with those of the representatives from the other German states. Aside from the delegates from West Berlin, the total membership of the Bundesrat is 41. The seating arrangement is alphabetical by state delegation.

The party composition of the Bundesrat depends upon the political party control in each of the Länder. The deputies from each state vote in a bloc as instructed by their state governments. To the extent that the Bundesrat is important in national politics, therefore, it is incumbent upon the national parties to seek control of Land governments. In actual practice, state election campaigns frequently have been dominated by national issues rather than matters of state concern. Thus, paradoxically, making the Bundesrat a more federal body than the American Senate has resulted in nationalizing state politics—that is, reducing the importance of purely regional and local political questions.

Turning to the Bundestag, the largest occupational group by far is civil servants. (This is a bit misleading since the term includes school and university teachers, who typically have civil service status.) Civil servants can take leave from the bureaucracy to serve in an elective office and later return to their administrative position without any loss of status. This helps to explain why well over 40 percent of the Bundestag are civil servants of one type or another. White-collar workers account for not quite a seventh of the membership as do also political party and trade union officials. Self-employed and professional people each constitute one tenth of the membership. Despite the strength of the SPD, manual workers make up only two percent of the membership. At the same time, well over half of the members belong to a union.

Although a woman served as the presiding officer of the Bundestag from 1972 to 1976, the proportion of women members has declined from 1 in 12 in 1961 to 1 in 14 in 1976. The educational level of the members has risen over the years. Whereas formerly only about half had university degrees, now about three fourths do.

In recent years there has been a trend toward younger members in the Bundestag. The average age of members in 1957 was 52, but had declined to 47 in 1976. Associated with this decline has been an influx of new members. Almost one third of the members elected to the Bundestag in 1969 were serving for the first time. The same was true in the 1972 election. After that election there remained only ten members of the Bundestag who had served in the first post-World War II legislature elected in 1949. The rapid rate of turnover declined in 1976 with less than a quarter of those elected serving for the first time.

Salaries for Bundestag deputies are generous. Until 1976 the salary was tax exempt, but in November 1975 the Federal Constitutional Court ruled that deputies must pay tax on their legislative income. To compensate members for this, the salary was almost doubled in 1977 to 7,500 DM a month (well in excess of $3,000). A typical deputy will have a net income of over $26,500 a year. In addition to the salary, deputies receive other benefits, such as an annual tax-free expense allowance of over $23,000. Furthermore, deputies can claim up to $1,000 a month more to pay for secretarial and other office assistance.

ORGANIZATIONAL STRUCTURE

As do other legislative bodies, the Bundestag and the Bundesrat have standing orders of procedure, presiding officers, committees, and established modes of doing business. Because of the basic differences between the two bodies, notably the absence of a significant role for political parties in the Bundesrat, the organization of the two bodies is somewhat dissimilar.[1]

The physical arrangement of the Bundestag has been the subject of debate. For the first several years it was housed in a lecture-hall type of chamber, with the members of the Cabinet sitting on a raised platform at the front. Deputies wishing to speak could not do so from their seats but had to proceed to the front of the chamber. Under the urgings of its president, the Bundestag in 1961 decided to remodel the chamber so as to resemble the British House of Commons (to a degree) by arranging to have the majority party and opposition parties face each other; this would have enabled the deputies to speak from their seats. The Cabinet would have had a special area on the majority side. Partly because of the narrowness of the vote, and partly because of plans to build a huge new parliament building, the exact nature of the chamber was left to be determined later.

---

[1] For the standing orders of the Bundestag and Bundesrat see John C. Lane and James K. Pollock, *Source Materials on the Government and Politics of Germany* (Ann Arbor, Mich., 1964), pp. 60–67 and 70–72.

Although the new building containing offices for the members of the Bundestag has been completed, the meeting chamber itself was only slightly redesigned. The seating arrangement has not been altered fundamentally; the members sit at desks arranged in a fan shape, like the American House of Representatives, instead of facing each other on benches as in Britain. Unlike in the United States, however, members of the Bundesrat are permitted to sit as spectators at the front of the chamber facing the Bundestag from behind a long desk to the president's right. And the Chancellor and the Cabinet are located similarly to the president's left. Until recently the Chancellor and the Cabinet physically looked down upon the Bundestag, since their seats were raised above floor level. In 1969, as a symbolic gesture indicating that the executive was not to domineer over the legislature, the Cabinet's seats were lowered to about the level of the Bundestag's.

The presiding officer of the Bundestag, known as the president, is elected by that body from among its own members by secret ballot, and serves until a new Bundestag is elected. Thus far, he or she has been a member of the ruling coalition or majority party. His or her authority extends to such things as the rights, prerogatives, and internal order of the Bundestag. He or she is vested with vague police powers, which have been interpreted as granting authority to exclude unruly deputies from sessions of the Bundestag up to 30 days at a time. Unlike the Speaker in the House of Commons, the president of the Bundestag is an active party leader. Assisting the president are four vice presidents and a number of recording secretaries, also elected by the Bundestag from among its members.

The key organizational unit of the Bundestag is the party group or *Fraktion*. Usually all the deputies of a given party, the SPD, for example, combine to form a *Fraktion*. Standing orders stipulate, however, that a group with fewer than 15 members cannot qualify as a *Fraktion*. The significance of this rule is that individual deputies or deputies who represent a small party will not have much influence in the legislative process unless they can combine with enough others to meet the minimum. This provision is of little practical importance now, since even the FDP, the smallest of three parties represented in the Bundestag, has well over twice the minimum number. In the first couple of Bundestagen, however, the situation differed. In 1949 the Communist party had exactly the minimum number, while the Center party and the Union for Economic Reconstruction both fell short. The rule is another example of the steps the Germans have taken to hamper small parties and avoid the splintering of the party system that helped to weaken the Weimar Republic.

Only *Fraktionen* are entitled to committee assignments and are permitted to introduce legislation. Furthermore, debate time is alloted to *Fraktionen* on the basis of their relative strength in the Bundestag. The *Frak-*

tionen in turn decide which of their members are to receive the committee posts allocated to the party group and which of their members are to be granted what segment of the debate time given the group. Hence, despite Article 38 of the Basic Law, which states that deputies are ''not bound by orders and instructions and are subject only to their conscience,'' they can exert influence only if they belong to a *Fraktion*.

An important power center is the Council of Elders, a type of steering committee. It is a permanent committee of 28 members, composed of the Bundestag president (who presides over the Council as well), the vice presidents, and representatives designated by each *Fraktion* in proportion to its strength in the Bundestag. The Council of Elders meets weekly to set the agenda for the Bundestag and determine the time to be allowed for debating each subject. It is responsible for securing cooperation among the *Fraktionen* to facilitate the work of the Bundestag. The Council of Elders also appoints the presiding officer of the various legislative committees. While the Bundestag can override any of the decisions of the Council of Elders, this rarely occurs.

The Bundestag has 19 permanent subject matter committees, ranging in size from 17 to 33 members with 27 being the typical number. Each *Fraktion* is represented in proportion to its strength in the Bundestag. In an interesting departure from American practice, committee heads are allocated among all the parties according to their legislative strength. Thus, for example, in the 1972–76 Bundestag the SPD and the Christian Democrats each headed nine committees, the remaining one going to the FDP.

The various party groups seek to assign members to committees in accordance with the special competence of their deputies, but the standard of performance varies a good deal from committee to committee. One reason for this is that at times a bill may be referred to as many as three committees, with all the consequences that divided responsibility may bring. On the whole, however, parties seem to work better in committees than they do in the Bundestag. Antagonism between Cabinet and the Opposition is far less in evidence in committees, perhaps because committee work is not open to the glare of publicity. Also, as mentioned above, the Opposition holds a number of chairmanships and deputy chairmanships, which may make for a greater sense of responsibility.

Committees are empowered to call in expert witnesses, and on important occasions their sessions are attended by appropriate ministers and their assistants. In this way, committees have the benefit of the Cabinet's point of view when it is needed most. Representatives from West Berlin who are assigned committee posts participate fully, including the right to vote.

The Bundestag performs most of its significant legislative work in committee. As a result, it spends much less time in regular sessions than do most legislative bodies. The Bundestag sits for little more than 300 hours a year, which is little more than a quarter of time which the U.S. Senate spends in such meetings.

An interesting innovation was the Bundestag's creation, when the new German army was established, of the post of Defense Commissioner. The Commissioner is elected by the Bundestag to investigate all complaints about possible violation of the basic rights of soldiers or of the principles of internal leadership in the military forces. The Commissioner has access to pertinent papers and other necessary information and may refer complaints to appropriate sources for settlement. The Bundestag intends the Commissioner to serve as a watchdog guarding against the development of antidemocratic sentiments in the military. The Defense Commissioner has served in several instances to alert the Bundestag to practices that it wants to eliminate.[2]

Like the lower house, the Bundesrat does the bulk of its work in committee. It has only 13 committees with each of the ten Länder being represented equally. West Berlin is permitted to send an observer to each committee, but this person is not allowed to vote. The presiding officer of the Bundesrat, known as the president, is elected annually. The practice is to select a new president each year, rotating the office so that over a period of years each of the Länder will have held the presiding officer's chair.

POWERS AND PROCEDURES

Legislative powers are divided between the central government and the governments of the Länder. The constitution specifies that in some areas the central government has exclusive jurisdiction, while in others there is concurrent authority. The central government has exclusive legislative power (Article 73) in such matters as foreign affairs, citizenship, freedom of movement (passports, immigration, and so on), fiscal regulations (currency, money, coinage, and so on), customs and tariffs, posts and telecommunications, national railroads and air traffic, the legal status of persons in the service of the central government, industrial property rights (patents, and so on), cooperation of the national government and the Länder in the field of criminal police, and in matters concerning the protection of the constitution. In the areas of exclusive national power, the Länder can legislate only if, and insofar as, they are expressly so empowered by law by the central government.

---

[2] Klaus Bolling, *Republic in Suspense: West Germany Today* (New York: Frederick A. Praeger, Inc., 1964), pp. 184–85. Also see Lane and Pollock, *Source Materials on the Government and Politics of Germany*, pp. 127–28, and Walter Stahl, *Politics of Postwar Germany* (New York: Frederick A. Praeger, Inc., 1963), pp. 260 ff.

The constitution sets forth a long list (Article 74) of matters that fall in the realm of concurrent powers, matters over which the Länder are empowered to legislate as long as, and insofar as, the central government does not use its legislative power. The constitution stipulates, however, that the central government can act in these areas only insofar as national regulation is needed because the Länder cannot act effectively or because action by one or more Länder would injure the interests of the other states or the nation as a whole. Finally, Article 75 lists several matters for which the central government may issue general directives, but must leave detailed control to the Länder. Other articles round out the division of powers between the central government and the states. Significantly, education and cultural affairs are left primarily to the Länder. Moreover, administration, even of laws passed by the central government, is left largely to state officials.

Bills may be initiated by legislators or by the Government. They may start in either house, except that Government sponsored bills must begin in the Bundesrat, which sends them to the Bundestag via the Cabinet. In this way, the Bundestag knows the views of the Bundesrat, which is to say the Land Governments, on the Cabinet's proposals as well as the Cabinet's reaction to the Bundesrat's position. Bills which originate in the Bundesrat are submitted to the Bundestag via the Cabinet, which must attach a statement of its views on the proposal.

The process of passing a bill from this point on can be clarified by referring to Figure 21–1. Bills are considered by the Bundestag in three readings. On first reading the basic principles are discussed and a vote taken. If the vote is favorable, the bill goes to committee. As noted previously, party lines are more fluid in committees than on the floor of the Bundestag. Thus bills receive thorough consideration before being sent back to the chamber. Some of the Cabinet ministers have close contact with various of the committees. Should some aspect of the proposed legislation which they favored have been eliminated from the bill by the Cabinet, such ministers may take their case to their legislative allies on the committees.

When the bill is returned from committee it receives a second reading, a time when the detailed provisions of the bill are debated and amendments considered. Discussion on third reading is largely confined to a general debate of the main features of the bill, although amendments are also in order if supported by at least 15 deputies. On third reading, each deputy may speak a maximum of one hour unless the majority, by resolution, accords him or her more time. In urgent circumstances, all three readings of a bill can take place in a single day provided there is unanimous agreement. After passage in the Bundestag, all bills are transmitted to the Bundesrat.

Voting in the Bundestag is by a show of hands or by standing. In case of

FIGURE 21–1
West German Legislative Procedure

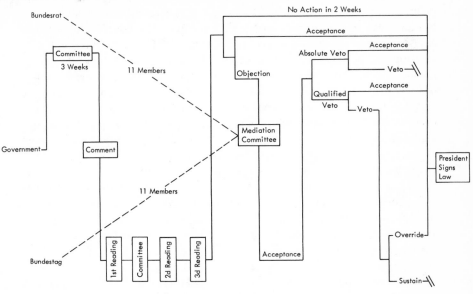

doubt, there is a division, similar to the one employed in Britain, in which deputies file through doors past counting clerks. If as many as 50 members request it in advance, a roll call vote is taken.

On the motion of 30 members, closure can be voted upon and debate is terminated if a majority wishes to do so. This rarely is necessary, however, since the debate in the Bundestag tends to be too limited rather than too lengthy. In the 1961–65 Bundestag only 40 percent of the members ever spoke at all and only 6 percent spoke more than three times. One third of all the speeches made by Christian Democrats were made by only 8 percent of their members and over half of the speeches made by Socialists were made by only 11 percent of their members. Over 60 percent of all the bills passed by that Bundestag went through all three readings without being debated at all. And of those that were debated, almost one quarter were discussed for less than ten minutes. Less than 6 percent of the bills enacted were debated on the floor of the Bundestag for more than three hours.[3]

The reason for this is that the Germans tend to regard the legislative process as an activity which brings legal expertise to bear on a proposed statute so that it will be properly worded. Thus, extensive discussion of

---

[3] Wilhelm Hennis, "Reform of the Bundestag: The Case for General Debate," in Gerhard Loewenberg, ed., *Modern Parliaments: Change or Decline?* (Chicago, Aldine-Atherton, 1971), pp. 75, 78.

the general principles involved in the bill by those lacking legal knowledge is not regarded as useful. Furthermore, since various deals or compromises have been worked out among the concerned interests when the bill has been in committee, further discussion on the floor of the Bundestag seems superfluous. The problem is that the Germans have not fully grasped the importance of debate and discussion in the legislature as a means to legitimate the policy output of the government. People are much more willing to accept distasteful rules and regulations if they feel that the various alternatives have been considered fully and that the particular point of view they favor has had a chance to be heard. Related to this legitimating function of the legislature is its educative function. Through debates on the principles of legislation, a parliament has the opportunity to air the most prominent views on the leading public issues of the day. Even limited reports in popular newspapers of such debates help to educate and inform the citizens. The Bundestag, however, apparently regards performance of this function as either unnecessary or unimportant. To this extent, there remains something of an elitist orientation to the German political process.

The Bundestag still lacks an imaginative and aggressive group of well-educated and politically trained members who realize that their chief task is to depict and explain things as they are and, in the process, to win the people's support for future policies. Many energetic deputies have spent much time on committee work and in trying to compete with the bureaucrats in mastering details. And while this is not to be deplored, it often has been done at the expense of debating the main issues of policy. The deputies seem to be groping to develop a style suited to their system, but the downgrading of debate in the Adenauer era hampered that development.

But to return to the process of a bill through parliament and Figure 21-1, when the bill reaches the Bundesrat it usually is sent to a committee. Thereafter it is considered by the entire house in a single reading, where all voting is by roll call of the Länder. As indicated earlier, each state casts its three to five votes as a bloc. If the Bundesrat accepts the bill or fails to act within two weeks, the bill becomes law. Should it object, however, the process becomes rather complicated.

When the Bundestag and the Bundesrat disagree, a Mediation Committee meets to promote a workable compromise. Unlike conference committees in the U.S. Congress, which are established for particular bills as the need arises, this one has permanent status. It is composed of 11 members from each body. Aside from ministers of the national Government, no one else is permitted to attend its meetings except by express decision of the Committee. In order to provide continuity, the standing orders permit no more than four changes of membership during the existence of a single Bundestag.[4] Unlike the situation in the Bundesrat itself, Bundesrat members of the Mediation Committee are not bound to vote as their respective state governments would like them to. The record of the Mediation Committee, judged by the agreements it was successful in promoting, has been impressive. During the first three legislatures (1949–61), 181 bills were submitted to it, and of these 177 were passed by the two houses in the form recommended by the Committee.[5]

Helping to promote the success of the Mediation Committee is the fact that the Bundesrat has two kinds of vetoes—absolute and qualified. In matters affecting the interests of the states, the approval of the Bundesrat is required before a bill can become a law; should it not assent, the bill is dead. An example of a bill of this type is a taxation law providing, as frequently in the case in Germany, that a portion of the revenue raised is to go directly to the states. Bills on administrative matters affecting the states also are subject to absolute veto. Since most federal law in Germany is administered by the states, this encompasses many legislative proposals. In all, about half of all the bills considered by Parliament are subject to the absolute veto of the Bundesrat—must have its approval to become law.

On bills not involving the interests of the states, the Bundesrat has only a qualified veto. If it objects, the Bundestag can override it and make the bill law anyway. If the Bundesrat has rejected the bill by a simple majority, a majority in favor of it in the Bundestag is sufficient to override. Should the Bundesrat have voted against the bill by a two-thirds margin or greater, however, the Bundestag must vote for it by at least two-thirds.

As we have noted, conflict usually does not come to this pass, since the Mediation Committee is so successful. When the Bundesrat has a qualified veto it may, and usually does, call the Committee rather than voting against the bill. When the Bundesrat has an absolute veto, the Government or the Bundestag also can call the Committee. In either event the compromise worked out by the Mediation Committee tends to favor the Bundesrat's position.

Thus the Bundesrat, which is to say the state governments, usually can get what it wants. Since its members, as state executives, are involved in the administration of national legislation at the Land level, their knowledge of local conditions equips them to tell the national ministers, as well as Bundestag members generally, what will and what will not work, and how legislation should be drafted so as to achieve the best results. Furthermore, it must be stressed that since Government legislative proposals

---

[4] For the standing orders of the Mediation Committee, see Lane and Pollock, *Some Materials on the Government and Politics of Germany*, pp. 73–74.

[5] Alfred Grosser, *The Federal Republic of Germany* (New York: Frederick A. Praeger, Inc., 1964), p. 45.

go to the Bundesrat first for comment, the Government consults extensively with the Bundesrat in drafting legislation so as to avoid adverse comments from that house.

The constitution provides that the national government must keep the Bundesrat informed of the conduct of affairs. In order to do this, the Ministry of Bundesrat and Länder Affairs was created, although informing the Bundesrat is not its only task. Approximately once a week, the minister meets the permanent representatives from the Länder and tells them about Cabinet policies. Since he or she usually attends Bundesrat meetings and remains in close touch with its members, he or she is in a position to convey back to Cabinet colleagues the views of the Land representatives. Given the variety of means, then, that the Bundesrat has for influencing legislative output, it is not surprising that it has made less and less use of its power to initiate legislation.

The Bundesrat is one of the world's strongest upper houses. It helps to make the German legislature a significant element in the policy process and to balance the distribution of power between the executive and the legislature.

BIBLIOGRAPHICAL NOTE

Two studies of the German national legislature are Gerhard Loewenberg, *Parliament in the German Political System* (Ithaca, N.Y.: Cornell University Press, 1966), and R. K. Ullmann and Stephen King-Hall, *German Parliaments: A Study of the Development of Representative Institutions in Germany* (London: The Hansard Society, 1954). Also of interest are certain chapters in Karl Deutsch and Lewis Edinger, *Germany Rejoins the Powers* (Stanford, Cal.: Stanford University Press, 1959). For an examination of the role of the upper house see Edward Pinney, *Federalism, Bureaucracy and Party Politics in Western Germany: The Role of the Bundesrat* (Chapel Hill, University of North Carolina Press, 1963).

Policy-Making Structures

Germany follows the traditional parliamentary pattern of having a dual executive—that is, both a head of state and a head of Government. The head of state, whose position largely is ceremonial, is known as the President. The head of Government, who is the equivalent of a prime minister, is called the Chancellor.

THE ROLE OF THE PRESIDENT

Contrary to practice under Weimar, the President is not popularly elected. This is to help restrict the President to only a ceremonial role; a President cannot claim to embody the popular will as fully as does Parliament. The President is chosen instead by a body known as the Federal Assembly, which is composed of the members of the Bundestag plus an equal number of persons chosen by proportional representation by the legislatures of the states. Any German qualified to vote who is at least 40 years old is eligible for the office. Unlike the American Presidential Electoral College, the Federal Assembly does meet as a group to cast their ballots for President. But debate or campaign speeches before the voting is not allowed. An absolute majority is required for election on the first and, if necessary, second ballots. On the third ballot a plurality suffices, so that the election cannot drag on interminably.

Only in 1969 did a Presidential election go to the third ballot. Theodor Heuss was elected on the second ballot in 1949 and was reelected five years later virtually unanimously on the first ballot. The second President, Heinrich Luebke, also was elected on the second ballot and reelected by a substantial margin on the first ballot. The third President, Gustav Heinemann, outpolled his opponent by only six votes on the decisive third ballot. The current President, Walter Scheel, elected in 1974, not only became the first President to be elected on the first ballot but received more votes—530—than any other President had on first being elected to the office.

The President serves for five years and may be reelected only once. He or she must, upon election, resign from other public offices and from offices in profit-making organizations. He or she may not be a member of Parliament nor of the legislature of one of the Länder, and may not practice a profession while in office. President Heuss even resigned his membership in his political party after his election.

The parties almost seem to be rotating the office among themselves. Heuss was a Free Democrat, Luebke a Christian Democrat, and Heinemann a Social Democrat. Heinemann's party affiliations were a bit out of the ordinary, however. Originally a member of the CDU, he resigned in 1950 to oppose the party's policy of rearming Germany. For a time he headed a somewhat neutralist splinter group before joining the SPD. In any event, one may wonder whether the cycle is beginning again since Scheel is from the FDP.

The President may be impeached for "willful violation of the Basic Law or any other Federal law." A vote by one quarter of either house of Parliament is sufficient to introduce the motion for impeachment. Then a two-thirds vote is required to bring the President to trial. The case is heard before the Federal Constitutional Court, which decides whether the President is guilty and, therefore, removable from office.

There is no vice president in Germany. If the Presidency becomes vacant, the president of the Bundesrat serves the remainder of the term. During necessary absences of the President, he or she performs many of the President's functions.

The President's functions largely are ceremonial. Unlike the situation in the Weimar Republic, the President cannot dismiss the Chancellor nor authorize the use of any emergency powers. All his or her political acts, except for designating the Chancellor, must be countersigned by the Chancellor or another appropriate minister. Nonetheless, the President does have some discretion of action and the powers of the office are ambiguous to some extent.

After each Parliamentary election the President offers a candidate for Chancellor to the Bundestag. If no party has a majority, there is some choice in this selection. Should one party have a majority or clearly predominate, however, the President has little alternative but to choose the leader of that party. Thus, the simplification of the German party system has tended to reduce the President's discretion in these matters.

If the President's nominee gains an absolute majority, then he or she becomes Chancellor. But if this does not happen, then the Bundestag may elect anyone Chancellor by an absolute majority. Should it fail to do so within two weeks, then it can choose a Chancellor by a plurality. But at that point the President has an option. He or she may accept the Bundestag's choice as Chancellor or may call for new Parliamentary elections.

The point of these provisions is that the President cannot force his or her choice for Chancellor upon an unwilling Bundestag. But at the same time the Germans want to be certain that the Chancellor has fairly broad support. If this is not clearly the case, the President has the opportunity to call the electorate into the process. Thus far in Germany, these provisions have not been necessary. The President's nominee always has received an absolute majority. But in 1949 the vote was close. Adenauer had not a single vote to spare even when three votes were counted which had his name on them rather than "aye," which was the proper vote on the motion of whether he should become Chancellor.

In the 1961 elections the Chancellor's party failed to win a majority and had to make considerable concessions to the Free Democrats, with which it had been in coalition, in order to stay in power. Obviously, the President must, as in other parliamentary states, have due regard for the political complexion of the legislature when designating the head of the Government. In 1961, he waited until an agreement had been reached between the strongest party and its coalition partner, thus ratifying the informal choice that the leaders of the majority in the Bundestag had already made.

Among the ambiguities of the President's power is the matter of a veto. The Basic Law does not give this power, but does say that the President must sign laws before they are effective. The signature was expected to be automatic and simply indicate formally that the law had been passed. President Heuss, however, withheld his signature in some cases. He questioned, for example, whether a particular tax law that had been passed by the Bundestag alone needed as well the approval of the Bundesrat. When the Federal Constitutional Court ruled passage by both houses was required, Heuss refused to sign the bill and as a result it was not enacted. While this is not exactly a veto, it did have the effect of killing the bill.

Although the point in question was one of correct constitutional procedure, there was a substantive issue also. The Government and a majority of the Bundestag had favored the tax law on its merits. In blocking it, the President was becoming involved in politics. And to the extent that this was true, he would be less able to discharge his ceremonial role, for to do the latter successfully he must appear above politics so as not to repel the supporters of any party. One of the main duties of a ceremonial leader is to be a symbol of national unity.

Despite such conflicts, the Presidency under Heuss acquired considerable prestige. He proved to be human and accessible, combining dignity and an unassuming manner. He was ready and willing to participate in all activities which in his opinion served to advance the intellectual and political interests of his country. Luebke was not as capable or effective a President, in part because toward the close of his second term questions were raised about some of his activities during the Second World War and whether he had compromised with the Nazis. The election of his successor was held a few months early so that he could leave office sooner. Heinemann, on the other hand, despite serving for only a single term, performed the ceremonial functions well, particularly in his contacts with other countries.

Scheel is the most experienced politician to hold the office. He was leader of the FDP, Foreign Secretary, and, in effect, Vice Chancellor, immediately prior to his election as President. As had his predecessors in office, he has indicated his desire to expand the President's influence by exercising the office's limited powers fully. He has not transformed the President's role, however.

Basically, then, the influence of the President, like that of the British monarch, depends upon the qualifications and initiative he or she possesses, and the prevailing political circumstances. Heuss said that the President "may not . . . take part in the practical decisions of day-to-day politics, but he is permitted to help in improving the atmosphere and in facilitating the putting into effect of certain quite simple, reasonable, and generally accepted points of view." At times the President may be influential. Nonetheless, the Chancellor, like the British Prime Minister, need not accept the advice of the head of state; the Chancellor, not the President, is the key maker of policy.

CHANCELLOR DEMOCRACY

France has seen a shift in power from the Council of Ministers to the President as it moved from the Third and Fourth Republics to the Fifth. Similarly in Germany the distribution of power within the executive branch in the Bonn Republic is different from that in Weimar. The shift, however, has been in the opposite direction—from the President to the Chancellor. As we noted in Chapter 14, the power shift in France is not just a matter of altering the constitution, but also of the personality of the first President of the Fifth Republic. In Germany, as well, the personality of the first Chancellor, in addition to the changes in the constitution, has affected significantly the present powers of the office. Just as the Fifth Republic sometimes has been referred to as the de Gaulle Republic, so also the Federal Republic of Germany has been labelled Chancellor democracy.

The Chancellor is chosen by the process discussed in the preceding part of this chapter. Once the appointment has been confirmed, the Chancellor selects Cabinet colleagues, whose formal appointments are signed by the President. Members of the Cabinet may be, and usually are, members of the Bundestag. Cabinets have varied from 15 to 20 members. The President may advise the Chancellor on these appointments, but, as the first Chancellor demonstrated, such advice easily can be ignored.

The Basic Law provides for a deputy chancellor, but for approximately the first 20 years the office remained largely a figurehead. This was in part because Adenauer dominated the Government for most of this period. In 1966 when the Grand Coalition between the CDU and the SPD was formed, however, the SPD leader, Willy Brandt, obtained the position. When subsequently the SPD and FDP formed the governing coalition, the latter party supplied the deputy chancellor so that first Walter Scheel and then Hans-Dietrich Genscher have held the position. Thus the political situation, rather than constitutional provisions, have made the office more significant in the last decade.

The Basic Law strengthens the executive by providing that the Bundestag may not increase expenditures or taxes over what the Cabinet wants. This corresponds to the control over finance long exercised by the British Cabinet and, more recently, by the French Council of Ministers. The Cabinet or its ministers may issue decrees having the force of law but only when statutes already in effect, which the decrees must cite, so authorize. Moreover, the decree power may not be used by the central government to avoid the constitutional requirement of Bundesrat consent for certain types of legislation. In these areas, decrees by the central government or its ministers require the approval of the Bundesrat. Emergency powers are provided for, but are carefully limited as discussed in Chapter 18.

The German Cabinet is intended to be a very formal body with elaborate operating rules.[1] These specify the number of ministers needed for a quorum and require formal votes to reach decisions. When the Cabinet is divided, the majority is to rule, except in some key instances. On financial matters, for example, the Chancellor and the Finance Minister are allowed to have their way even if the rest of the Cabinet is opposed. All this differs considerably from the practice in Britain, where the Cabinet is governed by informal procedures that have grown up over the years, rather than by written rules, and where the Prime Minister normally ascertains the sense of the meeting by going around the table to "collect the voices" rather than calling for a formal vote.

Despite the German Cabinet's elaborate rules for joint decision making, collective responsibility for Government policy has been limited. The Basic Law makes the Chancellor alone, not the entire Cabinet, responsible to the Bundestag. Furthermore, Article 65 says that the Chancellor

---

[1] For a translation of the text of the standing orders, see John C. Lane and James K. Pollock, *Source Materials on the Government and Politics of Germany* (Ann Arbor, Mich.: George Wahr, 1964), pp. 42–45.

"determines, and is responsible for, general policy." Adenauer interpreted this provision to mean that he did not need to consult the Cabinet in making policy. He regarded the Cabinet as a board of experts whose role was to assist him only on his request. Should he so desire, he might consult them for information on which to base *his* decisions, but this might not be necessary, since he established a system of research committees responsible to him alone. Thus, when he presented his proposals to the Cabinet, he would have the weight of independent, expert opinion on his side. Although at times he used his ministers, the net result was that his personal research network tended to make his position stronger than that of the rest of the Cabinet and, thereby, reduced the ministers' authority.

Further aiding Adenauer in dominating the Government was the Federal Chancellery, provided for by the Cabinet's standing orders. The Chancellery's administrative staff perform primarily two types of functions. First, they issue relevant instructions, in the Chancellor's name, to all ministries and thus decide many important matters before they reach the Cabinet. Second, they act as coordinators by settling many disputes between ministries. Only those disputes which they cannot resolve go to the Cabinet for settlement. The head of the Chancellery, titled an undersecretary, is the personal appointee of the Chancellor. During the Adenauer period this undersecretary was, in a sense, second in command and more powerful than any one of Adenauer's Cabinet colleagues. Although the Chancellery's influence has diminished since Adenauer's time, it remains an important source of power for the Chancellor.

Adenauer did not hesitate to criticize publicly his Cabinet colleagues when he disagreed with the positions they had taken in speeches. On the other hand, he was reluctant to dismiss even inefficient ministers, if they were loyal to him personally. He tended to relate to his Cabinet in much the same way as an American President treats his Cabinet. Again this contrasts sharply with British practice, where the Prime Minister, although *primus,* still remains *inter pares.* This contrast is the more remarkable because Germany, like Britain, is a parliamentary, not a presidential, system. Such was Adenauer's dominance, however, that some observers felt that the true nature of the German political system could not be grasped by terming the Bonn Republic simply a parliamentary system. They began referring to Germany as a Chancellor democracy.

After serving as Chancellor for the first 14 years of the Bonn Republic, Adenauer resigned in October 1963 at the age of 87. His role in the evolution of German democracy has been both criticized and applauded. Generally speaking, his positive contributions stand out, particularly when viewed in the light of the times and problems that confronted him. He commanded the respect of even those who did not like him. His image was tarnished to a degree, however, because he stayed on too long. There was a general consensus, even in his own party, that he should have retired at least two or three years earlier. In the last years he antagonized many people, including his closest associates, and became somewhat of a burden and a liability. After 1960 his power and prestige declined, and his retirement in 1963 was part of the price exacted by the Free Democrats for joining the Christian Democrats in coalition after the 1961 elections.

Perhaps the most prominent of Adenauer's defects as Chancellor was his dislike of criticism, most of which he took personally. He often cast suspicion on the opposition Social Democrats, who in his view were not too different from Communists. He did not seem to understand that, despite differences of opinion, the Government and the Opposition could cooperate in many matters. His attitude toward the Opposition gave the impression that he was treating the Bundestag in a condescending manner, and its reputation suffered thereby. He did not seem to appreciate that a successful parliamentary democracy requires the collective wisdom of a cabinet, subject to the collective judgment of a parliament. It is also true that he often treated many of his colleagues coolly and perhaps even unfairly, and demanded unanimous approval from them. And he discouraged the introduction of democratic practices in the CDU. Some of the blame for his autocratic behavior must rest with his party and colleagues, however, who simply capitulated to him.

Chancellor democracy had its pragmatic merits. Adenauer faced the problem of holding a number of diverse elements together in the CDU. He did a good job of mediating among all the groups. Although he was criticized for apparently not wishing to offend any major one of them, he hardly was playing merely a passive role. He prevented any one group from dominating the CDU and thus narrowing its appeal, which would have been unfortunate for the development of the German party system.[2]

He exercised his powers cleverly and carefully built up his personal prestige. Though he exploited to the limit the opportunities that the constitution provided, he rarely was charged with violating it. Adenauer's prestige was enhanced considerably by his handling of foreign affairs, especially in the early years of the new regime when he was its sole spokesperson. Even his opponents admit that in those years he won considerable international position and prestige for his country by knowing when to be patient and when to display firmness and tenacity. In brief, he was imaginative, flexible, and statesmanlike in the pursuit of Germany's national interest.

Most importantly, by providing a stable and effective government, Adenauer demonstrated that democracy and authority are not mutually exclusive. In this way he contributed significantly to the German acceptance of democracy, a considerable accomplishment in a nation lack-

---

[2] See Klaus Bolling, *Republic in Suspense* (New York: Frederick A. Praeger, Inc., 1964), especially chaps. 4 and 7.

ing a democratic tradition. He was given considerable credit for the rapid economic recovery and general prosperity, which stood in sharp contrast to the ruinous inflation of the early Weimar period and to the subsequent economic collapse. In short, Adenauer's strong leadership and clear-cut policies, together with the attendant prosperity, gave the Germans reason to believe that democracy can be a success. Had his political style been more democratic, his historical contribution to German democracy would not have been as great. Clearly, he possessed the attributes appropriate to the times.

Neither Ludwig Erhard nor Kurt Kiesinger, the Christian Democrats who followed Adenauer as Chancellor, proved to be strong leaders. Erhard was hampered by the fact that, through most of his three years as Chancellor, Adenauer remained the leader of the CDU and sought to prove that Erhard was less able than he himself had been. Furthermore, because some people had been alienated by Adenauer's arrogance, Erhard sought to be more congenial and to consult his colleagues more adequately in decision making. As a result, he was derided for being a "rubber lion." Nonetheless, during his time as Chancellor relations improved with the opposition Social Democrats and the Bundestag generally. In his first official statement as Chancellor, he said: "I regard the opposition as a necessary element of full standing in a parliamentary democracy and hope that our discussion and disputes, which are bound to arise, may be conducted in this spirit." In addition, Erhard stressed the importance of popular participation and public opinion in a democratic society.

Erhard's inability to deal with economic recession in Germany in 1966, however, forced him to resign. He found himself unable to marshall the necessary political support to make decisions and implement them. His failure to deal with an economic crisis seemed particularly damning, since he had been Minister of Economics under Adenauer. He had been identified closely with the CDU's social market economy and with the economic miracle of Germany's recovery. Thus, it seemed to some that his policies had failed in the long run. Furthermore, if he could devise no solution for a problem in the area of his supposed expertise, how could he be expected to deal adequately with problems in other areas?

The Government formed to replace Erhard's carried the CDU's acceptance of the SPD a step further, to a stage that Adenauer would not have countenanced. The new Chanceller, Kiesinger, formed a Government that included both the CDU and the SPD—an arrangement labelled the Grand Coalition. (This coalition was formed to secure the agreement of both major parties on the steps required to deal with the economic problems Germany encountered in 1966). The leader of the SPD, Brandt, became deputy chancellor and Foreign Minister. Since Kiesinger often had to accept the views of the rival party to maintain the coalition, he did not appear, during his almost three years in office, to have the strength of Adenauer.

After the 1969 election, the movement of the Free Democrats back toward the center had progressed sufficiently far for them to enter a coalition with the SPD. During almost five years as the Bonn Republic's first Social Democratic Chancellor, Brandt demonstrated that he preferred to reach decisions more collectively than did Adenauer and to discharge the responsibilities of Chancellor in a more democratic style. Nonetheless, Brandt's prominence within the Government and the SPD was such that no one thought of him as a weak Chancellor. His authority was enhanced considerably when he was awarded the Nobel Peace Prize in 1971 in recognition of his efforts to improve relations between Germany and Russia and Eastern Europe through *Ostpolitik*.

Only a few years after the Nobel prize, Brandt resigned as Chancellor because a high-ranking official in his Chancellery proved to be an East German spy. Brandt accepted the blame for not having prevented the spy from seeing secret documents. He also felt that he no longer could be effective in improving relations between East and West Germany. There also is some indication that his SPD colleagues pressured him to resign because they feared that he might become an electoral liability. The voters might come to believe the Christian Democrats' charge that the SPD was too gullible in its dealings with the Communists. The key point is that despite Brandt's sources of strength, he still was driven from the Chancellor's office. The German Chancellor is powerful, but remains accountable.

With Helmut Schmidt, the Chancellor since 1974, Germany almost has come full circle back to the Adenauer style. Schmidt has a reputation for bluntly speaking his mind regardless of the consequences and for pursuing his own goals without much consultation with others. His detractors call him Schmidt-Schnauze—big-mouth Schmidt or Schmidt, the lip. Nonetheless, since the SPD can remain in office only with the support of the FDP, Schmidt must compromise at times and pay some attention to views expressed in the Cabinet. This was especially true after the 1976 elections reduced the SPD-FDP majority in the Bundestag to only five seats.

LEGISLATIVE-EXECUTIVE RELATIONS

Legislative leadership is largely in the hands of the Cabinet, if one is to judge by the measures introduced and enacted. Approximately three fourths of all bills have been initiated by the Cabinet. Initially, many bills were introduced by ordinary members of the Bundestag, but this number has declined considerably. Furthermore, only about 40 percent of the bills introduced by Bundestag members have become law. Legislative initiative has shifted toward the executive. This has been due partly to the strong lead the Chancellor has given and partly to the influence of the expert bureaucracy which has the relevant information; bills are drafted in executive departments by experienced lawyers, whose services are not directly available to the Bundestag. Party discipline in Parliamentary voting is high, which is further evidence of executive leadership in the legislative halls.

In an effort to obtain the executive stability which the Weimar Republic lacked, while still maintaining a parliamentary, instead of presidential, system, the Basic Law provides for a procedure known as the constructive vote of no confidence. Under this procedure, a Chancellor defeated in Parliament, even by an absolute majority, is not required to resign. The only way in which the Chancellor can be forced out of office is for the Bundestag to designate a successor by an absolute majority. This prevents a negative majority, of say the extreme left and right, from voting a Government out of office when all they can agree upon is that they do not like what the Government has been doing. The only way to get a new Government is for a majority to agree upon what they want to see in the place of the old Government.

A Chancellor may seek to mobilize support by making an issue a matter of confidence. Regardless of who raises the question of confidence, 48 hours must elapse before the vote. Should the Chancellor fail to win an absolute majority after asking for a vote of confidence, he or she may request the President to dissolve the Bundestag and call for new elections. This is the only situation in which elections can be called before the Bundestag has served its full term. This means that the German Chancellor lacks the maneuverability of the British Prime Minister in seeking to schedule elections at a time when the public opinion polls indicate that the Government parties are doing well.

No attempt was made to pass a constructive vote of no confidence until April 1972, when the Christian Democrats sought unsuccessfully to remove Brandt from office. The fact that some members of the FDP had defected from the Government coalition made the Christian Democrats think that they might succeed. These defections continued to cause a problem, since they meant that the Government had lost its majority and now had no more votes in the Bundestag than the Opposition had. Thus it was clear that new elections would have to be called. Since the Bundestag's term had another year to run, however, this was not easy to do.

Despite the clear wording of the Basic Law that the Chancellor could call for new elections if he failed to get an absolute majority on a vote of confidence, the prevailing view came to be that Brandt needed to be *defeated* in the Bundestag for elections to be called early. The danger was that once the defeat occurred the Christian Democrats would attempt again to elect a new Chancellor under the constructive vote of no confidence procedure. Should they manage to do this before the President responded to Chancellor Brandt's request to dissolve the Bundestag, the elections would not occur and a Christian Democratic Chancellor would replace Brandt in office. In the event, the SPD contrived to defeat Brandt in the Bundestag by withholding some of their votes; the Christian Democrats did not try to elect one of their members Chancellor before the President called for new elections.

Although these provisions of the Basic Law have come into play only in this instance, this does not mean that they otherwise have been unimportant. The entrenched position of the Chancellor has permitted some flexibility in party discipline in the Bundestag. Bills which the Government did not favor have been passed and the Government did not fall, as would have been the case in Britain. On occasion the SPD and part of the CDU have carried a bill against the opposition of another part of the CDU. While this is common enough in the American Congress, in most parliamentary systems it would result in the Government's resignation because it no longer had the loyal support of its followers and could implement its legislation only with the aid of the Opposition. Yet, again, in Germany the Government survived.

The Germans were aware that, although they had devised a procedure which gave the Chancellor an entrenched position, they really had not thereby dealt with the problem of enabling the Government to get its legislative program through Parliament. A deadlock could develop if the Bundestag would not support the Chancellor, but could not elect a new one, while the Chancellor felt that the political situation was inappropriate for calling new elections. In that case he or she might simply resign because he or she could not get the program through Parliament and the whole purpose of the constructive vote of no confidence to secure executive stability would be defeated.

Therefore, in Article 81 provision was made for a so-called legislative emergency. The procedures involved can best be understood by referring to Figure 22–1. If, in the circumstances outlined in the previous paragraph, the Bundestag rejects a bill labelled urgent by the Government, then the Government may ask for a declaration of legislative emergency. If the Bundesrat opposes this, the matter is killed. But if it agrees, the request goes to the President. How much discretion the President has is one of those ambiguities in Presidential powers noted earlier in this chapter. By saying that he or she *may* declare a legislative emergency, the Basic Law seems to imply that he or she could decline to do so. If the President signs the declaration, then an obstructionist Bundestag may be bypassed in the legislative process. Any bill that it rejects or fails to act upon within four weeks becomes law anyway, if the Bundesrat approves it. This means that 21 people, a majority of the Bundesrat, can enact a law. The legislative emergency remains in effect for six months, unless the Bundestag elects a new Chancellor.

FIGURE 22–1
West German Legislative Emergency Procedure

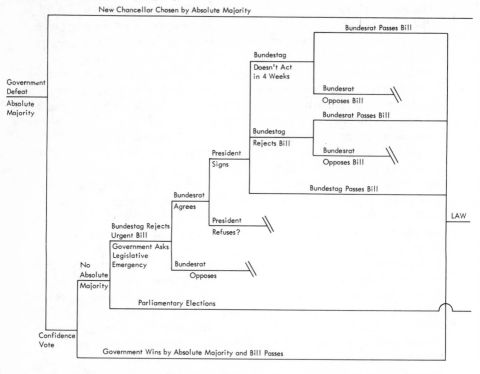

One of the safeguards on this procedure is that once the emergency expires another one cannot be declared until elections are held. This provision is intended to be simply a temporary aid and, if it does not solve existing problems in a few months, the voters must be asked to sort things out between the Chancellor and the Bundestag. Furthermore, during the period of legislative emergency the Basic Law cannot be amended, repealed, or suspended.

Admittedly this is a very involved procedure. But it must be understood as part of the Germans' effort to correct the deficiencies of the Weimar Republic so that this time democracy could survive. The search for executive stability through the constructive vote of no confidence necessitated some procedure like that of Article 81. At the same time, because abuse of emergency powers in Article 48 of the Weimar constitution had helped to undermine democracy, safeguards had to be written into the Basic Law. All this has made the provisions very complex.

This is a perfect example of what it means to respond legalistically to pressing problems. The drafters of the Basic Law, operating within traditional German governmental values, believed that a viable democracy could be produced if only the governing law—the constitution—were drawn up properly and contained all the right provisions. Few understood that this was more a political than a constitutional or legal question. And this is why Article 81, which has not been used to this point, is likely to remain vestigial. The important development has been the simplification of the party system. The fact that two leading, near majority parties have emerged means that the circumstances for which Article 81 was drawn up are unlikely to arise. Deadlocks such as it envisioned may occur in fractionalized party systems, but not in a two-party system with the tradition of party discipline common in Germany.

The constructive vote of no confidence is not the only means of calling the Government to account. As noted in the previous chapter, however, the debates on the floor of the Bundestag do not serve this purpose very effectively. And Adenauer's refusal at times to permit Cabinet ministers to appear before Bundestag committees—despite the provision in the Basic Law requiring this—weakened as well enforcement of responsibility through the committee system.

The procedures for questioning ministers, however, have been strengthened. At first only one hour a month was set aside for questions, and written notice well in advance was required. But since 1960 the procedure has been more like the British practice. Now deputies question ministers at the start of each meeting of the Bundestag; they need give notice of their questions only three days in advance (in exceptional circumstances only one day). In addition, supplementary questions may be asked from the floor. Should the normal question hour be inadequate to deal with all inquiries, other question sessions can be scheduled. Deputies are limited to three questions a week. Unfortunately, they may not question the Chancellor.

In 1965 the Bundestag initiated a new procedure of a topical hour. The aim was to discourage ministers from making statements to the press and television before discussing a subject with the Bundestag. If 30 members so request, the Government is required to make a statement to the Bundestag on a specified subject. Should only 15 make the request, then the Bundestag votes to determine whether a statement will be required. Statements come immediately after the question period. They are followed by an hour-long debate on the topic, with each speaker limited to five minutes.

Despite the various procedures available, the Bundestag has not energetically enforced control over the executive. During the formative Adenauer period, deputies became used to acquiescing to the Cabinet's arrogance in ignoring some of the views of the Bundestag. The practice under subsequent Chancellors has improved only partially.

Germany, like France, seems to have solved the traditional European political problem of executive instability without departing from a democratic framework, as too often has occurred with past such solutions. Interestingly, the two countries have achieved this result in differing ways. France has strengthened that part of the executive which is not responsible to the legislature (nor much to anyone else), while Germany has entrenched the one that is responsible. Furthermore, the legislature has not been downgraded as much in Germany as in France. Despite the Adenauer tradition, Governments in Germany have had to make some concessions, have had to seek some consensus in carrying out their programs. In both countries developments in the party system have been at least as important as institutional reform in explaining the success of their current political systems in dealing with long-standing defects in the political process.

BIBLIOGRAPHICAL NOTE

There are no books in English dealing exclusively with the German executive. Klaus Bolling, *Republic in Suspense: Politics, Parties and Personalities in Postwar Germany* (New York: Frederick A. Praeger, Inc., 1964), contains much valuable commentary on executive leadership. The following biographies are a source of some information: Terence Prittie, *Adenauer* (London: Stacy, 1971); Rudolf Augstein, *Konrad Adenauer* (London: Secker & Warburg, 1964); and Hermann Bolesch and Hans Leicht, *Willy Brandt: A Portrait of the German Chancellor* (Tubingen: Erdmann, 1971). See also Konrad Adenauer, *Memoirs* (Chicago: Regnery, 1966).

Policy-Implementing Structures

Increasing governmental activity in the economic and social fields has made administration more vast and complicated in virtually every country. Even apart from this trend, however, administration long has been a significant element in the German political system. The Germans very early established a systematically organized civil service as one of the twin pillars on which the state rested. The other was the army. Administration in Germany differs from that of Britain and France because Germany is a federal system and vests some significant powers in Länder, or states.

STAFFING AND ORGANIZING THE BUREAUCRACY

The German civil service in the 19th century earned the reputation of being competent, incorruptible, and objective. Since recruitment was based on expert training and knowledge, and since higher education generally was unavailable to the lower classes, membership in the higher civil service tended to be limited to the sons of the upper classes. Furthermore, civil servants who expressed liberal or democratic views endangered their positions. Consequently, the civil service developed into a conservative class system. But precisely because of their prestigious background, civil servants were looked up to by the general population. The high-level civil servant seemed to typify all that was best in German national character. Added to this was the orderliness of the bureaucratic system itself, another quality attractive to most Germans. Thus, in general, the Germans were willing to allow the bureaucrat to exercise great power.

In the United States most people tend to regard the bureaucrat as aloof and see the politician as the defender of their interests. In an interesting reversal of perception of roles, Germans tend to regard the politician as remote and the bureaucrat as sympathetic to the average person's problems. This is because the term civil servant has a broader scope in Germany. It includes such diverse occupations as those of meter reader, railway conductors, and teachers. All of these are considered employees, and thus representatives, of the State. Furthermore, in Germany most administrators are employed by state and local governments instead of by the national government. Thus, instead of being way off somewhere in the capital city, they are nearby and in contact with the population.

During Weimar, an attempt was made to liberalize recruitment to the civil service, with some decline in quality as a result. In the Nazi period, civil servants whose loyalty to the new order was in question were removed. Recruitment also was controlled carefully. The net result of the Nazi period was also a decline in quality. At the end of World War II, there was an attempt to denazify the service and to rebuild it. After the somewhat uncertain period of the first postwar years, the general quality and competence of the service has improved steadily.

The present status of the civil service is regulated by the Federal Civil Service Act (1961).[1] This law sets up three classes in the civil service. These are the higher service, the intermediate service, and the ordinary service. In order to qualify for the higher service, a person must have a university education and have passed the initial examination, which is followed by three years' experience in the service and the passing of a second examination. The intermediate service requires a secondary education (or its equivalent), plus three years in the service and the passing of the intermediate service examination. The ordinary service requires an elementary school education or its equivalent and an apprenticeship period.

Traditionally, legal training was required to qualify one for the higher civil service. Under the present law this has been broadened to include degrees in economics and political science. The class composition of the civil service has been broadened somewhat also. Yet most recruits still are sons either of the wealthy or of civil servants. Contributing to a continuation of the class bias is the fact that few civil servants are promoted to the top positions from lower ranks. Entry into the higher civil service normally is directly at that level. Thus, only those with the proper education (and the German educational system tends to be biased toward the upper classes) can secure the top positions.

The Germans have a national school of administration for the specialized training of civil servants, in addition to at least one Land school

---

[1] For partial text, see John C. Lane and James K. Pollock, *Source Materials on the Government and Politics of Germany* (Ann Arbor, Mich.: George Wahr, 1964), pp. 114–16.

(Hamburg). The national school was set up initially by the French at Speyer in what was their occupation zone. The school now serves the whole of the Federal Republic and its costs are borne by the national government and the governments of the Länder. Young candidates for the civil service spend three or four months there, usually between their initial and second examinations. They study history, political science, economics, and the principles of public administration. In addition, they have an opportunity to visit governmental institutions at work and to associate with colleagues from all parts of the country.

The Federal Personnel Committee regulates conditions of service and appointment. Its members are chosen from different branches of the bureaucracy as well as from nominees of the trade unions, including the civil servants' union. Working closely with the Personnel Committee are the personnel committees of the Länder. Grievances are handled by councils set up for such purposes. Civil servants may belong to trade unions, but have no right to strike.

The civil service law requires bureaucrats to be the servants of the people, not of any political party, and to carry out their tasks impartially. They are subject to the law and must support the democratic order. Their conduct is supposed to be exemplary; they are expected to so order their lives as to bring respect and trust to their profession. By and large, they live up to these demands. Graft, bribery, and other types of improper conduct are rare, both in the national bureaucracy and in local administration.

Germany was the first nation to accept responsibility for the wrongful acts of officials while performing their official duties. Part of the reason may have been that state ownership of various enterprises occurred earlier in Prussia than in most other countries. In any case, the present constitution acknowledges this legal responsibility and authorizes administrative courts, similar to those in France, to deal with such cases.

In discussing the British civil service we stressed the limits placed on the bureaucrats' political activity in an effort to ensure their neutrality; only then, the British feel, can the civil service be trusted to serve whatever party currently is in power. Germany, like France, however, has not been concerned to draw a sharp line between political and administrative service of the government. Civil servants may enter national politics freely without resigning their office. Those who are successful simply take a leave of absence. When they cease to be members of the Bundestag, they are reinstated in the civil service. Moreover, nothing prevents a civil servant from participating actively in politics on the Land or on the local level. In most cases, however, those elected to a state assembly take a leave of absence, but with the right of reinstatement. Because of this right, and hence the very real possibility of going back, civil servants tend to continue their official associations.

Also blurring the line between politician and civil servant was some ministers' practice of sending bureaucrats to address the Bundestag in their place or to respond during the question period. In addition, they often asked bureaucrats to participate in committee decisions and even to sign unpopular orders. Such deliberately fostered confusion made it difficult to distinguish clearly between the responsibility of ministers and that of civil servants. Because of some ministers' failure to consider themselves accountable, the public at times centered its fire on the civil servants.

In 1967, however, partly as a result of the negotiations that led to the Grand Coalition, the above situation was altered by the creation of parliamentary undersecretaries in the larger ministries. These appointees, who are similar to junior ministers in Britain, must be members of Parliament. Their primary duty is to stand in for ministers at Parliamentary question time, a practice that makes for an element of ministerial responsibility. In turn, the career civil servants have become a little like the permanent secretaries in Britain in that they do not become involved in party politics.

German ministries are staffed entirely by permanent civil servants. Ministers are, of course, political appointees, and each minister usually appoints one undersecretary, known as state secretary, although some departments have two.[2] The state secretary is the equivalent of the British permanent head of the department. Although state secretaries are usually promoted from the ranks of the higher civil service, the law permits the Chancellor to appoint a few without any restrictions.

A number of observers have criticized the German civil service for being unimaginative, authoritarian, and enslaved by routine and rules. This does not mean that its personnel are neo-Nazis, although denazification did not remove all those who were officeholders under Hitler. Rather the point is that one cannot expect in a crisis situation any great support for democracy from this quarter. The civil service is not antidemocratic; it simply lacks any democratic tradition. We noted in Chapter 18 that younger Germans seem to be more committed to democratic values than their elders are. The same holds true in the civil service; the younger bureaucrats are more democratically oriented. Thus, significant changes are under way in this segment of the political system as well.

THE ROLE OF THE STATES IN NATIONAL ADMINISTRATION

Except for defense, railways, and the post office, the national government in Germany employs only about 10 percent of the total number of

---

[2] The German term *Staatssekretar* (state secretary) is also used to denote the highest rank in the civil service. This is in addition to the parliamentary undersecretaries mentioned above.

civil servants. About one third of all administrators work for local governments and over half are employed by the states. National ministry staffs number only about 100,000 persons. Of these more than 8,000 are in the higher civil service. They occupy the top positions in each department and include the chief secretaries, bureau chiefs, and immediate staffs.

German ministries have little administrative machinery of their own. For the most part, the actual implementation of the law is left to the bureaucracy of the states. The constitution provides that the Länder "execute the federal laws as matters of their own concern insofar as this Basic Law does not otherwise provide or permit." Even where state and national government ministries exist side by side, the national ones are concerned chiefly with drafting uniform legislation and in seeing that the administration by the Länder conforms with the statutes and the constitution. National ministry offices usually are small and compact, with supervisory offices in the major cities. The bulk of detailed administrative activity occurs in the counties and municipalities under the direction of the Land governments.

It should be recalled from Chapter 21 that Bundesrat members serve in both a legislative and an executive capacity. They participate in the passage of national legislation, but as officials in their respective Länder they are engaged in administering not only the laws passed by their Land legislature but also those passed by the national Parliament. Thus, they administer laws which they themselves have helped to pass, or, alternatively, had voted unsuccessfully to defeat.

Unlike Britain and France, Germany is a federal system. This means that there is a division of powers between the national and constituent units of government which cannot be altered unilaterally. In Chapter 21 we discussed this division of powers, noting that only a few areas were the exclusive province of the national government. Residuary or reserve powers rest with the Länder. These are relatively few, the most important being education and cultural affairs. The great bulk of governmental powers are concurrent—either the national or the state governments can legislate in these areas. Should there be any conflict, the national government's action would take precedence.

These provisions give the national government such extensive powers that some observers have questioned whether Germany is anything more than a quasi-federal system. The national government appears to be by far the most dominant element of the system. Evaluating German federalism just by looking at the distribution of legislative power, however, is not adequate.[3] Unlike the American states, the German Länder play a major

---

[3] See the following two articles in the *American Political Science Review* 53 (September 1959): Karlheinz Neunreither, "Politics and Bureaucracy in the West German Bundesrat," pp. 713–31, and Peter Merkl, "Executive-Legislative Federalism in West Germany," pp. 732–41.

role in administering laws passed by the national legislature. And in implementing these laws Land administrators have a fair amount of discretion.

This immediately raises the question of how diversity bordering on chaos can be avoided and how national-state conflict can be resolved. Clearly the national government of the United States would have been naive to leave the racial integration of the public schools in the hands of the relevant state officials in many Southern states. The national government in Germany can issue administrative regulations which are binding upon state administrators. But these require the approval of the Bundesrat, which means that at least half of the state governments must agree. The national government also can send its agents to investigate the quality of a state's administration. Should this be deficient, the national government can demand improvement and compliance. But again this requires the agreement of the Bundesrat. Given the ample opportunity for input from the states in the national legislative process, as discussed in Chapter 21, conflict over administrative matters rarely comes to this point.

Most observers believe that the state governments have made an enviable record. They handled the difficult problems of administration in the postwar reconstruction period before there was any national government. Moreover, interparty cooperation has been more common at the state level, with less bitterness and a greater inclination toward compromise, than at the national level. State legislatures have tended to be more lively and less formal than the Bundestag. In all there is little doubt that the Länder have provided excellent training for self-government in Germany; a number of Bundestag members served in a Landtag before coming to Bonn.

One astute observer has given three main reasons for the general success of governments in the Länder. First of all, the political leaders in the Länder gained their experience at a time of great emergency, when only people of ability, courage, and character could succeed and could rise above petty political considerations. Secondly, the major issues of policy that divide people sharply (foreign policy, rearmament, and so on) are not the concern of leaders at the state level; hence they do not impede cooperation. Finally, the caliber of leaders at the state level has been every bit as high as that of the people in national politics, and higher if they are to be judged in terms of adequacy in dealing with the type of problems with which they have been faced.

BIBLIOGRAPHICAL NOTES

The following are useful on various aspects of German administration: Gordon Craig, *From Bismarck to Adenauer: Aspects of German Statecraft* (Baltimore:

Johns Hopkins Press, 1958); Herbert Jacob, *German Administration Since Bismarck* (New Haven Conn.: Yale University Press, 1963); Edward L. Pinney, *Federalism, Bureaucracy, and Party Politics in Western Germany* (Chapel Hill: University of North Carolina Press, 1963); Roger H. Wells, *The States in West German Federalism: A Study in Federal-State Relations, 1949–1960* (New York: Bookman Associates, 1961); and Hans-Joachim Arndt, *West Germany: Politics of Nonplanning* (Syracuse, N.Y.: Syracuse University Press, 1967).

24

The Judicial Structure

The German judicial system, as are the systems in other continental countries, is similar to the French pattern. The law is code law instead of case law, although precedent has become increasingly important in Germany. Moreover, the judiciary is identified with the State more than in Britain or the United States. This is largely a matter of emphasis, for courts everywhere are in a sense instruments of the State. In Britain and the United States, however, they are viewed as protectors of the individual, both from private and governmental actions. In Germany and in other continental countries, on the other hand, they are viewed as dispensers of justice, seeing to it that justice is done from the point of view of society at large, with less concern for the individual person. Finally, court procedure under the Roman law system, as already discussed in Part III on France, differs from the Anglo-American pattern.

JUDGES AND COURT ORGANIZATION

Although Germany did not become a democratic state until after World War I, the German courts gained considerable independence as early as the first quarter of the 19th century. The Prussian constitution of 1850 had even proclaimed the rule of law principle, including the idea that courts were free of executive influence. As in the higher civil service, judicial positions were open only to university graduates (typically law degrees), a qualification that only the sons of the wealthy could hope to meet. This meant that judges were drawn from the conservative strata of society. It is not surprising, therefore, that most German judges developed a conservative political orientation, which became particularly evident in the Weimar and Nazi periods, when they did not seem to grasp the nature of the Nazi movement.

As in France, the German judiciary is supervised by the Ministry of Justice. Judges are recruited from law school graduates who seek a judicial career. They must first spend some three to four years in probationary and preparatory service, following which they must satisfactorily pass a final examination. Appointments are made by the Minister of Justice, who is assisted by nominating committees at both the national and state levels. The nominating committees are selected by the respective legislatures. Promotion is through seniority and merit, and is handled by the Minister of Justice and a committee of judges.

Judges are independent, but they must not violate the principles of the constitution. They hold their positions during good behavior, and may only be removed by their fellow judges through procedures regulated by law.

Judicial procedure in Germany is much like that in France, with the judge dominating the proceedings. It is his or her job to ascertain the truth, and to this end to admit or exclude evidence. As in France, the rules of evidence are relatively flexible. And again as in France, there are pretrial investigations, with the accused seldom released on bail, although pretrial detention is reviewed periodically. In case of acquittal, however, the defendant may seek indemnification for the detention prior to the trial. The Basic Law abolishes the death penalty.

As tends to be the case in France, legal proceedings in Germany are not excessively expensive. Lawyers' fees usually are set rather than being a percentage, and appeals costs often are geared to the minimum money value of the case. Those who cannot afford trial costs are provided court-appointed legal talent paid for by the government. In general, justice in Germany is accessible, fair, and not too cumbersome.

Although Germany is a federal system, its state and national court systems do not parallel and partially overlap each other as is true in the United States. Instead there is a single integrated system of regular courts. The three lower levels of the court system are all state courts. As is the practice for administrative matters, the state courts are used to try federal as well as state cases. Thus, virtually all cases in Germany start in a state court. The top level courts are national courts. Uniformity is obtained despite this structure by the fact that all courts are regulated by national codes, both as to procedure and as to the bulk of the substantive law which they apply. Moreover, all legal judgments and instruments are applicable throughout the nation. The law does not vary from state to state, as is so often true in the United States.

At the bottom of the court hierarchy are the local courts (*Amtsgerichte*), presided over by a single judge. In the smaller places he or she hears all types of small civil suits and minor criminal actions. In larger towns, the court may have several sections or categories of cases, each presided over by a single judge. In both instances the judge is joined by two lay assessors, and in certain criminal cases a second judge is added. The assessors are chosen by lot from lists of local inhabitants. An American-type jury is not used.

Standing above the local courts are the district or provincial courts *(Landgerichte)*, serving both as courts of original jurisdiction and as courts of appeal. They are divided into sections, or chambers, some concerned with appeals and others with original jurisdiction. On the civil side there is usually a section that hears appeals cases and another section that hears those original cases over which local courts lack jurisdiction. On the criminal side there are two appeals sections (little chamber and big chamber) and two original jurisdiction sections. One of the original jurisdiction sections is also called the big chamber, and the other the assize court, which tries the more grave criminal cases, such as murder.

All sections of the district court have three judges, except the little chamber, which has one judge and two lay assessors. The judges in the big chambers are also assisted by two lay assessors. The assize court, however, has a six-member jury, which votes jointly with the three judges. Although decisions are reached by majority vote, the judges exercise preponderant influence.

The superior courts *(Oberlandesgerichte)* have two sections, civil and criminal. The civil section, staffed by three judges, reviews judgments of district courts and may alter them. The criminal section has a little and a big chamber; the little chamber has three judges and the big has five. These decide points of law; they do not try cases but may order retrial in a lower court.

Decisions of the superior courts may be appealed to the Federal High Court *(Bundesgerichtshof)*, which has approximately 100 judges. It is divided into sections of five judges each, some dealing with civil matters and others with criminal. The Federal High Court must review all cases submitted to it. Consequently, most of its work is concerned with appeals, and hence its major function is to insure uniformity of legal interpretation among the courts of the Länder. Because some crimes are exclusively national, however, there is a criminal section which has original jurisdiction over them. An example of this would be cases of treason. The judges for this court are selected by the Minister of Justice in connection with state legal officials and an equal number of members of the Bundestag. The Federal High Court is the final court—even in cases of treason, which originate there—unless a constitutional issue is raised. In that situation the case goes to the Federal Constitutional Court, discussed fully in a moment.

There are several special courts in Germany, the most important of which are the administrative courts. Other special courts deal with labor relations, commercial disputes, tax disputes, and social security cases. Moreover, there are special disciplinary courts for actions against officials of the Länder, and the legal framework exists for the establishment of national disciplinary courts to hear proceedings against officials of the national government.

As in France, the government accepts liability for the wrongful acts of its officials while performing their official duties. Unlike the situation in France, however, claims against individual officials, as well as salary and other pecuniary claims of civil servants, go to the ordinary courts. But judgments are handed down against the state and not against the offending officials. The bulk of claims against public authorities, as well as conflicts between them, are heard, however, in separate administrative tribunals which have been set up for this purpose. There are administrative courts in the Länder, and there is a supreme administrative court at the national level.

BASIC RIGHTS AND THE CONSTITUTIONAL COURT

Remembering what had happened to their basic rights under the Nazis, the Germans were anxious to provide all possible legal safeguards against losing them again. The first section of the constitution, consisting of 19 articles, deals with the people's rights in detailed fashion. At the outset the constitution declares that the ''dignity of man is inviolable'' and that it is ''the duty of all state authority'' to ''respect and protect it.'' The enumerated basic rights are said to ''bind the legislature, the executive and the judiciary.''

Elsewhere, the constitution forbids extraordinary courts, double jeopardy, and retroactive laws. The right of habeas corpus is also preserved. The police may not hold a person longer than the end of the day following arrest unless he or she is charged with a crime. The judge's decision in a habeas corpus proceeding is subject to appeal to higher courts. Also, provision is made against mental and physical ill-treatment of detained persons. And due process and the equal protection of the laws are declared to be part of the constitutional order.

Aware of how the guaranteed rights of free speech, free press, and free assembly were abused by both the Nazis and the Communists during the Weimar Republic so as to subvert democracy and destroy these rights, the framers of the Basic Law sought to shield the political system from the abuse of freedom. Article 9 prohibits associations whose aims and activities are in conflict with criminal laws or are directed against the constitutional order. Article 18 asserts that ''whoever abuses freedom of expression of opinion, in particular freedom of the press, freedom of teaching, freedom of assembly, freedom of association, the secrecy of mail, posts and telecommunications, the right of property, or the right of asylum, in order to attack the free democratic basic order, forfeits these basic rights.''

In order to defend the liberties specified in the Basic Law, the Germans, although lacking a tradition of judicial review, readily accepted American insistence upon it. A Federal Constitutional Court was established, and experience over the past quarter century indicates that the Germans have taken to these procedures quite readily. Not only is the Federal Constitutional Court generally accepted, but similar courts function extensively at the state level to review state legislation.

The Federal Court consists of two panels of eight judges each. To be eligible for appointment one must at least be 40 and of proven legal ability. But one need not have made a career as a judge; a legal degree is sufficient. Thus although more than 40 percent of the appointees to the Constitutional Court have been judges, more than a quarter have been civil servants with most of the rest being professors or lawyers. Appointees serve a 12-year term and cannot be reappointed.

The Minister of Justice maintains a list of potential nominees to the Court. Included are the top judges and others suggested by the Federal Government, a state Government, or a party in the Bundestag. The Bundesrat and the Bundestag alternate in filling vacancies on the Court from this list. For this purpose the Bundestag appoints a 12-person committee whose political composition is the same as that of the house itself. Eight votes are required to select a judge. The Bundesrat makes the selection itself with a two-thirds vote required for appointment.

Again it is interesting to note from an American standpoint the extent of influence given to the states in this matter. The states have a chance to suggest possible judges and half the time actually appoint the judge to the Court. As in the United States, the Court has as one of its duties the settling of disputes between the national and state governments. The procedure used for selecting the personnel of the Court in Germany gives the states an opportunity to defend what they conceive to be their vital interests by selecting judges sympathetic to their views. This is not to suggest that the judges of the Federal Constitutional Court are biased. But obviously approaches to interpreting and applying a constitution differ from one judge to another—some are strict constructionists and others are more liberal. And in Germany the states have some opportunity to get judges with the orientation they prefer onto the Court. Thus the German Länder are less likely than the American states to see the highest court in the land as being a hostile element of another level of government. The Federal Constitutional Court is more likely to be regarded as an impartial arbiter.

One panel or senate of the Constitutional Court deals with questions of the violation of civil liberties and constitutional rights, while the other senate hears all the other cases within the Court's jurisdiction. Examples of these would be conflicts between two or more states or between a state and the national government. Although the first senate deals only with cases of one general type, it has had the heavier work load.

The Court has three types of jurisdiction—concrete, abstract, and constitutional complaint. In concrete jurisdiction the Court considers an actual case that raises a question of constitutionality. This is the way that the American Supreme Court operates. If it is claimed in a case in the regular court system that the Basic Law has been violated, the case goes to the Federal Constitutional Court. Should it be a violation of a state constitution that is claimed, the case goes to the constitutional court of the appropriate state.

Under abstract jurisdiction, it is possible for the Court to rule on a constitutional question when there is no actual case before it. As noted in the discussion of the form of judicial review practiced in France, this is a procedure which the U.S. Supreme Court has refused to follow. In Germany, however, the Federal Government, a state Government, or one third of the total membership of the Bundestag can request that the Court rule on the constitutional validity of a law before that law actually is implemented or, should it be in effect already, before any case has arisen questioning the law. The comments, made in Chapter 16 on the appropriateness of this procedure in a code law system are relevant here as well.

Unfortunately, whatever party is in Opposition in the Bundestag has tended to use this power as a political weapon. When legislation that it strongly opposes passes, it seeks to thwart the majority by moving a political conflict into a legal forum and getting the Court to throw out the law. As the German newspaper *Sueddeutsche Zeitung* commented recently,

> there is no longer almost any law of great political, economic or social significance that goes into effect without checking by the highest court. In principle, there is nothing to complain about this, although the growing danger is not to be overlooked, that political decisions in the final analysis have to be made by judges on the Constitutional Court. In this manner, there comes an element of insecurity in the application of laws, particularly, to the degree that they affect economic life.

The constitutional complaint is similar to abstract jurisdiction but broader in scope. Anyone in Germany can challenge any law on the grounds that it infringes rights guaranteed by the Basic Law. There are no court costs for this procedure and the challenger need not even hire a lawyer unless he or she wishes to do so. Thus in Germany when someone says, "I'll fight it all the way to the Supreme Court," it is not quite the idle threat that it is in the United States.

Constitutional complaints are far and away the great bulk of the matters brought to the Constitutional Court—1583 of 1647 cases in 1974, for example. In all, in a quarter of a century the Court has had around 30,000 constitutional complaints. Given the Germans' litigious nature the procedure clearly would get totally out of hand unless some limits were imposed. Normally, one must go through the regular court system before getting to the Constitutional Court. Furthermore, the Court has a screening committee, which can reject a request to hear a case. Thus about 98 percent of the constitutional complaints never are heard by the Court, having been rejected as inadmissible for lack of legal merit. Nonetheless, in a quarter of a century well over 400 such complaints, about 1.5 percent of the total filed, have resulted in overturning a law, regulation, or previous court decision. To that extent, rights which would have been infringed in some way, have been protected.

As noted in Chapter 18, the Court is empowered to rule on petitions by the Cabinet or the Bundestag that a political party be banned because it seeks to overthrow the established democratic order. Under this power a neo-Nazi and a Communist party were declared illegal. The Court also has ruled, however, that a person cannot be punished for membership in, and service to, a banned political party at a time before the party was prohibited.

What the Germans have sought to do is to strike a viable balance between liberty and license. On the one hand they wish to protect basic liberties from the violation they suffered under the Nazis. Yet they also want to avoid the Weimar situation where freedom was used in an abusive fashion so as to undermine the democratic system. Thus they have included in the Basic Law provisions aimed at protecting the State from those who would seek to subvert it. In the end these concerns interrelate, for those who seek to destroy the democratic order would abolish individual liberties were they to succeed. A constitutional court is no guarantee against this happening, but it can make the rise of a dictator more difficult and can play a major role in educating the public to the importance of basic freedoms. It can contribute significantly to the establishment of a tradition of liberal democracy.

BIBLIOGRAPHICAL NOTES

Published information on the law and the judiciary in present-day Germany is meager and scattered. Some information is to be found in several of the general books on Germany. For a discussion of the Constitutional Court, see Donald P. Kommers, in Joel B. Grossman and Joseph Tanenhaus, *Frontiers of Judicial Research* (New York: John Wiley & Sons, Inc., 1969), and Edward McWhinney, *Constitutionalism in Germany and the Federal Constitutional Court* (Leyden: Sythoff, 1962).

Part V

PROSPECTS FOR EUROPEAN DEMOCRACY

Durability and Change in Response to the Challenge of Eurocommunism

"A specter is haunting Europe," so wrote Karl Marx in the middle of the 19th century as the opening words of the world's most influential pamphlet, *The Communist Manifesto*. Now over one and a quarter centuries later something more substantial than a specter is troubling Western Europe—Eurocommunism, the heir (or is it the illegitimate offspring?) of Marx's Communism. Eurocommunism is a major factor in the domestic politics of France, Italy, and Spain. And although not of direct and immediate importance in Britain and Germany, it significantly affects the foreign policy calculations of both countries.

The prominence of Eurocommunism in European politics of the late 1970s is not just a matter of the size of Communist parties and the extent of their popular support. The French Communist party's share of the electorate was considerably larger 30 years ago, and for the first time since the end of World War II the party now actually is less popular than the Socialist party. Nor is it a matter of Communist nearness to a share in government power. In 1946 and 1947, both the French and Italian Communists held Cabinet seats and thus shared in governing France and Italy.

Instead, the basic issue is whether the way that we in the West have learned, through a couple of decades of Cold War, to perceive Communism is correct or needs to be altered. Eurocommunism confronts us with the crucial question: Are all Communists fundamentally the same? From this basic concern flow a number of subsidiary queries. Are all Communist parties controlled by the Soviet Union? Are they, as Guy Mollet observed during the debate on where the PCF should sit in the French legislature "not so much Left, as East"? Do they all approve of using violence to gain power from existing legitimate governments that have been popularly elected? And should they, by whatever means, come to power, would any of them be willing to permit full political competition to continue in their country so that a free election might vote them out of office? And should this happen, would they be willing to accept the electoral verdict and relinquish power rather than claiming that it was only a mistake or a fraud that had cost them the victory they deserved? These are the questions on which the voters and politicians in France, Italy, and Spain, and the Foreign Secretaries in Germany, Britain, and the United States have to make up their minds.

The basic issue raised by Eurocommunism goes back to June 1948 when the Russians expelled the Yugoslav Communist party of Marshal Josip Tito from the Cominform, the international Communist organiza-.tion. Although the Russians accused Tito of failing to conform fully to Marxist ideology, the real issue was his refusal to accept the Soviet Union as the model for political and economic development of all Communist parties and states and to accept Russian "advisors" in Yugoslavia to guide that country in the task of "building socialism." There was no question in the eyes of the Western democracies, nor, for that matter, in the mind of Tito himself, that he was not a Communist. Although the Yugoslav political system may not have been as fully repressive as was the Russian, yet it clearly was a one-party dictatorship. Industry and agriculture were being collectivized rapidly and the capitalist West was denounced as an enemy. Nonetheless, to the Russians Tito was an heretical nationalist, not a Communist, because, in saying that Yugoslavia was not willing to be governed from Moscow, he had denied that only the Russians were entitled to interpret Marxist ideology and decide how it was to be implemented concretely.

Subsequent events amply demonstrate that the Russians were entirely correct in some senses. Maintaining a coherent, unified ideology is impossible if no one single locus of authoritative interpretation exists. Grant that more than one entity can decide what a doctrine means and you grant diversity and weaken central control. It is as though we would permit each state in the American federal system to decide what the U.S. Constitution meant within their own borders. This country had to fight a civil war to establish that such a step was a certain recipe for disintegration of the political system. If Yugoslavia could decide for itself what Communism was, then it could decide to act domestically, and, more importantly, internationally in ways that the Russians would not prefer. And if Yugoslavia could do this then why could not other Communist systems? Thus the Russians clearly had to oppose any step toward diversity or pluralism within the Communist movement.

But Tito, with aid from the West (which figured that anything which annoyed the Russians must be a good thing), survived. Within a decade and a half the Russians concluded that Tito was not the worst thing in the world. Much more serious was the unwillingness of the Chinese Communists to comply with Russia's wishes. By the mid-1960s relations between China and the Soviet Union had reached the point that experts were speculating on the prospects of war between them—a possibility that only a few years earlier would have been dismissed as evidence that anyone suggesting it was totally ignorant of Communist affairs. What made the Chinese defection especially embarrassing to the Russians was their claim that they were the true Communists and that the Russians were heretics because they had gone soft on the need for violent world revolution to destroy imperialist capitalism. Although the Chinese and the Yugoslavs were moving in different directions, both were moving away from the Russians and toward greater diversity within Communism.

Even before the Russians and the Chinese had begun huffing and puffing at each other publicly, another event even more relevant to this topic had occurred, although it was little noticed at the time. In June 1956 in an interview, Palmiro Togliatti, the leader of the Italian Communist party said, "The Soviet model should no longer be obligatory . . . the complex of the system is becoming polycentric, and in the communist movement itself one can no longer speak of a single guide."[1] This was the origin of the doctrine of polycentrism—the true parent (although it is an Italian idea, we resist calling it the godfather) of contemporary Eurocommunism.

Togliatti did not want to abandon Marx, because he felt that Marx's analysis, despite its age, remained basically correct. Class struggle and exploitation continued to be useful concepts in understanding the political process. But Marx, who, after all, wrote *The Communist Manifesto* almost a quarter of a century before Italy was unified into a single nation, could offer little guidance for specific policies in the present Italian context. Furthermore, although the Russian leaders, unlike Marx, were alive and not dead, they were Russians, not Italians. Few, if any, of them ever had been within the borders of Italy for even a few hours. Obviously they could have little knowledge or understanding of the political and economic situation within which the Italian Communist party must operate. Thus they must permit the PCI to decide for itself how best to pursue the goals of Communism in Italy.

That Togliatti should have been the one to develop and propagate such a doctrine is surprising. During the period of Facist control of Italy he had lived in exile in the Soviet Union, returning home in the spring of 1944 to build the PCI into a major postwar political force. He had been one of the early leaders of the Comintern. And in 1949 he condemned Tito. Immediately after World War II the PCI was regarded widely as perhaps the most extreme Communist party in Western Europe. It was well armed from helping to drive the Nazis from Italy during the war and many thought

---

[1] Quoted in Stanley Henig and John Pinder, eds., *European Political Parties* (London: Allen & Unwin, 1969), p. 206, n. 1.

that it might try to seize control of the government by force in the late 1940s. In 1956 it approved the Soviet Union's crushing of the Hungarians' revolt against their Communist government. Nonetheless, even a party such as this soon began to want to run its own affairs without instructions, to say nothing of control, from Moscow.

As these attitudes began to spread, European Communists became less willing to accept Soviet behavior which formerly they had approved. When in 1968 Alexander Dubcek tried to liberalize Czechoslovakia's regime to create "Communism with a human face," the Russians sent in tanks to crush his reforms. Unlike their response to similar action against Hungary a decade earlier, the Italian Communists condemned the Soviet Union, as, but with great reluctance, did the French Communists.

During the 1970s reliable information has become readily available about the ways in which the Soviet system represses its political dissidents. (Discussed fully in Chapter 32.) Those whom the Russian leaders dislike are not permitted to travel outside the Soviet Union and may be exiled to a forced labor camp or a mental hospital. As denying that such things occur has become increasingly difficult, Western Communist parties have felt forced to criticize such practices to avoid losing all credibility in the eyes of West European voters.

The Russian leaders' intolerance of criticism has led them to respond with charges of anti-Sovietism, thus further undermining their relations with West European Communists. Only leaders as paranoid as the Russians could have made such an error. The West European Communists had not said that if forced to choose between Russia and the West, they would prefer the latter. They do not want to replace Communism in the Soviet Union with capitalism any more than the Russian leaders do. But they could see what the Russians could not—brutal domestic repression of dissidents is silly because it is unnecessary. The number of dissidents in the Soviet Union is so small that they have little prospect of overthrowing the system. There is, in short, no threat against which the Soviet Union needs to be defended, in contrast to relations with the West where a strong opponent does exist. The West European Communists simply were refusing to defend the Soviet Union against imagined enemies, not against real ones.

The embittered relations between the Soviet Union and the Eurocommunists have become almost comic at times. In 1974 the French Communists joined with the Socialists to support Mitterand for President. During the course of the campaign the Soviet Ambassador to France, Tchervonenko, called on the conservative candidate Giscard, but had no time to see Mitterand. The Communists felt that the Soviet Union deliberately had undercut them. Since then Georges Marchais, the leader of the French Communists, has refused to see Tchervonenko. When Kirilenko of the Soviet Politburo attended the French Communist party congress in

1976, he was not allowed to speak. Furthermore, Marchais refused to attend the meeting of the Soviet Communist party in Moscow in February 1976, thus breaking with past custom. When Leonid Brezhnev paid a state visit to France in June 1977, he talked with several political leaders, but not with Marchais. Just who was avoiding whom is not clear.

Enrico Berlinguer, the leader of the Italian Communists, did attend the party Congress in Moscow. When he addressed this important gathering of Russian and other Communist leaders, however, he spoke out for human rights and democracy. He made it clear that not only did he accept Italian membership in NATO, but that he saw it as a means of preventing foreign interference in Italian affairs. Berlinguer was implying that even a Communist Italy might be invaded by the Soviet Union, just as Hungary and Czechoslovakia had been. Thus, a Communist Italy would need NATO to protect itself from its comrades in the Soviet Union.

Berlinguer's position is not accepted by all Eurocommunists. A senior member of the defense policy committee of the Italian Communist party indicated in an April 1977 interview that were there an international crisis between the Soviet Union and the West, the Italian Communists would support the Soviet Union or, at best, be neutral. The Spanish Communists oppose Spain's entry into NATO, and their leader, Santiago Carrillo, despite being clearly anti-Soviet, hardly has greater sympathy for the West.

The French Communists continue to be strongly anti-German and anti-American. When de Gaulle was President of France he was so concerned about maintaining France's sovereign independence that he took the country out of the military aspects of the NATO alliance. Subsequent Presidents, however, have been moving back from this extreme position to cooperate in some military matters. The French Communists have opposed these moves. Until 1976 they had denounced France's nuclear deterrent, even though de Gaulle had developed it under the slogan of "defense to all horizons" to indicate that the weapons were not directed solely against the Soviet Union. Having spent a year in reconsidering their policy, the party announced in the spring of 1977 that they accepted the French nuclear striking force. This did not mean that the PFC had become pro-West; rather, it was additional evidence of the party's traditional nationalism. As one scholar has observed, "Marchais is the poor Frenchman's de Gaulle."[2] While extreme nationalism can be a problem for NATO cooperation, as de Gaulle and others have shown in the past, yet it hardly is helpful either to the Russians in their efforts to direct an international Communist movement. The more nationalist the French Communists are, the less likely they are to accept instructions from the Soviet Union.

[2] Neil McInnes, *Euro-Communism*, The Washington Papers, vol. 4, no. 37 (Beverly Hills and London: Sage Publications, 1976), p. 70.

Some people have wondered whether the Russians welcome the growth of Eurocommunism, representing a step forward in extending Communism over the entire globe, or fear it because of the diversity of views and loosening of Soviet control which it brings to the Communist movement. Whatever the answer, the Russians clearly are anxious about the development and are laboring to keep the Eurocommunists within their control.

In June 1977 a Russian Communist magazine reviewed the book which Carrillo, the Spanish Communist leader, had written on Eurocommunism. He was harshly denounced for supporting an idea designed to split the international Communist movement. The review reasserted "internationalist solidarity" (Russian control of all Communism) and declared that there could be only one true Communism. Carrillo was reviled for speaking "of our country and our party in terms that even the most reactionary writers do not often venture to use." Significantly the Russians had waited until after the Spanish elections to attack Carrillo. Since his party had received only 9 percent of the vote, the Russians apparently felt that he could be challenged more easily than either the French or Italian Communists, who have two to four times as much support in their countries.

The Russians' tactic of dividing the Eurocommunists by selective attack succeeded only partially. True, the Italian Communists said little to defend Carrillo and the French Communists were even quieter. Neither of them wanted so to antagonize the Soviet Union as to call down its wrath on their heads as well. But Rumania and, to an even greater extent, Yugoslavia opposed the Russians' action. Rumania maintained that each Communist party had a right to work out its own policy. The Yugoslavs saw the attack as a repeat of their conflict with the Soviet Union in the late 1940s. They asserted that the Russians were violating the agreement reached at the summit meeting of Communist parties from all over Europe held in East Berlin in 1976, which was supposed to have devised an acceptable compromise on the question of Russian leadership of the international movement. The problem for the Russians resembles that of trying to stamp out a fire; just as the blaze seems to have been extinguished at one point, it breaks out at another.

Whether in an international crisis the Soviet Union could count on the loyalty of the Eurocommunists is a matter of concern, of course, for both the Russians and the leaders of the Western alliance. Of more immediate importance to many Europeans, however, is the question of what would happen to their countries were the Communists to come to power there. Would their lives become like those of the East Germans and the Poles?

On the question of changing a nation's economic system, the Italian Communists are much more moderate than the French. In fact, it is not at all clear that the Italians want to do anything that any responsible party should not favor. They recognize that existing state-owned enterprise is operating so badly in Italy that they do not want to nationalize anything else. They concede that straightening out Italy's economy will require severe measures that may result in a lowering of the standard of living. They oppose trade unions' striking for unrealistic pay increases, which only are eaten up in galloping inflation. And they recognize that transferring some labor to more productive uses may result in greater short-term unemployment. One observer has gone so far as to say, "Economically, the Party's line is somewhat to the right of the French Socialists."[3]

The French Communists have not shown the responsibility of the Italians. The PCF is pressing its Socialist allies to support even more extensive nationalization than the two parties agreed to in 1972. Their object is to have all fundamental production plus credit facilities in the hands of the state within three months of coming to power. They support huge increases in the minimum wage, old age pensions, and the allowance each family receives for every child. This is to be achieved, despite cutting working hours, by increasing the taxes of those with higher incomes and having industry absorb some of the costs. Putting these measures into effect would produce a catastrophic inflation rate of 35 percent. In short, the French Communists' economic proposals are not so much tyrannical as they are stupid.

More serious is the question of whether the Eurocommunists on coming to power would accept parliamentary democracy or would try to establish a dictatorship. In November 1975 Marchais went to Rome to meet with Berlinguer. At the end of their talks they signed an agreement promising to exercise power by democratic means and emphasizing the need to protect all liberties. This agreement was especially significant because the two parties were, in effect, pledging to support each other in the conflict which they expected to occur over Eurocommunism at the international meeting of Communist parties scheduled for early in 1976.

A little over a year later in March 1977, the two leaders went to Madrid, to meet with Carrillo. This meeting, more than any other event to that time, seemed clearly to identify Eurocommunism as a separate current. The Declaration of Madrid, which the three leaders signed, not only committed them to a detailed list of rights, but, by virtue of the ones it mentioned, clearly criticized the Soviet Union's treatment of its citizens. The Eurocommunist leaders committed themselves to

> the respect, guarantee, and promotion of individual liberties of every kind: freedom of thought and of expression, of the press, of association, of meetings and demonstrations, the right of free movement within and beyond national boundaries, trade union freedom and independence, the right to strike, the inviolability of privacy, the respect of universal suffrage and of the opportunity of the majority to change the government democratically,

---

[3] James Goldsborough, "Eurocommunism after Madrid," *Foreign Affairs* 55 (July 1977): 807.

freedom of worship and of the expression of philosophical, cultural, and artistic opinions and trends.

Not surprisingly, the government-controlled press of Eastern Europe and the Soviet Union gave the Declaration only limited coverage. Only an East German paper printed it in full.

Many of the rights listed in the Declaration of Madrid had been included in a Declaration of Freedoms issued by the French Communists in May 1975, although their statement was even more extensive. Like the Madrid document, it also was a disguised attack on the Soviet Union.

Not only have the Eurocommunists declared their support for human rights. They are also not committed to the term Marx used to describe how the shift in power would be consolidated after the revolution—the dictatorship of the proletariat. Although past leaders of the Italian Communists have expected significant changes in the power structure when a new class attains power, they never supported the idea of an illegal, dictatorial phase. Thus, the PCI never has talked about the dictatorship of the proletariat. The French Communists had used the phrase but have said little about it since the late 1960s. Then in January 1976 Marchais announced that the party officially would drop the phrase, a step that was approved by the party Congress the next month. Before dismissing this event as a painless exercise in semantics, one should reflect on how tenaciously some people in the United States cling to a literal reading of the American Constitution. And in Britain, Labour party Leader Hugh Gaitskell had to abandon his efforts in the late 1950s to get the party to revise its statement of principles because of the strong opposition of left wing traditionalists.

When the Eurocommunist leaders said in the Declaration of Madrid that they supported the right of the electorate to change Governments, they were only restating what they had been saying for well over a decade. From the late 1950s on, the parties had accepted parliamentary democracy with its requirements of peaceful pursuit of office and acquiescence in the electorate's decisions. Admittedly, they had qualified their position by warning that if the wealthy classes resisted social change, conflict would occur and the resulting turmoil might preclude complying with all constitutional procedures. Such warnings have disappeared gradually. Nonetheless, the Italian Communists, although willing to accept the electorate's verdict, still find it hard to believe that once the workers truly attain power anyone would want to go back to the bad old days when a wealthy elite ran things.

On the whole, then, although some doubts always will continue to exist about any speculative situation, the evidence available does not make the Eurocommunists seem to be an automatic threat to European democracy. Such a conclusion leads one to ask what still is Communist, what is distinctive or unique, about these parties. One comprehensive study of

Eurocommunism has answered this question by saying that these parties believe that they continue to be Communists, regardless of how their policies shift, as long as they retain "the Leninist party machine, the practise [sic] of democratic centralism and absolute rule by a small group around the secretary-general who can change tactics brusquely and without explanation."[4]

In this respect the Eurocommunists have changed least. The Italian Communist party has a reputation of being more willing than other Communist parties are to tolerate internal pluralism and diversity of opinion among party members. McInnes maintains, however, that this is a mistaken view. He contends that only a few leaders, not the average party member, can question the party line. Furthermore, disagreements between the leaders are not settled democratically by vote of the rank-and-file. Thus he questions whether the PCI is any more democratic than is the PCF, which long has had a reputation for rigid internal discipline. In the past those who wanted to liberalize the policies of the PCF often have been expelled from the party. More recently with the shift toward Eurocommunism, it has been the Stalinist traditionalists who have been expelled. But in either case the message has been the same: Dissidents are not welcome within the Communist party.

Communist party organization makes repressing internal diversity relatively easy, and not only because members can be expelled. The basic party unit, the cell, can communicate only with the level of organization above it, not with other cells. Views that depart from the party line simply are filtered out at the level above the cell and are not transmitted on to the party leaders. Furthermore, the lack of communication between cells makes organizing any sizable opposition bloc extremely difficult. Dissidents remain isolated in small groups which the top leaders can defeat easily.

The key issue is whether a party that is so undemocratic in its own internal affairs can be trusted to abide by the rules of parliamentary democracy in the national political system. This is a legitimate concern, but it also is somewhat naive. No political party is fully democratic, although many of them do better in this regard than do the Communists. As we have argued earlier at various places, the test of whether parties deserve to be called democratic is not the nature of their internal power structure, but their willingness to accept democratic competition in their country's political system.[5] The basic function of political parties is not to provide a channel for mass participation in the policy-making process, but to offer the voters a choice between sets of leaders who have been recruited,

---

[4] McInnes, *Euro-Communism*, p. 28.

[5] It would be well at this point to review the end of the Participatory Structures Section of the Introduction, the end of Chapter 4, and the end of Chapter 20.

apprenticed, and qualified through the parties.[6] Thus, if the Communists wish to cling to a highly elitist, rigidly disciplined internal organization this need not be fatal to a nation's democracy. The key concern is their willingness to accept the electorate's decisions, rather than whether they abide by their members' wishes. ·

As we have seen, the Eurocommunists do profess acceptance of electoral verdicts. The 22d Congress of the PCF, for example, in February 1976 specifically acknowledged that the electorate should remain free to vote Communists out of office. Of course, until that actually occurs no one can be completely certain that the Eurocommunists mean what they say. But it is worth noting that things do change, even in Communist parties. A new generation is coming to power. Of those who were on the Central Committee of the PCF prior to World War II, only three remain. More than half of the Central Committee (66 of 121) have attained this party office since 1970. Approximately the same is true of the Politburo; 10 of its 21 members have been selected since 1970. And as for the PCF membership as a whole, 70 percent is under 40.

Although, contrary to what some young people seem to believe, no evidence establishes that all young people are democrats and all older people tyrants, yet young people are a force for change. Thus as older leaders depart it is not implausible that some Communist parties should begin to move in new directions. To dismiss Eurocommunism out of hand as, at best, semantic exercises and, at worst, the most Machiavellian Moscow conspiracy thus far would be a mistake. It would be an example of precisely the rigidity of thought of which the Communists often are accused.

In focusing on the challenge of Eurocommunism, we have been talking in a vacuum to some extent. The lines along which any political movement develops are affected greatly by a country's history, political culture, and governmental structures, among other things, as we discussed in the Introduction. The Nazi party did not come to power in Germany in 1933 because a majority of Germans suddenly decided to hate Jews. Germany's political, social, and economic problems were not being solved effectively. People so despaired of any useful action by the existing political structures that they were willing to support new faces that offered hope and seemed to have a remedy for society's ills. Thus we must turn to a summing up of the political systems of Britain, France, and Germany. Only in this way can we understand fully the context within which the challenge of Eurocommunism occurs.

Britain was the first country we analyzed in this book. This was for the good reason that American scholars long regarded Britain as the model for

---

[6] The crucial question of the purpose of parties in democracy is examined thoroughly in Leon Epstein, *Political Parties in Western Democracies* (New York: Frederick A. Praeger, Inc., 1967). This book is essential reading for any study of parties.

all things good politically. If only American government and politics could be more like the British, we all would be better off, they said. France and Germany had had troubled histories and hardly could be considered models of democracy. Britain offered a standard of excellence against which these two countries and others could be compared to ascertain the shortcomings of their political systems. Thus, because of the longevity and stability of the British political system, we began with Britain as a model of parliamentary democracy and then went on to France and Germany as alternates to or variations on the themes we found in the British political system.

A recurrent theme in the chapters on Britain was accountability or responsibility. A second theme often touched on, although not so explicitly noted, was concentration of power. The essence of the British political process can be summarized in terms of the way in which these two themes relate to each other.

Concentration of power easily can be a great danger, as will become quite clear in Part VI when we analyze the Soviet Union as an archetypal dictatorial system. But in a political culture like that of Britain's with a traditional deep respect for democratic values, concentration of power can be a decided asset, for its means that responsibility is concentrated as well. In dictatorial systems this is not a relevant point, for they provide no way of enforcing this responsibility—the leaders are not accountable to the people. But in Britain they are.

So long as accountability is maintained, the British have been content to allow political leaders to exercise political power relatively unencumbered, for *the* limitation on power is not a written constitution, but the fact of accountability. Nor is there a system of checks and balances like that in the United States to defend freedoms.

The power structure of British government can be understood only in terms of the presence of accountability. Neither the monarch nor the House of Lords is accountable, and thus they cannot be allowed to exercise any real power. The judiciary is somewhat more accountable, since its members are appointed by the Government and can be removed by Parliament, but it is subject to little control. Thus its power, too, is circumscribed; British courts lack the power exercised by American ones.

The civil service, at its upper levels, clearly does exercise power and thus must be accountable. A special means of achieving this must be devised, which will not jeopardize the benefits of efficiency and merit selection. Thus the British have developed the doctrines of the political neutrality of the civil service and of ministerial responsibility. The nationalized industries also are centers of power and must be accountable. In this case the problem is to avoid losing the advantages of commercial efficiency. The public corporation is an attempt to satisfy the demands both of efficiency and accountability in this area.

The key structure in this system, in the traditional view, is Parliament. The people cannot by themselves call all the government's officials to account. The job is too vast; it requires full-time effort. Therefore the task is delegated to elected legislative representatives. These representatives are directly accountable to the people and everything else is accountable to the representatives. British parties, unified and cohesive, help to clarify where responsibility lies and thus aid the electorate in calling their representatives to account.

The Cabinet wields considerable power. Therefore, it is essential that it be accountable. This explains why the Government must keep Parliament informed of its plans and actions, why these must be debated fully there, why the existence of an official Opposition is essential, why the Opposition is consulted in planning the Commons' agenda, why the Government allows time for censure debates, why the Government submits daily to questioning of its actions and policies.

These are devices to make the Government more accountable and responsive to the people. And here we return again to the matter of concentration of power. Government may be accountable to the people, be subject to their control and yet not be very responsive to their desires because power is too fractionalized, is concentrated insufficiently to enable it to carry out their wishes or meet their needs.

In Third and Fourth Republic France and not infrequently in the United States, government has not seemed to be very responsive. In those French political systems the voters did decide who would represent them in the legislature. In the United States we decide this and, as well, who will be the chief executive. But given the normal diffusion of power in all these systems, the electorate really has not been able to decide who would be the Government, who would exercise governing power without being able to shift blame for failures or inaction.

In Britain the voters were thought to have precisely the power of determining who would govern. And should they decide that the party currently entrusted with this power was doing a bad job, then at the next election they could sweep them from office and get a change in policy. No other rascals need be turned out, no other strongholds of power assulted. The party in power had no excuse for failures because the domestic power structure contained no obstacles to thwart a Government from carrying out its program.

While these comments summarizing the virtues which the British political system long has been thought to possess continue to be true to some extent, yet the picture they present increasingly has come to be recognized as highly idealized. The atrophy of the doctrine of ministerial responsibility has weakened the accountability of both the political leader and the top bureaucrat. The cautious attitude of the civil service militates against utilizing new methods and knowledge which may be essential to coping with contemporary problems. The device of the public corporation has not insured properly the responsibility of nationalized industries to Parliament. Nor, despite British membership, does Parliament have effective control over the decisions taken in the European Economic Community.

Most grave of all, Parliament's ability to control the Cabinet is seriously in doubt. Question hour seems to have become little more than a minor irritant to the Government instead of a significant means of Parliamentary control. Party cohesion is a double-edged sword. While it can help to locate responsibility, it also can make enforcement of accountability more difficult. The Government can order its disciplined supporters to maintain it in office despite the failures of its policies. Increasingly during the 1970s not only experts, but even the average Briton seemingly has come to feel that the activity of the House of Commons is neither effective nor very important.

Given their traditional positive attitudes toward their political systems, one hesitates to assert that sizable numbers of Britons now are alienated politically. Nonetheless, disenchantment, at the very least, is widespread. The discontents generated by current political issues have contributed to this negative mood. Agitation, demagoguery, and hostility stemming from continued nonwhite immigration into Britain (especially the Ugandan Asians in 1972), and the virtual civil war in Northern Ireland that continued to drag on with little prospect of settlement have depressed and embittered political attitudes.

Even more serious was the feeling which grew from the late 1960s on that neither a Labour nor a Conservative Government could do anything to solve Britain's economic problems and to halt soaring inflation. Government, Parliament, parties—all appeared to many Britons to be ineffective. Many people began to wonder whether interest groups had attained such positions of influence in the British political process that controlling the wage demands of the trade unions had become impossible. Given Britain's dependance on international trade, discussed in Chapter 1, the economic situation was extremely critical. Thus, although Richard Crossman and others had argued that the Prime Minister had come to dominate not only the Cabinet, but also the entire political process, real political power appeared to lie not with him, but with Jack Jones and Hugh Scanlon, Britain's two leading trade union officials.

Some people saw a glow of hope for Britain's economy in North Sea oil, which began to be developed toward the close of the 1970s. To others this was a mirage that would make little difference. And should Scotland break away to independence, where would the oil revenues be then? Totally apart from the economic aspect, the thought of losing a sizable territory that constitutionally has been part of Britain for almost three centuries troubles many Britons. In the meantime the rise of nationalism in Scotland and Wales combined with the persistence of the Liberals so has changed the British party system that no party seems capable of winning a working majority in the House of Commons. While this may make the actions of Parliament more significant than many people thought they had become, it does little to enable the Government to cope decisively with pressing problems. Thus, one can see why some question whether the British political system is able to endure under such a load of burdens.

Accountability and concentration of power can serve as useful themes as well in analyzing the French political system. The basic problem for much of the Third and Fourth Republics was diffusion of power. No single party could command a majority in Parliament. Often not even a coalition of parties could do so. Opposition similarly was fractionalized. Thus, although Governments often were defeated in the legislature, no alternative Government existed—that is, no majority party or group with alternative coherent policies existed. Political groups combined readily to oust a Government, but could not agree upon what should be done thereafter. The legislature was unable to formulate policies. Affairs drifted on until problems reached crisis proportions before the system was galvanized into brief action. Instead of focusing accountability, one of the basic rules of game in this political system was to avoid responsibility at all costs. De Gaulle was determined to transform this situation in the Fifth Republic. Despite his anti-Americanism, the political position that de Gaulle sought for himself was not very different from that enjoyed by President Franklin Roosevelt. So successful was de Gaulle in bringing strong leadership to France that many people felt that the executive had become too dominant in the policy process. Such concerns hardly were unique to France. In the late 1960s and early 1970s a good deal was heard in the United States about "an imperial Presidency." We have noted previously that some students of the British political system believe that system is becoming "presidential," that the Prime Minister overshadows the rest of the Government. Few would disagree, however, that during the decade 1958–68 de Gaulle dominated French government and politics far more than other democratic leaders did their countries' political system.

De Gaulle was disinclined to associate Parliament and the parties in the tasks of governing. People held positions of responsibility in the Government because they enjoyed his confidence and not because they represented powerful groups in Parliament. In some ways his system resembled that which had prevailed in Germany under the Second Empire, a period which, as we have seen, did little to nurture the values essential to parliamentary democracy. De Gaulle had little or no interest in the political competition normal to a democracy; he refused to lead any political party. Often he seemed to be concerned only with lofty principles, expecting the administrative apparatus to devise the means of achieving them. The public seemed content to let him shoulder the nation's burdens and attempt to devise miraculous solutions for nearly insoluble problems. The opposition parties assailed de Gaulle but offered little in the way of coherent alternative programs.

The Fourth Republic, like the Third, was criticized for engendering popular apathy. People were unaware, or, worse, indifferent to political crises. De Gaulle's style of governing prevented the Fifth Republic from doing much to remedy this. Reliance on de Gaulle seems to have given people even less of a sense of participation and involvement in the political process. All political parties in France have considerably fewer members than they did in the late 1940s.

De Gaulle's principal bequest to France would seem to have been strong and stable executive leadership. By the late 1970s, however, questions had arisen even in this area. His strong leadership seems to have been based not so much on a reformed constitution, but on his personality and, ironically, given his dislike for parties, changes in the party system. That is to say that it was based on things more ephemeral than permanent.

President Giscard is not a Gaullist. His own party, the Republicans, is a relatively minor force in the National Assembly. The Gaullist party, the dominant force in the National Assembly, only lukewarm toward Giscard to begin with, has become increasingly hostile under the leadership of Jacques Chirac. By 1977 the true governing power clearly lay with Chirac, who held no national government position of any kind, rather than with President Giscard. Furthermore, should the Left coalition of Socialists, Communists, and Radicals win the approaching Parliamentary elections, as widely was anticipated, Giscard's power and influence would be undercut further. Recall that the French system is something of a cross between a separation of powers system and a fusion of powers system. To this point the latter characteristic has been more in evidence. The best guess for the future is a shift in the other direction. Thus, although we have discussed at length the problem of executive domination in the Fifth Republic, the future well could see a return to the ineffective government of the Third and Fourth Republics as Parliament clashes with a seriously weakened President.

As for Parliament itself, a splintering of parties back to the legislative fractionalization of the Third and Fourth Republics has become a greater danger. Both the Left and the Right are experiencing internal conflicts and tensions. As the *New York Times* French correspondent has commented, "While the fight on the left is over important political issues and the right is bickering mainly about personal ambition and tactics, both disputes are so intense and emotional that only a truce, not a peace, seems within reach of either side."[7]

---

[7] Flora Lewis, "Feuds among French Leftists . . . ," *New York Times,* June 30, 1977, p. A3.

In Germany a dominant personality began to bring strong, stable leadership a decade earlier than in France. Konrad Adenauer, like de Gaulle, had much about him that was irritating and unlikable. Both were arrogant and high-handed. Despite their elite orientations, however, neither was an authoritarian at heart. Both were dedicated to molding their countries into strong, yet free, nations. Adenauer's domination of German democracy during its formative years was precisely the style of government that was needed. The belief that equated democracy with weak leadership, as had been true in the Weimar Republic, had to be laid to rest. As a paternalistic figure, Adenauer was attractive to many Germans, especially in a period of considerable economic and political uncertainty. When all else was in doubt, he provided a rock of stability. One could have democracy *and* a strong leader with a sense of purpose. Under Weimer the Germans had .been forced to choose between these; under Bonn they could have both.

Germany's political achievements are not based on Adenauer's contribution alone, great as that may be. The Bonn Basic Law contains a more democratically attractive solution to the problem of excessive executive turnover than does that of the French Fifth Republic. The German executive is entrenched, but, unlike the French chief executive, remains responsible and accountable.

That Germany has departed further than has France from a fractionalized party system is even more significant. The concentration of political forces makes avoiding weak, deadlocked Governments easier. In contrast to Weimar the main parties no longer are narrow sectional organizations, but broad groupings of diverse interests. Ideology matters less in German politics today than it does in French. In France old conflicts and attitudes can continue to affect political behavior even when they have ceased to be very relevant to contemporary affairs. In Germany this is less likely to occur.

One reason that Germany has progressed further than France in this regard is that it does not have to deal domestically with Communism—Euro or other varieties. Communism has little electoral appeal for Germans. Nor are extreme political views at the other end of the spectrum any more popular. Thus the political views of the overwhelming majority of Germans can be accommodated by one of the three main parties, all of which are, to one degree of another, middle of the road. And even should Franz Josef Strauss decide to organize his CSU throughout Germany rather than remain confined to Bavaria, most observers would be surprised greatly if this led to an unraveling of the party system back to the fractionalization of Weimar.

The assertion that initially was little more than whistling in the dark has become true beyond doubt—Bonn is not Weimar. The Weimar Republic lasted less than a decade and a half before being replaced by a monomaniac's nightmarish vision, which was highly attractive to many and terrified few. The Bonn Republic has lasted twice as long as Weimar.

Although democracy is not the automatic product of prosperity, there can be little doubt that economic success is the overriding reason for the health of German democracy today. Within a generation Germany has gone from desolation to recovery to prosperity as one of the major economic powers of the world. Unlike Weimar, Bonn has had no problem of widespread unemployment, and inflation has not been excessive by the standard of other countries' current experience. The incredible inflation of Weimar, when restaurant meals literally changed in price while they were being eaten, has not been repeated. While Germany has had considerable outside help in recovering economically, its people rightly can feel that their industriousness and abilities were the major factor in rebuilding the country.

Had the Bonn Republic not been successful economically, commitment to the democratic political system would be considerably weaker. As we noted in Chapter 17, one of the reasons few people cared to defend the Weimar Republic from its attackers was its inability to deal with Germany's economic problems. Inflation, unemployment, and economic despair were so prevalent that people were ready for almost any change, thinking, incorrectly, that nothing could be worse than the situation in which they found themselves at the moment. Thus, what the prosperity of Bonn has done is to create an opportunity for democracy to take root. Had things gone wrong economically, democracy never would have had a chance in contemporary Germany, despite all the efforts to draft a democratic constitution. The Weimar experience had demonstrated the futility of relying on legal defenses alone.

France, also, has done well economically since the end of World War II. While not nearly as successful as Germany, it has overtaken Britain in most measures of economic achievement. Despite its political inadequacies, the Fourth Republic did make substantial economic gains. Had this not been true, its collapse probably would have come even sooner. This progress continued under de Gaulle, as vested economic interests opposed to modernizing the economy were routed in many instances. The antidemocratic threats experienced by France during the last third of a century would have jeopardized parliamentary democracy far more than they did had not the economy been developing soundly.

Speculating about what a difference the prosperity of Germany or even of France would have made to Britain is interesting. We have evaluated the British political system more qualifiedly, more guardedly than do traditional writers. Almost all of Britain's problems and danger points, the dissatisfaction and anxieties of her citizens, can be traced back to a malfunctioning economy. Had Britain, like Germany, had an economic miracle, we could have repeated unhesitatingly the traditional praise of its political system. The impact of Britain's poor economic record has meant that we have had to be as concerned to point out political shortcomings as to identify political virtues.

And yet we should avoid being too quick to condemn Britain for economic failure. An increasing number of economists is beginning to challenge the belief that pursuing the maximum possible economic growth is a desirable social policy. Foremost among them is Fred Hirsch of the University of Warwick in England, the author of *Social Limits to Growth*.[8] As he makes clear, continued economic growth is limited not so much by physical, technological restraints as it is constrained by social considerations. The essence of his argument is that until recently economic advance made possible increases in the standard of living for most everyone. We all could advance together. Not at the same rate, perhaps, or equally far, but at least in the same direction. But now economically advanced nations have reached the situation in which my gain can come only at your expense. Everyone cannot have a top job. If everyone and anyone can live in an exclusive suburb, it ceases to be exclusive. If too many people have vacation cabins in the woods, the population crush will be as great as in downtown Manhattan. Therefore, he feels that the alternative to a permanent division of society is a frontal attack on economic inequality.

His detailed proposals need not be discussed here. He does offer an insight, however, that is very relevant. He comments,

> The paradox noted by so many American journalists and visitors to Britain, that the poor record on the standard of economic indicators goes along with a gentle society and a more relaxed life style, is no paradox. It is the trade-off. Britain is far from having the balance exactly right. But its experience does indicate some of the real choices that modern society has to make.

Britain is not doing well economically, but this may be because it has chosen to pursue other, equally desirable goals. A visit to Britain totally dissolves the picture conveyed by the American news media. The country is not about to collapse economically or politically.

Study of the British system reveals a set of political structures that are highly institutionalized and durable. It is a system in which tradition is immensely important, yet one which is not rigid and brittle. The British have shown great talent in adapting old institutions to new functions, in shifting power and reforming society in generally acceptable nondislocative ways. They have demonstrated a knowledge of the fact that one who wants to retain the legitimacy of a political system must recognize that there are limits to the role of rationality in politics. It is wiser, although intellectually less satisfying, to allow for sentiment and tradition by means of piecemeal reform than to implement major structural changes recom-

---

[8] Published by Harvard University Press, Cambridge, Mass., in 1976. See also his two articles in the *New York Times* of May 26 and 27, 1977.

mended mainly by their abstract intellectual brilliance and the demands of some that all problems must be solved at once.

While the British have not solved their past fundamental political problems at a single stroke with an elaborate logical plan, they have evolved piecemeal responses tested by experience. This approach frustrates the impatient and frightens the anxious, but it has proven to be extremely successful. It would be a rash person who would wager now that this procedure should be abandoned as ineffective. The British genius for adaptability has not run out.

As for France, more than most countries, it seems always to be either on the verge of a crisis or at some major fork in the road. The Fifth Republic has coped with a number of the country's basic problems. In some instances these seem to have been disposed of permanently, but in other instances the solution may be only temporary. The current system of government continues the administrative tradition of strong executive rule. But France's competing tradition of Assembly government also has a long history. And if the Left comes to control Parliament but not the Presidency, it is certain to stress the tradition of legislative dominance even though it may be prepared to live with some of the reforms of the Fifth Republic.

Despite all that de Gaulle did during the 1960s to shape and establish the institutions of the Fifth Republic, its future development remains uncertain. Events of the late 1970s will demonstrate whether the more accurate label for this system is the more transient one—de Gaulle's Republic—or the more permanent one—the Fifth Republic.

We began our analysis of the German political system by noting the curious fact that, although Germany has had the characteristics conducive to or associated with democracy, it has lacked the democratic tradition so essential to a viable parliamentary democracy. We conclude our comparative assessment with the equally curious, or at least unexpected, judgement that prospects for stable democracy currently are at least as good in Germany as they are in France. The Weimar Republic was launched amid considerable enthusiasm in much of the world, if not in Germany itself. A sound, democratic constitution was thought to be sufficient to maintain a democratic system. The hope proved to be short-lived, the expectation naive.

Thus, the Bonn Basic Law and the system which it created have been regarded with considerably more caution. No one can predict with certainty the future of any system. Nonetheless, Germany clearly has made a success of the Bonn Republic. Of course, problems remain in Germany. We have pointed out the failure of the Bundestag to perform adequately the function of educating the public and legitimating the government's policy output. The civil service still lacks a strong commitment to democratic values, although younger, more democratically oriented bureaucrats are changing this. The judiciary, like the bureacuracy, continues to exhibit a conservative, upper-class bias. Yet even here things have changed. Unlike the response of the judges under Weimar, the courts in the Bonn Republic have on several occasions acted against those whose commitment to democracy was questionable and who posed a threat to the system. Democracy has taken root in Germany and the creation of a democratic political tradition where none existed before is well under way.

These three major European democracies vary from each other in many respects. Yet all of them are fundamentally alike in being democracies. However the principle may be qualified in practice, in each of them the governing political power is responsible to the people. Those who wish to control that power both can and must compete for it openly, with the electorate deciding to whom the victory goes. Each system has its inadequacies and shortcomings, but, nonetheless, more often than not lives up to its ideals. This situation contrasts sharply with that prevailing in the Soviet Union. Thus, our analysis of that political system in the final part of this book should help to clarify the overriding virtues of the democracies, whatever their defects, and to point up their fundamental similarity with each other and contrast with dictatorial systems.

BIBLIOGRAPHICAL NOTE

Eurocommunism has developed so recently that there has been little time for extensive scholarly analysis. An informative report is James Goldsborough, "Eurocommunism after Madrid," *Foreign Affairs* 55 (July, 1977): 800–14. A more detailed and thorough analysis is Neil McInnes, *Euro-Communism*, The Washington Papers, vol. 4, no. 37 (Beverly Hills and London: Sage Publications, 1976). About all that one can do beyond this is to watch for future articles in the quality press.

A sampling from the following titles will provide a taste of the doubts expressed and the questions raised during the 1960s concerning the effectiveness of the British political system. Arthur Koestler, ed., *Suicide of a Nation?* (London: Secker & Warburg, 1963); C. A. R. Crosland, *The Conservative Enemy* (London: Cape, 1962); Brian Chapman, *British Government Observed* (London: Allen and Unwin, 1963); John Mander, *Great Britain or Little England?* (London: Secker & Warburg, 1963); Michael Shanks, *The Stagnant Society* (Harmondsworth: Penguin, 1961); Ian Gilmour, *The Body Politic* (London: Hutchinson, 1969); and W. J. Stankeiewicz, *Crisis in British Government: The Need for Reform* (London: Collier-Macmillan, 1967). During the 1960s Penguin published a series of books entitled *What's Wrong with . . . ?* dealing with such subjects as industry and unions. The most relevant one to this chapter is the one on Parliament by Andrew Hill and Anthony Whichelow. Probably the first stone thrown in this barrage was Michael Young's 1960 pamphlet *The Chipped White Cups of Dover*.

The most recent comprehensive examination of current trends in British politics is Dennis Kavanagh and Richard Rose, eds., *New Trends in British Politics: Issues for Research* (London and Beverly Hills: Sage Publications, 1977). See also

Chapter 6 in Jock Bruce-Gardyne and Nigel Lawson, *The Power Game* (London: Macmillan, 1976).

Publications in English about France and Germany comparable to those mentioned above are not available. Portions of Roy Macridis, *French Politics in Transition: The Years after De Gaulle* (Cambridge, Mass.: Winthrop, 1975) do touch on topics relevant to these matters, however.

Part VI

THE SOVIET UNION

26

The Context of
Soviet Politics

The U.S.S.R. (Union of Soviet Socialist Republics), no less than other nations, is conditioned by the past, by her geography, by her people, and by her political and social heritage. While a detailed examination of that past is beyond the scope of this book, the author believes that even a cursory survey of the past will contribute to an understanding of the country and its political system. In this chapter we shall be concerned with presenting a few basic facts about the country's physical setting, its ethnic diversity, and its heritage of political autocracy. In the next chapter we shall consider the changing foundations of Russian politics in the decades before the Communist seizure of power. In this way, the Communist effort to impose a revolutionary system on the country can be viewed in the appropriate context, and the modifications in that system can be seen, in part at least, as the result of a need to compromise with social forces which have their roots in the past.

THE PHYSICAL SETTING

The present territories of the Soviet Union constitute about one sixth of the inhabited land surface of the world, or about 8.5 million square miles. This represents an area as large as the United States, Canada, and Mexico combined. It stretches from the Baltic Sea to the Pacific Ocean and from the Arctic to the frontiers of Iran, Afghanistan, and China. Much of the area was acquired in a rapid expansion to the Pacific. Russia's march eastward across Siberia was as rapid as America's westward march to the other side of the Pacific.

The country is divided into 15 republics. By far the largest is the Russian Soviet Federated Socialist Republic (RSFSR), accounting for approximately three fourths of the nation's total area and over one half of its population. It stretches from the Baltic to the Bering Sea. The other republics, in order of the size of their population, are: Ukraine, Kazak, Uzbek, Belorussia, Georgia, Azerbaijan, Lithuania, Moldavia, Latvia, Kirghiz, Tadzhik, Armenia, Turkmen, and Estonia.

Nearly all of the area of the Soviet Union is north of the 50th parallel (that is, north of the United States), although the most southerly parts reach below the 40th. For all its continental nature, it is largely landlocked, except for the Arctic. It has the longest and perhaps the most useless coastline in the world. All seas and rivers are frozen part of the year. The great rivers flow to locked seas. The only ice-free port, prior to the acquisition of Königsberg, Memel, and Liepāja (Lepaya), was Murmansk. Vladivostok is kept open year-round with icebreakers.

For the most part, the Soviet Union has a cold climate, which is to be attributed more to its continental position, away from the moderating effect of oceans, than to its northerly latitude. There are extremes, nevertheless, ranging from the frigid Arctic to the intense heat of the deserts of Central Asia, with some areas having moderate to semitropical climates. Generally speaking, however, large areas of the country are unsuited for agriculture, and the amount of new land that can be opened up is limited. Summers are brief; frosts occur late in the spring and early in the autumn. Conditions for the planting of winter wheat or rye are not favorable because of the intense cold and the poor snow cover. Moreover, the quality of many of the soils is poor, and irrigation possibilities are limited. Because of variations and unreliability in rainfall, even the more favored regions experience great difficulties.

One of the most striking geographical facts about the U.S.S.R. is the immense Russian Plain. Across this plain flow a number of great rivers which have been, and to this day remain, important avenues of transport, commerce, and conquest. The low watersheds and short portages between the rivers have made it possible to connect them with canals. There are more than 180,000 miles of navigable rivers, although winter freezing prevents year-round use. The Volga is the most important single river, carrying half the country's total river freight. It drops less than 1,000 feet in some 2,300 miles. The great rivers of Siberia are of considerably less value, since they flow north into the frozen Arctic. Mountains in the Soviet Union are for the most part to be found along the periphery. The Urals, a low, eroded chain, are the one exception.

The importance of the rivers as arteries of commerce ought not, however, to be overemphasized, for the railroads still carry the bulk of the freight traffic. Roads are a rarity in the countryside, with mud prevailing for several months of the year. Although more than twice the area of the

United States, the Soviet Union has 0.25 million miles of paved roads, compared to 4 million miles in the United States. Moreover, the peasants do not own their own cars or trucks.

From the Arctic southward, there are five zones, each with a characteristic soil and vegetation. The tundra of the far north, with the subsoil perpetually frozen, does not provide much vegetation or opportunity for its development. Gradually, it merges into the forest zone, which covers nearly half of the total area of the Soviet Union. It is the largest forested area in the world and contains a mixture of trees. South of the forest zone is the famous steppe region of Russia, extending from the western boundaries all the way to the Altai Mountains in the east, an area that is, on the whole, rich but often lacking ample rainfall. The semidesert and desert zone lies partly in southeast European Russia and in areas of central Asia. The smallest, as well as the most southern, of the five main zones is the subtropical. It covers some 190,000 square miles along the Black Seacoast, the Caspian Seacoast, the Crimea, southern Transcaucasia, and the mountains of central Asia. Vegetation in the seacoast areas is extremely thick because of the humus soil and heavy rainfall. Central Asia, with its mild winters and hot summers, has sometimes been referred to as the Imperial Valley of the U.S.S.R.

In natural resources, the Soviet Union is perhaps the richest nation in the world. She has all the raw materials necessary to contemporary civilization, although there is reason to believe she does not have all that she needs of each. These resources are scattered widely, although some areas seem particularly well endowed. The Ural Mountain range has a variety of minerals; the Ukraine has coal and iron ore; the mountains of central Asia and the Far East have many of the rare metals, including uranium; the Caucasus have an abundance of oil; Siberia has iron ore reserves greater than the United States, Britain, and France combined; and the natural gas fields of western Siberia are said to be the largest in the world. The supplies of timber are large, although for the most part considerably removed from the principal population centers. Similarly, there is a great hydroelectric potential, which is only partially developed. Because so much remains unexplored, it is possible that the Soviet endowment in natural resources may prove richer than present estimates indicate.

ETHNIC DIVERSITY

The population of the Soviet Union, according to 1977 estimates, is about 260 million, most of it concentrated in European Russia, and more than half (60 percent) of it is in urban areas. More than 100 distinct and different ethnic groups are represented in this total, although the number of major groups is considerably smaller. More significant, however, is the fact that almost three fourths of the population is Slavic, making for a greater ethnic unity than is sometimes supposed, although this does not mean that political unity necessarily follows.

Numerically, women predominate in the Soviet Union, making up 54 percent of the population. This disproportion stems in part from large losses in World War II, but it is perhaps even more attributable to the purges conducted over several decades by the Soviet regime. One recent study concludes that over 20 million deaths were caused by Stalin's terror.[1]

The Russian Slavs are subdivided into three main groups. The most numerous are the Great Russians, who account for one half of the total population.[2] The Ukrainians, sometimes called Little Russians, number over 40 million. The White Russians (Belorussians), not to be confused with the political White Russians (as opposed to the Red), number over 9 million. In addition, there are Slav minorities, chiefly Poles, Czechs, and Bulgarians. Traditionally, most Russian Slavs have been Orthodox Christians, although the Uniate Church, which had a connection with Rome and which for the most part was to be found in the Ukraine, was not insignificant. Protestant sects made little headway in Russia, with the exception of the Baptists, whose actual membership is not known but is estimated to number more than 200,000.

The second largest ethnic group on the U.S.S.R. is the Turkic or Turko-Tartar people, who number around 30 million. Predominantly Moslem, they are in the main the descendants of the Asiatic warriors who were led westward by Genghis Khan and Tamerlane in the 13th and 14th centuries. In this group are to be found the Uzbeks and the Kazaks of central Asia, the Kazan and Crimean Tartars, the Azerbaijanis of the Transcaucasus, the Kirgiz peoples who live in central Asia along the Chinese frontier, and the Yakuts in eastern Siberia.

In the third largest ethnic group are the Transcaucasian peoples, who number some 8 million. Prominent among these are the Georgians, the Azerbaijani, and the Armenians, together with smaller but closely related groups. They are of mixed religious affiliation, although preponderantly Christian at the time of the Revolution in 1917.

A fourth and final major ethnic group, the Finno-Ugrian, is linguistically and ethnically related to the Hungarians, the Turks, and the Finns. They number about 5 million. These peoples are mostly Estonians, Udmurts, Chuvash, Finns, and Karelians.

---

[1] Robert Conquest, *The Great Terror: Stalin's Purge of the Thirties* (New York: Macmillan Co., 1968).

[2] The first mention of Slavs seems to have been made in the sixth century. There is no agreement on the root meaning of the word "Slav." In certain West European languages, it is synonymous with "slave." In the languages of the Slavic peoples, however, the word means "praiseworthy" or "choicest."

In addition to the main divisions already listed, the 1970 census reported more than 2 million Jews living in the U.S.S.R. Most of these are scattered, although some are concentrated in the special Jewish autonomous region known as Birobidjan. One of the larger national minorities was the Germans; about 1.5 million of them lived on the Volga, but were relocated to Siberia during World War II.[3]

It has been popular in some circles to explain the behavior of the Soviet regime, as well as its very existence, in terms of traits to be found in the Russian character.[4] There is no doubt that certain characteristics or traits tend to stand out more in some people than in others. Efforts to relate the collective behavior of peoples who are today gathered together in nations to traits of national character ought not to be minimized. At present however, the state of knowledge in this area is insufficient to justify firm conclusions.

The Russians have on occasion been depicted as loving, or at least easily accepting, authority.[5] It is true that they have often appeared to put up with a lot. On the other hand, they have at times demonstrated an independence of mind, a boldness of spirit, and outright resistance. The more one looks into the matter, the more one becomes convinced of the inevitable complexity and indecisiveness of national character. While certain traits may offer clues to a people's collective behavior, it is impossible to assign such traits any specific or precise weight.

Traits do not originate in something called the national makeup of a people but in the historical experience of those people. Human actions frequently are reactions to conditions of life which reach back into the past. The legacy of history, economic and social dislocations, the flow of new ideas, and cataclysmic events such as wars all play their part in shaping a nation's future as well as the attitudes of the people toward that future and toward their ultimate destiny.

LONG HISTORY OF POLITICAL AUTOCRACY

It has often been pointed out that Russia's geographic vastness, coupled with the building of the Russian state largely in isolation from the

---

[3] Soviet policies toward religion and national minorities will be treated in subsequent chapters.

[4] For example, see Edward Crankshaw. "Russia in Europe: The Conflict of Values," *International Affairs,* (October 1946), pp. 501–10, and Dinko Tomasic, *The Impact of Russian Culture on Soviet Communism* (Glencoe, Ill.: The Free Press, 1953). Also see Joseph K. Folsom and Nikander Strelsky, "Russian Values and Character—A Preliminary Exploration," *American Sociological Review* 9 (June 1944), pp. 296–307.

[5] See Geoffrey Gorer and John Rickman, *The People of Great Russia: A Psychological Study* (New York: W. W. Norton & Co., Inc., 1962).

West, resulted in a physical and a psychological separation from the influences that in Western Europe served to do away with, or at least to modify, political autocracy. The influences of the Renaissance, the Reformation, and the Counter-Reformation simply did not penetrate Russia. And Western liberal-democratic ideas of the 17th and 18th centuries did not make any significant inroads until the 19th century, and then in limited and often perverted form. It is noteworthy that throughout Russia's long political past no institutions that could limit or channel autocratic power took root. Isolation from the West, however, may have been only one factor, because institutions that might have shared power were created (for example, Zemsky Sobor, Senate, State Council), but they did not succeed in assuming a role comparable to that of similar institutions in the countries of Western Europe.

Russia's long pre-Soviet history may, for the sake of convenience, be divided into four periods. The first is the pre-Mongolian period or the time of Kievan Russia, dating from the ninth century to about 1240. The second phase is the era of Tartar rule or the Mongolian period, which lasted nearly 250 years. The third period represents the resurrection of the Russian state, the rule of Ivan IV (the Terrible or the Dreaded), and the Time of Troubles, an era covering some 130 years. The fourth period represents the rule of the Romanov dynasty (1613 to 1917). This somewhat arbitrary division of Russian history provides a mere chronological framework, although a convenient one, within which Russia's development and expansion can be viewed.

One of the outstanding features of Russia's long history is her growth and expansion into a great empire. This was far from a steady and firm development, for there were many setbacks. Although Russia of the Kiev period was strong enough to maintain and preserve the nation for some 400 years, she was considerably smaller and weaker than the Russia of later epochs. The ruling princes of that period were powerful, but a great deal less so than the later tsars.

The epoch of Tartar rule, and particularly its disruption, was accompanied by the growing predominance of Moscow. With the division of Russia into many principalities during the Mongol period, the princes of the Moscow area gained in power, mainly by obeying the Tartars and through their friendship with church leaders, which resulted in Moscow's becoming the spiritual capital of Russia.[6] Gradually, Moscow gained a powerful economic hold over the small rival principalities. In 1340, the Khan singled out the Moscow prince as the Great Prince, making other princes subordinate to him. The succession of princes of Moscow, whose power and domain grew in comparison to the other principalities, provided a unifying force once the Tartar yoke was loosened. By the 16th century Moscow had become the political capital of Russia.

---

[6] Russia had accepted Christianity in the tenth century.

The unification of Russia in the post-Mongolian period was in no small part the work of Ivan IV. His official rule dates from 1533 to 1584, although, in effect, others ruled for him in the early years, since he came to power as a child, when Russia was in considerable turmoil due to quarrels among the princes for supreme control. By his determination and utter ruthlessness be became a powerful ruler and succeeded in unifying his country. With his death in 1584, however, Russia entered the Time of Troubles, a period of strife, palace intrigue, and civil war—a period which also witnessed the attempt of the king of Poland to make himself tsar of Russia. This era came to an end with the election of the first Romanov as tsar in 1613.

The rule of the Romanovs, spanning some 300 years, was the period of Russia's greatest expansion and the era of her rise to a position of power among the nations. But most of Russia's achievements as a nation in this period were associated with a few of her rulers. Clearly predominant is Peter the First (the Great), although the works of Catherine the Second (the Great) and Alexander the Second also stand out. Peter, who ruled between 1682 and 1721, set out to Europeanize Russia within his lifetime. Russia was to be westernized deliberately and expeditiously in order that she might become a powerful nation. He brought Russia to Europe by building a new capital on the swamps where the Neva River flows into the Baltic, which he called St. Petersburg, later to be called Petrograd and now Leningrad. He traveled to France, Holland, Denmark, England, and Austria, and everywhere he went he gathered information and recruited artisans to build industry in Russia.[7] All of Russia's resources were harnessed to the building of a powerful westernized nation. Even the church, with the creation of the Holy Synod, was brought under state control.

Some 40 years elapsed after Peter's death—years characterized by uncertainty, intrigue, and palace revolutions—before Catherine II came to the throne. She is regarded as a follower of Peter in that she sought to carry out his westernization policies. During her reign (1762–96), the Russian empire was enlarged and solidified. The non-Russian nationalities, however, constituted an internal weakness which was to plague Russia's rulers and which the Communists were to exploit at a much later date.

Although the Russian empire continued to grow, it was not until Russia's involvement in the Napoleonic Wars that it acquired the status of a first-rate power. From that time on it was to play a significant role in European affairs.

"The heart and core of the old Russian state was the autocracy, born under the Mongols, cradled in the Muscovite period, and reaching maturity in modern times."[8] This is a succinct and apt depiction of Russia's political

---

[7] It may be argued that this was an inauspicious beginning, for it set the pattern of state intervention in the development of the economy, which at a later date tended to prevent the development of an energetic and imaginative system of free enterprise.

[8] S. R. Tompkins, *Russia Through the Ages* (New York: Prentice-Hall, Inc., 1940), p. 1.

past under the tsars, although subsequent sections of this chapter will refer to some challenges to the autocracy and to attempts to modify it.

A few cursory observations about the development of autocracy in Russia may suggest the futility of seeking an easy explanation for its existence. One need but mention such things as the vast and interminable Russian Plain, which at one and the same time presented no barriers to foreign invaders and was conductive to free movement of people away from the center. In such circumstances, it was virtually impossible to maintain a compact, homogeneous nation without autocratic authority. Moreover, these factors, together with Russia's geographic vastness, combined to produce a country in large part isolated from the rest of the world. This was especially true during the period of Tartar rule, when "the new Russia of the backwoods (the Moscow area) . . . was thus politically cut off from Europe."[9] And isolation certainly played a part at a later date in keeping out moderating influences and liberal ideas which flourished in Europe and tended to modify the more objectionable aspects of European autocracy.

A noted historian has suggested that "it was not because of any alleged innate sympathy of the Russian soul to autocracy that the Tsardom of Moscow came into being but out of the stern necessity of organizing a military force sufficient to overthrow the Mongol yoke and then of securing control of a territory vast enough for strategic defense . . . Political freedom was sacrificed for national survival."[10] Another historian has asserted that tsarist autocracy was accepted as a necessary evil, in preference to the autocracy of the Polish nobles or other foreign rulers.[11]

There is some disagreement as to which of the Moscow princes was the first to assume the title of tsar (Caesar), but it is most often associated with Ivan IV (the Terrible or the Dreaded).[12] The beginning of autocratic rule in Russia is often associated with him. It was during his reign that the *Oprichnina*, a forerunner of the modern secret police, was established. It was also during his rule that slavery was introduced and a new nobility created. Ironically enough, it was during his reign that the *Zemsky Sobor* was established. This assembly gained in power during the Time of Troubles (1584–1613); in 1598 it elected Boris Godunov tsar and in 1613 elected the first Romanov, whose descendants were the ruling family until 1917.[13]

---

[9] Bernard Pares, *A History of Russia* (New York: Alfred A. Knopf, Inc., 1926), p. 73.

[10] George Vernadsky, *A History of Russia: Kievan Russia*, vol. 2 (New Haven, Conn.: Yale University Press, 1948), p. 17.

[11] Edward Crankshaw, *Russia and the Russians* (New York: Macmillan Co., 1949), p. 52.

[12] D. S. Mirsky, in C. J. Seligman, *Russia: A Social History* (London, 1931), p. 137, and M. T. Florinsky, *Toward An Understanding of the U.S.S.R.* (New York: Macmillan Co., 1939), p. 7. However, Pares, p. 89, and Tompkins, *Russia Through the Ages*, p. 110, assert that Ivan III was the first official tsar.

[13] No Sobors were held between 1654 abd 1682, and after 1698 no Sobors were ever summoned.

Other tsars who have stood out in Russian history for the most part continued in the traditions of Ivan IV, although their autocratic rule was not always accompanied by the degree of ruthlessness and brutality that is associated with Ivan and Peter I. Moreover, those who are known for their liberalization policies, such as Alexander II, did not accept limitations on their absolute power. Even the weaker tsars did not willingly accept limitations on their autocratic authority.

The Russian Orthodox Church, over the years, became the most vocal defender in Russia of tsarist absolutism. Christianity was accepted in the 10th century by the Russian ruler, Vladimir. Since the parent body was the Eastern Church, the Russian Church was from the beginning under the nominal control of the Patriarch at Constantinople. In time, the Moscow princes gained influence in the selection of the Russian Metropolitan, the head of the Russian Church. With the fall of Constantinople to the Turks in 1453, or about the time the Mongol domination ended in Russia, the Russian Church was completely severed from its Byzantine ties. Thereafter, the church fought for the unity and independence of the Russian Metropolitanate.[14]

With the establishment of the Holy Synod during the reign of Peter I, the church came under state control. The new princes of the church, especially the Ukrainian prelates, not only became subservient but also labored long to produce learned vindications of the new secular authority. "Thus, with the approval of the higher clergy, the Russian theocratic monarchy was transformed into a secular absolutism of the western type."[15]

The fact that most European countries had accepted Christianity from the Western Church (Rome) made the West appear hostile to the Russians. This helped to make the Orthodox Church an ally of Russian nationalism. Hostile actions of Western countries came to be viewed by the Russian Church as attacks upon Holy Russia, the true interpreter and defender of Christ.

It was not until the late 19th century, however, that a full-blown exposition of the Russian version of the divine right of kings doctrine was produced. Its author was Pobiedonostsev, the former tutor of Alexander III and Procurator-General of the Holy Synod. Not only did he defend tsarist autocracy in terms of divine origin of the tsar's authority but, in addition, he argued that Russia could be saved from the corrupting influence of foreign ideas only by a complete autocracy of state and church.

During the long history of Russian autocracy the most persistent issue was serfdom. Popular concern with political, legal, and other reforms was

---

[14] Vladimir had from the beginning "made use of the higher clergy as counselors," and "the priests, as the only literate persons, were invaluable for civil purposes; for the keeping of records . . . for embassies and for other public services." See Pares, *A History of Russia*, p. 30. The priests also brought a system of law to Russia.

[15] Mirsky, in Seligman, *Russia*, p. 184.

important, especially in the 19th century, but clearly secondary. The main preoccupation seemed to center on the injustices of serfdom and the crying need for a solution.

It was during the reign of the Romanovs that serfdom became a firm and fixed institution. Land grants which had been made to the service gentry in payment for military service included the peasants who lived on the land. Many of these, however, made successful escapes to the more remote regions of Russia. In 1646, all squires who owned land were required to register it, together with the names of each of their peasants. These and their future descendants became legally attached to the land. Serfdom became hereditary. A code in 1649 confirmed serfdom as a state institution. By 1675, the sale of serfs apart from land, although illegal, had become so widespread that it received legal sanction. Moreover, punishment for escape and for aiding fugitives became increasingly harsh.

But serfdom was more than an economic and social problem, with its legacy of economic backwardness, poverty, illiteracy, and human indignity. It was also a political problem in that it engendered attitudes of suspicion and distrust toward political authority and the agents of that authority. Serfdom was but the most notable symbol of Russia's peasant heritage, a heritage with which even the Soviet leaders have had to contend.

Despite a growing awareness of the acute nature of the problem of serfdom, and despite studies ordered by various rulers, no really significant step was taken to deal with it until the reign of Alexander II. What was done from time to time, even under Alexander II, left much more undone. It is a simple unadulterated fact that no tsarist regime found an acceptable solution to the most acute problem of Russian society.

Russian autocracy, along with serfdom, did not go unchallenged indefinitely. Protests took several forms. In the earlier years they consisted chiefly of limited peasant revolts, along with two revolts of major proportions led by nonpeasants, which attracted considerable support. In the 19th century the protests were mainly political and literary, although limited peasant uprisings continued to take place.

The first of the major rebellions was led by a type of freebooter, a Don Cossack by the name of Stenka Razin. The rebellion continued for four years (1667–71), but in the end it was suppressed and Razin was executed. A hundred years later (1773–74) another major rebellion broke out which for a time gained considerable headway, even threatening St. Petersburg. It too was brutally put down and its leader, Emilian Pugachev, executed. For the most part these were unorganized, spontaneous reactions against the oppressions of serfdom and the government's tax and other policies. Besides drawing support from the peasants, these revolts attracted outlaws and other elements which sought to profit from participating in them.

The first major political protest against tsarist autocracy is most fre-

quently referred to as the Decembrist Revolt.[16] During the Napoleonic
Wars, Russian soldiers had seen something of Europe and had absorbed
some disturbing ideas. The result of these new ideas was a liberal movement which contributed to the uprising that occurred in December 1825,
after the death of Alexander I. It was led by officers of the guard regiments, some of whom had been in France after the defeat of Napoleon.
They formed outside the Council of State, shouting for "Constantine and
Constitution." Constantine was a brother of Alexander and in line for the
throne, except that he had abdicated his right years earlier, although this
fact was kept secret. Upon Alexander's death, Constantine proclaimed
his younger brother Nicholas as Tsar. Certain regiments refused to take
the oath to Nicholas, who thereupon opened his regime with a ruthless
suppression of the Decembrists. The Decembrist uprising was not a peasant revolt. It was led by the nobles and a few liberals, loosely organized in
secret societies. Although they lacked a coherent political program, they
did talk of republicanism and of free speech. And they all agreed that
serfdom was a crying injustice.

The intellectual atmosphere which helped make the Decembrist uprising possible was but the beginning of a literary protest against the evils of
tsarism. This protest was to gain momentum during the 19th century—a
century which produced Russia's greatest writers. Among these are
Pushkin, Lermontov, Gogol, Herzen, Turgenev, Chekhov, Dostoyevsky,
and Tolstoy. Most of these became absorbed with contemporary political
and philosphical problems, much to the dislike of the ruling group. Censorship and imprisonment awaited those who advocated change. Gradually, however, they acquired boldness and experience, managing to circumvent the censors and to increase their popular following.

Nicholas I had inadvertently contributed to the rise of a generation of
revolutionary writers. During his reign, the reorganization of the universities revealed the lack of competent instructors. Promising young intellectuals were encouraged to travel and to study abroad. Many of these
went to Germany and upon their return were brimming over with ideas
they had acquired from Hegel, Fichte, Schelling, and other philosophers
and writers.

One result of the 19th century Russian intellectual activity was the
development of a cleavage between those who saw Russia's future in
western ideas and ways of doing things and those who believed in indigenous solutions to Russia's problems. These schools of thought came to
be known as Westernizers and Slavophiles. After the reforms of Alexander II, this controversy tended to die down. As Alexander's regime
moved on, however, a period of reaction set in, in part motivated by the
Polish revolt and the various attempts on the tsar's life. The dissillusion-

---

[16] See A. G. Mazour, *The First Russian Revolution, 1825* (Berkeley: University of
California Press, 1937).

ment with some of his reforms and the recall of Russian students from abroad contributed to the renewed spread of revolutionary doctrines.

The intellectual protest against tsarism and the evils of serfdom was but the forerunner of political activity in its various forms. New ideas and new political doctrines took root and were disseminated. Political organizations were being established, and political programs formulated. These and related questions will be discussed in subsequent pages. Suffice it to say at this point that these developments are but another indication that autocracy was being challenged, and, as we now know, the end of its long history was approaching.

BIBLIOGRAPHICAL NOTE

Among the studies that discuss the characteristics of the Russian people, some of the more informative are : Raymond A. Bauer, *Nine Soviet Portraits* (New York: John Wiley & Sons, Inc., 1955); Clyde M. Kluckhohn, Raymond A. Bauer, and Alex Inkeles, *The Soviet System: Cultural, Psychological and Social Themes* (Cambridge, Mass.: Harvard Univeristy Press, 1956); Sir John Maynard, *Russia in Flux*, edited and abridged by S. Haden Guest from *Russia in Flux and The Russian Peasant and Other Studies* (New York: Macmillan Co., 1948); Klaus Mehnert, *Soviet Man and His World* (New York: Frederick A. Praeger, Inc., 1962); and Wright Miller, *Russians as People* (New York: E. P. Dutton & Co., Inc. 1961). Two excellent recent books of general interest are Robert G. Kaiser, *Russia: The People and the Power* (New York: Pocket Books, 1976), and Hedrick Smith, *The Russians* (New York: Quadrangle/New York Times, 1976).

27

The Changing
Foundations of Russian
Politics

STEPS TOWARD REFORM

From what has been said above it should not be assumed that tsarist Russia took no steps toward reform. Although the various reforms in the end proved insufficient, many of them gave considerable promise at the time of their adoption. In a way, many of them can be looked upon as truly great advances, particularly those taken by Alexander II. Unfortunately, however, many of the promising reforms either were nullified by succeeding rulers or were not carried forward. Others, although significant, fell short of what Russian conditions demanded.

Russia at the beginning of the 19th century was a country of contrasts, a phenomenon which prevails today. She had attained the position of a first-rate power on the continent and yet she was one of the most backward countries in the world. As the century wore on, however, the weaknesses became predominant. This was to become glaringly evident at the time of the Crimean War and later during the Russo-Japanese War at the outset of the 20th century.

Economically and socially, Russia was a picture of backwardness at the beginning of the 19th century. Although the small gentry class lived relatively well, the serfs were living in poverty and their number was increasing. Moreover, the serfs were virtual outcasts. There was mass illiteracy. Non-Russian nationalities, especially the Jews, were oppressed. Nowhere in the social or economic picture could one point to progress.

Politically, Russia entered the 19th century no less backward. There was no semblance of self-government or even a widespread discussion of it. The church and state were united behind the tsar-autocrat. The tradition of absolutism and authority characterized the Russian political scene. The first two tsars of the 19th century were brothers who ruled for 54 years, a period divided almost equally between them. Steps toward reform during their reigns were so few and so lacking in their approach to Russia's basic problems that there is a danger of overemphasizing them.

Alexander I (1801–25) was primarily interested in foreign affairs, which occupied most of his attention. He seems to have favored the establishment of a constitutional monarchy, but only one of several projected constitutional reforms ever came into effect, and it was only partially realized. A State Council established in 1810 possessed only advisory powers. Its existence, therefore, constituted no effective limitation on autocracy.

Nicholas I (1825–55) is regarded by many historians as the most reactionary among the tsars. He came close to establishing a police state. His Russification program among the non-Russian nationalities was symbolized by the concept "one flag, one government, one church, one people." He ordered the opening of new schools to prove that the people did not want to go to school. When he was proved wrong, severe limitations were imposed on what was to be taught. Chairs of history and philosophy were considered dangerous. Many writers were placed under house arrest. Moreover, censorship generally became more stringent. His reign could appropriately be described as one long rearguard reaction against new ideas.

Some reforms, however, were inaugurated during the rule of Nicholas I. The most notable among these was the codification of the laws under the direction of Count Speransky, who had been responsible for the 1810 reforms establishing the State Council. Speransky completed his monumental task of codification of the laws in 1833.

The most promising steps toward reform were those that were taken by Alexander II (1855–81). These included: emancipation of the serfs (1861); reorganization of the institution of local government, the *Zemstvo* (1864); reform of the judiciary (1864); budget reforms (1862); reorganization of municipal government (1870); and the introduction of conscription on a nonclass basis (1874). Moreover, at the time of his assassination (1881) he had approved the project of Count M. T. Loris-Melikov for the creation of an advisory council to work with the State Council.

The emancipation of the serfs was hailed as a great and courageous act, which earned for Alexander the title of Tsar-Liberator. The emancipation, however, was only partial, and it was qualified. The state undertook to buy only one half of the land from the squires which was to be given to the peasants, who would be given 49 years in which to pay for the land. The village assembly, the *Mir,* was given the responsibility of collecting the payments. Until all the payments were made, the peasant could not consider himself an owner of any part of the land. As time progressed, the peasants found the redemption payments an almost unbearable burden. At the same time, it was becoming increasingly evident that the lands originally purchased were proving insufficient for the number of peasants needing land. The liberation had been a great step forward, but other steps had to be taken if the peasant problem was to be dealt with successfully.

The reform of the *Zemstvo* was at least in part the consequence of the emancipation of the peasants. Earlier, the landlords had governed the local community, but now the newly liberated peasants wanted some voice in local affairs. The reorganization of the *Zemstvo* provided that the local government assembly be elected on a nonclass basis. Similarly, prior to the liberation the landowners had dispensed justice. In the changed circumstances, this could hardly be continued. Among the reforms in the judiciary was the introduction of juries and lawyers.

Among the other reforms, the requirement that the nobility serve in the army also seemed to recognize the greater equality acquired by the peasant. Some reforms, like the granting of a considerable amount of self-government to the universities (1863) and making the budget public for the first time in Russian history, were of a more general nature.

None of these reforms, be it noted, limited the autocratic powers of the tsar. They did, however, teach the people something of local self-government, and they gave them some real hopes for the complete extinction of serfdom.

It should be noted that Alexander, as well as others who sought reform, labored under severe handicaps. The nobility was determined to defend its economic interests. And the peasantry, in whose innate political virtues the intelligentsia reposed such unjustified confidence, was something less than capable of assuming its newly acquired responsibilities. Moreover, Alexander had to rely on an unenlightened and often inept bureaucracy to carry out his policies. As a consequence some of his messages "never arrived," and others were "not understood." In the light of such circumstances, it is perhaps surprising that considerable progress was achieved.

The assassination of Alexander II doomed the prospects of further reform, and ushered in a period of reaction. Even the Loris-Melikov proposal, prepared during his reign as a modest concession to public opinion, was never promulgated. The new tsar, Alexander III, agreed with his antireform advisers. Among the most influential of these was his former tutor, Pobiedonostev, who was now Procurator-General of the Holy Synod. Although the official terror was fairly general, it was most felt in education and the press. The university autonomy, gained under Alexander II, was revoked. Student clubs were banned. A number of measures further restricted newspapers and their editors. A program of intensified Russification was begun. A new set of officials, called rural chiefs, was introduced to direct the work of the locally elected institutions of government. Extraordinary measures, ostensibly designed to deal with revolutionary organizations and their activities, enabled the political police, the *Okhrana,* to exercise far-reaching oppressive powers.

Economically, however, Russia experienced considerable growth during the latter half of the 19th century. Industrialization moved along at an increasing rate. Cities and towns grew apace, as did the number of their inhabitants. The most notable achievement in the transportation field was the building of the trans-Siberian railway.

BEGINNINGS OF CONSTITUTIONALISM

In 1900, Russia was a stronghold of absolutism. By contrast, in the United States, England, and a number of Western European countries the democratic system was widely accepted. Democratic ideas were spread elsewhere. Even in Germany and Austria, democratic institutions were making some inroads.

Although political activities among Russian citizens were limited in 1900, a political ferment was in the making. The political movements which could function openly, and which therefore were not regarded as a threat to the government, were few. The most important of these were the *Narodniki* (populists), an intelligentsia-led revolutionary group that sought to enlist the support of the peasantry by "going to the people." Their movement had begun in the early 1870s. Much to their dismay, "the youthful agitators discovered that they could not arouse the people's 'pent-up revolutionary energy' . . . [some] were stoned out of the villages and turned over to the tsarist police by the indignant peasants. The first waves of the go-to-the-people movement had broken against the wall of popular indifference and police repression. . . ."[1]

These failures tended to turn many of the youthful revolutionaries toward more and more direct action. The result was a split, out of which two rival organizations emerged, the terroristic *Narodnaya Volya* (the people's will) and the antiterrorist *Chernyi Peredel* (the black partition), a defender of the *Narodniki* tradition. One of the great movers in the *Chernyi Peredel* was George Plekhanov, who was to become one of the leading Russian Marxist theoreticians. By 1900, the *Chernyi Peredel* was a respectable organization.

A number of other political organizations were formed in secret and continued to function underground. Among these were: the agrarian Social Revolutionaries, whose ideas were a combination of Marxism and the

---

[1] Leopold H. Haimson, *The Russian Marxists and the Origins of Bolshevism* (Cambridge, Mass.: Harvard University Press, 1955), pp. 13–14.

teachings of the Utopian Socialists; the *Kadets* (constitutional democrats), made up primarily of the liberal and moderate intelligentsia, which desired the gradual and peaceful displacement of autocracy by a constitutional form of government; and the Social Democrats, who were the Russian exponents of Marxism.[2]

The Russian Marxists emerged from the underground revolutionary ferment in the 1880s. Many of those who had been identified with *Narodnaya Volya* and *Chernyi Peredel* were converted to Marxism. Despite police repression, the Marxian movement continued to grow and to remain active, although underground. The Russian Social Democrats were far from united, as exemplified by their split in 1903 into the Bolshevik and Menshevik wings.

The political ferment which flourished in the years around the turn of the century was given a considerable impetus by the evils stemming from industrialization, which came to Russia at a considerably later date than it did to the Western European nations. When it did come, industrialization came in a rush and brought about evils that have accompanied industrialization elsewhere (poor working conditions, long hours, inadequate pay, no organizations to speak for the worker), except that it produced them more precipitously. Neither society nor the industrial owners were in a position to cope with these conditions, nor did they seem to feel any particular responsibility for doing so, although there was some progress toward efficient and enlightened management prior to the revolution. The growth of industrial enterprises, the rapid increase in the number of industrial workers, the great increase in the population of the cities and towns, together with the evils associated with industrialization everywhere—all occurred in Russia at a time when fresh Marxian ideas were attracting a large audience in European countries.

In 1905, a revolution was triggered by the disastrous consequences of the Russo-Japanese War (1904–5). Previously, the protest against autocracy was, in the main, by individuals and small groups. In 1905, however, the Russian masses were moved to action on a large scale. To the impact of an unsuccessful foreign war were added the consequences of domestic hard times and the constant urgings of revolutionary parties, working in part through the *Zemstvos*.

The *Zemstvos*—the local government assemblies whose work the government had in many ways sought to impede—had gained considerable respect and popularity among the people. Among other things, they had done much in the field of public health and education, and they had organized relief during the famines in 1901–3. In November 1904 the first all-Russian Congress of *Zemstvos* met in St. Petersburg. It put forward a number of demands, including the recognition and guarantee of civil liber-

---

[2] Marxian ideas are discussed in detail in Chapter 30.

ties, the elimination of class and racial discriminations, and the establishment of a representative assembly with real legislative powers.

The situation was made more acute by the massacre of several hundreds of peaceful petitioners, led by Father Gapon, who on Sunday, September 22, 1905, moved toward the Winter Palace, carrying portraits of the tsar and singing religious and patriotic songs, to present the grievances of the workers and to ask for the tsar's intervention and help. The immediate result was an increase in tensions, which found expression most frequently in strikes. Disturbances continued throughout the summer, aggravated by the returning soldiers after the formal conclusion of the war at the end of August.

The tsar's promise in June to a joint deputation of the *Zemstvos* and municipal councils that he would call together a national assembly, "as soon as possible," to set up a new regime in which the public was invited to participate had not quelled the disorders. When it was announced in August that the projected legislature—the *Duma*—would be elected on the basis of a narrow franchise and that it would have only consultative powers, the growing unrest spread to the Baltic provinces and the Caucasus. The situation continued to deteriorate, culminating in a general strike in October.

In the face of these conditions, Nicholas gave in. Although martial law was the tsar's reply to the revolution, he simultaneously proclaimed a moderate constitution, providing for a national legislature, the *Duma*, which was to be elected on the basis of universal manhood suffrage. It was to have legislative initiative and the right to pass on projects submitted by the tsar.[3] A bill of rights guaranteed the freedoms of speech, assembly, and conscience. A cabinet of ministers was made responsible to the *Duma*. The proclamation embodying these concessions by Nicholas came to be known as the October Manifesto. Count Witte, who had a considerable hand in convincing the tsar to grant the constitution, was made the first responsible prime minister. Russia, at least in theory, became a constitutional monarchy.

In this new-found freedom, the pre-1905 secret societies blossomed forth into political parties. The most active of these were the Social Revolutionaries, the Kadets (Constitutional Democrats), and the Russian Social Democrats, who about this time had split into the Bolshevik and Menshevik wings. All of these parties sponsored an exceptionally active discussion of current political, social, and economic problems. They held meetings, published newspapers and political tracts, and in other ways sought to propagate their programs and points of view.

Russia's political experience under the constitutional monarchy is not easy to evaluate. The legislative beginnings were not auspicious, partly

---

[3] See Serge L. Levitsky, "Legislative Initiative in the Russian Duma," *American Slavic and East European Review* 15 (October 1956), pp. 313–24.

because of a lack of experience on the part of the participants. More important, however, is the fact that a number of the tsar's acts were clearly in violation of the constitution. In the midst of the uncertainties came World War I, which was to loom so large in the destiny of tsarism and Russia's future.

The first *Duma* convened in 1906, but was dismissed after a brief period of less than three months, most of which time had been spent in conflict with the government. It was dominated by the Kadets, "who devoted their full energy to expounding the indignation and disappointment experienced by the country at large at the inadequate reform and demanding a constitution on the English and the American pattern."[4] It thus earned the name "the *Duma* of the National Indignation." Count Witte was dismissed as prime minister and replaced by Peter Stolypin, who, until his assassination in September 1911, ruled the country with an iron hand.

The second, and newly elected, *Duma* was convened in March 1907. It met a similar fate after an existence of less than four months. Unlike its predecessor, it contained a strong group of Social Democrats, who had boycotted the first elections and who accounted, in part, for its hostile and revolutionary attitude. It achieved nothing in a parliamentary or legislative sense. When the *Duma* refused to consent to the arrest and trial of 16 Social Democratic members, who were charged with conspiracy and sedition, it was dissolved.

A third *Duma* was elected in the same year, but only after the electoral law had been changed without even consulting the *Duma,* as the constitution provided. The revised electoral law did away with universal manhood suffrage. Some of the non-Russian nationalities were disfranchised, and severe limitations were put on the electoral rights of the peasantry. The whole electoral procedure was involved and complex. Thus, by a clever manipulation of the electoral regulations, the Government was able to manage the election of a conservative *Duma,* dominated by the propertied classes and the large landholders. It served its full term.

During the period of the third *Duma,* the Government introduced two significant reforms. One was the law calling for a gradual introduction of compulsory education for all children in the primary grades, a clear departure from past policies. The second important law introduced the Stolypin land reforms (1906–10), the completion of which was prevented by the outbreak of the war. Stolypin's aim was to free many peasants from their bondage to the *Mir* and to make them free farmers. While this policy was attacked as discriminating in favor of the relatively well-to-do peasants, it was, in fact, designed to create a group of free peasants who would feel that they had a vested interest in the established order so that they would defend it.

---

[4] Edmund A. Walsh, *The Fall of the Russian Empire* (Boston: Little, Brown and Co., 1928), p. 85.

The fourth and the last *Duma* convened in 1912. Like the third, it was conservative and docile. For a brief period during the war, it rose to a position of leadership simply because its members were appalled by the decay in the government and because they sensed the approaching doom of tsarism.

The period of the *Duma* (1906–17), while representing a significant step toward democratic government, left much to be desired. The tsar, as noted above, was far from being a constitutional monarch—that is, above politics. Not only did he from time to time exercise real political power, but, in addition, he violated the constitutional rights of the *Duma*. Also, he elevated the State Council, an administrative body, to the position of an upper house. Moreover, administrative officials were often found abusing the emergency powers still on the statute books. More important perhaps is the fact that the *Duma* really never acquired many of the essential powers associated with a true parliamentary legislature. For example, it never gained a really effective control of finance; and its power to call ministers to account and to vote them out of office if need be was not recognized in practice.

WORLD WAR I AND THE DISINTEGRATION OF THE OLD ORDER

A noted historian has said that Russia by 1914 was making such progress in the economic, social, and political realms that in another ten years "the possibility of a revolution in Russia would have been very slight."[5] Russian industry, in all its branches, experienced a remarkable and a sustained upsurge in the final decade of the past century and in the pre-1914 years of this one. During the same period, no other nation approached Russia's economic growth rate. While workers were limited in what they could do to improve their lot, their economic position was nevertheless improving. Westernization and modernization reached also into the countryside. In brief, social and economic change, although creating problems in its wake, was proceeding at a rapid rate. But the promise of this period was cut short as the nation plunged into war in 1914. This is not to suggest, however, that Russia could have stayed out of the war once it came, for vital national interests were at stake.

The initial reaction of the people to the declaration of war was favorable and even enthusiastic. The German declaration of war aroused the people to a high sense of unity and dedication in carrying out their duties. This lasted for a long time. Moreover, despite tremendous losses and lack of equipment, the Russian soldiers fought well. It is now generally agreed

[5] George Vernadsky, *A History of Russia* (New York: New Home Library edition, 1944), p. 214.

that the efforts of the Russians saved France from collapse in the west. When news of reverses at the front became known at home, however—particularly news of shortages of military supplies, news of bungling and inefficiency, together with a seemingly general ineptitude—the mood of the people seemed to change.

The attitude of the people was influenced in part by conditions on the home front. There was a feeling that much of the bungling was due to inept administrative personnel and to the ministers in charge. The influence of Rasputin, a self-appointed "man of God," on the domestic scene is not to be underestimated. His influence was in large part due to the tsarina's belief that Rasputin could cure her son, the heir to the throne, of hemophilia. Because he seemingly had certain magic healing powers, the tsarina looked upon him as a man sent by God, and abided by his advice in the political and military realms. Constantly, she urged Nicholas to follow the advice he was getting from Rasputin. Many Russians noted that the result was the removal of able men whom the tsar had appointed in the summer of 1915. After several plots on his life, Rasputin was finally killed in December 1916.

The regime's answer to popular dissatisfaction with the way things were going in the military as well as in the domestic field was to send Nicholas to the front to take personal command of the army. Aside from the fact that Nicholas had no military training, his departure for the front resulted in his being politically isolated. The Bolsheviks, for their part, were spreading defeatist propaganda and making the most of a revolutionary situation.

It was at this time that the *Duma* requested the appointment of a responsible cabinet and the inauguration of much-needed reforms. Army commanders, *Zemstvos,* and the general public joined in the *Duma's* request for the appointment of a responsible cabinet. But the tsarist regime seemed to have been oblivious to any danger.

The beginning of the collapse of Tsarism came in the form of food riots in the capital in March 1917. Actually, food was not in short supply, but the distribution was bad and people had to wait long hours in queues to get their rations. Troops of the Petrograd garrison were asked to put down the disorders, but they refused to do so, and in a day or two went over to the side of the rioters. Thus, the revolution and the collapse of Tsarism came without much bloodshed.

The *Duma* leaders, who were witnessing the collapse, finally asked for the tsar's abdication. When asked, he abdicated in favor of his brother, who refused to become tsar unless the position were offered by a constituent assembly. In these circumstances, the *Duma* leaders (liberals and moderate socialists) created a provisional government, and thereby made the Revolution complete.

The *Duma* leaders realized that they did not possess the authority to create a new government, but nevertheless proceeded to do so because they were convined that it would be done by the leaders of the Petrograd Soviet of Workers' Deputies, which had come into existence even before the tsar's abdication was announced. Indeed, the Soviet, whose name was soon changed to include soldiers' as well as workers' deputies, lost no time in challenging the provisional government, and in a few months was to become the vehicle for the Bolshevik seizure of power.

Once established, the provisional government faced two basic decisions. The first had to do with the question of war—whether to continue it or to make a separate peace with Germany. The second was the question of domestic reform—whether it should be initiated or postponed. The government decided to carry on with the war and to put off reform until a later date. These decisions were to contribute to its downfall. In themselves, they would not have been disastrous if the government had possessed real authority. From the beginning, however, it was to be harassed by the Soviets of Workers' and Soldiers' Deputies which were springing up throughout the country.

It was on the home front that things began to deteriorate first. The first decree of the provisional government, among other things, had proclaimed a general amnesty; established freedom of speech and press, the right to strike, the right of universal suffrage; and had declared for a summoning of a constituent assembly. These freedoms permitted the socialist parties to begin agitating anew. Many of their leaders who had been imprisoned on various charges in 1915 were released by the provisional government. Since the land problem was not yet solved and since the army was composed mainly of peasants, the demoralizing effect of this socialist propaganda was disastrous. But it must not be forgotten, however, that the offensives of 1917 on the Austrian and Rumanian fronts, although successful in their initial stages, were a serious drain on the resources of the provisional government, and hence contributed to its weakening.

On the same day that the provisional government had issued its first decree, under pressure of the Petrograd Soviet, the Soviet issued its famous Order Number 1, which "was the principal agency in the destruction of the Russian army."[6] Under this order, soldiers' committees were to be set up in each military detachment and all weapons were to be under their control and not that of the officers. Moreover, each detachment was to obey the political decisions of the Soviet and only those orders of the military commission of the state *Duma* which did not contradict the orders of the Soviet. Since the collapse of the Russian army came after the Revolution, not before, it could be said that the collapse was the result of the Revolution, but that would be an oversimplification, for the Revolu-

---

[6] Vernadsky, *A History of Russia*, p. 236.

tion was in part made possible by reverses at the front and the impact of these reverses on the domestic scene.[7]

It is obvious, therefore, that from the first days of the Revolution there were two governments in Petrograd—the provisional government and the Soviet of Workers' and Soldiers' Deputies. The struggle for power between them was to continue from the spring of 1917 until the Bolshevik seizure of power in the fall of 1917. Initially, the Bolsheviks were skeptical of the Soviet. In any case, they were a minority in the soviets of Petrograd and Moscow, as well as elsewhere. Moreover, the Petrograd Soviet was, in their opinion, too friendly toward the provisional government. When it was clear, however, that the soviets were following a course increasingly independent of the provisional government, and with Lenin's agitation in favor of a seizure of power, the Bolsheviks began working inside the soviets in pursuit of their aims. After a time, they succeeded in winning a majority of the delegates, first in the Petrograd Soviet and then in the Moscow Soviet. Subsequently, upon Lenin's urgings, the Bolsheviks were instrumental in having the Petrograd and Moscow soviets establish "military revolutionary committees," which were to be instruments for the seizure of power.

Meanwhile, the First Congress of Soviets was held in June 1917. At this Congress the Bolsheviks and their allies had but a scant fraction of the total number of delegates.[8] The Social Revolutionaries had by far the largest number of delegates, with the Mensheviks next. Despite their lack of strength, the Bolsheviks proposed that the soviets should seize power. This proposal was defeated, mainly by being ignored. Shortly after the Congress had adjourned, the Bolsheviks became the leaders of the abortive July insurrection, which resulted in the arrest of many of their prominent leaders. Lenin, however, succeeded in escaping to Finland, from where he attempted to direct the second layer of leaders in their agitation and their work of organizing the workers and soldiers.

Simultaneously, the provisional government resumed the war effort with the launching of the July offensive. Initially a success, the offensive ended in failure. This failure and the growing inflation, plus the Soviet-inspired demands for reform and withdrawal from the war, resulted in increasing difficulties on the home front. More and more workers were becoming Bolshevik followers. The peasants, too, were becoming increasingly restive. At the same time, some of the national minorities were getting restless, partly because of the provisional government's failure to enunciate a nationality policy.

A radical effort to deal with the situation on the home front took place

---

[7] See John Shelton Curtiss, *The Russian Revolutions of 1917* (New York: D. Van Nostrand Co., Inc., 1957), pp. 29 ff.

[8] Curtiss, *The Russian Revolutions of 1917*, p. 41, says that the Bolsheviks and their allies had 137 out of 1,090 delegates.

in September. This was the famous Kornilov affair. General Kornilov, the commander-in-chief of the army, was persuaded by his advisers and by emissaries of Alexander Kerensky, head of the provisional government, to bring a detachment of troops to Petrograd in order to put an end to the inimical activities of the Soviet. His mission, however, was subsequently viewed by Kerensky as an attempt to seize power. Thereupon, Kerensky appointed himself Supreme Commander and sought to dismiss Kornilov, who refused to be dismissed and marched on Petrograd. Kerensky appealed to the Soviet for help. Spurred on by the Bolsheviks, who otherwise detested the provisional government, the Soviet responded to Kerensky's call to fight a common battle against Kornilov. The net result was Kornilov's defeat and arrest, as well as a strengthening of the Soviet in its struggle with the provisional government.[9]

THE BOLSHEVIK SEIZURE OF POWER

After the Kornilov affair, the growing strength of the soviets throughout the country was accompanied by an increase of Bolshevik power and influence inside the most important soviets—those of Petrograd and Moscow. The Bolshevik party had at the beginning of 1917 some 30,000 members. By October, the number had jumped to 200,000. Their strength was also reflected in their gaining control of factory committees and of some trade unions. But most importantly, they gained majorities in the Moscow and Petrograd soviets, and were soon to gain control over others.

In spite of their growing strength, the majority of Bolshevik leaders were not optimistic. Lenin was the exception. From nearby Finland, he urged preparation for an immediate uprising. Bolshevik leaders in Petrograd did not believe that power could be held, even if they were successful in seizing it in the capital. As if in desperation, Lenin returned to Petrograd in disguise (in late October) to urge acceptance of his position personally. Within a few days, he succeeded in winning over to his position all except two of the important Bolshevik leaders.

Employing the military revolutionary committees of the Petrograd and Moscow soviets, Lenin and his collaborators prepared to seize power on the eve of the meeting of the Second Congress of Soviets. In the night (November 6–7), they seized the important buildings (palace, railway stations, and telephone and telegraph centers) in Petrograd and in Moscow, and arrested the members of the provisional government who had not succeeded in fleeing. The next day (November 8), they appeared before the Second Congress of Soviets with the request that their actions

---

[9] For Kerensky's latest reflections on the situation, see his *Russia and History's Turning Point* (New York: Duell, Sloan & Pearce, Inc., 1965).

be endorsed. This the congress did, vesting power in a Council of People's Commissars, headed by Lenin.

Although in power, the Bolsheviks and their allies permitted the elections for the Constituent Assembly to be held. These had been scheduled by the provisional government, after considerable prodding by the Bolsheviks and their allies in the Soviets. In one sense, the results were disastrous for the Bolsheviks, for they received a relatively small portion of the delegates. In view of the party's small membership, however, polling one fourth of the total vote could be interpreted as a moderate success. The Social Revolutionaries won a majority. Nevertheless, the Bolsheviks permitted the Constituent Assembly to convene in January 1918. When they were convinced that the Assembly would not do their bidding, the Bolsheviks disbanded it with force after its first day in session. The Assembly was never to be heard from again.

Once in power, the Bolsheviks were forced to deal with several problems if they were to consolidate their authority. In the foreign realm, they had to liquidate the war with Germany and the Allied intervention which was to follow. Domestically, they had to liquidate the tsarist system and to build one of their own. Moreover, they had to embark upon the building of a new society.

The Bolsheviks, who had clamored for an end to the war, had little choice but to make peace at almost any price. At Brest-Litovsk in March 1918, they signed such a peace, with great losses of territory.[10] The signing of a separate peace by Russia was viewed by the Allies as little short of treasonous. The first thought in Allied circles, even before they could know the nature of the new Russian government, was how to prevent Allied munitions and other materiel which had been sent to Russia from falling into the hands of the Germans.

The Allied landing of marines at Murmansk in the early part of 1918 was the beginning of an Allied effort to deal with the consequences of the Russian withdrawal from the war. Later this move was to acquire the label "Allied Intervention," and the Bolsheviks as well as many non-Bolsheviks were to ascribe to it a purely political motive. Although there was no political motive initially, within a brief period after its inception the intervention did acquire a political motive.

As opposition to the Bolshevik regime developed into a civil war, with many troops and officers of the old Russian army forming units to fight the hastily organized Red Army, some Allied assistance to the anti-Bolsheviks was forthcoming. Additional Allied troops (although the total was never great) were landed in European Russia and in Siberia. In Siberia some Allied forces were much more concerned with watching the

---

[10] See John W. Wheeler-Bennett, *The Forgotten Peace: Brest-Litovsk, March 1918* (New York: St. Martin's Press, 1939). See also George F. Kennan, *Soviet-American Relations, 1917–1920: Russia Leaves the War* (Princeton, N.J.: Princeton University Press, 1956).

Japanese than with any attempt to overthrow the new Bolshevik regime. A comprehensive study, however, concludes that the intervention in Siberia was directed at neither the Japanese nor the Bolsheviks, but against the Germans.[11] It was believed in the West that a large number of German (Austrian) prisoners in Siberia were given arms by the Bolsheviks (at Germany's bidding) and that they were about to take large parts of Siberia.[12]

Although one ought not to underestimate the psychological impact on the Bolsheviks of the intervention, particularly when one remembers that Allied troops were landed in Russia as late as January 1919, one cannot overlook the fact that the Allied victory in November 1918 really knocked the heart out of the intervention. Allied troops, aware of the original intent of the intervention, soon became restive and had to be withdrawn. If one looks at the intervention with a balanced view, it is difficult to escape the conclusion that while it was a political fiasco it was, at least partially, a military success because it "played its part in stopping the flow of German troops from east to west."[13]

One needs also to remember the so-called American intervention in the years 1921–23, which was primarily a mission of mercy and good will. It took the form of the American Relief Administration, a private organization which responded to the urgent appeal of the Russians. Later, the U.S. Congress joined in by appropriating millions of dollars. This intervention saved millions of Soviet citizens from starvation.

Closely related to the intervention was the civil war which was precipitated by the Bolshevik revolution. Although Bolshevik intentions and aims had been well advertised, their strength had been consistently underestimated by the provisional government. Having awakened to the rude realities of the situation, the opponents of the Bolsheviks rallied around certain tsarist army generals who organized fighting forces to challenge the new regime. In the end, although they fought for approximately three years, they could not reverse the tide.

In the meantime, the newly formed regime was occupied with the task of liquidating the tsarist political order and building one of its own. Smashing the old order was easier than building a new one, for Marxian theory had provided virtually no guideposts for the new order. Lenin had said that it had to be a dictatorship of the toiling masses, but he had not worked out any detailed plan. There was much improvising to meet the demands of the moment. The Red Army had been hastily organized to meet the threat to the regime posed by the civil war and the intervention. Equally

---

[11] Christopher Lasch, "American Intervention in Siberia: A Reinterpretation." *Political Science Quarterly* 77 (June 1962), pp. 205–223. In July 1918, local Bolsheviks in Yekaterinburg liquidated Nicholas II and his whole family.

[12] Ibid.

[13] Sir Edmund Ironside, *Archangel, 1918–19* (London: Constable, 1953), p. 220.

hastily, the new regime organized a security police, first known as the Cheka—the so-called extraordinary commission for combating counter-revolution, sabotage, and dereliction of duty.

The Red Army and the secret police were initially conceived as instruments to guard against the revival of the old order, although, as time was to prove, the new regime came more and more to be based on force and terror. While the one-party state was not immediately instituted, the Bolsheviks lost no time in beginning the liquidation of other political parties, even those that had initially collaborated with them. Moreover, the problem of organizing a competent and loyal bureaucracy did not prove so easy as Lenin had predicted.

The overriding consideration in all of the new regime's efforts was the vast and complex problem of building the new society. One economic and social system had to be displaced by another.[14] The initial period of the attempted rapid transformation has come to be known as war communism (1918–21). In this period, the efforts of the workers to run factories and of the government to force the peasants to deliver their produce to government-owned enterprises were soon recognized as failures.

This initial period was followed by a compromise with capitalism or, as described by some Soviet spokesmen, a strategic retreat. This was the period of the so-called New Economic Policy, which was to terminate about 1928 with the launching of the new "socialist offensive" in agriculture and the beginning of the era of successive five-year plans. This was also the period of Lenin's death and the first major struggle for power.[15]

BIBLIOGRAPHICAL NOTE

Among the general histories that may serve as an introduction are: J. D. Clarkson, *A History of Russia* (New York: Random House, Inc., 1961); N. V. Riasanovsky, *A History of Russia*, 2d ed. (London: Oxford University Press, 1969); and Hugh Seton-Watson, *The Russian Empire, 1801–1917* (Oxford: Clarendon Press, 1967).

Bertram D. Wolfe, *Three Who Made a Revolution*, rev. ed. (Boston: Beacon Press, 1955), is a valuable discussion of the events leading up to the Revolution; while Edward Halett Carr, *A History of Soviet Russia* (New York: Macmillan Co., vol. 1, 1951; vol. 2, 1952; vol. 3, 1953; vol. 4, 1954), is a scholarly treatment of post-Revolutionary events. See also Robert V. Daniels, *Red October: The Bolshevik Revolution of 1917* (New York: Charles Scribner's Sons, 1968); and Adam B. Ulam, *The Bolsheviks: The Intellectual and Political History of the Triumph of Communism in Russia* (New York: Macmillan Co., 1965).

---

[14] For a perceptive discussion of the major problems that the Bolshevik leaders had to face in this regard, see Barrington Moore, Jr., *Soviet Politics—The Dilemma of Power* (Cambridge, Mass.: Harvard University Press, 1950), p. 85 ff.

[15] See Chapter 29.

28

Expression of Collective Interest: Marxism

The ideological foundations of the Soviet political system are to be found in the writings of Karl Marx, Friedrich Engels, V. I. Lenin, and other Marxists. As the word Marxist suggests, the common body of doctrine is known as Marxism or, in the Russian version, Marxism-Leninism. It is necessary to have a working knowledge of this body of doctrine if one is to understand the Soviet system. What follows is designed, understandably, to provide a summary only of the most essential elements of that doctrine.

HISTORICAL DEVELOPMENT OF SOCIALIST IDEAS

All socialists agree in the desirability of securing a fairer and more satisfactory apportionment of wealth and economic opportunity through some substantial limitation on the private ownership of property. This idea is not new; its historical roots can be found in the Old Testament. In different epochs, however, the arguments in its behalf have varied and the emphases and motivations of its proponents have not been the same.

Early socialism was motivated by religious and moralistic considerations. Each person was viewed as equal in the sight of God and therefore entitled to share relatively equally in the fruits of this earth. In the early modern period (about 1500), socialism became a combination of social revolt and religious zeal. Even as increasing importance was being attributed to economic life through the development of trade and so forth, socialistic ideas were, for the most part, still utopian, idealistic, and visionary. The primary motivation among the pioneers of socialism was an

418

urgent desire to get people to realize the good, rather than the bad, that is in them.

Although all beginnings are more or less relative, especially in the field of social history, the year 1848 may be viewed as the birth year of modern socialism. The Industrial Revolution had by the 19th century considerably altered the economic order in the West. Large-scale industry had developed, and with it a large class of propertyless wage earners, the proletariat. These developments were accompanied by evils (inadequate housing, poor sanitation, poor working conditions, long hours of work, absence of safety measures, and so forth) which came in the wake of the industrialization of modern society. In 1848 Karl Marx and Friedrich Engels published the *Communist Manifesto*, which not only sought to explain these evils but, in addition, to put forth a program of why and how they were going to pass from the scene.

Marxism is often described as scientific socialism. It is, in part, the result of two converging developments—modern science and the Industrial Revolution and its attendant consequences. While there is no effort here to pass judgment on modern science, its development enabled Marx to say, in effect: let us not be led down the mythical paths of the past if we are to explain social phenomena; let us put society under the microscope in order that we might get a scientific answer to the question of what makes it tick. Modern science had pointed the way to a mundane and realistic approach to the study of society.

Society itself had provided many of the tangible and visible factors which would enter into the analysis. There was the development of steam and machinery, with the replacement of manpower by steam power. There was discovery, exploration, and commerce. There was the trading merchant class, the bourgeoisie, which rose to a position of dominance. There was the proletariat. There were the glaring evils accompanying this economic and social revolution.

Since these evils had their gravest impact upon the proletariat, it is perhaps not unusual that socialism, since about the time of the publication of the *Communist Manifesto*, should have concerned itself primarily with the interest of hand laborers in industrial society. This will become even more apparent as we comprehend the nature of the Marxian analysis concerning the rise and development of capitalism, as well as its projection of the impending future evolution of capitalist society.

Before setting forth the basic ideas of Marx, however, it is well to be clear about the meaning of the terms *socialism* and *communism*, for when they are used in different contexts they have considerably varied meanings. Historically, over the past hundred years or so, they have come to be associated with different means of approaching a similar goal. The word *Communism* came into use in 1840. From 1840 to 1872 it came to imply revolutionary action aimed at the violent overthrow of capitalistic society. Socialism, on the other hand, was employed to designate constitutional activities aimed at the reform of the economic system through national control of the means of production. Between 1872 and 1917, however, the two terms became more or less synonymous, or, more precisely, the term *Communism* was dropped. Within 25 years of the writing of the *Communist Manifesto*, its authors were referring to themselves as socialists or social democrats. With the seizure of power in Russia by the Bolsheviks, the old distinctions were revived and even accentuated. In more recent years, the degree to which the economy should come under collective ownership or direction has also tended to distinguish Communists and socialists.

As employed by the Russians and their allies, the term *socialism* is frequently used to designate a stage in the transition from capitalism to the new society. It is the period in which the government has taken over the economy but one in which the ultimate stage of development has not been reached, the ultimate stage being Communism—a classless and stateless society.

The term *Communism* has been used to designate the Marxian doctrine, particularly as it has been modified and applied by the Russians. This has perhaps been done more frequently by non-Russians, although the Russians have also used the term quite extensively to signify the same thing. The Russians seem to prefer to use "socialism" or "Marxism-Leninism" when referring to the doctrinal ideology on which their system is based. Non-Russian socialists, even when they accept the Marxian analysis, prefer not to call the Russian system socialist, whereas Russian leaders do not recognize any system but their own as truly socialist. The Russians, however, use the term *Communist* freely when talking of their party and party leaders.

As employed in the pages that follow, unless otherwise indicated explicitly or in context, the term *socialism* will refer to the ideology or doctrine as expounded by Marx and other Marxists. When speaking of the political and economic system built up by the Russians, it will be more appropriate to speak of Communism or Bolshevism. The important thing to note, however, is that the reader should be aware of the different ways in which the terms *socialism* and *Communism* are used. The person using the terms, on the other hand, ought to make it quite clear how they are being used.

MARXISM AS A MATERIALISTIC CONCEPTION OF HISTORY

By far the greatest part of Marxian writings can be said to consist of an interpretation of capitalism. To be sure, Marx and his disciples concerned themselves about the establishment and the nature of the future society. But the bulk of their literary output deals with the laws of social evolution, and particularly with the factors governing the rise of the bourgeoisie, the modern capitalist class, and its "inevitable" demise. Therefore, Marxism is, first of all, an interpretation of capitalist society, in other words, an effort to define its place in the spectrum of long-range social development.

Different philosophers have sought an answer to the question of what is the moving force in history. Some have found it to be the will of God; others became convinced that the culture cycle was the law of history. Marx, on the other hand, concluded that on the basis of his researches societies rise and develop along a well-established path—the path of dialectical materialism.

The word dialectics was employed originally in ancient Greece to refer to a method of argument or disputation. A logical presentation of a point of view, or thesis, would provoke an opposition, or an antithesis. As a result of such a clash of views, the opinions of the disputing parties underwent a change, with the result that something new, higher, or more profound developed—a synthesis. There was a negation of the old and the creation of the new. Marx contended that the dialectic was at work in the social order, that each social order provoked or created an inner opposition. The result was a new and better society, which itself would become the new thesis and, in turn, create a new opposition, and so forth and so on.

What is the moving force in the dialectic process? Earlier, the German philosopher Hegel had argued in favor of the dialectic process, but he believed ideas to be the moving force in that process. Marx, on the other hand, concluded that the material factors in life were primary and all-important. They were the original force, while ideas, art, religion, philosophy, forms of political organization, and so forth, were but derivative forces. They were not even autonomous forces, but were dependent upon the material conditions of any given society.

According to the materialistic conception of history,[1] people make history by trying to satisfy their needs, which are originally imposed by nature but later modified by the artificial environment. These needs (food, clothing, shelter) are satisfied by people's productivity, which consists of extracting things from nature, in working them up, and in adapting them to their needs.

The productive forces (scientific and technical know-how) which people have at their disposal to satisfy their needs will determine all of their social relations. "The organization of any given society is determined by the state of its productive forces" (Plekhanov). In other words,

---

[1] One of the clearest expositions of the materialistic conception of history is to be found in a brief essay by one of the earliest Russian Marxists, George Plekhanov, "The Materialist Conception of History," originally published in 1897.

"occupational activities determine the fundamental modes of social behavior and in this behavior are formed ideas, attitudes, and habits which express themselves in other fields of culture" (Marx and Engels). It follows, therefore, that as the nature of the productive forces changes, the organization of society will also change. For example, the change in the state of the productive forces under capitalism resulted in the building of urban communities, with the consequent need for urban services (garbage collection, fire protection, and so forth). This, in turn, required a change in the organization of society so as to bring about these services. Urban local government with which we are familiar would have been unthinkable 2,000 years ago, for the state of the productive forces then available created no need for it.

Moreover, the Marxists argue, the prevalent mode of economic production in any society gives rise to definite interests, which are essentially antagonistic, thus dividing society into classes. These interests become expressed in law. "All positive law is a defense of some definite interest" (Plekhanov). For example, at a time when horses were domesticated and economically useful (for hunting or transport), the owners of horses needed a law against horse stealing. But all interests cannot be protected equally, for they are in fundamental conflict. The net result of the conflict of interests between antagonistic classes is a state organization (government, law, etc.) whose function is to protect the interests of the dominant group or class. The state is therefore an organization of class domination, an organ of oppression of one class by another.[2]

When new productive forces evolve, the existing social institutions—government among them—do not permit their proper utilization. In the end, the class struggle becomes more and more acute and logically can only be resolved by revolution. Thus, revolution is the inevitable result of the contradiction between the new scientific and technical know-how and the inability of social institutions to bring about the creative potentialities that the new forces of production offer.

To substantiate their theory, Marx and his followers cited historical examples, the most notable being the feudal system, which was overthrown when it stood in the way of the proper utilization of the new productive forces (the Industrial Revolution) of bourgeois capitalism. Capitalist society, therefore, was not only a necessary step in social evolution, but also a beneficial one in relation to the past. In relation to the future, however, it is an evil that will be destroyed.

The basic law of social development, according to the Marxists, has been stated above. But what are the proofs of its operation in capitalist society? First and foremost, not unlike the societies which preceeded it, capitalism creates within itself an inner opposition. Just as feudalism

---

[2] While Engels did not disagree with this analysis, he did concede that there were brief periods when the warring classes were so nearly equally balanced that the power of the state for the moment assumed a certain independence in relation to both.

created an inner opposition, bringing forth the bourgeoisie to destroy it, so the bourgeoisie bring forth the modern wage-earning class, the proletariat, which is to overthrow bourgeois society. Capitalism brings forth the proletariat because it needs it to operate the factories and other means of production. But it exploits the propertyless wage earners, for they cannot buy back all that they have produced. They do not get paid for all that they do; some is held back.[3]

Secondly, the position of the worker gets worse as time goes on. The rich get richer and the poor get poorer. Economic power tends to centralize, and wealth accumulates in large fortunes. This centralization of wealth robs the proletariat of purchasing power, which results in crises—overproduction, unemployment, economic depressions, and panics. These crises, Marx was convinced, would destroy the entire capitalist systems, for not only does the lot of the workers become more and more unbearable but, in addition, the ranks of the proletariat are greatly enlarged by more and more of the bourgeoisie being pushed out and forced to make a living as wage earners. Thus, revolution becomes imminent as capitalism ripens.

Finally, bourgeois society is doomed, for it has not done away with class antagonisms but has established new classes, new conditions of oppression, new forms of struggle in place of the old.[4] While the "history of all hitherto existing society is the history of class struggles,[5] earlier societies had many classes. "In ancient Rome we have patricians, knights, plebeians, slaves; in the Middle Ages, feudal lords, vassals, guild-masters, journeymen, apprentices, serfs. . . ."[6] The epoch of the bourgeoisie, however, has simplified the struggle. Instead of many classes, there are only two, the bourgeoisie and the proletariat.

Moreover, as Plekhanov was to suggest, the evolution of bourgeois society would result in a more enlightened proletariat, and hence one ready to revolt.[7] There is an immense difference, he observed, between being conscious of the restrictiveness of laws and consciously striving to abolish this restrictiveness. Where people do not strive to abolish old institutions and to create new ones, there the way for the new system has not been properly prepared by the economics (the productive forces) of the society. But as science and technology reduce ignorance, people will better understand natural phenomena. As a consequence, they will better understand social and economic phenomena. When they do they will revolt.

---

[3] This is the Marxian labor theory of value—that is, labor produced capital as well as the actual goods of consumption. This idea was not original with Marx.

[4] *Communist Manifesto* (New York: International Publishers edition, 1932), p. 9.

[5] Ibid.

[6] Ibid.

[7] *Essays in Historical Materialism* (New York: International Publishers edition, 1940), pp. 36–37.

V. I. Lenin, who was to become the leader of the Bolshevik Revolution, is the immediate doctrinal authority for the Russian Communists, as well as for many other Marxists. The Russian Communists almost always speak of Marxism-Leninism when referring to the ideological doctrine by which they profess to be guided. Although other Russian Marxists, notably George Plekhanov, preceded Lenin in laying the doctrinal foundations for Russian Marxism, Lenin has come to be regarded by the Russian Communists as the true interpreter of Marx.

Lenin made two principal contributions to Marxism. The first adds to the analysis of capitalism, while the second concerns the question of techniques for the overthrow of bourgeois society.

Lenin condemned capitalism for all the evils Marx had attributed to it, and he added others. In its later stages of development, capitalism, because of its monopoly controls, fostered scarcity at home. The reduced domestic buying power sent capitalists in search of markets abroad, which led to imperialism. Consequently, capitalism produced competing imperialistic ventures by the capitalist countries, thus leading to war.[8] At the same time, the state machinery was strengthened, with a notable growth of the bureaucracy and the military. Simultaneously, repressive measures against the proletariat were on the increase.[9]

Closely related to this idea was Lenin's argument that the proletarian revolution did not need to wait until society had gone through the evils of the capitalist phase, although this was contrary to his earlier thinking on the subject. The peasantry, he said, could be allied with the industrial workers to bring about the revolution. In his change in outlook, he may have been guided by his desire to consummate the proletarian revolution in Russia, which was still a backward country and not yet developed as a bourgeois society. The Russian peasantry, because of the lingering evils of serfdom, was, in his "more mature opinion," ready to join with the workers in seeking power.

Lenin's other contribution was his development of the concept of the professional revolutionary. Marx had viewed the proletarian revolution as inevitable. Lenin accepted Marx's analysis but was more insistent upon the need for leadership to bring it about. Marx and Engels paid little attention to the idea of a communist political party. Lenin, on the other hand, talked constantly about the need of a party of professional revolutionaries, and devoted more than 20 years to building that kind of party. While Marx and Lenin agreed that capitalism prepares the way for the revolution, Lenin was somewhat skeptical about the proletariat's rising spontaneously. Consequently, he argued that a small, tightly organized party of dedicated and trained revolutionaries was needed. These people would lead the proletariat in its successful revolution.

---

[8] See his *Imperialism, the Highest Stage of Capitalism* (originally published in 1916).

[9] *State and Revolution* (New York: International Publishers edition, 1932), p. 29.

MARXISM AS A POSITIVE PROGRAM

Although Marxists are first of all preoccupied with an interpretation of capitalism, they utilize this interpretation as the foundation upon which their positive program rests. Unlike other philosophers who have sought to explain the world, the Marxists also seek to change it. Once their analysis of the existing order is made they see two tasks confronting the proletariat. First is the seizure of political power, or converting their potential superiority into an actual one. Secondly, once political power is secured, the proletariat must go about the task of building the new economic and social order.

Marx argued that while history produces a revolutionary situation, it would be necessary for the proletariat and history to work together. The proletariat must have a program whose function is to show the workers how they can achieve political power. In democratic countries, they should organize politically to win the battle of democracy. In countries where the democratic process was forbidden to them, they should use organized force. Thus, Marx's program was at once both evolutionary and revolutionary.

Lenin, who was impatient to witness the revolution in Russia, placed a greater emphasis on action. Every step in the real movement is more important than a dozen programs, he declared. Moreover, he insisted that it was impossible to win by democratic means so long as the bourgeoisie commanded the army and the police. He frequently emphasized that unless revolutionary theory is combined with revolutionary practice, it is not Marxism but opportunism.[10] "The replacement of the bourgeois by the proletarian state is impossible without a violent revolution."[11]

Lenin, moreover, was much more preoccupied than Marx with the form of the new political authority once political power had been captured. While asserting that the bourgeois state must be destroyed root and branch, Lenin insisted that the Communists would for a time need the state. This new workers' state would function during the period of transition from capitalism to communism. Its functions would be to suppress the bourgeoisie and to build socialism. It would be a dictatorship of the proletariat. So as not to leave any of his followers in doubt, Lenin declared: "He who recognizes *only* the class struggle is not yet a Marxist. . . . A Marxist is one who *extends* the acceptance of class struggle to the acceptance of the dictatorship of the proletariat."[12]

The dictatorship of the proletariat would do away with the bourgeoisie by nationalizing capital—that is, by seizing all income-producing property, including natural resources as well as capital industries. Those who

---

[10] See V. Adoratsky, *Dialectical Materialism* (New York: International Publishers, 1934), especially chap. 6.

[11] *State and Revolution*, p. 20.

[12] Ibid p. 30. Italics his.

sought to resist would be liquidated. Nothing must stand in the way of the new proletarian authority "to abolish all exploitation," to crush "the resistance of the exploiters," and to guide the masses "in the work of organizing the socialist economy."[13]

The gains from the productive property, now in state hands, would accrue to the entire community and be distributed by public authority. Presumably there would be private property in income, although this could not be invested for the purpose of making a profit. Although there are contradictory statements among Marxists as to the relative equality of reward, Marx and Engles in the *Communist Manifesto* asserted that the ultimate objective was a society in which everyone would contribute "according to his ability" and in turn be rewarded "according to his need." Lenin, although speaking of immediate aims, was more specific when he talked of paying workingmen's wages to managers, technicians, bookkeepers, and government officials.[14]

As conceived by Marx, however, the dictatorship of the proletariat would not be a dictatorship of one person or a few. As he envisioned it, the proletarian state would be a dictatorship of the majority (proletariat) over the minority (bourgeoisie), and hence in reality a democracy.

MARXISM AS THE CLASSLESS, STATELESS SOCIETY

The struggle between the capitalists and the proletarians, according to Marx and his followers, represents the last historic clash between classes. With the abolition of private ownership of the means of production, the basis for the existence of classes will disappear. Everyone will be in the same "class," or more correctly, classes will disappear, for the concept of class has no meaning unless there are two or more of them.[15]

Since the state is the oppressive instrument of the dominant class, according to Marxian theory, there will be no need for it in a classless society. Therefore, the state will "wither away," but Marxists have not been too precise as to how soon this would take place. In 1918, Lenin thought of the transition period in terms of "ten years or perhaps more." A year or two later, he admitted that perhaps he had been overly optimistic, and for a time dwelt on the need for strengthening the state in the transition period. But he does not seem to have departed from his assertion

---

[13] Ibid pp. 22–23.

[14] Ibid, p. 43.

[15] In 1957 the Chinese Communist leader, Mao Tse-tung, revised Marxian doctrine to the extent of admitting that "contradictions" existed in China, that there were differences between the Communist government and the people. The Russians, however, have denied that such contradictions exist in the Soviet Union.

in *State and Revolution* that what the proletariat needs is "only a state which is withering away, *i.e.*, a state which is so constituted that it begins to wither away immediately. . . ."[16] In any case, irrespective of the time it took, Lenin expected the withering away of the state to be progressive and continuous.

Assuming the disappearance of classes and the withering away of the state, it still remains to be asked how the classless society will be organized and how it is to function without state authority. Here the Marxists are even more vague than in the matter of the duration of the dictatorship of the proletariat. Somehow, all production would be concentrated in the hands of vast associations of the whole people. The administrative functions normally associated with the state would become part and parcel of the productive process. Presumably, the people would choose representatives who would determine the basic policies to be pursued. They would plan the utilization of the material resources for the good of all. In essence, everyone would be a member of a cooperative commonwealth of the world in which cooperation would take the place of compulsion. The profit motive would give way to the service motive and people would do the right thing because it was the right thing to do.

If the classless, stateless society seems utopian and unrealistic, the Marxists would be the first to deny it, on paper at least. "We are not Utopians," said Lenin, "and we do not in the least deny the possibility and inevitability of excesses on the part of *individual* persons, nor the need to suppress *such* excesses. But . . . no special machinery . . . is needed for this; this will be done by the armed people itself, as simply and as readily as any crowd of civilized people even in modern society, parts a pair of combatants or does not allow a woman to be outraged."[17] In practice, of course, the Russians have yet to produce any evidence of the withering away of the state, although they are now in the seventh decade of the dictatorship of the proletariat.

CRITIQUE OF MARXISM

The foregoing discussion of Marxian theory is far from being exhaustive. Our main aim has been to concentrate on those aspects of the theory that would be most meaningful to a student of Soviet politics and government. Similarly, an extensive evaluation of that theory is beyond our scope here. Yet some critical analysis seems in order.

Unquestionably, Marxist writings have had an important impact on the world. There are elements of truth in these writings, else they could not

---

[16] Page 22.

[17] *State and Revolution*, p. 75.

have had such influence. However erroneous he may have been with respect to his predictions of future developments or however naive he may have been with respect to a future Communist system, Marx did contribute to man's knowledge about the past. By tracing social and especially political institutions to their materialistic or economic bases, he at least called our attention to the importance of materialistic factors, although most of us would not agree that they were always the decisive ones. Moreover, his exposition of the conflict between the proletariat and the bourgeoisie gave us an added insight into social relationships. And his demonstration of some of the instabilities of capitalism has contributed to more meaningful insights with respect to the workings of a free-enterprise economy. Finally, because of his many assertions, other researchers have been challenged to probe deeper, in order that they might contribute to a better understanding of our social order.

First among the criticisms that might be made of Marx's theories concerns the basic assumption that materialistic forces are primary in the shaping of all human development, that all other forces are derivative and secondary. The findings of most modern social scientists indicate that society is much more complex than the Marxian formula assumes. There is evidence that ideas and other considerations do motivate people, quite independently of materialistic forces. Moreover, Marx did not say that technical changes (inventions, etc.) were governed by materialistic forces alone. Why, it might be asked, does creativity in human affairs have to be limited to the technical sphere?

A second criticism that might be made of Marx's analysis is that the consequences of the Industrial Revolution which he saw are not to be associated with capitalism alone.[18] The Industrial Revolution, whether engineered by private enterprise or by the state, as in Russia, creates new social classes. State-initiated industrialization produces an industrial working class, while the bureaucracy, sometime euphemistically referred to by the Russians as the "toiling intelligentsia," becomes the ruling class.[19] The plight of the workers under state-engineered industrialization, in the sense that they are materially exploited and emotionally disoriented, is not unlike that of the Western European workers during the early capitalist period. Exploitation of the workers, therefore, is not the result of capitalism or of socialism but of the early stages of the Industrial Revolution.

Thirdly, Marx did not foresee that when the Industrial Revolution had

---

[18] See the series of articles by Hugh Seton-Watson in the *Manchester Guardian Weekly*, January 28, February 4, 11, and 18, 1954, under the general title, "Some Myths of Marxism."

[19] See Milovan Djilas, *The New Class* (New York: Frederick A. Praeger, Inc., 1957). For an excellent recent critique of Marxian theories, see his *The Unperfect Society: Beyond the New Class* (New York: Harcourt, Brace & World, Inc., 1969).

run its course the lot of the worker would improve and a certain social balance would be achieved. The position of the proletariat improved for several reasons. Free speech and a free press, by making possible a thorough discussion of workers' grievances, aroused the social conscience of the educated people. In addition, workers were able to organize in unions and thus push their demands. Moreover, they gained the right to choose members of legislative bodies and were influential in securing legislative enactments favorable to them. Without denying the great influence which capitalism wielded, it can be seen that political liberty and representative institutions enabled Western democracy to evolve a system characterized by a considerable balance among social classes.

Another defect in Marxian theory lies in its underestimation of the strength and flexibility of capitalism. Instead of impoverishing the middle class and driving more and more of its members into the ranks of the proletariat, capitalism has enabled the middle class to become more prosperous and to grow in numbers. Moreover, it had demonstrated a remarkable ability to adjust to public regulation of some of its important activities. By making concessions, it has provided untold opportunities for the middle class and for the workers, demonstrating a dynamic flexibility.

In their revolutionary appeal for unity among workers of the world, Marx and his followers underestimated the strength of the appeals of nationalism. National loyalties have proved to be stronger than loyalties to class, something which is true of the capitalist class as well as of the proletariat.

Finally, the Marxists erred in their assumption that workers would act, and act rationally, in given circumstances. Studies in the political behavior of human beings, indicate that people are often exceedingly irrational in their political choices. More important, perhaps, is the fact that people are seldom moved to action. Thus, Marx was wrong when he assumed the revolutionary character of the workers, as well as when he assumed that they would act rationally in support of their class interest.

As Djilas has written, "Marx became a Communist first and founded Communist doctrine afterward. . . . [He] searched the British Museum for objective laws that would justify his prophetic zeal."[20] Elsewhere he has written that "Communist ideas did not spring forth from the working class," and that "Communists have never anywhere fully understood the working class."[21] And as Robert Wesson has said, what distinguished Marx and other socialists was his proclivity for revolution, which explains much of the success of his doctrines.[22]

[20] *The Unperfect Society*, p. 116.

[21] See his articles in the *New York Times*, July 31, August 1, 2, 1972.

[22] Robert G. Wesson, *Why Marxism?: The Continuing Success of a Failed Theory* (New York: Basic Books, 1976), p. 25.

With respect to the Soviet Union, Marxism, or Marxism-Leninism has meant whatever the Soviet leaders have chosen to have it mean. In the first place, the men who set up the dictatorship, aside from a few educated Marxists such as Lenin, could not have known much about Marxism. Many peasant lads, like Nikita Khrushchev, who joined the party in 1918, were barely literate. Secondly, Soviet Communist leaders, including Lenin, Stalin, Khrushchev, and their successors, have never hesitated to revise Marxist postulates when it was thought necessary to defend certain policies or programs. By and large, the Soviet leaders have been guided by their cardinal aim—the abolition of private property. To achieve this, they have found it necessary to strengthen the state and, in the process, to protect the interests of the dominant class—the party apparatus.

Stalin's main contribution to Marxism-Leninism is the idea of "socialism in one country." When the Bolshevik revolution was not followed by similar revolutions elsewhere, Stalin saw in the outside world a threat to the Soviet system (the so-called capitalist encirclement). To meet this threat, Stalin believed that the Soviet state had to be strengthened, and this could be done, in his opinion, only by a rapid transformation of the Soviet economic system. This required forced industrialization, which in turn called for collectivization of agriculture in order that the new proletariat be fed. Marx had stressed the importance of the proletariat. Lenin had put greater emphasis on the party. Stalin sought to merge the party and the state so as to make the Soviet Union the chief instrument of proletarian revolutions.

From the notion of "socialism in one country" flowed certain other ideas. The dictatorship of the proletariat had to be viewed as the dictatorship of the one-party state. This dictatorship had to be strengthened in the so-called transition period, and especially the army and the police as guardians of that dictatorship. Moreover, the period of this dictatorship was to be relatively long, during which the economic and cultural prerequisites for "socialist victory" were to be created. These ideas led to the destruction of all opposition and to the strengthening of the monolithic character of the regime. The withering away of the state was, for all practical purposes, forgotten.

Stalin's idea of "socialism in one country" had other interesting implications and consequences. For example, revolutionary movements in foreign countries would be staged or called off depending upon whether Soviet foreign policy was furthered thereby. Similarly, in order to increase labor productivity Stalin introduced significant wage differentials and worker-discipline legislation. Moreover, he departed from Lenin's emphasis on internationalism, stressing the achievements of the Russian state, claiming Russian firsts in inventions, and elevating heroes of Tsarist Russia to positions of veneration. Although a member of a minority nationality (Georgian), Stalin became more Russian than the Russians.

Khrushchev, although not much of a theorist, advanced three ideas to which reference should be made. Allegedly correcting Stalin's errors, he in effect revised Lenin when he asserted that war between the Communist and non-Communist camps was not inevitable. Similarly, he revised Lenin when he proclaimed that it was possible for proletarian revolutions to be achieved by nonviolent means. More interesting than either one of these notions were his observations on the withering away of the state, which revised Marx as well as Lenin. Instead of being the last stage in political development prior to the establishment of the classless and state-less society, the dictatorship of the proletariat gives way to the "state of all the people." Instead of ceasing to exist, the state apparently dissolves itself slowly into organized society. In this organized society, the Communist party will replace the government and therefore its role will become even more important than in the past.

Khrushchev's successors have contributed little that can be classified as theory. The only possible exception is the so-called Brezhnev doctrine, the essence of which is that the Soviet Union has the right to intervene in the affairs of any Communist state when the Communist political order is threatened from within or without. This doctrine was proclaimed as a way of justifying the Soviet invasion of Czechoslovakia in August 1968, but it may also have unpredictable implications for the future.

MARXISM: RELEVANCE OF THE IDEOLOGY

At one time Marxism was an understandable human response to poorly understood, rapid, and threatening change that came in the wake of the Industrial Revolution. Today, however, Marxism has nothing to say about most of the great problems facing the world—the danger of nuclear war, the population explosion, the depletion of renewable energy resources, and the various threats to the environment. Moreover, there is some question about the relevance of Marxian ideas even in the system which purports to be based on those ideas.

Among the so-called experts there is some disagreement about the role of ideology in the Soviet system. A few maintain that it is a body of "ceremonial political functions," a type of Sunday creed to which most Communists pay lip service. A much larger group contends that ideology is a guide to action, a type of instruction manual of pragmatically extracted precepts from Marxist teachings, which permits the greatest flexibility in the practical implementation of fundamentally inflexible principles. This means that each Marxist-Leninist postulate expresses the position of the Communist party concerning some specific question at a particular time. When a goal is reached or circumstances change, the postulate loses validity, and the party's ideological position can be changed.

Thus, adherence to traditional concepts can be interpreted as faithfulness to the party line or as dogmatism. Readiness to modify such concepts can be interpreted as revisionism or as creative Marxism. Similarly, peaceful coexistence can be "a form of the class struggle on a worldwide scale" or "downright capitulation." As a guide to action, therefore, ideology is viewed less as a collection of dogmas and more as an instrument of communication and leadership.

Other experts, while agreeing that ideology as a guide to action assists the leaders in coping with practical needs, whether economic or political, maintain (correctly in the opinion of this writer) that ideology has an influence on policy beyond these needs. As a guide to action, Marxist-Leninist teachings are utilized to enhance and extend the role and power of the Soviet Communist party, but these teachings also reflect the party's world outlook. In this ideology are found most of the basic teachings of Marx: the class struggle, the overthrow of capitalism, and the establishment of a system of social (collectivist) production. Ideology in the Soviet Union is thus "a continuous process resulting from the interplay of Communist theory and practice, affected at times—perhaps continually—by the interests of ruling groups, by Communist internecine struggles and by the personal characteristics of dictators, but with a logic of its own."[23]

In spite of the fact that most of Marx's predictions have been falsified by history, Soviet leaders continue to spout the old arid formulas. In any conflict between ideology and power, however, the former always gives way.

It is interesting to note that many Marxists outside the Soviet Union have recently found comfort in Marx's earlier writings, especially those dealing with the concept of alienation; that is, people were alienated because their work was sold. The ideal society of those early writings was one in which it was possible for a person "to do one thing today and another tomorrow, to hunt in the morning, fish in the afternoon, rear cattle in the evening, criticize after dinner . . . without ever becoming hunter, fisherman, shepherd or critic."[24] Thus, alienation would disappear only when the division of labor had given way and when people worked for the fun of it. As Wesson has pointed out, "the naivete of this nostalgic dream is striking. But the idea has had a remarkable appeal for many modern readers. . . ."[25] It is not surprising, however, that Marxism-Leninism in the Soviet Union has no room for the concept of alienation.

---

[23] C. Olgin, "What Is Soviet Ideology?" *Bulletin: Institute for the Study of the USSR,* 11 (November 1964): p. 9.

[24] Cited in Wesson, *Why Marxism?* p. 15.

[25] *Ibid.*

BIBLIOGRAPHICAL NOTE

There are several editions of Marx's writings; among them, one of the more convenient brief collections is *Capital*, *The Communist Manifesto*, *and Other Writings* (New York: Modern Library, 1932). Among Lenin's numerous works, several deserve mention: *What Is to Be Done; Two Tactics of Social Democracy; Imperialism: The Highest Stage of Capitalism;* and *The State and Revolution.*

Analyses and critiques of Marxism include those of H. B. Acton, *The Illusion of the Epoch: Marxism-Leninism as a Philosophical Creed* (London: Cohen & West, 1955); Sidney Hook, *Marx and the Marxists* (Princeton, N.J.: D. Van Nostrand Co., Inc., 1955); John Plamenatz, *German Marxism and Russian Communism* (London: Longmans, Green, 1954).

Especially interesting are two books already cited: one by a one-time Marxist (and one-time member of the Politburo of the Yugoslav Communist party), Milovan Djilas, *The Unperfect Society;* the other by Robert G. Wesson, *Why Marxism?*

29

The Communist Party
and Its Role

The Communist party is the driving force in the Soviet system. It is the dictatorship, not really *of* the proletariat, but *over* the proletariat and over all other groups in Soviet society. It has a complete monopoly of political power; no competing groups or influences are tolerated. The Soviet "Government" is not a government in the Western sense, for it is not an autonomous force. It cannot function independently of the party. As Stalin once said, "Not a single important political or organizational question is decided without direction from the party. . . ." The party makes the decisions, while the governmental apparatus serves as the party's agent to carry out these decisions.

In any study of the Soviet system, therefore, the key role of the Communist party must remain in the foreground, but, as a subsequent chapter will show, this role is not confined to the spheres of economics and politics. Every phase of human endeavor is within the scope of its all-embracing authority and concern.

BACKGROUND OF RUSSIAN COMMUNIST PARTY

The early Russian Marxists, as did those in Western Europe, thought of themselves as social democrats and initially called their party the Russian Social Democratic Labor party. As a consequence of internal quarrels, the faction that was to gain dominance called itself the Russian Social Democratic party (B).[1] In 1918, they changed the name to Russian Com-

---

[1] The "B" stood for Bolsheviks; for discussion of Mensheviks and Bolsheviks see below

munist party (B), and in 1925 it became the All Union Communist party (B). After the 19th Party Congress in 1952, the official name became the Communist Party of the Soviet Union (CPSU).

Russian Marxism grew out of a split in the *Narodnik* (populist) organization, referred to in Chapter 27. The *Narodnik* movement was initiated by intellectuals who hoped and expected the peasantry to be responsive to their agitation—that is, to their explanations of the peasants' plight and their suggested remedies. When the peasantry proved unresponsive, and indeed hostile, many of the *Narodniki* turned more and more to direct action and violence. They acted through an organization called *Narodnaya Volya* (the people's will). Those who opposed violence established a rival organization, called the *Chernyi Peredel* (the black partition). Subsequently, leaders of the peaceful group, such as George Plekhanov, became convinced that the peasantry was a nonrevolutionary, conservative, and indifferent element. After searching for a new faith, they embraced Marxism, and founded the first Russian Marxist organization, called the Emancipation of Labor.

Declaring its disillusionment with the peasantry, this group, under the intellectual leadership of Plekhanov, declared that the revolutionary movement in Russia could triumph only if it were based on the working class. This constituted a break with the important *Narodnik* idea, which they had once shared, that Russia could skip the capitalist phase of development. Plekhanov and his cohorts were in effect saying that Russia was launched on the course of capitalist development, which would produce the working class, and which in turn would overthrow Russian bourgeois society.

Marxism, however, meant different things to many Russians who professed to be Marxists.[2] Some equated it with industrial development, others with traditional trade unionism, still others with idealistic reforms and opportunism. Plekhanov and his pupil, V. I. Lenin, viewing themselves as orthodox Marxists, sought in the 1890s to defend the orthodox Marxist analysis and particularly to reassert its revolutionary content. They agreed with the *Communist Manifesto* that the proletarian revolution would come in the wake of capitalist development. Because Russia was industrially backward, they believed that the initial task was to facilitate a bourgeois-democratic revolution in Russia. While Plekhanov remained loyal to his position to the end, Lenin was to find it increasingly inconvenient, for it got in the way of his activist bent. Other Russian Marxists were to find themselves similarly divided.

The Russian Social Democratic Labor party, founded in 1898, developed a split of major proportions at its second congress, held in

---

[2] See Leopold H. Haimson, *The Russian Marxists and the Origins of Bolshevism* (Cambridge, Mass.: Harvard University Press, 1955).

London in 1903.[3] Out of it emerged two distinct groups of Russian Marxists, the result of a split which had been in the making for several years.
The groups came to be known as Mensheviks and Bolsheviks. These
words are derived from the Russian words *Menshe* and *Bolshe,* meaning
less and more, respectively. The split between the Mensheviks (or minority men) and the Bolsheviks (or majority men) continued to widen in the
years ahead, leading to their complete and formal separation in 1912.

The Mensheviks and Bolsheviks found themselves divided on two primary and several subsidiary questions. The first of the major questions
concerned the political implications of Russia's industrial backwardness.
The Mensheviks, led by Plekhanov, held to the orthodox view that
socialism would come to Russia only after the bourgeois-democratic revolution, and this was to be a long-term affair. The opposite view, often
identified with Leon Trotsky, originally a Menshevik, held that the
capitalist class was not strong enough to bring forth the bourgeois revolution. Hence, the proletariat should bring on the revolution and keep it
going (in "permanence") until the proletarian revolution should be completed. This would mean telescoping two revolutions into one. While
continuing to pay lip service to the orthodox doctrine, Lenin and the
Bolsheviks were in spirit close to the latter group. Subsequently, Lenin
was to add his own contribution to Bolshevik theory by suggesting an
alliance with the peasantry so as to give the proletariat a broader base. By
the tactical combination of the proletariat with the peasantry to complete
the democratic revolution, and subsequently with the village poor to bring
on the proletarian revolution, industrial backwardness, in Lenin's view
(and later Stalin's) could actually be turned to the advantage of socialism.

The second major question in the split among the Russian Social Democrats involved the nature of the party. Lenin, as leader of what was to
become the Bolshevik faction, argued for a relatively small, closed party
of carefully selected and dedicated revolutionaries. This would be a disciplined organization run from the center. While sympathizers would be
encouraged, they would not be members of the party. The leaders of what
was to become the Menshevik faction, on the other hand, argued for a
broadly based party which would admit all who believed in its program.
Such a party would of necessity have to accord some voice to the rank
and file. Moreover, such a party would collaborate with other parliamentary parties when it was in its interest to do so, something that was
anathema to Lenin. Although initially in a minority, Lenin, through tactical maneuvers, gained a majority of the delegates for his side. In the years
ahead, he did all in his power to consolidate his position of leadership and
to rebuff all challenges to his authority.

---

[3] The first congress had met secretly at Minsk, but the principal participants were arrested before anything could be done beyond the appointment of the Central Committee and
the decision to publish a party organ. The second congress had to be held abroad; originally
it convened in Brussels, but soon transferred to London for fear of police pressure.

The definitive split in 1912 resulted in no small part from Lenin's precarious hold on the leading committees, which he was afraid he could not maintain, and therefore directed the formation of a separate Bolshevik organization with a separate central committee. The Bolsheviks, however, resisted his suggestion that they call themselves Communists, a name they adopted only after their seizure of power.

The collapse of tsarism and the establishment of the bourgeois-democratic provisional government seemed to favor the Menshevik position. The gains of the Bolsheviks, however, and particularly their seizure of power in November 1917, irrevocably settled the argument in favor of the Bolsheviks, at least insofar as Russia was concerned. The Menshevik arguments were answered by revolutionary action. The events of 1917, for all practical purposes, resolved the Bolshevik-Menshevik controversy in favor of the Bolsheviks. The Mensheviks, as well as others, continued an uneasy and harassed existence as opposition parties until the end of the civil war, when the Bolsheviks put an end to opposition groups.

The history of Russian Marxism in the early part of this century, and particularly the history of what transpired in 1917, has provided us with the major clue to Bolshevik success. In no small measure, their success may be attributed to the elasticity of their tactics. Their firm dedication to the goal of achieving political power was certainly important. Perhaps other political groups were equally dedicated to their respective goals, but they had none of the ingenuity or the willingness of the Bolsheviks to alter their methods, to change their positions, or to take seemingly contradictory positions when doing so would advance them toward their objective.

Lenin, for the most part, was the master tactician in all Bolshevik maneuvers. The elasticity of his tactics enabled him to bring the peasants into his theories because he believed that their discontent could be channeled to Bolshevik ends. Similarly, he was convinced that the discontent among the non-Russian nationalities could be harnessed in the interests of the proletarian revolution. His changes in attitude as to whether or not the Bolsheviks should participate in the Soviets, whether they should take part in the Duma elections, and so forth, further confirmed his influence on Bolshevik tactical elasticity. Lenin's dedication to this principle has by and large been observed by his party successors.

BOLSHEVIK CONCEPT OF PARTY

Out of this factious and discordant background and out of the experience of governing in subsequent years, the Bolsheviks developed a concept of party which embraces certain definite characteristics. In the main, these characteristics are identified with questions concerning what the party is supposed to be and what it is supposed to do. The answers to these questions have not varied materially during the period of Soviet rule.

The early formative years gave the party an indelible cast. That cast was in the nature of a monolithic revolutionary elite. Lenin was especially insistent upon the elitist principle: only the most qualified and dedicated persons should be permitted membership. They all must be of one mind, or at least capable of accepting iron discipline and obedience once the party line had been handed down. No deviations were to be permitted; in other words, no internal factions could exist. The party was to speak with one voice and to act as one unit. Sympathizers (fellow travelers) were encouraged to cooperate and to lend themselves to party ends, but they would not be permitted to become encumbrances on the party's disciplined and monolithic machine.

All of these ideas, predicated upon the assumption that the party would be the instrument for the seizure of political power in the name of the proletariat, were reinforced under the leadership of Lenin's successor, Joseph Stalin. By comparison with Stalin, Lenin's intolerance of disagreement and compromise was mild indeed. Rigidity in the interpretation of the party line increased constantly during Stalin's reign. Slightly varying points of view became known as major and treasonous deviations, which were punished with increasing severity.

Stalin's successors, although making certain modifications in the Soviet system, have not departed from basic Bolshevik tenets concerning the nature of the Communist party. It continues to be viewed as a monolithic, highly centralized, and disciplined organization. There has been no suggestion that factions be permitted within the party or that top leaders of the party be subject to criticism any more than they have been in the past.

The Russians have described the Communist party as the most conscious segment of the working class, whose role it is to lead and to speak for the proletariat. As the all-wise and only true defender and expounder of socialism, the party is supposed to know what needs to be done during the period of transition from capitalism to communism. Since no one else can be trusted with this task, the party becomes not only the source of all initiative, but also the all-wise judge of human actions and motivations and of good and evil. Moreover, the party not only assumes the role of guarding and protecting the interests of the proletariat against all other movements that would seek the favor of the proletariat but, in addition, prevents the formation or operation of any group whose aim is to appeal to any segment of society for support.

In other words, the party is the main, if not the sole, instrument for the totalitarian remaking of society. The party organization is charged with facilitating the execution and acceptance of the policies of the party's high command. Moreover, it must from time to time assimilate into its ranks various individuals, while at the same time making sure that their devotion to the party is unquestioned, so that the party may continue to be a trustworthy instrument of its leaders. The party, in short, operates as a machine of the party leadership for the total reconstruction of society.

The Bolsheviks have often defended their totalitarian dictatorship by arguing that democracy prevails inside the party. They have said that until the party takes a position on a certain question, party members are free to discuss and debate the various aspects of that question. Moreover, they have asserted that even after the party line has been established, rank and file members, as well as those at the top, are encouraged to engage in criticism and self-criticism.

In practice, as a subsequent section of this chapter will show, dissent within party ranks was discouraged from the outset, and progressively repressed until it came to an end. The criticism which remains today is a controlled criticism, directed from the top. The lesser figures in the party and their work are the invariable objects of this criticism. On occasion, a more prominent figure is accorded the "opportunity" of indulging in self-criticism, admitting his sins, and bringing down wrath upon his own shoulders. But high party leaders, as well as party policies, are immune from criticism from below, unless for some reason these leaders decide that a change is needed and that it would be facilitated by controlled and directed criticism.

But even controlled criticism does not assert that the party erred in a given situation. As a general rule, the criticism centers on bureaucratic inefficiency, venality, and outright refusal to carry out assigned tasks. Sometimes governmental officials are charged with being unimaginative, slow, and inept in adapting party policies to the circumstances at hand. Other times they are accused of misinterpreting party directives. Such criticism, the leaders hope, will have the effect of diverting attention from them as well as from the party when things go wrong.

Party leaders who die or are removed from office may be subject to criticism. This has been true even of top leaders such as Stalin and Khrushchev. But the contention is always made that their misdeeds are not the fault of the party. In the downgrading of Stalin, for example, it was even asserted that other party leaders had no choice but to carry out his evil directives. The system which permits or enables a personal dictator to arise is seemingly never at fault.

ORGANIZATIONAL STRUCTURE AND AUTHORITY WITHIN THE PARTY

The Russian Communists have by and large adhered to Lenin's precept that the party should be kept relatively small. The party has grown numerically, but for the most part this has been a controlled growth. The years of World War II were somewhat of an exception. Because casualties among party comrades were particularly high, recruitment policies were liberalized, with the result that Russia came out of the war with the party membership nearly doubled. New members were often taken in more because of their contribution to the war effort than for their knowledge of and dedication to Marxism-Leninism. In 1977 party membership totaled nearly 16 million, including candidates for membership. Most of the candidates are among the 35 million members of the *Komsomol* (Communist youth organization). In a total population of some 260 million, the Communist party is still a relatively small and select organization, comprising about 9 percent of the adult population. In absolute numbers, of course, 16 million constitutes a sizable organizational force.

In the light of Marxian theory, one might expect to find the Communist party the party of the proletariat. Soviet industrial workers, however, while constituting an important core of the party membership, are by no means in a majority. In fact, they account for approximately 40 percent of the total. The rural areas account for something less than a fourth of the total, although Soviet statistics in this area are exceedingly meager.[4] The remainder is made up from the "toiling intelligentsia," or the bureaucracy, which, together with the workers, enables the party to retain its predominantly urban character.

The really important development in party membership is to be found in the shift in emphasis from the workers to the technical and administrative intelligentsia. Party membership among the workers and among farmers has been in relative decline, while among the growing class of technicians, factory managers, engineers, and party and government bureaucrats, party membership has been on the increase. This has had the effect of raising the intellectual level of the party membership. It has also resulted in the wielding of an increasing influence by the new Soviet administrative and intellectual elite, with a corresponding decline in the influence of the workers and the farmers. It is interesting in this connection that Khrushchev in 1961 observed that in time there would be no need to divide party members into workers, farmers, and white-collar workers.

At least two things need to be noted about social composition. First, a person's social background is based on the category listed at the time of an individual's recruitment into the party. Thus, party head Brezhnev is listed as a worker. Moreover, in recent years junior office workers were transferred to the category of workers. Secondly, workers and peasants are represented only nominally in positions of real political influence.

For a long time rank and file representation in the party of various

---

[4] Soviet authorities have admitted that as late as 1958 some collective farms had no party units, while on others they were small and weak.

nationalities favored the Slavs, especially the Great Russians. This was especially true in Stalin's time. In recent years, however, there has been a considerable redressing of the balance, with the avowed aim of bringing the percentage of party membership among the non-Russian nationalities up to that of the Russian Socialist Soviet Federal Republic (RSFSR). While this goal has in a large measure been realized, the Great Russians still seem to enjoy a disproportionate representation in the party's top leadership groups.

From time to time party ranks are purged of "undesirables."[5] The Russian Communists have looked upon the purge as a rational and desirable way of keeping the ranks pure by cleaning out the undesirable elements. This is in conformity with the Leninist notion that the party should be a monolithic organism. The need for the purge presupposes that the rigid process for admission to the party is not foolproof, that some persons will get in who should have been excluded. At the 24th Party Congress in 1971, Brezhnev announced that party membership cards would be recalled and new cards issued on the basis of meritorious behavior and performance. This exchange of party cards began in March 1973, and represented a mild purge of undesirables from the party ranks, resulting in the expulsion of some 347,000.

In the struggles for power within the party, however, the concept of the purge was broadened to include mass expulsions and a large-scale liquidation of party leaders at all levels.[6] Purges to this end could hardly be defended as merely a cleaning out of persons of doubtful dedication to Marxism-Leninism, for some of Lenin's most devoted followers perished in the purges.

Where the penalty is mere expulsion, on the other hand, many members deliberately become undesirable, for being thrown out is by and large the only way out of the party. Once a person becomes a party member he dares not give thought to leaving the party on his own volition. To leave, or to suggest leaving, is tantamount to treason. Yet some persons have found it difficult to continue living a lie—that is, to pretend to believe the party's propaganda. The way out for some of these people is expulsion, which can sometimes be induced by failure to pay dues, attend meetings, or perform assigned tasks. Excessive consumption of alcohol may also produce undesirables, and hence candidates for expulsion.

Ostensibly, the Communist party is organized on the basis of the prin-

---

[5] For an excellent work on the purge as a technique of Soviet totalitarianism, see Zbigniew K. Brzezinski, *The Permanent Purge: Politics in Soviet Totalitarianism* (Cambridge, Mass.: Harvard University Press, 1956).

[6] The struggle for power within the party is discussed in a subsequent section of this chapter. Milovan Djilas says that Stalin's tyranny "devoured . . . some seven hundred thousand Communist party members. . . ." See *The Unperfect Society: Beyond the New Class* (New York: Harcourt, Brace & World, Inc., 1969), pp. 150–51.

ciple of democratic centralism. This means, as Soviet spokesmen have explained it, that the party is a pyramidal organization. At the bottom are some 370,000 primary units, once called cells. Above these are several layers of intermediate bodies; each layer has fewer units until the top is reached, where there is one supreme party organization. This setup is allegedly democratic because, in theory at least, members of the lower units in the pyramid elect persons to the unit above, and these, in turn, are responsible to those who elected them. The centralist aspect is to be found in that it is incumbent upon the lower layers to obey the directives and to carry out the orders of the units above them.

In Soviet practice, however, the accent has been on centralism. First of all, the elective principle has been largely meaningless, for so often members have been co-opted—that is, named by someone above, a practice admitted by the Russians, although in the form of a criticism. Secondly, the leaders at the very top, so long as they stick together, are in no danger of being ousted, and they in turn can virtually dictate the selection of those immediately below. These, in turn, because they have the confidence of the top leaders, can dictate the selection of those below them, and so on down the line. The one possible exception involves local party secretaries, some of whom have been ousted after the introduction of the practice of voting for each member of the local committee individually and by secret ballot. Secretaries of city and district committees must be approved by committees of higher units, which sometimes means that approval from top leaders is necessary. Finally, the practice of ruthlessly punishing dissenters has discouraged members from questioning the adequacy of individuals whom they have "elected."

Moreover, party rules protect members of the executive bodies at all levels from disciplinary action by the respective primary organization to which they belong. Punishment can be inflicted only if a two-thirds majority of the executive body concerned, meeting in plenary session, gives its consent. In this way the leaders run no risk, if indeed one ever existed, of being embarrassed by a "defeat in their own precinct."

Democratic centralism, as theoretically conceived, operated only at the beginning—while the Bolshevik party was in the process of organization. Even then the leaders were in large measure self-appointed, reaching the top through ability and the force of their personalities. Once the top group was fairly well established, the members of that group, and not those below, determined who should join them in positions of leadership. From that time on, democracy gave way to centralism and to authority.

The party congress, according to party rules, is the "supreme organ" of the party. In practice it is anything but that. Prior to 1971 it was supposed to meet at least once every four years. In fact, between 1939 and 1952 no congresses were held. Since 1952 there have been six congresses: 1956, 1959, 1961, 1966, 1971, and 1976. At the 1971 congress the rules were changed to require a meeting every five years to coincide with the introduction of new five-year plans.

Aside from the infrequency of their meetings, which, in any event, last but a few days, congresses are handicapped by their sheer size; recent ones have had several thousand delegates. Moreover, their proceedings give every outward indication of being carefully prepared in advance, with no dissenting debate and all decisions being taken unanimously. Party congresses are, in reality, huge manifestations or rallies of the party faithful who merely sit, perhaps also listen to, and applaud the party leaders. Conversely, the congresses provide a platform for the leaders to extol their alleged accomplishments, to call for renewed efforts on behalf of old or new goals, and to proclaim changes in the party line.

Far more important than the party congress is the Central Committee, ostensibly elected by the congress and meeting at least once every six months. Its membership has been characterized by large turnovers from one congress to another. The greatest turnovers occurred in the 1930s, after the great purges, but more recent changes have been quite extensive. At the 20th Party Congress in 1956, for example, 133 members were elected, over a third of them for the first time, while of the 112 candidate members over half were chosen for the first time. At the 22d Party Congress in 1961, the membership of the Central Committee was increased to 175 members and 155 candidate members. Among these the holdovers constituted approximately 37 percent. These large turnovers have not resulted from actions freely taken by the respective congresses, for no one is elected to the Central Committee unless his name is proposed by the top leadership of the party. In 1966 the Central Committee was increased to 195 members and 165 candidates. In 1971 it was increased to 241 members and 155 candidates, and in 1976 it was 287 members and 139 candidates.

The Central Committee is charged with directing the work of the party between congresses, and its powers, at least on paper, are extensive. Aside from its authority to manage party resources, appoint editors, and set up various party institutions, the Central Committee "directs the work of central government bodies and social organizations of working people through the party groups in them." While basic directives are issued in the name of the Central Committee, in actuality these functions are performed by and under the direction of the Politburo (or policy bureau) and the Secretariat (discussed below). While the Central Committee was relatively important in the 1920s, it rarely met during the latter years of Stalin's rule and, according to one-time party secretary Khrushchev, it was never called into session during World War II.[7] In more recent years, the Central Committee has held fairly regular sessions. For example, it

[7] *New York Times,* June 5, 1956.

met 16 times in the five years between the 23d and 24th party congresses. There is no evidence, however, to suggest that it has seriously impeded the proposals or programs of the recognized leader or leaders. Because many of its members are prominent in the governmental bureaucracy, in science and technology, in the military, and in the cultural field, the Central Committee serves as a link between the party elite represented in the Politburo and the Secretariat and the important scientific-technical-administrative apparatus that supervises the operation of the Soviet system.

For most, if not all, of the Soviet period, the most powerful party body has been the Politburo (between 1952 and 1966 known as the Presidium), which has generally numbered about a dozen men. In 1952 it was merged with the Orgburo (organizational bureau), making it a body of 25 members and 11 candidates. After Stalin's death in 1953, its membership was cut to its former size. In recent years its size has fluctuated between 10 to 15 members and six to nine candidates. In 1976 it numbered 15 full members and six candidates. As the group that is supposed to direct the work of the Central Committee between its plenary meetings, the Politburo is the supreme policy-making body in all spheres of Soviet life. Although elected by the Central Committee, Politburo members are chosen only upon recommendation by the Politburo—a recommendation that in the past originated with the recognized leader.

The Secretariat is a type of management board of the party apparatus. In recent years it has consisted of 5 to 12 secretaries (several of whom are also members of the Politburo) who are chosen by the Central Committee in much the same way as the members of the Politburo. With a staff of approximately 100,000 full-time party professionals, the Secretariat is charged with directing the current work of the party. This means that it selects personnel for positions of responsibility in various parts of the Soviet system, and that it verifies fulfillment of party decisions in all fields—political, economic, social, propaganda, and so on. In this way, the Secretariat not only serves to implement policies but is at the same time the eyes and ears of the Politburo.

In the Politburo and in the Secretariat there is a broad division of labor. These general areas of responsibility include foreign affairs, heavy industry, agriculture, party affairs, agitation and propaganda, political administration of the armed forces, and other spheres of activity with which the party is concerned.[8] Because of their intimate association with the party, state, military, and police apparatus, the members of the Secretariat are now thought to be in a position to exercise a decisive influence in the

---

[8] See Figure 29–1. For an excellent discussion of the various reorganizations of the Secretariat, see Merle Fainsod, *How Russia Is Ruled,* rev. ed. (Cambridge, Mass.: Harvard University Press, 1963), pp. 190–208.

Politburo on all matters of high policy.[9] But in the end the Politburo decides.

Although party rules have emphasized the principle of collective leadership, the general tendency in the Soviet system has been toward one-man rule. This was true in Lenin's day, but much more so after Stalin consolidated his power in the late 1920s. It was Stalin's position as general secretary of the party and his determination to use that position to the utmost that enabled him to rise to a position of unquestioned ascendancy. Nikita Khrushchev, although never using the title of general secretary (merely first secretary), was able to rise to one-man leadership in a brief span of time. His successor, Leonid Brezhnev, also assumed the title of first secretary, but the party Congress in 1966 restored the title general secretary.[10] The political significance of this change has been far from clear.

One other organ of the Central Committee, the Control Committee, deserves mention. Its task is to check on members to see that party discipline is observed, that its rules and its program are loyally adhered to, and, in case of violations, to punish the guilty. In addition, it passes on appeals from disciplinary actions of the central committees of the republics.

It is important to note that most of the men who have reached the top of the party hierarchy in recent years have spent most of their lives in administrative and organizational work. Most of the men in the Secretariat and in the Politburo have had long careers in the party apparatus. Aleksei Kosygin, an economic administrator who was named Chairman of the Council of Ministers in October 1964, is the only exception. Some of the men at the top have been consistently identified with a single area of competence, while others have had responsibilities in a number of fields. Most of them were graduated from institutions of higher learning, and a majority have only narrow, highly specialized technical training.

In the 1976 Central Committee the situation is not too different. Almost half (45 percent) of its full membership is made up of men whose primary background is work in the party apparatus. The next largest group (26 percent) represents men who have devoted most of their adult years to the state bureaucracy. The third largest group has primarily a military background. In view of these facts, it is perhaps not surprising to find that approximately 85 percent of Central Committee members whose careers have centered in the state bureaucracy have had a technical-scientific education, while 78 percent of members whose careers have been primar-

---

[9] Abdurakhman Avtorkhanov, "The General Implications," *Bulletin: Institute for the Study of the USSR* 11 (December 1964): p. 15. Also see Leonard Schapiro, *The Communist Party of the Soviet Union* (New York: Random House, Inc., 1960), pp. 563, 580.

[10] For a discussion of one-man rule versus collective leadership, see the subsequent sections of this chapter.

ily in the party apparatus have had such specialized training. Some 9 percent have had no higher education, while the remainder have had military or general educational training.

Some observers have suggested that younger party members are unhappy about the power exercised by the older generation. The group that controls the majority part of the party's apparatus in Moscow, for example, tends (on the average) to be about 60 years of age, with an average of 40 years of tenure in the party. In 1977 the average age of Politburo members was 67. Both government and party leaders in the provinces average from 50 to 55 years of age. These facts are particularly telling when we note that about one half of the 16 million party members are only now approaching 40, with an average tenure of ten years in the party. This younger group has few if any representatives in the higher organs of party power.

The party governing bodies at the national level, as the above suggests, are by all odds the most important. Each republic, except the largest, the RSFSR, has governing bodies that correspond to those on the national level. In almost every instance the names of the institutions are the same: congress, central committee, and so forth. Below the national level, however, the executive of party committees is called a bureau instead of a politburo. Party organizations below the national level are subservient to the national organization of the party, where all the important decisions are made as well as many of lesser significance.

The party organizations of the various subdivisions of the RSFSR report directly to the governing bodies of the national party. The desire of certain leaders in the RSFSR to establish a separate organization for their republic led to the celebrated Leningrad case, following World War II. The result was the purge and liquidation of a number of party leaders, including one Politburo member. In 1956 the 20th Party Congress established a special Bureau of RSFSR Affairs in the Central Committee, but this was abolished in 1966.

The first duty of party organizations in the republics is to see to it that the decrees and instructions emanating from the Central Committee in Moscow are carried out. The Central Committee seeks to ensure that this will be done (1) by specifying in great detail the duties of party organizations at all levels, and (2) by providing extensive controls in the party apparatus from top to bottom.

The bureaucratic apparatus of the party is vast, although the exact number of individuals engaged in full-time paid party work remains a secret. Various estimates have run from 100,000 to 500,000, with the first figure probably being more accurate as of this writing.[11] After 1956 there was a conscious effort to reduce the number of full-time party

---

[11] See Schapiro, *The Communist Party of the Soviet Union,* pp. 572–73.

functionaries, and Brezhnev announced at the 24th Party Congress in 1971 that the party apparatus had decreased by over 20 percent during the preceding 14 years. However, there are indications that most of the cutbacks occurred during the Khrushchev era and that the apparatus actually had increased by 10 to 20 percent during Brezhnev's tenure as top party leader. In addition, the number of part-time unpaid party workers has increased considerably.

The initial core of *apparatchiki* (men of the apparatus) emerged from the Bolshevik pre-tsarist conspiratorial underground organization. Stalin's rise to supreme power can in large part be attributed to his close association with this group. In the early years of the Soviet regime, his chief party work was in the Orgburo, which constituted his first base of operations. From that position, he built, shaped, and controlled the party's bureaucratic apparatus. It was in connection with this work that in 1922 he was named to the post of general secretary, a position that has come to be regarded as that of unchallenged supreme authority in the party.[12]

The party's bureaucratic machine serves to make the authority of the dictatorship effective. As the long arm of the dictatorship, operating under the respective sections of the party Secretariat, it handles the detailed work of the party. It transmits directives and orders, supervises local party organizations, checks on fulfillment of tasks, assigns personnel, calls party secretaries to render an accounting of their work, and reports its observations to the appropriate party leaders in Moscow. Figure 29–1 depicts a partial organization of the Secretariat of the Central Committee into various departments. It must be noted, however, that changes in the organization of the Secretariat have been made periodically and these have not always been publicized. Because of this fact, no scheme such as the one above can be up to date.[13]

In November 1962, the Central Committee approved a proposal by the party's first secretary, Khrushchev, to reorganize the party structure into two hierarchies, one to be concerned with agriculture and the other with industry. The resulting hierarchies of party committees would be coordinated for the first time at the republic level, where only one central committee and only one politburo existed. The avowed reason for this reorganization was to make more effective the party's control function—that is, in seeing to it that the policies and programs of the top leadership were carried out. This scheme did not produce the desired results and was probably a major reason for Khrushchev's ouster. In any case, his successors declared it a failure and abandoned it, going back to the territorial principle of organization.

---

[12] For an excellent summary of the growth of the party apparatus, see Fainsod, *How Russia Is Ruled,* chap. 6.

[13] For a detailed depiction, see Abdurakhaman Avtorkhanov, *The Communist Party Apparatus* (New York: Meridian Books, 1968), pp. 201–6.

FIGURE 29–1

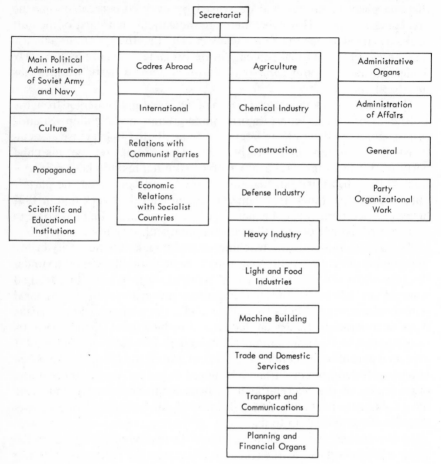

THE STRUGGLE FOR POWER WITHIN THE PARTY

In the writings of Marx, Lenin, and other Marxian theorists, there is the presumption that unity of purpose would characterize the dictatorship of the proletariat. The Russian experience has demonstrated, however, that irreconcilable differences arose. This should not have been too surprising in view of the ideological splintering that has prevailed during the past century in the whole socialist movement, including its Russian component. Uncompromising from the outset, the leaders of the Bolshevik faction, once in power, were determined not to tolerate factions inside the party. To this end, they embarked upon a course of cleansing the party, which in turn led to the physical liquidation of party dissidents, high and low. In the end, the purge was transformed into mass terror under Stalin; the unity of the dictatorship of the proletariat became the unity of the graveyard. Under Khrushchev and his successors the purge was continued, but it has been largely bloodless.

Lenin remained the unquestioned leader of the young Communist regime until his death in 1924, but he laid the psychological basis for purging party ranks, which was to become the decisive instrument in the struggle for power within the party. His utter rejection of compromise and his equating of disobedience in party ranks with treason left room in the party only for those who unquestioningly accepted the party's course as it was defined by the leader. During Lenin's lifetime, however, the purge of party ranks meant no more than expulsion from the party.[14] More frequently, discipline took the form of transferring the person to work in more remote regions of the country. But the groundwork for more severe measures was laid in his lifetime.

In the initial years of Lenin's rule, some party members believed that a certain amount of opposition within the party was possible. In 1920 a group calling itself Democratic Centralists appeared at the Ninth Congress of the party and, among other things, accused the Leninist Central Committee of being a "small handful of party oligarchs" who were exiling comrades because of their "deviant views." Simultaneously, party rank and file unrest developed into the so-called Workers' Opposition, which demanded that industry be controlled and managed by the trade unions.[15]

Lenin's answer to the Democratic Centralists and the Workers' Opposition, his one-time supporters who were turning against the regime, was to get the Tenth Party Congress (1921) to declare these and similar groups dissolved and to prohibit the formation of groups which were critical of the general line of the Central Committee. Moreover, he insisted on a proviso, kept secret for a time, which in effect forbade agitation against the party line even by leading members of the party. Although Lenin on occasion employed threats which clearly implied physical violence, he did not punish dissenters with anything more severe than expulsion from the party. But his suppression of all opposition within the party inevitably led to resolving struggles for power by force and violence.

In his position as general secretary of the party, Stalin had laid the basis for consolidation of power in his hands. This consolidation proceeded slowly. For a time, while Lenin lay dying and for two or three years thereafter, power seemed to be shared by a triumvirate in the Politburo,

---

[14] The outbreak at Kronstadt in March 1921 among the Red Navy sailors, one-time supporters of the Bolshevik revolution who demanded, among other things, civil liberties and the end of the party dictatorship, was nevertheless crushed with armed force. This cannot, however, be viewed as a party purge.

[15] For an excellent summary of party opposition under Lenin, see Fainsod, *How Russia Is Ruled*, pp. 141–48.

composed of Stalin, Lev Kamenev, and Gregory Zinoviev, who had banded together to keep Trotsky from succeeding Lenin. In response to Trotsky's open criticism of the state of things, Stalin's two cohorts demanded firm action (including arrest) against Trotsky, while Stalin appeared to be moderate and restrained. Gradually, Trotsky was removed from one position and then another until he had no power left.

In the meantime, differences between Stalin and his two cohorts had been developing. But Stalin had been preparing for a showdown. As general secretary, he was building a faithful machine of party workers who would increasingly control delegations to party congresses. Secondly, he was forging a coalition in the Politburo against Kamenev and Zinoviev, which included Nikolai Bukharin, Aleksei Rykov, and Mikhail Tomsky. Step by step, Stalin was able to isolate Kamenev and Zinoviev to such an extent that they abjectly confessed their errors and promised to abide by party discipline. But they were expelled from their positions and from the party, although they were later readmitted.

Once the so-called leftist deviationists (Kamenev et al.) were subdued, Stalin borrowed their program (collectivization of agriculture and intensive industrialization) and introduced it as Soviet policy. The so-called rightists (Bukharin, et al.) became restive. Stalin alleged that he had discovered a plot of the right-wing group to consolidate forces with the remnants of the leftist faction. Under Stalin's attack, Burkharin, Tomsky, and Rykov capitulated; they confessed their sins and asked to be permitted to do battle against all deviations from the general line of the party. But they were soon removed from the important positions they had held.

At the beginning of 1934 Stalin could boast of complete victory. "The anti-Leninist Trotskyite group has been defeated and scattered. . . . The anti-Leninist group of the right deviationists has been defeated and scattered . . . the national deviationist groups have been defeated and scattered . . . the party today is united as it has never been before."[16] Thus, in his struggle for absolute power, Stalin narrowed the margin of permissible dissent for the opposition until it disappeared.[17]

Throughout the period when he was consolidating his power, Stalin and his henchmen repeatedly declared that the need of purging party ranks increased after the proletariat had gained power. Power, they said, tended to attract opportunists, many of whom were able to conceal their real motives. Moreover, the bourgeoisie had not accepted defeat and was instead resorting to all sorts of vicious means in an effort to undermine the Soviet system. The opportunists in the party became convenient and ready tools of the class enemy. Therefore, said the Stalinists, the party had to be vigilant against the wrecking activities of these elements.

---

[16] Stalin, *Problems of Leninism*, pp. 515–16.

[17] For a more detailed discussion of Stalin's consolidation of power, see Fainsod, *How Russia Is Ruled*, pp. 148–60. Also see Brzezinski, *The Permanent Purge*, especially chaps. 3 and 4.

The road of repression moved from expulsion to arrest and imprisonment in the late 1920s and early 1930s. By the mid-1930s it had led to the extermination of the old Bolsheviks and to mass terror. A most revealing document concerning the Great Purge of the 1930s is the speech of the one-time party secretary, Nikita S. Khrushchev, to a closed session of the Twentieth Party Congress in February, 1956.[18] Although questions remain, Khrushchev's speech provided many previously unknown details of a purge whose main features have long been known.

The Great Purge ostensibly had its origin in the assassination in December 1934 of the Leningrad party secretary, Sergei M. Kirov, by a fellow Communist. The circumstances surrounding his assassination remain vague, or, to use Khrushchev's words, "inexplicable and mysterious." Khrushchev clearly asserts that there are grounds for believing that the killer was aided by people inside the secret police, and he asserts that the leaders of the secret police in Leningrad, after being given light sentences for their negligence, were shot in 1937 "in order to cover the traces of the organizers of Kirov's killing." This would seem clearly to implicate Stalin.

In any case, "the next four years claimed victims in the hundreds of thousands."[19] Trotsky had been exiled, but Kamenev, Zinoviev, Bukharin, Rykov, and countless of their alleged followers paid the supreme penalty. The blood bath also engulfed other important party figures and many more lesser ones. Tomsky committed suicide, as did a number of lesser figures. Many who escaped liquidation were sent to camps in Siberia, from which few returned. Expulsions from the party were on a mass scale. One fifth of the total membership was expelled; in the Ukraine one out of four was turned out.

The Great Purge also devoured many officers of the Red Army. Among those who perished was the chief of staff, Marshal Tukhachevsky. A number of generals and many lesser officers shared his fate.

Scarcely a segment of Soviet society remained unscathed. Many of those who perished, both inside and outside party ranks, were innocent, even by Stalin's admission. But since the infallible Stalin could not be responsible, the liquidation of innocent people was attributed to "enemies of the people," who had infiltrated party and police ranks. In any event, a momentary halt to the purge was called, while many of the purgers were purged. In the meantime, Stalin continued to liquidate those who became suspect, but at a somewhat slower pace and with less attendant publicity.

Originally, the purge was associated with the difficulty of coordinating

---

[18] For a purported text, see *New York Times,* June 5, 1956. Also see text published by the *New Leader* under the title, *The Crimes of the Stalin Era,* and annotated by Boris I. Nicolaevsky. Also see Bertram D. Wolfe, *Khrushchev and Stalin's Ghost* (New York: Frederick A. Praeger, Inc., 1957), and Roy A. Medvedev, *Let History Judge: The Origins and Consequences of Stalinism* (New York: Alfred A. Knopf, Inc., 1971).

[19] Fainsod, *How Russia Is Ruled,* p. 150.

Communists in the making of policy. Lenin's answer was the authoritarian formula, which under Stalin developed into an unbridled liquidation of all opposition or competition in matters of policy determination within the party. Simultaneously, the party purge provided an opportunity for the regime to sweep away all opposition, party and nonparty, real and imagined.

In the absence of institutional or other limitations on the dictatorship, the purge gained momentum. As it progressed it created the impression of a huge and continuing conspiracy against the regime, suggesting the need of extending the purge. This intensified already existing tensions and uncertainties. Fear bred fear. Had not a temporary halt been called, the purge might very well have consumed the system.

After a brief lull, during which many of the purgers lost their lives, the purge was resumed. Perhaps what we have come to refer to as "the purges" should be characterized as the violent eruptions of a purging process that is in continuous operation. Professor Brzezinski, in his cogently written book, concludes that the purge has become a permanent institution.[20] In his opinion, it serves to release or absorb tensions, conflicts, and struggles for power within the system. It facilitates the circulation of elites in a monolithic system where competition and free choice do not prevail. Moreover, it provides a way of maintaining revolutionary fervor by periodically weeding out corrupt and careerist elements.

Nikita Khrushchev's ascendancy to supreme power in the years after Stalin's death (1953), as well as his ouster in 1964, may have opened a new chapter in the struggle for power within the Communist party. Khrushchev's rise to a position of unquestioned leadership was somewhat reminiscent of Stalin's.[21] Within a month of the former dictator's death, he was the senior secretary of the party and not long thereafter was made first secretary. Almost simultaneously came the execution of Lavrenti Beria, Stalin's head of the secret police, and a number of his associates. Using his position as first secretary, Khrushchev asserted his leadership by assuming the role of the party's spokesman in the Central Committee and by becoming head of the government. At the same time, he sought to disassociate himself from the evils of the Stalin regime, primarily through his denunciation of the former dictator's misdeeds in a speech (discussed below) to a closed session of the party congress in February 1956. Moreover, he moved to discredit his principal rivals, Stalin's and his

---

[20] Brzezinski, *The Permanent Purge,* see especially pp. 168–75. Other and different views of the purges are to be found in such works as Isaac Deutscher, *Russia in Transition and Other Essays* (New York: Coward-McCann, Inc., 1957); George Fischer, *Soviet Opposition to Stalin: A Case Study in World War II* (Cambridge, Mass.: Harvard University Press, 1952); and Robert Conquest, *The Great Terror: Stalin's Purge of the Thirties* (New York: Macmillan Co., 1968).

[21] For a detailed discussion of Khrushchev's struggle for power, see Fainsod, *How Russia Is Ruled,* pp. 161–75.

one-time associates in the Politburo. He was challenged briefly in 1957, but succeeded in outmaneuvering his foes and removing them from the party Presidium (Politburo) and the Central Committee. The "collective leadership" was dissolved.

By the end of 1958 Khrushchev's leadership was beyond challenge. While condemning Stalin's personality cult and extolling collective leadership, he had built a personality cult of his own. He had achieved primacy without much bloodshed, it is true, and to a degree persuasion replaced preventive terror. Following the 21st Party Congress in January 1959, however, Khrushchev launched a widespread purge of the party and governmental apparatus. He set the stage for the new purge by telling the congress that changes in the party hierarchy were necessary in order to make better use of young party members, to free old members from excessive burdens, and to replace those officials "who have remained behind the times."

In October 1964 Khrushchev was replaced by some of the same men whom he had placed in positions of responsibility. The change resembled a palace revolution. An established Communist dictator was toppled for the first time as a result of a high level plot on the part of his associates. Perhaps one of the consequences of the Khrushchev era may be that struggles for power at the top levels can take place without the danger of participants' losing their heads. And it may be that the ouster of Khrushchev signified the replacement of a personal autocracy by a bureaucratic oligarchy, even though such a development would be contrary to past Soviet history. If that should be the case, however, the problem of extending intraparty democracy will still remain. But predictions are hazardous.

The overthrow of Khrushchev did not seem to be based on fundamental disagreements concerning the party's domestic and foreign policies. Rather, the disagreements seemed to involve the methods by which these policies were executed, as well as Khrushchev's general style of leadership. At the same time, Khrushchev became a convenient scapegoat for the political and economic failures of the system.

Leonid Brezhnev seems to have moved to the position of "first among equals" a little more slowly than Khrushchev before him. This may have only seemed that way because Aleksei Kosygin continued in the position of Chairman of the Council of Ministers. Brezhnev became General Secretary of the party in 1966 and his power and influence have been constantly on the ascendant, despite periods of apparent ill health in recent years. The celebration of his 70th birthday in December 1976 and his elevation in June 1977 to the presidency (Chairman of the Presidium) of the Soviet Union gave ample proof of his primacy in the Soviet system.

Because of Brezhnev's age and his apparent ill health, there has been more than the usual amount of speculation concerning his successor. Of the sixteen Politburo members all but three were born prior to 1917. It is conceivable that should Brezhnev leave the scene anytime soon, he might be replaced, at least temporarily, by one of his senior colleagues. The three "youngsters" are Fedor D. Kulakov, Vladimir V. Shcherbitsky, and Grigori V. Romanov. The first two were born in February 1918, and Romanov was born in February 1923. Should one of these succeed Brezhnev, the odds would seem to favor Kulakov or Romanov, mainly because they are Russian, while Shcherbitsky is Ukrainian.

THE DOWNGRADING OF STALIN AND ITS MEANING

After the death of Stalin in March 1953, his successors set about downgrading their former hero. Their efforts were by and large imperceptible until December 1953, when they liquidated Lavrenti Beria, for many years head of the secret police under Stalin. The first direct and extended criticism of Stalin was presented by Khrushchev at a closed meeting of the 20th Party Congress in February 1956. Although the Soviets did not publish it, a purported text was released by the United States.[22] In this speech, Khrushchev paid Stalin a tribute for his role in the Bolshevik Revolution and civil war and for his fight to build a socialist society in the U.S.S.R. But most of the speech was devoted to a criticism of his shortcomings and the grave consequences which ensued from them.

The principal criticism of Stalin, in the Khrushchev speech, centered on the so-called cult-of-personality charge. Stalin had become a personal dictator. Unlike Lenin, he did not tolerate collegiality in leadership or in the work of the party and government. He ignored his colleagues in the Central Committee and even those in the Politburo. Often he did not even bother to inform them of important decisions he had made. The cult of one-man rule, said Khrushchev, was contrary to the Leninist principle of collective leadership.

Moreover, the development of the cult of personality, according to Khrushchev, was promoted by Stalin himself, for he took an active part in the campaign of praise. Unlike Lenin, he was not a modest man. By taking credit for the achievements of the collective, Stalin arrogated to himself the attributes of an infallible superman. Stalin's vanity resulted in the establishment of many "monuments to the living" in the form of huge statues, busts, portraits, Stalin prizes, and so on. All of this, said Khrushchev, was foreign to Marxism- Leninism.

More serious than the un-Leninist nature of the cult of personality were its dire consequences. It was the "source of a whole series of exceedingly

---

[22] See *New York Times*, June 5, 1956.

serious and grave perversions of party principles, of party democracy, of revolutionary legality.'' Whoever opposed Stalin's concept of leadership or attempted to argue against it met with moral and physical annihilation. The result of Stalin's arbitrariness was the killing of countless thousands of innocent party comrades.

In describing the fabrications against his party comrades who perished, Khrushchev dealt in the main with the principal personalities—those who had achieved high positions.[23] In addition to citing individual cases by name, he reported that ''of the 139 members and candidates of the party's Central Committee who were elected at the 17th Party Congress, 98, or 70 percent, were arrested and shot.'' And more than a majority of the nearly 2,000 delegates to that Congress were arrested.

Stalin originated the concept ''enemy of the people,'' which ''made possible the usage of the most cruel repression . . . against anyone who in any way disagreed with Stalin, against those who were only suspect of hostile intent. . . .'' Many of those who in 1937–38 were branded ''as 'enemies' were actually never enemies, spies, wreckers, and so on, but were always honest Communists.'' Many were shot without trial, but trials were not too significant anyway, for convictions were made on the basis of confessions, which ''were gained with the help of cruel and inhuman tortures.''

Arbitrary behavior by one person, said Khrushchev, encouraged and permitted arbitrariness in others.

Khrushchev, however, did not criticize Stalin's struggle against dissident factions within the party. On the contrary, he praised his fight against the left deviationists (Trotsky, Kamenev, Zinoviev) and against Bukharin and other representatives of the right. Even Lenin had criticized the actions of Kamenev and Zinoviev, but, said Khrushchev, there was no suggestion on Lenin's part that they should be arrested and certainly no thought of shooting them.

The second major criticism in Khrushchev's speech, although he did not dwell on it, was aimed at Stalin's theory of the class struggle during the period of the dictatorship of the proletariat. The terror of the middle and late 1930s was defended by Stalin as a necessary retaliation against the class enemy. The use of extreme measures against the class enemy is perfectly justifiable and right, said Khrushchev. But, he added, this repression came after socialism was fundamentally constructed and the exploiting classes generally liquidated. It came at a time when ''there were no serious reasons for the use of extraordinary mass terror.'' And in any case, he added, this terror was not directed at the defeated exploiting classes, ''but against the honest workers of the party and of the Soviet state.''

---

[23] At one point, he made reference to over 7,000 persons who, upon investigation after Stalin's death, were posthumously rehabilitated. Also, see Footnote 6, above.

The third major criticism was directed at Stalin's role in World War II. In the postwar years, he was pictured as a "military genius" who was singlehandedly responsible for the success of the Soviet armed forces. This, according to Khrushchev, was far from the truth. Initially, he said, Stalin was not alert to the many warnings from foreign and Soviet sources that Germany would attack the Soviet Union. The failure to heed these warnings and to prepare for the attack had disastrous military consequences for the Soviet armed forces. Moreover, the earlier liquidations of the cream of the army's officer corps had left the Soviet Union in a weakened position. Secondly, the military reverses in the early part of the war immobilized Stalin. He ceased to lead. He was convinced that all was lost, that everything Lenin had built was lost in a brief period of time. Only when other Soviet leaders told him what must be done did he resume leadership.

When he did resume command of the war effort, however, he often hampered it. He interfered with field commanders, to the detriment of the army. Even urgent pleas from the front by Khrushchev and others for orders that would save the situation were ignored. He even refused to come to the telephone to talk to Khrushchev, who was desperately calling from the front. The net result was huge losses to the Soviet army.

In addition, Khrushchev criticized Stalin's wartime policy of deporting and exiling minority populations (such as the Volga Germans) who were near the front. This resettling was indiscriminate. Even Communist party members and their leaders among these nationalities were deported and exiled with the rest.

The successors of Stalin, by their criticism of a man theretofore depicted as infallible, set in motion forces which were difficult to control. Their criticism of Stalin reverberated around the world, and within a brief period of time produced crises at home and abroad.[24] The most immediate impact of the criticism of Stalin was the ideological crises in Communist parties in the non-Communist countries. French, Italian, American, and other Communists suddenly discovered that their hero had feet of clay, and worse. For years they had been engaged in perpetrating a hoax. And this on the authority of Moscow itself! This was not easy to take, for it was perhaps the rudest shock experienced by the foreign apologists of the Soviet Union. Some left their respective parties. Some asked where Khrushchev and his colleagues had been when all the evil deeds were being done. Others fell in with the new party line without outward questioning. Fellow travelers, although not all, fell by the wayside in great numbers. But the crisis was not to end there.

The way had been prepared for the ideological crisis in the world

---

[24] This analysis is in part based on A. Avtorkhanov, "Current Soviet Political Problems," *Bulletin: Institute for the Study of the U.S.S.R.* 4 (January 1957), pp. 3–14.

Communist movement by Khrushchev's revision of Lenin in his opening address to the party congress. By declaring that there were various roads to socialism (that is, by declaring that force and violence was not necessarily the only means, that war is not inevitable, and so forth), he appeared to be revising Stalin, but in effect he was revising Lenin also. This was far too flexible an interpretation for many comrades in the various Communist parties, and some openly declared that such flexibility would deprive them of the very thing that distinguished them from other workers' parties. The theoretical revision of Lenin and the personal condemnation of Stalin were bound to keep the world Communist movement in a certain amount of ideological turmoil.

The crisis in Communist ranks was not confined to party comrades in the non-Communist world. The beginning of a series of political crises in Eastern Europe followed quickly on the heels of Khrushchev's declaration about "different roads to socialism" and his revelations of the abuses under Stalin's rule. The restiveness of the satellite countries exploded in the autumn of 1956 into a full-blown revolt in Hungary, together with more peaceful changes in Poland. In both instances the revolt was against domestic Stalinists and, by implication at least, against Russia's Stalinist methods in dealing with the satellites. The Hungarian revolution soon assumed a general anti-Communist character. It was phenomenally successful until crushed by Soviet troops which were sent into Hungary for that purpose. Open Soviet intervention in Eastern Europe came again with the invasion of Czechoslovakia in August 1968, because of an avowed desire of the Czechoslovak regime to follow the path of a more humane Communism.

The events in Hungary served to make more acute the psychological crisis which had been developing inside the Soviet Union in the wake of Khrushchev's revelations about Stalin. The Soviet rulers took note of unrest among their own students and workers some time before the blowups in Poland and Hungary. After the Hungarian revolt had occurred, Soviet citizens were warned in the party press about their criticism of the party and the government, while "hiding behind the slogan of the struggle against the cult of the individual." University students were seemingly most vocal, and Khrushchev was moved to tell the dissatisfied: "If you do not like our methods, then go to work and others will come to study in your place."[25]

In assessing the Khrushchev denunciation of the cult of Stalin, Avtorkhanov notes three main contradictions in it. The first is practical: Stalin's methods were declared to have been illegal and not in the best interests of the party, and yet it would have been impossible to maintain the Communist system without them. The second is theoretical: Stalin's theory of

---

[25] *Pravda,* November 10, 1956.

the class struggle during the period of the dictatorship of the proletariat was denounced; yet, these theories were indispensable in justifying Communist practice. The third contradiction is moral: Stalin's treachery, suspiciousness, and hypocrisy were depicted as personal traits, whereas these qualities are an essential feature of the Communist system. It should be noted, however, that some scholars accept the first two points but not the third.

The various crises which followed in the wake of the criticism of Stalin could not but put a strain on the collective leadership. Suggestions to this effect were met with evasive denials until July 1957, when it was revealed that such old Bolsheviks as Molotov, Kaganovich, and Malenkov, as well as other members of the top leadership, had been removed from their posts because of their deviationism—that is, their attempt to oppose party policies as conceived by Khrushchev and his collaborators. Attacks upon this "antiparty group" have been repeated several times. At the 21st Party Congress, the names of several other former party leaders were added to the antiparty roster, along with a demand for an explanation of their parts in the plot. At the 22d Party Congress in October 1961, Khrushchev, as well as his collaborators, returned to the attack, with further revelations concerning the crimes of the Stalin era. This time he portrayed the members of the "antiparty group" as accomplices of Stalin. It remains to be seen if one day his name may also be associated with those crimes.

Apparently disturbed by the erosion of discipline caused by de-Stalinization, Brezhnev and Kosygin have allowed a partial rehabilitation of Stalin. Thus, while allowing some criticism of certain aspects of Stalinism, including the Stalinist aspects of Khrushchev's leadership, they have intensified repressive measures against writers and intellectuals who present a severely negative portrayal of Stalin. And several pieces have been published which present at least some aspects of his rule in a positive light. It would be hazardous to guess how far this "rehabilitation" will go.

Younger party members, better educated than their elders, display some evidence of a critical stance. Their right to question and to criticize is very much on the agenda. They are more inclined to ask for explanations than to accept commands. The response of the leadership has been to appeal for unity, while at the same time hinting that those who express criticism from "unprincipled" positions (that is, disagreeing with the official party line) might have to be purged from party ranks.[26]

---

[26] Speech by General Secretary Brezhnev, *Pravda*, March 30, 1968.

BIBLIOGRAPHICAL NOTE

The best work on the Communist party is Leonard Schapiro, *The Communist Party of the Soviet Union* (New York: Random House, Inc., 1960). Insight into the role of the Communist party in the Soviet system may also be gained from: Merle Fainsod, *How Russia Is Ruled,* rev. ed. (Cambridge, Mass.: Harvard University Press, 1963); Barrington Moore, *Soviet Politics: The Dilemma of Power: The Role of Ideas in Social Change* (Cambridge, Mass.: Harvard University Press, 1950); and Adam B. Ulam, *The New Face of Soviet Totalitarianism* (Cambridge, Mass.: Harvard University Press, 1963).

More recent and interesting studies include: Abdurakhman Avtorkhanov, *The Communist Party Apparatus* (New York: World Publishing Co., 1966), and Michel Tatu, *Power in the Kremlin: From Khrushchev to Kosygin* (New York: The Viking Press, 1970). Much valuable information may be gleaned from the two volumes of *Khrushchev Remembers* (Boston: Little, Brown and Co., 1970 and 1974), as well as from Roy A. Medvedev, *Let History Judge: The Origins and Consequences of Stalinism* (New York: Vantage Books, 1971).

30

Policy-Making Structures: Governmental Institutions

Since the Party is the decision-making body in the Soviet system, government is mostly a matter of administration. Governmental forms, as well as the whole fabric of organizational and institutional life in the Soviet Union, constitute the administrative apparatus for implementing party policies and party aims. An appreciation of this basic fact is indispensable to an understanding of the Soviet system. All else is secondary. Soviet governmental forms, as well as the theories that ostensibly govern their functions and powers, must ever be viewed as subordinate to the party hierarchy.

DUALISM OF PARTY AND GOVERNMENT

Formally, the party and government structures are separate and independent.[1] Organizationally, they are similar, except at the lowest level. They are in the nature of twin pyramids or dual hierarchies. The governmental hierarchy parallels that of the party (described in Chapter 29) in that the Supreme Soviet of the U.S.S.R. corresponds to the party congress, the Presidium of the Supreme Soviet resembles the party Central Committee, and the Council of Ministers is similar to the party Politburo. A governmental hierarchy corresponding to that of the central government exists in each one of the union republics. At the lowest level, gov-

---

[1] The governmental and party changes announced immediately after Stalin's death in March 1953 were, however, allegedly decided upon at a *joint* meeting of the party's Central Committee, the Council of Ministers of the U.S.S.R., and the Presidium of the Supreme Soviet of the U.S.S.R.

ernmental powers are vested in a soviet of working peoples' deputies, whose executive and administrative organ is the executive committee.

In theory, authority is wielded by the constitutionally established governmental bodies. In practice, however, party predominance is guaranteed by the existence of the party pyramid, which parallels the governmental structure at every level, and by the knowledge of all those in the governmental hierarchy that their basic task is to carry out party policy. Party and nonparty individuals in government offices are aware of and consult with party officials at their respective levels of authority. No governmental decision of any consequence is made except upon order or approval from competent party officials.

FIGURE 30–1
Intersecting Pyramids of Party and Government Organization

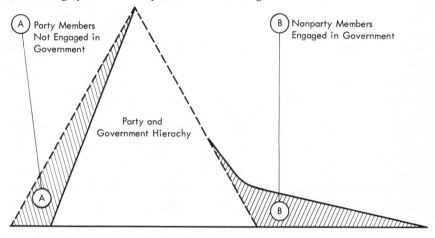

As implied above, party predominance is also guaranteed by an interlocking directorate of party members who simultaneously hold governmental and party posts. Party members who occupy governmental positions but do not serve as party officials are nontheless aware that they are primarily engaged in performing tasks pursuant to party decisions. Nonparty governmental employees are for the most part to be found in lesser jobs, but they, too, realize that the governmental structure is but an appendage of the party.

The Soviet constitution of 1977, to be discussed below, even more than its predecessor (the so-called Stalin constitution of 1936) openly recognizes the predominant position of the party. The preamble speaks of the party as the "vanguard of the whole people," and Article 6 says that it "is the *leading and guiding force of Soviet society and the nucleus of its political system, of all state and public organizations.*"[2]

BUILDING A GOVERNMENTAL STRUCTURE

When the Bolsheviks seized power they had little idea of how to organize the dictatorship of the proletariat. There was no ready-made Marxian blueprint for a governmental organization in a workers' state. Lenin, to be sure, had gone a long way toward developing the idea of the dictatorship of the proletariat, but he had not gone beyond generalities. Consequently, Bolshevik efforts to fashion a governmental structure were largely a matter of trial and error.

The soviets (councils) of workers' and soldiers' deputies which arose in 1917[3] were to become the pattern for the Bolshevik organization of the state. Initially the Bolsheviks had frowned upon participating in the soviets, for the soviets appeared to be cooperating with the provisional government. The soviets, in any case, were under the firm control of the non-Bolshevik revolutionary parties, a fact not calculated to induce Bolshevik cooperation. Before long, as noted in Chapter 27, the Bolsheviks saw in the soviets the one potential instrument for the seizure of power. After having served this purpose, the soviets became the organizational pattern for the Bolshevik state, and governing bodies at national, local, and intermediate levels became known as soviets.

The soviets under the Communist regime differ markedly from their earlier prototypes. Initially they were loosely organized democratic bodies. Members of several different revolutionary parties engaged in free and vigorous debate. Decisions were reached by majority vote. There was no attempt to suppress minority opinion. Once the Bolsheviks had taken over, however, they were determined to make of the soviets monolithic organizations. The more moderate revolutionary groups soon withdrew, for they were not anxious merely to serve Bolshevik ends. By the summer of 1918, all non-Bolshevik representatives had withdrawn or been expelled, leaving the Bolsheviks in complete control.

The Bolshevik approach to a constitution is entirely different from that to which we have been accustomed. Constitutionalism in the West has been identified with limited government. Initially, it constituted a way of curbing and regulating the powers of kings and other monarchs. Once this was done, the next step was to deny certain powers to the new democratic governments, in accordance with the consent of the governed, and to provide procedural safeguards in the exercise of those limited powers

---

[2] Italics added.

[3] These were patterned on the short-lived Petrograd Soviet of 1905.

which were granted to popular governmental authorities. This view of constitutionalism is foreign to the Soviet leaders, for their constitution neither imposes limitations upon government nor provides for meaningful procedural safeguards against the abuse of authority.

If the Soviet constitution does not serve the purposes normally associated with constitutions in the West, why, it may be asked, did the Russians bother with a constitution at all? There would seem to be at least two main reasons. First, a constitution makes the governmental-administrative structure explicit, providing for a smoother operation of the bureaucracy. Second, a fundamental law that stressed the rights of workers and peasants and proclaimed their participation in the government would serve Communist propaganda objectives at home and abroad.

In the early months of the Bolshevik regime there was no constitution. When they had seized power, the Bolshevik leaders went to the Second All-Russian Congress of Soviets, which was then in session, with a resolution decreeing a temporary government, bearing the name "Council of Peoples' Commissars." The resolution was adopted, including the naming of Bolsheviks to all leading posts in the government. This government was to last until the convocation of the Constituent Assembly, which had been promised by the provisional government. The Bolsheviks set the election for November 25, 1917, but, as noted earlier, the outcome was not favorable to the Bolsheviks. Nevertheless, they permitted the Constituent Assembly to convene in January 1918, but when they realized that it was not susceptible to manipulation by them, they disbanded it by force after it had been in session only one day.

A Bolshevik-framed declaration, setting forth the basic principles for the organization of the new state, which the Constituent Assembly refused to adopt, served as the basic law of the Russian state until the formal adoption of a constitution in July 1918.[4] The constitution, adopted by the Fifth All-Russian Congress of Soviets, provided a governmental structure for the Russian Socialist Federal Soviet Republic (RSFSR), by far the largest of the present 15 soviet republics. For the most part, this constitution ratified the evolving structure of soviets, setting forth specific provisions concerning the composition and powers of soviets and their central executive committees, the organization of the Council of People's Commissars, the powers of the central and local governments, and electoral rights. The revolutionary functions of the constitution were said to embrace the establishment of a dictatorship of the urban and rural proletariat (including the poorest peasantry), the establishment of socialism, and the suppression of the bourgeoisie and exploitation.

By 1921, under Bolshevik guidance, socialist soviet republics had been

---

[4] This declaration, in effect, became the preamble of the constitution. For texts of the declaration and the constitution, see James H. Meisel and Edward S. Kozera, *Materials for the Study of the Soviet System* (Ann Arbor, Mich., 1950), pp. 57 and 79.

set up in Belorussia, the Ukraine, and Transcaucasia, which had entered into a treaty relationship with RSFSR. In 1922 a Union of Soviet Socialist Republics was created, and in 1923 the constitution was revised to reflect this change.[5] The new constitution, formally ratified by the Congress of Soviets in January 1924, followed closely the RSFSR model of 1918. All powers of any significance were vested in the central government, leaving the union republics exceedingly little authority.

By 1936 the number of soviet republics had grown to 11.[6] In addition, a drastic social and economic transformation had taken place in the years 1929–35. A new constitution was needed, said Stalin, in order to bring the fundamental law into conformity with those changes. Allegedly, classes had been abolished and society transformed. Therefore, it was possible to introduce universal suffrage, direct and secret elections, and to eliminate inequality between workers and peasants. But, said Stalin, the new constitution "preserves unchanged the present leading position of the Communist party," which provided "democracy for the working people, that is, democracy for all."[7]

The widespread discussion throughout the Soviet Union of the draft of the 1936 constitution, and particularly the publicity surrounding this discussion which the Soviet leaders purveyed abroad, suggests that foreign (as well as domestic) propaganda may have been the dominant motive behind the new constitution. Soviet leaders, anxious to find allies among the capitalist democracies against the Nazi, fascist, and Japanese threat, were eager to demonstrate that the 1936 constitution was proof of an evolving democratic system which enjoyed the support of the Soviet peoples. Therefore there existed a common bond between the capitalist democracies and the Soviet Union in the face of the fascist threat.

In the post-Stalin period a new constitution was promised for several years. First, Khrushchev announced the appointment of a large committee to draft the new constitution. After his downfall in 1964 little was heard of the project until Brezhnev made known that he had reconstituted the committee. There were some expectations that it would be ready for consideration at the party Congress in 1971, but at that time Brezhnev announced only that a new constitution was in preparation. Those expecting a new constitution were again disappointed when at the party Congress in 1976 Brezhnev simply reported that work was continuing on it. Finally, in June 1977 a draft of the new constitution was published, with the aim of having the formal adoption coincide with the 60th anniversary of Soviet power in November 1977.

The 1977 constitution differs little from the 1936 one. The preamble

---

[5] For text, see Meisel and Kozera, *Materials for the Study of the Soviet System*, p. 152 ff.

[6] The Uzbek, Turkmen, Kazak, Kirgiz, and Tadjik republics were added, while Transcaucasia was divided into three republics—Georgia, Armenia, and Azerbaijan.

[7] "On the New Constitution" in *Problems of Leninism,* pp. 578–79.

declares that Soviet Union is no longer a dictatorship of the proletariat but a "state of the whole people," a formulation first put forth by Khrushchev. Second, the new constitution makes the exercise of basic rights much more dependent upon the fulfillment of duties. Third, the organization and operation of the economy is spelled out more fully. Fourth, the formal executive is augmented with the creation of a vice presidency. Finally, there is a chapter (new) on foreign policy.

GOVERNMENTAL STRUCTURE: FEDERALISM AND ELECTIONS

The governmental forms through which the party dictatorship is exercised resemble those to be found in a democracy, at least superficially. There is great emphasis on "popularly elected" legislative assemblies (soviets), which choose their respective executives and to which these executives are supposedly responsible. Moreover, the Soviet Union claims to be a federal state, with a distribution of governmental powers between the central government and the 15 republics. These governmental forms, upon closer examination, will stand revealed as a type of democratic facade behind which the party dictatorship functions. At the same time, something of the party's tactics in the operation of that dictatorship will be brought into sharper focus.

Ostensibly, the U.S.S.R. is a federal state, formed on the basis of voluntary association of equal republics. Any impartial study of the Soviet system will reveal, however, that this is not the case. A governmental system cannot be called federal unless (1) the distribution of powers between the central government and its component subdivisions provides the subdivisions with some real substance of power, and (2) the central government is prevented from altering this distribution of powers through its actions alone. The Soviet system meets neither of these two tests, either in theory or in practice.

Moreover, the 1977 constitution seems to strengthen the central government further. Article 3, for example, says: "The Soviet state shall be organized and shall function in accordance with the principle of democratic centralism. . . ." (see previous chapter for discussion of this principle). In addition, this constitution, as the one before it, grants powers to the central government which are so all-embracing as to leave the republics with no real substance of power. Finally, as in the past, the power to amend the constitution is vested in the central government alone; the republics are not required to ratify amendments.

Yet ironically enough, the constitution asserts that each of the union republics has "the right freely to secede from the U.S.S.R." Moreover, it provides that each union republic has the right to enter into diplomatic relations with other countries. These are not the attributes of a federal state but of a confederation.

In practice, however, the Soviet Union is neither a federation nor a confederation. The republics have neither the powers usually associated with component units of a federation nor can they exercise the powers normally enjoyed by members of a confederation. None of the republics has been permitted to establish diplomatic relations with foreign countries. A British proposal in 1947 to exchange diplomatic representatives with the Ukraine was rejected. Additional Moscow disrespect for the "rights" of union republics was demonstrated when in 1956 the Karelo-Finnish Republic was abolished without any seeming effort to obtain its approval, although the constitution asserted that the boundaries of a union republic may not be altered without its consent. Again, it cannot too often be emphasized that the U.S.S.R. is a highly centralized dictatorship where authority is wielded by the leaders of the Communist Party, a unitary organization. Moreover, it is a sound generalization that a one-party dictatorship is a poor place to look for federalism, to say nothing of a confederate arrangement.

The Soviet nationality policy is the basis for Moscow's claim to federalism. This policy, ostensibly one of autonomy, was based on the need to weld together the diverse fragments of the Russian empire which had fallen apart with the Revolution and which the Red Army was bringing into the fold. Lenin had sought to harness minority discontent to the aims of the Revolution; hence a departure from tsarist policy was imperative. The departure was in the direction of autonomy and it was an improvisation.

From the outset, however, it was evident that there would be no national autonomy in the realm of political power or in the matter of social or economic organization of society, although for some years that followed many continued to hope. In May 1918, Stalin, who was made chairman for nationalities when the Bolshevik government was established, stated that Soviet authorities were "for autonomy, but only for an autonomy where all power rests in the hands of the workers and peasants." In 1925 he depicted Soviet nationality policy goals as being "proletarian in content and national in form." During World War II, however, even the basic right of autonomous existence was violated when several nationalities were uprooted from the Caucasus because of alleged disloyalty.[8]

Similarly, it was made clear from the outset that the "right freely to secede" was meaningless. In 1920, Stalin reaffirmed the right, but at that stage of the revolution, he said, a demand for secession would be regarded as counterrevolutionary. Moreover, the history of Soviet nationality policy is replete with purges of party and nonparty "nationalists" in the

---

[8] In 1957 it was announced that five of the nationalities would be rehabilitated, and in 1965 it was announced that the Volga Germans had not really been disloyal.

Ukraine, Belorussia, Armenia, and several of the other non-Russian republics. Under Stalin, deliberate systematic efforts were made to eradicate "local chauvinism." Many of those who were purged were charged with harboring a desire to detach their respective republics from the Soviet Union, although the constitution presumably gave them this right.

What remained of the national autonomy, therefore, was largely linguistic and cultural. Soviet leaders, in their propaganda, made much of their policy of encouraging minority nationalities to advance themselves culturally through the use of their native language and through the development of their native cultural heritage. But the basic aim of the party leadership in Moscow was not cultural advancement for its own sake. Rather, they saw in the native language, educational system, and culture the means through which the party could more effectively sovietize the minority peoples. This takes on added significance when one remembers that these means could not be utilized by any other group to pursue a different or contrary aim.

It is also of interest to note that after 1948 the Jews were not recognized as a minority, although an autonomous region (Birobidjan) was set aside by Stalin for Jewish colonization. Ironically enough, however, they are a minority even in Birobidjan. In the early years of the Soviet regime many of the leading Communists were Jews, but Stalin purged most of them. In the last years of his life it was practically subversive to speak or write in Yiddish. Jewish schools, newspapers, and periodicals were closed down. Even Jewish prayer books were unobtainable. Articles in the official press were clearly derogatory.

Throughout the Khrushchev era and since, there has seemed to be an increasing harassment of Jews. More than a few anti-Semitic books and articles have been published, although some were critically reviewed in the Soviet press. Moreover, articles in the press emphasized that Jews were involved in a large share of the economic crimes committed by Soviet citizens. In addition, Soviet newspapers reported that a number of Jews were arrested on espionage charges, allegedly having given state secrets to Israeli diplomats. In August 1972 emigration taxes were imposed on Jews wishing to emigrate from the U.S.S.R., requiring them to reimburse the state for the cost of their education before they could obtain an exit visa. As United States-Soviet relations seemed to improve after 1973, these taxes seemed to have been quietly dropped, although the desire of Jews to emigrate continues to create all sorts of unpleasant difficulties (for example, loss of job, questioning by the police, difficulties for relatives, and so forth).

According to the constitution, all members of the various legislative bodies (the soviets) are elected "on the basis of universal, equal, and direct suffrage by secret ballot." If one goes beyond this formal proviso, however, any initial impressions of popular democracy are quickly dispelled. First of all, when the Russian voters go to cast their ballots they find only one list of candidates; there is only one candidate for each office to be filled. There are no alternative candidates to vote for, although by invalidating the ballot the voters can in effect cast a vote against the official list.[9] In practice even this demonstration of opposition has become difficult, simply because Soviet election officials do not require voters to enter the voting booth before casting their ballots, and hence they destroy the secrecy of the ballot. To vote for the list one need not mark the ballot, but one must do so if he or she is to invalidate it. Faced with the spectacle of certain voters' openly demonstrating their loyalty to the regime, other voters, who may or may not be inclined to invalidate their ballots, are discouraged from entering the voting booth before casting their ballots. Moreover, many voters believe, rightly or wrongly, that the voting booth itself does not ensure secrecy, since the officials have ways of detecting those who invalidate their ballots. In view of these considerations, the reports that official lists receive more than 99 percent of the votes cast can better be understood.

Secondly, popular democracy is lacking in the nominating process. Soviet propagandists have defended the single list of candidates on the ground that these are chosen after long and thorough discussions, which allegedly characterize the nominating process. The right to nominate candidates is accorded to Communist party organizations, trade unions, cooperatives, youth organizations, and cultural societies. Since the Communist party is the sole guiding force in all of these associations, there is no possibility of a person's being nominated if he or she is in any way repugnant to the party. Prior to an election, meetings of voters are held to discuss the various nominees. It is here that the party's view of who should be the candidate is made amply clear. No one will take a position against the party, although it does not follow that the nominee will be a party member. Often the party finds it expedient, particularly in local soviets, to have nonparty candidates. These are nontheless persons whom the party can trust.[10]

Finally, if need be, the Communists can control the results of elections, for they count the ballots. Who is to question the accuracy of the count? There are no challengers, no demands for a recount, no critical press, or political opposition to reveal irregularities. Even if 99 percent of the voters did not cast their ballots for the official list, as reported, the election officials could make it so.

That the party should be in complete control of the nominating and electoral process is perfectly consistent with the Communist view that in

---

[9]According to the Soviet electoral law, an election is not valid unless the list receives at least 50 percent of all the votes cast.

[10] In the Supreme Soviet of the U.S.S.R., the percentage of Communist party members and candidates approaches 72 percent, while in local soviets it falls below 50 percent.

their system only one program can exist. If no alternative to Communism is to be tolerated, why permit the nomination or election of persons who may oppose Communism? But then, the question may be asked: Why have elections at all? Why are they necessary; what purposes do they serve? Why is there such a determined effort to get all eligible voters to the polls?

An analysis of the Soviet system suggests that, from the Communist point of view, the elections serve several purposes. They provide a plausible façade by means of which the regime can claim popular support, especially in its propaganda abroad. Moreover, they constitute a technique by which the regime hopes to instill in the broad masses a sense of involvement in Communist undertakings. For those who do not cherish such an experience, their participation in Communist elections serves to create a climate of futility, moral despair, and hopelessness. No one who hates Communism can go through the symbolic approval of what he or she hates without a sense of personal degradation, of having destroyed one's own personal integrity. In addition, Communist leaders find elections soul-satisfying, especially when they register such overwhelming majorities. The lesser Communists, on the other hand, are afforded an opportunity by the elections to show their importance and to experience a feeling of power. The efforts of thousands, if not millions, of party workers are required during a national election campaign. Finally, elections provide an excellent peg on which to hang domestic propaganda messages. Periodically they furnish the regime with a convenient opportunity to praise itself, to explain away shortcomings, and to exhort the people to make new sacrifices.

Soviet leaders have admitted the propaganda function of their elections. One of them wrote openly: "The Soviet election system is a mighty instrument for further educating and organizing the masses politically, for further strengthening the bond between the state mechanism and the masses. . . ."[11] Similar statements are to be found in the Soviet press and in party pronouncements, especially in the days preceding an election.

GOVERNMENTAL STRUCTURE: LEGISLATIVE AND EXECUTIVE

The Supreme Soviet of the U.S.S.R. is a bicameral[12] body, consisting of a Soviet of Union and a Soviet of Nationalities. The Soviet of Union is chosen directly by the people in electoral areas on the basis of one deputy per 300,000 inhabitants. The Soviet of Nationalities is designed to repre-

---

[11] Andrei Y. Vyshinsky, *The Law of the Soviet State* (New York: Macmillan, 1948), p. 722.

[12] Soviets of the republics and other subdivisions of the U.S.S.R. are unicameral.

sent nationalities, with deputies distributed as follows: 32 to each union republic, 11 to each autonomous republic, 5 to each autonomous region, and 1 to each national area. They are also directly elected. Each chamber has about 750 members. Both chambers are elected for five-year terms and are said to have equal powers.

The Supreme Soviet, according to the constitution, is the highest organ of state authority; it is the exclusive wielder of the legislative power of the central government. Despite these constitutional declarations the Supreme Soviet cannot qualify as a parliamentary body as that term is generally understood. This conclusion would be valid on the basis of any objective analysis of the Supreme Soviet's activities, even if one did not take into account the predominant role the Communist party plays in the Soviet system.

First of all, the Supreme Soviet is supposed to meet twice yearly. An examination of the record in several post–World War II years reveals that it met only once yearly in the years 1947–52, inclusive. More important, however, is the fact that each annual session averaged no more than five days. Could anyone seriously suggest that the Supreme Soviet, with a membership exceeding 1,500, would be capable of legislating in the vast areas of authority which the constitution theoretically grants it by sitting five or ten days a year?

Moreover, a cursory examination of its activities during these brief sessions indicates that the Supreme Soviet engages in little deliberation or debate, to say nothing of dissent. The rank-and-file members play a simple role. They sit quietly while government and party leaders deliver a series of speeches, they applaud at the appropriate moments, and they cast unanimous votes for all government proposals. Unrehearsed and free debates are out of the question. The members are well rewarded, however. They receive a monthly salary approaching that of a skilled worker (this is in addition to what they receive in their regular jobs), plus free annual passes on all railway and water transport facilities. During the sessions of the Supreme Soviet they receive a liberal per diem.

From the Communist point of view, this is perhaps as it should be. The Supreme Soviet, a large and unwieldy body, is the governmental counterpart of the party's congress. In both cases, these large gatherings serve essentially similar purposes. Their function is not to debate and discuss but to applaud and assent. In a 20-year period (1937–58), for example, the ministers enacted, through decrees and resolutions, some 390,000 pieces of "legislation," while the Supreme Soviet and its Presidium (discussed below) were passing some 7,000 laws, resolutions, and decrees. Moreover, many of the acts of the Supreme Soviet merely confirmed decisions already promulgated by its Presidium.

The Soviet Union may be said to have a dual executive, although a comparison with other countries in this respect would be misleading.

There is the Presidium of the Supreme Soviet, a collegial executive body elected by the Supreme Soviet, which is a permanent nucleus of the Supreme Soviet. It consists of a president (formally, chairman) a first vice president, a secretary, 15 vice presidents (one for each of the union republics) and 21 members. It has become customary to elect the presidents of the presidia of the union republics to fill the vice presidential posts. Several top party leaders are always members. The president or chairman of the Presidium performs many of the functions of a formal executive in a parliamentary state. He receives credentials and letters of recall of diplomatic representatives, awards decorations, confers titles of honor, ratifies treaties, convenes sessions of the Supreme Soviet, exercises the right of pardon, and appoints and recalls diplomatic representatives. Decisions concerning these matters are made by the Presidium collectively, understandably on the initiative of the party.

At the same time, the Presidium is said to have powers which would make it correspond to a legislative body. In the interval between sessions of the Supreme Soviet, it performs many of the powers of the parent body. It has the power to issue decrees, to declare war, to order general or partial mobilization, to annul those decisions of the Council of Ministers of the U.S.S.R. and of the union republics which do not conform to law, to appoint and remove the higher commands of the armed forces, to proclaim martial law, and to appoint and remove ministers. The last is subject to confirmation by the Supreme Soviet. The Presidium also has the power to interpret the laws of the U.S.S.R. and to conduct nationwide polls (referenda) on its own initiative or on the demand of one of the union republics.

The Supreme Soviet also chooses the Council of Ministers, which is composed of the heads of the usual departments plus those ministries responsible for various parts of the economy.[13] The number of economic ministries was quite large at one time but was considerably reduced in 1957, when the Communist leadership decided to decentralize the actual implementation of party economic goals. Formally, the Council of Ministers is selected by the Supreme Soviet, but the real ministerial assignments are made by the party leaders. As might be expected, the Council of Ministers is engaged not so much in policy discussions as in the means of implementing policies already arrived at. Even the constitution refers to it as an "executive and administrative organ."

The Council of Ministers also has a "presidium," or a type of cabinet, consisting of the chairman of the Council of Ministers, his or her deputies, and personal appointees of the Council, in 1977 totaling 14. This body was not mentioned in the 1936 constitution, although even prior to 1953 there

---

[13] For a good account of the evolution of the Council of Ministers, see Julian Towster, *Political Power in the U.S.S.R., 1917–1947* (New York: Oxford University Press, 1948), pp. 272–76.

had been a "presidium" of the Council of Ministers and even a "bureau of the presidium," but without having been identified publicly. They were no doubt made necessary by the unwieldness of the Council of Ministers, which by 1952 had exceeded 60. Although drastically reduced in the reforms of 1953 and 1957, it grew rapidly in the 1960s. As of 1977 there were 62 ministries and 19 state committees, whose chairmen have ministerial rank. These, plus the 15 chairmen of the councils of ministers of the union republics, who are ex officio members, and the 14 members of the presidium of the Council (allowing for four persons counted twice) make for a grand total of 106 who are entitled to sit as the Council of Ministers. The 1977 constitution, however, leaves the determination of ministries to future sessions of the Supreme Soviet.

The administrative powers of the ministers are vast and far-reaching. One can appreciate how far-reaching they are only if one bears in mind that in addition to the normal bureaucratic apparatus of a large industrial nation there is added a bureaucracy to direct and administer the whole economy of the country. In such circumstances it is inevitable that the Council of Ministers be the source of much rule making as well as legislative proposals. Apparently, the decentralization projected in 1957 was at least in part based on the sheer inability of the ministries in Moscow to direct and supervise this huge bureaucracy in minute detail.[14]

There are two types of ministries represented in the Council of Ministers—all-union and union-republic. All-union ministries are ministries of the central government which operate directly through their own bureaucracy down to the lowest level. Union-republic ministries, on the other hand, are said to function indirectly through corresponding ministries in the republics. Often in the past, however, they have exercised direct control over certain enterprises. Moreover, the union-republic ministries have occasionally controlled and directed the work of purely republic ministries, which are supposed to be the sole concern of the individual republics.

Although ministers are technically responsible to the Supreme Soviet and, in between its sessions, to the Presidium of the Supreme Soviet, they are in reality responsible solely to the top party leaders. Most of these leaders are, of course, members of the party Politburo, and many of them are also members of the Council of Ministers. There is no such thing as collective responsibility of the cabinet, nor are there any resignations of ministries as a whole. There are no motions of censure, no political attacks on the ministry in the legislature, and no votes of confidence. As long as individual ministers can satisfy the top party leadership, they have no reason to fear incurring the wrath of anyone else.

---

[14] For a discussion of the administration and the bureaucracy, see Chapter 31.

GOVERNMENTAL STRUCTURE: JUDICIARY AND CIVIL RIGHTS

The judicial system in a dictatorship cannot be looked to as an instrument for limiting the arbitrary acts of the wielders of dictatorial power. More than that, Soviet courts have often been told publicly that it is their duty to act as faithful servants of the dictatorship. The provision in the constitution that the judges are independent and subject only to the law has been interpreted publicly to exclude any thought of political independence on the part of judges. On the contrary, it has been pointed out that the key phase is "subject only to the law," and this means Communist law. Moreover, it should be noted that in the Stalinist period the secret police were not responsible to the courts or subject to the law, even Communist law. Reforms instituted in the Khrushchev era were allegedly designed to establish "socialist legality," but Soviet leaders were quick to point out that this did not mean they were concerned with the rights of individuals. To them "socialist legality" means strict observance of the law by government agencies and by individuals alike. This does not imply, however, that the regime is bound by the law as defined and enforced by the courts, for in the final analysis Soviet courts are the servants of the party dictatorship.

As a general rule, laws and the means employed to enforce them are but a reflection of the ideas and principles which characterize any given political system. In this respect, Soviet laws and Soviet courts hold true to form. The Marxist-Leninist doctrine, upon which the Soviet system is founded, insists that law is not based on some abstract concept of justice. Rather, all law reflects the will of the dominant class. Accordingly, Soviet leaders have made it amply clear that their law and their courts are the instruments of the dictatorship of the proletariat, designed to strengthen and to defend the conquests of the Bolshevik Revolution as these are interpreted by the top party leadership. Therefore, the primary objective of Soviet laws and Soviet courts is to preserve the Bolshevik regime and its achievements and to aid and protect those who faithfully seek to carry out its programs. Conversely, the Soviet judicial system is to strike down all those who constitute a barrier to these ends.

In view of these basic concepts and in the light of the party's extensive program in all fields of human endeavor, the need for a centralized, uniform, and disciplined judicial system becomes strikingly evident. That system must be studied and judged in this context, for to condemn it solely on the basis of the results and thereby leave the impression that it conceivably could come near our own standards of justice while remaining an integral part of the dictatorship would be misleading and meaningless. Soviet law and the Soviet judiciary cannot be studied apart from the political system they serve and whose instruments they are.

The provisions in the Soviet constitution concerning the rights and duties of Soviet citizens are completely in harmony with basic Soviet ideas about law and justice. Contrary to the belief of many persons, who apparently have not bothered to read the constitution of the U.S.S.R., Soviet citizens *are not* guaranteed the basic rights of free speech, press, and association in the way that these are secured for the citizens of democratic countries. Article 50 of the constitution defines these rights so narrowly as to make them meaningless in any true sense. Their guarantee is prefaced by the following clause: "In conformity with the interests of the working people, and in order to strengthen the socialist system. . . ." This is the identical formulation found in the 1936 constitution. Hence, these rights could not, even in theory, be said to guarantee a person the right to advocate anything except the socialist system. And the party is the all-wise judge of what that system is and what will or will not strengthen it.

Similarly, Article 51 states: "In conformity with the aims of building communism, citizens of the U.S.S.R. are guaranteed the right to unite in public organizations. . . ." It cites examples, such as trade unions, cultural and scientific societies, youth organizations, and others. It would be difficult, therefore to defend, even in theory, a right to any type of organizational life except that which accords with the party's wishes and desires.[15]

Moreover, several articles in the 1977 constitution further limit the exercise of basic rights. Article 39 says: "The exercise by citizens of rights and freedoms must not injure the interests of society and the state. . . ." Article 59 says: "Exercise of rights and freedoms shall be inseparable from the performance by citizens of their duties." And Article 62 states: "The citizen of the USSR shall be obliged to safeguard the interests of the Soviet state, to contribute to the strengthening of its might and prestige." In addition, Article 66 specifies that parents have an obligation to prepare children "for socially useful labor," and "to raise worthy members of the socialist society."

Other articles speak of the right to rest and leisure, to education, to housing, medical care, and to maintenance in old age. They also refer to equality of women and the equality of the races. The freedom to worship or to engage in antireligious propaganda is recognized, but there is no recognition to a right to engage in propaganda in favor of religion. There is "the right to work," but there is not the right to stop working—that is, the right to strike. Moreover, the inviolability of homes and of the person is guaranteed, but the actions of Soviet authorities have frequently made a hollow mockery of this alleged guarantee.

---

[15] For a discussion of how the Soviet regime utilizes its concept of civil rights to harness the masses to the dictatorship, see Chapter 32.

The other declared duties of Soviet citizens include military service as an "honorable duty" and the defense of the U.S.S.R. as a "sacred duty." It is the duty of every citizen to abide by the constitution, to observe the laws, to maintain labor discipline, to safeguard and fortify public, socialist property as the sacred and inviolable foundation of the Soviet system.

Taken as a whole, therefore, the so-called Bill of Rights not only specifies the purposes for which certain "rights" are to be utilized but, in addition, asserts that the defense and furtherance of these purposes and aims are among the fundamental duties of Soviet citizens. What gain is there, many Soviet citizens might ask, in being given the right to speak, to write, to organize in order to defend a system they may not like? Or in being told that it is their duty to do so? Yet, in reality such is the Soviet Bill of Rights.

In the Soviet Union each republic has a court system, consisting of local and intermediate courts and a supreme court. In addition, there is the Supreme Court of the U.S.S.R., which is the highest court of the nation. Moreover, there are special tribunals, such as military courts. Some special tribunals have received little publicity, such as those in the concentration camps, and there may be others whose existence is known to only a limited number of people in the Soviet Union. On the other hand, the special transport courts, which had jurisdiction over crimes affecting railroads and waterways, were abolished in 1957.[16]

The basis of the Soviet judicial system is the people's court, established in each district and consisting of a popularly elected judge and two people's assessors, chosen at a general meeting of persons at their place of work, residence, or military unit. The judge, who is supposed to have legal training but often does not, is selected for a term of five years, while the assessors are chosen for two-year terms.[17] There are no juries. These courts exercise original jurisdiction in various kinds of civil cases and in minor criminal cases.

A variety of courts are to be found between the people's courts and the supreme courts of the republics. These are based on territories, areas, regions, autonomous regions, and autonomous republics. The judges of these courts, five in number, are elected for terms of five years by the soviets of the respective geographic units. All these courts have panels of people's assessors, but they are utilized only in cases of original jurisdiction, and not in appellate cases. All these courts may review cases originating in the people's courts, and they possess original jurisdiction in the more important civil and criminal cases.

The supreme court of each republic, consisting of five judges and a

---

[16] At the same time it was also announced that a "people's assessor," a representative of the public, would in the future sit on military courts.

[17] Assessors at upper levels in the judiciary are selected by the respective soviet which appoints the professional judges.

panel of assessors elected by the republic's supreme soviet for a term of five years, exercises both original and appellate jurisdiction. It has original jurisdiction in civil and criminal proceedings of major importance. It exercises a certain supervisory function over the courts below it and can set aside any of their verdicts. In 1957, the load of the supreme courts of the republics was increased when the Supreme Court of the Soviet Union was restricted largely to appellate functions.

The Supreme Court of the U.S.S.R. is elected by the Supreme Soviet for a term of five years. Presumably because it has been restricted mainly to appellate jurisdiction, its size was reduced in 1957. In 1970 it consisted of a chairman, 3 deputy chairmen, and 16 members, plus the 15 chairmen of the supreme courts of the union republics who serve ex-officio. In addition, there were 45 assessors, who served when the court was exercising original jurisdiction in civil and criminal cases of exceptional significance. The 1977 constitution does not specify the exact number of members. The court rarely sits as one body; in the performance of its actual work it is divided into several colleges.

In addition to its other functions, the Supreme Court of the U.S.S.R. is charged by the constitution with the supervision of the judicial activities of all the judicial organs of the U.S.S.R. and of the Union Republics. This power has been exercised to ensure a centralized, uniform, and disciplined judiciary. The restoration in 1970 of a national ministry of justice signified additional central control over the court system.

In the late 1950s and in the 1960s extrajudicial institutions of law enforcement were considerably augmented. These in the main consist of (1) comrades' courts, (2) voluntary citizens' militia, and (3) children's commissions. The first have been in existence for a long time, but their jurisdiction and powers have been extended in recent years. The latter two are of relatively recent creation. All of them seem to be based on the assumption that direct public action is more effective in the case of certain offenders than the regular courts are.[18]

Comrades' courts may be created in places of residence (apartment building, collective farm, and so forth) or in places of work (factory, office, and so forth). The members are elected by the respective collective for a period of one year. The size of the court is not specified, except that the members choose a chairman, vice-chairman, and a secretary from among their number. Comrades' courts concern themselves with violations of labor discipline, drunkenness and other improper social behavior, violations of apartment or dormitory regulations, petty theft, and similar offenses. Originally, they could impose reprimands and assess small fines. In 1965 they were empowered to impose fines up to approxi-

---

[18] For an excellent account of crime and its study in the Soviet Union, see Peter Juviler in Henry W. Morton and Rudolf L. Tökés, *Soviet Politics and Society in the 1970s* (New York: The Free Press, 1974), pp. 200–238.

mately $55 and to demand full repayment on damaged property. They may also decide to transfer a case to the regular courts. Decisions of comrades' courts may not ordinarily be reviewed by a court, although a trade union committee or the executive committee of the local soviet may suggest that the case be heard over again.

The voluntary citizens' militia, or public-order squads, came into being when the antiparasite laws were being passed. Initially, these public-order squads were designed to combat drunkenness, rowdyism, and other breaches of the peace by patrolling the streets, usually during the evening hours. They work under the guidance of party organizations as well as the police. A significant portion of their membership comes from the ranks of the Komsomol. There have been reports of many abuses of authority (beatings, invasions of privacy, and so forth) by the voluntary citizens' militia, but Soviet authorities insist that the streets have been made safer.

Children's commissions handle lesser crimes or infractions by juveniles. These most frequently involve thieving and group violence (fist fights, malicious mischief, joyriding), as well as drunkenness and running away from home. A majority of juvenile crimes are apparently committed while the perpetrators are intoxicated. As a preventive measure, the Soviets have experimented with imposing evening curfews.

In the late 1950s and in the 1960s the Soviets experimented with another form of extrajudicial law enforcement—the so-called antiparasite tribunals, which were not really courts but mass meetings of the local population. The antiparasite laws provided for the exiling to more remote regions of the country persons who evaded socially useful work or who lived on unearned income. Sentences could be up to five years, with forced labor at the place of exile and possible confiscation of property not acquired by labor. In 1970 a new version of the antiparasite law was enacted which dropped the reference to exile but tightened up on other penalties, including a mandatory one- or two-year prison sentence or corrective labor. In effect, the duty to work was laid down as a legal obligation which the state would enforce. While some of the antiparasite laws may still be on the books, their enforcement seems to have been taken out of the hands of ad hoc gatherings of neighbors.

The prosecutor-general is vested with supreme advisory power to insure the strict observance of the law by all ministries and institutions subordinated to them, as well as by officials and citizens of the U.S.S.R. generally (Article 163). Appointed by the Supreme Soviet for a period of five years, he or she in turn appoints the prosecutors-general of the republics, territories, regions, and autonomous regions, who serve for five years. Area, county, and city prosecutors are appointed for a like period by the prosecutors of the republics, subject to the approval of the prosecutor-general of the U.S.S.R.

The powers of the prosecutor-general in the enforcement of laws are vast. According to the constitution, all officials of his office are in no way subordinate to any local organs of authority. In discussing the judicial reforms in 1957, however, Soviet officials revealed that a "special council" of the Ministry of the Interior, which included the secret police, had existed and had given instructions to the courts. Ostensibly, the full powers of the prosecutor have been restored, and the court system has been divorced from the secret police.

Many Soviet judicial procedures have over the years come under considerable criticism in the democratic countries. Perhaps the most telling commentaries on these procedures, however, have been the admissions by Stalin's successors that many innocent persons were imprisoned or executed during the Stalin era. It is now alleged that some of the notorious judicial practices have been or are being abolished. It still remains to be seen, however, to what extent this will be done. In any case, it does not seem likely that Soviet judicial procedures will be modified to such an extent that they will meet democratic standards of justice.

One of the most repugnant of Communist judicial practices stems from the absence of habeas corpus. The result is long pretrial incarceration and investigation. This period may last for months or even years, during which the imprisoned person may not be told why he or she is being held. Friends and close relatives may have no idea where the person may be or why. The 1961 RSFSR Code of Criminal Procedure empowers the prosecution to hold a suspect up to nine months without filing charges. According to the announced judicial reforms of 1957, the right of counsel was to be accorded at some stage in the pretrial investigation, but the legal codes adopted in December 1958 limit this right to minors. Moreover, the persons conducting investigations are to be less subject to the orders of the prosecutor than heretofore. While these reforms, if actually put into practice, may result in an improved situation for some unfortunate persons, they do not go to the heart of the problem. The absence of habeas corpus, particularly in a society where the public cannot know who is being held or for what period of time, continues to perpetuate fear and uncertainty.

Another repulsive practice, perhaps made partially possible by the absence of habeas corpus, is the forced confession, the sole basis of countless convictions. Long pretrial imprisonment has given the police authorities ample time to torture and to wear down victims to a point where they will sign anything. This has made possible the fabrication of a case against the accused which was false from beginning to end. Stalin's successors have admitted this, although the more specific references were to party comrades who were liquidated and not to the ordinary citizens, who must have received even less consideration. Allegedly, proof of guilt will in the future require more than a confession. While this may be a modest gain, depending upon what weight courts continue to give to confessions, it does not do away with long pretrial imprisonment nor with the techniques for obtaining confessions. Nor does it forbid the use of such confessions in court.

The Soviet judicial system operates on the inquisitorial approach. In countries where democratic legislative bodies and a free press stand as guardians against the misuses of the judicial process, the inquisitorial approach has achieved high standards of justice. In the Soviet Union, however, it has made it possible for the judges to browbeat witnesses and to create an atmosphere of fear in the courtroom. The accused, who are obliged to take the stand and be grilled by the judge, often present a sorry spectacle. Even the so-called defense attorneys are often afraid to attempt a real defense, particularly in instances of the so-called crimes against the state. After the downgrading of Stalin, some Soviet jurists advocated the discarding of the presumption of guilt doctrine and the acceptance of the principle that a person is assumed to be innocent until proved guilty. While present statutes do not recognize this principle explicitly, they do state that the burden of proof rests on the prosecutor.[19]

In a somewhat similar situation are the ostensible guarantees to a public trial and to defense counsel. As in the past, the right to a public trial would not seem too meaningful, for the constitution permits legislation to deny it. Consequently, innumerable trials have been secret. It is possible, however, to overemphasize the value of public trials in the Soviet Union, for they have not been a barrier to miscarriages of justice. The right to defense counsel has in the past left much to be desired. By not being familiar with the case in the pretrial investigative period, defense attorneys have rarely had time to prepare a defense in the allotted time. Moreover, in certain types of cases neither the defense attorney's nor the defendant's presence was required for conviction. It still remains to be seen whether significant reforms are instituted in this area.

Also of concern to many students of the Soviet judicial system is the absence of any protection against double jeopardy. Acquittal does not prevent additional trials for the same alleged offense. Similarly, moderate sentences may be appealed to higher courts and stiffer penalties imposed. It is altogether possible for a person to receive a moderate sentence in the court of original jurisdiction, thereby conveying a favorable impression of the Soviet judicial system, only to have a much more stringent sentence imposed by an appellate court without this fact's becoming public knowledge. Now, however, appeals from acquittal or mild sentences must be made within a year.

Two procedures, said to be abolished in 1957, were not even a part of Soviet law, and therefore all the more repugnant. One was the practice of holding a person in violation of the criminal code in cases of minor negli-

---

[19] Harold J. Berman, *Justice in the U.S.S.R.: An Interpretation of Soviet Law*, rev. ed. (New York: Vintage Books, 1963), p. 71.

gence and other administrative offenses not foreseen by the law. Administrative officials, usually in the Ministry of Interior, imposed penalties, some of which banished the person for several years. The second practice permitted the holding of a person in violation of the criminal code for crimes by analogy—that is, for acts that were analogous to illegal acts. These practices are allegedly no longer in existence. A similar procedure, also allegedly discarded, permitted punishment of relatives for crimes committed by their kin. The family of a soldier who deserted abroad, for example, was held collectively responsible for this act. A new type of offense has been added, however. Particularly dangerous state crimes committed against any other workers' state are now punishable under a new law.

Reports of improvements in Soviet judicial practices must, however, be tempered with the fact that the party has always reserved the right to go outside the law if considerations of policy demanded it. The setting up of the voluntary citizens' militia and the decree of the Presidium of the Supreme Soviet in 1961 authorizing a retroactive application of the death penalty for speculation in currency, are examples.

It should also be remembered that new laws can be made any time that the regime's leaders desire them. At the time of the 1958 reforms, for example, the "counterrevolutionary" crime of "agitation or propaganda" against the Soviet system was retained, which is punishable by up to seven years' imprisonment. And while the worst abuses of the Stalin era have apparently been eliminated, it may be significant that the death penalty has been extended in recent years to several new categories of crimes. Among these are serious economic crimes, illegal transactions in foreign currencies, large-scale bribery, and resistance to a policeman which results in his death.

It is necessary also to note that Soviet courts are not impartial in dispensing justice. Party members usually receive more lenient sentences than nonparty citizens. Moreover, the Soviet press has from time to time printed stories indicating that prosecutors have been reluctant to bring party members to court at all. That some favoritism toward party members exists cannot be questioned, but its extent and prevalence are far from clear.

Finally, it needs to be noted that where there is no free press as a guardian of men's liberties, the existence of dubious judicial practices and procedures cannot be brought to light in a way that will have a serious impact upon the rulers. Moreover, where there is a corresponding emphasis upon secrecy, many odious practices can exist for years without becoming known to the most astute observers. Freedom would seem to be the first prerequisite for the type of judicial standards to which free men aspire.

THE MILITARY IN THE SOVIET SYSTEM

In Marxist eyes, the army was the dreaded instrument of the bourgeois state, and, like it, had to be destroyed. But something had to be put in its place—an armed force of the new authority. But since the party was to become all-powerful in the Soviet system, it is quite understandable that the army (armed forces) could not become an autonomous force. New armed forces were established, but like their predecessors, they became the instrument of the prevailing political authority, only more so.

It needs to be reemphasized that the Communist party is regarded as the source of all wisdom and authority. Any efforts to set up alternate or competing centers of political discussion, and any questioning of the party's program, have been viewed as treasonous and treated as such. The army, like other institutions in the Soviet system, is supposed to be subservient to the party. It can have influence only to the extent that what it wants to do is also what the party wants to do. In the age of missiles and space technology, however, the technical specialist is in a position to exert considerable influence in the allocation of critical material and human resources. If the army ever achieved an independent status the result would probably be a military dictatorship and not a dictatorship of the party.

The party's aim, of course, has been to produce the type of military man who will see no conflict between his role as a military man and his role as a party member. More than that, the party has sought to raise the political educational level of the military commanders, so that they will act as loyal party men. It should surprise no one that over 85 percent of the officer corps is made up of party members and that the top command of the military forces is made up exclusively of party members. In other words, the military officer comes to this position imbued with the idea that the party is the most important part of the Soviet system and that he, as a party member and as a military man, owes his highest allegiance to the party. And the party, for all practical purposes, means the top leadership. Military men, therefore, are party comrades, and it would be unthinkable for them to challenge the authority of the party leaders in the hierarchy above them. To do so would be to challenge the Soviet system itself.

Nevertheless, the party has also developed other means of ensuring the loyalty of the armed forces. First of all, the officers in the armed forces live well, and rarely do they cherish the loss of the privileged positions they happen to occupy. Secondly, there is the authority of the superior officers, who are also trusted party leaders and upon whose good opinion promotion depends. In addition, the party's Central Committee has a special section whose responsibility is confined to political administration in the military forces, where the *zampolit* (deputy commander for political affairs), formerly political commissar, guards the party line. Moreover, the party organizations in the armed forces have independent chains of command. They report to the top party authorities and are not subject to the local party organization. Finally, the secret police operates within the military forces and, like the party organizations, is not subject to control by the local or regional party organizations.

As a result, loyalty in the armed forces has been maintained, although not without purges, some of which have been of considerable proportions. We do not know to what extent there was any serious attempt on the part of military men to overthrow the system, but we do know that they have expressed their displeasure with some decisions of the political leaders.

Khrushchev has revealed that there have been differences between the party leadership and certain highly placed officers. He has reported that one such officer made the party leaders uneasy, while another one criticized the party leadership in a private conversation with another officer.[20] He has also reported that Admiral N. G. Kuznetsov openly criticized the political leadership after its decision to put off building up the navy and to concentrate on the air force and missiles. For this he was relieved of his duties and demoted, even though this upset some military men, but, says Khrushchev, "we had to put an abrupt halt to any manifestation of Bonapartism among the military."[21] Khrushchev also reports that very early in his leadership he was made commander in chief of the armed forces, although this decision was not made public.[22] And in the Epilogue of his second volume, he warns that, while there is no military class in the Soviet Union, if "given a chance, some elements within the military might try to force a militarist policy on the government. Therefore the government must always keep a bit between the teeth of the military."[23]

There have been some indications, however, that political leaders have used the military leaders in their struggle for power within the party. In 1957, for example, when an effort was made in the party Presidium (later renamed Politburo) to oust Khrushchev, Minister of Defense Marshal Zhukov, who owed his appointment to Khrushchev, employed military aircraft in order to get members of the Central Committee to Moscow quickly, thus enabling Khrushchev to frustrate the efforts of his opponents in the Presidium. Thereupon Khrushchev ousted his foes and rewarded Zhukov by making him a full member of the Presidium—the first time a professional soldier achieved such a distinction. But Zhukov erred in thinking that he could curtail the work of party organizations in the military, and in a few months was ousted not only as minister of defense

[20] *Khrushchev Remembers: The Last Testament* (Boston: Little Brown and Co., 1974), pp. 16–17.

[21] Ibid., pp. 25–27.

[22] Ibid., p. 12.

[23] Ibid., pp. 540–41.

but also as a member of the Presidium and the Central Committee. Subsequently, the role of the party in the armed forces was strengthened through explicit orders and through a reaffirmation of the principle that the leadership of the military cannot be outside the control of the party. As long as the authority of the party dictatorship is maintained, therefore, it seems safe to conclude that the armed forces will be loyal to whichever leaders remain at the top of the political ladder.

BIBLIOGRAPHICAL NOTE

A general view of the structure of the Soviet government may be found in Fainsod, *How Russia Is Ruled* (cited in Chapter 29); Darrell P. Hammer, *The Politics of Oligarchy* (Hinsdale, Ill.: The Dryden Press, 1974); Frederick C. Barghoorn, *Politics in the U.S.S.R.*, 2d ed. (Boston: Little, Brown and Co., 1972); Joseph L. Nogee, ed., *Man, State, and Society in the Soviet Union* (New York: Frederick A. Praeger, Inc., 1972); John R. Reshetar, Jr., *The Soviet Polity: Government and Politics of the U.S.S.R.* (New York: Dodd, Mead and Co., 1971); Michel Tatu, *Power in the Kremlin: From Khrushchev to Kosygin* (New York: The Viking Press, 1970); and Milorad M. Drachkovitch, ed., *Fifty Years of Communism in Russia* (Univeristy Park: The Pennsylvania State University Press, 1968). More recent works that deserve mention are: Archie Brown and Michael Kaser, eds., *The Soviet Union Since the Fall of Khrushchev* (New York: The Free Press, 1975); Peter H. Juviler, *Revolutionary Law and Order: Politics and Social Change in the U.S.S.R.* (New York: The Free Press, 1976); Henry W. Morton and Rudolf L. Tökés, *Soviet Politics and Society in the 1970s* (New York: The Free Press, 1974); Roy A. Medvedev, *On Socialist Democracy* (New York: Alfred A. Knopf, Inc., 1975); Leonard B. Schapiro, *Totalitarianism* (New York: Frederick A. Praeger, 1972); Robert C. Tucker, ed., *Stalinism: Essays in Historical Interpretation* (New York: W. W. Norton & Co., Inc., 1977).

31

Policy-Implementing Structures: Administration

The Soviet state, more than any other political system known to man, is an administrative state. Soviet society is bureaucratized to the highest degree. Even the lives and daily decisions of individual Russians are guided by the decisions of the Communist party, as expressed in the all-embracing administrative system. A detailed treatment of this system is beyond the scope of this book. But it is important that its main features be examined, its formal organization depicted, and some of its major problems set forth.

NATURE OF SOVIET ADMINISTRATION

Prior to their seizure of power, the Bolsheviks, and especially Lenin, envisioned a new type of society without bureaucracy, police, or army. Anyone knowing the four rules of arithmetic, in Lenin's view, possessed the qualifications of an administrator. After the initial establishment of the new society, administration would need to be only a part-time affair. It was not long, however, before the Bolshevik leaders learned how indispensable was a highly organized bureaucracy to the orderly functioning of a modern state, especially a state bent on speeding industrialization and embarking upon large-scale social engineering. This became particularly evident when they started the U.S.S.R. down the path of successive five-year plans.

The scope and extent of public administration in the Soviet Union would be sizable under any political system. There is a huge territory to oversee, with varied climates, peoples, and problems to cope with. An authoritarian system, of whatever type, would need an extensive bureaucracy to make sure its edicts were obeyed and the empire held together. This is all the more true of a dictatorship which sets out to remake society and does not hesitate to run roughshod over everyone who might stand in the way.

Moreover, one can appreciate the size and scope of the Soviet bureaucracy if one keeps in mind the fact that virtually nothing in the U.S.S.R. occurs as a result of private enterprise. A notable exception are the private plots in agriculture, discussed below. The government runs or controls every form of economic activity—stores, factories, mines, farms, trains, ships, and all of the other things normally associated with private endeavor in other countries. In a broad sense, everyone works for the government.

The size and scope of the administrative machine becomes even more meaningful if one remembers that it is not merely a matter of a bureaucracy running the machinery of government it has inherited. Under its control nothing is supposed to happen by accident. Everything is planned and controlled. The bureaucracy not only runs things but, in addition, plans them and runs them according to the plans. Under such a system and in such a large country, the size and scope of the administrative appartus must be large indeed.

In the Soviet Union, therefore, the administration works within the framework of the policy guidance which the party establishes. From the beginning, it was the party which had to determine what the factories should produce; how raw materials, manpower, and machinery were to be combined so as to realize the planned output; and how that output was to be distributed. As an arm of the party dictatorship, the Soviet bureaucracy has the task of building a Communist society in accordance with the party blueprint. As such, the Soviet bureaucracy cannot be viewed as a nonpolitical and detached civil service. It is clearly partisan.

But the party does more than merely furnish policy guidance. It is constantly engaged in checking on the execution of its policies. The top political leaders must keep an eye on the bureaucrats, who have not been above falsifying records and engaging in a whole host of other "unsocialist" acts in order to receive material or political rewards from their superiors. The administrators all along the line have learned to expect the party's watchful eye, and to fear the attribution of political motives to some of their acts, with possible dire consequences, even when such motives may never have existed.

Simultaneously with checking on the fulfillment of its policies, the party is engaged in mobilizing popular support behind planned targets. This may range all the way from exhorting the workers to surpass planned output to urging a mass movement of people to an area where there is a manpower shortage; such exhortations very often are made without taking other circumstances into account, which may result in making matters worse. In short, the bureaucracy can expect to hear the party's voice at all stages of its operation.

As the above suggest, public administration in the Soviet Union is highly centralized, with control and direction from the center. The most important control agency is the party, which decides on the nature of all other controls. These controls have been altered so often that any description of them would soon be out of date. For example, the Ministry of State Control gave way in 1957 to the Commission of Soviet Control which, in turn, gave way to the State Control Commission in 1961. In 1962, Khrushchev reorganized the party into two hierarchies, one to check performance in agriculture and the other in industry. As a part of this reorganization, the State Control Commission was replaced by the Committee of Party and State Control. Khrushchev's successors abolished the dual hierarchy arrangement, and established a new control body—the People's Control Commission—which, however, has no jurisdiction over party affairs.

Other controls are exercised by the office of the state prosecutor and by the secret police. In addition, various ministries and the State Planning Commission perform control functions. Moreover, the party also makes use of advisory workers' committees and a corps of volunteer inspectors.

This multiplicity of controls must be viewed against the party's shifting standard of what meets or does not meet the requirements of theoretical dogma. What is perfectly acceptable today may turn out to be un-Marxian tomorrow. What supports the strategy of party leaders becomes an impediment when that strategy changes, and it has changed often during the life of the Soviet regime. When something does not produce the desired result, there are changes, often based on little more than the principle of trial and error, although the party leaders never admit this. In their words, each change is but another step toward the desired goal, a step which more appropriately corresponds to "the present stage of socialist development."

In their search for workable administrative arrangements, the party leaders have emphasized the desired objectives, usually to the exclusion of other considerations. To them, loyalty and adherence to party directives have been of the utmost importance. Efficiency is important, but secondary. The rights of individuals, on the other hand, are given little weight. The administrative machine, understandably, operates to achieve state-determined objectives and not to preserve abstract personal rights.

FORMAL ADMINISTRATIVE ORGANIZATION

Superficially, at least, the Soviet administrative organization bears a certain resemblance to that found in most other countries. There are ministries—until 1946, the Soviet leaders avoided this bourgeois term—and bureaus, offices, missions, and others. There is a civil service to staff these various offices. Moreover, from time to time there have been changes and reorganizations in the administrative structure. In other ways, however, the Soviet administrative organization is unique, which will become evident from what follows.

As noted in an earlier chapter, there are three types of ministries in the Soviet Union— all-union ministries, union-republic ministries, and republic ministries. All-union ministries are national ministries which operate from Moscow through their own employees down to the local level. The line of responsibility is vertical. Union-republic ministries are those ministries which exist on the national level and on the republic level. In other words, the ministries in Moscow which operate through corresponding ministries in each of the republics are known as union-republic ministries. The line of reponsibility, therefore, is both vertical and horizontal, although the vertical is more important. In both all-union and union-republic ministries, the final control rests in Moscow. Republic ministries on the other hand, are ministries which exist on the republic level, with no corresponding ministries at the national level. These are reponsible to their respective republics, although they may be engaged in carrying out programs determined in Moscow.

The number of ministries in the various categories has changed a number of times. The number of all-union ministries was increased and decreased several times. At the time of Stalin's death, for example, there were 60, but two days later these were reduced to 25. Within a year, the number had increased to 46, and by 1956 it was up to 52. This number dropped sharply after the 1957 reorganization, discussed below, but by 1969 the number of ministers at the national level increased to about 90. The 1977 Constitution, unlike that of 1936, does not list the ministries by name, but merely provides that this will be done subsequently by legislative act.

In 1957 the Soviet Union underwent a sweeping reorganization of its industrial-administrative structure. Most of the all-union ministries in the economic sphere, as well as many union-republic industrial ministries, were abolished. In their place more than 100 regional economic councils were set up, corresponding to the number of economic regions into which the Soviet Union was divided. In most instances, these regions coincided with the existing administrative and territorial divisions of the U.S.S.R. The regional councils, which were given authority to run the vast industrial empire, were, in theory, to be chosen by the governments of the respective republics, but Moscow retained a veto power over members of the councils as well as over council decisions.

In some circles this reorganization was referred to as decentralization of the Soviet economy. Soviet leaders, notably Khrushchev, insisted that it was, in effect, a more effective centralization. It was only the operative control which was being decentralized. Decisions concerning basic policy as well as planned targets were still to be made in Moscow. The regional councils and local authorities were merely to have more discretion in finding ways and means of carrying out basic economic directives. This meant that power once exercised by a departmental bureaucracy in Moscow had been transferred to the bureaucracy which was actually at the center of production. In addition, some of the powers previously exercised by ministries in Moscow had been transferred to local ministries and local party committees.

To insure basic control from the center, the functions (and to some degree the administrative apparatus) of the all-union ministries that were abolished were transferred to the reorganized State Planning Committee and to a whole host of other committees, which in a way resembled skeletal ministries. Most of the heads of the abolished ministries were made chairmen or deputy chairmen of these new committees, with the rank of minister of the U.S.S.R.

Less than a year after the 1957 reorganization went into effect, evidence began accumulating that all was not running smoothly. Complaints began appearing in the Soviet press that certain regional councils were putting local interests ahead of the national interest. After seeking to remedy the situation by providing bonuses for deliveries of goods to outside economic areas, the Soviet leaders found it necessary to resort to sterner measures. A decree was promulgated which made it a criminal offense to fail to deliver goods to other areas or to the government—a method of control that had been used in the past. Unless there was a valid excuse, the guilty would be subject to strict disciplinary measures or fines of up to three months of salary. Second offenders would be treated more harshly.

Further difficulties were evidenced by the fact that in 1960 a new agency, the Russian Council for the National Economy, was established. It was charged with coordinating the work of the 70 regional economic councils in the Russian republic (RSFSR). In 1962, a new reorganization divided the country into 17 major economic regions, each with a council to be concerned with the development of resources and with the coordination of planning and production among the management bodies under its jurisdiction. In 1963 the Supreme National Economic Council was established to coordinate the planning and management of industry on a nationwide basis. The authority of the regional councils was further reduced when in 1965 several state committees, notably in the defense field, were converted into full-fledged ministries and thus removed from the jurisdiction of the councils. By late 1965 the Soviet leaders had abolished the regional councils altogether, thus continuing the search for more efficient ways of organizing and operating a vast planned economy.

At the top of the formal administrative structure is the Council of

Ministers of the U.S.S.R. During most of Stalin's reign this was a large and unwieldy body, which really never decided anything important as a body. Really effective power was exercised by a small group, sometimes referred to as the Presidium of the Council, which consisted of the chairman and the deputy chairmen of the Council. With the abolition of many national ministries, the Council initially decreased in size, but in more recent years the number of national ministries has again risen appreciably.

The Council of Ministers is the directing agency of the administrative machine. It is supposed to have the main responsibility in supervising the carrying out of the industrial plans. As such, it can overrule the councils of ministers of individual republics. It exercises wide decree powers in finance, taxation, pricing, and foreign trade. It is also empowered to issue decrees in the realm of military affairs, and it can promulgate measures to protect socialist property. Important decrees are often issued jointly with the Central Committee of the party. Sometimes there is a joint promulgation of decrees by the Council of Ministers and by the All-Union Council of Trade Unions. The All-Union Council has been empowered to issue binding decrees, especially in the labor legislation field, subject to approval by the Council of Ministers.

Centralized economic planning became an essential feature of the Soviet economy by 1921, although it is usually associated with the beginning of the era of the five-year plans. Established in 1921, *Gosplan* (State Planning Committee) did not come into prominence until the launching of the first five-year plan in 1928. That year also marked the consolidation of the Stalin dictatorship and the final abolition of private economic enterprise.

The principal aims of the five-year plans during Stalin's reign centered on the building of a heavy industry and the collectivization of agriculture. The former involved a series of successive drives to build new capital goods factories and plants at an ambitious rate. The latter was ostensibly aimed at increasing agricultural production by seeking to convert small and often scattered peasant holdings into large-scale mechanized units. These were monumental tasks, and in the industrialized sector there were some substantial gains, but the human and material costs in both were huge.

Centralized planning and direction are still the responsibility of *Gosplan*, which is to determine the direction and rate of economic development. It coordinates its efforts with those of planning committees in the respective republics, who in turn coordinate with various enterprise directors, as well as with the directors of the economic ministries.

The planning operation is an involved and complicated affair. It begins with the aims and goals of the party, transmitted via party and governmental channels from top to bottom. *Gosplan* and the subsidiary planning bodies at the republic, regional, and local levels must work out the detailed plans in collaboration with other governmental authorities as well as with economic ministries, regional officials, and individual enterprises. These plans involve not only planning for a set number of years but, in addition, planning for each year and each quarter of a year. The more detailed planning involves targets and timetables for each month.

The precise number of people in the Soviet bureaucracy is difficult to determine, mainly because there is some question as to who should be included. Should one include, for example, the people who work full time in the trade unions, the party apparatus, and the youth organizations? Depending upon how one conceives the bureaucracy, its estimated size runs from 10 to 15 million.

The vast army of civil servants is recruited under the watchful eye of the Communist party, which is the final judge in all personnel matters. The party's concern with personnel is understandable, for the highest duty of the bureaucracy is to carry out party policies. For years the party's concern with personnel was exercised through the Cadres Administration of its Central Committee and through similar party organizations at all levels of government. Now, however, individual ministries recruit people at the lower levels, usually from the universities, where they can prescribe certain courses, or from schools that are attached to certain ministries. But as one moves up the bureaucratic ladder, the transfer and movement of personnel is subject to increasing party control.

The government (party) can shift personnel at will. Although the 1940 decree on the compulsory transfer of personnel was repealed in 1956, the government can employ other coercive means to achieve the same end. For example, it can appeal to the trade unions, the party, or the youth organization to send its members to new industrial sites, the virgin lands, or elsewhere. Uncooperative persons can be expelled from these organizations, a circumstance fraught with serious practical consequences for the persons concerned, such as the loss of job, position of responsibility, or privileges attendant to membership. Moreover, the government can, and does, promulgate new decrees at will. And it can, and often does, act without the benefit of any legal sanction.

As the above paragraphs suggest, the bureaucracy is first of all responsible to the party. In actual practice, control of the bureaucracy is complicated. The People's Control Commission has vast powers to investigate and to institute measures of correction, to reprimand, and to dismiss. The Council of Ministers exercises powers in the same realm. The Presidium of the Supreme Soviet can modify and interpret decrees and decisions of administrative bodies. The police, the courts, and the prosecutor's office, to say nothing of the "volunteer" inspectors (who are publicly encouraged), exercise a type of cross control. Finally, there is the criticism and self-criticism voiced through the press, in editorials, or in letters to the editor. Despite the fact that the party ostensibly provides the necessary guidance, the nature of the control apparatus lends itself to confusion and abuse. And the Soviet press continues to assert that the work of the control organs is far from what it should be.

So as to deal more effectively with the large number of lawsuits between state economic enterprises, the Soviet leaders have established a system of so-called state arbitration tribunals. They have the power to summon witnesses, to request the submission of documents, to appoint expert examiners, and to issue decrees which must be obeyed. They are appointed by, and are subordinate to, the supreme executive bodies of the areas in which they function, and their decisions may be reversed or altered by these same executive bodies. The chief arbitrator is attached to the Council of Ministers of the U.S.S.R. He supervises the arbitration work of state arbitrators at all levels, and issues general instructions to them. He is also empowered to review their decisions.

In the settlement of disputes, the state arbitration tribunals are supposed to protect the ''property rights and lawful interests of enterprises.'' At the same time they are to protect the basic concerns of the state by declaring invalid all contracts between enterprises which do not conform to Soviet law or which run counter to the plans of the State Planning Committee. Most of the disputes between economic enterprises concern alleged breaches of contract, which may involve late or nondelivery of goods, poor quality of goods, or their delivery in poor or damaged condition. Some disputes concern prices and terms of payment. Other disputes involve damage claims resulting from the delivery of allegedly defective materials or machines. Arbitration tribunals are also called upon to resolve precontract disputes, where enterprises are legally required to enter into contracts and yet cannot agree on the terms.

MANAGEMENT OF GOVERNMENT ENTERPRISES

Lenin believed that capitalism had simplified and routinized industrial methods to such an extent that socialized industry could be operated by anyone who could read and write. ''The ability to observe and record and to make out receipts—this, with knowledge of the four rules of arithmetic, is all that is required.'' Soviet leaders were to learn the hard way, however, that the role of management was much more important than that.

For years, the great problem in Soviet management was the lack of freedom to manage. The first phase in Soviet industrial management was characterized by the power of factory committees and the trade unions. They had to be consulted on virtually everything. But neither the factory committees nor the trade unions were trained to deal with problems of supply, manufacturing, and distribution. Consequently, Soviet industrial production dropped sharply. For a time, in the era of the New Economic Policy (NEP), many of the capitalist managers were called back. By the time the Soviet leaders were ready to launch the five-year plans (1928), they were convinced that the managerial concept must be accepted.

The philosophy behind the five-year plans was production at any cost. In order that nothing should interfere with the pursuit of the announced goals, the factory committees had to go. The five-day week and other labor gains also had to go, while the trade unions were made a part of the governmental machinery, with assigned roles to play. Their chief task now was to ride herd on their members in order that management might reach its assigned production quotas. To achieve the goals of the five-year plans, the managers needed to have the power to manage, and with minimum interference even from party organizations.

The purges of the 1930s, however, dealt the managerial concept a hard blow. Many old Bolsheviks who held high administrative or party posts were liquidated or displaced. Managers of various ranks were removed by the thousands, and many of them were shot or sent to slave labor camps. The net result was a widespread fear of making decisions. The safe way was to refer everything, even ridiculously minor matters, to Moscow. Soviet management was to suffer from this malady as long as Stalin lived. Since his passing, however, there have been indications that the new Soviet leaders have been engaged in restoring the power of management to the managers.

The acceptance of the importance of the managerial role was accompanied by a trend toward capitalist-type incentives. In the early years of the regime, when the trade unions sought to protect the workers, the five-day week was the rule, and there was a trend toward equality of wages. With the launching of the five-year plans, however, the previous trade union attitude was viewed as defensive and negative. Increasingly, the practice of rewarding people in proportion to their output became the rule of the Soviet society, receiving constitutional recognition in the fundamental law of 1936.

To the end that people would be rewarded "according to their work," the salaries of managers jumped phenomenally, for their work was regarded as much more important than that of the ordinary workers. In addition, managers were given bonuses for overfulfillment of planned goals, as well as compensation in kind, such as good apartments, special food, a radio and even a private automobile. The work of engineers, technicians, and skilled laborers received similar recognition, with corresponding gradations in salary and rank.

Differentiation was also made even among the unskilled workers. Piece rates and production quotas were established for them, with increasing rewards for those who surpassed the so-called norm of production, which was raised steadily as more and more workers surpassed it. Those who consistently produced above the norm were designated as *stakhanovites* (shock workers), after a coal miner named Stakhanov whose work output was allegedly phenomenal. In setting wage scales in the Soviet Union, familiar capitalist principles, such as education, experience, and the arduousness, complexity, and exactness of work, are given weight. The net result is wider differentials and inequalities of reward than in the United States, where legal enactments and union activity have served to narrow the gap.

Those workers who are judged to be particularly deserving are awarded medals, trips to Moscow, special vacations, and other honors. Negatively, the capitalist type of reward was accompanied by rigid controls, applicable particularly in the case of the less cooperative worker. Movement from job to job became almost impossible. Absenteeism without an acceptable excuse was punished progressively in wages, ration coupons (during rationing), and, ultimately, in the loss of job and dwelling quarters. Drunkenness was also punishable.

The drift toward capitalist patterns of reward was not, however, accompanied by any visible trend toward a free market as a regulator of the economy. Production and distribution were determined by the plans, as were the costs and profits. The plans were enforced, for the most part, by changing the rate of the turnover tax, a type of sales tax, which is also the prinicpal source of government revenue. By increasing or decreasing the rate, the government can effectively encourage or discourage certain types of economic activity. It could, for example make shoes expensive and television sets inexpensive. In brief, this is the way the party's arbitrary decisions concerning the allocation of resources were carried out.

Under this system the preferences of the consumer were ignored. Moreover, the producing enterprise had no particular incentive to turn out quality goods. The result, all too often, was an accumulation of poor quality goods that went unsold. In order to remedy this situation and to combat a malaise in the economy, Kosygin in 1965 announced a new set of economic reforms designed to shift considerable operational control to enterprise managers while keeping the system of centralized planning. Cautious approaches were made to the use of certain market mechanisms such as interest charges, profits, and consumer demands. The central planners continued to set basic targets, but most factories were to be given greater authority in carrying out the plans. It was reasoned by the leadership that requiring enterprises to pay interest on the money they borrow and permitting them to share in the profits would, in effect, reward those enterprises that made desirable goods at a reasonable price and punish those that turned out goods no one wanted. In this way, enterprises were encouraged to make an effort to discover what the consumer liked and desired. Similarly, the new system was to encourage managers to improve the efficiency of their operations.

This shift toward the employment of market mechanisms was associated with a Soviet economist, Liberman. He argued that enterprises would improve production, make better goods, and increase efficiency if they were charged interest on the money made available to them, provided they could also share in the profits. The implementation of his ideas initially led to modest successes, but serious problems remained. The government did not permit sufficient flexibility in prices, and suppliers often did not live up to their contracts, in terms of both delivery times and quality of goods. In addition, it began to appear that the leadership had second thoughts about the reforms, because of both opposition from central agencies and ministries and the apparent timidity of the managers themselves in exercising the promised new authority.

In 1973 and 1974 new rulings were issued, but the 1965 statute has not been officially amended or repealed. For all practical purposes, however, the 1965 reforms have been negated in practice. The attempt to utilize economic levers was handicapped from the outset by centrally determined prices and the ever-present detailed instructions from above. The appearance in January 1977 of a new journal, which is to deal with such problems as who is entitled to give directions to managers of production associations and enterprises, seems to focus on the need to regulate more precisely the legal position of various agencies connected with Soviet economic life.

As the Soviet industrial empire grew, the importance of the technical-administrative intelligentsia became more and more evident to the Soviet leaders. Increasingly, members of this group rose to higher and higher posts in the administrative hierarchy. During Stalin's dictatorship, however, they were sufficiently terrorized that they could not openly challenge party dictates, even when these were obviously faulty. By 1957, on the other hand, a number of them felt sufficiently secure to argue publicly against some of the theses put forward by party leaders. This became particularly evident in the discussion of Khrushchev's theses concerning industrial reorganziation. Atomic energy specialist Kapitsa, metallurgist I. P. Bardin, and others pointed out that in their particular specialities the Khrushchev proposals would not work or at best they needed modification.

It is, of course, impossible to tell if the discussion of Khrushchev's reorganization scheme by technical specialists is to be repeated in other contexts. Observers have for several years been noting the growing importance of the technical-administrative intelligentsia in the party membership itself. Most indications point to the growing importance of this group in Soviet society, although some observers have asserted that one of the aims of Khrushchev's economic reorganization plan was to reduce the power of the technical-administrative intelligentsia and to increase the party's control over the economic apparatus.

Moreover, during the Brezhnev years there was ample evidence that party leaders would be in full control of industrial developments at all levels. Nevertheless, some observers have called attention to a coalition of institutional interests, suggesting a limited institutional or bureaucratic pluralism. In the 1970s, as if to counter this, party representatives in ministries were given increased powers to check on the work of the ministerial apparatus. In sum, the party has the last word if it wants it.

MANAGEMENT IN AGRICULTURE

Despite the revolutionary cry of "all land to the peasants," the Bolshevik leaders did not intend to promote private ownership of land. In the early years they attempted, in effect, to confiscate agricultural produce through compulsory deliveries, a practice highly resented by the peasants. During the NEP period, however, the peasants were free to produce and to sell. The more enterprising ones leased land and even hired labor, practices which led to the growth of a moderately well-to-do group of peasants, subsequently called kulaks. In 1929 the party leaders called a halt and embarked on a program to collectivize agriculture. Through heavy taxation, refusal of credit, making it illegal to own or lease farm machinery, and, in the final analysis, through physical liquidation of the recalcitrants, the regime conducted its farm revolution, which was virtually complete by 1932. The original plans had called for the collectivization of 15 to 20 percent of the land during the first five-year plan. At least in part because of peasant opposition, this figure was boosted to 75 and subsequently to 90 percent.

Some form of collective ownership and operation of agriculture was required by the Marxian doctrine, although the details were far from clear. Seemingly of more importance to the Soviet leaders was the promotion of greatly increased agricultural production, which was necessary to feed the growing industrial-urban population. This could be achieved by mechanization, but there was some question of how effectively machinery could be used on the small and often scattered pieces of land—hence the conclusion that mechanization would only be effective on large-scale agricultural units. Parenthetically, however, it might be noted that during the entire period of Stalin's dictatorship productivity per acre was not raised. Increased yields were achieved only by adding acreage.

Agricultural land in the Soviet Union is in the form of collective farms (kolkhoz) and state farms (sovkhoz). The state farms are government owned and operated; the workers on them are ordinary wage earners. The collective farms are also really government owned, but they resulted, in the main, from the merging of neighboring farms, under rules set forth by the government. Hence, the people who live on them have a right, at leas in theory, to their exclusive use. Under rules handed down by the government, the members of the kolkhoz divide the profits of their labor, which made for a very uncertain income indeed. In more recent years the Soviet government established minimum earnings to go to each collective farmer. Moreover, in most instances the individual family dwelling was retained by the family, together with an adjoining household or garden plot of from one-half to three acres. The plot, theoretically, could be used as the family saw fit, but in practice the government could and does change the rules.

Over the years, it became increasingly evident to the Soviet leaders that these private plots were occupying a large part of the time of the collective farm members. Instead of planting a few vegetables and berries for the family table, the peasants were using these plots to grow major produce as well as to support the maximum livestock permitted (a cow and two calves, a pig, a few goats or sheep, and an unlimited number of poultry). Prior to World War II, the average member of a kolkhoz was earning approximately one half of his total income from these plots, a fairly good indication that collective farmers were not giving the collective effort a very high priority.

Soon after legalizing the private plot, the government began to hedge it in with restrictions designed to make it so costly that the peasant would ultimately abandon it. High taxes were imposed on produce from these plots. After World War II, the government increased compulsory deliveries on a portion of the produce, even requiring the delivery of milk, eggs, wool, and so forth, whether the farmer owned the livestock or not. Moreover, there was an attempt to reduce the size of the plots in 1950, during an amalgamation of small collective farms into larger ones. After a temporary relaxation in 1953–54, the regime returned to the attack. In 1956 it inaugurated a program designed to eliminate the private plots. In 1961 decrees urged consumer cooperatives to step up the purchase of surplus produce from the farmer, pointing to the elimination of the last remnants of a free market. By 1965, however, shortages in agricultural produce forced the government to encourage peasants to grow food on the private plots, and to sell the surplus at local markets, where supply and demand determine the price.

In the 1950s there were several developments indicating that the collective farm itself may be on the way out. A number of the smaller collective farms were amalgamated, with the result that the total number was reduced by more than one half. Almost simultaneously there was a move to promote the construction of *agrogorods* (agricultural cities), where the collective farmers would live, commuting to work. While this idea fell by the wayside after Khrushchev's rise to power, he nevertheless promoted the further merger of collectives as well as the creation of additional state farms at the expense of the collective farm idea. The 6 million acres of virgin land opened up in 1955, for example, were all organized on the state farm principle. Between 1966 and 1976 the number of collective farms dropped from approximately 36,000 to 29,000, while the number of state farms grew from about 12,000 to 18,000.

In the late 1970s the government seemed to be promoting a new version of the *agrogorods*, merging farms into gigantic agro-industrial associations. This could mean a resettlement of as much as 25 percent of the population. By bringing about an interfarm amalgamation, the government hopes to provide off-season employment and some of the amenities of urban living for those living on the land.

Generally speaking, the government has in recent years increased its investment in agriculture, provided higher prices for farm produce, and demanded lower prices for consumer items that the farmer needs. While the net result has been an increase in the standard of living of farm families, many problems remain, to which reference will be made below.

Ostensibly, the members of each collective farm meet in an annual assembly and elect a management committee to run the affairs of the farm for the year. In actual practice, the Communist party by and large controls all such elections. In any case, the management committee must operate under the general laws dealing with collective farms and it must fit its operation into the overall agricultural plan.

In accordance with the general rules, applicable to all collective farms, the land, farm buildings, draft animals, and major tools are owned in common. Credit and other things furnished by the government must, of course, be paid for by the collective. Each able-bodied adult is required to put in a minimum number of days in the collective effort, which means about one half of his annual work time. But, in view of the fact that a large part of agricultural work is seasonal, this normally means much more than half time. Income to the peasant depended upon how well the collective farm did at the end of the year. Because of the understandable uncertainties in such a system of reward, the regime has in recent years sought ways to guarantee a minimum wage to the collective farmer.

Prior to 1958 the collective farms were not allowed to own the major agricultural machines. These were leased by the government through the Machine Tractor Stations (MTS), which were important instruments of political control. They also acted as effective collecting centers of agricultural produce, for each collective was obliged to sell a certain proportion of its produce at a low government-established price. In 1958, however, all of this was changed. Collective farms now own their own machinery. In place of the MTS there is now the Farm Machinery Association, whose job it is to sell and repair machines and to sell fertilizer and other farm needs. The practice of obligatory deliveries of farm produce at low prices has given way to a more realistic price system.

The day-to-day operation of a collective farm is under the direction of the manager or farm chairman. Assisting him is an administrative staff—bookkeepers, brigade leaders, watchmen, storekeepers, day and night guards, an agronomist, and the manager of the livestock unit. Obviously, by American standards Soviet collective farms are top-heavy with administrative personnel.

While there have been some improvements in Soviet agriculture in recent years, enormous problems remain. First of all, productivity is low, except for the private plots. The growth of agricultural production has barely kept pace with that of the population. In per capita terms, Soviet agriculture, with all its technological advancement, is scarcely more productive than the backward agriculture of pre-1914 Russia. The average Soviet farmer produces food for only 7 persons as compared to the Amercian farmer who produces for 46 persons. The private plots, on the other hand, with less than 4 percent of all arable land, contribute about 25 percent of the Soviet Union's gross agricultural product (if we include meat and animal products from private livestock holdings). The private plots contribute 40 percent of the vegetable product in the largest republic, the RSFSR.

A second problem concerns hidden costs. At harvest time, for example, a large number of trucks, tractors, and personnel are "borrowed" or "commandeered" from industrial enterprises and/or the army. Moreover, there is inadequate machinery, and the problem of spare parts has not been resolved. For example, when milking machinery breaks down, there is an urgent need to employ milkmaids.

Third, there is a shortage of manpower, particularly those trained to operate agricultural machines. Only one youth in 20 wants to stay on the farm; 50 percent of farm labor consists of older women. One reason is that farm life is considered dull and boring. At certain times of the year there are no roads; mud cuts farms off from towns and even from one another. There are few diversions or entertainment, especially for the young.

Finally, the Soviet leaders seem to have realized that centrally controlled prices and procurement plans, as well as other forms of interference, have had an unfavorable impact on production. It remains to be seen, however, whether they can liberate themselves from old ways. Two recent developments would seem to be positive. The first of these is the experimentation with the so-called "link system." In this system, seven to ten people, often members of the same family, are allocated certain lands and machinery, and they are paid according to their output. It is not uncommon for a link member to earn two or three times what a collective or state farm worker does. The other development concerns the assistance being given by the government to private plot production, but without advertising it openly. In order to increase milk and meat production, for example, the government will provide fodder for cows and pigs, and will even help the farmer in the marketing of his produce. It is necessary to emphasize that these are recent developments, which could be merely temporary concessions.

SOME CONCLUSIONS ABOUT SOVIET ADMINISTRATION

It is difficult to evaluate the effectiveness of the Soviet administrative apparatus. First of all, the operations of the Soviet government are treated with such great secrecy that we are not sure just how much of the picture we do not see. Secondly, there is the matter of what yardstick should be used in passing judgment. And finally, we have no way of balancing the costs against what the Soviet citizen would be willing to pay for the services he receives. In spite of these difficulties, however, it is possible to make some reasonably sound observations about the administrative machine, based in large part on revelations in the Soviet press.

Contrary to Lenin's expressed hope that the organized state bureaucracy would dwindle and ultimately disappear, it has actually grown. There would seem to be several explanations for this trend. First of all, Stalin found in the bureaucracy the only firm foundation of his power. Under his rule, the Soviet regime operated on the premise that no one could be trusted, including the more seasoned party members. Consequently, a system of checking and crosschecking required the services of countless people. Secondly, the sheer size of the country and the assumption that the party should direct or at least have its eye on all developments required a huge bureaucratic machine, often resulting in duplication and endless paper work. Finally, there has been a tendency toward overstaffing in government agencies, due in part to an inefficient distribution of manpower and in part to the growing tendency of people to prefer office employment to work on farms or in factories. Moreover, the shortage of qualified personnel in the earlier years of the regime encouraged establishments to recruit and to hang on to more people than they actually needed.

While there may be other reasons which would explain the growth of the bureaucratic apparatus, the essential fact remains that it has grown to considerable proportions. And equally important is the fact that this development is at variance with the promises of the regime when it came to power, a consideration which would seem of no small consequence to the citizen who pays the bill.

There is no clear-cut line of responsibility in the Soviet bureaucracy. Technically, responsibility is vertical to the Council of Ministers, which, in turn, is supposed to be responsible to the Supreme Soviet. In practice, the picture is far from clear. The bureaucracy is, in the end, certainly responsible to the party, but the party has set up various channels of control, with no clear lines of authority. The trade unions and local soviets are told, for example, not to interfere in the management of government enterprises. At the same time, they are told to assist enterprises and to oversee their work, creating a situation which often leads to a conflict in jurisdiction. Simultaneously, the *Komsomol* organizations are urged to be vigilant, and the secret police is expected to be ever watchful.

For the most part, it seems that the party wants it this way. By avoiding firm and set channels, the party leadership is able to skip intermediate control centers and to go directly to the lowest level if intervention seems necessary. Knowing this, and believing that party officials will ultimately hear about it, managers tend to take their problems to party committees rather than to the appropriate governmental agencies. One consequence of this is that there is an absence of a close working relationship up and down the bureaucratic ladder. Such a close relationship exists only with immediate superiors and immediate subordinates.

On the whole, however, the party is probably in a position of firmer control than it was a decade ago. This is especially true in agricultural management, where party organizations and party members have come to play a more decisive role. In industry, too, as state enterprises have expanded, so has the party. Moreover, by institutionalizing the practice of frequent promotion, demotion, or transfer of local officials, the party seeks to minimize the opportunities for local arrangements that might be detrimental to its basic objectives.

The demands upon the administrative apparatus are such, and the bureaucratic restrictions so confining and often contradictory, that responsible administrators have found it necessary to go outside the law if they are to achieve what is expected of them. This means finding informal ways of bypassing technical bureaucratic requirements. More specifically, it involves asking for favors, which beget requests for favors in return. Sometimes it is necessary to falsify reports or to employ other means of concealing the real situation. Often the net result is a whole network of protective evasions, which the Soviet press has sometimes labeled "the building of family relationships."

Such extralegal arrangements are officially condemned, but despite its secret police and its other means of control, the regime has often seemed helpless to cope with them. Paradoxical as it may seem, the administrative apparatus, as it has grown, has to a certain extent been able to resist manipulation at the same time that it was becoming more and more indispensable to the Soviet dictatorship.

Since the people do not have any control over the administration, the absence of popular trust in it is not strange. This is particularly true when we remember that the Soviet regime has made countless promises which it has subsequently failed to fulfill. Even such solemn obligations as the repayment of loans made to the government have been broken. Soon after

World War II, the government, without warning, proclaimed a currency reform, as a result of which the citizens received one ruble for every ten. A similar reform was promulgated in early 1961. Similarly, in 1957 it was announced that the government would postpone payment of state loans for 20 to 25 years. Moreover, no interest is to be paid on this money. This is all the more repugnant to the holders of government securities, for although their purchase was theoretically voluntary, almost no one could avoid "investing" less than one month's salary annually in these loans.

These are but some of the more obvious ways in which the Soviet administration has broken faith with its people. Reference has already been made elsewhere concerning arbitrary administrative acts, such as arrests and imprisonment. Various citizens of the U.S.S.R. could no doubt provide an endless catalog of administrative acts which have caused them to lose confidence in the regime. But the Soviet regime is not dependent upon popular support, and most of the available evidence suggests that popular support is not very high on the regime's list of desired goals or priorities.

SOME OBSERVATIONS ON THE SOVIET ECONOMIC REVOLUTION

Irrespective of what has been said in the foregoing about the Soviet system, one cannot deny that it has been able to produce some desired results. There has been an economic revolution in the Soviet Union. Through a series of successive five-year plans, the economy has in large measure been industrialized. The regime was ruthless in its takeover of the economy and in its direction. It appropriated the means of production and distribution. Nothing was permitted to stand in the way of the government's aims. As a result of the regime's determined and impatient approach, there has been considerable progress, particularly in those areas where the best talent and the best materials were allocated. Generally speaking, however, the trial and error method resulted in huge costs, both material and human. But the country was moved ahead, and this is what the leaders wanted.

The motivation behind the industrialization drive was largely political. There was a firm conviction that the economy should be exploited for political purposes, for example, to build a strong industrial and military state. The prolonged emphasis on the development of heavy industry and a large military establishment, together with the extremely low priority accorded to consumers' goods, was ample proof. Consequently, the building of socialism became a distinctly secondary consideration.

At the same time, the Soviet leaders had to provide incentives to those who were made responsible for the achievement of the regime's goals. To some extent, these persons, as loyal party functionaries, could be relied upon to carry out the party policies in any case. But social and economic inducements were seemingly more important. The managerial class was provided with better wages, better living quarters, bonuses, and increased opportunities for promotion and recognition. The method of positive and negative incentives was applied with considerable success.

BIBLIOGRAPHICAL NOTE

Among the more useful of the numerous studies of Soviet economic policy are: Abram Bergson, ed., *Economic Trends in the Soviet Union* (Cambridge, Mass.: Harvard University Press, 1963) and *Soviet Economic Growth* (Evanston, Ill. and White Plains, N.Y.: Row, Peterson & Co., 1953); Philippe J. Bernard, *Planning in the Soviet Union* (New York: Pergamon Press, Inc., 1966); Alex Nove, *The Soviet Economy: An Introduction*, rev. ed. (New York: Frederick A. Praeger, Inc., 1968); Karl W. Ryavec, *Implementation of Soviet Economic Reforms: Political, Organizational, and Social Processes* (New York: Frederick A. Praeger, Inc., 1975).

Specialized studies of agricultural administration include: Fedor Belov, *The History of a Soviet Collective Farm* (New York: Frederick A. Praeger, Inc., 1955); Naum Jasny, *The Socialized Agriculture of the U.S.S.R.* (Stanford, Cal.: Stanford University Press, 1949); and Roy D. Laird, *Collective Farming in Russia* (Lawrence: University of Kansas Press, 1958); Karl Eugen Wädekin, *The Private Sector in Soviet Agriculture* (Berkeley: University of California Press, 1973).

Useful discussions of Soviet labor, trade unions, and industrial management are: Jeremy Azrael, *Managerial Power and Soviet Politics* (Cambridge, Mass.: Harvard University Press, 1966); Joseph S. Berliner, *Factory and Manager in the U.S.S.R.* (Cambridge, Mass.: Harvard University Press, 1957); Emily Clark Brown, *Soviet Trade Unions and Labor Relations* (Cambridge, Mass.: Harvard University Press, 1966).

Information on local administration is included in: Merle Fainsod, *How Russia Is Ruled*, rev. ed. (Cambridge, Mass.: Harvard University Press, 1963); W. W. Kulski, *The Soviet Regime, Communism in Practice*, 4th ed. (Syracuse: Syracuse University Press, 1964); John A. Armstrong, *The Soviet Bureaucratic Elite: A Case Study of the Ukrainian Apparatus* (New York: Frederick A. Praeger, Inc., 1959); William Taubman, *Governing Soviet Cities: Bureaucratic Politics and Urban Development in the U.S.S.R.* (New York: Frederick A. Praeger, Inc., 1973).

32

Policy-Implementing Structures: Instruments of Control

One of the most perplexing and, at the same time, one of the least adequately answered questions encountered by persons seeking to understand the workings of a Communist regime concerns the methods and techniques by which the masses are mobilized to do the regime's bidding. Since the number of persons belonging to the Soviet Communist party does not exceed 9 percent of the adult population, how do they manipulate the other 90-odd percent? Part of the answer is to be found in the fact that Soviet leaders have never operated on the assumption that it is sufficient not to have people against you. They must be for you. It is not enough to prevent undesirable acts. It is essential that people act positively. It is imperative that the people do the things that the party wants done, even if these are deeply repugnant to the people who are forced to do them. Explaining how the party gets the masses to do its bidding is the task of this chapter.

FORCE AND FEAR

From the outset, the new Soviet regime employed the instruments of force and fear to compel obedience, a practice that has been copied by every other Communist regime. Over the years these instruments were developed and applied with increasing refinement. And, although they were supplemented by various efforts at persuasion, behind each such effort there always lurked the possibility of a serious if not a frightful sanction.

Following Lenin's dictum that the Communists should not be

503

squeamish about spilling blood, the wielders of the new authority lost no time in imprisoning and executing their opponents, real or imagined, even though they had violated no law. Those considered most dangerous to the new regime were put out of the way, often without benefit of any type of trial. In the initial years, it was the "class enemy" (former owners of productive property and persons who had been associated with the tsarist regime) that felt the brunt of the terror. In subsequent years, however, the terror was to seep into all segments of society—workers, peasants, and even the Communist party.

Those who were not considered dangerous enough to warrant physical liquidation were imprisoned for varying terms. People were banished to concentration camps for years on a no more serious charge than that they were found to be "socially dangerous," although there was no definition of social danger. Proceedings against a person did not have to be public, nor was it necessary for him or her to be present or to be represented by counsel. In some cases, sentences of people sent to camps contained the proviso, "without privilege of correspondence." The authority to pass such judgments was vested in special boards of the secret police, and they were in no way bound by provisions of the criminal code, nor were they responsible to the courts.

To take care of a vastly larger number of individuals whose loyalties were suspect, but who were not considered dangerous enough to liquidate or to imprison, the new Soviet regime created a secret police.[1] Initially it was known as the Cheka, extraordinary commission for combating espionage, counterrevolution, sabotage, and speculation, but subsequently it was known under a variety of initials (OGPU, NKVD, MVD), reflecting changes in name and, to some extent, changes in function. In August 1954, its powers allegedly curbed, the secret police became the Committee for State Security (KGB), and was made responsible to the Council of Ministers. Khrushchev's successors, however, seem to have enhanced the role of the KGB.

Agents of the secret police are to be found in all segments of Soviet society, in the offices, in the army, in schools, in recreational clubs, and in collective farms, but most people can only surmise as to the identity of the agents. They move about freely and are not subject to local control of any type.

People who are something less than enthusiastic about the regime are made aware of the existence of the secret police in a variety of ways. Some are asked to report to the local office, where they may be questioned about remarks they or their associates have allegedly made. Or

---

[1] See Simon Wolin and Robert M. Slusser, *The Soviet Secret Police* (New York: Frederick A. Praeger, Inc., 1957), and Ronald Hingley, *The Russian Secret Police: Muscovite, Imperial Russian, and Soviet Political Security Operations* (New York: Simon and Schuster, 1971).

they may be asked to explain their absence from parades or other manifestations sponsored by the authorities. Or they may be held for a few hours or a day, with no hint as to the reason. Subsequent invitations to appear may follow, and one never knows when a more permanent stay may result.

When the authorities wish to go beyond intimidation, a person may be held for days or months, or even years, and without knowing the charge. Such imprisonment is usually accompanied by endless interrogation, particularly if a confession is desired. The methods used to extract confessions have been so adequately described in recent years that further comment would seem superfluous here. Suffice it to say that the methods of torture, mental as well as physical, have been systematically refined and developed. Once caught in the web, even high party dignitaries become helpless.[2]

In recent years there has been a notable increase in the regime's use of psychiatric hospitals to isolate and punish citizens who express unorthodox religious or political views. It is estimated that the number of persons declared insane without medical justification and confined in psychiatric wards without having been formally arrested or charged with any crime runs into the hundreds.

The tactics of secret police agents are many and varied. Often the agents are provocateurs, posing as enemies of the regime and urging the creation of antiregime organizations. When the desired persons have been implicated, the net closes and the agents become star witnesses in court, admitting all. At other times, they are placed in prison to talk about their "crimes," and in the process they learn as much as possible about the past activities of their cell mates, only to become more convincing witnesses at the trial.

Secret police agents cannot be everywhere at all times. Hence, there is need for a sizable net of informers if surveillance is to be reasonably complete. Wherever a few people come together, for work or pleasure, there is certain to be one or more secret police informers. Everyone knows they exist, although they are not known even to one another. Since people do not know who the informers are, they are led to suspect everyone, including close friends. The result is a general feeling of isolation and distrust.

Most informers are recruited, but there are those who volunteer, hoping thereby to build some good will with the authorities against the exigencies of more difficult times. Often enough the informers find that they are pitted against each other to ensure a thorough reporting job. Failure of one informer to report even a minor matter results in his or her

---

[2] See Khrushchev's speech to the 20th Party Congress (February 24–25, 1956) for some notable examples (*New York Times*, June 5, 1956).

integrity's being questioned. Once having begun to inform, the informer is at the mercy of the secret police. Even more onerous tasks are demanded, and should he or she hesitate, the question of changed loyalties immediately arises. Even past performances are examined for hidden and disloyal motives.

The end result of the techniques of force and fear is to eliminate or to cow and terrify all those who would be capable of offering an alternative to the Communists. The effect of the terror apparatus is made more frightful by virtue of the feeling that anyone could be next. It matters not whether the threat is real or not; it is sufficient that the people think so.

MOBILIZING PUBLIC OPINION

Supplementing force and fear in harnessing the masses to do the bidding of the dictatorship are a host of elaborately developed techniques for mobilizing and monopolizing public opinion. Unlike democratic governments, the Soviet regime is not interested in satisfying popular demands. But it knows that people will continue to do some thinking even if they cannot make their views known publicly. It is imperative, therefore, that the Soviet leaders learn something of the people's frame of mind so as to be able to channel their thinking more effectively along desired lines. In order to do this, the regime exercises complete and active control over the public opinion media and, in addition, seeks to exclude all competing influences.

The extent of the government's monopoly in the public opinion field cannot be appreciated unless one bears in mind that there are no privately owned newspapers or press agencies in the Soviet Union. There are no privately owned stocks of newsprint or printing presses. There are no privately owned movie theaters, film producing, or film importing enterprises. There are no privately owned or operated television or radio stations, or privately produced programs. There are no privately owned theaters or privately produced plays. There are no privately published or privately imported books. It is illegal to publish anything privately, even with a mimeograph machine. In short, Soviet citizens are not to attempt to spread their ideas except through channels the government provides. And the official censor guards the access to these channels.

Nevertheless, in the last few years there has been a great deal of underground private dissemination of typewritten or duplicated materials (*samizdat*, which means "self-published"). Perhaps the most notable of these has been the *Chronicle of Current Events*, a publication which has reported on the regime's restrictions on civil liberties and its persecution of dissidents.

In general, however, the government's control over the instrumentalities of public opinion enables the leaders to control what the public is to know. Visitors to the Soviet Union never fail to be astounded at the extent of popular ignorance about world events that are well known to people in the democratic world. Even Lenin's testament was not published in the Soviet Union until some time after Stalin's death, 30 years after its publication in the outside world. Moreover, ignorance is compounded by a great deal of misinformation which the regime regularly purveys.

From time to time, the party leaders' ideas as to what the public should know change, and history needs to be rewritten. For example, one-time Politburo member Lavrenti P. Beria was, like Orwell's Winston, "lifted clean out from the stream of history." After his execution in 1953, the official state publishing house supplied subscribers of the Soviet Encyclopedia with four pages on Friedrich Bergholtz and pictures of the Bering Sea, recommending that the four-page article on Beria and his picture in Volume 5 be cut out and replaced with this new material. Beria will never have existed! Stalin is barely mentioned in the new Soviet Encyclopedia. To the surprise of many, Nikita Khrushchev received the same treatment, and before his death in 1971 had become an "unperson."

Control over what the public can read or hear extends also to the outside world. The number of publications from non-Communist countries is pitifully small, and these are permitted to come in only after the most careful screening by the censorship. Foreign radio broadcasts, especially those from the United States, were jammed prior to 1963 by an array of Soviet transmitters. More recently, jamming was reintroduced. In addition, Soviet citizens have not been free to travel outside their country except on official missions, a practice which was seemingly modified in a limited manner after 1956. Likewise, foreign visitors to the U.S.S.R. were pretty well excluded during the heyday of the Stalin era, and their contact with Soviet citizens was extremely dangerous to the latter. Since 1956 it has been much easier for foreigners to visit the Soviet Union and to talk with Soviet citizens, although the length of their stay and the areas they can visit have been rigidly limited.

The protective curtain against outside ideas has also been used to keep undesirable information about Soviet society from reaching the outside world. The few foreign news correspondents who have been permitted in the Soviet Union have not been permitted to gather news freely.[3] They have had to rely, for the most part, on official handouts. Moreover, until 1961 their dispatches had to be submitted to the censor, with no knowledge at the time of what was passed and what was deleted. More recently, the Soviets have permitted correspondents of foreign radio networks to

---

[3] See the books by Hedrick Smith and Robert G. Kaiser, referred to in the Bibliographical Note to Chapter 26, for first-hand accounts of newsgathering in the Soviet Union.

broadcast from Moscow. In all cases, however, the government has felt free to expel correspondents if what they reported met with official displeasure. The representatives of one American network were even expelled because that network produced, in the United States, a television show which was regarded in Moscow as being "anti-Soviet propaganda." Although news-gathering in the Soviet Union is still not free, the outside world gets considerably more news from there than it did some years ago.

Owning and controlling the existing instrumentalities of public opinion, however, does not satisfy the Soviet authorities. They are determined that all segments of society should be involved in the regime's propaganda effort to create an atmosphere of assent for the party's aims and policies, and especially for its current programs. To this end the Soviet leaders have created a welter of new and different propaganda instruments.

These propaganda instruments are designed to reach groups and individuals who could normally avoid political polemics. Scientists, teachers, musicians, writers—all are given a propaganda outlet, which they are expected to utilize by way of praising the Communist way of life and the opportunities it affords them. Writers who might have pleaded that it was inappropriate for them to contribute to clearly political papers, such as *Pravda,* the official organ of the Communist party, discovered that the regime had created a newspaper for writers alone, *The Literary Gazette.* Writers could be reminded that in tsarist days they were unable to find an outlet for their views. Now, the government has set up a special newspaper for them wherein they can write about the great opportunities for writers and artists in a Communist society. Here was a means of expressing their gratitude. Here was an outlet for their views. Here were printing presses and stocks of newsprint—and here were party-furnished texts of what they should like to say. How much easier could it be!

Similarly, other groups in Soviet society are provided an outlet of their own. A biology professor, for example, cannot claim that it would be inappropriate for him or her to write in political journals. There is no need to. The government provides a special and dignified platform, a specially created newspaper for professors. And the party is generous in providing themes to write about. If the professor can demonstrate that official duties do not leave enough time, someone will be found to write a piece for him or her. The greater the professor's reputation the more important it is, from the regime's point of view, to have his or her name associated with the party's goals and programs. The same can be said of the scientists, musicians, actors, engineers, and others.

Members of some groups are more effectively involved by various public meetings. Engineers and other respected personnel in a plant or other economic enterprise are asked to take part in party-sponsored political meetings or other propaganda manifestations. If they cannot always be prevailed upon to give a speech or to take some other leading role, they are asked "just to sit on the platform," and so on. In this way the rank and file can observe a visual connection between party leaders and the respected persons in their enterprise. In other words, the regime does not want to leave uncommitted anyone in whom the rank and file could see a leadership alternative to the Communists.

Since everyone cannot be counted upon to read the party's program or even to listen to it over the radio and television, the Soviet leaders have developed face-to-face agitation to a fine art, a technique always regarded as paramount. It has been estimated that the Communist party enlists the part-time services of some two million persons in face-to-face agitation.[4] Formerly known as "Agitators," they are now called "Politinformers." They speak to groups in factories or on collective farms. They visit homes and small gatherings of apartment dwellers. In this way no one can escape getting the party's propaganda message, perhaps in several different forms.

The primary responsibility for directing the Communist party's propaganda is vested in the Central Committee's agitation and propaganda section, commonly referred to as Agitprop. It must see to it that all propaganda outlets do their job. It issues directives and suggestions. And it furnishes various materials. Moreover, it sees to it that those who fail or falter are criticized for their shortcomings.

Twice a year (on the anniversary of the Bolshevik Revolution and on May Day) Agitprop develops and the party issues officially a large number of slogans, which constitute the keynote of the party's policies for the coming months. They are the principal guideposts for the various propaganda outlets. These are modified by subsequent party declarations on various subjects. In the absence of official party declarations, the party's different official organs offer ample clues as to the current party line on any subject. And, of course, there are the confidential instructions from Agitprop.

One or two examples of the more detailed work of Agitprop may be instructive. The face-to-face agitation, for example, is systematically organized. At regular intervals, Agitprop publishes the *Agitator's Notebook,* which contains materials for speeches and themes to be stressed. Generally speaking, there are several brief articles, some dealing with domestic problems and some with foreign affairs. Thus the agitator is furnished a steady and current stream of propaganda materials. Moreover, the so-called letters to the editor, which are often depicted by Soviet leaders or their sympathizers as examples of freedom of expression in the Soviet Union, are for the most part organized and controlled by Agitprop or its agents. Closely related to the letter writers are the so-called worker, peas-

---

[4] See Alex Inkeles, *Public Opinion in Soviet Russia: A Study in Mass Persuasion* (Cambridge, Mass.: Harvard University Press, 1950).

ant, youth, and soldier correspondents, who are trained and paid for their contributions. The various newspaper staffs are instructed in how these correspondents are to be trained and how they are to go about their work. In editorial conferences with these correspondents, there is often a party representative to give advice and guidance. Sometimes the party calls conferences of correspondents to discuss the important themes to be dwelt upon. Hence, it is obvious that these correspondents and letter writers deal only with those topics deemed appropriate by the party. Their function is to help the regime mold public opinion and not to express it as it actually exists.

This does not mean that ordinary persons do not write letters, because indeed they do. Most of the ones published, however, are fairly harmless from the regime's point of view. They deal with alcoholism, with the husbands' responsibility in helping working wives, with whether more failing grades should be given in Soviet schools, and so forth. There are letters that are critical, but these are more often than not anonymous, and they are usually not published. Periodically, secret police officials go through letters received by a newspaper, and some are taken away, usually the anonymous ones.

THE MASS ORGANIZATIONS

In addition to the instruments of force and fear and the techniques of persuasion, the Soviet leaders have developed numerous organizations through which everyone is involved, in one way or another, in helping to carry out the party's program. Whereas the instruments of force and fear are employed to destroy opposition and to instill fear, and whereas the public opinion media have been developed and organized to make sure the party's propaganda message gets to everyone in a variety of contexts, the numerous party-sponsored organizations are designed to harness the masses to the dictatorship by having them help the party to realize specific and concrete aims. All mass organizations have been referred to by Soviet leaders as "transmission belts," linking the party with the masses. Not only are people not allowed to oppose or to stand aside; they must actively assist in carrying out Communist party programs.

The most far-flung of the mass organizations are the soviets. Although they constitute the administrative apparatus for carrying out governmental policies, they are also the principal means by which mass participation in community activities is secured. The majority of the members of local soviets, unlike those at the top, are not members of the Communist party; hence, the idea of popular control in administration is conveyed. But, as noted in an earlier chapter, the soviets are organized on a pyramidal basis, with effective party control at all levels. Moreover, even the selection of nonparty members for local soviets is decided upon by the party.

Because they are a part of the governmental structure and therefore have the authority of the state behind them, the soviets reach out to include a large number of people. They have officially been depicted as "the mass organization of all toilers." Because they are so described, no citizen can refuse to help the soviets in carrying out their tasks.

Supplementing the soviets are the trade unions. Unlike those in democratic countries, Soviet trade unions are not expected to hold views that are essentially different from those of the employer. They were described by Stalin as "the mass organization of the proletariat, linking the party with the class primarily in the sphere of production." But in the Soviet Union the interests of the proletariat are not judged to be in conflict with the interests of any other group. Initially, the trade unions did conceive workers' interests more narrowly and sought to represent them as against the narrower interests of management. But within a brief period of time they were brought into line. The workers were depicted as being also the owners. If they should strike, therefore, they would be striking against themselves.

As are other organizations in a Communist state, trade unions are organized in a pyramidal fashion, with authority being wielded by the All-Union Central Council of Trade Unions, which is at the apex of the pyramid. At the base of the pyramid is the factory committee, elected by the union in each factory. Between the base and the top are a number of intermediary committees at the district and republic level. Throughout the trade union organization, however, the real wielder of authority is the Communist party. In various enterprises, party control is achieved through the appointed director, the primary unit of the party, and the shop committee. The shop committee is nominally an agency of the trade union, but, in the past at least, it has been more of an adjunct of management than a representative of the workers.

Therefore, the trade unions have in the main functioned as instruments of the party in seeking to attain higher production quotas, labor discipline, efficiency, and other regime goals. Beyond this, in actual practice their principal area of action has been in the social welfare field. They have been charged with the administration of social insurance and labor benefits. Interviews with Soviet workers who have left the U.S.S.R. show that they regard Soviet trade unions solely as instruments of the party and of factory management.

In 1957 the Soviet leaders took steps that indicated they wanted the trade union representation on the disputes commissions to at least uphold the legal rights of the workers. At the same time, they revealed that in the past a worker's complaint did not get much of a hearing, often none at all. Rights of appeal were narrowly limited. Often the union members of the disputes commissions had sided with the actions of management, even when they ran contrary to the law. While not suggesting that the trade unions defend traditional workers' rights, they were told that they should at least defend those legal rights which the workers in the Soviet Union do possess.

Mass organizations also embrace the youth. It has been evident for a long time that the Soviet leaders, although jealously guarding top leadership positions, have staked everything on youth. The future of Communism is in their hands. Not only must the new leaders come from the youth but, in addition, new generations of supporters for the regime must be won there. The Communist way of life cannot be perpetuated unless a steady stream of new adherents can be recruited who are enthusiastic enough to want to perpetuate it.

Consequently, the Soviet leaders have left no stone unturned to develop the most elaborate network of youth organizations.[5] These include the *Octobrists* for small children, the *Pioneers* for adolescents, and the *Komsomol* (union of Communist youth) for the young adults. All children are *Octobrists*, but there is progressive elimination as one goes up the ladder. The cream of the youth, from the party's point of view, is to be found in the *Komsomol*, which in turn is the principal recruiting ground for new party members. Similarly, leadership is from the top down. Party members lead the *Komsomols*, which in turn are responsible for work among *Pioneers*, while *Pioneers* are supposed to help the *Octobrists*. The party, of course, is the final judge in all matters of youth organization and action. The activities of these youth organizations are carefully planned and supervised. In the case of the *Octobrists* and *Pioneers*, it is mostly a matter of implanting attitudes, but in the case of the *Komsomols* there is more serious work to be done. Broadly speaking, the work of the *Komsomols* can be said to comprise four basic functions: (1) assisting in the ideological training of youth, (2) setting an example, by hard work, which will help the regime realize its economic aims, (3) helping the regime to spot trouble or disloyalty by maintaining a sharp lookout at all times, (4) assisting the regime in realizing its objectives in the armed forces. Moreover, *Komsomol* members are required to play an active role in the quasi-military civil defense agency (DOSAAF), which is directed by top-flight reserve officers of the Soviet armed forces. Here they are taught first aid, given shooting practice, trained to operate and manipulate parachutes, taught about guided missiles, and subjected to further political indoctrination. To achieve their varied goals, the *Komsomols*, some 35 million strong, have the unstinting support of the party, which spares no effort in their behalf. In order to realize the ideological tasks of the *Kom-*

---

[5] The Soviet schools, as devices for harnessing the masses to the dictatorship, are treated separately in a subsequent section of this chapter.

somols, for example, special courses, schools, and study groups are organized. Here the youth study the history of the party, the biographies of Soviet leaders, and the works of Marx, Lenin, and others. In addition, over 200 youth newspapers and magazines are published with a total circulation of over 20 million copies.

Moreover, there are a number of other techniques designed to capture the youth for the regime. Among these are youth theaters, youth physical culture centers, and youth homes and recreation centers. To the end that new generations must be won for Communism, leisure as well as work time of young people is carefully planned, supervised, and directed by the Communist party.

But there are indications that all is not well in the *Komsomols.* Soviet newspapers continue to carry accounts of poor and unsatisfactory work in the youth organizations. The *Komsomolists* are negligent of their leadership duties among the *Pioneers.* Many of them are calculating careerists, using the *Komsomol* organization to advance personal ambitions and goals, being indifferent to everything that does not affect their careers. Many have fallen for bourgeois tastes in music, literature, art, dress, and manners. Many have not responded to special appeals to engage in various volunteer projects. Many who have completed their university or technical studies find ways of remaining in the larger urban centers and thus avoiding service in the more remote provinces. Many have raised embarrassing questions about the regime's promises and declared goals. Soviet leaders have spoken of "unhealthy moods among the youth," and official *Komsomol* newspapers have written of "ultrarevolutionary demagogues," "apolitical persons devoid of ideals," and "nihilists, carrying out a reappraisal of values."

While it would be difficult to speak of opposition to the regime among youth because it is impossible for opposition to organize or be manifested openly, it is possible, at least, to speak of a passive dislike for the regime.[6] There is a revulsion against the constant interference in the personal lives of young people. There is dissatisfaction with the material state of things. There is a feeling of isolation and a yearning for contact with the outside world. Even among the privileged youth, the system of completely limiting the individual tends to produce moods of depression.

Bits of evidence stemming from informal gatherings in private homes, apparently not so hazardous as in Stalin times, reveal a general desire for political and spiritual freedom. Although political topics are for the most part studiously avoided, unorthodox views on other matters are fre-

---

[6] See Georgie Anne Geyer, *The Young Russians* (Homewood, Ill.: ETC Publications, 1975). For an earlier view of a former Soviet student, see David Burg, "Soviet Youth's Opposition to the Communist Regime," *Bulletin: Institute for the Study of the U.S.S.R.* 4 (April and May, 1957): pp. 41–47, 44–50. Also, see Hedrick Smith, *The Russians* (New York: Quadrangle/New York Times, 1976), pp. 171–96.

quently expressed. Further testimony of the yearning for freedom is provided by the fact that the names of several underground student magazines have found their way into the Soviet press. Far from creating new generations of unconditionally obedient robots, devoid of feelings and ideas, the Communist party may, in the long run, produce the exact opposite.

In the late 1950s and early 1960s, young *Komsomol* members were openly asking some difficult questions. They were asking what the society they were supposedly building will look like in the future. Having come face to face with the contradictions and injustices in the Soviet system, they were seeking an answer from their leaders as to the nature of the future society. Aware of the inequalities of the Soviet class structure, they wanted to know if Communism would mean the end of these inequalities. The regime's answer was the new party program (1961), which reiterated many old promises and had the avowed goal of catching up with the United States in 20 years. By 1980, according to the program, Soviet citizens could look forward to certain free services, including most utilities, municipal transport, midday meals, education,[7] medicine, and rent-free housing. By 1970, however, this program was conveniently "forgotten" and went unmentioned.

There are other bits of evidence of generation gap difficulties between the party leadership and the *Komsomol* membership. In 1968 a considerable shakeup of the *Komsomol* leadership took place. The extent to which changes were made is illustrated by the case of a man who had not been involved in *Komsomol* work for ten years, and yet was elected secretary of a provincial *Komsomol* organization, directly in violation of *Komsomol* statutes. Moreover, the party leadership has stepped up its campaign against proponents of "bourgeois ideology," who are allegedly attempting to subvert the Soviet intellectual community.

Writers and artists in the Soviet Union, too, cannot escape being mobilized. They are expected to develop and to utilize their talents in order that they may more effectively support the Communist political system. There is no freedom to create except as the creation assists the party in mobilizing support for the regime. The Soviet bill of rights gives writers and artists the "right" to create, but only for the purpose of defending and strengthening the socialist system. And the party leaders are the sole judges of what that system is and what strengthens it and what does not.

From time to time the party conducts a literary purge, during which certain works and their authors are severely criticized and the magazines

---

[7] The 1936 constitution proclaimed education to be free, but shortly before World War II tuition charges were introduced for secondary and higher seducation. The 1977 constitution merely refers to the right of education.

which published their pieces are censured. Sometimes the authors are expelled from the Union of Soviet Writers, an organization which serves to keep would-be mavericks in line. During Stalin's reign, many writers also went to prison camps. The usual criticism is that literary and artistic works are ideologically harmful, apolitical, imitative of bourgeois Western concepts, or based on the notion of art for art's sake. In the Communist party's view, Soviet art, literature, music—in short, all forms of artistic expression—must serve to glorify the Soviet system, the Soviet leaders, and the domestic and foreign policies of the Soviet Union.

But the party does not simply wait to judge artistic and literary works in a sort of postaudit. Through its official organ *Pravda,* the *Literary Gazette,* and other media, the party frequently sets forth tasks for writers and artists. They are told to stress the efforts of workers and peasants in the realization of the current economic plan, or some other objective with which the party is currently concerned. Occasionally, the party bemoans the absence of a great poem, novel, opera, or other work depicting some Soviet scene, and calls for the production of such a work. In other words, great art or great literature is what contributes to the realization of whatever goals the Communist party is pursuing at any one time.

For those who live up to the party's expectations there are generous rewards. Artists of all types, but especially writers, actors, and singers, are held in high esteem by the regime and consequently receive considerable note in the press and other publicity media. Moreover, they are the highest paid people in Soviet society, which makes the material rewards perhaps more important than the recognition. Soviet writers and composers receive royalties, which means that some of them are millionaires. Actors and singers, if considered good, are given special engagements for extra pay, even though their regular salaries are high. Finally, the better artists have an opportunity to travel abroad, they have better clothes, and they have good housing, which is scarce everywhere. If an artist is willing to have his talents exploited for political purposes, therefore, he gets recognition from the regime and usually can be assured of excellent material rewards.

After Khrushchev's 1956 revelations of the crimes and abuses of the Stalin era, party publications called for an end to the narrow political approach to art. The Stalinist cult was held responsible for a debased cultural life. Certain writers who were sent to prison during the Stalin period were released, and some who had met a worse fate were posthumously "rehabilitated." Within a year a tremendous change had occurred in the Soviet literary and artistic output. No longer was there an effort to hide or to avoid the facts of Soviet life, including illegal arrests, the prison system, and the fate of former colleagues. In print, on canvas, and on the stage, Soviet artists and writers were presenting ambitious and greedy party officials and government bureaucrats as the villains of their pieces.

Their heroes were simple people, often not even party members. Some writers, cautiously hopeful, were stressing the need for freedom of creative endeavor.

The victory of the anti-Stalinists in Poland, and more particularly the Hungarian Revolution, forced the Soviet leaders into a reappraisal of their new attitude toward art. Reportedly, there followed stormy sessions of writers' and artists' associations, where the political leaders sought to reassert the party line in the artistic and literary fields. The meeting of artists fell in line, adopting a resolution in which they promised to reflect in their works "the beauty and grandeur of Communist ideals," and pledged to combat the infiltration of alien influences. Reports of the meeting of writers, however, indicated that the party leadership was not too pleased with the results. The author of the most controversial work of fiction at that time (Vladimir Dudintsev, author of *Not by Bread Alone*), far from confessing his errors, defended his work, despite the fact that the party leadership was displeased with it.

In 1957, before he knew that his novel, *Doctor Zhivago,* could not be published in the Soviet Union, Boris Pasternak arranged for its publication outside Russia by an Italian publisher. The publisher, an alleged Communist, refused to suspend publication when, as a consequence of the decision that it would not be published in the Soviet Union, he was asked to do so. The book was translated into several languages, and in 1958 Pasternak was awarded the Nobel prize in literature. Before Soviet authorities could act, Pasternak signified acceptance of the award, but subsequently declined when he was bitterly attacked in the Soviet press, expelled from the Union of Soviet Writers, and threatened with exile.

In the early 1960s there seemed to be room for optimism. The refreshing nature of Yevtushenko's and Voznesensky's poems, as well as those of other poets, and the forthright prose of Nekrasov and some of his colleagues gave rise to hopes of increasing relaxation. The publication of Alexander Solzhenitsyn's *One Day in the Life of Ivan Denisovich,* depicting life in one of Stalin's concentration camps, seemed to improve opportunities for critical realism. In 1963, however, Krushchev made it clear that the party was on the side of those who insisted on maintaining ideological purity in the arts.

In the last years of the 1960s, the Soviet leaders appeared to be turning back the clock. First came the trial and imprisonment in 1966 of Andrei Sinyavsky and Yuli Daniel for having published works abroad under pseudonyms—works allegedly harmful to the Soviet regime. Then came the arrest and imprisonment of several other writers, seemingly for having protested the actions against Sinyavsky and Daniel, and in turn new protests generated new trials. And in 1966 an article was added to the Russian Republic Criminal Code making it a crime to spread "deliberate fabrications defaming to the Soviet state and public order." This was ready-made to use against the dissidents.

The Soviet military invasion of Czechoslovakia in August 1968 brought further difficulties. Many important Soviet writers refused to fall in with the official party line. Scientists, educators, and other intellectuals also refused to lend support for the Soviet intervention. A few of the most outspoken protestors were brought to trial, again generating new protests.

There followed an increasing number of trials similar to those in the Stalin era (that is, no evidence for the defense permitted and no cross-examination of prosecution witnesses). Those who protested these proceedings were often arrested and tried themselves. The transcripts from some of these trials, circulated by *samizdat*, reveal that many of the defendents spoke out even in court. For example, the writer Andrei Amalrik, tried and convicted in 1970, charged that his trial reflected "the cowardice of a regime that regards as a danger the spreading of any thought, any idea alien to its top bureaucrats." Before he served out his term he was sentenced to another three years by a labor-camp court. In 1976 he was given permission to leave.

One of the most notable writers to protest against censorship and the restrictions on individual freedom is the 1970 Nobel Prize winner, Alexander Solzhenitsyn, who could no longer get his works published in the Soviet Union. His *The First Circle, Cancer Ward,* and *August 1914* were published in the West. In 1969 he was expelled from the Writers' Union, but answered back with a devastating criticism. Thereupon the regime intensified its public attacks on Solzhenitsyn, branding him a traitor and defaming his character and the conduct of his personal life, but the writer continued to openly condemn the government for its harassment and persecution of dissident intellectuals. Following the publication abroad in December 1973 of his accounts of Soviet concentration camps *(The Gulag Archipelago, 1918–1956),* he came under severe attack in the Soviet press, and in 1974 was expelled from his homeland.

Other writers who have voiced protests against or violated the government's censorship policies have found themselves expelled from the Writers' Union or removed from their positions with literary journals. And persons who defended the writer or editor under attack were often punished as well.

Clearly, censorship of creative literature has been more rigorous and more consistent under Brezhnev than under Khrushchev. In brief, there has been less cultural freedom, although there has been more freedom of discussion in the scientific-technological sphere, especially where the aim has been to improve the economic performance of the system. But economic reform can be closely linked to political reform, so that those who propose economic change need to be cautious.

In the light of these developments, the future of literary and artistic expression in the Soviet Union seems unclear. For a brief moment, at least, Soviet writers felt a release from the deadening conformity into which they had for years been forced by the Stalinist dictatorship. They were able to experience a modicum of creativity, which they had not known in the years before. Perhaps the tide cannot be completely reversed. Only time will tell.

*   *   *   *   *

The mass organizations discussed in the preceding pages are the ones which seem to get the greatest attention from the Communist party, and are, therefore, perhaps the most important in helping realize specific and concrete tasks. But other organizations also have important roles to play. There are sports groups, an association of railway workers, an organization for war veterans, an association of collective farmers, reserve military organizations, and so on. All of these have their periodic meetings, at which they examine their problems, their past work, and, in the end, inevitably pledge to do their utmost to come up to the expectations the party holds out for them.

The net result of the whole scheme of mass organizations is that nearly every person, at least in the cities, is caught up in the vortex of Communist organizational life, often belonging to several organizations, each of which strives to bend him or her to fit the Communist mold. The composition of each group may vary with changing occupational or avocational groupings, and the techniques may be altered by party edict, but the end is always and forever the same. The Soviet citizens, despite everything they can do, become entangled in the Communist web. In addition to their regular jobs they find themselves going to meetings and conferences, taking part in parades or other manifestations, and being involved in one or more so-called voluntary projects. Physically they find themselves exhausted and resenting the time spent at propaganda meetings. Psychologically, if they do not like the Communist system, they see themselves compromised, involved as in a huge conspiracy, contributing to a perpetuation of the system, yet seeing no way out of the web in which they have become enmeshed.

ORGANIZED DISSENT

Dissent has become increasingly organized, if loosely, over the past decade, despite reprisals. It was provoked in part because the Brezhnev regime made it impossible to continue publication of criticism of the Stalin years, as well as by government reprisals against a few intellectuals who had protested the Soviet invasion of Czechoslovakia in 1968. In 1969 the Action Group for the Defense of Civil Rights in the U.S.S.R. was formed, but its leader, Pytor Yakir, was soon convicted on the charge of anti-Soviet activities and imprisoned. In 1970 another group, the Committee for Human Rights, was formed by two leading physicists, Andrei Sakharov and Valery Chalidze. Both groups, but especially the latter, attracted a number of notable writers, scientists, and other intellectuals.

The latter group has been particularly active in seeking to monitor Soviet violations of that part of the Helsinki accords (signed in 1975) which deals with human rights and which gave the dissident movement unexpected new life. Most of the leaders of this group have been imprisoned, with the exception of Sakharov. Chalidze, while on a trip to the United States in 1973, had his passport taken away by Soviet diplomats. The same thing happened to Zhores Medvedev in August 1973, while doing scholarly work in Great Britain. A well-known geneticist, Medvedev spent some time in 1970 in a psychiatric hospital because of his dissident views. This "treatment" has been meted out to a number of dissident intellectuals in recent years.

The employment of psychiatric hospitals to "treat" persons with dissident views suggests that Soviet authorities are substituting selective persecution for mass terror. It is interesting to note that even as the climate of repression has grown worse, the 1977 Soviet constitution could assert that "persecution for criticisms shall be prohibited" (Article 49). But even a cursory reading of the constitution as a whole provides ample evidence that the permitted criticism is narrowly defined, and that governmental authorities can easily interpret any criticism as anti-Soviet and therefore prohibited.

What do the dissidents want? It is difficult to generalize, except that all of them want freedom which they now do not have. Some want greater freedom within the system, while others would like to replace the system. Some of them are religious and some not. Some believe in a socialist order and some do not. Artists and writers want freedom to create and do not like to be bound by the canons of "socialist realism." All of the dissidents seem concerned with problems facing Soviet society, as well as those facing other societies, and the impact of all of this on the international order. They would like to be able to travel freely, to discuss with citizens of other nations problems of common concern, and to do this without fear or government-directed hindrance. As of this writing (1977), the Soviet authorities are not sympathetic to these aspirations.

SCHOOLS IN A STRAIT JACKET

Along with the youth organizations, the Soviet Communist party looks upon the schools as the main instruments for shaping the new generations. Since the launching of the first Soviet earth satellite in 1957, the Soviet educational system has received a good deal of attention in the West from educators and political leaders alike. It is beyond the scope of this book, however, to examine the Soviet educational system in all its ramifications. We are primarily interested in it as an instrument in the hands of the party for molding new generations to fit the requirements of its political leaders.

As do all other institutions in the Soviet Union, the schools have a definite role to play. In addition to providing the type of training desired by the party, mostly professional and technical, the schools are supposed to turn out young citizens who will be enthusiastic supporters of the Communist system. The attempt to reeducate older generations has not borne much fruit. Hence there is an urgent need, from the point of view of the party, to redouble the effort to guide young people along the desired path. Therefore, little is left to chance. All educational programs are carefully planned with definite political objectives at all levels.

As might be expected, there is a desire to get to children at an early age. The much-advertised nurseries, or day-care centers, where working mothers may leave their young ones, offer the first such opportunity. Here, in picture, song, and story, the young ones learn to glorify Soviet leaders and their achievements. In most instances the young one returns to the mother at the end of the day, although there are a growing number of centers which return the child to the parents only for the weekend.

Understandably, the party sets the educational goals of the Soviet schools and assigns important personnel to check on their realization. Basic directives are usually in the form of resolutions of the party's Central Committee, which may be spelled out in greater detail by the Council of Ministers. Key articles from the party press or in educational journals offer further guidance. In addition, there are the ministries of education in the republics. Moreover, important school officials (administrators and teachers) are party members and presumably familiar with the party line on education. Through all of these channels Soviet teachers are told, time and again, that all education must be based on the one and only true science, the science of Marxism-Leninism.

To this end textbooks and other teaching materials are expected to conform, with increased emphasis on ideology as one moves up the educational ladder. Moreover, the general tone is set by the most important general reference work for all citizens, the Large Soviet Encyclopedia, which is regarded as the final authority and the undisputed source of information on all subjects. It was produced on the basis of a political directive which in 1949 declared that the second edition ''should widely elucidate the world-historical victories of socialism . . . in the U.S.S.R. in the province of economics, science, culture, art.'' And ''it must show the superiority of socialist culture over the culture of the capitalist world.'' All articles are thus written from the point of view of the Marxist-Leninist world outlook. This concept of an encyclopedia is foreign to the Western world, and foreign to the traditional concept of what an encyclopedia should be.

In their propaganda aimed at the outside world, Soviet leaders have expressed considerable pride in their educational system. Among other things, they have on innumerable occasions pointed to the banishment of illiteracy as one of their great achievements. While not denying this, an objective observer must also ask: What achievement is it if the purpose is to enslave the mind? What gain is it for an Armenian or a Ukrainian to have the party organ, *Pravda*, translated from the Russian into one of his own tongue? This is not to suggest that banishing illiteracy is not a desirable goal, but to point out that in the Soviet system it is not an unmixed blessing.

In their domestic output, in contrast to what is said about the educational system in propaganda destined for abroad, the Soviet leaders are frequently critical of the shortcomings of their schools. On the one hand, there are the material deficiencies, poor or inadequate physical facilities (necessitating double and even triple shifts), inadequate housing and work space for teachers, and the like. On the other hand, and seemingly more important, are the undesirable results. Too many students are receptive only to the type of learning which will get them into institutions of higher learning, while these institutions can admit and accommodate only a portion of them. Moreover, many of the university graduates are often pictured as ideologically unprepared, enamored of cosmopolitan views and tastes, and, in general, not possessing the ideological outlook the party leaders expect and desire.

In late 1958 and early 1959 the regime launched an organizational overhaul of the Soviet school system, which came to be known as the "Khrushchev School Reform." Its avowed goal was to channel only a relatively small proportion of young people toward higher education. The remainder were to be trained for a specific niche in the labor force, while giving them a modicum of general knowledge. In support of his plan, Khrushchev observed that it was unwise and unrealistic for so many young people to aspire to a higher education, particularly when many of them did so because they found the idea of manual labor repugnant.

The objectives of the Khrushchev School Reform were to be achieved through an eight-year compulsory school, followed by on-the-job training for two or three years. While for some, on-the-job training consisted mainly of going to school, 80 percent of the university admissions quota was reserved for persons with at least two years of work experience. While on the job, these youngsters would prepare themselves for institutions of higher learning through special classes, night schools, or correspondence courses. Under this plan, Soviet authorities would be able to determine at an earlier age than before who would go to the university, to the technical institutes, or to the mines and factories.

This aspect of the Khrushchev School Reform was not enthusiastically received by a number of educators, who doubted the wisdom of interrupting the educational careers of promising students. It came under fire in the Soviet press soon after Khrushchev's ouster in 1964, and in 1965 it was altered so that quotas would be in proportion to the number of applications received from high school graduates and from young workers.

In 1966 the Khrushchev School Reform was abolished in all but name, leaving young people from industry at a severe disadvantage in competing for university places. In 1972 the party and government issued a joint decree calling for greater stress on combining traditional school subjects with production, including student excursions to factories and farms, as well as some work experience during the school year and during vacations. A ten-year program of compulsory school was set up, but shortages of school buildings, textbooks, qualified teachers, and other facilities have hindered achievement of this goal.

There are great disparities as well as inequities in Soviet education. Some schools are blessed with good equipment and excellent instructors and others are not. Getting into the better schools depends in part on connections and favors. Children of the educated have a much better chance of making it to the university than children of workers or farmers. Only one out of seven graduates of secondary schools can get into institutions of higher learning, and if one gets expelled from one university it is impossible to get into another one. According to the Soviet census of 1970, fewer than half of all adults had gone beyond the seventh grade, and fewer than 6 percent had any education beyond the secondary level.[8]

ATTACK ON COMPETING INFLUENCES

In seeking to create the new socialist man, the Communist party found it necessary to combat those influences which ran counter to its ideological position. As noted earlier in this chapter, foreign influences were in large measure excluded by policies which came to be referred to collectively as the Iron Curtain. Domestically, at the time the Communists seized power, the family and the church were the most powerful influences in shaping new generations. Consequently, Soviet leaders lost no time in devising ways of eliminating or minimizing these influences.

Marxian theory had explained society and the nature of its development in a "scientific" way and without the need of a deity. Previous political systems, according to Marx, had made use of religion to enslave the people more effectively. Religion was an opiate which served to divert the worker from his earthly woes. It was, in essence, one tool in the hands of the bourgeoisie for keeping the proletariat in its place. In view of the

---

[8] An interesting study is by Susan Jacoby, in *Inside Soviet Schools* (New York: Hill and Wang, 1974).

close association of the then prevailing faith (the Russian Orthodox Church) with tsarist autocracy, this analysis must have seemed plausible to many Russians. In the new society, said Marx and his followers, religion will be relegated to the museum.

Soviet leaders were unwilling, however, to wait for the day when the people would discard religion as no longer useful. Consequently, they embarked upon the task of destroying churches. Countless thousands of them were physically demolished, although a few of the more impressive ones were left standing. Most of the churches were stripped of their religious appurtenances, including gold-covered Bibles, silver and gold crosses, the more impressive icons, robes, and other things of value. Many of these were placed in museums. In many instances, regime partisans prevented the use for religious purposes of the churches left standing. These gradually deteriorated over the years, although some have been refurbished since World War II. In most instances, however, they are not used for religious purposes, but are labeled as "architectural monuments." Their preservation at state expense is justified on the ground that they are examples of architecture of a certain period and therefore historically important to the nation. Some of the churches left standing were converted into atheistic museums.

The physical destruction of churches was accompanied by a corresponding attack upon the clergy. The more important ones were quickly liquidated, unless they succeeded in escaping. Others were imprisoned or herded into labor camps. Those who were neither liquidated nor imprisoned were mocked and persecuted. All sorts of indignities were heaped upon them. Moreover, they were left without any means of support, for they were forbidden to plead for any type of aid for themselves or their churches. They were forced to rely on voluntary and usually surreptitious gifts.

The 1936 and 1977 Soviet constitutions proclaim freedom of religious worship, but the right to propagandize about religion is limited to those who are against it. As the regime evolved, new church leaders came into being, but these swore allegiance to the new regime. During World War II, Russian church leaders prayed for Stalin and for the victory of the Red Army. Since that time, the Russian Orthodox Church, as well as a few Protestant churches, have been able to function in a limited way. In many areas there are no churches or clergymen, and even in cities like Moscow and Leningrad, they are few and far between. A few synagogues have also been permitted, although during the latter years of Stalin's reign a calculated anti-Semitic policy—never identified as such—was in effect. As of 1976 there were only four seminaries for training Orthodox clergymen, and the number of new students who may enter each year is severely limited.

Religion is not regarded as a private affair in the Soviet Union. For members of the party and the *Komsomol* it cannot be, for both are dedicated to oppose actively all non-Communist ideological influences, especially on the young. Numerous visits to Russian churches by American tourists in recent years revealed an almost total absence of representatives of the high school and college generation. Women and older people tend to stand out in any church congregation, although there is a fair sprinkling of persons in their 30s and 40s, and some in their late 20s.

In the case of the youth, the party and *Komsomol* organizations have an active campaign of providing them with other things to do on Sundays and other religious holidays. There are special parades and manifestations, youth work projects, visits to libraries, museums, and historical places, as well as circuses and carnivals. Religious instruction for the young is not permitted, while youth publications attack religion in all of its manifestations. In brief, the party will endeavor to make sure that the church cannot compete successfully for the allegiance of the young. As a totalitarian and materialistic philosophy, Communism cannot tolerate effective competition for people's minds from a spiritual force.

Moreover, by the time most youngsters reach adulthood they are made all too clearly aware that advancement in their society depends upon the party. The most desirable jobs, as well as promotions, are controlled by the party. Young persons soon learn that their attitude toward the party and its policies can be decisive. Consequently, they are not likely to jeopardize their future knowingly. And they know that if they go to church or if they become known as religious persons, these matters will be noted in their *dossiers,* or personnel files. In such circumstances, some jobs will certainly be closed and promotion in others impeded. Consequently, these are compelling reasons for avoiding even the appearance of being religious.

Finally, the party keeps a close watch on whatever religious activities are permitted. Official governmental councils for church affairs have been established to regulate the spiritual safety valve. There is something cruelly ironical in an avowed Communist's being the supervisor of the Orthodox hierarchy. Like other organizations in the Soviet system, churches are expected to serve Communist propaganda purposes and to endorse the party's political decisions. From the regime's point of view, the basic battle has been won; only mopping-up operations remain, and the vestigial remnants of worship will eventually dwindle to nothing.

On the other hand, regime actions in recent years suggest a growing concern about religion. During the Khrushchev era, for example, antireligious activities were stepped up considerably. Additional churches, monasteries, and seminaries were closed or turned into museums. Many clergymen were arrested under pretexts of fraudulent manipulations, insanity, or the exploitation of believers. A retroactive income tax was imposed on all priests. Antireligious publications, antireligious lectures, and other antireligious activities were markedly multiplied. A special institute of atheism was established, and a course in atheism was introduced in the schools. Prizes were announced for literary and artistic works that most effectively conveyed antireligious messages. It is perhaps significant that while the struggle against religion in the early decades of the regime was carried on by semiliterate party agitators, in the Khrushchev years it was performed by scholars, scientists, writers, and poets, who were mobilized in the antireligious crusade.

In spite of this systematic attack, there are indications of rumblings beneath the surface. While it is not possible to speak of a religious revival, there is some evidence of hostility toward a system that does not regard religious attitudes as matters of personal and private concern.

In the early years of the new regime, youngsters were encouraged to inform on their parents as a means of discovering anti-Communist sentiment. Many parents stood in fear of their children, and many went to prison because of them. As the years wore on, and particularly as young citizens came to realize the hollowness of the regime's claims and promises, and as they began to experience the same material fate, informing by children dropped off sharply. But by that time, the regime had consolidated its position, won many new recruits, and refined its techniques for controlling the masses.

At the same time, however, the number of the disaffected grew. To young fathers and mothers a great deal of the ''old-fashioned nonsense'' they had learned from their parents now seemed to make sense. Consequently, parental disillusionment with the regime has continued to be of constant concern to the Soviet leaders. Inevitably, children were hearing things in the family during their formative years which, in the opinion of the leaders, must be unlearned.

It is in the light of this situation that one must look at the party's intensive campaign among the young, in and out of school. It is in this light that one must, at least partially, view the use of boarding schools and the effort of the Soviet leaders to "reform" the family which does not do its job "correctly." Thus a 1969 law promises that the state will help with the "communist" upbringing of children but emphasizes that it is the parents' duty to perform this role. If the parents fail, the child may be transferred to a boarding school or adopted.

Aside from all the other things discussed in this chapter, as ways of influencing and controlling the people's minds, there are two primary means of countering family influence. One is to get hold of the child as early as possible in his life, and the other is to monopolize his waking hours or, negatively, to leave as few days and waking hours as possible in which children can be with their parents.

In contemplating the future, it should be noted that in recent years naked force and violence have been less in evidence than in the past. Some observers feel that former inmates of Soviet prisons, many of whom now occupy important governmental posts, give the society an inner toughness and constitute a substantial barrier against the rise of a new police terror system. Some even suggest that the day of the informer may be past, and that Soviet society is no longer controlled by fear. This does not mean, however, that the Soviet leaders have rejected force and violence as instruments of political control or that they will not resort to them if less violent means fail to keep the people in line and thereby threaten the security of the regime and its leaders. Force and fear, along with persuasion, are ever present in varying combinations.

BIBLIOGRAPHICAL NOTE

An understanding of the extent to which force and fear are utilized under the Soviet system may be gained from F. Beck and W. Godin, *Russian Purge and the Extraction of Confession* (New York: Viking Press, 1951); Zbigniew Brzezinski, *The Permanent Purge, Politics in Soviet Totalitarianism* (Cambridge, Mass.: Harvard University Press, 1956); Arthur Koestler, *Darkness at Noon* (New York: Macmillan Co., 1941); Nathan Leites and Elsa Bernaut, *Ritual of Liquidation, The Case of the Moscow Trials* (Glencoe Ill.: The Free Press, 1954); Simon Wolin and Robert M. Slusser, eds., *The Soviet Secret Police* (New York: Frederick A. Praeger, Inc., 1957); and Ronald Hingley, *The Russian Secret Police: Muscovite, Imperial Russian, and Soviet Political Security Operations* (New York: Simon and Schuster, 1971).

Alex Inkeles, *Public Opinion in Soviet Russia: A Study in Mass Persuasion* (Cambridge, Mass.: Harvard University Press, 1950), is a pioneering study of the Russian use of the mass media and of their role in public opinion formation. Insight into *Komsomol* activities may be gained from Ralph Talcott Fisher, Jr., *Pattern for Soviet Youth: A Study of the Congresses of the Komsomol, 1918–1954* (New York: Columbia University Press, 1959). Also see William Taubman, *The View from Lenin Hills: Soviet Youth in Ferment* (New York: Coward-McCann, Inc., 1968), and Georgie Anne Geyer, *The Young Russians* (Homewood, Ill.: ETC Publications, 1975).

On dissent and dissenters, see the books by Hedrick Smith and Robert Kaiser, cited in Chapter 26. Also, see Andrei D. Sakharov, *My Country and the World* (New York: Vintage Books, 1975); Aleksandr I. Solzhenitsyn, *Letter to the Soviet Leaders* (New York: Harper & Row, 1974); Alexander Solzhenitsyn et al., *From under the Rubble* (Boston: Little Brown and Co., 1974); and Anatole Shub, *The New Russian Tragedy* (New York: W. W. Norton & Co., Inc., 1969).

33

The Soviet Challenge

Because Western democratic politcal systems rest on popular approval, some people are apt to think of other political systems as having the consent of the majority of their respective peoples, at least at the time of their initial establishment. This is not true, however, of the Soviet or any other Communist system. In no country has a majority voted freely in favor of Communism, either before or after its inauguration. And yet the Soviet leaders (and their ideology) assert that all other countries must sooner or later go their way. This is the Soviet challenge, in its most elemental form, to the non-Soviet world. Although this chapter deals with the Soviet challenge, the reader should bear in mind the evolving challenge of other Communist systems, notably that of China.

UNIVERSALITY OF THE CHALLENGE

All societies around the world are told, in effect, that the laws of historical development are pushing them inevitably toward revolution and the proletarian dictatorship. The all-embracing Marxian ideology not only professes to explain the basic laws of social development, and thereby to predict the shape of the future society but, in addition, it seeks to provide the instruments with which the transformation is to be brought about. In the hands of Soviet and other Communist leaders, this ideology and the systems they have built constitute a type of declaration of war on the non-Communist world. Hence this world finds itself, whether it wishes it or not, in the midst of a life and death struggle.

There are three aspects to this struggle. The first is essentially domestic—that is, the challenge (or threat) that the Soviets will provide a viable political, economic, and social system which best meets the needs of the members of society and provides the greatest measure of social justice. Or, to put it in question form: Will they succeed in building a social order which, by its sheer success in meeting human and social problems, will constitute a powerful attraction and a persuasive argument for conscious imitation?

The second aspect of the struggle—really a part of the first—is the challenge to the non-Soviet world to establish and maintain a social system (or systems) that will continue to be superior to anything that the Soviets may devise. By and large, this is a dual problem. On the one hand, there are the highly developed industrial nations, which have, in the main, established viable social systems, but which must be able to adjust to the changing needs of evolving industrial societies. On the other hand, there are the nonindustrialized nations, sometimes referred to as under-developed countries, which find themselves in varying degrees of economic and political development. The challenge to these two broad groups of non-Soviet nations, although related, is of considerably different magnitude for each.

The third aspect of the struggle concerns the militant effort of the Soviet leaders to utilize the power of the Soviet Union and her allies to alter the international status quo in their favor. To this end, they are employing a variety of means. Because of the nature of modern weapons of war, this aspect assumes major proportions, for it is here that the life and death of nations and peoples may hang in the balance.

HOW VIABLE A SOCIAL ORDER?

An evaluation of a changing social order must remain tentative. While Stalin was alive, an appraisal of Soviet society was less difficult. But gone are many of the rigidities of that era. Although many things remain as before, some changes are taking place, and any current estimate must take this into account. This is not to suggest that extraordinary departures are expected, but merely to call attention to the fact that Stalin's successors are less resistant to experimentation.

Without doubt, great strides have been made in the Soviet Union toward industrializing a backward nation. The rate of economic growth in the 1950s was particularly impressive, but it had slowed down considerably in the late 1960s. The world has witnessed dramatic proof of the achievements of Soviet science and technology. But progress has been uneven; some aspects of the economy have received much more attention than others. And the human and material costs have been high. The judgment of a onetime Soviet citizen is still valid: there has been considerable progress for those who survived. Also, there is a marked contrast between new buildings and equipment and the lack of proper maintenance.

Moreover, there is a marked contrast between the growth in industrial production and the slow pace in agriculture. In most food items, production per inhabitant is below that of 1913. In December 1958 Khrushchev admitted that "the agricultural situation was grave" and that some earlier Soviet agricultural statistics had been a "fraud" and a "deception"—an interesting description of official data by a Soviet leader. In the same year, he admitted that to produce a unit of milk the Soviet farmer put in three times as many man-hours as the American farmer. And in the case of wheat it was seven times the man-hours. In the ensuing years he continued to express dissatisfaction with the results of Soviet agriculture, frequently accompanying his declarations with changes in farm management. In 1963–64, in 1972–73, and again in 1975, the Soviet Union was forced to buy large quantities of wheat, mainly from the United States and Canada. Because of the huge purchases (19 million metric tons in 1972–73 and 13 million metric tons in 1975 from the United States alone), an agreement was reached in October 1975 which would enable them to buy six to eight million metric tons per year over the next five years.

On the whole, the Soviet Union has a low standard of living. Most, if not all, European countries have a higher one. This means that the Soviet rate of national economic growth has not been reflected in such consumer items as food, clothing, or housing. Rather, it is to be found in the buildup of capital goods industries and in the Soviet military establishment. It needs to be noted, however, that in the Khrushchev years there was a far greater emphasis on consumer goods and services than in the preceeding years, resulting in an increased standard of living, particularly in the urban areas. The rise in real incomes in the past decade mostly benefitted those who had been less well off, thus cancelling out some of the improvement.

The boasts about surpassing the United States standard of living are not apt to materialize in the near future. Substantial increases in consumer items cannot be brought about without encouraging individual initiative, providing better living conditions, and increasing agriculture production. At present, the low agricultural output still ties up about one third of the Soviet labor force, which is in sharp contrast to the 4 or 5 percent of the United States labor force which produces large agricultural surpluses. Housing is far behind nations in the west and medical services, while free, suffer from serious shortages of space, equipment, and drugs. For the privileged, however, there are special clinics and hospitals where care is excellent.

The low standard of living is coupled with an uneven distribution of consumer goods. The "new class," the privileged in Communist society, gets the most of what there is to get. But within other groups in Soviet society (for example, the workers) there is also a large disparity in rewards. The gap between the low and high paid in virtually every group is greater than gaps within similar economic groups in the United States. In any event, and however else the Soviet Union may be described, it certainly is not an egalitarian society.

Moreover, the Soviet standard of living, such as it is, is in part dependent upon the work of many women. Although there are laws on the "protection of female labor," a substantial percentage of steam furnace stokers, metal welders, blacksmiths, and stevedores are women. Moreover, they handle hot asphalt, lay bricks and stone, handle ties and rails in railway construction and repair, and unload coal, cement and grain—to say nothing of their work as janitors, street cleaners, and farm workers. What may be even more important is the fact that the percentage of women in the Soviet labor force has increased over the years.

While there are some uncertainties as to the ability of Soviet society to achieve a large measure of balanced economic growth and to provide its citizens with an improving standard of living, no such uncertainties are to be found in the political realm. Barring a cataclysmic upheaval, the Soviet Union seems condemned indefinitely to dictatorial rule. The Communist party remains an all-powerful elite, and its leaders are determined to keep it that way. For the foreseeable future, therefore, there is no indication that the Soviet Union will be anything except a one-party dictatorship.

This means that whatever aspirations for political freedom the peoples of the Soviet Union may have—and there are various indications that such aspirations exist to some degree—will go unrealized. It means also that the secret police and other instruments of totalitarian control will continue to function. It seems ironic that an ideology whose avowed and declared purpose was to liberate people should produce the opposite. Over the past century and a half, man's personal liberty has increased in many countries, but in the Soviet Union, as in other Communist states, it has become more restricted.

Nevertheless, certain contradictions beset the leaders of the U.S.S.R. On the one hand, they may be able to make concessions in a number of areas, but they will not be able to make them in the one significant area of giving people a voice in deciding who should govern. To do so would be to invite the people to replace them with someone else. This they can never do. Moreover, it is doubtful if they can even permit open and free criticism, for to do so would be to pave the way for the next step in the democratic process—that is, to throw out of power those leaders whose policies and programs are the bases of the criticism.

On the other hand, the leaders are beset with demands, particularly from young people, that there be a more realistic discussion of the nature of the future society. To the young people the single most intriguing aspect of Communism is the promise that goods are to be distributed in conformity with the principle of "to each according to his needs." The young people, even the Communists among them, have come face to face with the contradictions and injustices of the Soviet system. The less fortunate, particularly, are anxious to know if there is going to be an end to the inequalities with which they are so familiar.

That the young people are asking questions and arriving at independent answers suggests that they are unwilling to accept what they are told by their leaders. The leaders would rather not discuss such questions at all. But they know that whether they wish it or not, these discussions will "go on without us, without our intellectual influence." Consequently, they have attempted to provide answers. From the reactions their answers have provoked, however, they must know that the young people are far from satisfied.

The absence of the most significant freedom—political liberty—has its crucial implications for all other freedoms. As was pointed out in Chapter 32, a dictatorship of the modern totalitarian variety seems to need control over all aspects of human endeavor, and cannot, therefore, permit unbridled freedom in any area. From time to time it may be able to make some concessions. But without political freedom, people cannot feel secure in any of their other liberties.

The period of liberalization (1955–57) in literature and other forms of cultural expression is instructive in this regard, although far from conclusive. Subsequently, the all-powerful government was able to reimpose more rigid controls and to get pledges of reform and rededication from artist and literary associations. But it does not seem likely that the educated younger generation, which responded so favorably to the liberalization, will be easily reconciled to the Kremlin's reimposition of orthodoxy. The Soviet public, as one Soviet writer pointed out to an audience of critics, is tired of "the same steam shovel, the same dam, the same road." Moreover, for a time there was reason to believe that the Brezhnev-Kosygin leadership team would be forced to seek an accommodation with the increasing desire of writers and artists to be free of the fetters of socialist realism, but their actions have not given reason for much hope.

VIABILITY OF THE NON-SOVIET WORLD

What the above suggests is that Soviet society is far from being a viable social order. But viability is a relative matter. The crucial question, particularly in the long run, may be: Does the non-Soviet world present examples of a more viable social order or oders? In this respect it is difficult, if not impossible, to speak of the non-Soviet world, or even of the Western world, as if it were one. Many of the nations of the non-Soviet world vary a great deal from each other in their historical and cultural heritage, as well as in their political, economic, and social experience.

For the purposes of this discussion the countries of the non-Soviet world may be divided, although somewhat arbitrarily, into the industrialized or developed nations and the underdeveloped countries. It must be kept in mind, however, that some nations will not fit into either category or, rather, they will fit both categories partially. They are the countries which are either in transition or experiencing serious social crises.

For the most part, the countries in the first category (United States, Great Britain, France, Canada, Germany, Italy, Japan, Switzerland, Scandinavia, and the Low Countries) are sometimes referred to as the free nations. Most of them have experienced political freedom long enough to appreciate keenly what is at stake, what there is to lose. Most of them, too, have evolved in the direction of an improving standard of living for their peoples. They want to remain free, but some of them have serious economic problems.

There is some question, however, if even these nations are fully aware of the nature and extent of the Communist challenge and what they must do to remain free. Certainly, there is some division among the peoples of these countries on this question. When the domestic Communist party is weak or nonexistent, it is difficult for many inhabitants of the country to perceive the danger. Similarly, when the Communist movement is gaining ground in another country, people who are somewhat removed from the scene do not become excited easily, especially if what is taking place is in little known areas and in countries which have only recently achieved their independence.

Most western leaders have long believed that Communist victories anywhere constituted a threat to the free world. They viewed such victories as enhancing the power of the Soviet Union and its allies, and thereby reducing the actual or potential area of the free world. This view was not shared by certain nations, sometimes labeled neutralist, whose leaders deliberately sought to avoid involvement in great power controversies. In recent years, as differences among Communist states evolved, significant segments of opinion in democratic countries have questioned the earlier views of their leaders.

To meet the Communist threat in various parts of the world, the major nations in the free world have embarked upon programs of economic and other aid, particularly to underdeveloped countries and especially to those which are seeking to establish or perpetuate democratic political systems. The hope is that such aid will help these countries to make the transition from backwardness to industrialization without sharp and violent political and social upheavals.

In many of these countries the situation is favorable to the Soviet Union. Among large segments of the people there is mass ignorance, backwardness, resentment of the wealth the West holds, and little or no experience with political freedom. There is great impatience to get things done; slow growth has few supporters. Moreover, their political leaders, often naïve and almost always ambitious, are attracted by the Soviet experiment in radical social and industrial engineering. They are impressed by the rapid transformation of peasant Russia into an industrial and military power.

Moreover, the Soviet Union has embarked upon its own aid program to certain underdeveloped countries. Because they need not account to an electorate, the Soviet leaders can dispense aid irrespective of cost. Even if they cannot win people over to their side, the Soviets can foment unrest or augment already existing trouble. Sometimes, however, Communist actions have helped the West by betraying Soviet bloc intentions. The ruthless suppression of the Hungarian Revolution and the invasion of Czechoslovakia are but two examples.

MILITANT SOVIET EFFORTS TO CHANGE THE STATUS QUO

The Soviet challenge to the non-Soviet world is made particularly acute by the militant campaign waged by the Soviet leaders and their allies to change the international status quo. Their violations of World War II agreements, which were designed to guarantee free and unfettered elections to the countries of Eastern Europe, are well known. And Korea and Vietnam are a matter of record. Recently, there have been some signs that Soviet foreign policy is becoming less militant, but such indications can be easily overemphasized or misinterpreted.

While the objectives of Soviet foreign policy and the means for their implementation are in large measure dictated by the Marxist-Leninist world outlook, it would be a mistake to ignore the influence of historical and other factors that antedate the Soviet era. The Soviet leaders inherited tsarist Russia's geography, population, natural resources, and its drive to gain access to warm-water outlets to the sea. Although the Bolsheviks consented to great losses in territory in the German-imposed treaty of Brest-Litvosk, they waged a concerted and largely successful military campaign to regain the tsarist patrimony after Germany was defeated in the west. Among the first foreign policy ventures of the new regime, therefore, was the one to reclaim the fruits of tsarist expansionist policies. Soviet leaders may deny the influence of the tsarist inheritance on their foreign policies, but in this case actions speak louder than words.

Marxian theory tells the Soviet leaders that the world is in a process of conflict and change. This process, the same theory tells them, will lead to proletarian revolutions in all nation states, and the overthrow of their capitalist social orders. Most Soviet leaders have been convinced, however, that this process needs assistance. Consequently, they have believed that one of the missions of the Soviet regime is to promote revolutions. In other words, world revolution is the maximum goal of Soviet foreign policy, the minimum goal being the survival of the U.S.S.R.

In pursuit of this goal (or goals) the Soviet leaders have utilized a variety of means. At varying times, they have employed espionage networks, infiltration, foreign trade, propaganda, domestic Communist parties, the secret police, and such organizations as the Comintern and Cominform. And finally, they have utilized their military establishment. For them, war and diplomacy are two sides of the same coin, but they distinguish between just and unjust wars. Among the just wars are wars of liberation from colonialism and capitalism. By definition, any war engaged in by the Soviet Union would to them be a just war. By the same token, wars waged by capitalist countries, particularly the leading ones, would be unjust wars.

Soviet leaders have on many occasions insisted that Marxism teaches the inevitability of violence as the final arbiter in international affairs. They have no faith in the idea that Communist and non-Communist states could exist side by side, with common legal principles or moral precepts regulating their relations. This, combined with the Marxian notion of the inevitability of proletarian revolutions, the Soviet doctrine of just and unjust wars, and the Kremlin's possession of nuclear and other capabilities presents the remainder of the world with some unpleasant prospects.

In more recent years, however, the Soviet leaders have said that "peaceful coexistence is an objective necessity," a point of view not shared by their Chinese comrades.[1] Meanwhile, they have not hesitated to exploit the universal fear of war to gain some of their objectives without war.

It has been argued that once the Soviet regime achieves the basic objectives of Communism at home, the need to foment revolutions will fade or disappear. A more persuasive argument, it seems, is that the preservation of the totalitarian system at home will be more difficult to justify as the objectives of Communism at home are met. In order to continue exacting sacrifices and denying basic freedoms, the Soviet leaders will need to show that this is required in the interests of aiding the Soviet brand of Marxism to advance in the world at large, as well as of protecting the Soviet Union from dangerous ideas coming from the outside world.

From time to time, Soviet leaders have said that they believed in the coexistence of differing social systems. In Stalin's time, such expressions

---

[1] These and other differences in the Communist camp are discussed below.

were meant for foreigners and not for the Soviet public. Moreover, such declarations did not speak of permanent coexistence, nor of the conditions for its establishment and maintenance. On the contrary, a careful examination of those statements revealed that the basic condition would be the willingness of the non-Soviet world to yield to the Kremlin's world revolutionary objectives. Coexistence, from Stalin's point of view, was the time the Communists needed to achieve superiority—the period during which the Soviet Union would seek to destroy or weaken the military and political solidarity of the free world.

There is reason to believe that Stalin's successors have been forced to alter his concept of coexistence. Available evidence suggests that they do not accept nuclear war as a realistic means of achieving their objectives, although some experts are convinced that the Soviets are not above engaging in nuclear blackmail if they should find themselves in a favorable military position. Moreover, the new Soviet constitution has a section on foreign policy, which asserts that the Soviet Union supports "peaceful coexistence of states with different social systems," and pledges "noninterference in internal affairs" of other states (Articles 28 and 29). In the same place, however, the Soviet Union is pledged to support "the struggle of peoples for national liberation." In addition, the 1961 party program states that "Leninism teaches and historical experience confirms that the ruling classes do not yield their power voluntarily." And in their instructions to writers, the Soviet leaders have made it quite clear that political and military coexistence does not mean that there should be ideological coexistence.

In this, as in other areas, the Soviet leaders have demonstrated that while they may be inflexible where goals are concerned, they are exceedingly flexible in strategy and tactics. They do not believe that their system can be safe so long as free nations exist as beacons of hope for those who live in tyranny. Yet if they reject nuclear conflict as a means to an end they can be counted on to work harder in the exploitation of other instruments to reach the same goal. Therefore, it ill behooves a world that is tired of conflict to accept at face value the disarmingly attractive doctrine of peaceful coexistence. If it is to have any real meaning for the non-Communist world, peaceful coexistence, as a concept, will require further modification by the Communists so that it constitutes a genuine effort on both sides to reach a workable accommodation.

SOME OBSERVATIONS ON DÉTENTE

In recent years the Soviet Union has indicated a strong interest in improving relations with the West, especially the United States, seeking at least a relaxation of tensions, which has come to bear the name détente.

The Soviet leaders have even boasted in some conferences of Communist states that détente has borne more fruit than the policy of confrontation. They have indicated a desire to improve trade relations with the West, openly recognizing that the Soviet Union is a long way behind in modern technology, especially in the computer field. Since they have little in the way of goods that the West needs, a relaxation of tensions would seem to require some demonstrated willingness to reach accords on disarmament or on other problems, but the Soviets have resisted. As of this writing (1977), disarmament discussions between the USSR and the United States are moving along at a snail's pace.

The height of détente was represented by the agreements signed in Helsinki on August 1, 1975. These accords recognized the existing territorial boundaries in Europe, provided for mutual notification by NATO and Warsaw Pact nations of upcoming military exercises (including the invitation of observers), and committed the signatories to respect human rights and fundamental freedoms.

In 1976 and 1977 the "Public Group for Furthering the Implementation of the Helsinki Agreements in the USSR" reported that, from their observations, the Soviet government has not and does not intend to fulfill its obligations in the area of human rights. The group reported that the practice of psychiatric repression has neither been condemned nor stopped, and that there has been no improvement for those who want to emigrate. The Soviets have reacted to the unfavorable publicity given these reports in the West by insisting that since the Helsinki agreement also spoke of noninterference in internal affairs, other nations have no right to criticize anything that is happening in the Soviet Union. Moreover, as indicated in the previous chapter, most members of the above-mentioned group have been arrested on one charge or another, and all of them have been subject to persecution in varying degrees.

The rulers in the Kremlin seem to resent the fact that the human rights issue has become a stumbling block on the road to increased economic cooperation. For the foreseeable future, therefore, relations between the Soviet Union and the West are apt to be characterized by elements of conflict and cooperation. The Kremlin's difficulties are also compounded by the attitude of Communist parties in Western Europe (see chapter 25), whose public attitude toward human rights is not to the liking of Moscow.

THE COMMUNIST CAMP

The seemingly monolithic nature of the Communist camp in the early post-World-War-II years proved to be deceptive. The first open break came in 1948, with the public airing of differences between Yugoslavia and the Soviet Union. For a time a form of unity was reestablished with the "isolation" of Yugoslavia. After Stalin's death in 1953, and particularly after Khrushchev's denunciation in 1956 of many of the actions of his predecessor, the bonds between Moscow and its Eastern European satellites began to loosen. While varying degrees of attachment to Moscow are to be found in these nations, signs of independence have been notably on the increase. In the main, however, most of the Communist regimes in these countries, including Yugoslavia, support the Soviet Union in its approaches to foreign policy.

The Soviet invasion of Czechoslovakia in 1968, however, raised the question of whether the Soviet Union could ever put in order its relations with the East European states. The so-called Brezhnev Doctrine, enunciated in connection with the invasion, asserts the right of the Soviet Union to intervene in the internal affairs of any other socialist state when socialism is threatened. Since the Soviet Union presumably decides when such a threat exists, the sovereignty of these states would seem to be in perpetual jeopardy. It might be interesting to speculate whether the Brezhnev Doctrine might at some time in the future be invoked to justify Soviet action against China.

The most acrimonious discord in the Communist camp has involved the Soviet Union and China. Apparently, there are four major issues in dispute. The first concerns the question of leadership of the international Communist movement. The Chinese have stressed the equality of Communist states and they have accused the U.S.S.R. of "great power chauvinism." The Soviets have at least paid lip service to the principle of equality, but at the same time they have pointed out that power and responsibility cannot be separated. At a time when the Communist camp must ultimately rely upon the power of the Soviet Union, the Kremlin leaders believe that the decisive voice should be theirs.

The second question at issue concerns the matter of revolutionary tactics and strategy. The Chinese leaders want the Communist camp to pursue global revolution; they stress the point that Communists should not be deterred by nuclear blackmail. They have attacked the peaceful coexistence policy of Moscow as being un-Marxist and un-Leninist, and therefore devoid of theory. They criticized Khrushchev bitterly for his withdrawal of Soviet missiles from Cuba in 1962 and for his signing of the nuclear test-ban agreement in 1963. The Soviet leaders view the position of the Chinese leaders as devoid of an appreciation of practical realities. They have asserted that the prevention of nuclear war is feasible, and have pointedly asked the Chinese if they really thought that all bourgeois governments lacked all reason in everything that they did. The Moscow leaders are convinced that their knowledge of what is possible in foreign affairs is superior to that of the comrades in Peking. They are convinced that the Chinese strategy for global revolution could easily result in global suicide.

The third problem dividing Moscow and Peking involves the nature and form of intrabloc assistance. The Chinese leaders have complained that the newer Communist states, notably China, have not received sufficient aid or even the right type of aid from Moscow. They have criticized the Soviet leaders for their reluctance to provide massive aid for the Chinese industrialization program. And they have been critical of Soviet aid to such non-Communist states as Egypt. Moreover, they have charged that Moscow has used its aid to exert political pressure. To all these charges, the Soviet leaders have replied by citing statistics on the extent of their assistance (military and economic), made at great sacrifices to the people of the Soviet Union. In addition, the Kremlin has on occasion pointed out the uneconomic nature of certain plans of the newer Communist regimes. Finally, the Soviet leaders have made it quite clear that, in the current stage of development of their society, it is necessary to provide greater and greater material incentives to their people. In addition, they have maintained that it was their international duty to so build Communism at home so as to provide their foreign comrades with an appealing example.

Finally, the Chinese leaders have been critical of some of the consequences of de-Stalinization. They insist that they see the reemergence of capitalist forms in several of the smaller Communist nations and in the U.S.S.R. itself. Liberalization, they believe, will lead to the liquidation of Communism. Their own experience in China leads them to conclude that they cannot build the new society without the employment of Stalinist tactics which, they assert, had been necessary in the Soviet Union also. And those tactics, they argue, must be justified by reference to doctrine. De-Stalinization tends to rob them of the necessary doctrinal support.

While the above would seem to be the major elements in the disagreement between China and the Soviet Union, there may be others. There have been heated disagreements over territorial boundaries. And Peking has publicly suggested that the Kremlin rulers regard noncaucasians as something less than equal to the whites. Whatever else may be at issue, it should be noted that nationalism is still the great force of our age. Communist national states, not too much unlike non-Communist nations, are beset with different internal problems, and their views of their respective national interests are far from identical. Consequently, they have different ideological needs. In this atmosphere of diversity, the discord in the international Communist camp is not likely to be resolved in the near future.

Moreover, the Soviet Union may one day have to confront the problem of the various nationalities in its own empire. Nationalism remains strong in the Ukraine and in the Baltic republics, where some demonstrations and strikes have taken place in recent years. In addition, there have been indications of an aroused nationalism in Georgia and Armenia. On several occasions, Soviet leaders have demonstrated that they see the nationalities question as potentially dangerous, although publicly they always insist that all nationalities in the Soviet Union are equal, and therefore the problem does not exist. In their more rational moments, however, they must realize that time does not stand still and that change is the law of life.

BIBLIOGRAPHICAL NOTE

The attempt to evaluate the Soviet challenge on the international front may be facilitated by the following works: Vernon Aspaturian, *Process and Power in Soviet Foreign Policy* (Boston: Little, Brown and Co., 1971), and *The Soviet Union in the World Communist System* (Stanford, Cal.: The Hoover Institution, 1966); Frederick C. Barghoorn, *The Soviet Cultural Offensive: The Role of Cultural Diplomacy in Soviet Foreign Policy* (Princeton, N.J.: Princeton University Press, 1960); Milorad M. Drachkovitch, ed., *Comintern: Historical Highlights, Essays, Recollections, Documents* (New York: Frederick A. Praeger, Inc., 1966); Louis Fischer, *Russia's Road from Peace to War: Soviet Foreign Relations, 1917–1941* (New York: Harper & Row, 1969); J. M. Mackintosh, *Strategy and Tactics of Soviet Foreign Policy* (New York: Oxford University Press, 1963); Marshal Shulman, *Stalin's Foreign Policy Reappraised* (Cambridge, Mass.: Harvard University Press, 1963); Adam B. Ulam, *Expansion and Coexistence: The History of Soviet Foreign Policy, 1917–1967* (New York: Frederick A. Praeger, Inc., 1968), and *The Rivals: America and Russia since World War II* (New York: The Viking Press, 1971); and Robert G. Wesson, *Soviet Foreign Policy in Perspective* (Homewood, Ill.: The Dorsey Press, 1969).

The following more recent works are recommended: Frederick C. Barghoorn, *Détente and the Democratic Movement in the USSR* (Riverside, N.J.: Free Press, 1976); Robin Edmonds, *Soviet Foreign Policy, 1962–1973: The Paradox of Super Power* (New York: Oxford, 1975); Charles Gati, ed., *Caging the Bear: Containment and the Cold War* (Indianapolis: Bobbs-Merrill, 1974); Roger E. Kanet, ed., *The Soviet Union and the Developing Nations* (Baltimore: Johns Hopkins Press, 1974); Daniel Yergin, *Shattered Peace: The Origins of the Cold War and the National Security State* (Boston: Houghton-Mifflin, 1977).

INDEX

Index